Ruth Hamilton was born in Bolton and has spent most of her life in Lancashire. Her novels, *A Whisper to the Living*, *With Love From Ma Maguire*, *Nest of Sorrows*, *Billy London's Girls*, *Spinning Jenny*, *The September Starlings*, *A Crooked Mile*, *Paradise Lane*, *The Bells of Scotland Road*, *The Dream Sellers*, *The Corner House*, *Miss Honoria West* and *Mulligan's Yard*, are all published by Corgi Books and she is a national bestseller. She has written a six-part television series and over forty children's programmes for independent television. Ruth Hamilton now lives in Liverpool with her family.

For more information on Ruth Hamilton and her books, see her website at:
www.Ruth-Hamilton.co.uk

WITH LOVE FROM MA MAGUIRE

Ruth Hamilton

CORGI BOOKS

WITH LOVE FROM MA MAGUIRE
A CORGI BOOK : 0 552 13616 6

Originally published in Great Britain by Bantam Press,
a division of Transworld Publishers

PRINTING HISTORY
Bantam Press edition published 1990
Corgi edition published 1992

10

Set in 10/11pt Plantin by
Colset Private Limited, Singapore.

Corgi Books are published by Transworld Publishers,
61–63 Uxbridge Road, London W5 5SA,
a division of The Random House Group Ltd,
in Australia by Random House Australia (Pty) Ltd,
20 Alfred Street, Milsons Point, Sydney, NSW 2061, Australia,
in New Zealand by Random House New Zealand Ltd,
18 Poland Road, Glenfield, Auckland 10, New Zealand
and in South Africa by Random House (Pty) Ltd,
Endulini, 5a Jubilee Road, Parktown 2193, South Africa.

Printed and bound in Great Britain by
Cox & Wyman Ltd, Reading, Berkshire.

For David and Michael Thornber, my two wonderful sons.

Also for Aunts Rachel Lundy, Agnes Sexton, Dorothy and Gladys Girling and in memory of Uncle Jack Girling who died during the preparation of this book.

Acknowledgements

Many thanks to: Heather Jeeves, agent and friend; the Bolton Library Service for unflagging tolerance; the *Bolton Evening News*; and my cousin Eileen Murphy who helped greatly with research.

Part One

1904

Chapter 1

Somewhere above it all, a watery sun was setting. Here and there a few brave rays found access, allowing the scene a strange and eerie light, a mixture of greys and pale sepias that blended well with old brick and stone. School Hill, known far and wide throughout Bolton as 'Little Ireland', caught its corporate breath at the end of another Monday, a dawn-to-midday struggle with sheet and quilt, copper and fire, tub and mangle. Now, at six in the evening, the back alleys were denuded of billowing whites and no Irish or Lancashire voice cried out against the coming of a ragman's cart. But although a thousand chimneys had begun to cool, their legacy hung over the houses, mingling with sulphuric fumes from nearby factories where paper, leather, machine parts and, above all, cotton were produced.

As a church clock chimed the hour, Delia Street came out to await the event which had been the sole topic of gossip all day. In twos and threes they gathered beneath lamps as yet unlit, while every doorway was open and occupied by an aproned female figure. Little noses were flattened against windows smeared with drawings shaped by sticky fingers in mists of breath. Whispered messages passed along the row, words 'mee-mawed' by women used to communicating without sound during their childfree days in the mills.

'I'd have swore it were bound to rain about tennish and me with nowt dry enough to iron. Hey – are you sure he took everything with him, Edie?'

'Took all his own, I reckon. Her'll have a paddy on tonight, I'll bet. She's told him to go often enough, 'cos I've heard it all through me back wall.'

'What'll she do?'

11

'Nay, don't ask me, lass. Who can tell what that one'll do? Never talks to nobody, never lets on in the shops and that. I stood behind her only last week in the tripe queue and she never batted a lid and me her next door neighbour. But she lets on at him, I can tell thee. I'll swear she throws flat irons or summat at him. Mind you, happen he asks for it. Some of 'em do, you know. We can't be sure what goes on behind a closed door, though I've heard her lose her rag a fair few times.'

'Aye. Well, same as I've always said afore, you can't treat a man like that for ever, Edie. Mine'd smack me one in the gob if I tret him that road. Who's she think she is anyrate? All airs and graces, never a good word for nobody. Have you seen her furniture when that door's open? Table on its own's worth a few bob. How'd he manage that just selling bottles of rubbish what she throws together in the back scullery?'

'I've heard as how it's not all rubbish, though. Her black tonic's supposed be a right pick-me-up according to Elsie Shuttleworth. That eldest lad's never looked back since he were dosed . . . '

'Shurrup, Edie – she's coming!'

Every head turned towards the tall figure which materialized, or so it seemed, out of the fog created by the day's many labours in mill and scullery. Casually, they leaned against wall and jamb, each pretending not to notice the woman, every last one of them apparently engrossed in studying a pavement crack or a wedding ring.

As soon as she reached the end of the street, she felt the atmosphere, knew that she was somehow the centre of attention. They didn't fool her, not for a minute. Like a painting forever frozen behind glass, the stillness of the tableau was unreal, unnatural. So lazy they looked, slumped motionless in doorways, yet she knew that any one of them could outrun a galloping racehorse if it meant saving a sheet on a wet washday. She paused at the corner outside the clogger's where the tap-tap of hammer on nail and wood suddenly ceased as a row of barefooted customers rose in unison to peer through the window. When the woman

12

turned to face them, they backed away from her steady blue gaze, a stare that seemed to penetrate the dimmest of evenings.

Course, they weren't really a-feared of her. She was just another Irish immigrant, one among many, no better or worse off than the rest of them except for her house being a bit on the grand side. But there was something about her, right enough. For a kick-off, she was a sight taller than many of the men and it wasn't natural for a woman to keep her head so near the ceiling. She must have been not far short of five foot nine or ten, straight as a die and with an odd beauty that was in itself slightly unnerving in an area where the women aged young. Not a line on her face, though she must have been all of twenty-five. But it was the eyes that put most folk off. Never a word, yet she looked straight through a person, as if she could see what he was thinking, as if she knew the deepest and best kept of secrets, the darkest corner. And the way she made a body feel – well, it wasn't easy to express in normal language. Three years she'd lived here and hardly a cough or a spit out of her. Aye well. She'd be getting her comeuppance any minute now. But who would tell her? Which one of them, man or woman, would dare come forward and say . . . ?

They sank on to the bench as the clogger wiped his hands and came round the counter. 'Mrs Maguire?'

She hesitated fractionally before stepping through the front door and into the small room. 'Yes?'

'A word in the back workshop if it's convenient, like . . . '

One of the men on the bench swallowed audibly, blushing under layers of miner's dust. Like many of the poor Irish in this community, he hid his superstitions, laughed at them over a pint in the vault at the Bull, denied the folklore that seemed to follow travellers across dividing waters. But here was a woman as near a witch as any good man would care to get. Wasn't it said by many that her granny had been given special healing powers and the ability to place the odd curse? And didn't this one here brew weird teas and potions, wasn't she known for her strange silences? All those pots in her back yard too, full of queer-looking plants, they were, stuff she

13

used for her funny medicines that her husband was supposed to hawk about the streets.

The temporary silence was broken as 'Pey' Peter rounded the corner, his high-pitched voice raised in its familiar cry, 'Peys! Come and get your hot peys! Black ones, green ones, fetch the jug, Missus!' and the scutter of clog irons was heard as children and women arrived to buy peas for supper. Most of the pea purchasers craned their necks to peer into the clogger's, but the subject of interest had already disappeared into the back workshop. Those waiting for clog repairs sat rigidly in a line near the wall, incapable of leaving the shop until they were re-shod.

' 'Er won't take this job well,' muttered an old Bolton weaver who had just popped in on his way off shift to get a new half-set of irons. 'I reckon 'er's not reet in the 'ead.'

'Shush!' whispered the Irish miner. 'Hasn't she the whole street to face just now? This will not be easy for her.' Aye, there was pride in that bonny face, sure enough. And temper too. Hadn't he himself seen Seamus Maguire beating it hell for leather down the street on several occasions as if the devil were on his tail? The four men in the shop seemed to stop breathing as they strained fruitlessly to overhear something – anything at all – from the back room, for wouldn't their wives be agog with it when they got home, mithering over what had been said and how did she take it?

She emerged after several minutes, neither hair nor feature out of place. 'I'll be thanking you then, Mr Chadwick,' she said, her voice firm and clear. 'I knew he'd be going home sooner or later – in fact, I told him to go. Do not fear on my account, for Seamus will send money. He has . . . interests in Limerick, you see.'

Freddie Chadwick watched the ramrod back as it left the shop and sailed off up the pavement, that familiar Spanish-galleon posture proclaiming her advancing pregnancy. He shook his large head sadly. A fair few comings and goings he'd seen in this street, midnight flits, births and deaths, families near murdering one another when the strain got too much for them. But this was a right bad do, this was. 'Interests in Limerick?' he mumbled to no-one in particular. 'That one's stuck his fingers in more pies than they've got in Tattersall's bakery. She's all right, is Mrs Maguire. Just over-proud, is all. Eeh well.' He lowered himself on to his stool. 'Kiddy coming, no money and no work. There'll be nowt down for that poor lass once the child's born.' He picked up a clog and tore off the irons angrily, then filled his mouth with a dozen or so wooden plugs, thus ending his monologue.

There was no merriment in the clogger's that night. He was usually good for a laugh or two, was Skenning Freddie, who had acquired his nickname because of crossed eyes. Yet, in spite of this affliction, he could peg a nail hole with the best of them, while his handmade footwear was reputed to be the finest for many a mile. But this evening he stuck to his work, not a smile nor a joke on his lips.

Philomena Maguire entered her house and sank slowly on to the cold stone floor, her back resting against the relative comfort of the wooden door. It had taken every ounce of her fast-diminishing courage to walk the length of a street where unfinished sentences hung on the air like icicles, each one snapping off abruptly as she approached. Caps had been doffed as she passed a lamp, but not one word of greeting had reached her ears. Now they began, cackling and chattering along the terraces, no doubt discussing how Seamus had left with his sack of possessions, probably embroidering the tale to a point where it might become legendary. Oh yes, she listened to them many a time while she did her washing on a Saturday afternoon in preparation for her week in the mill. Everyone's dirty linen was aired over the backs while she scrubbed her own. Yes, they'd have Seamus's parting words engraved in stone like a new set of commandments by this time. It was a disgrace, the final disgrace for a woman. 'Can't keep her man for two minutes on the trot' and ' 'course, he left at the finish and who could blame him?' For a second or two, she felt like beating a hasty retreat just as Seamus had, gathering her bags and making off for home. Aye, but to what? Mammy with her gimlet eye and even sharper tongue lashing out because another mouth – soon to be two – would

15

require feeding? All those endless acres of marsh, no movement save for animals and children at play, backbreaking days of dawn milking, churning, mucking out, cleaning? No! Better the mill than that; better still the plan she had laid for the long term, an idea that might give her a business of her own once she got on her feet.

She stirred herself to light the lamp in the centre of the table. If the house remained dark, then those outside would have more gossip to serve up with the black peas for supper. In the brass-framed mirror over the grate, Philomena caught sight of her reflection and she listlessly dragged a few strands of cotton waste from her thick black hair. Another day over. She lowered herself into the good leather armchair and stared unseeing at grey coals. Whatever now? Oh, it had been coming anyway, the end of her time at the mill. Her belly grew bigger by the day; soon, she wouldn't be able to bend and stretch to tend the mule and piece her ends. And she'd been so lucky with her job, for how many women became minders in charge of four part-time piecers after just a few years? It was probably on account of her being so hefty and strong. So much to give up, all that security! But with a baby on the way, no doubt the job must go. Which would have been all very well with a husband in the background, a regular income to fall back on.

And yet, her feelings were mixed like a ball of tangled wool just now. She was almost sorry he'd gone, sorry for the fatherless child, for herself with all the responsibility to shoulder. And she was concerned about the future, though she'd calculated long enough against this almost inevitable eventuality. But mingled with the mild grief, shining out like a silver strand among plain threads, was a strong sensation of relief. No more worries about how and where he earned his money, no more waiting for a knock at the door, no more watching as he heaved his drunken body across rooms and up stairs. Yes, she was her own mistress now. Alone. Completely alone in a street of strangers.

Oh, if only she'd turned to her neighbours more easily! Not a one of them would stop to help her now, she knew that. But she'd been so ashamed of Seamus and his carryings-on, all that buying and selling, things hidden all over the house, deals made no more than a whisker's width inside the law. And the rows, those terrible endless arguments because she'd known all along that he saw himself as the poor man's hero, stealing from the British to provide funds for his Fenian causes. How could she ever invite a neighbour in with the parlour filled to bursting at times with stuff he couldn't adequately account for? Bolts of good brocade, joints of meat, pots and pans bought as a job lot from 'some feller over to Manchester'. Each working dawn, he would load this contraband on to his handcart, carefully hiding it by spreading a blanket over which he always placed his wife's ointments and medicines. When folk in the mill asked, 'And what does your old feller do?', she answered, as coolly as she could, 'He sells my herbs and other things on markets and the like.' Oh, Seamus sold things all right. Things that made their way as if by magic from Liverpool docks, things that got found before they were ever lost. Or before they were missed, that was more like it.

She shifted in the chair as the child kicked. Thank God for the man's drunkenness at least, because she'd managed to filch enough from his pockets as he slept, a sum sufficient to preclude immediate worry about rent and food. He'd never a notion of how much or how little money he had, so she'd taken advantage of this particular stupidity. Over months, her store had grown to almost forty pounds which she'd hidden in a small box behind a loose brick in the wash-house. So, for a while at least, she would manage.

The noise in the street started up again. In and out of one another's homes by the minute, they were. Pity they'd nothing better to occupy themselves . . . But no, there was a different quality to the commotion this time, the sound of fear interspersed with shrieks of panic and desperation. Whatever was going on at all? Still, she'd herself to see to, a fire to light, an unborn baby to feed . . .

Someone tapped hesitantly at the door. 'Missus? You in there?'

17

She leaned forward and gripped the arms of her chair. 'Who is it?'

'Come out, Missus! Old Mother Blue's gone missing again, likely up to her armpits in gin, shouldn't wonder. We need some doctoring!'

She strode across the room and threw open the door. 'Then fetch the doctor, child.'

A pair of dark brown eyes stared out of a pale, underfed face. 'We've not paid doctor's man for weeks,' mumbled the boy. 'And we can't find Mother Blue.'

Philomena folded her arms across her chest. Oh yes, she knew of Mother Blue, right enough. A filthy old woman with a black cloth bag who went from door to door 'doctoring'. The drunken fool in her navy straw poke bonnet caused many a mischief, going straight from laying-out to childbed with her hands unwashed, the nails decorated by rims of dirt, her numerous layers of stained clothing reeking of sickroom smells. 'Then why do you come for me, boy? Answer, for I shall not bite. Though I'm still in want of a supper.' She attempted a smile. 'Why me?'

He swallowed, glancing over his shoulder towards a house across the street. 'Because . . . because you're a . . . a . . . wi—We know you make cures and that . . . Because me mam says as how you know things, like.'

'I do. Sure enough, I know things. We all know things, don't we now? But I'm not a witch, son—'

'I never said—'

'Indeed, you didn't. You didn't say a thing. So, let's away and see what's to be done just now.'

She took the startled child's hand and led him home. The smell at the front door was enough to confirm her worst fears. How many more would perish of this dreaded summer sickness and May not yet over? The room was crowded with inquisitive neighbours and family members. Philomena pushed her way through to the couch where a pale woman lay, legs drawn up to her chest with cramp. A clawlike hand reached out. 'Can anyone help me? The baby gone with it, now it's taking me . . . '

'What has she eaten?' The whole room fell silent as soon as Philomena spoke.

'Pobs,' replied the little boy.

'Bread and milk? Holy Mother . . . Look child, how many are you in the house?'

'Seven with me dad.'

'Then the six of you will remain upstairs except when it is unavoidable. Stay out of this room.' She turned to face the small crowd. 'Will one of you go into my house and fetch my fly killer? It's an odd contraption made by my husband – a sort of rubber ball fastened to a stone jam jar. Don't spill the contents on your skin. And I suggest that the rest of you go out of this place and pray.'

The visitors turned to leave, but she continued to shout after them, 'Clean your drains every day, kill flies and burn old food. Put fire ashes down the closet morning and night . . .'

They were gone, melted into the dusk. Grimly, she rolled up her sleeves and set to work, washing the fevered woman on the couch, boiling a pan of water for drinking after it was cooled, searching dingy cupboards for necessary ingredients, then finally laying-out the tiny corpse of a baby girl.

She turned from these unpalatable tasks to find Edie Dobson standing behind her.

'I've . . . er . . . fetched your contraption, Mrs Maguire.'

'Thank you.' Philomena took the item, a crude spray made up of tubes, jar and metal funnel. 'It's a bit hit and miss, but it kills a fair few of them.' And she squirted the vile-smelling droplets into the room. ' 'Tis the flies bring the illness, Mrs Dobson. And in your condition, you had better be going home.'

'But . . . what about you?'

'I've had a touch of it, so I hope I'm still fighting. The mill, you see. I keep the house clean, but the spinning room's a breeding place for this sort of thing. And I'm strong, Mrs Dobson. How many babies have you lost? Didn't you give up your place at the loom to carry this one?'

'Aye. But I didn't know you knew . . .'

'I hear things, I'm not deaf. But let me tell you now – if

19

you want that child in your belly to thrive, keep Mother Blue out of your house.' She turned to stare at the writhing figure on the couch. 'The old woman delivered this last one, I believe. And I've no doubt she killed it too.'

'I'd . . . best be off, then.'

Philomena followed her neighbour to the door. 'Leave some things on the step for me, would you? Go into my kitchen and fetch pearl barley, some lime water and the arrowroot. I shall be here till morning.'

Edie Dobson turned on the pavement. 'But what about your work, Mrs Maguire?'

'Ah, no matter. I've been up many a night at a calf-birthing and with my own mother's labours too. There's no rest for the wicked, is there now?'

'Right enough.' Edie paused and studied this odd, tall person who had been labelled 'queer' and 'witch'. 'Only you're not wicked, are you?'

Philomena smiled. 'Ask my husband – if you can find him. Good night now.'

She sat for an hour with the delirious patient, spooning drops of boiled water between parched lips to prevent a total drying out. With no outward sign of revulsion, she cleaned away the constant messes and sponged the fevered body with cool cloths. At eight o'clock, she went to the foot of the stairs. 'Master?' she called. The man of the house, a thin, sad-faced creature, presented himself on the small landing. 'I've placed a pan of boiled water on the stairs. You and the children will drink from it. If it tastes a bit sour, sure that's only a drop of lime added in. You will eat nothing for two days.'

'What about me work?'

She shrugged her shoulders. 'If you want to give this sickness to your fellow men, then I cannot stop you.'

'And the kiddies are clemmed – can't they have some bread and milk?'

'Not before Wednesday night. And no milk at all this week, for milk can be a killer. But a body never died for two days without nourishment. Keep the closet clean and let me know if anyone else becomes ill.' She closed the stairway door firmly.

It was an endless night and from time to time it looked as if all might be lost, for the wretched soul on the couch had few resources to call upon. Malnourishment and poor housing had left her weak, while recent childbirth had also taken its inevitable toll. But by morning the fever had broken and a transparent hand reached out gratefully to encircle the visitor's wrist. 'I'm reet now. I'll not forget thee, Missus. You've saved me, God knows.'

'Not yet, I haven't. You're still weak as a kitten from childbed. Now, listen to me carefully. See these three cups? This is all you can have today. This large one is plain boiled water – take as much of that as you can hold. Then I've brewed up some pearl barley and here's a nice lime drink. No food at all, especially milk. I'll be back to see you after work.'

Philomena Maguire made her weary way across the street. It was five-fifteen and her shift would begin at six. When she opened the front door her breath was taken away by what she saw. A small fire burned in the grate, the copper kettle bubbled on the hob while the table was set with bread and Lancashire cheese for breakfast. She sank on to a chair, tears coursing freely down her cheeks. How did they know that the woman had survived? Ah yes, news soaked through walls in this street. If you sneezed twice, the clogger at the other end would get to know.

The front door opened and Edie Dobson's head poked through the gap. 'Are you alreet, lass?'

She dried her streaming eyes. 'Yes, thank you.'

'Don't fret thyself, for we shall see you right, Missus. "Pey" Peter's going to take you to work on his cart, save you walking. Can I come in?'

'No! I've the disease on my clothes.'

'Oh.' The young woman hesitated before continuing. 'I'll be baking today, later on, like. Will tatie pie and peas do you a supper? Only I know you'll be busy seeing to Mrs Critchley . . .'

'Mrs Who?'

'The lass you've been all night with! Eeh, to think you've likely saved her life without knowing her name!'

21

'Death and illness don't know any names, Mrs Dobson. And I'll be glad of your pie, just as I'm grateful for this.' She waved an arm towards the fire. 'The . . . the baby's body is in a box in the back yard. I meant no disrespect, only to save the rest of them . . .'

'Aye. It'll all get seen to, don't you fret. No need for tears, Mrs Maguire.'

'My name's Philly.'

'Is it? Like a young horse?'

'Yes. Like a young horse.'

'Bet you feel ninety this morning though, eh? I'm Edie, by the way.'

'I know.'

'Oh.' The small round face broke into a hesitant smile. 'I'd best get going, then. See you later, eh?'

'Yes. See you later.'

As she stripped off her clothes for a wash in the scullery, Philly Maguire found herself humming quietly in spite of tiredness and the sound shocked her to the core. Singing? When did she last have a tune in her? She looked round the whitewashed brick walls and all along the shelves where her bottles and jars sat. And in that moment, she recognized that she was happy because she was at home. Philly belonged, would make a place for herself. For the first time since her marriage, she had stopped feeling alone.

The morning was long, tiring and tedious. By the time eight o'clock arrived with its half-hour breakfast break, Philomena was too exhausted to eat her meal of bread and butter. Everyone else sat round the edges of the room, some on skips, others on the floor, eating their food on the oil-covered boards, using as tools fingers thick with heavy yellow grease. Her stomach heaved and she made a mad dash for the toilet. There was only one on each floor, so she was forced to stand and gag while others took their turn. When at last she closed the door and relieved herself, she noticed, not for the first time, the degree of infestation in the tiny room. A particularly vile type of cockroach – a strange and unusually huge beast – patrolled this area in vast numbers and she

22

reached for the worn-out brush that had been placed here to keep these foragers at bay. It wasn't right, any of it. Fifty-five and a half hours a week she worked in this place for a few paltry shillings, out of which sum she was forced to pay her little- and side-piecers, children who would break their backs for a chance of an extra penny. For what hellish reason? For them all to finish up sick or dead, killed off by accident or by disease carried on the backs of rodents and other vermin?

During the rest of that morning, Philly looked at the spinning room with newly opened eyes. Twelve-year-old half-timers slid about in thick oil, bare-feet skating to keep up with the work. From time to time a shrivelled little-piecer with the body of an infant and the face of an old man ducked under a mule with brush and wiper to clean, bent over double so as not to break the precious ends of cotton. Although she was paid by the draw, which meant she depended for her living on how many times her mule opened and closed, she deliberately slowed herself down to look around. It was a waking nightmare of dirt, noise, heat and damp.

Then, just before the dinner hooter was due, a minder across the room trapped his piecer when the mule returned to its creel. No screams were heard above the deafening noise of machinery, yet some instinct told everyone that something was amiss. Work stopped as the limp child was carried out in the minder's arms, then resumed as soon as the drama was over. With a living to earn and piecers to pay, no spinner could pause for more than a minute. Within half an hour, the child had been replaced and life continued as if the incident had never occurred.

When the dinner break sounded, Philly stopped her mule and walked over to the accident site. 'How is he?' she asked.

The man shrugged thick shoulders. 'Alreet. Lost a finger, though. I've had a look round, can't seem to lay me hand on it at all.' He grinned crudely. 'I'd have a job to find it round here, wouldn't I? Never mind, the mice'll happen get a good supper . . . '

She delivered a resounding slap to the side of his surprised face. 'I see it,' she said. 'And it will be eaten by no mouse.'

23

Philly stalked out of the room, her heart pounding loudly. Well, today was as good a time as any other to leave this infernal place, she reckoned. Boldly, she hammered on the manager's door.

'Come,' boomed a loud voice.

She entered the small office only to find no less a person than Mr Richard Swainbank himself, mill owner, landlord, gentleman farmer and respected citizen of these parts. He sat at the large desk, thumbs in waistcoat pockets, heavy gold chain across his chest, a diamond pin securing his silk tie. She took in all the trappings, the shiny black hat on the table, a silver-headed cane leaning against bookshelves, a pair of handsome grey kid gloves tossed carelessly on to a chair.

She hesitated fractionally, her hand resting on the door knob. Swainbank was a quantity relatively unknown, a being that passed occasionally through the spinning room with a time-piece in its hand. A spectator. A creature that escaped frequently to fresher and cooler air. This was a hard man, one whose supposedly regal posture commanded immediate respect and unquestioning obedience.

'Well?' he asked, a straight eyebrow raised towards thick brown hair. 'What can I do for you?'

With a bravado fed by anger, she fixed her eyes on him, although her knees seemed to have gone to jelly. The cotton barons of Bolton were a breed apart, a breed that defied both description and explanation. Here sat a gentleman who was not a gentleman, a monied person who owned lands and cattle without ever touching plough or feedbag. Yet his vowels were often as flat as those of any winder, while his manner fell far short of the genteel. What was he, then? A self-made man? No. His money was old, passed down along the line from earlier generations of mill tyrants. But this man of means had been known to roll up his sleeves a time or two during epidemics, could kick a mechanical mule to life when every engineer in the town had signed its death certificate. Aye. She nodded slightly. Himself would work the mills until the day he died . . . A self-made gentleman? Was such a creature a possibility, even a fact? He was, she concluded with an almost imperceptible shrug, an improbability . . .

'What is it you want?' He folded his arms and leaned back in the chair.

It was the edge to his words that thrust her forward, propelled her through the space between door and desk. The tone, the very cadence of his voice, that mixture of superiority, condescension and . . . and amusement! With grim determination, she stared into eyes as black as hell itself, irises of a brown so dark as to leave the pupils unremarkable. Richard Swainbank was a man of great beauty, the sort of beauty that went beyond the merely handsome. In spite of more than forty summers, his face remained unmarked by time, while the odd combination of colourings with which he was endowed set him even further apart from the general run. Hair and whiskers were fair to mid-brown, while lashes and eyebrows echoed the darkness they so clearly framed. But Philly was not impressed by such arresting packaging.

'Well?' he asked impatiently.

Her hackles were fully risen by this time. He was known far and wide for his tantrums, was Mr Swainbank, had never been averse to on-the-spot sackings or wage dockings. But she didn't care, didn't choose to care! Straightening her shoulders, Philly slapped the grisly parcel on to his desk where, lying between inkstand and blotter, it slowly unwound to reveal the sad contents.

'I expected the manager, but I suppose you'll have to do. That, Mr Swainbank, is a severed finger. The child to whom it was recently attached is twelve years old with ricketty legs and not a pick of flesh to his bones . . .'

'Bloody hell!' He returned the woman's furious stare. She talked as if she were educated, as if she imagined herself to be his equal! 'And what, pray, would you have me do with this item? Shall I use it as a paperweight? If the damn fool lad can't run fast enough to save his hands, then he's no use to me!'

She leaned forward, tightly clenched fists pressing against the edge of the desk. 'You can shove it, Mr Swainbank!'

'Pardon?' The second eyebrow joined its twin.

'You heard me sure enough! Shove that and the job up your waistcoat front!'

He fought a chuckle that rumbled ominously in the region of his chest. What a fighter, eh?

'The poor boy is no use to anyone from this day! And that is your fault!' After a moment or two, she added a derogatory 'Sir' to this shouted accusation.

His whole countenance was suddenly darkened by a rush of colour as he jumped to his feet. 'Get out of here, Mrs . . . Mrs . . . '

'Maguire,' she spat. 'I was going anyway for my health's sake. This place is teeming with disease – do you hear? Tics, fleas, rats, mice, cockroaches as big as horses . . . '

'Silence!' He held up a large hand and she studied a heavy gold cufflink that peeped out beneath the sleeve of his jacket.

'All right then,' she whispered. 'Silence me, why don't you? I'm used to it, so I am, for me husband tried often enough – too often for his own good . . . ' Her voice was rising now, quickening in tempo, keeping pace with the temper that had long plagued her, a temper that would, according to her family at least, be her downfall one day.

'And so he should try!' shouted Swainbank. 'With you in the house, he'd need the patience of a saint!'

'He's not in my house any more. I have ways of ridding myself of vermin!'

They stared at one another for several moments of crackling tension.

'So have I!' he yelled now. 'Full name?'

'Philomena Theresa Maguire,' she replied at the top of her not inconsiderable vocal powers.

'Address?'

'34 Delia Street.'

'Good!' He glanced across at the workers' register which lay on top of the bookcase. 'You will be struck off the list as from this noon.'

'Ah no!' She wagged a finger dangerously near to the end of his nose. 'You will not strike me off, Mister, for I came in here just now to withdraw without notice!'

'Excellent. I don't need your kind here, Mrs Maguire. Barging around as if you own the place . . .'

'Own it? Own it? God help me, I live in it except when I'm asleep – which is more than you do!'

His pulses were racing erratically as he slumped back into the chair. It wasn't just her appearance, though that alone would have made her special in spite of her advanced pregnancy. No. It was something else, something beyond those intelligent blue eyes, that pale smooth skin, the fine high cheekbones, the glossy raven's wing sweep of her hair. This was a woman, a real woman with the ability to warm a room simply by being in it. She was magnificent. Insubordinate, out of order, uncontrollable and bloody magnificent!

'And keep off the port!' she snapped wickedly. 'It's killing you, all that good living. Here we die of starvation. Up on the moors, you're seeing yourselves off by over-indulging. From the colour of your face just now, I'd say you've ten years at best left, Mr Swainbank. And a good riddance too!'

'You . . . little . . . bitch!'

She laughed heartily at this and he marvelled at such a courageous display of nonchalance. 'I'm not little, Mister. And I'm no female dog to be running at your heel! Well now, did I upset you by answering back, by sticking out for me own rights? Isn't that a desperate shame?'

'You'll never work in this town again!'

'Away with your bother! I can take care of meself, Mister!' She marched to the door then turned, hands on hips, eyes flashing blue fire. 'A curse on you and yours, Mr Swainbank! And I bid you the worst of days.' She nodded slowly. 'I hope you live to rue setting eyes on me. But I suspect that you will not survive long enough!'

She slammed the heavy door behind her.

Richard Swainbank reached for his cane and threw it across the room. Bloody woman! How dare she? How dare she walk in here like the Queen of Egypt with all the colours of the Nile reflected in her eyes and . . . Oh, damn her! He rose stiffly and stared into a small mirror between the two high windows.

27

How would she look with the hair uncoiled? With a mighty roar, he turned and swept everything off the desk, his eyes fixed to a small bloody bundle as it tumbled across the floor. Fifty pounds. He would find the damned lad and give him fifty, that would be enough . . .

Philly stood on the landing, a hand pressed against the wall as she fought for air. He was wicked, the devil incarnate, so he was . . . Not one jot did he care for anyone, not for the poor lad with his finger gone, not for the sickly folk who forced themselves daily into this place of endless drudgery. Behind her he crashed about the room and she allowed herself a tight smile of triumph. He was off the horse for a minute or two and she must take credit for having unseated him.

The door flew open. 'Mrs Maguire?'

'Yes?' She quickly raised herself into an upright and steady position.

'Er . . . ' His eyes wandered down the stairwell while he pulled at his waistcoat, then he passed a hesitant hand through the mop of dishevelled hair. 'What . . . er . . . what'll you do?'

Philly put her head on one side while she studied his obvious discomfort. 'What do you mean?'

'Well . . . er . . . husband gone and . . . and . . . '

'Baby coming?' Her tone, in direct contrast to his deepening blush, was light. 'I shall take care of meself, Mr Swainbank.'

He thrust a large hand at her. 'Here,' he barked. 'Take it. It's what's due in wages and a bit on top – get yourself a perambulator or some such article . . . '

Her jaw must have been hanging open, for she heard it shut with a snap as she inhaled deeply. Was he going soft? Wages when she was walking out? Wages after she'd told him what he could do with his blessed job?

'Take it!' he snapped. 'I don't dole out spare cash every day of the week.'

Slowly she reached out and accepted the proffered notes and coins, her eyes widening as she realized that there must be all of six or seven pounds here. 'It's . . . it's charity,' she heard herself saying.

28

'If it's charity, then it's bloody history in the making too,' he replied with sarcasm in his tone. 'I'm not noted for good deeds. I shall see to the lad, him that lost the finger.' He stared at her for a moment or two, then, after walking back into the office, slammed the door firmly home.

Philly counted the money, placed what was due to her in a pocket, then posted the remainder through the brass letter-box in the office door. His curses were audible above the sound of dropping coins, yet he made no move towards the stairs. Again she smiled grimly. She would take what was owed, no more than that. If the man was feeling generous, he could give this small amount to some deserving cause. She turned away, a sudden sadness invading her heart, a new weakness making her catch her breath as anger evaporated. What was this picture in her mind? His eyes . . . so . . . so full of grief and . . . and was that loneliness? Still, he deserved to be lonely. No! She must not pity him, must not feel grateful or indebted! These wages she had sweated for, this money she would keep!

After composing herself, Philly descended the stairs until she was out in the open air. Across the mill yard, she caught sight of her own piecers on their way to half-time school. They ran to her side. 'What's up, Mrs Maguire?'

'I'm off for good. Tell the afternoon lads, will you? I shan't be back.'

'Aw, Missus. You were a good minder, sixpence extra we always got!'

'You know where I live. Take care of yourselves now!' She watched the weary boys as they made their way towards school where, no doubt, they would be severely beaten at some stage for sleeping at their desks after six long hours in the mill.

All afternoon, she wandered aimlessly about the town. In less than twenty-four hours, her life had changed completely. Seamus was gone for good, of that she felt sure. Now she'd thrown away her job, slapped it on the table with that poor little mite's finger – dear God, whatever next? Yes, she knew what next. It had to be done and she was the one to do it. Might as well get it all over in the one day.

After checking Bessie Critchley's progress, she ate a tasty meal brought in from Mrs Dobson's kitchen, then changed into one of her two good dresses, a soft ankle-length grey that wouldn't quite fasten because of her increased girth. To hide this gap, she picked a soft shawl from the drawer and folded it around her shoulders, pinning the edges together with the tiger's eyes brooch given her by Uncle Porrick many years ago. She smiled as she fastened the stiff clasp. Uncle Porrick had always been her favourite man, while she was his 'best girl'. He'd taken the brooch from a leprechaun, or so he always insisted – especially when his tongue was loosened by poteen. Ah well. If the stone really did have magic powers, which she sorely doubted, then she would need its help tonight!

Philly had never been in a public house before, so it was not without trepidation that she approached the Bull. A nauseating smell of stale beer hung in the air outside the two entrances and she hesitated before choosing which door to use. The flagged vault with its ever-open door did not seem the right place somehow, so she chose the door leading to two others marked 'Open Bar' and 'Bar Parlour'. She studied these legends for several minutes before making a decision. The door on the right was quite ornate, seemed a more likely place for a woman, so she entered and was surprised to find a pleasant room, thickly carpeted and with an open fireplace covered by a large brass fire screen. No-one occupied any of the seats. Philly made for the bar where a small woman was polishing glasses. 'Yes?' asked this red-faced female. 'What's your pleasure, Missus?'

'Well, I don't want a drink, thank you.'

'Really?' A sarcastic smile broadened the tiny features. 'This is a pub, love. Usually, folk what come in here want a drop of something or other.'

'I'm looking for somebody.'

'Missing persons? Try the police, dear . . . '

Philly bridled. 'I am looking for an elderly woman who calls herself Mother Blue. I don't know where she lives, so I came here.'

The woman placed glass and cloth on the counter, then beckoned Philly to come nearer. Dropping her voice as if the room were full, she mouthed silently, 'In the vault, love. She's as drunk as a bucket of tiddlers. Aye, I'm not surprised you don't know where she lives. Never goes home till closing, spends many a night rough, I reckon. If you'd take her off our hands, we'd be grateful . . .'

'I just want to see her. It's important.'

'Well, you'll have to go outside again. There's no public entrance to the vault from in here. You see, we keep the vault separate on account of it being a bit on the loud side.'

Philly thanked the woman, then went out into the street. Picking up her skirts, she entered the smoke-filled vault, a long narrow room with a single bench running round its edge. Sawdust and half a dozen strategically placed spittoons decorated the crude floor.

A foul-smelling man threw a heavy arm about her shoulders. ' 'Tha's what we need in here,' he muttered drunkenly. 'Bit o' class, bit o' good looking stuff.'

She pushed him away impatiently and drew herself up to her full height. 'I want to see Mother Blue,' she announced loudly. 'And unless you keep your hands to yourself, you'll be in the gutter a little earlier than usual!'

Silence descended on the room. Philly walked to the corner where the old woman lolled against a wall. 'Are you Mother Blue?'

'I am. Get us a gin, lass.'

'Get your own.'

The men gathered in a long line against the high bar. One of the main sources of amusement was women-fights, though they usually had to wait till Saturday for a good one. There again, old Blue was in no state, while this one had an unfair advantage, a hefty lass, she was. Some who recognized Philly slunk towards the door and watched from a safe distance. She'd sorted her old feller out more than once, the size of her.

Philly cleared her throat. 'You are spreading disease and death around School Hill, Missus. Your clothes are filthy and you take no care of those who pay for your services.'

31

'You what? You bloody what?' The old hag struggled to stand. 'How many in here were brought into the world by me, eh?'

'And how many died?'

Mother Blue swayed on uncertain feet. 'Aye well. There's always the odd one . . .'

'Yes! Especially when you go from the dead to the newborn without a wash! And when you carry fever on your hands and in your skirts. Bessie Critchley's baby died last night and where were you? In here drinking what the poor woman had paid you. Well, if I see you in my street again, I'll put my toe to you, that I will!'

'Oh aye? You and whose bloody army?'

'I shan't need any help, Missus. You're so near gone with drink, I reckon I could blow you over with a single breath! Just stay away from School Hill if you know what's good for you!'

With a strength that belied her obvious age, Mother Blue threw herself upon the intruder, fingers gripping hard on to Philly's coiled hair. Using just one hand, the younger woman lifted Mother off her feet, holding her in a vice-like grip for several seconds. With a yell of surprise, the old girl released her hold on Philly's head and found herself hurtling through the air and back on to the bench.

Philly dusted her hands together. 'Pick somebody your own size in the future,' she said quietly. 'And when the next baby dies, I'll be along for you, so watch your step.'

A loud guffawing laugh came from the throat of one of the men. 'No wonder her always wears t' bloody bonnet! Look, lads. Bald as a babby's bum!'

Mother Blue reached for her dangling hat and crammed it on to her head. In spite of all the gin she'd consumed, she knew her shame, recognized that her secret was finally out. 'I'll get thee,' she spat.

'Not if I see you first!'

Philly picked her way out on to the pavement while the men applauded loudly. As usual, news travelled on winged heels and by the time she reached home, quite a reception party had gathered near to her house.

'Were she really bald, Missus?'

'Did she curse thee? I'll bet your ears are fair ringing . . . '

'We got it after she come to our house. We all had it . . . '

'What's that you said about putting ashes down the netty?'

She held up her hand and voices were stilled as if by magic. For an awful moment, she didn't know what to say. Every eye was on her and she felt the colour rushing to her cheeks. 'I'm . . . I'm not much for talking . . . '

'Aye – we noticed!' The ensuing laughter made her easier.

'Though me mammy always said I'd talk the four legs off a table once I start. I . . . er . . . I have not been a good neighbour. But I've had me troubles and those particular troubles meant I had to keep meself to meself.'

'That's alreet, lass.' Skenning Freddie stepped forward, hammer still clutched in his hand. 'Only you'd best find your tongue, 'cos I've three full sets and one broken bottom waiting. They go through good clogs like a hot knife through butter round here.'

The crowd grew as Philly spoke. 'The flies go straight from privy pails on to your table. You'll find them particularly active after the night soil men have disturbed them by emptying the closets. The creatures are very taken by rotting food, so burn all you don't eat, any fruit that's marked. Keep milk cold and don't drink even good milk if the sickness gets you. With ashed-down pails, there'll be less soils for the flies to reach and they'll go off elsewhere to breed. If one of you can read and write, we can make a list of things to do against the summer sickness.'

'Have you got medicines for it?'

'I have, though 'tis better not to get the disease in the first place.'

A woman at the back spoke up. 'How come you know all this, eh? Where did you learn if you don't know your letters?'

Philly turned her steady gaze upon the questioner. 'From my granny. We'd no doctor for many a mile, so we found our own ways of keeping well. I use plants and oils, things I buy from the herbalist and some I grow myself. The main thing is not to get ill in the first place, which is why I keep telling you about the flies. They carry scarlet fever, diphtheria, consumption and even the typhoid fever.'

The small crowd muttered and mumbled for a while, then Edie Dobson was pushed forward as spokesperson. 'She was all we had, was Mother Blue. Some can't afford to be paying doctor bills all the while. Who'll see to our birthings and our dead? Will you?'

Philly nodded her dark head. 'I will. Indeed, I will.'

'And if you're at your work?'

'I'm finished at the mill. My living will be earned now by making and selling cures. You saw how I nursed Mrs Critchley, so tell your friends that Mother Blue is finished.'

Edie grinned. 'And Mother Maguire is just starting?'

Philly's brow creased into a frown. 'No. I don't like that. Let me see . . . ' She paced about the flags in front of her door. 'I know I'm a bit young for it, but I shall be called Ma Maguire. Yes, that has a good ring to it. Tell them all to come and buy Ma Maguire's tonics and cures . . . '

So Ma Maguire it was.

Edie Dobson stood in the middle of the floor brandishing a large wooden spoon in the air. 'It won't come right, Philly! Matter what I do, it's all curdled.'

'Oh, for heaven's sakes, beat it, woman! Stand it in cold water and hit it round the bowl. Let me look.' She peered into the earthenware dish. 'Ah well. If all else fails, we look to have dumplings for supper. Put a bit more of the powder in, that'll perhaps bind the oils. And don't be worrying, it's only for chapped hands – I'm not asking you to cure the plague of London single-handed. Now, where did I put me nipbone?'

By the end of the evening, the two flushed women had a dresser covered in bottles and jars, each one labelled 'Ma Maguire's Cure' with specific instructions for use printed beneath. Philly stared at these markings. She knew jars and bottles by their shape, contents by colour and texture. It had been Edie's idea to put the labels on, every one hand printed by children who gladly took a penny for doing a couple of dozen.

They sat by the fire, each clutching a welcome mug of tea. 'It amazes me how they all read,' commented Philly. 'So young and so clever, they are.'

'Well, I can read a bit. Arthur's the one, though. He reads the paper out for me, tells me all the news. Mind, he's usually that weary after twelve hours down the pit . . . eeh, I wish he'd find summat else, Philly. It's dangerous work, is that. Years I've tried to have this baby and I don't want to finish up a widow. I want me child to have a father . . . nay, I'm sorry, lass. Thine won't have a dad, will it?'

'No. He won't have a father, that's for certain. Seamus Maguire will keep out of my way, sure enough. If I'd had one more day of his nonsense, I'd have gone for the police. Here we are, sitting on chairs either stolen or bought with bad money. But this little feller won't need a daddy.' She patted her belly.

'Still sure it's a lad?'

'Indeed. Just as I know yours is a daughter.'

'Margaret. Molly for short.'

'Patrick. No doubt Paddy, also for short.' She sighed and wriggled in the chair, trying to find a position that granted some comfort. 'We're near time now, Edie. And I don't know how I'd have managed without you these last weeks. All the years I lived here never knowing that my best friend was the other side of the wall.'

Edie chuckled loudly.

'What is it?'

'We all thought you were right peculiar – you know – a bit daft in the head. Some said you were a witch making spells, especially the kids. It was 'cos you never said nowt, just sailed by with your head in the air.'

'Ah well now, isn't that interesting? Me granny could lay a fair curse at your door – didn't she cause all Mick Mulligan's cows to dry up and his hens to go egg-bound? Nobody ever tangled with Granny because of her powers. And I'm the spitten image of her, so I could be a witch after all. Then there's me Uncle Porrick and the big dish. He left it out every night so's the little people could have a bit of a swim on his kitchen table. He got up one morning and found all these tiny wet footprints and a brooch which he gave to me. "Philly," he said. "If ever you're in trouble, turn to the brooch and the little people will come." ' She smiled at Edie, her head waving mockingly from side to side. 'So there I was with me nose in the air and many of you waiting for me to stumble, is that right?'

'Aye. Till you saved Bessie across the way and gave Mother Blue that rollocking. Her's out of business now, by all accounts. Begs for a living down town.'

'I know. I give her sixpence a week.'

'You what?' Edie sat bolt upright, or as upright as her bulging belly would allow. 'Whatever for?'

'I feel a bit guilty, sorry for her too. No doubt she drinks my sixpence, but it helps me keep my peace with God.'

'You're a right good woman, Philly Maguire. You'd never do nobody a badness, would you?'

A sharp rapping at the front door caused Edie to struggle to her feet. 'I'll let 'em in, lass. Time I were off anyroad.' She waddled across the room and lifted the latch. 'Philly!' she called over her shoulder.

'What is it?'

'It's a feller in uniform with a posh carriage and all.'

Philly rose carefully, a hand to her breast. Not the police! Surely after all these weeks . . . ? 'Bring him in, Edie.'

The man entered, clutching a braided cap to his chest. 'Are you Ma Maguire?'

'I am.'

'You make medicines?'

'Indeed.'

He moved awkwardly from foot to foot. 'It's the Master,' he said finally. 'Got a sore on his leg what the doctor can't shift. Only me mam works in one of the mills, said as how you've got some stuff for leg sores. It's just that . . . ' His eyes moved warily about the room as if he expected to be overheard and punished. 'He's past living with, Missus. I mentioned your cures to the cook and she had a word upstairs. The mistress says any port in a storm, like. So here I am.' His eyes swept over the row of new bottles. 'Give us something, please. Like a bear running mad, he is. We're all copping it, specially me, 'cos I take him everywhere. If I go too slow, he moans. If I hit a bump, he cracks me one across the ear'ole. We shall all get the push soon . . . '

Philly leaned heavily against the table. 'Is the sore wet?'

'Aye, I think so.'

'Yellow? Does it smell?'

'It does, even through his clothes it stinks to high heaven if the weather's on the warm side.'

She nodded slowly. 'Then it wants drying, not drawing. Tell him no baths unless he leaves the leg over the side and out of the water. I've a powder for this somewhere . . . ' She opened a dresser drawer. 'Here we are. Keep a clean dry dressing on and plenty of this. It likely can't be cured, but we might ease it.'

'Thanks, Missus.' He grabbed for the package but she held it back.

'Who is your master?' she asked quietly.

'Swainbank. Mr Richard Swainbank.'

'Is that right now? Did you hear that, Edie? Mr Swainbank's got a weeping leg.' She turned her attention to the man. 'That will be one guinea, please.'

'What?' He staggered back. 'A guinea for a bit of powder?'

'I should perhaps make it two. It's not a matter of powders, young man. It's a matter of mills full of cockroaches and children without fingers. Twenty-one shillings, please.' She held out her palm.

'You're a hard woman,' he said as money and parcel changed hands.

'Am I now? Well, when your master's in need of more powders, tell him to drop in and see me. Say I don't deal with servants. Nothing personal, nothing at all, for you're a fine credit to your mammy, so you are. I've just a notion to see your master and look what can I do for the leg. After all, I can hardly treat what I don't see. Understand?' She smiled grimly, casting her mind back to their last meeting, him behind the desk and her standing like a child awaiting the strap. Should they meet again, she'd have the upper hand and he could do the worrying!

He nodded, placed the powder in his pocket and the hat on his head, then said a curt farewell to both women.

As soon as he had left, Edie grabbed Philly's arm and burst into gales of laughter. 'Hey – what I said before . . . '

'What? Don't make me laugh, we'll both be in labour . . . '

'About . . . about you never doing a mischief . . . to nobody . . . '

'Well?'

'I take it back, Philly. Six weeks' rent money for a bit of powder?'

'The powder and the money were not the point, Edie . . . '

'I know! But I still take it back, though!'

As the time for her own delivery drew near, Philly cut down on her house-calls. Those in need of medicines came to her, while births and layings-out were temporarily taken care of by other neighbours after intense instruction. She was well satisfied with her own progress, for hadn't she always been as strong as an ox? But Edie worried her. At thirty-four, she was carrying her seventh baby, the only one to have gone full term. Philly knew that come what may, she had to be up and about for Edie's confinement.

She sat in her comfortable home one balmy August evening, a half-finished baby garment in her lap, thinking how lucky she was. Her home was beautiful by most standards, larger than the rest too, having an extra downstairs room called the parlour. This was seldom used, but it was good to know it was there all the same. Seamus' money remained untouched; the doctoring and selling of cures brought in enough to pay rent and food bills. Yes, she was just about happy, contented with her lot. How many women found a job they could do at home and a good neighbour to help in the business? Between them, she and Edie had a good thing going, a trade they could continue after both babies were safely born.

Then suddenly Arthur was at the door, his face white with fear except where the coal-dust had eaten its way into skin to

38

mark it for ever. 'She's started,' he gasped. 'I've put her on the sofa, for I'd never risk stairs with her like that. What shall I do?'

Philly struggled to her feet. 'Stay here and make some strong tea. And get yourself a large Irish out of the scullery whether you've signed the pledge or no.'

'But—'

'Ah, away with your butting! If you want occupying, black-lead my grate for me. It's no place for a man, Arthur. There's nothing you can do for her now.' Then she picked up her bag and ran as fast as her condition would allow.

When she entered next door, she found Edie squatting in front of the fire with the baby born in her hands. 'Just a couple of pains, Philly! That's all I had, just a couple!' She began to cry, her whole body heaving with great sobs of pure relief. Philly took the child and gently forced her friend to lie on the rug. It was a perfect girl, round and plump, pink and screaming fit to crack plaster on the walls.

As she finished cleaning mother and baby, Philly felt her own first stab of labour. But she paid little heed to the fierce warning in her back, for she had an afterbirth to deliver and a baby to put to breast. When all was completed to her satisfaction, she stroked Molly's downy head and looked down at her exhausted neighbour on the horsehair sofa. 'It's my turn now, Edie.'

'What?'

'I've started. And please apologise to Arthur, for my waters have soaked the rug.'

'Oh, Philly! Why didn't you tell me? Who's going to help you, lass?'

'Ah now, don't excite yourself. We Irish can give birth in a field and carry on picking praties, so we can. I'll help meself, Edie.'

It seemed a long way home, such a slow and painful journey that she might have counted one brick's width with every step. Once inside her kitchen, she grabbed Arthur. 'Listen to me now. You've a fine daughter and I'm just about to have a son to make the pair. But I'm not happy with this pain – it's too strong too early. I'm sorry to spoil your special day, but would you kindly go down for the doctor?' Then she fell in a dead faint at his feet.

The poor man didn't know where to turn first. He was desperate to see his wife and child, yet he had this woman on his hands and a doctor to fetch. He flew next door and looked at his daughter. 'She's bonny, Edie. Only I have to go for the doctor, see—'

'Why? We're all right—'

'Aye, but her next door isn't. Her's on the floor like a bundle of rags, white as a sheet too.'

'Run, Arthur!' Her voice cracked as she screamed, tears of fear and panic welling in her eyes. 'For God's sake, run!'

'I will, lass. Thanks for giving me such a grand babby . . . ' He grabbed his cap and fled.

Philly dragged herself across the floor while red-hot knives tore ruthlessly at her insides. She'd never had a child before, but she'd seen enough to know that this was all wrong. A terrible scream was wrung from her weakening body as the pain increased to an unbearable intensity. Mercifully, she knew no more until a dark shadow loomed over her. 'Doctor?' she managed.

'That's right, dear. Lie still now.'

'I can pay! I'll give you double if he lives!'

She felt herself being lifted on to the table, heard the doctor saying, 'Support her head, Mr Dobson.' Then a sweet smell entered her nose, choking her until she faded away to a place without pain.

She came to in her bed, the doctor perched beside her on the edge. He smiled kindly. 'Well now. There's a first for me and for you, young lady. I never delivered a child by surgical means on a kitchen table till today.'

Her head swam. 'Surgical means?'

'Your son was born by Caesarean section, Mrs Maguire. Just like the king of Rome was delivered.'

'You . . . cut him out of me?'

'I did. It was a first for Mr Dobson too. He made a grand

40

nursing assistant. If I ever need a good man in the operating room, I'll look for a coalminer.'

'But . . . but why?'

'Well, your baby was not coping too well. There were some signs of distress . . . '

'Distress? What went wrong?'

He patted her hand. 'Best not to dwell on that, I think. He's very small, Mrs Maguire.'

'Will he live?' Her hands gripped the sheet. 'Please say he'll live, for I'll have no more!'

'It would be unwise for you to have more. Shall I send in a nurse? You'll not be up to caring for him yourself for a time, not while you've stitches to heal.'

She nodded slowly, her mind still drunk with ether. 'Get a nurse. And give me my child.'

With trembling fingers she held the delicate infant. He was unbelievably tiny, far too small for the clothes she'd made. But he was breathing well and making some small effort at the breast. And in that moment, Philly fell in love for the first time in her life. Her lips moved in silent prayer to the Blessed Virgin. In spite of the acute pain in her abdomen, her only concern was that this small creature should survive. 'If I don't make it, Edie next door will have him. She knows his name and will rear him Catholic even though she hasn't the Faith. Aye, they can be raised as twins, for they have the same birthday. But this one will do his best to live,' she pronounced finally. 'He has my determination.'

An hour after the doctor had left, a nurse arrived. She was a kind and matronly figure, a woman obviously used to caring for babies. Philly handed her child into large, welcoming arms. 'Bring me the bottle of water from the table,' whispered the new mother. With sobs choking her voice, she baptized her infant son with this priest-blessed fluid. 'Patrick Joseph Maguire. In the name of the Father, the Son and the Holy Ghost.'

'Amen,' said the nurse. 'But there was no need, lass. We'll have him chasing girls in no time.'

Philly smiled weakly. 'Yes. But just in case, Nurse. Just in case . . . '

'All right, Mrs Maguire. Now, get some sleep and I'll mind the little feller . . . '

'Give him a drop of boiled water till my milk comes in . . . ' Her voice was fading.

'I know my job, love.'

Philly mustered enough final strength to fix the woman with a look of iron. 'And so do I. So mind him well.' Then she fell, exhausted and grey-faced, into a sleep that would last for many hours.

One of Philly's first visitors, once she was well enough to receive while still enthroned in her bed, was the chief reporter from the *Bolton Evening News*. The paper's real interest lay not so much in the events of recent days – many people endured and survived surgery in conditions that were less than sterile. But Ma Maguire's fame had spread like wildfire throughout and beyond School Hill. Wasn't this a healer, a woman of good sense and vision? Hadn't she cleaned up a slum almost single-handedly, didn't she make good medicines from simple weeds and herbs?

Ma answered the man's questions with her customary terseness, aware however that this small piece of advertising boded well for the future of her business. Her baby had lived. For him she must do the same. No. To survive would not be enough. For Patrick, she must make a decent living. And so, towards the end of the interview, she smiled pleasantly and offered advice for the paper's readership. The man left with a pot of balm for his wife's corns and a bottle of licorice-flavoured tonic to keep him awake at his desk. Philly fed her hungry baby and crooned a Gaelic lullaby. Everything was going to be fine, just great . . .

Dr Flynn arrived, black coat discarded in deference to the heat, shirt sleeves rolled, handkerchief mopping his wet brow. 'This is a stinker of a day,' he breathed. 'How's the wound?'

'Mending in spite of the weather,' she answered. 'And I tell you now, I am out of this bed tomorrow, Doctor. How many weeks am I here? Me legs feel like they don't belong to me any more!'

'You'll do as you're told,' he snapped with mock severity. 'You're lucky to be here at all.'

'Why?' Her face was serious now. 'Tell me why, for it is all beyond my understanding. I'm a fine big woman, strong as a carthorse – never a day did I ail till this. So why?'

Dr Flynn passed a wise eye over this intelligent though rather impatient patient. 'There was no alternative. The cord was around the child's neck and the afterbirth had separated from the wall of your womb.' Yes, he could tell her. Most women would cringe at such outspokenness, especially from a man. Matters as delicate as these were seldom discussed even among females; birthing was an event to be whispered about, a mystery to be kept securely shrouded and hidden. Though not from this lady . . .

'But . . . but . . . ' Philly's face was white. 'How did you know? How could you tell?'

'I couldn't,' he replied honestly. 'Not at first. But I knew you were dying, Mrs Maguire.'

'Dying?'

He nodded quickly. 'You were showing all the signs of going into a fit. Even if you had survived it, you might have suffered fits for the rest of your life. We lose a lot of mothers due to stressful pregnancy. I . . . we were just lucky. I recognized your symptoms. As for me-lad-o here, I'd no idea of his trouble until I actually got my hands on him.'

'Dear God! How can I ever thank you, Doctor Flynn?' She held out her hand and shook his outstretched fingers gravely. ' 'Twas a fine thing you did, a wonderful miracle.'

'After what you've managed with these people, Ma Maguire, it was no more than you deserved. For long enough I've handed out lectures on hygiene – might as well talk to myself. But you've got them on the straight and narrow. For that, I shall always be grateful.'

'Oh dear, Doctor—'

'What is it?'

She pulled her hand back and placed it against her cheek. 'The babies I've delivered and never a thought to this kind of carry-on. What if I get a mother like myself? How will I know?'

'You'll know. It's not a common condition.'

'Aye. Yes, yes, I suppose I have learned something. Out of every evil comes a little good, eh?' She sighed deeply and lay back on her pillows. 'So we nearly died, the both of us. Mind, he's fine now, screaming fit to burst when he's hungry. But to think that I was all right one minute and at death's door the next. It's a funny old world, is it not?'

'It certainly is.' He turned to leave, then hesitated in the doorway. 'By the way, I owe you for a couple of stomach powders. That's powerful medicine you make, Ma Maguire.'

She began to chuckle, a hand against her belly where the scar still stung. 'On the house, lad. And if you ever need doctoring, you know where to come.'

'Yes. Yes, I certainly do.'

Patrick Joseph Maguire was ruined from the day he was lifted gently into the world and placed in a padded wicker basket out of draughts and well out of danger. His birth had been without effort and he seemed to expect the rest of his life to continue in similar vein. He screamed when hungry, hot, cold, wet or dirty. After a while, he learned to scream when there was nothing to scream about, especially when Philly was busy at her chores. Each time she lifted the tiny infant from his cradle, she heard the words she'd spoken so often to new mothers, warnings about spoiling the child, about making a rod for a family's back. Yet she still lifted him, though all the while she suspected that he was seeking entertainment, that she was a mere plaything to while away boring hours and minutes. Thus she continued, a happy slave to his whims and fancies, forever guilty because she'd failed to give him a 'decent start'. He thrived beautifully, nourished frequently on breast milk and an over-abundance of love. And it wasn't just Philly's fault. Arthur Dobson, who had been present during the operation, made almost as much fuss of Patrick as he did of his own daughter. As the little boy grew and became stronger, he spent much of his time next door with his borrowed father. Edie watched all this and said little, though she worried for her friend. The lad had been born weak and sickly, but this ruination would reap its own reward in time. She felt no jealousy at Arthur's interest in the boy, for he lavished love in equal amounts on both children. But Edie took care not to spoil her daughter all the same. One screaming brat between the two houses was enough, in her opinion.

Christmas Eve found the women in the town centre, heavily laden baskets weighing down their arms. Carollers stood in small groups beneath lamps, sheet music clutched in gloved hands, candle-lanterns adding to meagre gas lights. Most of the shops would remain open till midnight or until all the stock was sold, so intelligent shoppers left their purchases to the last minute, hoping for a bargain as butchers off-loaded stock which might otherwise spoil during the holiday break.

Philly and Edie stopped to borrow some heat from a small boy's winter warmer, a punctured cocoa tin containing smouldering cotton waste and bits of twig. 'I hope Patrick's all right,' mumbled the taller woman.

'Give over,' snapped her companion. 'Arthur's good with him, you know that . . . '

'But I've never left him before . . . '

'Aye.' Edie pulled her shawl around her chilled head. 'Happen it's time you did leave him. They'll be getting somebody else to do the nursing jobs unless you shape. And what'll you live on then, eh? Fresh air? You can't fool me, lass. I know that husband of yours never sends you a brass farthing to chew on. So I reckon we'll need to be shifting ourselves come New Year, get the stocks made up again. I can mind the kiddies while you go round the houses.'

Philly stopped and placed her basket on thinly-frosted ground. 'I never knew I'd care so much, Edie. When I look at him, me heart fills up, so it does. You think . . . you think I care too much, don't you?'

The small, top-heavy figure of Edith Dobson rested itself against a shop window. 'We've both only the one chick, Philly. But that doesn't mean we must ruin the pair of them past recognizing. Every time he yells, you run like the wind. That lad plays you like an old piano – and you know it.'

45

'But he's only four months old—'

Edie nodded briskly. 'Aye. So's mine.'

'But Molly never ailed!'

'He's over the worst! Will you be shifting for him till he's twenty-one? Pull out of it, Philly. Apart from owt else, you've a living to earn. Anyroad, let's not spoil Christmas. We'll talk about this in a week or two.'

They made their way homeward past traders who had come out into the streets now, a greengrocer with cut-price apples and cabbages, a butcher giving away 'two chickens price of one'. Edie stopped to negotiate with the fishman whose dishes of cockles and mussels were going for a quarter of the normal price.

Philly walked to the corner while her friend haggled over herrings and finny haddy. As she sheltered from the bitter wind in a doorway, a smart carriage drove up slowly and stopped at the junction. A broad and well-dressed man climbed down carefully and stepped over icy cobbles until he reached the pavement. 'Mrs Maguire?' he asked, his voice full of strength and confidence.

'Yes. Who's that?'

'Swainbank.'

She looked straight into his eyes, for the two of them were much of a height, he carrying the advantage of a mere couple of inches. Even in the lamplight, his handsome face was clear enough, straight black brows, a strong nose, eyes as dark as treacle, moustache and beard trimmed to perfection. Yes, he was a good-looking feller. When he wasn't in a purple rage, at least.

'And to what do I owe this pleasure?' Even if she'd tried, she would never have kept the edge from her voice.

'I understand that you don't deal with servants?' His tone too was trimmed with ice.

'I like to attend my customers personally.'

'I see.' He leaned on a silver-topped cane and swept his eyes over her body. 'Quite a celebrity, then? I saw the piece in the *Evening News*—'

'Have you been following us?'

Unaccustomed to such a direct approach, he stepped back a fraction before replying gruffly, 'I need more powders.'

'I have none.'

'But at home – surely you have some there?'

'No.'

Swainbank stroked his beard thoughtfully. 'Will you be making more?'

She shrugged her shoulders lightly. 'That I can't say, Mr Swainbank. You see, I've more urgent things to see to, children with severe disorders because of poor diet, children whose mothers can't afford to feed them well. Wages, you understand. Never enough to go round. Then there's the odd mill accident, I have to attend to that sort of thing. There's a lot of death and illness around. Hardly surprising with the long hours of work, is it?'

He opened his mouth to speak, but she cut him off quickly. 'And they start work so young, don't they? No. I've more important things than leg sores to deal with—'

'Then give me the receipt—'

'The what?'

'The formula. I'll have it made up.'

She shook her head vigorously. 'Can't do that. Family secret, you see. Handed down over generations . . .'

He put his head on one side. 'And you don't have it written down because you can't write?' There was heavy sarcasm in his tone.

Philly grinned broadly. 'No, I can't write. Can you make medicines?' Her heart was crashing about in her chest like an unbroken pony, heaving and pounding wildly against her rib cage. She hated this man, hated everything he stood for. The coolness of her voice belied her real feelings, for she would never allow him the satisfaction of knowing how much he truly disturbed her. 'My friend is coming, Mr Swainbank. I'll bid you good night.'

'Mrs Maguire . . . please . . .'

She stared at him with as much contempt as she could manage to convey through the thickening darkness.

'Don't make me beg. I need the powders . . .'

Philly sighed deeply, watching the frosted cloud of exhaled breath as it hung in the chilled air. He was standing badly, obviously depending on the one leg. 'See me at my house the day after Christmas. And don't be leaving your fancy carriage at my door, for the neighbours have no time for your kind.'

She walked away and joined Edie who was struggling with yet another set of parcels. 'A bit of nice haddy there for breakfast. Who was that?'

'Swainbank. Don't stare at him, for goodness sake!'

'What's he want?'

'Powders. Keep walking.' They marched away at speed, Edie almost having to run to keep up with her slimmer and longer-legged friend. When they reached St George's Road, Edie dragged at Philly's sleeve and implored her to slow down. 'What the heck's got into you at all? Like a cat with its tail roasting, you are. I know we're going to no bloody funerals, but all the same there's no fires either. Have you never heard of pacing yourself? Me bloody arm's ready for dropping off here . . . '

'Well, don't you be letting Arthur hear you swearing. And him with the pledge signed too—'

'Oh, give over with your mithering! Stand still while I look at you.'

Philly came to a halt and faced her friend. 'Right. Not that you'll see much in this light . . . '

Edie pushed the larger woman along a few paces until they stood beneath a lamp. 'Aye. He's got you going, hasn't he?'

'What do you mean "got me going"? If you mean I'm angry, then you're right. He expects me to drop everything – Christmas shopping included – to see to his almighty leg. The gall of the man, the cheek of him, the impudence . . . Why are you nodding your head like that, Edith Dobson? You look like the doll I bought Molly for Christmas.'

'He's got his eye on you, hasn't he?'

'What? Who?'

'Him! Mr flaming posh-neck Swainbank! I can tell with your physog there's summat going on—'

'Edie! There is nothing going on. He wants powder for his

48

leg sore, no more and no less than that. Except that his very existence annoys me past bearing, which is why I'm a bit . . . over-excited.'

Edie bent down to rearrange the parcels in her baskets. 'If you say so,' she muttered between chattering teeth. 'By, it's gone cold. Happen you were right to move fast.' She picked up her burdens. 'Well? What are you standing there for like cheese at tuppence? You're likely not the first . . . '

Philly dragged herself after her neighbour who seemed to have found new strength after the brief pause. 'The first what, Edie?'

'The first one he's had an eye on.'

'Is that so? Well, he can take his eyes and leave them elsewhere. And what makes you think he's interested in me?'

Edie raised her face to heaven as if seeking patience and guidance. 'For a kick-off, I'm not as daft as I look – I know he followed us all through town. For another, it'd take more than a flaming sore leg to get you so riled. And for extra time, he's still following us.'

'He's not!'

'He is. Go on – look. I dare you!'

'I'm not looking!' She quickened her stride. 'I don't want to look.'

'Why? Frightened of encouraging him?'

They reached Edie's door and placed their parcels on the paving stones. Philly gave her friend a stern look. 'Edie. I am a married woman—'

'Aye. And he's a married man.'

'I'm a good Catholic . . . Edie! It's not like that! I hated him the day I gave my job up, I still hate him to this day . . . '

'And you a good Catholic? Doesn't it say summat about loving thy blinking neighbour?'

'He is not my neighbour! He's a mill owner and I don't even like him!'

Edie lifted the door latch. 'Cup of tea?' she asked, her green eyes twinkling with mischief. She leaned over so that her face was nearer to Philly's shoulder and in conspiratorial tone she added, 'He's got piles of money, lass.'

'Edith!' But it was too late. The door was open, the kettle was on and Arthur was sitting with the two babies. Philly turned to pick up the shopping and there he was on the corner, hat in hand, stick tucked under his arm. He made a deep bow. 'A happy Christmas, Ma Maguire,' he called before disappearing alongside Skenning Freddie's shop.

Philly paused, a hand to her throat. Edie was right. There was a lot more to this than flaming leg sores.

Richard Swainbank could never work out why Beatrice made such a damned great fuss at Christmas. The rest of the year she was as miserable as sin, a face on her like an old clock in urgent need of an overhaul. Her enforced gaiety during the festive season was a great source of bemusement to all concerned. Even the servants had the odd laugh behind their hands – he'd caught them at it. What the hell he'd ever seen in her . . . Too late for all that now, he supposed. And he had to admit, however begrudgingly, that he'd had a fair run for his money, avoiding marriage altogether till he was thirty-five. But he'd expected things to be a bit different from this, a sight more cheerful. After all, she was fifteen years his junior, ought to be full of life and raring to go. But at twenty-nine, Beatrice was about as attractive as a worn-out carthorse. Maternity had done nothing to improve her appearance or her disposition. Not that he minded disposition in a woman – oh no, he liked a bit of temper. But he could do without the cold silences and the disapproving looks, that was for sure.

He winced as his leg started to play up again, then smiled to himself at the thought of seeing that cheeky young madam tomorrow. Now, there was a woman he wouldn't mind waking up with, somebody who'd keep the home fires burning on a winter's night. Aye, there was little enough to come back to here, wasn't there? Well, Beatrice could stick to her headaches and her vapours, because he'd done his duty by the line, two sons reared safely and no need for any more. Thank God. He pulled a solid gold watch from his waistcoat and studied the time. At least the infernal church business was over with, all that shuffling about in the family pew while

Nanny tried to control boys of six and four, each with a marked distaste for confinement and a definite desire to remain with his Christmas toys.

Lunchtime. And that was another good laugh, because the lads would never sit through half a dozen courses even when there was company present. Inevitably, there would be just himself and Beatrice enjoying the seasonal fare, one at each end of the long table, nothing to say to one another beyond the odd comment about how well the table looked and what a nice meal. Servants would flit about trying to look busy, then they'd make off with the food and have a good party in the kitchen. Of course, tomorrow promised to be even more hilarious, because on the evening after Christmas, the staff sat down in the dining room while Beatrice served them and handed out useless gifts. Well, he'd be long enough gone by the time that particular fiasco started. He'd make some excuse and clear off before the fun got under way.

He walked towards the dining room, his heart made heavy by the prospect of the next hour or two. Eat, drink, play with the children. After which happy sequence he would be allowed to read while Beatrice did petit point or tapestry in an overheated drawing room where they must remain together for the whole day. This was the law at Christmas and he dared not break it. Yes, he did! By God, he did!

In spite of his heavy leg, he spent the afternoon in the grounds, declaring to his shocked wife that he needed to walk off the meal. He watched her flitting about in the drawing room window, her mouth narrowed into that familiar thin line. After nine years of marriage, he had broken some holy tradition and by his calculations, this would merit a month or two of vapours and headaches. Ah well, to hell with her, he'd sooner bed down with the dogs and horses in the stables.

He sat on a low wall at the end of the terrace and surveyed his domain. Not quite as grand as Smithills Hall, but it was a fair enough statement of his wealth and success. The front of the house was of grey stone, very wide and imposing, six broad steps up to double front doors, six tallish windows to each side, pleasing in its symmetry. Ten bedrooms, two modern bathrooms, enough space to get lost in when avoiding a vinegary wife. Chase Farm at the back was also Swainbank property, tenanted and supervised by a dependable family. He should be happy with his lot in life, should rejoice in all this comfort and splendour. He leaned heavily on his cane as he struggled to rise. Happy? How could any man be happy while so damned lonely? This was Christmas, a time for merriment and togetherness, for fun and laughter. He inhaled deeply and turned to look at his vast garden, feeling even more isolated among its frost-crisped expanse of lawn and shrub. No man should be alone at Christmas. No man should reach the age of forty-four and still feel so desolate. Aye well. He had better go in and do his duty by the children. If only they would hurry and grow up! He'd little time for infant games, took no interest in the tedious milestones of childhood, teething, crawling, walking, speaking.

Beatrice looked up as he entered the stifling room. Her narrow face was grim. Even on this special day, the one time in the year when she tried to make some sort of effort, her bitterness shone through the thin veneer of bonhommie. To think that he would go outside alone on Christmas day! Whatever would the servants make of that?

He looked long and hard at her. To be as fair as he could manage, he had to admit feeling slightly sorry for Beatrice. He wasn't the best husband, wasn't often home when needed. She'd come from a country estate in Cheshire, born of a good but impoverished family with some remote connection to nobility. And he'd taken her on because the rest of the females had been good breeders. Aye. He dropped into an armchair. He'd bought carefully, chosen her just as he'd have picked a good brood mare. She'd not been bitter then, had she? His head drooped slightly as he tried to remember. But no, there remained no image, no concept of the girl he had led up the aisle such a comparatively short time ago.

'I'm a bit rough and ready for you, Beatrice, aren't I?'

She dropped her needlework, a look of astonishment invading her pallid features. 'Pardon?'

'I was just thinking while I walked – we're not really suited, you and I.'

She swallowed delicately, a hand to her thin throat. He'd never talked like this before, never a word about suitability. Or love. 'What are you trying to say, Richard?' Nervous fingers plucked at the threads in her lap.

'We should never have married. I don't like seeing anybody so downcast, let alone my own wife. It's with me being trade and you being gentry, I suppose. They'd no money, your lot, but they had class, you see. As for me – well, I dare say we'll never make a silk purse out of a sow's ear . . .'

'Richard!' She jumped to her feet, embroidery frame and cottons tumbling on to the carpet. 'This is Christmas—'

'I know. I just want the air cleared and I reckon Christmas is as good a time as any. We're coming to the end of a year, starting another . . . I think it's time we swept a few cobwebs out. I'm grateful for the two lads, glad you gave this house a future. But we don't love one another, do we? Be honest, Beatrice.'

'Honest? What would you know about honesty? How many . . . ?' She bit back the rest of this sentence before she went too far.

'How many women?' His voice was almost a whisper. 'One or two, that's about the size of it. But I never expected much passion from a wife, so it's not your fault. However, I thought I should let you know that there'll be no further need for you to make excuses, because I'll not be visiting your bedroom again.'

Her eyes narrowed into thin grey slits. 'I see. So this is my Christmas gift?'

'No. I gave you a pearl necklace, did I not?'

'Indeed. One you had sent up from London. You didn't take care to choose it, did you?'

'I haven't the time! The mills don't run themselves, my dear. Managers are all very well, but they need watching. If I weren't on their backs all the time they'd slacken off and let the workforce have a party every day. It's a delicate business, is cotton, with a fine line between profit and loss. I can't afford to take my finger off the pulse, or they'd all be spending their days leaning on walls. Can't trust any of them – they want paying for nothing, that's the top and bottom of it. There's no room for charity in my game . . . '

'And charity begins at home, doesn't it, Richard? Or does it begin with your mistresses?' She made for the door, her back rigidly straight. Part way across the carpet, she turned to look at him. 'I shall not make your life easy, Richard Swainbank, because you have ruined mine. Yes, I know I'm just a woman, a creature of no importance. You can cast me from your bed, but not from your house. No, you'd never live with the disgrace, would you? But let me inform you here and now that I am not terribly interested in you or in your sons. Yes, they are my boys too and if they had a different father, another surname, then I should probably love them. But whatever you do from now on will be no concern of mine.' She spoke quietly, evenly, not a trace of malice colouring her voice. In fact, she might just as well have been reading from a shopping list – or the Bible, come to that.

'Beatrice?'

'Yes?'

'Have you no spirit, no temper?'

She moved her eyes slowly down to his feet, an expression of disdain covering her face. 'I think I had spirit once. You killed it. Why should I waste time and energy on temper when I really don't care what you do or say? At least I tried, Richard. Perhaps my efforts have not been good enough, perhaps my unhappiness has shown through too easily. But for you to do this thing at Christmas, a time that has always meant much to me.' She shook her head. 'In future, I shall spend the season with my parents. They are civilized.'

He jumped to his feet and brought a heavy hand on to the mantel shelf. 'Can't you fight me, for God's sake? Have you no pride, no anger at all?' He stared at the woman he'd married, still thin in the face where she'd wanted flesh, yet wide around the hips where she could well have done without it. And a vivid picture of Philly Maguire flashed across his brain, obliterating all else in the room. Tall and grand of posture,

54

black hair coiled about her head . . . if ever a woman had been born to the wrong class, then that was the one, because any man would be glad of such a fine item to adorn his home and walk by his side.

'That smile makes you look ridiculous,' murmured his well-bred wife. 'Do as you wish, I shall not fight you. There is nothing to fight about.' She left the room, closing the door firmly in her wake.

Richard paced the floor, the ulcer on his shin stinging even more now that his temper was up. Aye, she'd never slam a door, would she? Whereas Philly Maguire would have had foundations shaking by this time. But he knew Beatrice well enough by now, recognized that she'd make him suffer one way or another. Devious, she was. Like a bad nut covered in sugar, the thin coating cracking here and there to let a bitter kernel show through. Whether or no he'd been the cause of her nastiness – well, he neither knew nor cared. But one thing was sure. He would reap the dubious benefits of today's brief episode of honesty. No matter how well a man kept his wife down, there was one area where she reigned supreme come what may. From this day, his life at home promised to improve not one jot.

She told herself that she was cleaning up for pride's sake. After all, he likely lived in a mansion full of statues and rugs from heathen parts, forty rooms of stately living and good taste. She took jars of goose-grease and bottles of olive and camphorated oils from the oven where they always sat warming except when baking was in progress, then flicked a final duster over her gleaming black-leading. No, she wouldn't take him into the parlour, because the small cast iron grate in there had never seen coal and she wasn't going to spoil those blue and white side-tiles just for him. All the same, he'd have been surprised, no doubt, to be shown all that grandeur in a mill-girl's house. In front of the parlour fireplace sat a beautiful tapestry screen with a stag woven into its centre. Then there was the piano with its twin candelabra all polished and bright, her aspidistra plants – firstly, the splendid monster in the centre of the table, then its two younger brothers in copper tubs on the hearth. Yes, it was a pity he'd never see her green velvet door curtain with matching mantel cover and tablecloth, all with hand-applied gold fringes. And the good mahogany chairs tucked up to the table, the shiny horsehair sofa along the wall.

She checked herself, tut-tutting aloud while she straightened the handmade rug in front of a roaring fire. Why on earth should she want to impress him at all? Was it that she needed to impress him, or did she simply seek to avoid his contempt – or his pity? She whipped off the starched linen cloth and smiled down at her kitchen table. Most women had a white scrubbed item to work on, but she was blessed with two good tables – or cursed when she considered where Seamus might have acquired them. This unusual piece was octagonal and inlaid with many woods, the pattern radiating from a rich red central block that formed the top of the pedestal. To work on it at all, she had to cover it with many layers of blanket and sheeting, so precious was its magnificent surface.

Everything was in its place. On the large dresser stood the Sacred Heart and the Virgin, each on a wooden plinth and encased under a polished glass dust-dome. Her few concessions to frivolity, including a boy with cherries and a porcelain crinolined lady, also sat on the burnished dresser, their reflected backs showing in the attached mirror. Before the fire stood two easy chairs, one upholstered in carpet, the other in leather. The flagged floor was covered by oilcloth, well-scrubbed and with the flag joints showing through like a pattern of large squares. A single rug, carefully pegged on winter evenings out of clipped-up clothes, was as clean as it could be, having had the life beaten out of it on the back yard line. Two brass candlesticks and a crucifix stood on the mantelpiece, always on display in a Catholic home in case Extreme Unction or a Mass for the sick should ever be required on the premises. Over these hung a brass-framed mirror, while various holy pictures decorated the rest of the walls. It was a good home, a clean home, one to be proud of. Well, at least he wouldn't be able to say he'd visited a slum dwelling the day after Christmas. She might have few rooms, but they were as clean as primitive conditions would allow and a sight cleaner than she was used to at home.

She sat by the fire, outwardly composed, forcing herself to think of her family, pushing Christmas wishes across the miles to a little rush-thatched cottage full of brothers and sisters. If only she could read; if only they could write. Yet she was not unhappy, for County Mayo was a closed chapter now. Her life was here and she accepted it gladly for what it was, comfortable, manageable, predictable. And the respect she got from the neighbours, that was indeed a blessing. After the holiday was over, she must set to and make new batches, go out on the rounds again, because she had used some of Seamus' money to pay doctor and nurse.

He didn't even knock. One minute she was alone, then the next brought a draught to her ankles and a chill to her shoulders. She stood and turned to face the door. 'Come in. I've himself in the cot by the stairs and he must not get cold.'

He closed the door and stared at her, noticing that she never lowered her eyes, never attempted to acknowledge his superiority. 'That's a fine fire, Mrs Maguire . . . '

'Sit yourself in the leather chair and roll up the trouser leg.' Her tone was terse and uninviting.

He faltered, his hand still on the door. 'Do you have to look at it?' No, he didn't want her as nurse, couldn't quite stand the thought of her seeing his vulnerability. And the leg, while greatly improved, was not one of his better features. 'Can't you just give me the powder? It seemed to be doing the trick . . . '

She folded her arms and shook her head slowly. 'It's entirely up to you, Mr Swainbank. Your bad leg is your concern, but if you want it mended . . . '

'Oh, very well.' He removed his heavy greatcoat and placed it with his hat on the table. Not a word was spoken as he sat in the chair, took off his boot and sock, rolled up the trouser leg and placed his foot on a nearby stool.

She squatted on the rug, her face reflecting the glow from radiant coals. 'That, Mr Swainbank,' she finally declared, 'is

57

what my next door neighbour would call a bloody mess and no mistake. Have you banged it ever?'

'Many a time while riding.'

'Then don't ride. These weeping sores are deep and imposs- ible to shift altogether. It's enough to have one without mak- ing it worse by riding and gallivanting like a young lad. What is your age?' She looked up at him. 'How old are you?' she repeated, as if to a child.

'Forty-four.'

'And you without the sense you were born with, I shouldn't wonder. Men! All the same, infants from cradle to grave every last one. Have you seen the blood vessels on this leg? Look for yourself, man. Like the cast-offs from a rope factory, all twisted and tangled past saving. You must walk less. Give yourself an hour every afternoon. Say to yourself, "This is my leg hour." Don't ride, don't drink, don't smoke and above all, don't bang this sore. And I'd suggest four or five small meals each day, no banquets. With luck, you could be healed over within six months.'

'And no operations?'

'Does your physician want to operate?'

'He'd like to use me as guinea-pig. Especially as I can pay well.'

'That's up to you.'

He stared hard and long at the lovely head of hair that was almost within reach now as she bent to study his leg more closely. 'If I can't ride, eat or smoke . . . '

'Or drink,' she interspersed quietly.

'Or drink? Then what the hell do I live for?'

She lifted her head and looked straight into his face. 'To make money, Mr Swainbank. To make money while your workers starve. Isn't that your hobby?' She jumped to her feet. 'Now, I'll dress this and give you plenty of spare powder. Don't get it wet at all . . . '

He watched her walking across the small room, a room where she definitely did not belong. A gem like this deserved a better setting among further finery that might embellish it and bring out the true lustre. 'I have the power to change your life completely, Mrs Maguire.' His voice was no more than a whisper, almost a caress. 'I can take you from this place and give you a beautiful home, a fitting place in which to bring up your son. Fields and flowers, fresh air and sunshine . . . '

'I've had all those.' She took bandage and powders from a drawer, heart in her mouth as she stared at her reflection in the dresser mirror. It wasn't just him! It was herself as well, for didn't she want to . . . ? Ah, she didn't know what she wanted to do with this hateful man. Best to get the nursing seen to and have him on his way.

Bracing herself, she knelt to dress his leg.

'You have a gentle touch. It feels better already.'

'Good. It's glad I am of that.'

'They call you Philly, is that right?'

With her head bent to her task she replied, 'I was baptized Philomena.'

'I see. Then what do I call you?'

'Mrs Maguire. Or Ma Maguire would be acceptable.'

While he replaced his sock and boot, she washed her hands at the scullery sink. 'Please make him go now,' she prayed inwardly. 'Dear God, let me not submit to this thing I don't understand. Give me the strength to fight what I am feeling, remove the temptation you have sent to me . . . '

Then she felt large fingers encircling her waist and moving up to cover her shaking body. 'No!' she screamed. 'No!' But expert hands turned her and she found his hard lips silencing the loud denial. For a second or two, she was overcome to the point where she almost began to respond in spite of shock and fear, then she pushed him fiercely away. 'Don't you dare,' she snarled. 'Whatever do you think I am . . . ?' She was cold, so unbearably cold, angry too because her disobedient body was screaming to be warmed. By him?

'Beautiful. And lonely too . . . '

'But I'm not an animal!'

He smoothed his dishevelled hair. 'What's wrong with animal instinct?'

'Nothing. If you're a dog or a horse. The thing that

separates us from the beasts, Mr Swainbank, is that we live for the future, not for the present.'

'Ah.' He took a step closer. 'A philosopher too, I see. Not content to be nurse and midwife?'

She reached into the slopstone and picked out a large knife, the one she used to trim fat from meat for beef tea. 'If it's a toss-up between my virtue and your life, then there's no contest, Sir.' This last word was spat venomously. 'You will go now from my house and you will never return.'

'You talk of the future, Philly. I can give you one, all the money you need, clothes, an education for the boy . . . '

'No!' She brandished the knife before his face. 'I don't want anything from you.' It was better to lie, that would be the smaller sin. Because she was lying. There was something here in this room, created by the two of them, uninvited, unwelcome, but compelling all the same.

'Really?' His lip curled. 'That wasn't the message I received a moment ago. Yes, like all women, you speak one thing while your body says another.' He gazed around the scullery, apparently unimpressed by the six inches of steel she was waving so carelessly. 'I can have you thrown out of here tomorrow. Your landlord's a friend of mine . . . '

'Oh yes? Well, see what do the neighbours say about that, Mr Swainbank. And not just in this street, but in many streets around. I'm useful here. I clean up the mess you make of their lives, treat cuts and bruises that should really be dealt with at the mill. All the illnesses you breed in those filthy holes are brought home and I cure them. Ask Doctor Flynn, why don't you? And see did I ever miss my rent, see does the landlord want me out. I tell you now that he does not, for I have brought cleanliness to these slums. You don't frighten me. A godless person never did frighten me.'

He looked her up and down. 'And I could relieve you of that knife in two seconds.'

'Do it, then.'

Their eyes locked in silent combat for several moments, then he turned on his heel and left the room. Swiftly, she followed him with the knife held out at waist-height, placing herself between him and the cradle that contained her sleeping son.

He snatched up his outer garments and made for the door.

'Mr Swainbank?'

'Yes?' He looked at her, his hand resting on the gleaming brass door latch.

'That will be two guineas, please. A guinea for the powder and another for my time.'

His lip curled into a snarl. 'Huh! And what would you charge a mill-hand?'

'Sixpence at best. But you need my medicine, don't you? In future, you need not come here. Just send your boy now that I have seen the sore for myself. And take care, because my curse still stands.'

He threw some coins on to the table. 'What curse?'

'The one I laid at your door. Did you not know I have a reputation as a witch?'

'Rubbish!'

'Is it? Aye well, think about it when you lie in your bed with the blood flowing so slowly through your veins that you fear the heart stopping. But then, there may be nothing in it with me such a good Catholic woman. Close the door as you leave, please.'

'Philly! Philly Maguire . . .'

'Yes?'

'You will live to regret this day.'

She stepped forward to pick up the money, her eyes fixed on his face. 'I think you'll find, Mr Swainbank, that the boot is on another foot altogether.'

Swearing beneath his breath, he opened the door.

'And while we're on about feet, I must warn you to watch out for the gangrene,' she said quietly. 'You'll recognize it sure enough, for the toes go black before they drop off. And I've no cure at all for that . . .'

He slammed the door behind him.

Philly placed the knife on the table and steadied herself with one hand on the back of a chair. Ice-cold fingers groped in her pocket until they found a rosary, then she fell to her knees beside Patrick's cradle. The sins of the flesh had not

61

needed consideration before, for she had never felt so drawn to a man. Yet so repulsed at the same time! How could dislike and desire be partners in a person's soul? How on God's good earth could she care for one who made slaves of decent working people, who turned a blind eye to want and deprivation, a fiend without compassion or warmth in his soul? She didn't understand any of it. For the first time ever, Philly had been a brief victim of passion. It had not been a comfortable experience and she would avoid it carefully in the future.

After feeding her child, she sat gazing into embers until the room became truly chilled. Would she ever feel warm again? There was no doubt in her mind now – Richard Swainbank was a force to be reckoned with. And so, because of her weaknesses, was Philomena Theresa Maguire.

Chapter 2

1905

It began with a headache, no more than that. As usual, Philly was on her rounds, pushing Seamus' handcart around the streets of School Hill, selling her wares with the rest of the street tradesmen. She was a familiar sight now and people listened for the high-pitched tinkle of her handbell, came out in droves to buy a penn'orth of tonic and a ha'p'orth of liniment. Occasionally, she would be stopped and brought into a house of sickness, while many a time a child would arrive breathless from running, 'Ma, me mam says she's started', then handcart and bottles would be abandoned for a household to mind until Philly's various crises ended.

She always patrolled the same area, though good sense told her that her medicines could sell anywhere. But the folk of School Hill depended on her now that Mother Blue's questionable assistance was no longer available, so she stuck rigidly to her own patch. In time, she got to know all the other traders. There was Billy Black who mended dolly-tubs, Old Sharpie – he honed knives and scissors on a dusty wheel, Hughie Burns who sold brushes, Tommy from the tripe shop with his basket of offal, black puddings and sausages, the ragman who traded small blocks of salt for old clothes.

It was March, still chilly enough, though the air held a muted promise of spring even here in the shadow of the mills. By three o'clock, Philly knew she had had enough. In spite of her extra shawl, she was shivering uncontrollably and her eyes seemed to be misting over with tiredness. She blinked several times to clear her vision, then pushed the cart, which suddenly weighed a ton, in the direction of home. When she reached Edie's house, she hammered loudly at the front door. Edie put her head through the opened lower half of the bedroom window. 'What's up with thee? Can't you open the door like everybody else?'

'I'm sick.'

'Aye, so am I! Your Patrick's been doing a fair imitation of the opening of Parliament here, all noise and no bloody sense.' She paused. 'What's matter?'

'I'm coming down with something. You'll have to hang on to him, Edie. I don't want him getting it too.'

'Keep him overnight, you mean?'

'Yes. You know I'd do the same if it was Molly.'

Edie brought her lips together tightly before she said anything. The lad was past dealing with some days and this was one of them. Seven months old and he carried on like the blinking Kaiser if he didn't get his own road all the while. 'Can I do anything for you, lass?' Aye, she did look a bit poorly, did Philly.

'Keep away, please! If it's what I think, you mind those babies till I'm over it and the house fumigated.'

'Bloody hell!'

'And don't swear, Edie.' Philly steadied herself against the cart. 'Get Arthur to shove this into the yard later on. I'm well past meself. If I bang on the wall, get the doctor.'

'I'll get him whether or not. Go in that house this minute, Philly Maguire.'

She staggered up the stairs, gripping tightly on to the cast-iron rail. Her head swam as if she were drunk, while all four limbs felt as if they were weighted with lead. Incapable of removing her clothes, she fell on to the bed and drifted into a tormented sleep.

As soon as Arthur came in, Edie ran from the scullery to greet him. 'Were it a bad day, lad? Well, it's not over, 'cos Philly's been took badly. You'd best get down for the doctor . . . What's matter, love?'

His head drooped as he fell into a chair. He took a deep shuddering breath before looking up at her. 'It's Bob – you remember Bob Hawkins, him as come round with his Missus when I'd no work?'

'That's right. He made a collection, didn't he? Gave us a

64

few coppers every week till your arm got right.'

'Aye, that's him. Well, he'd six childer up to last Sunday, four lads and two girls, a bonny lot too. By this morning, he'd got one left and that's poorly.'

A hand flew to her mouth. 'Dear God! Whatever is it? Scarlet fever?'

'Nay, lass.' He shook his head wearily. 'That doesn't kill many, just leaves them deaf and with weak insides. No, it's the other.' He almost choked as he whispered, 'They're saying it's the dip again, Edie.'

'Diphtheria?'

'Aye, that's what most of the doctors are putting it down as. Anyroad, they're falling like flies with it, streets of kiddies just wiped out.'

'No!' Patrick began to scream again and Edie looked anxiously at the two children on the rug. 'What if . . . ?'

'Don't think on it, lass. Just keep her in the house till it's all passed over.'

'But we've Patrick too! She says I have to hang on to him while she's ill. What if he's got it? What if he gives it to our Molly?'

'The Lord will look after us, Edie. He knows she's too precious – aye and Patrick too. Anyroad, I'll go and get the doctor for Missus next door.'

After he had left, Edie fed the two babies on thin stew followed by rice pudding then breast-milk. It was not uncommon for one woman to feed both children if the other was busy. She examined the infants carefully. They looked well enough and were weaning early, so happen they'd find the strength to fight whatever this was. She bathed them and put them to bed, glancing from time to time at the slow-moving clock, wondering what was keeping Arthur so long.

When at last he returned, his face was grimmer than ever.

'Did you get the doctor? Where've you been all this while?'

For answer, he threw his cap on to the table and rubbed a hand across coal-rimmed eyes.

'What is it, Arthur?'

'There is no doctor, lass.'

'No doctor? Why, is he out on a call?'

'Aye, you might say that, Edie. His last call.'

'Arthur!' She ran to him and threw her arms about his neck. 'Not Dr Flynn! No!'

'This morning. He'd been treating them, you see, so he caught it and passed away before dinner. I reckon Philly's been near it too, lass, so we must prepare for whatever comes.'

Edie burst into tears while her husband, whose own grief was not far from the surface, held her tight in his arms. 'There's nowt at all we can do, girl. I ran down St George's Road to see if I could find the other feller, only he'd the shutters up. Happen he's laying low and looking after his own.'

She pulled away from him, her eyes wide with fear and panic. 'What about Philly? We can't just leave her, yet I daren't go near in case I fetch summat home to the babies. Whatever shall I do?'

He reached for her hand. 'Make a brew while I think on. There must be a road round this . . . '

Two hours later, after scouring the town for medical help, Arthur returned once more to his wife. 'That's it,' he announced quietly. 'The doctors are all out or not answering, then the hospital said they were full up, no more room for isolation cases. But there again, we mun look on the bright side – she might not have it, Edie. Happen it's a chill or the scarlet fever. See, I'll go in . . . '

'No!' Edie's voice was fierce. 'She wouldn't want that, Arthur. She must have something bad, else she'd have been knocking on the wall or trying to get to see us. And if she's poorly, then for Patrick's sake and for our Molly, she'd never let us in.'

'She might be too poorly to know who's in and who's out . . . '

Edie shook her head determinedly. 'We're none of us going in there. You stop here, lad. I'm off to find the one person who will take this on for a few bob.'

'Nay . . . '

But she was already fastening the shawl about her head.

66

'It's our only chance, Arthur. And whatever happens, thanks for trying. You're a good lad and I don't know what I'd do without you.'

She was gone. Arthur washed himself down at the scullery slopstone then pushed his dried-up stew around the plate for a while. At about nine o'clock, Edie returned with a subdued and unusually sober Mother Blue in tow. After sending her husband upstairs, she dragged in the tin bath and ordered Mother to get a good scrub. By this time, Philly had been alone next door for many hours and Edie was once more anxiously watching the clock. Fortunately, the two women were much of a size and within another few minutes, Mother Blue was dressed in Edie's cast-offs.

Edie sat her down by the fire. 'Right. Remember what I told you. The food and your gin will be left on the doorstep every morning. If it's nothing serious, you'll likely be on your way in a day or two, but if she's bad, then you have to promise to stay in there with her till it's all over one way or the other. All right?'

'And three guineas of her money at the finish?'

'Four if she lives.'

'Right, Missus.' Mother Blue struggled to her feet. 'No gin, love. Just bring me black beer while I'm working. Save me a couple of bottles of the good stuff for after.'

Edie led the old lady to the door. 'Aren't you a-feared?'

Mother Blue laughed, toothless gums glistening pink in the lamplight. 'Me? I've seen more disease than you've had hot dinners, lass. Nay, I'm frightened of nowt, me. Mind you, Missus High and Mighty next door likely won't want me in her house . . . '

'That can't be helped, Mother. We can't find nobody else willing, so just do your best and we'll make it worth your while.'

'And I'll talk to you through the bedroom window at eight o'clock in the morning. Is that right?'

'Yes.'

When the old woman had left, Edie burned the filthy rags of clothing, allowing herself a sad smile as a picture flashed

67

across her mind, a vivid memory of Mother Blue in the bath with her bonnet still firmly in place. Anybody who'd keep the blinking hat on in the bath must be well away with the fairies and no mistake. Still, the old besom was their only chance, so there hadn't really been any other alternative, had there? Though God alone knew what Philly would say when all this was over! She called Arthur down for his cocoa and toast. They sat on opposite sides of the fire, both exhausted by the day's happenings.

'I hope the lass makes it,' said Arthur, his voice edged with sadness.

'Aye well, we'll know if and when she's on the mend. I reckon this house'll fall down when Philly sees Mother Blue. She'll go bloody mad!'

'Don't swear, Edie.'

'Sorry, love. But them two together – can you imagine? Mind, there were nowt else for it.' She sighed as she gazed into the fire. 'Say a prayer for our Molly, lad.'

'I will. And for Patrick too.'

'That's right. Let's not forget Patrick.' She dropped her voice. 'As if we ever could.'

'What?'

'Nothing, love. Just say one for all of us.'

She was choking, choking to death. Someone had rolled her over to the edge of the bed and left her hanging there face down with her mouth drooling on to the floor. Now she was lifted, heaved about like a sack of coal, pushed and pummelled past endurance. 'Breathe, you bitch,' whispered a female voice. 'Don't you dare bloody die on me, else I'll kill you!'

That, thought Philly, was a ridiculous thing to say. Then the owner of the voice was on top of her, straddling her body and hissing in sinister tone, 'Open your gob, Missus. Go on, open it.' Philly continued to drift in and out of consciousness until a sharp jab in the stomach made her mouth open involuntarily. Inflamed and swollen throat membranes were suddenly assaulted further when a foreign object entered her mouth, something smooth and long. Dear God! Somebody was pushing a snake down her throat! With a painful sigh she absented herself, put herself away where she was not reachable.

Mother Blue smiled at her small triumph. It hadn't been easy to work out how to feed this one, because the throat was near closed, but a bit of narrow and well-greased rubber tubing had done the trick something lovely. Mind, it was a bit dicey, was that. The only way of knowing that the tube was in the stomach was to check that the patient hadn't gone purple. But she hadn't, so all was well enough up to now.

She took a funnel and inserted it into the end of the tube, then poured milk and beaten raw egg into this receptacle. It was a slow process, but the law of gravity had its inevitable way in the end, leaving Mother with an empty jug and a smile of victory. That was a beginning now. After six days of no food and little water, the battle had looked to be lost. She would leave the tube in, drip a bit of nourishment down every hour or so.

It wasn't a bad life. A bit on the boring side with nobody to talk to, but plenty to eat laid on every morning by her next door, a nice full coal hole to provide fires in kitchen and bedroom, then a couple of pints of dark beer thrown in on top. Mind, as soon as this one popped her clogs, there'd be none of that. Which was why Mother had willed the young dragon to stay alive. At least, that was the idea in the first place, only now she'd gone and let herself get fond of the great lump of a girl. By God, she had some spirit, right enough. And she was a bonny-looking lass even with all the flesh gone off her – took some lifting even if she had lost weight. Happen she must have been made with a heavy skeleton, because she looked about as healthy as something left in the ashpit for a fortnight. Aye, it was all bone now – without the tube, there'd have been no better than a dog's chance. There again, this was Mother Blue's opportunity to prove herself once more, let everybody know that she could still do the job. The whole street was waiting to see if the famous Ma Maguire would stay alive with Old Blue in charge. Well, it was touch and go, but it wouldn't be for want of trying.

She poured a bit more milk down the tube, then went to the

window. Edie Dobson was waiting as always, hanging halfway out of the next door bedroom. Reports were due every hour on the hour now – and there was usually quite an audience gathered in the street.

'I got the tube down,' she announced to Edie and those assembled below. 'She's had raw egg and plenty of milk, so she'll come to no harm. How's her lad?'

Edie grimaced. 'Depends what you mean. He's healthy and horrible, I suppose.' The neighbours chuckled. 'Nay, I shouldn't be saying things like that with his mother so poorly,' she continued, a blush of shame colouring her cheeks. 'He's all she's got, poor soul.'

'Will she make it?' asked Bessie Critchley anxiously. 'Only she said you don't do things right, said as how you made me ill . . .'

'I'm doing me bloody best!' snapped the old lady. 'Anybody want to come up and see if they can do better? You're more than welcome to have a go, Missus, changing the bed half a dozen times a day, boiling sheets in the middle of the night, shoving bloody pipes down her throat. Any volunteers?' She paused, pretending to wait for an answer. 'No, I thought as much.' Then she slammed down the window, only to raise it again immediately. 'Hey!' she shouted to the next bedroom along the row.

Edie poked her head out. 'Yes?'

'I want some more eggs and a bit of brandy. And I fancy a nice lamb chop for me tea tomorrow.' Down went the window again and everyone dispersed until a further bulletin was due.

Mother turned and faced the bed. 'Eeh well,' she remarked quietly. 'Somebody been rattling the bars of your cage, eh? How long have you been awake? What's matter, nowt to say? Oh, I see. Some bad bugger's shoved a lump of rubber in your gob, what a bloody shame about that. Have I to fetch the animal doctor and have you seen to? Only it'd have to be him, 'cos the real doctors are a bit thin on the ground with this here epidemic. Nay, if I didn't know different, I'd swear them Irish eyes are laughing at me. Cheeky bugger! Listening to me at the window, were you? Anyroad, the lad's all right. No!

70

Don't you be pulling that there pipe out! It's all as is keeping you going and don't forget it. I know it's a bit hard to breathe – that's why I've got this pan of water on the fire with some of your balsam in. Stinks like the flaming farrier's when he's had all the brewery horses in. That's right, queen. You go off back to sleep now. No need to fret, Mother's here . . . '

The days blended into one another, became a week, then a fortnight. After the tube was removed and normal – if somewhat soft – feeding had resumed, Philly found herself still at the complete mercy of this little old woman, because her own chief weapon seemed to have been mislaid. Although her lips moved to frame words, nothing came from her voice box, so she was forced to listen instead to Mother's endless tales.

'I'm from Liverpool in the first place. Brought up by nuns, I was, miserable beggars too, the lot of them. Not that I know exactly where or when I was born, like. But I must have been just a young woman when I came here. Got carried away by a handsome Lancashire lad, you see. Only he got carried away to prison and I never saw him no more. Led a bad life, I have, no use pretending I've not. Went with men for money – there was nowt else to do then. Seems like a hundred years ago now. Lost me looks with the scarlet fever. And me hair too. Everybody else just shed their skin, ended up looking like boiled shrimp, but I had to go one better and finish up bald. So. Who wants a good time with a bald woman, eh? Anyroad, I took to midwifing and laying-out – did a bit in the mill too, cleaning up and that. Didn't like it. And I'm past it all now, too old for any of it.'

Philly smiled as broadly as she could manage. She was on the mend, but still needed rest and building-up. Was there no end to this lady's tales? On and on she went, stories of men she'd known and loved, how much they'd loved her, how much they'd paid to prove it.

'Am I getting on your nerves? Only it's not often I have a silent audience what can hear me, like. The only time I've ever been on me own with a woman, she's either been in labour or dead . . . '

Philly fought a painful chuckle as Mother relived a dozen

births and several excruciatingly funny layings-out. 'No bloody door to straighten him out on – they'd even burned the netty door for firewood . . . ' And, 'I've seen some ugly babies in me time, but this one made me wonder if the organ-grinder had lost his monkey . . . '

The younger woman looked up at the ceiling. Dear Lord, couldn't somebody or something stop Mother Blue? If Philly didn't laugh, she'd burst right here on the spot . . .

'You've gone all purple again. Am I being funny then? We're like that, Liverpool folk. We don't even know when we're being funny. Did I tell you about that one down Allinson Street? I swear to this day she poisoned him deliberate . . . '

Philly swallowed as carefully as she could. With this old dear in the house, she had better improve quickly. Lying here and hearing all these hilarious tales, lying here a prisoner, not even able to laugh properly . . . Well, she would choke to death on a giggle if this carried on much longer!

But it did carry on, endlessly, relentlessly . . . 'You were disappearing in front of me eyes. As sure as sixpence, if you'd fell on the floor, you'd have shot straight between a crack in the boards and into the downstairs oven. So I gets this here tube what him next door fetched from the ironmonger's . . . '

Mother Blue lifted Philly high on to her pillows and placed a cup in her hands. 'Put yourself outside of that beef tea. Take your time, we can always knit the odd blanket between swallows. And that lad of yours wants taking in hand, Missus. He's led them next door a fine dance after you've ruined him past mending. Start shoving him on his own, let him scream it out, do his lungs good. An idle little sod, he is, can't even shift himself to try and crawl while some soft woman'll pick him up. I've heard him through the walls, carrying on like destruction.'

Philly sighed and struggled hard to swallow the hot liquid. The woman was right, of course. Patrick was a torment – hadn't she listened to him herself these last days since she started picking up a bit? She must take a firmer stand with him in future.

'Then there's all them food parcels,' continued Mother Blue with hardly a breath as she changed subject. 'You've a mystery caller twice a week, leaves fruit and fancy tea on your step. Bloody tea tastes like scent, so I don't bother with it meself, but I reckon it's grand posh stuff like what the gentry has. Whoever brings that lot must come in the middle of the night, 'cos I've never seen nobody. Likely one of your customers with more money than brain. I'll catch the bugger one of these days, tell them to fetch proper tea. Anyroad, I'll give you a wash now, then you can settle for the night. You'll happen manage without me for once, though God knows I've nowt to go home for . . . '

Philly reached out a thin hand. 'Stay.'

'Good God! You sound like a back gate wanting oil. Shall I fetch the can and give you a squirt? And what do you need me for? I'm just a mucky owld woman full of gin and idle talk. You told me plain enough down the Bull . . . '

'Stay.'

'All right then. Just for a day or two . . . '

Swainbank was bringing the parcels, Philly knew that. Somehow, he had found out about her illness . . . How could a person be so kind and yet so cruel? Kind to her just now, probably to his family all the time. Yet so cold when it came to those who toiled day in and day out to make his living for him.

She watched the tired old lady as she fetched bowl and towel for the nightly bed-bath. If Philly had her way, Mother's day or two would be stretched to what was left of the old girl's life, which couldn't be much. And it wasn't just selflessness that prompted Philly to offer Mother Blue a home. With another adult in the house, she would be safe from Swainbank, safe from herself too. Not that she felt up to much at present, but no doubt the flesh would heal and temptation would return.

'You saved me . . . '

'Shurrup with your bother! I'm getting bloody paid for it! You don't think I'd have stopped here with you and the heavy breathing for nowt?'

'You can live here.'

Mother Blue dropped the flannel, a look of amazement covering her shrivelled face. 'Nay, lass. There's no need for that . . . '

'Please?'

Old eyes were suddenly filled with tears. 'I don't know what to say, queen. That doesn't often happen to me, not knowing what to say, though I'm more at home with the fellers down the vault than I am with women. It's just that you're grateful – and I understand how you feel. But I'll be all right. There's folk out there that'll see to me, stop me starving. And I couldn't live here, love. You'd be out of your mind with me coming in drunk and dirty. Tell you what – we'll talk about it when you're a bit brighter. Happen you're not thinking straight . . . '

But Mother Blue stayed. As Philly made her slow progress towards recovery, the old girl started to go out more, often coming back the worse for drink, though never once did Philly scold her. When sober, Mother was an asset, quickly learning how to make medicines and ointments, even taking the cart out a time or two in order to swell diminishing household funds. When Patrick came back to his own home, the old lady took him over, surprising everyone with the amount of control she achieved over this wayward child. If he screamed for no reason, she simply yelled at him to shut his gob – and shut his gob he did. Within a month, she had him eating out of her hand, because the little lad was fascinated by the strange lady in the funny hat.

Ma Maguire and Mother Blue, old adversaries and new allies, sat one each side of the fire one cool May evening. Philly hadn't been out yet, except to the back yard or to peg washing on her twin lines that stretched across the alley between ashpits. Any troubles outside of the immediate domestic environment had been kept from her by Mother and Edie who had decided that this was the best way to help recovery. But questions that had long been evaded would soon require answers – even the priest had been forced to lie in a negative sense by simply not telling the truth. Still, the time had come, thought Mother. Especially as Philly was asking now, 'Didn't Doctor Flynn come ever? I'd have thought he'd take a look at the babies, just to make sure. And he never came near me, did he? Not that I blame him . . . '

The faded blue bonnet nodded slowly. 'Brace yourself, queen. The poor man died the day you fell ill – went with the same bad throat as you had.'

Philly's face paled to an even lighter shade. 'No! Dear God, why ever was I not told? That wonderful clever man? The same who saved my life – and my son's too? Oh no, Mother! Say it's not true, for we need doctors like him!'

'It's true. This illness takes no notice of whether you're clever or not. Kills anybody from president to pauper, that's what they say, so it's not going to take much notice of a young doctor, is it?'

'But he saved others . . . '

'And neglected himself, just as you did. Aye, it's a cruel world, Philly Maguire. Twenty-odd children died these last weeks – and that's just round School Hill. A mate of Arthur's next door lost his whole family, wife and all. Went raving mad and chucked himself in the Croal. Oh, they saved him, 'cos the water wasn't deep enough to drown a kitten, but he's locked up now, gone crackers, see? Nay, we've kept you long enough in cotton wool, time now you realized what's been going on around you. Mrs Critchley over the road lost their Ernest a couple of days ago and he was right as rain but for the last few hours. I went over, but there was not a thing to be done, because his throat was shut as fast as your back gate. Long as I live, I'll never get used to seeing a child fighting for breath and the fear in his eyes.'

'Oh, Mother . . . '

'Yes, I know.' The old head wagged sagely. 'Thought I didn't care – is that it? Well, there's a big difference between not caring and not knowing. I never heard of germs till lately, never took no notice, didn't give a thought to getting scrubbed before a birthing. Now, it's too late. But I'm not going to blame meself for being ignorant.'

'Nor you should. You've been good to me, Mother Blue, and I'll not have you on the streets again. And don't start, for I will not take no for an answer. You'll live out your days here – there's that little bedroom and enough food and coal for the three of us.' She stood up and began to pace the area between rug and table. 'Doctor Flynn!' Her hands twisted together as if she were wringing out a dishcloth. 'A good Catholic man with a brilliant mind for medicine. What is this thing, Mother? This and consumption and all the fevers – why are we so plagued? He had some ideas, that man. He says – or rather he used to say – that one day, we'll all get a little dose of every illness, given deliberately on a spoon or in a pill to make our bodies fight. What'll we do without his likes? Who's to come now when we're ill? Some doddering old fool with no idea of how to treat us?'

'Oh sit down, for God's sake! Apart from wearing the floor out, you're getting on me nerves. And there's more to this, so listen to me, Missus.' She waited until Philly was seated once more. 'You've had a very near do, within that of death, you were.' She snapped finger and thumb together. 'Now, if what you say's right, if all these things can get carried on clothes and in coughs, what about the next time?'

'You mean . . . me bringing sickness home?'

'That's right, nail on the head. Say you go in a consumptive's house to do a bit of nursing. Next news, you could be passing it on to Patrick—'

'But I always get scrubbed—'

'You can't scrub a cough, you can't shift what's been breathed in!'

Philly leaned back in the chair and closed her eyes. 'So. You're saying I must give up the nursing. No doubt I shall still make a living selling my cures, but what about them?' She raised her lids and waved an arm towards the window. 'They can't afford doctors all the time. And anyway, we could catch a fever in a shop or at church, anywhere crowded.'

'Best not to tempt fate, though. Now listen to me, girl. I've had a word with Skenning Freddie, 'cos we none of us want you wandering about the streets with that cart, not after what you've been through . . . '

'And what, pray, can the clogger do to prevent that?'

76

Mother smiled knowingly, tapping a finger to the side of her nose. 'He's moving out. You know he's always lived upstairs and his meals cooked by next door? Well, he's met himself a fine widow woman and he's getting wed, got a nice little house down Arkwright Street way. So, he's going to give you half his shop. He'll use the upstairs for storing his stuff and the scullery for doing his makings. He reckons if he sets up two smaller counters, one facing the other, you could have two shops in one.'

'But what about his on the spot mending? And his bench for them waiting for clogs?'

Mother shrugged. 'You'll just have to squeeze in and put up with the din. He only wants two bob a week. If anybody's ill, they can send down for what's needed and you can tell the family what to do. It'll be safer, lass.'

Philly nodded slowly. 'Yes, yes, I see what you mean. I have to work, because I've a household to run. But there's no point in me looking for trouble, is there? A counter in the clogger's won't keep me away from illness, but at least I won't be meeting it head-on day after day. And I'd not have far to come for stock, would I?'

'That's right. You could nip home any time for a cup of tea and a look at the baby. As for me – well, I'll stop off the gin in the daytime, make sure the lad's minded. Unless you think her next door'll feel a bit pushed out . . . ?'

'Edie's not like that.' She thought for several seconds. 'I'll still have to take some risks, though. Births and deaths – they'll need me then. Unless I know for certain sure there's danger in the house, then I'll have to go.'

'Fair enough. Shall I tell Skenning Freddie he's on? Only he's bought all the wood for the new counters . . . '

'See! You'd it all planned behind me back . . . '

'Aye well. Somebody's got to put your head on straight, Ma Maguire. And if it takes the clogger and an old drunk to do it, then so be it.'

Mother Blue leaned forward to poke the fire to life under the kettle.

'What's your real name?' asked Philly suddenly. 'You

77

surely haven't been Mother Blue from birth?'

'I'm Kate. And since I was found, or so I'm told, out on a doorstep on a lovely clear day, they called me Katherine Sky. That was turned to "Sky Blue" and the rest just followed.'

'Well, go into the scullery, Katherine Sky and see what did Father O'Grady bring for you. It's a token of my thanks.'

The old lady bustled out, then, after a great many exclamations of joy and incredulity, she returned without bonnet and with a full head of mid-brown hair. 'Oh my goodness,' she cried at the mirror. 'What am I like? Dear Lord, I'll get a man at the finish just as I always said! A few pot teeth and I'm on, eh? Would you take a look at that, now! Where the hell did he get it?'

'From a nun.'

'From a nun? You mean I'm wearing a bloody nun's hair?'

'Yes,' giggled Philly. 'They have it cut off when they take the veil, then it's sold for wigs. So. That belonged to a very good woman. And it still does, for I'll vouch for you any day.'

The old woman began to laugh uncontrollably, bending double with the agony of it. 'I always said . . . when I was little . . . and they strapped me . . . never enough to eat . . . oh, I said I'd get me own back! But I never thought I'd be taking the head off one of them! Forget the tea, lass! I'm off down the Bull for a gill of black. Wait till they cop sight of this, eh? I'll tell them it grew back overnight with me saying me beads, like a miracle.' She threw a shawl around her thin shoulders. 'Thanks, lass,' she said, quieter now. 'These last weeks have been the best in me life.'

Philly stared into the fire for a long time, her mind filled with pain as she thought of all those terrible deaths. Because it was a terrible death, she'd been near enough to know that. Yet why did some in a house die while others remained untouched? He'd been keen on that theory, had Dr Flynn, the idea that living close to illness and getting a slight dose sometimes resulted in natural resistance. Wearily she prayed that other doctors would come along and pursue the same line of thinking. One day, it might be wiped out, all that awful suffering. But Dr Flynn would never know, would never make his contribution.

Edie came in unannounced with a plate apple pie. She studied her friend's careworn face. 'You know, then? About all the others, like?'

'Yes. I was lucky, Edie. I'm keeping her here.'

'I thought you might. She's not long, has she? I saw her in the wig, like a dog with two tails, she is.' She paused for a second or two. 'Any more parcels by the way? It was him. I spotted his carriage the other day.'

'None since Tuesday. I hope nobody sees him, for I don't want to be giving the wrong impression about me and himself.'

Edie crossed to the fire and sat opposite this shrunken version of Ma Maguire. The flesh seemed to have melted away from her frame, leaving her spare and gaunt, a much older woman altogether. But the eyes remained the same, incredibly blue, uncomfortably penetrating. 'Happen he'll not bother you no more, love. You're not the same girl,' she said with her customary bluntness.

'He never bothered me anyway, Edie . . .'

'Oh aye? Tell that to the cat.'

'I haven't got a cat.'

'I know.'

Philly looked down at her reduced body, noticing, not for the first time, how her clothes hung loose where once they fitted. 'Anyway, no matter what he wants, he won't get it here. He knows how we all feel about his mills and the slave wages he pays. So, if it's a friendly ear he's looking for, he must go elsewhere.'

Edie sighed loudly. 'It wasn't a friendly ear, love. It was you. You were beautiful and full of fight. His last one was a mill girl who clocked him across the bum with a yardbrush when he got a bit . . . interested, like. He set her up in a cottage, bought her all she needed . . .'

'And what became of her?'

'Oh, she's still there. Once he sets you up, he carries on paying even after . . . well . . .'

'After he's grown tired?'

'Aye, I suppose so. Mind, nobody bothers with her now . . .'

'So you wouldn't recommend it as a way of staying alive?'

'No. And I know you'd never take him on anyroad.'

'Then hush about Swainbank, will you? I believe I'm to start up in business under Freddie Chadwick's roof? Did you have a hand in that too?'

'Well I—'

'I thought so. Howandever, for once, I shall go along with the majority decision. There's something to be said for staying in the one place and doling out cures and advice. I can't be putting Patrick at risk, can I? He's improved of late, has he not? Less of the screaming.'

'Yes.' And not before time, thought Edie. Mother Blue had had a lot to do with Patrick's changed behaviour, because she never gave in to him. While this one here was like soft clay in his hands. Edie opened her mouth to speak, but bit back whatever she had been about to utter when Philly placed a hand to her own lips. With a level of agility that was surprising in one so recently ill, she bounded to the door and threw it open.

'Pick it up,' she said sternly.

Edie rose from her seat and crept across the room, peering as best she could over her neighbour's shoulder.

'Tell your master that I have no further need of his charity. Anything else he leaves here will be sent directly to the poorhouse, which is no doubt filled by weary worn-out souls who used to work in the Swainbank mills.'

Edie heard a hesitant male cough, then, 'Right, Missus. I'll tell him you're on the mend.'

'You come here just for powders from now on. Understand?'

'Aye, Missus.'

'And he'll get none of those if there's any further trouble. You tell him what I said, now. He'll understand.'

'Right.'

Philly closed the door and turned to her friend. 'Don't you say a word, Edith Dobson.'

'As if I would . . .'

She enjoyed every minute of her working day at Freddie Chadwick's. He was a gentle soul, but with a rapier-sharp wit that belied his rather strange appearance. Skenning Freddie had a shock of bright red hair that was receding fast, leaving a bushy fringe all round his head – from a distance, he would not have looked out of place in a monk's habit. Pale blue eyes seemed to fight each other for space next to a bulbous nose, while his whole countenance was covered by freckles and a huge ginger moustache heavily waxed at its tapering ends.

The shop was always filled with odd characters, some on business, others just 'dropping in a minute to get away from that lot'. The latter category was mostly female, harassed mothers driven to distraction by hordes of children, truanting grannies who, having been left to mind the kids while mother and father worked in the mill, had escaped for a moment's peace and sanity while young charges slept. It was here in Skenning Freddie's that Philly learned a vital lesson – that there was more to retail than just selling. Customers did not come simply to buy, for they also sought contact, affection, attention, counselling. Most of all, they looked for distraction, something to take their minds off the daily drudgery of cleaning, washing, mothering and trying to make ends stretch far enough to meet without breaking. The noise and clatter in the clogger's was obviously preferable to the sound of squabbling infants.

When she wasn't busy, Philly spent much of her time watching Freddie work, her eyes round with amazement as she witnessed his dexterity. Each clog was handmade from a wooden sole and leather upper, the whole fastened together by brass-topped nails which shone like gold when new. Philly never saw him make a clog, because actual manufacturing was performed at the back of the house. But to watch him mend was like seeing a work of art taking shape before her eyes. Quick as a flash, he would remove old irons, tossing them into a box beneath his counter. Then into his mouth he would throw a number of wooden pegs, pushing them out one at a time beneath his bushy moustache. Although his face never moved, each peg emerged pointed end first. With these tiny objects he filled old nail holes, then, after choosing a suitable iron from a wall-hook, he would throw small nails into his mouth and repeat the performance as he pinned the replacement items on sole and heel. The whole process lasted a matter of seconds. That such a performance should be taken for granted amazed Philly. Freddie Chadwick was a master craftsman, yet no-one ever commented on his skill.

Her own side of the business thrived, though the landlord had stepped in and put the rent up as soon as he heard of this new scheme. But even after she'd paid three shillings a week on top of her domestic rent, Philly had more than enough for herself, the old girl and Patrick to live on. Of course, the newly reformed Mother Blue insisted on earning her keep and she often left the baby with Edie so that she could push the handcart round the streets. The real reason for this, thought Philly, was that Mother wanted an opportunity to show off her new look, a look that was indeed original and quite startling. Apart from the wig, Mother Blue had acquired an exceptionally large set of dentures from a rag and bone man, swapped for a few old clothes and a broken metal fire-box. These terrifying teeth were on display at all times, for the simple reason that the old lady could not close her mouth when they were in position. During meals, Mother's 'furniture' went into a pocket because she could manage a great deal better without it cluttering up her small mouth. At night, the offending items sat on the scullery window sill, grinning hugely in a glass of water until morning came, whereupon they would be wedged once more between permanently parted lips.

But however odd the old soul looked, she had certainly done the business a lot of good by travelling further afield with the cart, thereby advertising Ma Maguire's Cures over a wider field and attracting more custom to the shop. Edie, Mother and Philly had to stay up late many a night while Arthur minded the babies, so great was the demand for various tonics and potions.

As time passed, Philly got her looks back, though she never quite regained the youthful sparkle she'd displayed before the illness. But she remained a fine-looking woman, more mature now, given less frequently to bouts of temper. In School Hill she was highly respected, while in Delia Street itself, she was undisputed queen. It seemed that her brush with death had been a mellowing experience, for she became kinder, more thoughtful and appreciative of her neighbours and clients. Yet even now, the occasional glimpse of an Irish paddy was sighted when she tackled a neglectful mother or a delinquent child. Such was her quiet power, that a mother only had to threaten a child by saying, 'I'll send you down to Ma's,' for the young person in question to hesitate and review his attitude. Yet although she was not averse to telling others how to rear their offspring, Philly's handling of her own son continued far from perfect. For this she was universally forgiven, because had she not almost lost him at birth? And she was, at least, more reasonable now, easier to approach, more patient and forgiving.

So it was a very surprised Delia Street that witnessed Ma Maguire's outburst at the end of August. Both she and Freddie had worked late and were ready to close when a carriage pulled up at the door. As the mill owner climbed down on to the pavement, those who recognized him doffed caps and stood open-mouthed while he entered Skenning Freddie's shop. Within minutes, Mr Swainbank was on the pavement again with Ma behind him, her voice gathering strength and volume as she spoke. 'Examine your leg? And why should I be doing that when I've been refusing to visit the really sick? Don't you dare come here! I've told you before, the servant can pick up your medicines—'

'But I wanted you to have a look . . . ' He seemed amazed, almost afraid of the tall woman who pursued him relentlessly to the edge of the flags.

'I don't do treatments any more, not even for my neighbours. Except, of course, in cases of extreme emergency where a doctor cannot be afforded. You, Mr Swainbank, can afford a doctor!'

'The doctor is no bloody good!'

'Well, that is no fault of mine! I cannot be stopping my business just to look at your leg, sir. You have no privilege here. This is our patch – yours is down the road among all that filth and grease . . . ' Her voice began to rise even higher in pitch and those who recognized the old symptoms backed away towards their own doors. 'See here, Mr Swainbank. See what did I save for you.' She reached into her apron pocket and pulled out a paper package. 'These are splinters taken by me from the feet of your child slaves. I could light the fire with them, so I could! This large one here . . . ' She held up a particularly vicious-looking item. 'This was wedged for three weeks in the heel of a child who dared not stay at home for fear of his mother starving. In the end, he was forced to have me cut it out of him and I have never seen so much poison before.'

He looked around at the silent crowd. 'Do you have to make a scene?' His voice was steely. 'Can't you act like a rational human being for once?'

'Get out of my street! Go on!'

It was obvious that he didn't know what to do next. If he stayed and argued, then the town would be buzzing with the tale by midnight. If he walked away, she would have won. Aye, a slip of a mill girl would have defeated him and he would never again hold up his head among the workers.

He decided to treat the matter lightly. 'Very well. If you can't accept having been sacked from the spinning room . . . '

'Sacked?' she screamed. 'I was never sacked! I told you where to put the job after that poor child lost his finger.'

He raised his cane and waved it at her. 'You were insubordinate and unemployable.' In spite of his fury, he could not help noticing how her eyes flashed, how her thick dark hair shone in the deep bronze of sunset. 'You are a bloody menace, woman!'

She grinned widely and nodded her head. 'That's right. And you need my powders, don't you? So you still employ me in a fashion, for you buy what I make.' She sighed loudly and raised her palms upwards in a gesture of dismay. ' 'Tis a funny old world now, is it not? There's me unemployable and you employing me all the same. That's a desperate strange thing.'

He brought the cane down from the air with force, whipping it across her cheek and she stumbled towards the wall, a hand to her face. Yet a look of triumph shone from her eyes as several neighbours stepped forward. They were scared of him, right enough, but if he was going to hit Ma Maguire . . .

'Well now,' she muttered, her tone dangerously quiet. 'Isn't that the giddy limit? This is an offence, striking me in the street. Wouldn't it look just great now if I got you prosecuted for such behaviour? And in front of witnesses too?'

He backed away slowly. 'You wouldn't dare—'

'Try me, Swainbank!' The crowd gasped as she spat out his surname, for no-one ever addressed a mill owner in such a way, not within his hearing. 'Hit me again and I'll have the eyes from your head. Will I tell them the truth? Will I tell them that you were after setting me up in a cottage like you did with other mill women—'

'That's a lie!'

'Oh, I know I'd never prove it, not in English law. But here, people know I never lie.' She turned to the crowd. 'He tried to buy me, wanted to turn me into a cheap trinket. Of course, he failed . . . '

Swainbank stumbled up the step and into his carriage, leaning forward to peer through the side window. 'You have made a dangerous enemy in me,' he whispered. 'I'll have you punished, Ma Maguire.'

'Don't threaten me! They hear you even when you whisper. If anything happens to me, they'll know where to send to get justice done. Away with you, Richard Swainbank! And watch your step tomorrow, because I have many friends in the mill and accidents can happen in those terrible places.' She picked up her skirt and went back into the shop. Skenning Freddie pushed her down on to the customers' bench. 'You fool,' he muttered as he examined her face. 'We don't cross swords with his kind.'

'One day, Freddie. One day . . . ' She fought the tears, swallowing hard to stop herself screaming her frustration and anger.

'One day what?'

'The workers will turn on him.'

He dabbed at her cheek with a cloth dipped in witchhazel. 'And what will they do then for a living?'

'Something . . . anything rather than bow to his likes.'

'It's a dream, Ma Maguire.'

'Is it? I don't think so, Freddie. They're reading and writing now, learning to count. All that education will make them clever, too clever to lie down under his dirty boots.'

'Go home, lass. Go home . . . '

She stood on the step and looked at the perplexed faces of those who trusted her, depended on her. Yet all she could see was the look on one man's face, the great sadness in his eyes when she'd turned on him. Like a fish rising to bait, she had felt herself being pulled into the net he was casting in such dangerous waters. Yes, he must have been desperate to see her if he'd resorted to coming here, because this was not a safe place for him. Oh, perhaps he had wanted his leg looking at, but she wasn't going to dance to the bosses' tune, lose face among her own people. Yes, he could have been simply seeking treatment. But as Edie had said all that time ago, there was a lot more to this than just a flaming sore leg.

Without a word to anyone, she held up her head and strode the length of the street where Edie waited to drag her into the house.

'Where's Mother?' asked Philly, trying to keep her voice even.

'Out. She's took the big pram with one at each end. I kept them out of bed with it being warmish, thought a late walk would do them good. Sit yourself down, you're as white as a sheet – except for that stripe he gave you.'

Philly put a hand to her burning cheek. 'Great fool of a man! What does he want to come here for? I've no time to be stopping just to look at his precious leg—'

'Philly?'

'What?'

Edie took a deep breath, her head shaking slowly from side to side. 'I never had no sisters or brothers, 'cos me mam died having me and me dad popped off a few years back with the drink. So I've never been close to nobody 'cepting you.' She paused as if deep in thought. 'He was all right, me dad – when he was sober – but he put Arthur off the bottle for good, made him feel he had to go down the mission and sign the pledge. I've never really had a family apart from Arthur and Molly. Till you, Philly. It's like I've known you all me life, like as if we was raised together.' She plucked at her white apron, her face pink with embarrassment. 'I love thee, lass, like I'd love a sister – and I know what you're thinking and feeling a lot of the time. Oh, I know you're a deep one, but it's plain to me that you love that man—'

'Edie!'

'You can't help it, Philly! You can't stuff your feelings in a box and put the lid on them! I mean, look at me dad. A right tearaway, he was, somebody to be ashamed of most of the time. But I loved him.'

'He was your father—'

'He was a drunk. There was times he beat me, times we had nowt to eat with him supping the lot. I never hardly went out, for I'd nothing to wear. He was not a good man, Philly. And I worshipped the flags he stood up on. When he could stand up, like. Yet all the while, part of me hated him so much . . . ooh, I could have killed him some days. Love's like that, Philly. What you feel for that man, all that hate . . . it's part of it, don't you see? You care about him—'

'I don't! Except as a good Catholic woman who'd care about any soul damned to perdition. I do not love him, Edie!'

'Aye well. He certainly gets you going, same as I've said before. And there's more to it than anger, a lot more. Why the hell do you think you said all that in the street, all that about him offering to set you up? It were nowt to do with shaming him, Philly Maguire! That were so's you'd keep yourself safe, stop being tempted by him. I might not be a particular clever woman, but I know what I see and I speak as I find. There's torment in your soul, love. He wants you and you want him. And you can't have one another.'

The two women stared across the space between them in silence for several moments.

'Don't worry, lass,' said Edie finally. 'The secret's safe with me. And you know what? Part of me envies you, even if I have got the best husband in the world, 'cos I've never felt

87

what you're feeling now. Nobody ever made me so angry, nobody ever made me so alive.'

'Even your father?'

'That were different. With Arthur, there's just been safety and kindness – I don't think we've ever had a real row. Don't get me wrong, I wouldn't swap him for any man, but there's never been a lot of . . . fire. You might not be able to feed your fire, but at least it's been lit.'

'I never asked for it. I never wanted . . . all that. It's confusing, Edie, because I hate him for what he does to people, for his . . . arrogance towards ordinary folk. But there's . . . oh, I don't know . . .'

'Something about him? Something you can't put your finger on?'

'Fire burns fingers. Fire's a destructive thing. I don't want to get consumed by it, Edie. I'll put it out if it takes every bucket of water in the town and all my life . . .'

'And I reckon it might, lass. Aye, I reckon it just might.'

Chapter 3

1910

Paddy Maguire hated school from the very first day. For a start, he was expected to work and work was something which held little appeal for him. And he was forced to be obedient, because if he misbehaved the punishment was swift and severe. At the beginning, in the baby's class, he would run home and tell everything to his mam, who would then take time off from the shop to come up and raise Cain with the teachers. She was great at that. If anybody laid so much as a finger on him, the classroom door would be flung open and there she would stand, hands on hips, eyes darting venom at the unfortunate soul who had dared to whip her precious son.

But after a while, this had to stop. For one thing, the other children started to laugh at him and for another, his mam got wise after a session with the headmistress, a terrible woman with a passion for catechism and the ten commandments. When, after well over a year at school, Paddy had learned none of his religious lists, Sister Concepta sent for his mother and told her straight that the lad was idle, shiftless and sinful. At about this time, Mam started to treat him differently, nagging him gently about his lessons, making him recite things at home and generally siding with the school.

He was fed up. The other children stopped calling him 'mother's little lad' and chanted 'dunce' after him in the street, so he pulled up his socks and learned to read in a week. Within a month he had won two catechism prizes and a medal off the priest for knowing his commandments. So, having shown his hand thus far, he decided to hang for a sheep and, after discarding the many layers his mother forced her 'weakly' boy to wear, he came first in the flat race, third in the hurdles and would have won the three-legged as well if his partner had shown a bit of sense.

Philly knelt nightly before her statue of the Virgin, a smile of thanks on her lips, a prayer of absolute gratitude in her heart. The boy was well at last. Hadn't he won all the races and learned his lessons, wouldn't he make a fine man? It had still not occurred to her that Patrick was simply taking the line of least resistance, that he would continue to do as he was told as long as it suited his needs, not one moment longer.

The main source of trouble with the two children was Molly, which surprised both women immensely. She had been a biddable baby, a sweet and charming child with a nature as sunny as a long midsummer day. But now she was suddenly a rebel, both clogs dug well in every morning because for the first time since birth, she and Paddy were separated by their schooling. Everyone said she would 'get used in time', but few had made room in their calculations for Molly's sheer determination. Time after time she escaped from the chapel school, walked the length of a main road and charged into Paddy's classroom. If he could go to the Catholic school, then so could she.

In the end, Arthur, a dedicated chapel man, decided to look into it. He had no real prejudices and was quite willing to allow Molly her way, but Edie stepped in. 'You're what? You're letting her go to St Peter's? Whatever for?'

'Because she wants to. They said she can stop out of the religious lessons, though I don't mind if she—'

'Arthur Dobson! We've never crossed swords before, but we shall now.'

'But why? What's wrong with her going to the same school as her little friend? They've never been apart before. Have a heart, Edie.'

She folded her arms beneath the ample bosom and raised her eyes to heaven as if seeking divine assistance in the face of such stupidity. 'Look, Arthur. That there lad has had his own road since birth. She's happen cottoned on to it, thinks she can do the same by creating. Well, she can't. I won't have her spoiled like him, that I won't. Little upstart, thinking she can have her own road by throwing the odd tantrum and shutting herself upstairs.'

'Nay, Edie—'

'Look. If she'd been a lad, I'd likely have tanned her backside before this. That's my daughter, Arthur. I'm the mother, I'm the one as has to see to her. If we'd had a son instead, then happen you would have had more of a say. But girls is a mother's responsibility and I'm seeing to it that she grows up decent and with a bit of respect for what's asked of her. She will not go to the Catholic school. Not that I've owt against them, only you're chapel and I'm not bloody bothered.' She held up a hand. 'And don't start on about me swearing – if I were going to reform, I'd have done it a while back.'

He sank into the wooden rocker under the window, hands folded together as if in prayer. 'She's unhappy, lass.'

Edie strode across the room and banged the teapot on to its stand. 'Unhappy? Unhappy's a thing she'll have to get used to. What's down for her, Arthur? A bit of reading and writing followed by years in a mill then kids of her own to worry about. It's a matter of discipline, I think they call it. Sooner she learns, the better for her.'

'And you won't budge?'

'That I won't!'

Molly crept out through the back door and shut herself in the new tippler netty, tears of fury just about held back by gritting her teeth hard. Mam didn't love her. If Mam loved her, she'd let her go to school with Paddy and all them nuns, so important they looked in their long black frocks and veils. And she'd be able to go into the church on holy days, look at the stained-glass windows and listen to the singing. Her own church was boring, just a bare room, songs about Jesus and picture slides showing drunk men coming home to hit their wives and babies. No statues, no nice smelly stuff in a big tin hung on chains, no feller in a long frock at the front giving out round bits of bread. There was little excitement at the chapel, just a bloke carrying on about drinking and smoking, as if she cared.

But she'd been. Only once, but she'd been all right to a do

called Benediction, smuggled in by Paddy when they were supposed to be playing on the rec. Oh, they were lovely, them songs. Summat about Tantum Ergo, all in a foreign language, everybody bowing and scraping as if it was dead important. And when they walked at Whit, all the brewery horses done up, banners flying in the breeze, statues held high by big proud men, little girls in white dresses and veils, brass bands and bagpipes . . . ooh, lovely, it was. Big, colourful, soul-stirring. And at the end, when they got to the centre, some man would sit on one of the stone lions under the clock, waving a flag while thousands of Catholics sang 'Faith of our fathers, holy Faith, we will be true to thee till death.' Grand, it was. Course, Paddy walked, but she was just a spectator with the rest. On a lucky year, they paid sixpence for box seats at the edge of the pavement, but she usually saw it all from her father's shoulder.

What now? Mam had put her foot down, so there'd be no point carrying on about it. She was only little, was Mam, but she always got her own road one way or another. Molly leaned against the whitewashed walls, heedless of the warnings she'd had about coming in covered in flakes of paint. Well, she'd just have to wait till she was thirteen. At thirteen, you left school and did what you wanted. Then she'd marry Paddy in that lovely church and walk every Whit. That would put Mam's nose out of joint and no mistake. Till that time, she'd better get on with it, be like Paddy and pretend to be good.

'Molly?'

She put her head round the door to find Paddy hanging over the back gate. 'Any luck?' he asked.

'No. We'll just have to wait till we can get wed.'

'All right.' He didn't look terribly worried about any of it. 'Coming out, are you?'

'Where are you going?'

'Away from me mam. She's after me with brimstone and treacle again.'

'Oh. Didn't you get dosed at Easter with all the street?'

'Yes. Our classroom was rotten that week, I think she'd done everybody in it. If you'd lit a match, we'd have gone up like a bomb. That's what Skenning Freddie says anyroad. But she's after giving me an extra lot, so I'm off.'

They fled down the back street, Molly happy because she was with Paddy, he happy because he had escaped, however temporarily, an extra spring-cleaning. They sat on a pile of bricks at the edge of a small recreation area commonly known as Butler's rec. Nobody knew who Butler was and few cared, never giving a thought to a man who had bequeathed this small island for children to play in.

'There's no fun,' moaned Molly, her little mouth down-turned. 'And we're still not seven, so we can't go nowhere. There's been nowt at all since Mother Blue's funeral. That was great, eh?'

'I liked her,' mumbled Paddy. 'She made me laugh. Mam's about as much fun as a punctured ball, never laughs no more. They were always fighting, her and Mother, but I reckon Mam misses her.'

'My dad says that was the finest send-off anybody ever got. All them black horses with feathers, crowds following – it was a bit like the walks only sad. Your mam went all to Liverpool, didn't she?'

'Yes. Some nuns' house, trying to find out how old Old Mother Blue really was. It come out at ninety-seven after they'd reckoned up. That means she were born in 1812. I can't imagine being nearly a hundred years old, can you?'

'How do you count so fast? Are you still top of the class?'

'Naw. Can't be bothered. I like reading books though, history books.'

'What are you going to be, Paddy? A teacher?'

He shrugged his thin shoulders. 'I'm not going down the pit and I'm not going in any mill. Me mam says I'll have to work outside on account of being weak in the chest. I'm fed up with being weak in the chest, but if it keeps me out of the pit, I shan't be right bothered. Happen I'll do summat with horses. I like horses.'

'Shall we have a farm, Paddy? Our own farm with pigs and cows and hens? And statues like what your mam has on her dresser and church every Sunday, proper church with candles?

And nobody to tell us where we can go and where we can't . . . ?'

'And no brimstone and treacle.' He sighed deeply. 'Thank God it's near Christmas and nowt to pick. She had me tramping three moors looking for comfrey a few weeks back, said the walk would do me chest good.' He stood up, hands thrust deep into the pockets of his knee-length breeches. 'I get a bit fed up with it. The house stinks of that balsam she makes and I daren't say nothing to her if I feel a bit ill. She sent me to school last week with a hot potato tied to me ear with a scarf, said she could tell with me face I had earache again. Course, I threw it away before anybody saw me. Same with all that bacon fat wound round me throat not long back – honest, I stank like Sunday's breakfast. She puts that much goose-grease on me chest . . . ' He pulled her towards the pavement. 'If I stop out any longer, she'll be looking for me.'

As they made their way home, each could hear the sound of child-calling from the close-linked alleys and streets. Every youngster recognized his own mother's call and it was not too long before they caught the familiar cry, 'Padd . . . eee? Padd . . . eee?'

'Brimstone and treacle,' he muttered quietly.

'Better than chapel,' said his companion. 'Anything's better than chapel . . . '

On Wednesday, 21 December, Paddy sat in class with the rest, everyone feeling slightly relaxed because school would close that afternoon. It had even touched the nuns, this festive spirit, and the lads at the back seemed to have got away with singing 'one on a trolley waving his brolly and one with a fat cigar' when it came to the three kings bit. It was near dinner time; once the sing-song was over, he'd be able to get out for a bit of fresh air. Smells got to Paddy. The close proximity of four dozen young bodies, many of them unwashed, almost made him gag at times. Not that he was a great one for washing himself, but he was glad he didn't pong like some of them did, all cabbage water and mucky socks.

Then he heard it above the singing, the frantic calling in the street, 'Special! Special edition! Read all about it!' but he took little notice as he was happily absorbed in making spit-balls out of paper, seeing how many he could make stick in the girls' hair.

As 'Silent Night' struggled its way to a discordant end, Sister Concepta bustled in and engaged in a short whispered conference with Miss Miles, after which the nun held up her hand, a signal that demanded and invariably achieved total silence. 'Does anyone here have a relative in the Pretoria mine?' she asked, her voice unusually gentle. Several hands, including Paddy's, shot into the air.

'Come out those of you with a father in that mine,' she said. Two boys stepped forward. 'And those with a brother – or a female relative working on the surface?' Three further children crept to the front of the class. 'Patrick Maguire?'

'It's me uncle – Uncle Arthur from next door.'

'Then come out here with the others. The rest of you will continue as normal until recess.'

They were led out into the corridor and down to the headmistress's office where they stood in a line before her desk. Without more ado, Sister Concepta opened her top drawer with a key and took out a large metal box. To each astounded child she handed a full silver shilling. 'Go home now, children, for you will be needed this day above all days. Give comfort to your loved ones, help your mammies with the family and take as much joy as you may from Christmas.' She turned away from them, but they could tell from the shaking of her shoulders that Sister Concepta, immovable, unlovable, indomitable, was weeping.

Not one of them dared ask questions. After whispering their terrified thanks, they fled from the school and into the street. Paddy and two of the others immediately collared the lad who was selling the special edition. 'What is it?' asked Paddy, though he knew the answer. Even at six years of age, these children knew what to dread.

'Pit's gone up,' replied the boy.

'Gone up?'

'Aye. Exploded – you know? Boom?' He walked away to continue selling the bad news.

The small group of frightened infants looked at one another for a second or two, then each set off homeward as fast as little legs would move.

Paddy's house was empty, so was next door. He flew down to Skenning Freddie's and found the shop closed for the only time within his memory. Perplexed, he walked back to wait for Molly who would be home soon for her dinner. Then fat Mrs Halligan from across the road staggered out to the middle of the cobbles. 'You've to come in ours, you and Molly.'

'Why?'

'Because . . . because I said so. And don't go telling nowt to that poor lass . . . ' She turned and wobbled back inside the house, a hand to her eyes. Paddy sank on to his doorstep, a lead weight in his chest. Uncle Arthur? He was the nearest thing to a dad Paddy had ever known, kind, generous, full of stories about getting stuck in the pit, about miners always helping one another like Christians should, about canaries and gas, pit ponies . . . And then there was Molly. For what was probably the first time in his young life, Paddy actually thought about someone else. He was her dad! Uncle Arthur was Molly's dad! Sometimes Paddy felt a bit mad about not having a father like most other kids, so how would Molly feel about suddenly losing one? Still, he happen wasn't dead. It might be only a few of them.

When Molly got back, he explained away the sudden change of dinner time venue, saying that the two mothers had gone to see a herbalist for some stuff. Mrs Halligan smiled at him across the table. 'And you can both stop here and help me with the baby this afternoon.'

'Why?' asked Molly, eyes wide with amazement.

'It's me legs.'

Molly nodded. She knew that Mrs Halligan suffered from something called 'melegs' because she was often called upon for messages and errands. While the little girl played happily with the baby, Mrs Halligan took Paddy into the scullery. 'Be brave, lad. It looks like they've all gone.'

'All of them?'

'Most, anyroad. Seems as if her's heard nowt anyrate.' She

nodded her head towards the kitchen. 'Keep it that way, son.'

'I will.' He brushed a tear from his eye. 'Where's me mam and Auntie Edie?'

'Gone up Westhoughton to the pit-head. There must be thousands on 'em up there by now. I don't know when they'll get back. Don't cry, lad. For Molly's sake, hang on till we know for sure.'

They brought out what was left of Arthur late in the evening. He lay under coal sacks with dozens of others, men and boys whose number would eventually total in excess of three hundred. Philly had to leave her friend with Freddie, because many of the rescuers were getting injured as they fought to reach their dead colleagues. She spent hours tearing up shirts and petticoats ripped willingly from spectators' own backs, bathing heads in water fetched from nearby cottages, giving out sweet tea and steaming soups. There was a strange silence about the behaviour of this vast but united crowd. Women wept noiselessly while men brought out one body after another, scarcely disturbing the scarred earth as they moved with their precious bundles of dead humanity. From miles around they came, faces set and grim, many just out of their beds and ready for a shift to begin, some coming from other pits after hours of toil.

When she knew that no more could be done, Philly returned to Edie and took her hand. 'Come on, mavourneen. 'Tis time we were home for the children.'

'What?'

'Time to go home.'

'Aye. There's Arthur's bath to get ready. Yes, we'd best hurry up.'

Freddie grabbed hold of Philly's arm. 'She's not took it in, love. Look, there's a flat cart over yonder going Bolton way. I reckon there's room for us three.' They lifted Edie on to the vehicle which held miners and many grieving widows. The man next to Philly was sobbing quietly, tears making twin white rivers on coal-blackened cheeks. She took his hand. 'God bless you all for trying.'

He sniffed loudly. 'Stock up on coal, Missus,' he muttered.

'What?'

'This is just the start. Seven months ago, we lost 136 lads up Cumberland. I reckon there's twice that gone here today and we've had enough, lass.' He wiped his nose on the sleeve of his coat. 'My lad's still down there.'

'I hope they get him out.'

He turned to look at her. 'What for? One burial place is as good as another. He's been buried alive down there since he left school anyroad, so what's the bloody difference? Nay, we've had it now. Mark my words, this time next year there'll be no coal for nobody. Mills'll shut and poor folk'll have to spend their nights picking slack off the heaps or chopping trees.'

'A strike, then?'

'Aye. And it won't just be us, neither. At the finish, we shall bring every bugger out and to hell with the bosses.'

'And not before time, Mister, not before time.' She looked at Edie who seemed to think she was out on a joyride, all smiles and giggles. Freddie put a heavy arm around the tiny woman as she shivered in the cold December frost. He shook Philly's sleeve. 'You'll have to tell Molly. This one's well gone with the shock. I don't know what you're going to do with her once you get her home. Have I to stop with you? Me wife won't mind, she's an understanding sort . . .'

'It's all right, Fred. The neighbours will all help for sure. He was such a good man. Why? Why, Fred?'

For answer, he simply shrugged broad shoulders and turned away, pulling Edie closer, trying to lend some heat to the frozen body. 'He's gone, lass,' he whispered. 'Arthur's dead, killed down the pit. You'll have to tell yon lass of yours.' Edie pulled the shawl tight about her head. 'By, it's cowld,' she said. 'Good job I've tripe and manifold in. He likes tripe and manifold with plenty of onion and a drop of vinegar. I wonder if there's enough swede to put to that carrot, though? Happen I should have got a penny swede today, Philly. A nice big one to put with his carrots . . .'

'He's dead, Edie!' screamed Philly while everyone else on the cart remained still and quiet. 'Get it into your head for

Molly's sake, your man is not coming home for his tripe and onions! Nobody's coming home! Nobody!' And she began to weep for all of them, howling their collective grief into a black sky.

When they finally reached St George's Road, Freddie helped the two women down and led them through the maze of streets until they were home. He took Edie into her own darkened house while Philly fetched the children from across the way. One look at Paddy's face told her that he already knew and she nodded her grim confirmation before guiding Molly to the leather chair. 'Sit down, child.'

'Where's me mam?'

'She's . . . busy. I wonder would you like to sleep here tonight? I'll be popping in and out to help your mammy, but you can bed down in Mother Blue's old room . . . '

'What about Monty? I can't sleep without him.'

'I'll get your bear when I go to see Edie. All right?'

The child nodded slowly. 'There's something up, isn't there, Auntie Philly?'

'Yes.'

Paddy stepped forward, almost pushing his mother aside. 'I'll look after you, Molly. I've never had no dad, so I know what it's like.'

The little girl swallowed hard. 'Me dad?'

'Yes,' replied Paddy. 'Gone to Jesus. He's gone to Jesus 'cos he's a grand man and Jesus wanted him for singing and that. They need good singers, specially at Christmas.' He had obviously given time and effort to the preparation of this short speech.

'Will he . . . will he come back? After Christmas, like?'

'No.'

Philly stepped back and watched her son doing the job better than she could have ever expected – and far better than she might have managed herself. He squeezed on to the chair at the side of his little friend. 'Your dad was chosen.'

'But . . . ' Her lip began to quiver. 'I want him. He's my dad and I want him here to tell me stories and play with me.'

'He can't be here no more – can he, Mam?' Paddy, beginning to flounder now, looked to his mother for help.

'That's true enough. He's gone to heaven, child.'

'He's dead? My daddy's dead?'

'Yes, Molly.'

'Killed in the pit?'

'Yes, I'm afraid so. It's very sorry we all are, Molly, for we shall miss him very badly.'

The little girl jumped up. 'I want me mam,' she sobbed.

Philly caught the small girl and held her tight against her own shaking body. 'Your mammy's taken it badly, love – she's not herself just now. You must stay here and look after Paddy, just as he will take care of you. Mammy's in dire need of my help just now. Paddy!'

'Yes, Mam?'

'Keep her here. I must away next door and see what does she need. Get some bread and butter from the scullery, put a bit of life into the fire and give this child a small glass of barley wine – that will make her sleep.'

She ran next door. Freddie was sitting by the dying fire, exhaustion plain in his eyes. 'Where is she?' asked Philly anxiously. Freddie pointed towards the scullery door where Edie was struggling to drag in the tin bath. 'Whatever is she doing?'

Freddie ran a hand over his balding pate. 'Nothing that makes sense, lass.'

'Go home, Fred. And thanks for everything.'

'Are you sure? What if she gets past handling?'

'She won't.'

After he had left, Philly sat and watched while Edie stoked the fire and filled the huge copper with water for her husband's bath. Not a word was uttered as the little woman pushed tripe and onions into the oven and set places for the customary evening meal.

'It's ten o'clock,' said Philly at last. 'Shouldn't you be thinking of your bed, Edie?'

The small woman looked at her friend as if noticing her for the first time. 'I never go to bed without Arthur. He's . . . he's happen having trouble getting home . . . '

'Yes.'

'With the weather so bad and it's a long way to walk up Westhoughton and back every day.'

'I know that.'

Edie leaned against the table. 'Have you noticed he's a bit bandy? His legs, like. I've often said we could drive a coach and horses between his knees.'

Philly smoothed her apron and watched her friend's quickening movements, table to dresser, dresser to door, door to table. 'Go on, Edie.'

'Did you know why he's bandy? Did you know? 'Cos he spends half his time doubled over in a little hole in the ground, hardly big enough for a kiddy to stand up in. Like a mole, he is, digging away, never stood up proper on his feet except when he's coming out. Or going in.'

'Sure, that's a terrible life now, Edie.'

The small round woman waved a hand towards the bath. 'I do this every day. I always scrub his back with Pinkabolic where he can't reach, then I take his clothes outside and bat them with me carpet beater. You should see what comes out! I could keep the blinking fire going with all that dust.'

'I'm sure you could.'

Edie took salt, pepper and malt vinegar from the dresser and placed them in the centre of the table. 'I told him it were tripe this morning. I said "You be home early for your tea," but he's not come, has he? I wonder if he's gone straight to meeting?'

'Not in his dirt, girl.'

Edie stared hard and long at her best friend, eyes locking into those bright blue orbs which contained that terrible message, the message she would not open her mind to. But she could not deny for ever such merciless honesty and in the end, her gaze was averted towards the fire. She steadied herself against the dresser, her face a mask of confusion and incredulity. 'He were a grand man, Philly.'

'He was indeed.'

'It's not true, is it? I mean, anybody can be a bit late. And it didn't really look like him, did it?' Her voice began to rise with hysteria. 'That weren't my Arthur! That were some

101

other feller with the same hair. And there wasn't enough of him . . . he's such a big feller . . . that one they brought out seemed so little . . . Oh God! Oh my God!'

Philly jumped up and grabbed this tormented piece of humanity, drawing her close against her breast. 'It was himself, Edie. And he was not alone, for hundreds of his fellows perished today.'

'No! No! It can't be right! I've his bath ready and his tripe . . . I don't like tripe, neither does Molly. He's got to come home and eat it else it'll go to waste.' Her mouth opened wide as she screamed, 'Who'll eat me tripe, Philly? Who's going to eat it now?'

The larger woman fought to swallow her own rising tide of grief. It was always the same with these Lancashire girls – probably the same with all grieving wives and mothers. In the end, it was something small that got to them, an empty chair, a cold pipe, an old sock on the bedroom floor. With this one it was a plate of tripe and onion and no man to eat it. She spoke gruffly into Edie's hair, bending to reach the tiny head. 'Remember Mrs Murphy's ginger tom? Arthur loved that cat, always fetched it in for a taste of his dinner. If Arthur could speak now, he'd tell you to give the tripe to old Ginger. Shall we do that? Then it won't be wasted?'

'All right.'

After steering Edie to a chair, Philly took the dish from the oven and placed it on the table.

'Some milk too,' said Edie. 'He likes milk, does Ginger.'

This strange procession of two made its way down the street to the Murphys' house and Philly knocked quietly. Pierce Murphy opened the door, his face still red with weeping. 'Ah, 'tis Mrs Dobson now. Come in.'

The women stepped into the room. 'We've brought Arthur's supper,' said Philly, her eyes fixed on Pierce's face as if telling him to simply go along with everything. 'Edie had a notion that Ginger might like to eat it.'

'To be sure, he would,' replied the burly Irishman.

'You'll have to pick the onion out.' Edie's voice trembled. 'Arthur likes . . . liked onion, but the cat doesn't.'

Philly left the dishes on the table and returned to her friend's side.

'I . . . was there,' mumbled Pierce. 'It's not my pit, but I went all the same. We all did, but there was nothing . . . '

'I know. We were there too. Come along now, Edie.'

Mrs Murphy appeared at the stairway door, her eyes still streaming. 'You poor woman!' she exclaimed before turning to run back to her children.

Pierce coughed self-consciously. 'She's thinking I'll be next. We're very sorry, Mrs Dobson.'

'Thank you. Don't forget to pick the onion out.'

It seemed that the giving away of Arthur's dinner had done the trick because as soon as they got back, Edie began to grieve in earnest, going about the house in a terrible rage, screaming at God and man alike as if she didn't know which to blame for the death of her husband. Philly allowed this to run its full course, using quieter moments to move the bath and make several brews of tea. She knew better than to try and reason with Edie; grief was not responsive to rational argument. When all the swear words had had a good airing, the little body slumped on to the sofa and drifted into fitful sleep.

Philly took the opportunity to run next door with Molly's bear, only to find the two children wrapped together in the big bed, both still fully clothed and tear-stained. She laid the toy on the pillow by Molly's head and left the pair of them to sleep out their shared pain.

Bolton saw too many funerals that week. In a strange way, those who had funerals were lucky, because many bodies remained undiscovered, some in places that would not be reached for months. Up at Westhoughton where the pit head stood, one street lost every man and boy, while almost fifty residents were taken from a single street in Daubhill. Arthur's was not the only death in School Hill, but there were sufficiently few for the funeral to be over in time for Christmas. Normally, a body would be kept in a house for several days, but in deference to Molly and Paddy, the two women did away with the niceties and hastened matters. It was a very plain affair, for Arthur had been a plain man, a chapelgoer

103

with no time for frills. There was no gathering after the simple burial, just the four of them together in Philly's house with a small meal of ham, bread and butter.

The two children retired to play quietly on the frozen pavement outside, making a few half-hearted attempts at sliding along the flags. It didn't seem right to play, but the mothers wanted to talk in private.

Philly poured yet more tea into two of the best cups and studied her friend and neighbour covertly. She was quiet enough, though the suffering was etched deeply into the round, plump face. There was little money, Philly knew that. Apart from the burial fund, no provision had been made against this terrible eventuality because the means to furnish such provision had never been available. 'What will you do now, Edie?'

'I don't know, I've not thought. He's only been gone two days and buried already – it's not decent. We should have sat with him—'

'Over Christmas and two children to consider? Arthur would never have allowed that and you know it. So. What next?'

She shrugged her shoulders. 'Christmas Eve tomorrow—'

'Don't be worrying about that now, for the neighbours have seen to the shopping and you will both eat here. I mean after Christmas, love. Whatever will you do about the rent with no proper wage coming in?'

'I don't know.' Nor did she care, from the sound of her voice.

Philly took a deep breath. 'I want you both to live here with me,' she said. 'There's the extra bedroom and we'll open up the parlour to give you a place to be a family.'

'Eh?'

'It makes sense, does it not? The house has three rooms upstairs, so you and Molly can share, leaving Paddy with the smallest one.'

'But . . . but I can't pay any rent.'

'Did I mention rent, now? Did you hear me asking . . . ?'

'No. But I'm not living on charity, even yours.'

Philly pursed her lips in frustration. 'You can help with the shop, take the cart out if you like – and there's the compensation fund, you will surely be given something . . .'

'I'll get a job off Swainbank. I worked there before, so he'll likely have me back, I were a good tenter. I may be newly widowed, Philly, but I've got me pride. That's your business, the medicines and—'

'But you've always helped me!'

'That were different, that were for extras! I'm . . . I'm the head of a family now, like it or not – and I've to earn keep for me and my daughter.'

'Will you move in here, though?'

Edie stared hard and long into the fire. 'Aye. The one thing as terrifies me is being on me own. Oh, I know I'd have Molly, but it's not the same as having somebody older, somebody to turn to. He were always there for me, you see—'

'I know.'

'You don't, lass.' She shook her head thoughtfully. 'You go up to any woman in this street and ask her how much her husband earns. She'll likely tell you she's no idea, 'cos she just gets what she's given and he keeps the rest. Most of these men look on their wives as servants – they never think to hand over more money when kids are born. So, the wives go on, another mouth to feed, then another, having to make the money stretch from here to bloody Manchester. After a few years, there's no love lost and no respect given, 'cos they've grown that far apart with him at work or down the pub and her tied to the kitchen. Aye, you wonder why the women gossip over the backs. Gossip's cheap, all they can afford, it's their entertainment.' She lifted her head proudly. 'We weren't like that. I got the full packet and he took what he needed, different every week according to what he wanted to do. If I needed more, he'd give me some back. We never lost our . . . dignity, me and Arthur. I'll not clap eyes on his likes again.'

'No.'

'It weren't . . . exciting or nothing, but it was . . . good.'

'I know that, Edie. I've eyes in me head. There's many a

time I've been glad of Arthur's reliable ways. But we've got to go on, make the best we can. I think he would have liked us to stick together.'

'He would. I've no family and neither has he. So. It's thee and me then, Philly Maguire?'

'If you can put up with Paddy.'

Edie smiled sadly. 'Nay, lass. This is his house. It's him as'll have to put up with me. And I've noticed how he's kept his eye on little Madam for me. Oh aye, I've not been completely blind these past days. I reckon we might make something of him after all.'

Paddy put his head round the door. 'She wants to go to church, light a candle for Uncle Arthur. I know he weren't a Catholic, Auntie Edie, but it's the same heaven, isn't it?'

Edie's tears flowed anew and she opened her arms to the small boy, pulling him tightly to her knee. 'Go and light your candles, lad. It's the same God for all of us, the same heaven.' After the children had left, she raised her haggard face to Philly. 'And the same hell, eh? Here on earth . . .'

Philly ran to her side. 'No! We might be different, but beneath it all, we're Christians and despair is a mortal sin in anybody's book, girl. If it had been you gone and Arthur left, do you think he'd have looked on the world as a bad place? No, he would not. There was hope in Arthur, always hope. Remember? How he'd say, "Never mind, lass, it'll all come out in the wash with a bit of soap and a few prayers"? He never missed a meeting, never gave up even though he worked on hands and knees under the ground every hour God sent him. We've a business, Edie. There's lemon and thick spanish to boil for coughs, oatmeal and comfrey to mix for poultices, your famous hand-cream to make! There's ever tomorrow, don't forget it.'

'I'll try, Philly,' sobbed the grieving woman.

'Of course you will.'

'Will it get better, easier?'

'Yes. After a while, you'll just think of him with gladness in your heart. But it takes time, Edie. Everything takes time . . .'

He hadn't seen much of her over the past few years. She sometimes walked through the market on a Tuesday, noticeable by being a head taller than most other women, stalking about as if she owned the place. His leg still plagued the hell out of him, but he sent the lad for powders now, wouldn't dare expose himself to that anger in the street again. And she'd kept herself so well protected, moving the old woman in, now her neighbour, so there was no point trying to reason with her over the doorstep. Bloody women! Especially that one with her airs and graces, well above her station, she acted. Why, she was nothing but another Irish fishwife, all mouth and flaming cheek, all dark hair, alabaster skin and filthy temper.

He paused at the corner of Market Street and took the watch from his waistcoat pocket. Well, he wasn't going to hang about for ever like a lovelorn idiot; she was likely at the shop anyway, though she did stock up on a Tuesday . . .

'Good afternoon, Mr Swainbank. How's the leg?'

Dear God, you never knew where you were with this one at all! Was that a part of being Irish, he wondered obtusely. They were supposed to be a bit fickle, rather changeable and unpredictable. Was this the same who'd hunted him out of the shop five or six years ago?

She rested a large basket on her hip and looked down at his cane. 'Is that for decoration or support? Did you lose your tongue, now? Come on, man, it's older and wiser we are now, the both of us. Isn't that all long forgotten? I've been giving the powders to your man—'

'Aye. For a price.'

'Well now, you can consider that your bit of charity, for your extra pounds go to help the poor of School Hill. You heard of last week's disaster, I take it?'

'I did.'

'My neighbour was taken. At times like this, Mr Swainbank, I always feel we should try to forget past quarrels. Life is extremely short.'

He coughed. 'The wife has moved in with you?'

Her eyebrows shot upwards in amazement. 'And how did you know that when we only yesterday told the landlord?'

'He's a friend. I told you before—'

'Ah yes.' She faltered now, because wasn't this evidence of his continuing interest? Surely, by now he had someone else, some other woman with whom he could while away his time? 'I'll be on my way, then. Look after that leg.'

'Wait!'

She turned and stared at him, noticing the grey in his whiskers, the many lines around his eyes. 'What?'

He moved closer, shifting his head around in order to ensure that no-one of import was nearby. 'It's ridiculous. I know it's ridiculous and so do you. But I've never got you out of my mind, not completely. It's like . . . like an obsession.' His cheeks glowed as crimson as those of a young boy making his first declaration. 'Philly, I've never told a woman that I—'

'Then don't do it now, please. Especially here in Market Street with the world and his horse passing by.' Her pulses were racing. Yes, it was still there and no, he was not the only ridiculous one. 'It's no good, Mr Swainbank—'

'No good?' His teeth were gritted. 'How do you know it's no good? And traffic like this doesn't run just one way. I must have felt something coming back from you to me—'

'You were mistaken, sir.'

'No.' He removed his hat to display a shock of thick greying hair. 'I have not been mistaken, Ma Maguire. Since that first time when you walked into the manager's office, I've known you were for me. Do you realize that if I could divest myself of my wife and ignore my sons, then I'd . . . I'd—'

'Marry me? I'm already taken.'

'By an absentee?'

'The Faith allows no divorce. I am married for life—'

'And therefore safe from me?'

She would never be safe, not from him and certainly not from herself until one of them died. Why, though? How could she feel so desperately drawn and yet so reviled? Then she remembered her granny, wise old bird, not a tooth in her head, yet with the wisdom of Job. '*Philly, we all get the one special temptation. Look at Jesus now. Did he not go with Satan into the wilderness and Him the Son of God Almighty? And*

108

Satan asked Jesus did He want the whole world, promised Him all the land and sea including Ireland, he did. Your special temptation will come across the waters, for I can see there's little here for you . . . ' Philly swallowed hard, dragging herself back into the here and now. 'I'll always be safe from you. Although you struck me once with your stick, I know that it is not in your heart to injure me again. I wish I could say you displayed the same concern for those who work for you.'

'Just tell me, tell me once that you feel something for me. That will have to be enough.'

She steadied herself against the wall. 'I will not lie any more, because there is no use in doing that. You are a handsome man and I always thought of you as . . . presentable. I don't like you and never will, but . . . '

'Yes?'

'There was something. With you, I always felt . . . matched. We could have had some fights, discussions at best. I sometimes had the cheek to imagine I might alter your ways, make you a better person. And . . . the animal thing, whatever that is, was there too.' She lifted her chin defiantly as she spoke these terrible words. 'But I'm a hard creature, Mr Swainbank. There has been nothing between us because I decided, I made sure.'

He brushed a hand across his eyes as if removing a tear. 'You're an honest woman, Philly. That's what attracted me, though God knows I've cursed you as a liar. Do I give you the satisfaction of knowing how unhappy I am? Will I tell you how drab my life is without you?'

'No. But you will give a thousand pounds to the miners.'

He threw back his head to laugh, then stifled the sound with a gloved hand. 'If ever a son of mine brings home a girl like you, I'll kill him! You'd have the shoes off my feet, wouldn't you?'

'If they fitted and suited a poorer man, I would.'

He held out his hand and she shook it solemnly. 'Give to the poor and get your reward in heaven, Richard.'

'Oh, Philly—'

'I know. It was never to be, fine sir. Now give me back my

109

hand and we shall part as near friends as we can ever be. Look to your wife and children and I shall respect you for that, at least.'

She walked away with her eyes blurred by unshed tears. He wasn't worth weeping for, surely? But there was so much sadness in the man, so much raw suffering . . . perhaps he hadn't had love ever. Perhaps he didn't know or understand what he did to his workers. Were they educated, these rich people? Could they not see what was about to happen, that the poor would unite, rise and bring everybody down like a house of cards?

Yes, it was coming, that day of reckoning. The Welsh miners were agitating and the echo had already reached Lancashire.

She turned at the corner for one last look at him. Had it worked then, that curse? So old he looked, so unbearably miserable. Was his house suffering because she had laid ill-wishes at his door? Surely not. Surely that was all a nonsense?

Their eyes met across several hundred yards and she suddenly shivered. A blinding knowledge entered her mind, a dreadful feeling of premonition. It was hard to define, yet she felt that the link between herself and him was forged in spite of her, outside of her. Somehow, his house and hers were fastened . . . were both houses cursed? She shrugged away the silly thought and made for home. As the English would say, it was all a load of Irish, nothing to take notice of, nothing at all . . .

Part Two

The Twenties

Chapter 4

It was all her fault. If only she'd said less about conditions in the mills, then Molly might have gone for a job with a sight more dignity, a little bit of self-respect at least. But no, Ma Maguire had to open her mouth as usual, open it wide enough to put both feet in and a pair of size twelve boots on top. Aye, there was more pride in tending a mule than there was in what Molly was doing now, bowing and scraping, fetching and carrying up at the big house. Swainbank's house too, with Madam in charge. From the sound of that one, it now came as no surprise that Richard had looked elsewhere for comfort and company. Ma sighed heavily and turned away from the parlour window, flicking a duster over the table before having a last look round. This had been Edie's room, piano sold for more space, fire grate used at last for its proper purpose, Edie's sewing box still sitting to the right of the brass fender. No fire now, though. No Edie, no Molly . . . She closed the door firmly behind her.

In the living room, she spread a heavy blanket over the octagonal table and got on with her makings, poultice mixtures and liniments for this week. It was hard without Edie, hard in more ways than one, because she'd been better than a help. Edie had been her friend and comforter, the only person in the world who truly understood her. Except for him. And the thing between him and her was what most folk round here would call daft, because nothing had ever happened, just a word now and then in town, a raised hat and a slight bow as he passed.

She threw down the bag of oatmeal and sank on to a straight-backed chair. Edie. Going off like that in her sleep without so much as a word of warning, no sign at all that she was ailing.

Eight years now. Eight years with two children to raise, one she loved and one she tried to love. It was hard admitting to herself that she didn't love her own son, harder still to acknowledge the fact that she cared more for Molly than she did for her Paddy.

Oh Paddy! How she had adored him, that scrap of an infant, that warm bundle of humanity . . . Now he was wayward, lazy and difficult, often putting her in mind of his father. Or was it her own fault? Had she protected him too fiercely, cared too much when he was young? He wasn't a bad lad. No, she couldn't call him bad. Just weak and stupid. Yet clever enough to get away with doing as little as possible, greedy enough to believe that the world owed him a living. If only she could push back time, return to the beginning, leave him to scream in his cradle, then, later on, let him fight his own battles. If only she might rekindle that flame, keep it out of the wind, nourish it instead of allowing the elements to extinguish the love while she wasn't looking!

Where was he anyway? Up at one of the farms more than likely, messing about with horses when he could have been earning a crust droving or slaughtering. Not that he'd ever been offered full-time work – oh no, that wasn't entirely his fault. After the war, there'd been few enough jobs to go round and he could only get the casual stuff. But he might do more if only he would try, she felt sure of that.

She dragged a hand through thinning hair and pinned it tight against her scalp. Molly had had to go. They were only seventeen, raised like twins too for the past eleven years, yet Paddy had wanted Molly even at fourteen, was now more determined than ever to make sure of the girl before anybody else caught sight of her. She was a lovely creature, sure enough. Light brown hair all waves and curls, creamy skin and green eyes just like her mother's. It was uncomfortable living with the two of them, him with his possessive vigilance, her forever trying to avoid him. She was strong-willed, was Molly. Blunt too, just as Edie had been. So there'd been nothing else for it. When Molly got the job up at Briars Hall, Ma had simply let go. All the same, it was a pity. The house just wasn't the same without Molly's cheek and laughter, would never be the same again. And Ma was lonely, so lonely that she sometimes felt chilled to the bone even on a hot day. Yes, she remembered the first time she'd experienced that sense of isolation, when she'd rejected Richard's advances in the scullery all those years ago.

Still, there was little sense in sitting here feeling sorry for herself. Self-pity was a sin and she'd no intention of indulging it. Gritting her teeth, she got on with the jobs just as she always did. Rain or shine, the rent wanted paying and plates needed filling.

The front door opened and Paddy strode into the room. He was a slender boy, tall and handsome in a delicate way, with Ma's dark hair and clear blue eyes. He threw his cloth cap on to a chair and stared at his mother.

'Whatever's the matter with you at all, Paddy? Have you done any work today?'

'I've been at Swainbank's.' His voice was cold, as if he were suppressing a great anger. Never mind, thought Ma. At least anger proved that he had some energy, some enthusiasm . . .

'She's been made up to parlour now. I never thought she'd do it, not with the old biddy keeping her in her place. So now she waits on at the table, serves fancy meals and wears a daft pinny with a frill on.'

'So what?'

'I don't know!' He waved his arms about in frustration. 'She's not the same any more. It was all right before, she used to come home and moan about old Mrs Swainbank making her stop in the kitchen. Only now, she'll likely stay there in her little attic bedroom – we won't see her no more.'

Ma dried her hands on her apron. 'Sit down, son.'

'I don't feel like sitting down!'

'Then stand up! Straighten your shoulders, for you've the look of a man with the world's troubles on his back. You don't know you're born, Patrick Maguire! Now, listen to me. You obviously don't know Molly as well as you should. She will not forget us. No amount of pretty frills will keep her away. What is keeping her away is you!'

He stumbled across the rug and fell into the leather chair, his mouth agape. 'Me? What the hell have I done?'

'You keep following her, Paddy. Every time she turns round, you're there—'

'I drive his bloody cows, don't I?'

'Don't you swear at me, young man! The cows are at the farm, which is not attached to the house – am I right?'

'Yes but—'

'And the animals do not get moved for slaughter every week. There are other farms, Paddy, other farmers who need you to do the droving. And John Preston from the slaughter-house was asking after you the other day – no doubt he has work for you. And where were you when you were needed? Up at Briars Hall spying on Molly.'

He hung his head and sighed. 'When we were kids, we always said we'd—'

'I know all about that, Paddy. But you are still children! Seventeen is no age to be thinking of settling for life. She needs a bit of freedom, lad—'

He lifted his chin defiantly. 'Aye. And so do I. I could do with a bit of freedom from you! All me life you've shouted the odds—'

'Then go, why don't you? See will some other silly woman act as your mother, look after your chest and your hands! I'm not standing in your way – you live here of your own free will.' She came round the table and sat in the carpet chair opposite her son. 'Look. The top and bottom is that you're not getting your own way. I've done this to you and that's the only thing I'm guilty of. For years I gave in to you, allowed you to get away with too much. Well, you're fast approaching manhood and if you don't start showing some sense, then you'll never amount to anything at all.'

He looked hard at her. 'I'm going to marry her, Mam.'

'So you say.'

'There'll never be another girl, not for me—'

'Then pull yourself together, why don't you? Get out and work, show you can make a living, for I won't always be here to provide. What about when children come, have you given that any thought at all? How can you look after Molly when you won't do a job? Wouldn't it be better to prove yourself first?'

'There's no steady work in my line.'

She shook her greying head slowly. 'If you'd stuck to your books—'

'I don't need books to work outside. You always said I had to work outside because of me chest. Do you want me fastened in an office?'

'There might be something to be said for that after all. At least we would know where you were all day. But to get back to the point, stop putting pressure on that poor girl, otherwise she won't be coming here on her days off. And I do not want to lose Molly because of your foolishness. Perhaps she will marry you in time, but that must be her decision, not yours.' She rose to her feet and gazed down at him. The only time he showed signs of life was when Molly was around and his almost perpetual stillness irritated her. 'Get down to Preston's and help him with the pigs.'

He swallowed audibly. 'I hate that smell. That's another thing, you getting me taken on for weekends at the slaughter-house when I was fourteen. I'd no choice, had I? You decided it was good for me, walking miles with animals then killing them. I don't like it—'

'You don't like anything that means getting up out of the chair! Well, I'm telling you now – and it's for your own good – unless you start bringing some decent money into this house, there'll be no plate for you at my table.'

Angrily, he jumped up, snatched his cap and slammed out of the house. Philly sank back on to the chair. Dear God, why had Edie left her with this mess? They'd been reared like brother and sister – she'd never given a thought to this sort of thing happening. And if Molly had any sense at all, she'd set her sights elsewhere, because Paddy was a wastrel, one who'd take the bread from anyone's mouth rather than bestir himself to go out and earn it.

Yes, Edie had been right. All that ruination had reaped its own reward. And Ma Maguire was now gathering in its dubious benefits. She turned and looked at the photograph of Edie and Arthur on the dresser. 'Edith Dobson,' she said quietly, what have you done to me? And how would you have managed this, eh? Would you have thrown him out and told him to leave her alone? 'Tis a desperate situation now. He was never one for work, you knew that. And with his head turned by Molly, he's worse than ever. Whatever shall I do, Edie? Whatever shall I do . . . ?'

John Preston stood in the slaughterhouse doorway, leather apron dripping, hands stained scarlet, face wet with sweat after recent exertion. He looked hard at Paddy Maguire. 'Listen lad. If you don't want the bloody job, just say so. There's no need to go carrying on at young Gizzer – he's nobbut doing what I pay him for.'

Paddy nodded slowly. Yes, Gizzer was well named, because he'd begged long enough at the door to 'gizzer go'. He enjoyed his work, did Gizzer, would likely have done it for no pay if push came to shove. 'There's no call for cruelty, Mr Preston. I still say they should be shot. He bloody enjoys pole-axing them poor creatures and cutting their throats.'

The older man sighed. 'I've told you before – bullets cost money. And we've had one feller with his leg near blew off when the pig shifted over . . . '

'Then do it my way, for God's sake! I've showed you often enough and it's quick. If you break the top of the spine, they feel nowt when you go through the jugular. That'll cost you nowt!' Aye, he had to admit to himself, however begrudgingly, that Ma was good for some things. She'd explained the method, the way she'd been taught by her own family in Ireland. 'It's my way or nothing, Mr Preston.'

John Preston took Paddy's arm and led him out into the middle of the yard where a red river poured into a shallow sough. 'You might not turn up every day and you're not the strongest to look at, but you're the best man I've ever had. I know you don't like doing it, son. Not many of us likes doing it. Only folk have got to eat, haven't they?'

Paddy stopped and turned to look at the cows waiting in the

118

small enclosure. 'They know,' he said quietly. 'Best we can do is to make it quick for them, give them an easier death. It's like a flaming massacre in there with that damned idiot. He hangs them up before they've gone proper—'

'All right.'

'All right what?'

'I'll get shut on him. If you'll promise me a full weekend every week, right to midnight Sundays, then I'll see him off.'

Paddy thought rapidly. If he worked here every weekend, then he wouldn't see as much of Molly, would he? Aye, but happen that might be a good thing if Mam was right. Happen Molly would think more of him if he worked regular and wasn't always there waiting when she got home. 'Right, you're on. But we kill the beasts proper.'

The slaughterman threw back his head and guffawed loudly. 'Who's the bloody boss, eh?'

'You are, Mr Preston.'

'I'm not so blinking sure of that! Hey – seems you've took after your mam after all, telling us all how to go about things. Does it run in your family, then?'

Paddy shrugged his shoulders lightly. It wasn't often he felt so strongly about things, but with animals – well, he cared. If somebody had to kill them, then it might as well be him, because at least he'd make sure they went quickly and with as little pain as possible. 'Naw. Me mam's the one for shouting on the Town Hall steps, not me.'

'Didn't she get locked up once? For turning a cart over when them Cornish miners come up to work the pits?'

'She got cautioned. They couldn't lock her up, Mr Preston. She'd have drove them all daft by morning – that's if she hadn't brought the building down.'

'Fine woman, though.'

'Yes.'

'All for the working man, isn't she?'

'I suppose so.'

'Then you'd best start work, hadn't you, Paddy?'

Paddy grinned. 'Aye. You're not wrong there, Mr Preston. I'd best start work afore she flays me.'

119

He took a deep breath before walking towards his personal nightmare, the one that plagued sleeping hours with monotonous frequency. The colours, the smells, all so clear as he slept. Awake, he always looked into their faces before he did it, always tried to communicate his mute apology before turning them into somebody's Sunday dinner. Asleep, he said the words and saw the sadness, the terror, then finally and worst of all, that awful resignation arriving in dark velvet eyes.

He rolled up his sleeves and donned the leather overall, watching covertly as Gizzer was led out of the shed. Ah well, there'd be no fun for anybody here today. At least he and John Preston did their best, didn't take pleasure in what had to be performed. He sharpened the murderous blade and brought in the first reluctant beast. Nobody could do better than their best.

Richard Swainbank sat at the head of the family table, eyes moving slowly over the occupants of surrounding chairs. Yes, it was true enough – a man could choose his colleagues and his friends, but a family just got visited on him, dumped like an uninvited package with no instructions as to how to make the best use of its contents. This was his birthday. Was he sixty or sixty-one and did it matter anyway? On the sideboard lay a pile of gifts, unsolicited items that he likely wouldn't live to use if his health didn't show some better signs soon.

He pushed a forkful of food into his mouth, not tasting, not enjoying, not even identifying its category. Eating was a thing he did to stay alive these days. He hadn't made a career of it, not like some folk here present.

Yes, what about this lot, eh? What was he leaving behind to pick up the reins and carry on in the famous Swainbank tradition of toil and trade? Oh, Charles was all right in his way, but . . .

He stared down the length of the room to where his wife sat at the opposite end of the table, ears dripping sapphires, neck covered by a collar of pearls, hair pulled back so tightly from her face that the skin of her forehead was stretched, as if held in place by rigid piano wire. Nothing modern about her, no concessions to the fashion of the day from that particular quarter. The servants called her Old Bea – he'd heard them often enough, complaining in audible whispers, going on about her shrewish temper and viperish tongue. Yes, she was an old b— they were right about that. Forty-six at most she was, yet she looked like an old woman, yellow and decaying, hands puffy with arthritis, face screwed up with pain and discontent. She could only get about with the aid of a stick now and her limitations improved her disposition not one jot. Bitter, she was. Like a lemon with all the juice squeezed out of it, a sour and empty sack devoid of life.

He glanced to her right where sat his elder son, Charles. A good enough lad, that one. The only way in which he'd managed to match his younger brother for daftness was by marrying young, far too young in Richard's opinion. If marriage was a life sentence, then good behaviour time should be taken first, before the door got locked and bolted. Still, Charles looked to have a fair head for business, seemed a sensible enough chap. Which was why Richard could not work out how the lad came to be stuck already with an ailing wife who couldn't even get downstairs for the party, too frail to leave her bed just because she was carrying a child. The place opposite Charles was empty. Amelia's place. Richard took a sip of wine and gazed thoughtfully at this unoccupied chair, almost praying that the girl would manage it somehow. Because if she didn't deliver a live child, then the bulk would go to . . . oh God forbid!

Harold. Richard stared at him hard and long. Aye, the young beggar had managed all right, a son delivered as if by special order nine months after the wedding day. Dear darling Alice sat across from her young husband – and what a sight that was, all bangles and beads but not much brain. Every time she opened her mouth a load of caramel-coated gibberish popped out, ten tons of rubbish each day, fast and high-pitched like an overwound music box. Skirts were going to be shorter, even the better class of lady could wear a 'smidgen' of powder, hair would be bobbed soon and London had taken to wearing a narrow scarf around its collective head. Boring, she was. And Harold had chosen her, which said not a lot for him, did it? Mind, they did match. Because Harold wasn't too much when you got right down to it, just a bundle of new clothes and two-tone shoes that were all the rage. All the same, sweet little Alice had produced a son, squawking Cyril as Richard called him on the sly. Even the baby was not likeable, had failed completely to stir any paternalism in the old man.

Richard inhaled deeply and glanced at the clock. Time this particular piece of nonsense was over and done with. 'I've decided to give you a house, Harold,' he said carefully, aware that the hornets would escape any minute now from their nest. 'I know there's plenty of space here, but you're a family now, you and Alice and young Cyril. As you all know, Briars has always gone to the eldest son, so I've had Greenthorne done up.'

Alice's dessert fork clattered into her dish. 'But Daddy! We adore living here with you – don't we, Harold?'

Richard gritted his teeth. Daddy! He'd be glad enough to see and hear the back of that one, sure enough. Aye, she liked living here all right, did young Alice. Servants, everything laid on, not a hand's turn required of her. And she enjoyed waving young Cyril under Charles' and Amelia's noses just to show there was an heir in case the older son's wife wasn't up to producing one. 'It's all settled,' he continued, his voice as carefully controlled as he could manage. 'Charles and Amelia will stay on here. You can move to your new home on Friday week. The place is fully furnished and I'm sure you'll have no trouble getting more staff.'

Harold jumped up, his face distorted by temper and disbelief. 'I'd have thought you'd have wanted us to stay on, Father—'

'Oh yes? And why should I want that?'

Harold seemed to shrink slightly, head dropping, cheeks reddening as he mumbled, 'Well – Cyril's the only grandchild, isn't he?' His voice tapered away, leaving behind an uncomfortable silence. Beatrice was the only one to remain unaffected, but no-one ever expected much reaction from her unless something major happened. Like the napkins arriving badly folded or a supposedly hot dish coming up cold from the kitchen.

Richard pushed back his chair and rose unsteadily to his feet. 'Right, lad. You just listen to me for once. Charles will have a son – probably more than one. You're like a pair of vultures sitting here waiting for Amelia to miscarry that child of hers. Well, I'll watch it no longer. If you want to feed off your brother's misfortune, I think we'd all be more at ease if you did it from a distance.'

'Please, Father . . . ' Charles reached out a hand. 'Don't spoil the party, for goodness sake—'

Richard raised his head and laughed mirthlessly. 'Party? Party, you say? More like a bloody wake if you ask me. Look at your mother – go on, look at her! She can't wait for me to shuffle off so she can get to Blackpool and live with her sister. She hasn't the guts to leave me in case she loses out at the finish.' Beatrice did not even raise her eyes from the plate during this. Richard turned on his younger son now, the full force of his anger apparent in the volume of his voice. 'You're sponging off me no longer, lad! At least your brother works, doesn't go mincing round town all day pretending to do business. After I die – and it won't be long now – I want a sensible chap living in my house, not some jumped-up dandy with a wife as daft as himself!'

Alice fled from the room howling like a banshee, all ideas of etiquette suddenly abandoned.

'Hadn't you better follow her?' Richard's tone was quiet and sarcastic now. 'Can't you even look after your own? I want you out by next Friday. And if you don't start bringing some orders in, there'll be no wages for you either.'

Harold stalked out of the room, flinging his napkin in the general direction of the sideboard as he left.

Beatrice, who had maintained her customary detached silence throughout, simply carried on eating, a task which occupied a great deal of her time these days as she loved her food and could not eat quickly because of rheumatoid fingers.

Charles stood up and walked to his father's side, gently pushing the old man down into the chair. 'Calm yourself, there's a good chap.'

'I'm not a good chap. Ask your mother, see if you get an answer. If you do, it'll be not far short of a miracle, since she's hardly spoken two words to you since you were born—'

'She's not well—'

'Not well? Not bloody well? She's been ill a long time, then.' He beckoned Charles to bend, then whispered in his ear, 'She hates the sight of all of us, Charles. And I hate the sight of her, too.'

The younger man straightened, trying not to smile. Not that it was really funny having parents who so obviously despised one another, but it was ludicrous the way Father carried on talking about her as if she were deaf or elsewhere. And the fact that Mother seldom responded added to the grim humour of the situation. 'You shouldn't get so heated – remember what the doctor said?'

'Heated? No wonder I'm heated with those two hanging about waiting to see if Amelia loses the baby. Greed, that's all it is. They know damned well there's sufficient to go round, yet they want it all for young Cyril.' He banged his fist on the table, causing a shiver of crystal and silver. 'No, it's not for Cyril they want it – it's for themselves.'

'Don't carry on like this! You're doing nobody any good, especially yourself.' Charles lowered his substantial frame into an adjacent carver. 'You'll be popping off before I've got the idea of running Swainbank's properly. How will I manage without you? It's no use making yourself really ill. And I'm sure Harold will improve in time . . . '

'Will he now? I'll lay odds they all said that about Judas, but he still sold out for a few coins, didn't he? I'm telling you now, Charles, watch your back while Harold's around. He's taken after his mother, that one – stab you in the back as soon as he gets half a chance, he will. Mind, there's neither of you had a decent upbringing. What sort of a start did you get from that one, eh? Yes, I'm talking about you, Beatrice! Just look at that youngest lad of yours—'

'And yours,' she replied calmly as she struggled with the dish of profiteroles. 'I merely carried them. They're Swain-banks through and through—'

'Oh, get on with your pudding!' He turned to Charles. 'Fetch me a nice fat cigar, lad.'

'You know what the doctor said—'

'Bugger the doctor! It's my birthday, so get me a smoke.'

While Charles found and prepared a Havana, Richard studied his wife as she carried on eating. It was a good job she could only eat slowly, otherwise she'd have been the size of a house by now. It was as if she'd invested her meagre supply of interest, imagination and energy in this one facet of her existence, because she lived solely for food. There was, in his opinion, neither rhyme nor reason to any of it. More than a quarter of a century fastened to that cold fish and what had he got to show for his penance? Just Charles. Thank God for Charles!

Beatrice struggled to stand, her supposedly regal posture considerably diminished by stiff limbs and a few drops of cream on her chin. Charles rushed to her side, but she pulled away from him. 'If I ever require assistance, then I shall ask for it—'

'Mother!'

But she dismissed him with a slight movement of her head.

The two men lingered over cigars and port, the door firmly closed against the rest of the household.

'You think it'll come, then?' asked the older.

'I do. The miners have been agitating for long enough, starving us of fuel, even closing some of us down at times. Since the war, they're more worked up than ever – past reasoning with, in my opinion. Yes, I think the colliers will bring everybody out in time—'

'Then they'll all bloody starve!' roared Richard. 'Where's the sense in that?'

'Like I said before, there's no reasoning with it. They know they'll suffer, but they'd rather that than feed us, or so they say.'

Richard heaved his leg on to a footstool, flinching as it came to rest on the upholstered surface. 'Unions? God, what do they know, eh? I'd like to see them keeping three mills open and a few hundred people housed. Words, that's all they know,

125

flaming words. And words put no meat in the pot, no bread on their tables. Do they think we don't work ourselves? Do they think we're as rich as we used to be?'

'I don't know what they think, Father. But that woman's been stirring them up again.'

'Ma Maguire?'

Charles nodded slowly. 'Yes. She was on the steps again last week talking about the dignity of labour. For somebody who can't read, she certainly manages to get her tongue round a few choice phrases. Honestly, you'd think we were murderers, the way she carries on. There were a few others with her, union chaps who read out figures – how many dead, how many mutilated. It read like a roll of honour for nearly an hour. Then there was a longish diatribe about conditions and facilities – they want canteens and first-aid posts.'

'Oh yes? And beds for a lie down after dinner? And slippers for their feet, gloves to save their hands? That woman! That bloody woman—'

'She's looked after your leg—'

'I'm aware of that.' His tone was heavy with sarcasm. 'And she's stirred them all up, riddled about like a poker in hot ashes, got herself in places where she's no right to be. She was at the back of that trouble up Daubhill when the pit owners brought in some willing labour, a few decent chaps who were prepared to go down and get the bloody coal. Oh yes, she was in the thick of that all right, turning a cart over and yelling at the . . . what do they call them?'

'Knobsticks. That's their word for strike breakers. But the unions are gaining in strength every day, Father. Soon, we shan't be able to breathe without permission and we own the flaming factories! And it's no good telling them to go and blame the bloody Kaiser, is it? They see an empty purse, a bare table, half a dozen starving kids – so they blame us! We're just the first in the firing line, that's all. But if it goes on, there'll be nobody wanting to invest in a factory. Why should we set ourselves up as targets, eh? We're probably a dying breed.'

Richard shifted his leg, wincing as he searched for a more

comfortable position. 'Aye. All I know is this. The steps of the Spinners' Hall are wearing thin with clogs to-ing and fro-ing with complaints. If they lose their false teeth through a shuttle coming off, then they're off down there with their heads wrapped in a scarf so we wouldn't recognize them with or without the blinking teeth. All I ask is for them to be reasonable. I can't be bothered employing a man to count every cut of cloth to see if Joe Soap's been underpaid by tuppence! Anyway, I reckon their complaints books are so full by now, they'll be able to start a lending library.'

Charles drained his glass. 'It'll all end in disaster—'

'Never you mind disaster, lad! You'll not shut my mills. Full or short time, they stay open no matter what.' He groaned loudly. 'This perishing leg will see me off, Charles. I feel as if there's a poisoned dart stuck in it, can't sleep, can't walk. Mind, she did warn me years ago.'

'Ma Maguire?'

The old man's features suddenly softened. 'I wish you could have seen her then. By, but she turned a few heads, did that one. She was about a foot taller than most, so she stood out in the crowd, made you stare at her. She walked into my office like the Queen of Sheba, hair wound round her head, eyes flashing, hands bunched up as if she wanted a go at me . . .' He grinned widely. 'By Christ, she didn't half curse me. I've forgotten what it was all about now – some daft lad got himself stuck, I think. She damned me to hell and back three times over – I could hardly get a word in edgeways. "A curse on you and yours," I think she said.'

'And you let her get away with it?'

Richard burst out laughing. 'Let her? You couldn't stop her, lad. She was like a steam engine out of control – she'd have mown down anything in her path! But she was a beauty, a real beauty. And that wasn't the end of it – oh no. After telling me I'd less than ten years to live, she spent the next few of them overcharging me for powders, kicking me out of her house, throwing me out of her shop – you've no idea, son. They broke the mould when they made her, believe me.' He sighed, his head wagging slowly from side to side. 'Pretoria

127

changed her, made her worse. Or better, depending which faction you're for, I suppose. But she's been a freelance member of every flaming union ever since, shouting her mouth off under the Town Hall clock, encouraging them to stand up for what she calls their rights.'

The timepiece on the mantel sang a melodic chime as both men gazed into the fire, each lost in private thought.

'I loved her,' whispered Richard, almost to himself.

'What? You loved old Ma?'

'She's not old, Charles. She'll never be old – even at ninety. That woman has bested me time after time, the only living soul who's ever managed it. There were occasions when I felt I could have killed her, strangled her with my bare hands. But I'd have had to catch her first.' He yawned and settled back into the armchair. 'I couldn't say it was love, but there again, I couldn't say it wasn't. But it was something I never got from another woman, especially your mother. Warmth, I suppose. Yes, warmth, a bloody good fight and loads of energy.'

Charles watched as the old man began to drift towards sleep, his own mind wandering back over an unhappy childhood in a house where love was never mentioned. Here, for the first time, he had heard his father speak of love, love for a woman. But not for his mother. No. No-one could ever love Mother because Mother cared about no-one, never had.

As he helped his father up the stairs, Charles found himself considering his own situation. Amelia was ill and fragile. For months he had not touched her, had maintained his distance in an effort to keep her calm and undisturbed. For how much longer could he endure this existence without the closeness of a woman?

He helped the old man on to his bed, then turned to go for the valet.

'Charles?'

He swivelled on his heel. 'Yes, Father?'

'I never touched her. Ma Maguire – there was nothing—'

'You don't have to tell me that. It's not my business.'

Richard struggled into a sitting position. 'Are you happy with Amelia?'

Charles studied his shoes for several seconds. 'I love her,' he said finally. 'It's . . . difficult at the moment, but I'm sure things will improve once she's up and about.'

'But you've an eye, haven't you? Like your old dad – come on, it's nothing to be ashamed of! Oh, I've watched you looking at the parlour maid. Do you know who she is?'

'No.' He could feel his cheeks reddening. 'I've no idea except that she's Molly Dobson.'

Richard smiled broadly. 'She's Ma Maguire's property, son. Like an adopted daughter, I suppose. That'll be where Molly got her fire from. Have you noticed how she glares at your mother? If looks could kill, old Bea would be six feet under and gone to dust by now. Anyway, take care, Charles—'

'I've no intention!'

'Intention hasn't a lot to do with it. I never had any intentions and look where I finished up. Three in cottages with a nice little income each, one I never got near who's bled me dry, heart, soul and pocket. A king's ransom I've paid just to stay on my feet and never even a proper kiss, just thanks for helping her bloody charities. And on top of that lot, I've got your mother. I shouldn't take too much notice of intentions if I were you. Just keep your mouth shut and your trousers fastened, that's all you can do if you want to stay out of trouble.'

Charles closed his father's door and walked across the wide landing towards his and Amelia's suite. They were quite detached if they chose to be, sitting room, two bedrooms, bathroom, even a little kitchen added on now. But with Amelia so ill, there was no question of detachment at present.

He met the maid as she came out of their quarters carrying Amelia's dinner tray. 'How is she, Molly?'

'All right, sir. She's had her soup and a bit of meat and veg. And she's laughing more—'

'Oh yes?' He leaned against the wall. 'You've not been at it again, have you?'

'At what?'

'Imitating all of us. Especially Mother and Cook.'

'Me, sir?'

'Yes, you sir! I've heard you when you've been setting the table, shouting at yourself with Mother's voice.'

She placed the tray on a half-moon table and faced him squarely. 'All right, I plead guilty. But I wouldn't do it in front of family, sir. I only do it to cheer meself up when Old Bea . . . sorry, I mean your mother's been getting at me.'

'I apologise on her behalf, Molly.'

Her chin jutted forward. 'She gets on me bloody nerves – ooh, I shouldn't swear, should I? But she goes for me every time I put a foot wrong. It's not fair . . . ' Her head dropped slightly. 'Sorry. I mustn't moan. If it wasn't for you, I'd still be in the kitchen buried under a pile of mucky pans.'

'Oh dear.' He shuffled about, trying hard not to laugh. 'You mean there's somebody in there – actually buried?'

She nodded quickly, mischief shining from her bright eyes. 'We don't even know her name, 'cos nobody's clapped eyes on her since she first come. We know she's there – the pots keep turning up clean. There's a rumour that she even sings at times, like a bird in a cage.'

'That's terrible, Molly. Shall I send in a search party? And how will we know her when we do find her?'

She shook her head with mock solemnity. 'It's not when, sir. It's if. You must look for red hands and a pasty face. Then there's her eyes, all screwed up with being kept in the dark too long. Still, it's either this or one of your mills, isn't it? And now I'm out of the kitchen, I'd sooner have this than spinning, 'cos I like a nice house and a glimpse of daylight now and then.'

He thrust his hands deep into trouser pockets and stared at the carpet for several seconds. 'What's she told you, Molly? Did Ma Maguire paint a grim picture of us, leeches sucking the blood from our workers?' He raised his head. 'Do you think we keep them all shut in the factories against their will?'

She looked boldly into his face. 'She told me to keep well away from all of you, said there's not a one of you can be trusted except to make money.'

130

'Then why are you here, Molly?' His eyes travelled over the straight young body, pausing fractionally on the round and supple breasts, finally resting on her face. Yes, the word for Molly was happy. Her eyes twinkled like emeralds, especially here in the artificial light, while her hair glowed with life in its bronze-streaked waves. She was beautiful. Beside her, Amelia would look pale and anaemic – no! He must not think like this! 'Why are you working for us when you've received such a clearly defined warning? Ma Maguire is very eloquent – I've heard her more than once.'

She inhaled deeply. 'Because I'm bloody-minded, sir.'

He took a step towards her. That was the sort of answer he was beginning to expect from this very unlikely source. It was difficult to think of her as a servant, for she bowed to no-one. Bold, blunt and straight to the point, that was Molly Dobson. 'You'll go far,' he said, his heart beating erratically as he looked into those deep green eyes.

'Do you think so? 'Cos I don't, sir. If I'm not back in the kitchen five minutes ago, I'll not even reach the front gate on me day off. Cook's all right, I suppose. She gives me leftovers to take home, but if she sings and I don't dance, there's hell to pay. I mustn't collect any more black marks, sir.'

'Black marks?'

'Aye.' She lifted up her hands and began to count on her fingers. 'One, I don't know a fish fork from a pudding one. Two, I wear me cap all wrong – rakish, she calls it. Three, I didn't turn the antimacassars last Thursday. Four, I broke a soup dish and that's a hanging offence. Shall I go on? Have we got all night?'

'No, Molly. Don't go on. Otherwise I shall never stop laughing. Tell me – how did you come to be so clumsy?'

She picked up the tray and arranged her features in a fashion she imagined to be serious. 'It's not easy, sir. I put it down to practice, meself. Years and years of practice.'

He watched her walking away, little head held high, rounded hips swaying as she minced along in an exaggeratedly careful way. He noticed darns where the heels of her shoes had rubbed against stockings, thick woollen stockings, cheap black shoes. Why, Amelia had a wardrobe full of things she never wore, outdated but still good, items that would doubtless be considered thoroughly passé by the time the pregnancy was over. Why not give the poor little maid some of those? Better still, why not fetch her a few odds and ends from the mills, fancies with a small flaw here and there, lengths she might make up herself in the sewing room? Molly was adept enough with needle and machine, a fact already proved by the many jobs she'd done here on curtains and cushions. Yes, he would do that, though he was still unsure of his motive . . .

He opened the door and crept in quietly to look at his sleeping wife, so pale and blonde, so absolutely untouchable. After tearing off his clothes with an anger for which he could not account, he lay beside her, scarcely disturbing the sheets in his effort not to rouse her. The child had to survive. And so, he thought as he drifted towards sleep, must Amelia. Because, although he dared not approach the stranger beside him, he still remembered her when she'd been real and tangible, an elegant lady on top and a bundle of fun underneath.

Slowly, silently, he turned to look at the light gold head on the pillow next to his, noticing how transparent and blue the eyelids seemed, how drawn and worried was the face, even in sleep. Why had he distanced himself from her so thoroughly? Surely he could still talk to her, enjoy her company, be her husband without making love? But no, it wasn't just him. Amelia had somehow turned herself into a chrysalis, a human pod invented simply to protect the life it contained. She wasn't Amelia any more, wasn't accessible. His thoughts became jumbled and confused with the onset of sleep. Was Amelia wrapped around the unborn child, or was it her protection, her armour against a husband she had ceased to love? When had she last said the words, when did she last sing 'Charlie is me Darling'?

Molly plagued his dreams, haunted every moment of his brief period of sleep. Dawn found him seated at the window, a cigarette in one hand, a brandy globe in the other. She'd be up and about soon, lighting fires, setting places for breakfast, polishing floors, doing whatever it was that housemaids did in the early morning. He drained the glass, allowing it to fall to the Persian rug as his hand slipped wearily towards the floor. No good would come of the way he was thinking just now. But Molly was alive and real, Molly was now. He glanced towards the bed, his eyes flicking over the motionless figure of his wife. Poor Amelia was a person of the past – and perhaps of the future. And now, right now, he ached with loneliness.

Ma Maguire studied her son's hand closely. He'd never toughened up at all, this lad. Why, in the winter time, he had cracks in his palms deep enough to stand a coin in. That was one of his party tricks, or so she'd been told, performed to an uncivilized audience down at the Bull, a place he was far too young to frequent anyway. Not that there was any doing much with him. Like his father before him, he loved a drink and would doubtless continue to get one whenever he so pleased. Well, this was a mess and no mistake. The wax wasn't working any more; nor was that most ancient of remedies – the application of his own urine – taking effect since things went so far. But how? And why him? Hadn't he enough ailments to cope with?

When the lump had first appeared some months ago, everyone had called it 'butcher's wart' and little notice had been taken of Paddy's latest problem. But the molehill had become a mountain now and the poor boy was having to undergo the most savage treatments at the hospital.

She looked into his pale face. 'TB, then?'

He puffed out his cheeks and blew noisily as she touched the tender raw spot. 'That's what they say. Bovine tuberculosis or summat. It's with slaughtering, Ma. I told you I wasn't cut out for it.' He managed a grim smile. 'Though me hand's being cut out for it now, eh?'

She tutted impatiently at this flippancy. 'But I thought you'd the cows tested for such things? Doesn't some feller have a look at the herd before you slaughter it?'

Paddy nodded. 'Aye and that's good for a laugh and all. If they find TB blood in the front glands and clear in the rump,

133

then they condemn half a cow. We burn the front and get the back ready for eating.'

Her jaw dropped. 'So . . . so we eat the diseased beef?'

'That's right.'

'That's wrong, Paddy. Doesn't it occur to these ignorant souls that the blood might circulate ever? Don't they wonder at so many of us getting this illness?'

He shrugged his shoulders. 'Just trying to save money and get round regulations, I'd say. There's many a pound passed over so a mouth will stay closed, Ma. This fair world you go on about doesn't exist, never has and never will—'

'We're all being poisoned!'

'Not from Chase Farm, we're not. They've burned the lot, fifty or sixty head all gone up in smoke.'

'Swainbank.' This was a statement, not a question.

'Yes.' He flinched as she refastened the bandage. 'Christ, Ma, that doesn't half hurt. I know I've not to take the Lord's name in vain, but honest, this would make a saint swear. They keep scraping away – every time it heals up, they open it again and cut chunks off me. And when they pour that stuff in I can smell me own flesh on fire. It's disgusting.'

'Get and see old Richard. Tell him his cows have almost lost you a hand. With a bit of luck, he'll see you right. Ask for compensation and a job on the estate . . . '

He smiled sheepishly. 'I've already done that, only I spoke to Master Charles. I hear the old feller's on his last and his temper's not the best.'

'Is he . . . dying?'

'So they say.'

'What of?'

'How should I know? Anyway, Master Charles said he'd learn me to drive once me hand's better. So as well as odd jobs, I'll likely get a bit of chauffeuring now and again.'

She tied the ends of the gauze dressing. 'And compensation?'

'They're looking into it.'

'I'm sure they are, Paddy. I often look into a mirror, but not a lot happens except I grow older. Just you keep on at them—'

'It might not have been their cows, Ma.'

'And it might well have been theirs. Whatever, take some money from them, son, for I fear you'll do little work for some time now. Did the hospital say when to go back?'

'Three weeks.' He threw himself into a chair, half-elated because he'd be doing no more slaughtering, half-worried on account of what the doctors had said. Not to him, oh no, never to him. But they muttered in corners, did doctors, went on about lupus bovine getting in his blood and killing him. Then they held him down, started scraping and tearing and messing about with creosote and acid till the place was near stunk out. Course, they kept a bucket handy now, because they knew he'd vomit every time. Aye, he'd come across some smells in his time, but the stench of his own skin and bone burning took the bloody biscuit all right.

He groaned self-pityingly. From now on he'd be forced to wear a glove on his unsightly right hand, keep it covered up so as not to put folk off. Molly mostly.

She entered the house as suddenly as she had entered his thoughts, all bounce and life and colour, a basket of food on her arm, a giant bunch of roses balanced on top of this bounty. 'Ma!' She threw her free arm around the tall lady. 'I've got some home-grown spuds and half a ham. The boss sends his best and the powder money. There's cake too . . . hello, Paddy.'

He grunted a half-hearted response, sick to death of forever being an afterthought. Always Ma first and him last. And she looked different, didn't she? He opened his mouth to speak, but the two of them were chattering away like magpies as usual, so he sat back to bide his time.

'I hear that the old man's ill?' Ma's voice was cool, though it hid a thousand emotions, feelings she could never have analysed or even identified in a lifetime.

'Yes. He doesn't go to work much now, but he spends hours on the phone shouting at somebody. He's funny on the phone, thinks he's got to be loud 'cos the folk on the other end are a long way down the road.'

'What's . . . er . . . what's his trouble?'

135

'Well, there's his leg as you know. Then he's got summat up with his blood, too much sugar in it, I think the cook said. He's not supposed to have anything sweet or a drink of brandy. Course, he takes no notice when it comes to the drinking, though he seems to have lost interest in food. His heart's not so good and he can't breathe proper. Nobody cares about him 'cepting Master Charles. I know old Swainbank's not a good man, Ma, but I don't like seeing anybody suffer like that.'

'No. No, I'm sure you don't.'

Paddy cleared his throat loudly. 'New frock?'

'Yes. Master Charles gave me a load of stuff from the mills, material that would have gone on the outside market as seconds. He said I could make it up in me spare time. Not that there's enough hours in a day what with Cook and Madam going on all the while.'

'Treating you all right?' Ma's eye travelled over the trim young figure in the crisp white dress. 'You look smart, sure enough.'

'They don't treat me exactly bad. You see, to be a good housemaid, you've got to be nearly invisible, do all the work in a way that's not noticeable. I just have to do me best to become invisible, that's all.'

'Well, you'll never disappear in that frock,' mumbled Paddy.

She rounded on him. 'I don't wear this at work, Clever Clogs. I wear me black frock and . . . '

'I know. A daft hat and a pinny with a frill.'

'Oh shut up, you miserable devil!' She turned her attention to Ma. 'They've all had a big row.' After placing the basket on the table, Molly seated herself opposite Paddy and beckoned Ma to join them by the fire. The older woman turned one of the chairs from the table and they sat in a semi-circle while Molly gossiped, her eyes ablaze with merriment as she imitated various members of the household. 'So Master Harold and Mrs Alice have been cast out into the cold, Ma. Oh, you should have seen it! Mrs Alice wept that many tears, we were thinking of following her round with a mop and bucket. The day they left, she'd sort of hardened up a bit – in fact, she'd a face on her like a clog bottom with new irons on when she sailed through that front door. Mind, I'm glad they've gone, 'cos young Cyril was a right pain in the neck and I was sick of hiding in corners trying me best to be invisible and not to laugh when she started, "Oh Daddy. Please let us stay here and look after you." Huh! The only one she'll look after is herself, I can tell you. But he's right hard-faced is old Mr Swainbank. I don't think he gives a thought to anybody, even his wife. Nobody up there cares, except Master Charles. Talk about a loving family – you could slice pieces out of the air with a butter knife when they're all in the one room. Ooh, but she's mean, that old Bea. I reckon if she had her own road, we'd be counting grains of sugar well past bedtime. Cook's all right, though. Always sends you a parcel, doesn't she?'

'And so she should,' said Ma. 'She staggered in here five years ago with ingrown toenails and I cured her, so she owes me the odd favour.'

Paddy leaned forward, his face grey with the pain in his hand. 'He's no call to be giving you cloth for frocks. What does he think you are – a bloody charity case?'

'Less of the language, Paddy!' Ma took a tiny box from her apron pocket and, after spreading snuff along the back of her hand, she inhaled deeply of the mustard-coloured powder. This new habit thoroughly infuriated Paddy who was forced, because of his chest, to sneak out to the yard whenever he craved a smoke. 'I wish you'd come to your senses and get home where you belong,' he said to Molly now.

'Leave her be.' Ma snapped the lid of the small tin. 'Isn't Charlie Swainbank supposed to be your friend at least? Wasn't he the one who promised you work when the hand's better? Aye and driving lessons too. Sure, he's only helping Molly because he knows what a desperate terrible woman she has for a mother.' She turned to her adopted daughter. 'And how's Mrs Amelia?'

Molly's face creased into a frown. 'I don't see much of her now, only I reckon she's in the dumps. Can't get out of bed, can't get comfortable because her back and heels are sore with lying down all the while. She's got a full-time nurse and she's still three months to go. Eeh, I think about her sometimes and wonder if it's worth it. All het up, she gets, in case she doesn't have a lad to follow on. There's nowt as queer as rich folk, Ma. I mean, as long as she's all right, why do they worry and make such a song and dance?'

Ma smiled grimly. 'It's the line, Molly. The old man likely wants a grandson off his eldest, because from what I've heard of Harold – well – he couldn't even produce a decent sneeze. And you say his wife's not up to much either, which won't please old Richard. Just don't waste your time trying to work them out, girl, for you'll never manage it. They're a different breed, that's all I know.'

'A breed you'd be best away from.' There was a hint of steel in Paddy's tone. 'It's all right for me to go and work for them – I can look after meself, stick up for meself. But I don't like the thought of you bowing and scraping to that lot all the while. Nobody in this house has ever been a servant before.'

Ma kept her counsel, bit back the ready reply which hovered so temptingly on the tip of her tongue. Every man was a servant – aye, and every woman too. A slave to a master, a husband, a wife, a child. Hadn't this son of hers ruled the roost from the very day of his birth and hadn't she allowed that? Weren't rich and poor alike the slaves of fortune, tossed this way and that on an ever-changing tide, victims every one of them, terrified of the bigger man, the fuller purse, the empty larder? And now Richard faced the final tyrant, the one over which no man had emerged victorious. In the end there was only the certainty of death. But these wise thoughts she kept to herself, knowing that the other occupants of the room were not ready to hear that life could be an endless prison, that the ultimate escape was essentially negative and finally destructive, that nothing could be done to hold back that tide.

She looked at the two youngsters and, realizing that the usual subject was about to rear its head, picked up the basket and carried it through to the scullery. It was obvious that Paddy had set his heart on marrying the girl for all he was only seventeen. And with his track record thus far, Ma would not be too surprised if he got his way simply by expecting to get it. She closed the door. This was one area where she would not interfere directly. She had said her piece and if he was still determined to pursue Molly, there was little to be done.

'I'm too young to get wed.' Molly smoothed the folds of her new dress. 'And so are you, Paddy. There's loads of girls out there . . . ' She waved a hand towards the window.

'Aye and they can stop out there and all. Come home, lass. We can live here and you could happen get something part-time if you want to carry on working. Then there's Ma and her medicines – you could help her. Since Freddie Chadwick shut the shop, she's been on her own here, nobody to talk to all day—'

'Don't, Paddy.'

'Don't what?'

'Well . . . getting me worried, making me feel guilty 'cos Ma's stuck here by herself. It's not my fault, is it? I went into service because I'd sooner that than the mill and I don't see why you should carry on like this. Why shouldn't I work? I went up to Briars Hall to better meself – I could end up a ladies' maid in London or somewhere interesting if I got trained proper.'

He stretched his legs across the peg rug and kicked her toe gently. 'To hell with London! You went up there to get away from me, didn't you?'

'No!'

'Course you did. You were feared in case I touched you, frightened I'd get you in trouble deliberate so's we'd have to get wed. I wouldn't do that. I wouldn't do anything to hurt you. There was no need for you to take on and run away like that . . . '

She jumped up, cheeks blazing with temper. 'I didn't run away! I went for a job, same as any girl would after leaving school. I didn't run at that age, did I? We'd no notions of getting wed at fourteen, for God's sake! Mind, you were getting a bit too interested even then, I will admit that much. Look Paddy, I've served three years in that bloody kitchen, three years past me elbows in grease and mucky water. Do you think I went through all that for nowt? I want to work me way up, happen be a housekeeper in time . . . '

'In somebody else's house?'

She stamped her foot angrily. 'What's the difference? Somebody else's house, somebody else's farm or factory? What do you expect me to do? Go out and buy me own business just like that?' She snapped finger and thumb together. 'You've always been a dreamer, Paddy—'

'So have you. When we were kids, you said every day that we'd get married. Mithered to death with it, I was, all about your long white frock and the matching rosary beads. Why have you changed? You never go to church no more – and you were all for turning. What's happened? Did the sky fall down and I never noticed?'

Molly leaned heavily against the table's edge. 'I grew up. We both did. Look, I'm not saying we won't get wed, 'cos we might. Only we should meet other people first, so we can choose, like—'

'What for? I don't need to pick one out, I've already chosen! If you don't marry me, Molly Dobson, I'll be like a priest all me life.'

She threw back her head and howled with laughter. 'You? Like a priest? Well, I've never heard a priest swear like you do, Paddy Maguire.'

'Hush – she'll hear you.'

'You're not still a-feared of your mam, are you? 'Cos I've never found her all that frightening.'

'Aye, well.' He drew in his chin and stared down at the rug. 'You never had a bad chest and funny hands, did you? Molly – listen to me.'

'I'm all ears.'

He swallowed. 'I might die.'

Molly paused fractionally. 'So might we all any minute. With Master Charles racing round the estate in his car and Master Harold leaping about on his horse, I could be a pancake three times a day.'

He leaned forward and held out the bandaged hand. 'See that? They said it can go into me blood and kill me. Well, when it does, I'll have the words printed on me gravestone, "Broken heart thanks to Molly Dobson". They'll come for

miles to read that and you'll be branded as a wicked woman.'
He attempted a smile. 'Could you live with that?'

She began to pace back and forth about the room, arms
waving wildly as she shouted, 'Give over, will you? I'll make
up me own mind in me own time. And if we do ever get wed,
it'll be nowt to do with your hand or with your mam needing
company.' She swung round to face him, checking herself as
she noticed the pain in his eyes. It was real pain, physical
hurt, not just from her words. The hand must be bad, really
bad . . . 'Please let me think, love. Give me time. Happen
when we're nearer twenty . . . '

Ma entered with a tray of ham sandwiches. 'Cook has done
us proud again, sure enough. Give her my regards, Molly.
Oh, and take the kettle off the fire and scald the pot, there's a
good girl.' She placed the tray on the table. 'Have ye settled
the differences or will it take an Act of Parliament?'

While Molly brewed the tea, Paddy stared sullenly into the
fire. With a tenderness she had seldom displayed in recent
years, Ma came to his side and laid a hand on his shoulder. 'I
know, son,' she whispered. 'You'll be fine.'

After the two young people had left, Paddy escorting Molly
back to her work, Ma took the beads from her pocket and
knelt before the Virgin, offering up decade after decade,
praying till her knees were sore and her back ached with
stiffness. She blessed herself and perched on the edge of a
dining chair, eyes still fixed on the statue. As always, once the
serious praying was done, she talked to Mary as if the two of
them were the best of friends. 'Help him, Mother.' She sighed
deeply and looked briefly at the ceiling, impatient with herself, not understanding her mixed feelings at all. 'What sort of
a woman am I, praying now for a man who wanted to sin
with me?'

But she could picture him in her mind's eye, that fine
strong man reduced to wreckage, the noble face shrivelled by
time and pain. And she remembered how he'd offered to buy
Paddy's pram, how he'd tried, in his own bumbling way, to
look after her, watch over her from afar. Richard Swainbank
had loved her . . .

Yes, she was for the workers, was Ma Maguire. A fighter, an orator, a troublemaker. Yet this one man had entered her heart, never invited, never properly welcomed. And she knew why he had this special place, just as she'd always known why. He might be a boss, a man of substance, yet right down to every single fibre and sinew of his body, Richard Swainbank was a worker. A cruel, lonely, sad, working man.

Tears ran unchecked down her cheeks as she pushed the rosary into her pocket. She turned to look at the Sacred Heart whose wounds were blurred now by the moisture in her eyes. 'Don't let him suffer, Lord. That's all I ask, that he should not suffer . . . '

In Molly's opinion, Charles Swainbank was a very handsome man, just as good-looking as a film star. In fact, he made the Rudolph Valentinos of this world seem a bit pallid and unadventurous, because Master Charles was big, heavy-muscled and colourful, a real swashbuckler striding out ready to take life by the throat, feared of nothing. She looked at him a lot these days, assessing him as if he were an object, something that would look nice in a certain setting, like on a stage or dressed up as a cowboy with a big white hat and a huge white horse. It occurred to her briefly that she was doing what men usually did to women, weighing him up for physical charm, looking at him as if she were about to buy him in the same way as she might choose a new lamp for the front room. But he was grand, right enough. At least six feet tall and with a bold, straight carriage, not like some lofty men who seemed to get round-shouldered through bending to talk down to shorter folk.

Like his father, Charles had unusual colouring in that his hair was quite fair – a sort of dark blond or light brown – while near-black eyes were fringed by thick dark lashes. The old man's hair was pepper and salt now, but the heavy black eyebrows had remained dark, just like his elder son's. Harold was a different kettle altogether, very like his mother, shorter than Charles and with more fat than muscle. The younger son was ordinary in comparison to his other male relatives – pale hazel eyes, fair skin, no real evidence that he was a Swainbank except for the completely straight eyebrows, fairer than those of the other two men, yet still geometrically perfect, as if drawn with the aid of a ruler.

Molly watched Charles now as he parked his car in the rear courtyard, so handsome he looked in his white silk scarf, like one of those blokes who flew planes during the day and drank champagne in clubs at night. The car was an Armstrong something or other, all shiny new paint and great silver head-lights stuck on the front, a real big monster of a thing, it was. The noise it made terrified and excited her simultaneously and she often wondered how it would feel to travel at such speed with the trees and houses flashing by, the world a blur of sound and colour.

She turned away deliberately, stifling that silly dream before it could start up again. Ridiculous, it was. Aye and so was she, imagining what it would be like to be a lady and married to somebody like Master Charles. It plagued her, annoyed her half to death some days, yet she still went back to it time after time. While the sensible side of her nature dictated that her status was already decided, some devil in her forced her to carry on, sitting at the big table when she was supposed to be polishing it, handling crystal goblets and china plates as if they were her own, posing before mirrors in one of the three new dresses she now owned, things she was allowed to wear in her few free hours.

She could hear his feet approaching, so she deliberately quickened her steps, telling her inward self sharply that it was no use, that even if he hadn't already been married he'd never have looked twice at her. She was a servant while he was a master and there was no mixing the two, ever.

'All right, Molly?'

'Yes, sir.' She looked into his warm dark eyes. 'Just taking me afternoon off, keeping out of the road in case Cook finds summat for idle hands to do. Last time I stayed here on me day off, she had me cleaning silver up to teatime, said it was good for me soul. I don't know about me soul, sir, but it near took the skin off me fingers.'

143

He slowed and matched his steps to hers. 'Why aren't you going home?'

She shrugged lightly. Oh no, she wasn't going to tell him about the real excuse for staying here, to keep away from Paddy and his mithering. Then there was the other daft reason, of course, best not spoken of to anyone at all. No, it was hard enough admitting even to herself that she was parading up and down at the back of the house pretending the place was hers, imagining she was some sort of princess that talked proper and had modern frocks and her hair cut like Mrs Alice. 'It's too far,' she muttered lamely. 'I can't be bothered there and back just for the afternoon. If I'm not in by nine o'clock, Cook sends the army out to find me.'

They stopped by the corner of the house, she preparing to walk towards the kitchen, he obviously undecided about continuing round to the front door. He fiddled with his driving gloves, eyes cast down as he said casually, 'I've a few hours off myself. Would you like a ride in the car? We could go up to Affetside or perhaps to Barrow Bridge.'

'Rivington!' She clapped her hands like a two-year-old. 'I've not been up the Pike for ages. We used to go when we were little, take our eggs up at Easter and roll them down. We used to roll ourselves down too – you know – lie down and turn over and over sideways till we reached the bottom where all the mothers sat with picnics laid out ready. My, we got in some bother for ending up stuck to folks' scones and jam butties, I can tell you.'

He cleared his throat. 'Very well. Rivington it is.' He paused, a hand resting lightly on her arm. 'Meet me at the end of the drive – out in the lane.' Brown eyes were slowly raised until they encountered the expression of puzzlement on her face. 'It isn't done, Molly,' he whispered. 'We know we're friends, but the other staff may become jealous if they think you are favoured.' His voice was husky, as if his throat had suddenly become dry and constricted.

She thought about this for several seconds. Wasn't she good enough then? Wasn't she fit to be seen in his precious car? She looked over her shoulder at this beloved possession of

144

his, torn between pride and the desire to tear along the roads at forty miles an hour. In the end, the latter won, though she told herself she was daft all the same. What was the point of getting a taste if you couldn't finish the plateful? But Molly's wisdom extended only as far as her youth would permit and she knew that she would have to indulge her exuberance this once. After all, how many of her kind got thrown a crumb, a chance to pretend that life went beyond the kitchen sink and the polishing of brasses? 'All right,' she said, chin raised defiantly. 'I'll just run in and fetch me coat. Will I tell Cook I'm getting the bus home after all?'

He smiled as reassuringly as he could manage. 'Yes, that's it. Say you're visiting family – that'll stop any chatter before it starts.'

She ran towards the kitchen like an elated child. He watched her quick movements, his heart racing as if to keep pace with her flying feet. She was an infant, probably untouched by human hand, as clean as the day she'd been born. What the hell was he doing? His eyes travelled up the gable end, upward and upward until they reached the windows of his and Amelia's quarters. The bedroom curtains were closed, shut fast against him. She didn't care, was too concerned about the child to wonder where he was, whom he was with, too bound up in herself to love him any more. But was that any reason for him to follow such a dangerous path? On his own doorstep too? Better some other woman, someone from the town, an anonymous face in an anonymous setting. No. It was Molly or no-one and he would do his best to make sure it would be no-one. Just a ride in a car, a bit of conversation, some fun . . .

Father was down at the mills for once, the leg giving slightly less trouble than usual. Yet still Charles heard his voice delivering that homily about intentions and fastened trousers. Oh, to hell with it all! Nothing would happen – he was just taking the girl out for a bit of fresh air. Angrily he cranked the car to life, jumped into the driver's seat and hurtled off down the driveway, dust and gravel flying in his wake. With fingers tapping impatiently on the steering wheel, he waited for Molly to arrive.

Then she was suddenly at the side window, smiling face bent to look at him, tiny hands fiddling excitedly with the door handle. He reached to release the catch and she jumped in, bringing with her the perfume of eternal springtime, the plain aroma of freshness and youth.

He took the Chorley road, driving quickly and almost furiously until he noticed whitened knuckles clamped tightly to the edge of the dashboard. With deliberation he eased the speed down and glanced at her ashen face. 'Frightened?'

'Never been in a car before, sir. It's worse than I expected – and better too. I keep thinking we're going to hit something.'

'We'll be all right. Just wait a few years till everybody has one of these things – that'll be the time to worry.'

'Yes, sir.'

'The name's Charles. Charlie to my friends—'

'Ooh, I couldn't! What if I tripped meself up and said "Here's your dinner, Charlie" back at the house? I reckon your mother would die of shock.'

'You're not quite so clumsy, are you?'

'I don't know about that.' She smiled wanly. 'If I can trip over a rug every other day, I reckon I can fall over me tongue. It's long enough at times. Ma says I could talk me road to Manchester and back twice over without stopping for breath.'

He made a careful left turn. Yes, there was Ma to consider, wasn't there? Dear God, what would that one say if she could see the pair of them together now, master and servant rolling merrily towards Rivington and heaven only knew what else? She'd probably explode on the spot, go mad at the very thought, because it would reinforce every one of her myths about the continuing cruelty of the bosses. Nothing would happen. He would make sure of that. Was he about to allow his masculinity to become so overpowering? Never! Or was his manhood weak, did it need scaffolding to support it, were his bodily hungers going to win over sense and reason? He gripped the wheel tightly. Why the hell did the girl have to be so damned beautiful? Servants should be ugly, ugly and characterless. They should not be people . . .

As soon as they reached the foot of the steep mound, she

leapt from the car and raced towards the Pike, scrambling here and there on hands and knees so that she might win some age-old race, a game that seemed to be bred into the working classes hereabouts. Show them the Pike and they would run for the top, climbing over each other if necessary, every one of them determined to be the first to reach the folly. He watched her for a while, enjoying the child in her, relishing the sight of this primeval joy, regretting somewhat that he'd never been a part of the Easter races, that his class and status had precluded so much pleasure.

He slammed the car door and chased after her, puffing and panting as he tried to match her swift progress. At the top they paused, both breathless after coping with such a steep gradient at speed. 'I beat you!' she gasped triumphantly.

He bent, hands on knees, fighting to regain an acceptable level of oxygen. 'You . . . cheated. Set off . . . before I did!'

'Aye. And you're about a foot taller than me.' She blew out her cheeks noisily. 'My little legs have to work twice as hard to get half as far.'

'Nonsense!'

'It's not! Stands to reason if you think on it. Are you all right?'

'Yes. I'm fine.' He straightened. 'No picnics today, eh?'

They gazed at the deserted area like a pair of monarchs surveying their domain, carpets of varying greens all lush with frequent rain, church towers in the distance, clumps of tree and shrub punctuating the rolling landscape. Everything was edged with the mellow tints of autumn, golds and reds made brighter by an unseasonably warm sun. The sky was stained here and there, streaked by the greyish emissions from faraway chimneys.

'Lancashire's beautiful,' he said quietly. 'People think it's all machinery and filth, but they've never taken time to look at these moors.'

'Aye. Only it's not all like this, is it?' Her tone was clipped. 'Most folk don't get chance nor time to come up here that often. They're too busy running the rest of it.'

'Oh, Molly.' He leaned against the small stone tower, hands

thrust deep in his pockets, brow creased into a frown. 'If it wasn't for the moors, there'd be no mills, no work. These hills keep the damp in. They help the cotton spin without breaking. There's no sense in resenting what's down there. What's down there is affluence and a way of life. Would you rather we all begged for a living?'

'No sir.'

'Charlie!' He tutted quietly and shook his head. She'd never use his Christian name, would she? 'Oh, I know what it's all about. There's us and there's you, the owners and the workers. Neither could exist without the other. Have you ever seen a picture of underwater life, Molly?'

'No. There's enough goes on up here without me being right bothered about the blinking sea. What's underwater got to do with it anyroad?'

'Well, there are fish down there the size of battleships. They could swallow a piano in one gulp – stool, sheet-music and all. Great mouths, they have, bigger than the Town Hall doors.'

'Really?'

'Really. Yet there'll be one particular little fish, a very ordinary sort of chap, swimming in and out of the big fellow's mouth, cleaning his teeth and eating up what he leaves. Does the big fish swallow the little fish? No. Never. Because he depends on the little scavenger for his life, you see, couldn't manage without him. They're interdependent – almost married to one another. The big fish would die without the little fish – and vice versa. It's called a symbiotic relationship. We have that – you and I.'

'Do we? How?'

He sank to the grass and squatted on his haunches. 'You serve my meals, clean my house. I pay your wages.'

'But you wouldn't die without me.'

'No.' He shook his head thoughtfully, wondering obliquely whether or not life would be worth living anyway without characters like Molly. 'I'd live on shop-bought bread and lumps of cheese if I had no servants. I don't know the first thing about baking and looking after a house.'

148

'Then you'd have to bloody learn, wouldn't you?'

'I haven't the time! It's the same at the mills – do you think I could run hundreds of mules and looms . . . ?'

'Without the little fish?'

'Exactly.'

She joined him, spreading out her yellow skirt as she sat. 'What I want to know is this. How do I get to be a big fish, 'cos I'm sick unto death of swimming in and out of other folks' gobs and feeling grateful for the leavings.'

'Molly.' He took her hand. 'You don't need to be a big fish to be necessary and important. Haven't you listened to a word I've said? Giant fish have mammoth responsibilities. First, they've got to take care not to swallow a friend by mistake and that takes practice . . . '

'I could learn . . . '

'Secondly, there are always even bigger fish with huge teeth lurking behind every rock. There's the bank manager fish – an ugly brute which eats everything in its path. Even he pales into insignificance at the side of the government fish with the kangaroo pouch on his belly for collecting taxes in. He's the real thief, everybody's enemy. Then there's the union shark – that one used to be a stickleback, but he grew while no-one was looking. It's not safe for any of us, my dear.'

'Then we'd best stop out of the water, eh?' His grip on her hand had tightened and she made some small effort to pull away, but he held on fast. 'Master Charles?'

'Yes?'

'Why are you holding my hand?' Her eyes were wide – not with fear, but with amazement.

'Because . . . because I like you. I like you very much. The main thing is for you to carry on being yourself, be sure of who you are and what you want.' He paused. 'Are you sure, Molly?'

'What about?'

'Well – what you want from life, where you're going . . . '

'Back to Briars Hall, I'd say.'

He knew then what it was about her that he loved. Was it love? Whatever, the thing that drew him was the way she

149

skipped from child to woman in a matter of seconds. She
knew nothing, yet she knew everything, was possessed of an
innocent awareness – if such a contradiction in terms could
be possible.

'I think we'd best get back, sir.'

Sighing, he let her go and rose stiffly to his feet. She
grinned at him. 'There's only one way down . . . Charlie.'

'Pardon?'

'Well, you said I'd to call you your proper name and this
once, I will. 'Cos up here, we're all the same with everything
being so . . . so big. But there's rules, see? You can't walk. It's
not allowed to walk. If you walk down, then you're a chicken.'

'Oh.'

'You wouldn't want to be a chicken, would you? Better a
bloody great fish than a chicken, eh?'

'If you say so.'

With no outward sign of embarrassment, she bent to tuck
her skirt into her knickers as if she were preparing for a
paddle in the sea. He caught a glimpse of thigh above a
gartered stocking, his heart skipping a beat at such arrant
provocation. Or was it?

She raised her chin and stared challengingly into his face.
'You see, you're on our patch now. This is all ours, not yours.'
She waved a hand across the view. 'Top of the Pike, you do as
we do. That there Lord Whatsisname . . . '

'Leverhulme . . . '

'Aye, him and all – he left this place for us, for the workers.
So now you have to do what I say, same as I'm forced to do at
the big house. Right?'

'Right.'

'Your clothes'll get spoiled. Mine are all right – they'll go
in the tub.'

'Fair enough.'

She looked down the steep slope. 'Now, there's a right way
and a wrong way of tackling this. Don't go head first –
Jimmy Pickles from our school did that and finished up in
hospital with a funny brain. Mind you, he were as daft as a
bucket of frogs before we ever kicked off. You go sideways.

Keep your head up when you're face down and your head down when you're face up.'

'Pardon?'

She put a hand to her forehead and whistled under her breath. 'Do you understand English or what? Would you sooner I talked Yiddish or rubbish? Listen. Watch my lips while I'm speaking. Keep your face out of the dog muck. Is that clear enough for you?'

'Yes.' A laugh was threatening in his chest, rumbling deep inside him in a place where he hadn't felt joy for months. 'Are you suggesting that I roll down this hill, Molly Dobson?'

'You can bloody fly down if you want. The rule is that you don't walk. If you can find any other way of getting to the bottom, then do it and welcome.'

He suddenly fell flat on the grass, arms folded across his chest.

'Hmm,' she muttered. 'I reckon you'll make a fair enough corpse once you set your mind to it. Ready?'

'Ready as I'll ever be. If I don't come out in one piece, make sure Harold looks after my car.'

She settled herself away from him, on a part of the slope with which she was familiar, a quicker route to the bottom. 'Any more last requests, then?'

'No irises at the funeral. Evil-looking flowers, they are.'

'Right. On your mark . . . get set . . . go!'

He tumbled into the abyss, bumped and jostled on uneven soil, his eyes assaulted by flashes of sky each time he turned. But he could understand why they did this thing every Easter, because it was exhilarating, joyous, unbounded by propriety, completely unfettered and free. When he reached the bottom, she was waiting for him, skirt correctly arranged, hair still pinned, not a mark on her. He struggled to his feet and looked down at the ruined suit. 'Why are you so clean?' he asked, amazed by the difference in their conditions.

'Oh. I forgot.'

'Forgot what?'

'To tell you that some places are better than others. And I know the good places. Sorry.'

'You're not sorry at all! This was deliberate, just to put me in my place. Molly Dobson—'

'Yes, sir?'

'Back to sir, is it?'

'Back to earth, sir.'

'This amounts . . .' He brushed at his muddy jacket. 'This amounts to an assault on my person.'

'I never touched you! Nobody forced you to come rolling down the blinking hill! What's a man of your age doing rolling down the Pike, eh? Ooh . . .' She bent double with laughter. 'If they could see you now—'

'Who?'

'Your mam. Your dad. The workers . . . oh God, I'll never walk again. Your face is all green. Is it 'cos you're sick or is it grass? And you've dirt in your hair. Oh, come here. I don't know. Whatever shall we do with you at all?' She pulled the grass and soil from his hair, then walked around him in a large circle as she examined his clothes. 'You'll have to say you've had an accident.'

'With what? A tractor or a herd of cows?'

'You could always—' She doubled over again.

'I could always what?'

'Say you've . . . got greenmould . . . oh, I'll never look you in the face again. Can you imagine it? Me serving your dinner and asking "any more greens?" Ooh, no!'

'Molly!'

'What? For God's sake, take me back before I go hysterical. You look like . . . like you've crawled out of that . . . underwater world. A big fish! Covered in seaweed!'

'Molly! Behave yourself or things will get really out of hand.'

She attempted sobriety, but failed immediately, sinking to the ground as she groaned, 'Out of hand? They've got fins, not hands. And I'm a giddy kipper aren't I? So that makes two of us . . .'

He pulled her roughly to her feet and into his arms. She was easy, so easy! Her mouth opened the second his lips touched hers and there was no rigidity in her tiny body. 'Molly, Molly,' he murmured as he released her. She stood round-eyed

152

and open-mouthed, hands still resting on his shoulders. 'What the bloody hell do you think you're doing?' she asked at last.

'Loving you. Celebrating. Oh, I don't know—'

'Well, you'd best find out, hadn't you? And when you have found out, happen you'll send me a telegram so's I can be in on the secret too. Put me down. I'm not going to fight you, 'cos I know it'd be no use, might as well set a mouse to flay a cat.' She drew away from him. 'Take me back. Take me back now, this minute, otherwise I start walking.'

'Molly! I love you!'

She turned and glanced sideways towards the village of Rivington. 'We've had a lovely day, Master Charles. A stolen day, it was, a day that should never have happened. You can't love me. You've a wife at home, a kiddy coming—'

'That's . . . different,' he said lamely.

'Is it?' She faced him squarely, hands on hips, head raised so that she could meet his eyes. 'So I'm for a cottage, am I? Like your old dad's bits and pieces, tidied away where I can do no harm? Well, you can shove that, Mister.'

He groaned his frustration. 'Look, you silly little girl. Perhaps I married the wrong one, perhaps it should have been you or someone like you. But I didn't know that then. Must I suffer all my life like my father did?'

'That, sir, is nowt to do with me!' She turned and ran, fleeing past the car and down the lane before he could react. Following an instinct that was purely animal, she threw herself into the ditch, covering her body as best she could with the long grasses and weeds.

She heard him, first shouting and running, then starting up the car. Back and forth he drove, up and down the lane until dusk began its descent. From time to time he left the vehicle and walked along the roadside calling her name. And still she remained in her hide. When at last he seemed to have abandoned the search, she began the endless walk back. It was too late now to worry about what Cook might say and do. And anyway, she had other and more pressing concerns, hadn't she?

The last lap was the worst, those final few hundred yards

along Stitch-mi-Lane, the lights of Briars Hall appearing now and then in gaps between trees. With eight or nine miles under her belt, she was exhausted to the point of collapse, yet still her mind worked on and on, going over the day in a series of pictures that flashed across her weary brain. She shouldn't have gone. He shouldn't have asked her to go, shouldn't have kissed her like that. And most of all, she should not have enjoyed that urgent embrace. Cool air fanned cheeks ablaze with embarrassment as she recalled how she had clung to him, the sweetness, the pleasure, the promise of further joys beyond her comprehension. She was, she admitted to herself as she furtively opened the rear door, too young for all this.

Cook turned from the table, arms akimbo, sturdy legs set well astride as she surveyed the returning prodigal. 'Well?'

Molly glanced quickly at the clock. A quarter to ten – not too bad, not as bad as she'd imagined while stranded on endless lengths of unlit road. 'I missed the tram.'

'Missed the bloody tram? It looks as if the tram never missed you, though. Or have you been set about by a gang of thieves and murderers?'

Molly looked down at her filthy ditch-stained dress. 'I fell over a stone in the lane.'

'Oh yes?' Cook's practised eye swept over the girl's dishevelled clothing. 'Aye, I reckon you could fall over your own shadow, you could. You'd best start framing yourself or you'll be breaking your neck afore long. But that's not new dirt, Molly Dobson. That there muck is hours old and you'll never get the grass stains out of the frock. I reckon the coat's seen better days and all. Been messing about with some daft lad, have you?'

'No, I haven't.'

Cissie Mathieson tapped the toe of her shoe on the stone floor. 'Happen you'd best get a bath and straight to bed, lady. There's cocoa in the pan if you want some.'

'No, ta.' Molly ran gratefully from the room.

Cissie sat up well into the night pondering. It didn't take much to put two and two together, did it? Mind, there was nowt worth proving, 'cos her job would likely be on the line if she opened her gob. But Sid Potter had been down earlier with Master Charles' suit, trying to sponge the grass marks out of it. Missed the tram? Christ, she'd be missing more than the flaming tram if Ma Maguire got wind of this capering on. What the hell was the girl up to? She seemed bright enough, sharp and quick to learn – quite the full shilling, in fact. Had her head been turned by a married man and a master into the blinking bargain? Oh, it didn't bear thinking of! And she wouldn't think of it, that she certainly wouldn't! Years of experience had taught Cissie Mathieson when to switch off, so she simply stopped thinking and went to her bed. She had heard nothing, seen nothing and would say nothing.

In her attic room, Molly lay staring at the ceiling, her body still glowing after a hot bath. She turned towards the window, a groan escaping from her lips. There was nothing else for it, she would have to leave the Hall, work somewhere else. Because she couldn't stop him, wouldn't stop him. Why, though? She'd been brought up proper, first by her mam and then by Ma, always told to keep herself to herself, forever instructed – especially by Ma of late – to avoid contact with men. But this fevered flesh was not caused just by the hot bath. Oh no. Whatever it was that went on between men and women had nearly happened to her. And she'd wanted it to happen, still did. Where was her loyalty to Ma, to Mrs Amelia, to herself? She stuffed a corner of the pillow into her mouth as she wept, choking back the noise of her grief. She would miss him, she really would. He'd been a good friend, kind and gentle. Still weeping, she fell asleep only for the torment to continue, because now she dreamed of him, felt his strong hands on her body.

By the time it stopped being a dream, it was already too late for Molly. When he roused her to partial wakefulness, she became instantly malleable and responsive, clinging to him, returning his kisses with an ardour that surprised and delighted him. He was tender, excruciatingly slow and careful, expertly leading her along a pleasurable path from which she had neither the strength nor the will to turn. She wept when he finally hurt her, but he smothered her tears with grateful kisses and words of comfort. Then it was over. The bed was narrow and hard and she found herself wedged between him and the low window, her body aching with tiredness and discomfort, yet still silently screaming for some kind of completion. Was that it, then?

He stood at the side of the bed, just a shape outlined against a cream-painted wall. Who was he? What had they done together and why did it hurt so much? Oh, this wasn't just a physical injury; this went a long way past the merely physical, because although she had co-operated fully, the thing that had happened would be with her for always. He could walk away and forget it, but it was in her, incorporated now, not mendable, not forgettable.

'Are you all right?' he whispered.

'No.'

'Can I . . . can I help?'

She lay back against her tear-soaked pillow. 'I reckon you're the last one who could help me, Charlie. Go away.'

'I'm sorry.'

'Aye, I dare say you are. And so am I.'

'Molly . . .'

A tremendous anger suddenly invaded her breast, obliterating exhaustion and fear. She leapt from the bed, hands clawing at his face, tearing and ripping, nails gouging deep into flesh. 'Bastard!' she screamed until his hand covered her mouth.

She fought him, kicking and punching till there was nothing left, no strength, little anger now, just a tearful desolation as temper evaporated simply because she had not the energy to refuel it.

'Be quiet!' he hissed. 'You'll have the whole house awake.'

'Happen that's what I want,' she said wearily. 'Happen they should know what you are, Charlie. A bastard. A dirty, rotten, evil bastard. Like your bloody mother. Aye, like him and all, filthy old bugger he is, with his bits of women all over the town.'

'But I thought . . . I thought you . . .'

'Thought I wanted it to happen? Listen, you. I might be only seventeen, but I'm old enough to know I'm not old enough. You guessed I liked you. You knew I thought you were handsome. Huh. We'll see just how handsome you are in the morning with them stripes I've given you. I should have listened to Ma.' With a surge of determination, she pulled away from him, tightening the nightgown against her shaking body. 'You'll pay for this, Charlie Swainbank.'

'I will. If it's money you want, I'll do anything—'

'For me silence? Pay me to keep the gob shut, will you? Coward! No, I'll take not one penny from you. But you'll pay in other ways. I'll get you, just wait and see.'

He stood by the door, a hand to his bloodstreaked face. 'I care about you, Molly! For God's sake, won't you listen? It's not just what we've done – that's only a part of it. You're alive and beautiful, a fine woman in the making. I want you with me—'

'As a member of your . . . what are they called? Harems? Is that it? Am I supposed to just lie here and let it happen, be grateful 'cos you're noticing me? I don't want to be that kind of special, lad! I want me own man to meself, not summat I share and pass round like a bloody plate of cakes!' There was pride in her tired voice. 'My dad was chapel, a God-fearing man with a heart you could never match. That was love, what him and me mam had. Love means . . . oh, giving things up, making room for one another, going without for somebody else's sake, living day to day and sharing everything. And if me mam was here now, she'd choke you with her bare hands for all she was four foot ten. Don't you ever forget, Charlie Swainbank, I've still got a mam, a mam as could bring you down by batting a single eyelash. There's plans. Marches, strikes, go-slows – the lot. Ma Maguire hates your kind.'

'Are you threatening me?'

'I am. Even a bloody great fool like yourself must see that! Don't ever come near me again.'

'You enjoyed it.' His voice was cooler.

'Did I? Well, I thought there was a bit more to it than that, to be honest. There again, I didn't notice half of it with being near asleep.'

157

Yes, she knew where to kick a man, didn't she? That innocent awareness again, that wisdom extending far beyond her years, way past her limited education. He found himself shaking, suddenly terrified of what he had done. All women valued their virginity, but this one had the brains to fight back now it was all over, was sufficiently fiery and unpredictable to make him shiver with fear. What was this power she had, this indefinable strength? And where had she got it? He smiled grimly at the rhetorical question in his mind. Would she tell the old girl? Would she run to Ma? He coughed quietly. 'What will you do?'

'That's for me to know and for you to worry and wonder over. Now, get out of this room or I scream the place down.'

'Molly.' He took a step towards her.

'Don't you know me yet, Swainbank? I mean what I say, always mean what I say. Do you realize I used to feel sorry for you having such a rotten family? Your mother's as ugly as sin, horrible from the inside, so bad it shows in her face. I'm glad she's crippled, glad she hurts. And the old feller's on his way – happen we'll get cleaner air when he's hopped it. They're in you like poison and I hate you too! So get out before I bring the slates off the roof!'

He slipped out of the room, too intent on escape to notice Cook's door slowly closing as he made his quiet descent. With his mind working overtime, he left the house and made for the stables. In the morning, he would say he'd heard a horse in trouble, would swear he'd been kicked to the ground, that his injuries were from falling among the cobbles.

In her room, Molly vomited violently, stomach heaving as she retched over the blue and white washbowl. Alone, she felt none of the courage she'd expressed to him, all that false strength dredged up from the bottom of her soul, the righteous anger she'd supported on a shallow foundation built of no more than self-esteem. But that was crumbling now. She felt dirty, ashamed of her willing participation. It was his fault, right enough, but she could have screamed earlier, should have put a stop to it.

What now? She dried her face and swept a glance over the

158

room that had become hers, a happy place where she'd read her penny dreadfuls and indulged her childish dreams. No more of those now, because she'd been dragged into womanhood, had allowed it, even welcomed it! What kind of person was she? Bad? Like him?

Noiselessly, Molly Dobson packed her few possessions in a battered cardboard case, deliberately leaving behind everything he had given her, stuffing the three dresses into a bottom drawer, pushing shoes, ribbons and scarves into the small cupboard. They could think what they liked. After a last quick glance at the bed, she picked up the bowl to carry out for emptying. But it slipped from uncertain fingers, bouncing silently on the bed, its nasty contents spilling over quilt and floor. She made some small attempt to clean up the resulting mess, using as mops the few handkerchieves she owned. It was hopeless. No way could she manage, not with her stomach still heaving menacingly. Doubtless the poor kitchen maid would be left to deal with the dirt, and this knowledge made Molly even angrier. What she needed now was fresh air. Fresh air and escape . . .

She sat on an upturned barrel in the courtyard, a thick shawl covering the flimsy coat. Although she wanted to get away, what remained of her senses dictated that she must wait for dawn. When he emerged from the stable, she remained stunned for several seconds before slipping quietly down against the wall among deeper shadows. Her heart pounded in her ears as he approached and she flattened herself against the cold stones, praying that he had not noticed her.

He stood within feet of her. In spite of her own almost deafening distress, she could hear him breathing heavily, sighing like some injured animal, groaning and mumbling into the black night. Then she heard a choking sound, followed by the unmistakable noise of sobbing. With a hand to her mouth, she forced back her own tears, listening as he whispered her name over and over. It was one of the most terrible things she had ever heard, yet worse than that was her desire to run to him and offer comfort, forgiveness, anything that might stem that dreadful tide of grief. But she held on grimly, knowing, just as she had always known, that he was a dream, a mere piece of imagination, like a character from one of the romances she used to read. Just as she would have closed a book, she shut herself off from an ending that could never be happy or even satisfactory.

He stumbled away towards the house, out of her life, but never far from her mind. Because Charles Swainbank took a piece of Molly Dobson with him, a part of herself that was irretrievable, irreplaceable. And she would never, ever allow herself to forget that.

Ma Maguire, though outwardly composed, felt about as stable as an unexploded bomb. Deep inside her chest the anger rumbled, occasionally threatening to erupt at the most unexpected times. Almost from the start she had known the truth, a truth that was too awful to face. Molly, like her mother, showed symptoms unbelievably early. With all her pregnancies, Edie Dobson had been sick from the moment of conception. Then there was the other thing, that almost imperceptible altering of facial colouring, a darkness on the cheeks and eyelids . . . No! It couldn't be, mustn't be true! But it was, oh yes, dear God, it was! She clenched her fists tightly as she heard Edie's voice echoing down the years, 'I always knew. Right from the bloody kick-off, I were sick as a pig – even before I'd missed. And me face used to go a bit brownish . . .'

Ma sat at the large square table watching Cissie Mathieson's fat red hands kneading dough, pummelling and punching the greyish substance as if she were attacking an enemy. This was a fine pickle and no mistake, but Ma realized that the woman knew something, that she was simply shielding herself to save the job. Well, Ma would hang on here till she got to the bottom of things – or as near the root as possible. She smiled at the busy cook. 'So. The feet are still fine, then?'

'Aye. I put the stuff on after a bath like you told me.'

'Good.' Ma placed the new pot of balm on the table. ' 'Tis Molly,' she said, knowing she would have to choose her words with care. 'Just came home without saying a word. I can get nothing out of her, so I thought you might shed a little light?'

Cook divided the dough with a sharp knife and threw it into three square tins. 'All I know is that the bed was covered with sick, so she can't have been so well.'

Ma nodded. 'Yes, I can see that. But if she was ill, how did she manage to pack up her things and get all the way back to Bolton?'

'I've no idea.' She carried the uncooked loaves across to the oven, then returned with a large teapot. 'Sugar?' she asked as she poured.

'Just the one, thanks.'

They sat in silence through two cups each, Cissie's face getting redder by the minute. 'It's nowt to do with me anyroad,' she said at last. 'All I know is she come in late and covered in muck. I gave her a bit of a roasting and packed her off upstairs.'

'Who was it, Cook?' Ma's voice remained even and careful. Perhaps Molly was the lucky one after all. Not many poor girls in her situation had someone by them to recognize the signs. And not many poor girls would show their condition so early on . . .

'I'm saying nowt, Ma. Look, you know how I'm fixed – no husband, no family. Where do I go if I fetch trouble round here, eh?'

'There'll be no mention of you, I promise that. And I'm a woman of my word, that you can be sure of.'

Cissie reached for a scone and a bit off a huge chunk, turning to food just as she always did in times of stress. 'I'm saying no names,' she mumbled, her mouth full.

'Somebody here in this house?'

The cook shook her head vehemently, crumbs spilling down her apron. 'Leave it, Ma. There's nowt to be gained—'

'Isn't there?' Ma's tone was grimmer now.

'No, there's not! I mean, she's never caught, has she? Even if she had, you'd not know this early on—'

'I know nothing, Cissie, except that my girl came here clean and left tampered with. If you won't tell me, then I'll have to go upstairs, won't I? Will I do that? Will I say you sent me up? Look, I don't mean to threaten, but I surely need to know who made her so ill. It's not her body that's sick, 'tis her mind. She sits all the day gazing through the bedroom window, not a word will she utter—'

'Don't go up! For God's sake—'

'And for yours.' She leaned back in the chair. 'Right. Let's be having some sense out of you now. Was it a servant, a member of the staff?'

'No.'

'A casual visitor, then? One of the farm workers, perhaps a drover?' Aye, it might even have been Paddy—

'It wasn't any of them.'

Ma's heart turned over in her chest. 'Family, then.' This was no question. The cook didn't move, didn't even bat an eyelid, just sat very still and stared into her empty cup.

'Right.' The visitor rose from the table, picking up Cook's payment for medication and placing it in her purse. 'This need go no further, Cissie. I know you can hold your tongue and I will surely hold mine. Thank you for the tea and I trust that your health will continue good.'

Ma Maguire stood in the grounds and stared hard at the splendid frontage of Briars Hall. Brick by brick, stone by stone she had cursed it in the past, would have brought it down with her bare hands at times given half a chance. It was built on blood, was this place, founded on sweat, tears and early death. People had starved in cellars while Richard's father had thrived in his newly acquired and extended mansion. Aye. She nodded sagely. In cursing this house, she had cursed her own too, because the link was finally forged. That Molly carried a Swainbank in her belly was beyond doubt. The father was Charles, giver of dress lengths and shoes, he who promoted maids from kitchen to parlour where they would doubtless be more accessible. Yes, it was Charles all right. Otherwise Molly would never have been parted from her pretty dresses and ribbons, would never have arrived home with the case half-empty, would never have arrived home at all.

By the time she reached Bolton, Ma's anger was fully fuelled yet cold, iced down by an iron will. This was one time when she must keep her head, suppress the strong urge to go for Charles with fists and shoes flying, stop herself from killing him no matter what the price. The plan was complete, finalized in her mind, needed no bits of paper to make it real. Not yet. Papers would come later . . .

The workers greeted her noisily as she stepped into the shed, warps and wefts temporarily abandoned while they shouted out to one of their dearest friends and supporters. Cries of, 'All right, Ma?' and 'Are we coming out, then?' reached her ears above the sound of machinery, but she merely waved a hand on her way to the office.

They were both in, the older man seated at his huge desk, the younger standing by a window with a sheaf of papers and a pen. Richard made an effort to stand as she entered, but she nodded curtly and said, 'Sit down, Mr Swainbank. You'll surely be needing all your energy with that terrible leg of yours.' She turned to stare at Charles, noticing how he flinched visibly beneath her steady gaze.

Richard smiled wanly. She was still a bonny woman, though her hair had thinned out a bit and there was a streak of grey here and there. Aye, for one in her early forties, she wasn't bad at all. 'Sit down,' he said, pointing to a chair opposite the desk.

She hesitated. He looked so ill, so shrunken and defeated by time. Dear God, if only she could stop feeling . . . concern for him! 'I might do that. In a little while.' She paused for effect, watching as the men picked up the frost in her tone. ' 'Tis about Molly Dobson I'm here.'

'Ah yes.' Richard spread out his hands on the desk. 'She left us in rather a hurry, did that young woman. Pity. She'd the makings of a damned good little housekeeper.'

'I'm sure.' Ma's eyes never moved from Charles' face. 'She didn't leave, Mr Swainbank. The girl fled for her life, came home looking as if she'd seen hell itself. There's no getting much sense out of her, so I'm here to ask you what you know about Molly's predicament.'

Charles riffled through the papers, averting his eyes from the woman's steely gaze. 'Shall I go and see to these, Father?' He glanced at his watch. 'We've a meeting in half an hour—'

'You've a meeting now.' Ma stepped closer to the desk. 'You've a meeting with me.'

'Oh.' Richard clicked his tongue in irritation. 'We've a deadline to meet, Philly – I mean Mrs Maguire. There's a contract wants signing by four—'

'You'll have more than a contract in your bonnet by four o'clock, Richard Swainbank. The child is pregnant, a condition she acquired while residing on your property.'

Richard's jaw slackened. 'She's what?'

'You heard me, sure enough. My ward – Miss Molly Dobson – is expecting a baby. She was not in that state when she last visited me, but she certainly is now.' She watched Charles as he sighed with relief. Yes, that was the only proof she needed, for he'd doubtless consider himself away and off the hook with a pregnancy already diagnosed. She allowed herself a sour smile. What did he think Molly was? Surely he'd known she was untouched till he got his filthy paws on her?

'You're not suggesting that one of my servants stepped out of line?' roared Richard.

'No.' Her tone was dangerously quiet.

'Then what the hell are you saying, woman? Come on, out with it!'

She lowered herself slowly into the chair. 'Your son has been messing about with my adopted daughter, Mr Swainbank.'

Richard cast a quick glance in Charles' direction. 'Who? This one or young Harold?'

Ma's fingers tapped delicately on the edge of the desk. 'Master Charles,' she said. 'The apple of your eye has ruined a good girl.'

Charles dropped his papers on to a side table. 'Pregnant, you say?'

'Yes.' She spat this single word.

'Then it's not mine, couldn't be.'

'Really?' Her eyes seemed to bore right through to his soul and he felt a sudden rush of colour to his cheeks.

'Really?' she repeated.

'But . . . ' He looked towards his father. 'It can't be! It's only a couple of weeks, three or four at the most—'

'Since you deprived her of her virginity?' Ma's teeth were bared now. 'I know it's only a short time, but some women get sick very early. She is sick, sick as a dog morning, noon and night. I've not been a midwife all these years for nothing, Charles Swainbank. And you know you were the first—'

He swallowed. 'Did she—'

'No. She said not one word, but it doesn't take a genius to work it out now, does it? She runs home leaving behind all the gifts you gave her, all those little things that were supposed to wear her down. And obviously did. Oh, I'm not stupid!' She looked straight at Richard. 'I've come across this before, haven't I?'

Richard rose stiffly to his feet and crossed the room to where his son stood. 'Is this right? Have you interfered with that girl?' For answer, Charles simply hung his head until his father reached out and grabbed him by the waistcoat. 'After all I said! You bloody fool! Look at me when I'm talking to you. Never once in my life have I spawned a bastard. Never once. Only idiots do that!' He finished by delivering a terrible blow to the side of the younger man's face.

Richard returned unsteadily to his seat, leaving his son in the corner, a massive handprint staining his cheek.

'Well?' he asked her now. 'What do you want?'

Ma picked up her purse. 'I want this filled for my grand-child.'

'Your grandchild?'

'Yes. If you co-operate, I'll marry her off to my son with a bit of luck and no-one need be any the wiser about it.'

'I see.' He took a cigar from a case on the desk and rolled it between finger and thumb. 'And if I don't do what you want?'

'Then I'm afraid Molly will have to become a sacrifice, a sort of heroine, if you like.' She nodded her head in the direction of the door. 'It won't take much from me, Richard, to get that lot on the march. If they realized what your son has done to my adopted daughter . . . well . . . ' She sighed dramatically. 'I couldn't hold them, I'm afraid. They're fit to burst as it is. If I wave your son's bastard under their noses, they'll have your hide. And his too.'

'You wouldn't.'

'Try me, Richard. Just try me.'

He lit the cigar slowly, giving himself time to think. 'If I go along with this . . . blackmail of yours, will you stay away from my mills?'

'No. I've a fancy to learn the weaving.'

'What?' He exploded in a bout of coughing. 'At your age? And would I let you in here knowing you'll have them on strike within a week?'

'I will not have them on strike. But I want to get out of the house, let her become the housewife. So, I'll need a job.'

'Then get a bloody job somewhere else.'

'I will have a job here.'

Charles began to walk towards the door, his steps quick and angry. 'Stop!' yelled his father. 'This is your doing and you'll stay for the finish.'

Ma took a deep breath while the young man hovered behind her. 'You've shops in town?' she asked lightly.

'Bolton? Aye, I hold a property or two round and about. Why?'

'I want a couple of adjoining shops. Not now, don't get excited. But I'll be needing the deeds or the lease – whatever – to some sort of business in . . . shall we say fifteen years? One shop for the child, one for the mother—'

'Bloody hell! Would you like the coat off my back as well, the bread out of my mouth?'

She shook her head. 'Nothing so unsavoury, thank you. I want your grandchild – my grandchild too in a way – to have a decent future. Would you like to see a Swainbank stuck amongst mules all day sweating for a living?'

'He will not be a Swainbank!' Richard's temper was about to erupt fully any minute now. 'A Swainbank is always born in wedlock—'

'What a happy accident that is.' She turned to glare venomously at Charles. 'Nothing to say for yourself?'

'I'm sorry!' he shouted. 'I love the girl—'

'Well, isn't that nice?' Ma said sarcastically. 'That makes everything all right now, doesn't it?' She looked at Richard again. 'Listen, you. If there's anything amiss, if she loses the baby or if I've been wrong in saying she's pregnant, then we'll forget the whole thing. But I want it done all legal and proper, a payment each month for the child, a future for him – or her – in business and no more said on the subject. Molly does not know I'm here. She doesn't even know what's wrong with her yet, though the penny will drop in time. If you agree, then I'll persuade her to marry Paddy and your son's name will stay out of it.'

'And what about your own flaming son? Can't he count? Doesn't he know it takes nine months for a baby?'

'That will be my concern, not yours. Babies have a habit of arriving premature when the air's filled with filthy smoke from your chimneys.'

He placed an elbow on the table and leaned his head against a closed fist. 'You know, Ma, if you'd been educated you would have been really dangerous.'

'Just because I don't read – that doesn't mean I've no brain. It's time you started looking out for my likes, Mr Swainbank. There's many of us could better you in an argument. Right.' She rose to her feet. 'I'll be seeing one of those lawyer fellers once I've sorted Molly and Paddy out. I suggest you do the same. Enjoy your meeting.' She made for the door, brushing hard against Charles as she passed him.

'Ma!' he said, his tone subdued.

'Yes?'

'Give her . . . my regards.'

She approached him until there was barely an inch of space between them. 'I'll give her nothing from you, boy. Don't you think you've already given her enough – a lifetime of grief and worry? She's a lot to hide from the world and I'll not burden her further by mentioning your name in my house.' Stepping back, she delivered a resounding slap to the other

167

side of his face. 'There,' she said, dusting her hands together. 'Now your face is more . . . what's the word? Even, that's it.' She opened the door. 'Even,' she repeated before stepping out into the corridor.

Right, it was done. The easy bit, anyway. Compared to Molly, those two were bunny rabbits, tame ones at that, eating out of her hand. Now the hard work must begin. She listened for a few moments as Richard screamed at his son, obscenities pouring in a seemingly endless stream out of his mouth and echoing throughout the office. Poor Richard. Whatever he was, he didn't deserve this. Neither did she. Most of all, poor little Molly deserved none of what was to come.

She made her way along Deansgate and turned left for St George's Road, shoulders rounded for the first time in her life. He looked ill, so very ill, did Richard. And what she'd perpetrated this day would not do much to improve the man's failing health. But those closest to her had to come first as always. Richard was not her responsibility, never had been. But that history should repeat itself in such a cruel way . . . Oh, life could be unbearable at times, making it easy to sink into the deadly sin of despair. At her front door she paused, hand poised over the latch. Now, she really would have to become a magician, persuade Molly to marry Paddy, get the pair of them down the aisle as soon as possible. And with Molly in her present frame, none of it promised to be easy.

Molly Dobson lay still as a stone, hands flat against the woven quilt, unseeing eyes staring out towards the nothingness that was her life. Three weeks she'd lain in here now, twenty-one days of emptiness and near-starvation, just a bit of bread and a sip of tea now and again. She knew it was three weeks because Ma had said so this morning. And she'd said a lot of other stuff and all, things about marrying Paddy before the neighbours started talking, about Ma not being able to allow them both to stay unless there was a wedding.

This sickness was an awful terrible mess, nothing Ma could put a name to. No fever, no spots, no sneezes or soreness in the throat. Her stomach felt as if it had been ten times through the mangle, not a drop of moisture left to squeeze out, just a dry and empty sack. What was it? She rolled her head and stared through the window. Everything outside seemed to be carrying on as normal, ragmen shouting, women gossiping, children playing their noisy games . . . Her heart suddenly lurched. Children playing. An appalling idea lurked on the edge of conscious thought, had sat there for several days now, a monster whose tentacles reached a little further with each passing hour, waiting for her to open her mind. It couldn't be! Not after just the once – oh no, not that!

As if propelled from a gun, she sat bolt upright in the bed, her head spinning from this quick movement. Yes! She was late, a week late. And she'd always been like clockwork up to now. Her hand moved slowly downward until it reached her abdomen, but there was no swelling yet. Nothing but this vile sickness, nothing at all.

She leapt from the bed and pulled on her clothes, tearing and ripping in her haste. There was no time to think, to consider the options – and anyway, there were no valid choices. Her life from this moment was dictated completely, had been mapped out in another moment three weeks ago. She slowed her movements deliberately, determined not to let the panic show. After fastening her dress, she sat on the edge of the bed for a few minutes, her last minutes of individuality and freedom. Yes, she'd watched what happened to women hereabouts, dragged down by children and hardship. What she had done so far was wicked; what she half planned to do in the future could only be described as evil. And so it must be.

Ma listened as Molly reached her conclusion, tuned in while the message finally dawned, heard the scuttling, the haste, then the quiet. Her heart went out to the poor girl, but she brushed away the tears savagely. This charade would have to be acted right through to its end, each member of the cast having a difficult part to play, some deceiving, some deceived. Little Molly would have to act as both victim and perpetrator, while Ma herself would doubtless be the sorceress, the one who made it all happen, the one who would be blamed should things go wrong.

'Ma?' The trembling girl stepped into her welcoming arms. 'I've decided to stop,' she sobbed. 'Me and Paddy can get wed as soon as the Father will do it. I'll . . . I'll turn later on, so it'll have to be mixed to start with—'

'That's fine then, child. Sure we can always ask for a papal blessing later on, after your baptism. We can get the banns waived – I'm sure of that. Not that there's any real need for haste,' she added quickly. 'Only you know how these streets are, everybody chattering as if I'm keeping a bad house with the two of you not married.'

Molly giggled hysterically. 'I think I should have told Paddy first, though.'

'Ah, he'll be in soon and I won't say a word. Make your announcement and I'll do me best to look surprised.'

Molly continued to shiver violently, the truth hovering on the tip of her tongue, for she felt she could never live with this deception. Ma patted the shaking back. 'It will all turn out well, pet. You know he worships the ground you walk on – didn't he fetch you that fearsome bunch of half-dead flowers just the other day? And did you ever see the likes? I wonder which graveyard he stole them from, eh?'

'Oh Ma—'

'Yes, he's a character. When I saw the roses wrapped in Saturday's sports page with all the footballers on it, I nearly keeled over. "Wherever did you get this lot?" I asked him. But he said not a word, just swapped the *Evening News* for a sheet of greaseproof. There's no bad in him, Molly. Sure, you're both a bit young for it, but the neighbours know he loves you and they're waiting for the wedding. So. I'll go up and visit the presbytery, get everything sorted out.'

'I don't want . . . I don't want a white frock.'

Ma pulled the girl closer. 'No. White is a very peculiar colour – no colour at all, really. I find it very drab myself. A little cream suit with a matching hat would be nice. How's your tummy?'

'A bit easier.'

'Good.' She drew herself away and gazed into the pale face, unable to quite meet the eyes where a terrible grief showed so plainly. 'Yes, the job was too much for you, Molly. I'm glad you had the good sense to leave when it made you so ill. I'll . . . er . . . go out a while, child. Better if you and Paddy are alone just now and I'm wanting some baking soda.' She reached for her coat.

'Ma?'

'Ah yes – there's me purse. Do you fancy anything special for tea?'

Molly shook her head.

'Try to cheer up a bit. I know you aren't too well, but this is supposed to be a happy time, is it not? Get a cold wash and comb your hair. When I get back, you'll no doubt be engaged to me-lad-o.'

Molly dropped into a dining chair. 'Ma?'

The older woman turned in the doorway. 'Don't get too tired now – leave the housework to me until this sickness passes. You'll be better soon, I'm sure of it.'

'But Ma!' The door was closing.

'I'll be back soon,' came the muffled reply.

Molly sat for an hour or so waiting for Paddy to come home, her fevered mind dancing about like a dog recently released from its leash, tearing here and there with no real sense of direction. There were choices. Somewhere underneath all this mess, she could catch the edge of them if she concentrated hard enough. She could leave, pack her things and throw herself on Charles Swainbank's mercy. Or she could stay and marry Paddy. Between these two opposing poles there was no space for compromise. But she might not be pregnant! And if she was, would Paddy guess, would Ma find out?

Her head sank until it met tightly clenched hands, elbows resting on Ma's green plush table cover. No. She couldn't go back to Swainbank, wouldn't ask him for help. And there were people a lot worse than Paddy Maguire – she knew that only too well now. But to have a child and pretend that it was his . . .

The door opened. Molly looked up expecting to see Ma who had been gone such a long time just for a bit of soda. She screwed up her eyes against the invasive light, then pushed herself to rise.

'Hello, Molly. Up and about again, I see?'

'Yes.' And she took those first few steps, steps she would never be able to retrace, into the arms of her future husband.

Ma lingered in a back pew, a carton of soda crushed between clenched fingers. To lie, even for a reason such as this, was not a natural part of her being. In fact, she was going against every principle in her book, doing the very things she preached against, manipulating people, trying to act like a boss. Like God Himself. She looked around the walls at the Stations of the Cross, so beautifully portrayed in this particular church, three-dimensional and coloured, each arrangement set on a semi-circular plinth. It was a lovely church, was this. Most just had plaques, flat stone etchings of Jesus' sufferings, not much more than a set of brownish tablets. But St Peter's was a proud church, immaculately clean and cared for, a credit to the poor Irish and Lancashire folk who contributed weekly to the support of their pastors.

Her eye finally rested on the figure of Simon trying to help Jesus carry the Cross up Calvary. Wasn't she just helping Molly up her hill? Didn't the girl have a terrible cross of her own to carry and wouldn't Simon of Cyrene have done exactly the same thing? Dear God in heaven, was life ever going to be simple at all?

She looked down at her fingers all covered in white powder now, the container flattened past mending. Still, no-one would starve for the lack of soda. There was a good thick stew in the pot – if only Molly would manage to eat a little and hang on to it. Yes, even the soda was a lie, a visible one spread all over her hands and down the front of her coat.

She got up, dusted herself off, then genuflected before going to light a candle in front of Mary. The small flame flickered then rose upward, a wisp of blue smoke preceding its ascent. 'Help us all, Mother,' she whispered. 'Make her

172

eat, make her laugh again. Give my Paddy just enough sense to look after her, but little enough to guess what is really happening. And forgive me. What I'm trying to do for this little unborn soul is not strictly honest, but you know I think the father should pay in some way.'

She turned and walked out of the church. This was just the beginning, the start of a lifetime built on lies. How on earth would she explain away the child's sudden wealth when the time came? Uncle Porrick and his leprechauns, a pot of gold found in a thunderstorm? She lifted her chin and strode deliberately in the direction of home. There she would find either an engaged couple or an empty room. From now on, Molly would be making decisions by herself, never realizing Ma's involvement. And, if the girl had decided to stay, keeping her in ignorance would take a lot of luck. Luck and not a little prayer.

'Molly, it's no use sitting there dreaming and getting morbid. That's a desperate unhappy face you're wearing these days – what happened to your laughter? The child will surely feel it too if you sit about long-mouthed and weary the whole day—'

'I've done the dishes and got your teas. What else would you like? A bit of clog-dancing, happen the can-can on the table? I'm hot, Ma, hot and heavy.'

Ma shook her head grimly. 'Tell me about it, why don't you? You'd know what hot meant if you'd been stuck with me in that inferno the whole week. It's like hell at times, yet I love the weaving – always knew I would.'

'I just wish it was all over and done with, Ma.'

'Ah well, isn't that perfectly understandable now? Every expectant mother loses her patience towards the end, for it seems to go on for ever.' And thank God it had gone on forever. Almost eight months married now. If the child came this very day, there'd be no cause for suspicion. 'I've had special permission for a week off,' she went on carefully. 'I told the manager you weren't very well. I think your baby will be here soon.'

Molly's face was suddenly filled with fear. 'Will it?'

Ma nodded, a comforting smile accompanying the quick movement of her head. 'I know the signs, love. There's but few go full term in these parts. That backache of yours is a sure enough sign that he'll pop out any minute.'

'He?'

'Young Joseph. Didn't we agree that we'd call him after my favourite brother? A caution, he was – and still is, I shouldn't wonder. We could never find him, because he was forever running off after the wild ponies. I still miss them all at home, you know. Family is very important, Molly. Life can be a desperate hard thing without the support of a family.'

'Yes.' Molly lifted a potato pie from the oven. 'But I think it's a girl. I don't know why, but I've always felt that way.' She placed the pie in the centre of the table. 'Janet,' she said, her voice stripped of emotion.

'Why Janet?'

The girl shrugged listlessly. 'It's as good a name as any, I suppose.'

'What about your mother's name? The child will be half Dobson, after all.'

'I don't like Edith. But I'll call her Janet Edith all the same. And if you're right and it's a boy, it'll be Joseph Arthur after me dad.'

'So be it. Then we'll just have to wait and see, won't we? Where's our terrible husband and son? Rampaging, is he?'

At last a tiny smile played over Molly's lips. 'He's out doing Swainbank.'

'He's what?'

'Him and the chap from Chase farm, him as runs it. They're out performing push-ups or summat with the boss's money.'

'Push-ups? What in heaven's name are they?'

Molly eased herself into the carpet chair, a difficult task as she was now hugely pregnant and her shortness of stature was a sore impediment. 'I don't rightly understand it, but they're making money. They get to the market early on and look for likely beasts. Then they make a low offer. If the offer's accepted, then some clever beggar forges a slip with the auctioneer's name on it, as if they've paid more and his fee on top. Paddy and the farmer split the difference.'

'Well!' Ma threw her coat onto the dresser. 'Isn't that stealing?'

'Paddy calls it surviving. Mind, they lose out at times. If the feller doesn't sell cheap, then they all agree on a price. Paddy and his own farmer do what they call a stand-in, keep bidding and pushing the price up. If it goes no further than what they agreed, then Paddy has to buy. But if somebody else bids more, then Paddy, the farmer from Swainbank's and the selling farmer all split the extra money.'

'Well! I knew he'd brains, sure enough, but I never thought he'd be following so closely in his father's footsteps. What if they get found out?'

'They won't. Paddy's too clever for that.'

The subject of discussion suddenly burst in at the front door, his usually pale cheeks ablaze with excitement. 'Ma! Molly! Guess what?'

'We know,' said Ma grimly. 'You're making a small fortune out of certain gentleman farmers who shall remain nameless . . .'

'No! I mean yes . . . only that's not it!'

'Paddy!' There was a stern warning in Ma's tone. 'Wasn't the two hundred pounds compensation enough for you? Not that it'll last, the way you drink . . .'

'Will you listen! I've got a surprise for you.'

'Have you now? Well sit down and eat this meal before it spoils, Paddy Maguire.'

He twisted his cap between nervous fingers. 'Is there enough for a visitor?'

'Of course,' said Ma. 'You know I would never turn away a friend of yours. Set another place, Molly, while Paddy brings in his visitor. I'm away to wash a day's dirt from my hands.'

When Ma returned from the scullery, she found herself face to face with a man she had never expected to find in her house again. Shocked to the core, she leaned heavily against the dresser, her eyes wide and staring. He hadn't changed that much, she thought to herself while her heart pounded loudly. Still long, lanky and pale, still mean around the eyes and lips. 'Get out,' she muttered between clenched teeth.

'Now, Philly. Don't you be starting off again with the lashing tongue. Sure, I always knew your bark was worse than your bite . . . '

'Did you now? Well it's plain you know little enough!' She turned on her son. 'How could you? Have you no sense, no feelings at all in that thick head of yours? Whatever are you thinking of?'

'I . . . I recognized him, Ma, 'cos he looks like me. Soon as I saw him, I knew who he was.'

'Have a heart now, Philly,' said the man, his tone wheedling. ' 'Tis a clever man recognizes his own father . . . ' His voice tailed away as he noticed the fierce expression on her face.

'A father?' she screamed now. 'A father, you say? What kind of a father would leave his child before it was ever born? And what's a father at the end of the day? Just an instrument, something that starts a life then ceases to worry. This is my son, my daughter-in-law and my house! So get out this instant before I get my neighbours to throw you out.'

Paddy took a hesitant step towards his mother. 'He's over selling cows, comes over nearly every year—'

'Does he now? Well, where's the child support due to me these last years, Seamus Maguire? I've seen a solicitor and you can be made to pay even now. Didn't you think to come and visit your son ever? Didn't you worry and wonder was he all right, was I all right?'

'I knew you'd be fine—'

'Ah well, isn't that just great, now? Will I go out and kill the fatted calf, invite the street in for the celebrations? Or would you prefer me to get the police, for there's an order out, a desertion order. An English court would be interested in you and your arrears.'

He blanched and backed away towards the door. 'No po-liss,' he muttered.

She nodded slowly. Strange how she hadn't noticed till now how much of her accent had disappeared, how

Boltonese her speech was becoming. Compared to this estranged husband of hers, she was practically English. 'In trouble again, I take it? Lighting fires and smuggling bullets, having a go at the innocent who cannot fend for themselves?'

He straightened. 'I am at war,' he declared clearly.

'Indeed?' She walked to the table and removed the extra place-setting, flinging surplus items on to the dresser. 'Where's your uniform? I thought war involved a few soldiers lined up and a bit of ground between them?'

'It's not that kind of war—'

'No,' she hissed. 'And it never will be, because you know the English would wipe you out in ten seconds flat. Not that I'm taking sides, mind, only I know I'm not on yours.' She turned to Paddy now. 'This hero is preparing to wipe out the British Empire single-handed.'

'I'm not on me own—'

'Ah no. I was forgetting the half dozen others hidden in the bushes. Paddy, they kill defenceless people—'

'We kill those who stole our lands! There's English parading up and down as if they own my country.'

'I'm not saying it's fair, Seamus Maguire! Life was never fair, but several wrongs do not make one single right!' She sighed, her head wagging quickly in exasperation. 'A hundred times we argued over this. After eighteen years, I'd have thought you might have learned a bit of sense at least! But no. You'll carry on planning and killing, a few years' breathing space then off again with your shenanigans. You cannot stay here. I will give no space to a rebel, just as I would give none to those you fight against.'

'Your own country.' He spat these words. 'Not a damn do you give, even for family. Did you know your mammy and daddy are dead?' He smiled as she slumped against the wall. 'And your brother Kevin sits in a Belfast jail waiting on what they call British justice? We've done nothing, nothing at all, but we will some day and then let the eejits watch out for us.'

Ma pulled herself together with difficulty. 'If you were a man, you'd have been to my house before this to tell me about my own people.'

He hung his head slightly. 'It hasn't been possible.'

'No.' Her voice was heavy with sarcasm now. 'Because you've been in prison yourself, no doubt. And I'll have you back there before morning unless you leave now.'

Seamus hesitated, then took a step towards his new-found son. 'Believe me, I've done nothing to be ashamed of—'

'Oh aye?' Paddy stared hard and long at this stranger until the room crackled with tension.

'I see I'm to be a granddaddy soon.'

Molly, who had not attempted to speak during all this, heaved herself out of the chair and moved towards the staircase. 'I'll see you later, Ma,' she said before opening the door.

'But . . . ' Seamus looked from Paddy to Ma. 'What's the matter with everybody? I'm his daddy, for God's sake—'

Paddy crossed the room and stood beside his mother. 'You are no relation to me and I'm sorry I brought you here. You'd best get out before I throw you out.'

'What?'

'You heard. I often wondered what you'd be like, specially when I was a kid. A kid you walked out on. Any idea what she's been through?' He jerked a thumb towards his mother. 'Worked herself daft, she has.'

'And turned you against me!'

Paddy shook his head vehemently. 'Never mentioned you. It was obvious you weren't worth talking about – I can see that for myself now. And I don't want my little lad or lass having a jailbird for a grandad, so you'd best be on your way.'

Seamus Maguire seemed to deflate suddenly, like a balloon with all the air released from its elastic casing. 'I need a place for now, just for the while—'

'Why?' Ma's tone was steely.

'Jaysus, woman – have ye no imagination at all? And did you never hear of the Risings? English poliss we have over to home, English bastards who blame the innocent for what's their own fault! Sure, if they'd leave us alone—'

'You'll not hide here, that you won't! You're gone all these years and never a penny in support for your wife and son, then back you come with your tail between your legs expecting me to protect you from the law!'

'For God's sake, Philly!'

She held up her hand. 'For Paddy's sake, for Molly's, for the child and aye – for myself too – I am ordering you out of my house. Your name is no longer on the rent book, so you have no right to be here—'

The door flew open. 'It's all right, Missus,' called a deep male voice. 'We're here to take the burden off you.' Three huge policemen jumped into the room. Seamus flattened himself against the dresser.

'You are Seamus Maguire?' No reply came from the cowering man's whitening lips, so the sergeant stepped forward, a truncheon dangling from his right hand. 'I arrest you for crimes against the State. Namely, that you did knowingly and wilfully smuggle illegal arms into Dublin, that you committed arson in a public building, that you caused the deaths of two policemen and nine civilians—'

Ma leapt across the room, hand raised to strike.

'No!' yelled the sergeant. 'Don't do it, lass, or he'll say it was us. I want him unmarked and pretty for when he comes up in front of the judge.'

Because she could find no other safe way of expressing her contempt, Ma spat into her husband's face, leaning back to watch as the spittle ran down his cheek. 'Hang him,' she said quietly. 'And keep our names out of it. No doubt the neighbours have noticed already that you are here to arrest him, but I want it made plain that I have not seen this man since before my son was born. In fact, this is the first time Paddy has met his father – if we can call him a father, that is.'

Paddy nodded slowly, his eyes wide with terror after hearing such a terrible list of crimes. 'That's right.' He took a deep breath. 'I have no father, never did have. Just take him away – I don't want me Ma and me wife upsetting any more.'

Molly had reached the upper storey and was lying on the bed, her breath coming in short gasps as labour pains began to rack her body in earnest. But she did not call for help; Ma had

179

explained that this stage might go on for hours and there was enough trouble in the house already without her adding to it before absolutely necessary. In spite of the pain, she grinned. She felt so proud of Ma. Yes, what was a father after all? Nothing. Ma had managed to rear a son alone. With Paddy's help and Ma's support, her child's real father could remain completely unimportant.

Downstairs in the street, neighbours lined the short route from house to police van as Seamus Maguire was carted off to prison. When the black vehicle had turned the corner, Ma addressed the onlookers. 'Yes, that was Himself, the husband whose life I made a misery all those years ago. Well, now you all know why, for he's a desperate sort who's going off now to where he rightly belongs.' She nodded wisely. 'Ah yes, those of you who are old enough will remember how I was treated, looked upon with fear because I hunted him away and made medicines – a witch I was called.' The small crowd sighed and nodded in unison. 'Well, he's gone now, so you can get back to your chores with the show over.'

Pierce Murphy stepped forward, cap in hand, coal-rimmed eyes shining over-brightly beneath heavy black brows. 'We've always known you were all right, Ma. Sure, you've stuck by us through thick and thin, given cures for free, picked coal off the heaps with the rest of them when the pits closed. There's not a man or woman here would condemn you for having a criminal for a husband.'

'Thank you, Pierce Murphy. I am grateful for such good neighbours. And now, if you will excuse me, I have a meal to eat and a bed to get to.'

She was hardly through the door before Paddy grabbed both of her hands tightly. 'Ma! She's started . . . Molly . . . hurry up . . . she's early, isn't she?'

'Don't be bringing the house down with it, Paddy! Haven't we had enough excitement for the one day? By all that's holy, I swear you've had the heart scalded out of me every minute since you were born—'

'But Ma—!'

'Away with your bother, man. She's healthy enough, a fine

strong girl—' She pushed him aside, her heart fluttering wildly as she once again made swift calculation in her head. Although she could not cope with abstract numeration, she could count all right. ' – And it's not that early, for heaven's sake. Didn't Bridget O'Leary go but six and a half months and the baby survived?'

'What can I do? Will I boil water or what?'

Ma opened the door wide. 'You will go, this time with my blessing and ten shillings from my own purse, into the vault of the Bull. Where, no doubt, you will drink yourself into unconsciousness by nine o'clock.'

'No!'

Ma leaned wearily against the wall. 'Look, Paddy. This day I have had two bad cuts off my loom, a husband returned who I never wanted to see again, I've learned that my parents are dead, that my brother is in jail and that my daughter-in-law is in labour. And now, to top it all, you're being a desperate trouble when I could do without it. So go.'

Paddy stepped out into the street and sat at the edge of the pavement. He wasn't going anywhere. Oh, he had to accept that he couldn't be with Molly, couldn't hold her hand and mop her brow when she most needed him. But he wasn't leaving the street. Should the doctor be required, he'd be on hand to fetch him.

A few interested passers-by asked why he was sitting there and when the answer was given, a dinner appeared as if by magic, then a jug of ale with a blue-rimmed tin cup to drink from, a packet of cigarettes, a cheap and rather flattened cigar. Doors were closed in deference to the activity currently taking place in number thirty-four and Paddy sat in splendid isolation well into the night.

He must have dozed off, because the next thing he knew was Ma shaking him by the shoulder. 'Come on now, Paddy. You've stiffened up like a corpse – get into the house.'

He got up slowly and stretched his limbs, then, as he became fully awake, he grabbed Ma's arm. 'Is it all over?'

'Most of it. But you can't go up yet, I've the afterbirth to deliver. I wouldn't have left her, but I saw you through the window stretched out like a side of beef.'

'The baby?'

'A boy.' As she spoke, the unmistakable sound of a new-born baby's cry came floating from the upper storey of the house. 'He's small,' she said. 'But fine all the same,' she added reassuringly.

They stared at one another in disbelief as another and quite separate sound reached their ears. 'Holy Mother,' whispered Ma. 'Is that my hearing gone already with the weaving, or—'

'No, Ma! I hear it and all! Go on! Go to her—' But Ma was already in the house and halfway across the kitchen.

She raced up the stairs and found Molly crouched by the bed, just as she'd found the girl's mother all those years ago. Ma's hand flew to her throat. 'Edie!' she said before she could stop herself. And she was momentarily back in next door's kitchen with Edie and the new-born Molly all over again.

This second child was stronger and larger than the first, screaming fit to burst although it was not yet fully born.

'What is it?' asked the young mother, tears and sweat mingling on her cheeks.

'I can't tell yet. Ah . . . it's a girl. We were both right. Come on now, get back into the bed this instant.'

When the babies were safe in their shared cot, Ma stumbled to the top of the stairs, her voice cracking as she called, 'It's twins, Paddy. One of each. Don't come up yet, lad. I'll tell you when it's time.'

After seeing to Molly's needs, she crept to the side of the crib and stared down at these two Swainbanks, Richard's grandchildren, tiny, blameless and beautiful creatures, they were. While their mother slept, she took holy water from the side table and blessed them as Joseph Arthur and Janet Edith Maguire, laying particular emphasis on the surname. After that, they were hers, hers and Molly's and Paddy's. No matter what happened, nobody could ever take them away.

As she watched Paddy fussing over 'his' babies, she backed away into a corner, a lump rising rapidly in her parched throat. Yes, they'd both cheated him, both she and Molly. But as long as he believed the twins were his, as long as he loved them and loved their mother, surely nothing but good could come of this arrangement?

Paddy looked across at his mother, tears making tracks down his haggard cheeks. 'They're a bit on the small side, Ma. Will they be all right?'

She nodded quickly, not trusting her voice.

'Ma?'

'Yes. They'll be fine.' She swallowed hard. 'The lad's the weakest, about four pounds, I'd say. But the little girl's strong, a good five at least. As long as we keep them warm, get them feeding—'

'What's up, Ma? Did Molly have a hard time?'

She wiped her eyes on a corner of the capacious apron. 'No worse than most, Paddy. It's just . . . oh, I don't know. Mammy and Daddy dead, two gone and two born—'

'But that's the way, isn't it? Some has to go to make room for others?'

'Yes. Yes, I dare say that's the way of it, sure enough. When I came in, after delivering the first, I found Molly on the floor giving birth in exactly the same way as her mother did. I suppose that upset me as well, realizing how much I still miss Edic.'

He crept to her side and laid an arm across her shoulders. 'You've still got us, lass. I know I'm not up to much, but you've Molly and the babies—'

She reached out and touched his face. 'Paddy, you are what the world made of you, no more and no less. Don't be putting yourself down, for I shall do that often enough with my sharp tongue. They're lovely babies, babies you can be proud of, son.' She walked towards the door then turned to look at him. 'God bless,' she whispered before disappearing on to the landing.

Paddy knew he was grinning from ear to ear, felt as if his face would split in half at any minute. At last, he'd done something right. He was a family man now, a man with responsibilities. He would change, aye, he would that.

Molly opened her eyes and stared at her husband, watched

the pleasure and pride in his face as he looked at the twins. 'Bring them here, lad,' she said quietly. 'Time we taught them how to feed, eh?'

'Oh.' He studied his shoes. 'How do I pick them up?'

She began to giggle. 'Not by the scruff and not by the feet, Paddy Maguire!'

He fumbled among the tiny sheets and quilts. 'There's not a right lot to get hold of—' He swung round and glared at his wife. 'What the hell's up with you at all? There's nowt to laugh at! I might be used to calves and such, but this here's a different job altogether. They keep wriggling.'

'Oh, Paddy!' She clutched her bruised belly and screamed hysterically. 'They'll not break.' It didn't matter any more. They were born safely, that was the main thing. And she was wed proper, so there was no need to tell the truth ever. The euphoria of new motherhood filled the whole of her being, put everything into a perspective that seemed so clear just then. Paddy, happy because she was laughing once more, joined in the merriment as he struggled to carry his precious cargo across the room.

'Thanks, Paddy,' she said finally.

'What for?'

'Well – for marrying me, for the twins – for everything.'

He shook his head in bemusement. 'And you weren't for getting wed, were you? Oh no, you were off for a ladies' maid down London till the job got you down. I'm right glad it did, Molly. Hey, have you seen the size of these fingers? You can hardly see the nails . . . still, that'll be with them being a bit premature, like. Ma says twins often come early.'

'Yes. Go and get me a cup of tea. I shall be needing fluids.'

He left the room reluctantly, capering about and dancing as he made for the stairs. Alone, Molly hugged her children and kissed their downy heads. Charles Swainbank would never know the happiness she felt at this moment, would never see or hold his children. Because they weren't his at all. From now on, they were definitely Paddy's.

* * *

184

It wasn't as bad as it used to be, though no doubt it could have been a deal better.

In the mill where Ma worked, cleaners had been taken on, a small army who came in during the night to move the worst of the day's wastes. But there was still just one lavatory to each floor, while lunchtime facilities consisted of a temperamental boiler from which the workers might take water for tea. Even this was an improvement on several other mills where the workers paid nearby cottagers a few pence a week for hot water, travelling back and forth with billies and jugs during the dinner time break.

In mute deference to frequent demands, a box had appeared on each landing, an old skip containing a few bandages and ointments. As no-one seemed to take direct responsibility for the refurbishment of these containers, Ma filled them up in her spare time, coming in early or staying behind to see what was needed. The bills were written out by Molly and these were always paid through Ma's packet, though no mention was ever made of the service she provided.

There was a pecking order in the mills, a sort of division of classes within the class, with breakers and carders coming somewhere at the bottom of the list and weavers wearing the crown right at the top. By 1926, Ma was a master weaver, having learned every function of her machines, every pattern card, every quirk of her looms. She'd kept her side of the bargain all right. No longer the prime agitator, she simply followed where the union dictated, made sure her mouth stayed shut and her hands remained clean. The workers had, at first, expressed dismay at this change in her attitude, but she explained it away by telling them to follow the real leaders now, the proper and educated stewards.

And now, in May of this year, what Ma had prophesied was about to finally happen. On the Friday night, every loom and mule shuddered to a halt and the workers moved among machines for a last wiping down and oiling. There was a grim silence about them; not a one could be heard rejoicing at the thought of England closing down for a whole week if not

185

more. 'Ah well.' Ma folded her final cut. 'I suppose we've seen it coming.'

Meg Butterworth clucked her tongue. 'Aye. Try telling that to my lot come next Thursday and no tea on the table.' As always, Meg's mouth twisted itself into exaggerated shapes as she spoke and Ma found herself wondering, not for the first time, whether or no she'd discovered the true origin of the Lancashire dialect. The noise in the mills was usually so loud that messages had to be mouthed and the Bolton folk seemed to have taken this habit home with them, lips stretching this way and that, faces changing shape constantly during speech.

'Eeh well,' said Meg now. 'No use mithering over it, I suppose. Best get home and stop in bed for a week. You don't feel so clemmed in bed. Mind, he'll be at home too, so I don't want to give him no ideas. Nay, if I'm not careful, we shall be having another mouth to feed. How's them twins of your lad's?'

'Fine, Meg. They're doing great, ready for school soon.'

'And Paddy?'

Ma looked up to heaven. 'Don't talk to me about him. I knew it wouldn't last, all that business about turning over a new leaf now he's a father. He's doing a bit of droving when it suits him, though he's not allowed to kill on account of his hand. Still spends a lot of time messing around with horses, going to fairs and the like with farmers. When he's sober, that is.'

Meg nodded sagely. Her own husband wasn't too clever when it came to drink and she often turned up with a black eye or a bruised cheek. 'They're buggers with a pint inside them. I've told him often enough, I might be only little but I'll get him one of these days.'

'What'll you do?'

'Poison his bloody dinner, grease the stairs—'

'You wouldn't!'

'Aye, I know I wouldn't. And so does he.'

Ma wandered towards the door, wondering how it was that Meg Butterworth carried on worshipping a husband who beat her mercilessly every payday. She stopped in her tracks.

186

Richard was being carried in on a chair, supported on one side by Paddy and on the other by his own son. She folded her arms and watched this sight, her head on one side as she considered the irony of it. The twins' grandfather being supported by both their fathers. If it wasn't so dangerous and tragic, it might be funny.

They set the chair down and she studied the man who hadn't been expected to live anything like this length of time. He was truly old now, shrivelled and shrunken, a shell of a man but with a light still burning brightly in the fevered eyes.

He nodded. 'Ma?'

'Good evening.'

Paddy removed the driving gloves and smiled at Charles. He'd done a fair bit of work for the Swainbanks lately, was becoming quite an expert driver, in fact. Perhaps he should have cards printed, 'Patrick Maguire Driver and Drover'. That appealed to him, he liked a play on words.

'What the bloody hell are they up to?' asked the old man now. 'Bring them all over here, Charles. Let's see what they're made of.' The two younger men went off to gather the weavers together.

Ma coughed self-consciously. 'Is this just for the benefit of our shed?'

'No.' His breathing was laboured. 'I've been in every room. If I could get on my knees, then I would—'

'It wouldn't do any good, for there'll be no coal—'

'We've stocks, haven't we?'

'For a month or two.'

'Enough, I'd say.'

She shook her head slowly. 'They'll be out a while, the miners. What can you expect when they've had wages dropped? The rest of us are just standing by them for a week or so.'

'Waste of bloody time,' he gasped, his cheeks darkening.

'You should be in your bed.'

'While you close my mills?'

'It's not me! This was a proper decision, a vote—'

'Philly?'

'What?'

'How . . . how are they?'

She bit her lower lip. 'They're well. But I'd feel more comfortable if Paddy wasn't getting so familiar with that son of yours.'

Richard coughed so that he might breathe more easily. 'What would you do, I wonder?'

'If what?'

'If I had our . . . little agreement wiped out? Would you hold them up as Swainbanks, poor little mites?'

'You know that I could not do such a thing. Not now that they're born and well grown.'

'You'd never have done it anyway, would you?'

'No.'

'Then you won't keep me to the deal?'

She looked at him for a moment or two. 'I suppose not.'

He grinned and she caught sight of the handsome man he had once been. 'It's all right, lass. We won't back out of it now. Charles is a good lad – two of his own now. Peter and John. He knows he wronged the girl, Philly. He'll not let the kiddies down.'

'It's glad I am to hear it.'

Richard delivered a somewhat breathless sermon from the confines of his chair, telling the assembled weavers and tenters how foolish were their ways, issuing the occasional veiled threat about closures and no work for the future. No one seemed too impressed. The old man was weak, his son promised to be a softer option than old Richard had been in his heyday. And when all came to all, right was on the side of the workers. Time these bloated capitalists got the odd lesson.

Everyone went home to a very strange week of silence, a holiday that wasn't quite a holiday because folk's future seemed to hang by such a slender thread these days. All the uncles did a roaring trade, queues stretching either side of the three brass balls every morning, everything from father's suit to the best brasses pawned against starvation. When it didn't rain, the skies were clear and beautiful; this was how life might have been in the valley if the mills had not sullied the

188

atmosphere each working day. But there was a listlessness, a feeling of unreality to it all.

An extremely strange lady called Sarah Leason came down from her house on the moors, stepping for the first time ever on cobbles, sending her man to call at the colliers' cottages she owned. She stood at the end of Delia Street where just four houses belonged to her. Ma Maguire came out of the end house, a tray of flour cakes held in her arms. 'Can I help you?'

'Are those for the strikers?' asked Miss Leason.

Ma indicated the affirmative, wondering what this posh-knob was doing hereabouts. 'I'm on strike meself too,' she said defensively.

'And so you ought to be, my good woman. Are you a spinner?'

'A weaver, Ma'am.'

'It's Miss. Miss Sarah Leason.'

'Oh. Yes.' They'd heard of her. She kept a very peculiar household by all accounts, barn door left open for tramps, then there were tales of cats, dogs and even donkeys roaming everywhere. And her dad had been a pit owner too . . .

'What's your name?' barked this eccentric lady.

'Maguire. They call me Ma.'

A thin hand in a fingerless black glove thrust itself forward and touched the tray. Ma studied the tiny creature in its cape and fusty grey dress, like a blackbird, she was. Or like something from another century altogether.

'I'm calling in my rent books.' Beady eyes fixed themselves on Ma's face.

'You're not . . . not putting them on the streets, Miss?'

A weak laugh escaped from thin pale lips. 'Not on your nellie, Ma! I'm letting them stop rent free until this bloody mess is over. You'll be back in a day or two, you and the others. But my lot won't. I've sold the pits but kept the cottages. They'll pay me not one penny while they're out and they'll have no empty rent book sitting on the table as a reminder of their supposed inadequacy.'

Ma stepped back, her breath temporarily taken away. So it was true, then. Not all the rich folk were against the strike.

And the way this one talked, like an ordinary woman – swearing too!

'My family killed dozens of men and children, Ma Maguire. This is my small way of making reparation.'

'Then God will know it.' There was a small catch in Ma's voice.

'Yes, well you can leave God out of it, because I've no time for fairy tales. I stopped believing in God after Pretoria. If there is such a being, then it's something that plays with the earth like a ball, bouncing it about from time to time to see how many of us fall off. No, I place my faith in creatures. We could learn a lot from them.'

Ma shifted the weight of the tray on to her right hip. 'You sound like my son. He won't eat flesh at all, lives on turnips and apples most days.'

'Sensible chap.'

Ma sighed. 'Aye, but there's another part of his diet I didn't mention. Stout and Irish whiskey . . . '

'A sure sign of sensitivity,' said Miss Leason. 'He can't face the inhumanity of it all. I'm the same myself. Got a fox at the moment, a poor terrified creature hunted half to death by silly great men. I don't know what to do with him, for he trusts me now and probably trusts all men because I've healed him. If I keep him, he'll pine for his own kind. If I let him go, then he'll be hunted right to a kill. The wildest of creatures, Ma.' Her eyes misted and her voice was small and hurt. 'Yet he would never damage his own. We kill. We kill all things living, ourselves included.' She brought herself together suddenly, clicking her tongue against her teeth. 'Bring this son of yours to me.'

Ma looked down at the tray. The small fierce gentlewoman snatched this item from Ma's hands. 'I'll hold to the bread for you.'

It was a meeting of minds. Ma stood aside while Miss Leason propounded her theories, heard while her son agreed to go up to The Hollies and help with planting and weeding and harvesting. All for no pay, all in his spare time and just for a few vegetables and fruits.

'Money's almost gone, you see,' snapped the tiny woman. 'I had families to care for, mining families – and no one to stop me doing what was right. I'm the last of an iniquitous line, Mr Maguire. The house has gone to seed and I need money to feed my animals. Any help you might give will be appreciated.'

'I'll help you, Missus.'

'Miss.'

'Right then, Miss. I've debts to pay too, 'cos I killed a lot of beasts when I was slaughtering. So I'll come up the odd weekend and give you a hand.'

Ma delivered her flour cakes, wondering all the time about Miss Leason who seemed not to have the price of a loaf for herself, yet who came down in her dusty carriage with her one remaining servant to reduce her income so drastically. That, concluded Ma, was what having principles meant. She felt honoured to have met such a lady.

All kinds of people showed their hands that week. Vicars and priests patrolled streets arm in arm while they gave out shillings and oranges. Councillors from both sides collected up money and distributed it throughout the poorer wards, doctors treated the sick without charge, shopkeepers gave 'tick' without knowing whether or when the debts would ever be paid.

At the beginning of the second week, everyone returned to work. Everyone except the miners. Ma hated this. She walked past Pierce Murphy's door on her way to the mill, head bent with the shame she felt, lips tightened against words she must never say. For she had promised that she would be 'good' in return for the weaving job.

Pierce chased after her. 'Ma?'

'Hello, lad.'

'Tell them . . . tell them we understand. Well, some of us do, at least.'

She laid a hand on his arm, her eyes bright with anger. 'Some of us must work to keep those of you who must not.' She glanced over her shoulder at the three further miners' houses. 'These four families belong to Delia Street and to

Miss Leason. You will be cared for. Others have landlords too. And did you know how much the churches take from coal? Did you know that colliery land is rented from the highest in the country, paid for by the pit owners? If the owners hadn't such high rents to pay for ground to work, then your wages would improve. Tell that to the Archbishop in London, for he's surely a very wealthy man. The miners must take all they can from whoever owes it.'

'I'll tell the committee—'

'They already know it. It's a fierce fight, for you've taken on some powerful people.'

'I feel sick to the stomach, Ma.'

'Molly will be down with your bread and soup. Don't give in, Pierce.'

They didn't give in. Thirty-six weeks they stayed out while other industries struggled on the brink of starvation for the lack of fuel. Attempts were made to break the strike, but strike-breakers themselves were broken repeatedly by determined opposition. People died, people survived. Slates at shops ran into impossible figures and few pledges were redeemed over those months.

When it was finally over, shattered men went back into the earth's bowels with little flesh on their bones and for not much pay. Ma Maguire watched the sun rise on the day that the four doors opened, saw the men greeting one another in the middle of the cobbles, noticed how they clung together in their relief and humiliation. Ma was on short time, would not be required until the afternoon. So she sat as the winter sun brightened the sky, her eyes filling with tears. Even the sun seemed to mock this morning. Even the sun held just an empty promise.

Fergus had got out somehow. He kept doing it, kept going off to look for a mate, came back every time he got hungry. Miss Leason and Paddy patrolled fields and moors, he whistling between his teeth every few seconds, she calling the fox's name in her silly girlish voice, a voice that certainly didn't belong to a woman in her sixties. A strange figure she cut, thought Paddy, in men's overalls and with great big wellies on her feet. They paused for a breather and a sup of luke-warm tea from the bottle he carried.

'Paddy.' She slumped against a wall. 'I think we have to let him go this time.'

'Aye,' he agreed with reluctance. 'Happen he's found a safe place, Sarah. He might have a Missus – babies too afore long. Try and look on the bright side . . . '

'I can't. They'll all be chasing him in their silly red coats, dogs tearing him to bits, some savage creature taking his brush as a trophy . . . '

'Stop it!' He took the arm of this lady who had commanded him to call her Sarah, who hadn't the price of a crust some days, who slept and lived in just one room of that crumbling mansion. 'Look. Pull yourself together, for God's sake. We're off home now, 'cos I can see you're worn to nowt. And when we get home, I'm down to see that auctioneer feller at the back of Deansgate. We'll get rid of all that bloody antique furniture of yours. And when we do, the money's for you, not for the animals.'

'Paddy—'

'Don't start. My mam set out to save the world a while back, but she had to give up at the finish. You'll die for lack of food. Who'll look after all your animals then, eh? Have a bit of sense for once.'

'All right, all right. Keep your bloody hair on . . . What was that?'

They stood in silence and listened. 'A horse,' said Paddy finally. 'And it's in bother.'

Paddy held on to Sarah's hand, marvelling at the roughness of it. This was a lady who could have had anything – everything, in fact. Instead of which she had reduced her reinstated cottage rents in accordance with pay cuts and what she called inflation. 'Stop here,' he said gruffly. 'I'll find him.'

But there was no shaking her off. They found the distressed animal lying behind a low hedge, his stomach ripped by thorns, a hoof dangling at an impossible angle. 'This one'll never get up,' pronounced Paddy. 'And where's his rider?' The horse was fully saddled.

Paddy looked around until he caught a flash of red among the brambles. He flew to the spot and paused, a hand to his throat. 'Sarah?'

She was engrossed in the suffering horse. 'What? I reckon we can fix this, Paddy—'

'He's dead.' The neck was definitely broken.

'Not yet, he isn't.'

'I don't mean the horse. I mean this feller here.'

The woman left the beast and walked towards Paddy, her eyes narrowing as she saw the huntsman's colours in a crumpled heap on the ground. 'An eye for an eye,' she said. Paddy thought this was not only irrelevant, but also irreverent. Especially as she had no faith.

'Don't touch him,' said Paddy.

'Harold Swainbank.' Her voice was devoid of emotion. 'Always was wild, especially on horseback. Glad to say his brother doesn't hunt.'

Paddy looked around frantically. There was no sign of the rest. Surely Harold hadn't been hunting alone? Didn't they go in packs with dogs and horns? 'What do we do?'

She stepped back. 'You go over to Briars and tell them what's happened. I'll get some warm covering for the horse.'

They turned to find that the animal had risen and was attempting to walk. Without further ado, Sarah ripped out the sleeve of her coat and bound the hunter's foot tightly, squeezing the crushed hoof into some semblance of the correct position. Wild-eyed and terrified, the animal stood throughout these painful ministrations, knowing somehow that it dare not panic in the presence of this particular human.

While Paddy ran for help, Sarah led the horse slowly towards her home. That such a fine and beautiful creature might be shot for its deformities – no, she would not allow it.

Evening found Sarah, Paddy and Ma in an outbuilding with the exhausted horse. 'Well, we can do no more,' said Ma. 'The vet says he'll live, but with a limp. And he's not yours, Miss Leason.'

'Sarah.' She sank on to a bale of hay. 'They know where he is. Let them come for him.'

As if on cue, Charles Swainbank appeared in the doorway, a broken shotgun angled over his arm. He looked at the three white faces. 'I . . . er . . . came for my brother's horse,' he said, looking meaningfully at the weapon. 'Sorry you were troubled. The rest of the hunt lost poor Harold, I'm afraid . . . '

'So you're here to shoot this terrified creature?' Sarah's tone was shrill.

'Well, he's not to be ridden again.'

'I see.' The little woman jumped to her feet. 'Useless, is he? Like me, I suppose. Well, you'll have to shoot me first.' And she placed herself in front of the animal. 'Five pounds I've paid to have this foot put right and his wounds stitched.'

'You'll be reimbursed, Miss Leason. The animal must go. It caused the death of my brother.'

'What?' she screamed. 'What? With him whipping it into a lather and forcing it to jump about over fences? Horses do not jump, Mr Swainbank. In the wild, a horse will go miles out of its way just to avoid clearing a wall or a fence! Your brother killed himself—'

Ma placed a restraining hand on Sarah's arm. 'Not now, love. The man's lost a brother—'

'Killing foxes too! Including my Fergus.'

Fergus chose this unfortunate moment to put in a rather sheepish appearance, cowering along the ground until he reached the safety of Sarah's boots. Showing no emotion apart from anger, suppressing the great relief she felt at the sight of the fox, Sarah bent to pick up her wild pet. 'Look at him! Go on – look! Thirty grown men to kill a beast this size. Thirty men and two dozen dogs. So will you shoot the horse to put all that right?'

Charles bowed his head. There was no use in trying to talk sense to Sarah Leason. She was known far and wide for the lack of that particular commodity. And this was hardly the time to argue over an animal. 'I'll have his papers sent over tomorrow. The horse is yours, Miss Leason.'

Deflated considerably by this sudden turn of events and deprived of her soapbox, Sarah let out a long sigh. 'Right. All

fixed up, then. Sorry he's dead, Mr Swainbank. In spite of
. . . well . . . know what I mean.'

Charles nodded. 'The animal is not gelded, Miss Leason.
The pedigree is excellent. You can perhaps make use of him at
stud. If Samson had been gelded, then my brother might have
stood a chance. But no. He would never ride a safe mount,
always had to have the stallion. Still. I'm glad I don't have to
use the gun. Never did enjoy killing an animal.'

Ma stepped forward. 'We're very sorry.'

'So am I, Ma. So am I.'

As she looked into those sad dark eyes, Ma realized he wasn't
talking just about his brother. 'How's . . . how's your dad?'

'Not too well. This hasn't improved him.'

'No. No, it wouldn't.'

'They didn't get on, but Harold was still his son.' Why was
he saying all this to strangers? 'Families.' He shook his head
grimly.

'We all have our cross to bear,' said Ma kindly. 'Look at me
now with a husband in jail and a son who spends half his time
looking after animals and the rest as drunk as a fiddler's
elbow. Miss Leason has the best of it, I think. She chose her
family, four-legged every last one of them. She may be poor,
but at least she gets no smart answers from her children.'

Sarah Leason stroked Samson's nose. 'Will you come in for
a glass of wine, Mr Swainbank? All home made from my own
vegetables.'

'No thanks.' He studied his boots. 'I'll have to get back,
Father's expecting me. And my wife isn't too happy about
letting me out of her sight just now, though I did tell her
lightning never strikes twice.'

Ma smiled. Had he mentioned his wife deliberately, just to
let her know that he never thought of Molly? Ah no. Not
now, not at this time. There was too much grief about to be
reading meanings into folks' words.

He left the three of them to comfort horse and fox. As
the light failed, Sarah brought out the ancient trap and told
George, the one-armed ex-miner who looked after her, to take
her friends home.

They rode down country lanes towards Bolton, Ma leaning exhausted against her son's shoulder. After a day in the mill, the tending of a sick animal had been no repose.

'Ma?'

'What?'

'I'm not drunk half the time.'

'Not quite.'

'Then why did you say it? Why do you always say it?'

'In the hope that I'll shame you into mending your ways.'

He sighed loudly. 'It's our Joey as needs his ways mending. Have you heard the latest? He set a fire in next door's back yard while they were at work.'

'What for?'

'To bake spuds in. He wanted to sell baked potatoes to the other kids.'

Jesus, Mary and Joseph! She'd known there'd be trouble from that one. But not so soon! Please God, not so soon!

The knock at the door came just after eight o'clock on a cold December night in 1927. Ma was mixing a poultice base while Molly stitched Joey's torn jumper yet again.

'Come in,' called Ma. 'Unless it's money you're after . . . ' Her voice tailed away as Cissie Mathieson entered the room.

'He's going,' said the cook briefly. 'And he's sent for you.'

Molly turned her face away towards the fire, hoping that her blushes did not show. Did Cook know? Had she worked it out? 'Don't go, Ma,' she muttered. No good could possibly come of Ma going up to the Hall. What if somebody said something? It was bad enough already, Paddy hanging around the Chase Farm stables . . .

'Why shouldn't I go?' Ma's voice was clipped. 'Has he had the doctor, Cissie?'

'Aye. No hope. It's double pneumonia and his heart won't tackle it. I reckon the poor old beggar's suffered enough anyroad. Oh, I know he was a tartar, but all the same . . . ' She sniffed audibly. 'Missus has gone off to Blackpool for Christmas as usual. Mrs Amelia's took bad with a chest cold and poor Master Charles doesn't know whether he's fish or fowl at the minute.'

Molly gazed into the flames. A big fish, that's what he was, a big underwater creature with little fish cleaning his teeth for him. Bigger than ever now, with the old man on his way out. Rivington Pike. Aye, she'd taken the twins up there last Easter to roll their eggs. His children. Her heart turned over as she pictured them as they were now, rosy-cheeked in sleep, untroubled, ignorant of all this. 'I don't see why you should be at his beck and call, Ma. You never worked at the house.'

Ma pulled on her coat. 'I saw to his leg all these years, Molly. He probably wants to see can I do any more for him . . . '

'You can't! He's bloody dying!'

'Molly! Just stay here and do your sewing. If and when Paddy gets home, tell him where I'm gone to. And don't be worrying now. Sure, everything's fine.' She glanced at poor Molly, knowing only too well what troubled the girl. 'I'll be back soon.' Then she left with Cissie and climbed into the large black car, surprised to find Charles at the wheel. But then, she asked herself, who did she expect? Paddy and the other fellow only worked days and then just on a casual basis. She knew now why Cissie had come. If there'd been an employed driver, then Cissie wouldn't have been needed. At least Charles had enough sense not to set foot in the Maguire house.

'He's not expected to last till morning,' said Charles as they drove through the town.

'Have you told your mother?' asked Ma.

'No point.' He pushed a hand through his hair. 'She's in so much pain it would be cruel to move her again from Blackpool before absolutely necessary.'

'Is there a nurse?'

'He won't have one. I've been seeing to him – with a lot of help from the staff.'

'So. He's conscious?'

'Off and on,' said Cissie. 'Says some funny things, things a child might say. He was asking for his mam this morning. Heartbreaking, it is.'

Ma pressed the whitened knuckles of a closed fist against her mouth as she gazed at the frosty countryside. Such a fine man to be reduced to babyhood, wet beds and spoonfeeding. Such a tyrant in his time. Such a lovable, arrogant rogue.

As she passed through the front doors of the great house, Ma was unaware of the finery surrounding her. And yet afterwards, when it was all over, she could have described the tiniest detail, right down to the patterns in the thick-piled carpets. Charles led her upstairs to his father's door. 'He wanted to see you alone,' he said gruffly. 'And before you go in, I must warn you that he looks very unlike himself. It's as if . . . ' His voice broke. 'As if he's slipping away a bit at a time.'

'I understand.'

'Yes. Yes, of course you do. I'd forgotten how much nursing you've done.'

'It's one of the easier deaths. Pneumonia.'

He wiped a tear from his cheek. 'So I understand. As long as the patient's unconscious. But he won't let go. Not till he's seen you.'

'I'll go in, then.' She turned the handle.

'Ma?'

'Yes?'

He swallowed. 'After he's gone, things will . . . carry on. Support payments, future plans and the rest—'

'Good. Just don't expect me to be grateful. Now, I must go and see this man. He has meant a lot to me, Charles. In a way you'd never understand.'

'Do you understand it?' he asked unexpectedly.

'No.'

'Thank God for that. I was beginning to think you knew everything, Ma Maguire.'

She smiled sadly. 'Not quite everything. Just nearly.'

The room stank of human sickness, though it appeared clean and tidy on the surface. But no soap or polish on earth could wipe out this particular odour, the one that so often preceded a death. The figure on the bed lay still as a stone, hands and face as white as the linens on which they rested.

She approached the bed cautiously. 'Richard?'

199

Near-black eyes suddenly shone forth, twin pools of life in a waxlike effigy. 'Philly. I couldn't. Not without seeing you. One last time.' He paused between words, rasping breaths fighting their way into congested lungs.

'I'll sit with you.' She dragged a chair near to the pillow and perched on its edge, her hand grasping his pale fingers. 'I'm sorry,' she whispered.

'Are you? Didn't you curse me? I hear. My heart. Slow. Like you said. Too slow. No blood.'

'There now.' She stroked the hot brow. 'We can just sit here and talk until you fall asleep. I've missed you these years. Nobody to fight with. Not that you ever answered me back when I accused you of mistreating the cotton workers.'

'No point.' The death mask grinned. 'You never listened.'

'Didn't I?'

'No. I loved you, Philly.'

She fought the tears. 'And I loved you. It was something I couldn't deny, something I just had to live with.'

'We lived without.'

'Yes. Yes we did.'

'Tell me about it, Philly. Tell me.' His eyes closed.

She paused fractionally before beginning. 'In the scullery that night, I wanted you. When I threw you out of Freddie's shop, I wanted you. Edie knew. She was my neighbour. She said a fire had been lit between us, between you and me. A fire she had never known the like of. All those years I needed you to keep me warm, Richard Swainbank. And I couldn't have you. I had to stay away from that nice warm fire.'

'Fool,' he muttered, eyes still closed.

'Am I? Look what happened with Charles and Molly. That was foolishness, Richard.'

'Different kind . . .'

'Ah yes. But what would have become of us? You'd have visited, I'd have missed you. My religion would have gone by the board – and my self-esteem too. We would have quarrelled—'

'We did . . .'

'Yes, but about other things, things separate from us. We

200

never got tired of one another, never killed the love. It's still there. I feel now as if you're my husband lying in this bed.'

'Do you?'

'Yes. Though himself is very much alive, languishing in some jail either in Manchester or over to Dublin. Our love, mine and yours, was of the spirit, Richard.'

'It wouldn't have been.'

'I know. If you'd had your way. Don't waste your breath.'

He groaned. 'I'm going any minute, I know it.'

'Will I bring Charles?'

'No. No, he'd never handle it. The death. The moment. You understand?'

'Yes.'

He was slipping. Through her hand she could almost feel the life ebbing away out of his fingers, as if he were letting go, as if a decision had been made between the two of them.

'Richard?'

'Yes?' No more than a very weak whisper.

'I love you.'

'Keep . . . keep . . . saying—'

'I love you, Richard Swainbank. I loved you when you followed me through town at Christmas, when you came into my house, when you met me in Market Street and you all poshed up in the hat and gloves. Beautiful, you were. I've always loved you. I'll go to my grave loving you. You were the finest and most handsome man I ever met. I wanted to lie down with you, Richard. I wanted to live with you and look after you. I needed you. I still need you. Don't go! Please, please don't leave me!' she heard herself crying.

But she couldn't hold him. Nothing could hold him now. There wasn't even a death rattle. He just drifted away leaving a very lonely woman in a very empty room.

She stood at the window of the house she had cursed, great sobs shaking her body from head to foot. Was it a sin to wish now that she'd given him her love just once? So lonely. She looked back at the bed. Yes, he was lonely too, had always been lonely in spite of everything. He had lived and died alone, locked into a situation from which there could never

201

be an escape. Just like she was locked, trapped, caught in life's web. And at the end, what was there? A sigh, an empty shell, a soul gone to find its first, last and only freedom.

She shook herself fiercely, took hold of her body and rocked back and forth in an effort to rid her mind of these sombre and hopeless thoughts.

Charles entered, a tea tray in his hands. 'We thought you might like—' He stopped in his tracks.

'He's gone,' she said simply.

'When?' The cup and saucer shivered.

'Just now. It was sudden in a way. Quiet, but very sudden.'

He placed the tray on a side table. 'Didn't he ask for me?'

'He asked for nobody. I don't think he realized it was quite the end,' she lied. 'And that's probably the best for everyone.'

Charles walked to the bed and looked down at his father's shrunken body. 'He told me he loved you,' he said eventually.

'Did he now?'

'Yes. He said you were the only woman to make him feel alive.'

'I see.'

He coughed away his tears savagely. 'Are you sure he's dead? He doesn't look any different—'

'He's gone all right.'

'And you've been crying.' A statement, not a question.

'Yes. It's funny. I hated what he was and loved who he was. Though we never—'

'I know. Father told me a while ago. There's something for you – it's in the drawer.' He fumbled in the cabinet next to the bed, then held out an envelope.

'I can't read,' she said simply.

'Oh. Oh yes, of course. What shall I do with it then?'

'Read it to me. No one else can. Only Edie knew, you see—' She turned and stared through the window again. 'When you and Molly . . . well, it was like . . . like him and me. Except we managed not to. We loved enough not to—' Her voice cracked and she pulled a handkerchief from her pocket. 'You'll never understand in a million years. But read it to me all the same.'

He opened the envelope and cleared his throat. 'It's very personal.'

'So what?' She shrugged her shoulders. 'What's to lose or gain now, eh? The man is gone, so there's nothing to hide.'

He spoke in a whisper. 'It's a poem. Called "To the Girl with the Long Black Hair".'

'I'm listening.'

He rustled the page. 'Must be years old – the paper's yellow.'

'For goodness sake, read it!'

'Right. Here goes.

> "If at night I hear a sound
> A creaking on the stair
> O Lord, I pray, please let it be
> The girl with the long black hair.
>
> "I stare at fields and miles of sky
> In weathers wild and fair
> But all I see is the lovely face
> Of the girl with the long black hair.
>
> "Those Irish eyes are mocking me
> A smile and then a glare
> She's haunting all my days and nights
> The girl with the long black hair.
>
> "I'll love her till the day I die
> And then more days to spare
> Because she is the heart of me
> The girl with the long black hair." '

Ma turned to face the reader. 'Is that it?' A sob escaped from her lips as she saw that Charles was weeping openly now.

'Yes. Not much of a poem, but—'

'I wouldn't know one poem from another. I thought it was very pretty. And very, very sad.'

'Oh Dad!' He flung himself to his knees at the side of the bed, his face buried in the white coverlet. She brushed away her tears and joined him, a rosary in her hands.

'He really cared about you, Ma. He must have. I've never known him read a poem, let alone write one.'

'Hush now. We've a soul to pray for.'

She knelt there the whole night, moving only when the doctor came to make Richard's death legal and proper, then when the undertaker arrived in the morning.

It was freezing. She slipped out at the front door without making any goodbyes. The one important farewell had been said and she had no wish to linger. Two small white faces were pressed against an upstairs window. Richard's grandchildren. Richard's official grandchildren. She clutched the poem in her pocket and set forth for home.

In spite of the bitter cold, a lone figure sat on a bench in Queen's Park, a crumpled paper in her hand, all thoughts of work and family commitments set aside for now. She didn't feel the cold. It was as if she were stocktaking, going through her life, remembering, regretting, savouring the few good times.

No, it hadn't been all bad. Oh definitely no. She smiled as she remembered Mother Blue and the terrible teeth, Edie and her lumpy handcream, Paddy and his crafty ways of getting out of school work. And Richard. Richard Swainbank had loved her. Would he have loved her if she'd gone for a cottage like his other women? Or would he have tired of her? There was no point in any of these unanswerable questions, because she'd never have gone for a cottage no matter what.

She looked towards the town where smoke already rose to colour and stain the sky, where hooters sounded and clogs were no doubt pounding along worn pavements in that daily effort to beat the clock. A clock Richard had set, a clock that had finally beaten him.

What did it all mean? And how could a poor middle-aged Irish woman work out the meaning when she was frozen to the bench and hadn't the sense to realize it? She rose as Swainbank's hooter sounded again, a long mournful wail pouring out into the crisp bright morning. That was the announcement for the town. After a few moments the answers came, each factory sending back a drawn-out signal of sympathy.

In the silence that followed, Ma made her way homeward, head bent against a sudden bitter wind. Yes, he was gone. And the world would be colder without him. A bad man, a wicked man, a user of the poor. Where was the boy without the finger, she wondered suddenly. Had he found work, was he fed, was he happy? Oh, Richard. If only he'd been different. If only she'd been different. If only it wasn't so blessed cold! If only . . .

Part Three
The Thirties

Chapter 5

The sun was cracking the flags. Michael had already been sent to bed once for having a go with three good back rashers and a couple of eggs, trying to fry them on the pavement because he'd heard somebody say it was possible to cook like that in this fierce heat. Of course, he'd been allowed out again. Most people could get round Mam if they put a sorry face on and wailed a bit about unfairness and cruelty to children.

Molly sat in the kitchen, a hand to her heated brow. They were getting out of hand and she knew it, all four of them running as daft as screw-necked chickens just because their dad was out of flunter. He wasn't much use at the best of times, but the kids always played up when he wasn't around to threaten the two lads with a beating. Paddy seldom carried out his threats, but the children were learning fast that there was a first time for everything, especially since Ma's bad do. Yes, that was affecting them and all, because they missed her sharp tongue, weren't as biddable without the old girl ranting all over the house.

The four of them fell in at the door, a tangle of limbs, skipping ropes and whips for spinning tops. She looked at them sadly, exhaustion nagging behind her eyes where lurked the promise of a sizeable headache. It occurred to her briefly that she now had six children if she thought about it. Not that she ever had time to think. This lot she'd birthed and the other two she'd collected by accident along the way. Two accidents – him with his TB hand and his mother with the stroke. And the washing was still out and all . . .

She lined up her offspring in front of the long fireguard, giving Joey a premature clip round the ear for good measure before she started. 'What the bloody hell's going on now?' she asked quietly, dropping her voice in case she was heard swearing again. Though Ma Maguire couldn't say much about anything at the moment, she still had the power to skewer you to the floor with a glance.

'Nowt Mam – honest!' Joey dug their Janet in the ribs but got no response. Janet stared at the floor, her toe straightening the centre of the peg rug.

'Nowt? It doesn't seem like nowt! Organize your face, Joey Maguire, before I smooth it out for you with the flat of my hand! Now.' She began to pace the room, arms folded closely about her chest. 'All I know is this. I've got your Granny in there . . . ' She waved a hand towards the parlour then folded her arms again, hoping to look severe. 'Your poor Granny who needs everything doing for her. Then I've your dad upstairs ranting and raving with fever.' She turned at the window and glared at them. 'So. I open my own front door and what do I find?' She paused for effect. 'Well?'

'We . . . we don't know, Mam,' lisped Daisy. 'Acos we wasn't here.'

Molly sucked in her cheeks bravely. She wouldn't laugh. Not this time, she wouldn't. If the kids went wayward while she was in sole charge, then she'd get blamed from all sides. And anyway, nobody laughed with a headache. 'I'll tell you what I found. Bella Seddon with a face on her like the Town Hall clock stopped at midnight. "Mrs Maguire," she says, all sweetness and light. "I think as how you ought to know that your Joey and Janet have been at it again." And when I ask her what she means, she comes back with "the usual, Mrs Maguire." So I think an explanation's called for.'

Joey opened his mouth to speak, but Molly shook her head. 'No, I'll have it off our Janet. Happen I might get a penn'orth of truth out of her. You wouldn't know an honesty, Joey, if it hit you across the chops in broad daylight.' She turned to her daughter. 'Come on, lady. Out with it!'

Janet glanced sideways at her twin before answering. 'I . . . we . . . I mean, it was just a few apples, Mam.'

'Where from?' Molly continued to fight the urge to smile.

Michael stepped out of the line. He was only six, but he

already displayed the courage of a lion on such occasions. 'We all done it,' he announced.

'All of you?'

Michael nodded seriously. 'Yes. We done it to the baddie fruit-cart man, not the nice one with the red wagon. See, our Daisy laid herself down in the road and pretended to be dead—'

'What?' Molly's mouth gaped. 'Dead?'

'Not really dead,' said Daisy. 'Only pretend, only a bit dead—'

'Then, when he stopped the horse, our Janet and our Joey reached the good apples off the back, the ones he never sells . . . ' Michael's voice tailed away as Joey pulled him back into line.

'But that's stealing!' cried Molly.

'Never is!' Joey's colour rose as he shouted. 'You bought a bag of rotters off him last time, Mam. We just got our own back, that's all. Mind, he went mad when our Daisy hopped it good as new.'

Molly swivelled on her heel and faced the dresser. Exhausted as she was, she'd have laughed outright if she'd looked at her children for one moment longer. 'Where . . . where are the apples now?' she managed at last.

'All ate up,' came Daisy's plaintive reply. 'And I've got the belly-ache.'

Molly reached into her pocket and brought out a large white handkerchief, covering her nose and mouth against the bubble of mirth in her throat. 'No more than you deserve, all of you,' she mumbled. 'Now get in that scullery for a scrub, then it's up to bed with the lot of you. And mind you keep quiet while your father's badly.'

The four of them scuttled away while the going was good – no point in getting Mam riled up proper. Molly stood by the table and listened as they fought in whispers for space at the slopstone.

Ah well, she'd better get the washing in. But she wasn't going through the scullery, oh no, she didn't want the cheeky little beggars seeing her near doubled up laughing. She removed the five steel curlers from the front of her head, smoothed her hair and walked out through the front door. All the houses sat right on the pavements, but she was luckier than most because theirs was an end house, so as well as the extra downstairs room, there was the added advantage of a short walk round to the backs.

Course, Bella Seddon was lurking about, head poking out of the next gate, eyebrows raised as Molly collected her sheets. She tore them from the line almost angrily, suddenly remembering her own mother standing exactly where Bella stood now. Aye, Edie Dobson had been a different kettle of fish altogether, nothing like this know-it-all.

'Bit late with it today, Mrs Maguire?' The voice was coated with a false sweetness. Molly gritted her teeth and shoved the pegs deep into her pinny pocket.

'They'll be past ironing, I shouldn't wonder. Happen you'll have to damp them.'

'Aye, happen I might.' Ooh God, why couldn't she mind her own business for once? Bella Seddon had been trying to take over from Ma ever since the stroke. Not that there was any danger of her managing it, oh no. There was only one queen in this street . . .

'How's Ma then?'

'Fair, ta.'

'Want a hand with the folding?'

'I'll manage. Janet'll do it when I get in.'

Mrs Seddon stepped out into the narrow alley. 'Is she talking yet?'

'Our Janet never stops talking, never has.' Molly, knowing she was being deliberately obtuse, allowed herself a tiny smile.

The woman's brow tightened. 'I meant your mother-in-law.'

'No. No, she's not talking.'

'Walking at all?'

'No.'

'Eeh dear.' The shaking head was suddenly bowed as if in deep mourning. 'Such a fine figure she was, too.'

'And will be again, Bella Seddon. It'll take more than a bit of clotted blood to put a stop to our Ma.'

'Aye.' She backed away, heeding the warning contained in the use of her full name. After reaching the safety of her own domain, she paused on the clog-flattened step. 'How about the kiddies?'

'They're all right, thanks.'

'But . . . but the fruitman, Mr Greenhalgh – he said they'd been up to a bit of bother on St George's Road—'

'Mistaken identity, I think that's called, Bella Seddon. My children are not thieves. Truth is, they were down at the fish-market getting a nice bit of finny haddy for Paddy's tea.'

'Oh aye?' The head shot forward, causing the row of steel curlers that peeped from beneath a scarf to clank together as she declared, 'And I'm a monkey's granny!'

Molly fixed a wide imitation of a smile on her face. 'Oh dear. Well, we can none of us help our relatives, can we? And it wouldn't do for us all to be organ-grinders.' She turned and walked away with her bundle, leaving Bella Seddon with her jaw dropped so far you might have driven a coach and four across her bottom lip.

Molly entered the house and leaned against the door after slamming it loudly. These street-wars, almost a relic from previous centuries, still prevailed on School Hill and she was sick unto death at times of being stuck in the middle of it all. Ma had to get better, she really had to. If Bella flaming Seddon took over, then life wouldn't be worth living one day to the next. Why, that one would treep you out that black was white and wet was dry. Not with Ma though. Bella Seddon had seldom argued with Ma over anything. She daren't. Nobody did.

Almost immediately to the right of the front door was the entrance to Philomena Maguire's room, a room the old lady hadn't left for two months now. Not that Ma was really old, but life had got to her somehow, dried her up and finished her off before she'd even got to sixty. Molly shook her head slowly before walking across the kitchen and placing her washing on the table. Ma had started all this, setting herself up as boss of the neighbourhood, making sure everybody abided by her rules and reached her standards. Oh well. Molly had better have a look at her, she supposed. Between Ma downstairs and

Paddy upstairs she was practically off her feet, running about like a scalded cat dawn till dusk, day in and day out.

She opened the door to what had been the best room quietly in case Ma was asleep. But she wasn't, of course. The face was shrivelled and dry while claw-like hands, one curled permanently into a clenched fist, rested on a woven yellow quilt. Philomena Maguire's hair, once her pride and joy, was thinly spread now over the pillow in grey wisps like a fine cloud partly blown away in the wind. But the eyes had not changed. Although one was nearly closed, the lid frozen at half-mast, all the wisdom, wit and humour of the old country were visible in those bright blue depths.

Molly carried a straight-backed chair to the bed. 'Oh Ma,' she whispered as she sank on to the seat. 'I wish I could help you. It's not the same without you and your blarney all over the house. The kids are playing me up again, trying me on for size. Our Michael's a scream – I can hardly look at him some days. You know how I am, Ma, can't keep a straight face to save me life. Then there's that old bitch next door – ooh, I'm sorry – I know you don't like language. But she's driving me twice round the bend, is that one. She's watching the kiddies for what she calls behaviour and she's had the rent man out twice. That was your job, Ma. You kept the street decent. She'll turn it into a free-for-all, I shouldn't wonder.'

The left hand on the bed moved and Molly reached out to grip it. 'I know we've not always got on, Ma, I know we sometimes don't see eye to eye, but I do love you. Funny how you can live with somebody for years and never say how you feel, isn't it? But I'd never have made it without you after me mam died. Fighting with you has been part of me life – aye and losing most times. If only you could write. Even though it is your best hand gone, you'd happen have scribbled the odd message with the other. We should have found time to teach you some reading. What is it, Ma? What is it?' The old lady's mouth was twitching as she strove to speak and Molly bent her ear close to the pillow.

'B . . . br . . . o . . . o—'

'Try! Please, keep trying!'

'M . . . my—'

'Yes?'

'My . . . bro . . . o—'

'Your brooch? The one with the tiger's eye? Blink once for yes, Ma.'

The left lid winked slowly.

'Is it in the box?'

Again the eye closed. Molly reached under the bed and brought out a heavy miniature chest. No-one ever touched this. Ma's box was absolutely forbidden territory – even her only son would never have dared to interfere with its private contents.

Molly smiled as she fingered the carved lid. 'We're back to Uncle Porrick, are we? I remember you telling me about the leprechauns and the tiger's eye. Didn't Uncle Porrick say the little people would come and help you if you wore the brooch? Shall I get a bowl on the table same as he did, leave it out so they can call in for a swim?'

'N . . . no . . . !'

'All right then.' Molly prayed silently that the poor old thing was not going to put too much faith in this brooch. After all, there'd been enough novenas and masses said, enough prayers to move a mountain never mind a sick woman. If prayer couldn't do it, then some stupid Irish folk tale never would.

The key to the box was on a chain with an Immaculate Conception medal round Ma's neck and Molly unfastened the clasp hesitantly. It seemed strange, going in the box like this. As if . . . as if Ma wasn't here any more. After undoing the lid, Molly paused, a hand to her throat. The chest was filled to the brim with papers and small leather pouches. Her fingers crept round one of these and felt the coins inside. 'Ma,' she gasped. 'Is this . . . money?'

'L . . . eave . . . lea—'

'All right, don't worry, I'll not touch it. But where . . . I mean whose . . . ?

But that look was in the sharp eyes again and Molly removed several sealed envelopes before finally closing her fingers around the brooch. 'Here it is. Will I pin it to your nightie?'

The eye signalled yes.

Molly replaced the contents, locked the box and pushed it under the bed before fastening the chain, with its key and medal, around her mother-in-law's throat. 'You've got secrets in there, haven't you? Don't worry, I'll not let on to Paddy. If he knew you'd money, he'd make a miraculous recovery and we wouldn't see him again until he'd drunk the lot. Aye, once he gets over this fever, he'll find his thirst again, I don't doubt.'

She looked down at the brooch, turning and twisting it in her fingers. It was a large item, about the size of an infant's hand, all silver filigree except for the centre where the tiger's eye glowed yellow, smooth and rounded. 'I hope this helps you, Ma.' She pinned the brooch to Ma's high-necked night-dress and immediately the old lady's eyes softened and filled with grateful tears.

'I'm doing all I can.' Molly patted the waxlike right hand reassuringly. 'Doctor says you'll likely talk a bit in time, though he's not all that sure about your hand and your leg. Still, we keep on doing the exercises, don't we? Mind, I'm wondering whether we're going about it the right road, because I made them up meself. Only it stands to reason that if we don't jiggle you about from time to time, then you'll go to waste. Tell you what – how would you like our Janet to come in and read to you? Happen she could teach you some of your letters for when you're better. Would you like that?'

'Yes.' The left hand closed over the brooch. 'Yes.'

'Well!' Molly's face beamed. 'That was clear enough, wasn't it? I reckon you're on the mend, Ma Maguire. And may God help Bella Seddon the day you walk out over that doorstep.'

'Mo . . . ll . . . ee—?'

'Yes?'

'G . . . good . . . g . . . g . . . girl.'

Molly stared down at the poor diminished creature on the bed, her eyes swimming with unshed tears. 'I'm not a good

216

girl, Ma. There's things about me you don't know – things I hope you'll never know. Just hurry up and get better.' She rubbed the end of her nose on the heel of her hand. 'Paddy's took the fever again. I don't know what they think they're doing at that blinking hospital, only he's no better. Mind, I think he brings a lot of it on himself – he'd be best out working. Smashed the bedroom up good and proper this time, he has. I've hid all the best stuff in your little room, shoved it in the bottom of your chest of drawers. I'd have nothing left worth keeping else.' She sighed deeply. 'He'll never be no different, I know it. Not that he was up to much before – aye, that's one thing you and I have agreed about, isn't it? But whatever he's got comes back over and over, plagues him out of his mind at times. And when he's well he's drinking, so it's all the same whichever way.'

She leaned forward and straightened the top quilt. 'I'll do your heels and your back with some spirit in a bit. You know, I'm sure he'd pick up if he could get some work. When I tell him to go and look for a job, he curses me for mithering. I don't know what to do. Happen I'll get took on as unskilled in the mill – I can fold and knock the sizing out of quilt fringes, do a bit of cleaning . . . '

The left hand closed about Molly's wrist. 'N . . . no . . . nee . . . d. No.'

'But Ma . . . '

'No!' There was energy in this monosyllable.

Molly rubbed her chin thoughtfully. 'Where did you get all that money, Ma? What's it for? How long have you had it – they're sovereigns, aren't they? Did they force your husband to pay up at last?'

Ma Maguire gazed steadily at her daughter-in-law. Even if she had been able to speak up, she wouldn't have told, not just now. No, the time wasn't right yet. Not quite.

After Molly had left, Ma lay staring at the ceiling for a long time. The words in her mind had come back, most of them anyway. Sometimes she looked at a thing and couldn't quite remember the name for it, then it would jump into her head at an unexpected moment. Silly, it was. How could she look at a

217

chair without knowing it was a chair? Still, life was a little clearer now. But what use was it to know that a chair was a chair if she couldn't speak? Might as well be an elephant or a giraffe, anything with four legs. Chair, table, bed, curtains. All arranged in her mind, all collected and relearned. And not an ounce of use without a voice.

She was sick to death of the sight of this room, it was beginning to feel like a prison cell. She had counted the flowers on the wallpaper a dozen times, firstly to get her brain working, secondly to use them as a rosary while she remembered her prayers. And the damp patches over the window were getting on her nerves too; that idle son of hers needed a boot on the backside to persuade him to put the house to rights, for as sure as damnation awaited sinners, the landlord would never spend another halfpenny on these dwellings.

The landlord. She concentrated for a long time, sweating with the effort of remembering his name. How long had she lived here? For ever! He owned a mill, that she recalled vividly. Yes, the mill stood at the end of the street in another street. Now. What was the name of that street? No, it wasn't a street she was looking for, it was a man's name. Which man? Concentrate! The landlord. Cows. Something from a cow, that's what he was called after. Milk? What else? Cheese? Cream? She smiled a lopsided smile of victory. Leather. His name was Leatherbarrow and he hadn't much hair, just a few long strands pulled across his head to fill in the gaps.

The box. Aye, she knew what was in the box all right. It was to do with Janet and Joey and she'd have to see to it soon. She drifted away, her hand clasping the tiger's eye.

'Hello there, Philly!'

'Uncle Porrick!' The young girl ran across the muddy yard to greet him.

'See what did I fetch for you.' The big man opened his pocket and drew out a small package. 'From the little people.'

'Is it?'

And he told her the story of the dish left out, the tiny footprints on the table, the brooch left for his favourite girl.

'Can I keep it for ever, Uncle Porrick?'

218

'You can indeed. In times of trouble, you just turn to it and the little people will come.'

'Always?'

'Always and anywhere.'

They never had come. Even so, Philly had worn the brooch in times of stress, just to feel nearer to such a grand man, a man who took time from a busy life to tell stories to a young girl. Ah but she'd give her right arm for the sight of Uncle Porrick again. Yes, her right arm had been given at last . . .

The door flew open. 'Granny!'

The two times blended together and Ma found herself in bed, half-paralysed and with the damp patch still over the window.

'Granny? Are you awake?'

Janet. I'd talk to you if I could. Is it fifteen you are now? You and Joey, so like himself the both of you. But specially Joey.

'Mam says I've got to learn you how to read. I'm lucky – the others have to stop upstairs as punishment. Dad's raving fit to burst again – I think he's got a bottle of rum in the bed with him. So we're all in trouble one way or another.'

That's the way of it, child. The biggest trouble, all that explaining, is yet to come . . .

'We got nearly mangled off Mam for pinching apples from the back of Greenhalgh's cart. Mam was mortified to death, 'cos her next door came round in a big huff. It was our Joey's idea. He wanted to get his own back for all the bad stuff we've had off that cart. Mam was all riled up only she'd a job on not to laugh.'

Yes, laughing was always your mother's problem. Up at the big house, I bet she laughed, kept them all going. She used to do turns, didn't she? That's right, she had a lot of voices. That would be what attracted the other feller, him who brought all the big trouble to this house. She probably made him laugh too with all her voices. Wish I had just one voice, any one would do. She doesn't giggle like she once did, hasn't since you were born. When she was your age, I used to wonder how she managed to be so happy and her an orphan.

Janet threw herself into a chair and thrust a slate under Ma's nose. 'See. I've wrote all our names down. Now, this long one is you – Philomena. It should really begin with an F but them two letters stuck together make the F sound. These are Molly and Michael – they have the same beginning letter. Now Janet and Joey – they start with a J. Daisy is a D, though she should be another M with her real name being Margaret, then Paddy is a P, only it's not the same as yours with having no H after it.' She paused for breath after this long speech. 'It's not as bad as it looks, Gran.'

Janet, this English is a desperate difficult language written down. I'm tired just now and I keep drifting off back home. Sometimes I'm fourteen, walking along the edge of a bog with Uncle Porrick, then suddenly I'm an old lady going on sixty. Mammy and Daddy are dead, I know that for sure. And I've a husband Seamus probably still in prison. Things from long ago are coming back, so perhaps I'll get to grips soon with more recent events. I'm trying so hard. But it's all in little patches like a crocheted blanket, all squares that need sewing together.

'Our Michael's got to go to church every day,' Janet was saying now. 'On account of what happened last Sunday. He was fishing, see, early on, caught a couple of sticklebacks down the pond in the park. Anyway, comes time for church and all the bells ringing like mad, he's mucky as a chimney sweep and carrying this jam jar. Oh, it was so embarrassing, Gran! He gets to the church and drops the jar outside, picks up the fish and dumps them in the font of holy water by the door. I've never known anybody who can show you up like our Michael can. None of my friends have brothers like him. Not fit to be seen half the time, always covered in mud and with his clothes hanging off him.'

Ma's face broke into a half-smile. That boy was so lovable, so misunderstood . . .

'They were all blessing themselves as they came in, then this lady started shrieking as if the world was ending. Course, our Michael was only worried about the blinking fish. Black as a pot, he walked right down the church, grabbed a collection dish and scooped his sticklebacks up in the holy water. I could have died with shame on the spot. I kept hoping it was just a dream and I'd wake up in a minute. He'd his hair stood on end as if he'd just seen a ghost, the socks pushed down like a couple of wet dishcloths and his shirt was hanging behind him like a loose nappy. And everybody knows he's my brother! Anyway, he's got to polish two pews every morning and get trained for an altar boy. Can you see him? Dressed up in white and helping the priest? He'll never do it. There'll be incense spilled, bells ringing at the wrong time and he'll never learn his Latin responses. Oh, the shame of it. I think I'll start walking to St Patrick's.'

Yes, you're getting to that age now, aren't you? The age when things matter, when everything has to look right. Don't be ashamed of us. We are your family. Your real family . . .

'I'll read to you from the paper.' She rustled the pages of the *Evening News*. 'Some folk say there's going to be another war on account of that Hitler feller getting too big for his boots. Me dad says not. He says there was enough bother last time and nobody can afford to fight.' The page turned as Ma began to fall asleep, lulled and comforted by the sound of Janet's voice.

'Man up Daubhill's murdered his wife. Well, they say he did, but he says he never 'cos he was in the pub at the time playing darts. Coal's going up tuppence. Births and deaths are pretty well full up again – ooh, here's a big one. Bet that cost a bob or two. "Tragically, as the result of an accident on June 14th 1937, John and Peter, beloved sons of Charles and Amelia Swainbank." Isn't that awful? I wonder how old they were? Aren't they the big mill-owners, the Swainbanks? Granny? Gran, are you asleep?'

Don't shout, love. I was just getting into it. Now, where was I? Oh yes, if I buy fourpennyworth of fish and a tuppeny swede, that will be sixpence. Out of a shilling, I shall get another sixpence change. Now, I'll have to go on to something harder, up to half a crown. Leatherbarrow. Yes, that was his name.

Janet rushed into the scullery. 'Mam! She's talking!'

Molly turned from the slopstone where she was peeling potatoes. 'Aye, she mumbled a bit at me. Just yes and no, then a few odd words—'

'No, not mumbling, In her sleep, she talks. Plain as day I

heard her say something about Leatherbarrow and sixpence change.'

'Must be raving, then. Nobody ever got change out of Leatherbarrow. He's about as generous as old Scrooge on a very bad day.'

'But she still said the words, Mam. Honest.'

'Are you sure?'

'Yes! I was reading to her out of the paper, just bits and pieces, then she started talking – proper like she used to.'

'With a brogue as thick as a new clog bottom, you mean.'

'But she's talking in her sleep, using words. If she can talk in her sleep, then she can talk awake, can't she?'

Molly dried her hands. 'I'm not so sure about that, lass. Asleep, she doesn't have to think about talking. Happen when she's awake and trying too hard she just can't master it. But it's a good sign, our Janet. You must spend more time with your Granny. From the sound of things, it looks as if you might be doing her some good.'

Janet sidled along the edge of the small scullery table. 'Mam?'

'What?' She recognized the wheedling tone in her daughter's voice.

'Can we come down? It's only five o'clock. Think of all the winter days when we have to stop in.' She sighed dramatically. 'Seems a shame that children should miss the best weather.'

Molly puffed out her cheeks and blew noisily. 'Will you behave?'

'Course! We'll play jacks and bobbers on the six flags.'

'No stepping over?'

'Cross me heart.'

'All right then. But steer clear of that one next door. She'll be fetching the landlord up next news, getting us evicted as not fit to live in the street.'

Janet's chin jutted forward. 'Only 'cos Gran stopped her squeezing the lodgers in.'

'Aye well. Just don't push your luck till Granny's up and about. She's for taking over, is Mrs Seddon, so give no cheek and make sure you stick to playing on your own patch.'

'Ta, Mam.' Then she was gone with the pigtails flying behind her. Molly wiped the scullery table, her mind busy with something she was having trouble pinpointing. There were goings-on, things she needed to get to the bottom of, yet at the same time didn't want to know about. What was this niggle at the back of her mind?

She took in a sharp breath. All that money, all those papers Ma couldn't even read. But wait – what about that time she'd spotted Ma – ooh, about five or six years ago – yes, just before Daisy was born.

Molly walked to the slopstone and filled a pan with water for the spuds. That was right. Ma Maguire scuttling out of that lawyer's place on St George's Road, said she'd been seeing after a cleaning job. Why, Ma had been full-time weaving then. And when Molly had questioned her, the answer had been that Ma was considering giving up at the mill, taking a little job so she'd be around to help with the new baby. That had never been true, not in a month of Sundays.

She poured salt into the pan then set it to boil on the gas ring. Aye, they were legal documents in that box, seals and all they had on them. What was going on and why all the secrecy?

Paddy was banging on the floor again, likely feeling sorry for himself and after a bit of attention. Resignedly, she poured him a pint of tea and carried it through to the kitchen. The door to the stairway was in the corner, diagonally opposite the front door and well away from the best room. But even from the foot of the stairs she could hear Ma talking. Not the words, but she could tell that phrases were being strung together. He banged once more and she began her ascent, wondering what she'd find this time.

He was on the floor, head in hands and weeping again.

'Back into bed now, Paddy.'

She placed the large mug on the mantel shelf and went to help him to his feet.

'Nobody bloody cares,' he wailed. 'I feel as if there's spiders walking all over me body—'

'Aye and pink elephants doing a waltz in the middle of the ceiling, I shouldn't wonder.'

'You're a hard woman, Molly Maguire.'

'Am I? Well, I've had some good teachers, Paddy. You, your mother and bloody life. Now. Are you getting in that bed or do I get you packed off to the infirmary again? I will! I'll do it!' She snatched the empty bottle from beneath his pillow. 'How can you expect to get over this illness with poison all through your system? Weren't you told not to drink?'

'Oh shut up! You'll have me joining the chapel and signing the pledge next news.'

'What? They wouldn't have you, Paddy Maguire. For a start, you're a Catholic. And for another, you're never going to make teetotal and they know it. Do you think they'd let you in the door after all that bother you caused at their temperance meeting? You and Bobby McMorrow falling up the steps pie-eyed and bloody legless?'

He attempted a look of remorse. 'Well, we made a mistake. Anybody can make a mistake, even me mother. We thought it was an Orange Lodge—'

'Good job it wasn't. Otherwise, you'd have got home in a box instead of on a policeman's back. Now, get in that bed before I fetch the doctor, the priest and any other bugger with a chance of talking sense into that thick skull!'

He climbed on to the mattress and fell breathless against the pillows. 'You don't love me any more, Molly.'

'Oh, don't be starting up with all that again. What do you want me to do, eh? Open the window and shout "I love him" to the neighbours? Or will I go down the Town Hall and print it in purple paint on the front door? Here – drink your tea, it might flush the other out of you. Speaking of which, you can get down the yard in future, buck yourself up. I've enough with your mother without emptying your jummy and all—'

'Aw Molly . . . Molly—'

'Aw Molly Molly nothing! I've no time to waste. Do you think them four kids fetches themselves up while you lie here in all your muck and glory? For God's sake, lad, your hand's healing again, you're coughing looser. I'm sure a nice bit of droving out in the fresh air would be just the job, clear your head and cool you down. And Miss Leason could do with some help – you know she gives you the odd shilling now she's sold up.'

'I get me bit of pension off Charlie Swainbank—'

'That's not a pension, Paddy! That's a retainer so's you'll hold yourself ready when he sends a message. Anyway, I'd sooner you worked elsewhere. Cars is dangerous, let him drive his bloody own.'

'He'll have to. I don't feel fit to drive—'

'Fit enough to drive me! Round the bloody bend! It's all in your head, Paddy. Doctor told me plain as day, you haven't got the bovine in your blood.'

'It's in me bones,' he muttered sadly. 'I know it is, in the bones of me arm. Eating me away and all you can do is mither and create.'

She stared for a few moments at this father of her children and a temporary contempt for him flooded her being. He was stupid, spineless, lazy . . . Other men in the street worked in spite of incapacities. Pierce Murphy, going on sixty now, was known to spit blood, yet he still went down the pit every day. Bella Seddon's man had died at his work, a massive heart attack while shifting heavy hides down at the tannery. She checked herself. No, she didn't want that, didn't want him dead. But if only he would show some willingness! Before she could scream at him any more, she turned on her heel and left the room. He was stupid at times, but she'd been glad enough of that in the past. Did she want her bread buttering both sides?

Molly sat with a cup of tea in the kitchen, watching her children at play on the six big flags that marked their own immediate territory. Janet was doing double-unders with a bit of washing line, the rope swishing as she whipped it twice under raised feet. 'One-a-penny, two-a-penny, three-a-penny, four . . . '

Joey stood by and watched his twin, admiration for her dexterity plain on his face. They were growing up, these two – nearly fifteen now. Ma had made them stop on at school for the extra year, had organized private bookkeeping lessons for them, saying that education always came in handy no matter what. Funny old besom, was Ma. What would they want with fancy bookkeeping in the mill or the engineering shop?

Janet had stopped skipping now and was sharing a whispered and obviously amusing secret with her darker-haired brother. Yes, they were separated from the other two by more than just age, for they had always chosen to be apart, apparently needing and depending on one another almost totally. Though Janet was now showing some signs of throwing Joey off, thank God, but the poor lad hadn't got the message yet, or so it seemed. They'd be working soon. Joey had a half-promise on an apprenticeship down the engineering where they made machine parts for factories and the like. And Janet – well, she'd probably go in the spinning room with the rest of her classmates.

Little Daisy perched on the edge of the step with her doll. She'd likely get her frock covered in donkeystone, but Molly, unwilling to break the spell, said nothing. Michael crouched at the pavement's edge with the jacks and bobbers, a diablo by his side. Although she couldn't see his face, Molly knew it would be furrowed with concentration. He was a character, was Michael, a real fighter. Nearly seven and nearly ready to instigate and orchestrate the next world war.

She smiled sadly. A mixed bunch, they were, but what could she expect? She sat longer than she'd intended, almost mesmerized by this picture of her children framed in the doorway. If only she could pick it up, stick it in an album, keep them as they were now, safely protected from the world and its savagery. But no. Part of being a mother was letting go. And letting go of Joey and Janet was going to be the most testing thing she'd ever faced.

Philomena Maguire lay listening to the sounds of life going on around her and without her. It had been an odd few weeks – was it weeks, or was it longer? No. It was just weeks, because the twins hadn't had their birthday yet. She would have noticed a birthday. The sums were up to ten shillings now. She could work out a pound of stewing beef, a cabbage, carrots, turnips and how much change. Faces in shops were coming back to her, the butcher, the grocer, Tommy from the tripe shop. He didn't have a bike now. Tommy was in charge, striped apron and straw hat with a red ribbon. So proud of herself, she felt. After all, only a few days ago, she'd scarcely known her own name – even the family had looked unfamiliar for a while.

She'd nearly died. Twice she'd floated off and looked down at herself, watched Molly weeping or knitting as she sat patiently by the bed, such a good girl, she was. Both times she'd heard Uncle Porrick telling her to go back, so she'd gone back. Funny, these dreams after a stroke. Were they dreams? Whatever, they'd been powerful enough to make her ask for the brooch, specially after Granny had spoken to her. 'Away and see to that family,' she'd snapped, clay pipe wedged between gums.

The smell of cooking came under the door from the kitchen. Molly would be doing a hotpot or an Irish stew in the range. Amazing how that girl always managed to make a sixpence do the work of a shilling. Howandever, it would all be put right soon, just a bit more strength and Ma Maguire would be on her feet again and raring to go. But it could have been so easy to simply float away into eternity, no more worries, no more debts or promises.

Molly came in to feed her. 'You've been chattering in your sleep, Ma, talking as plain as you ever did.'

Dear God, what have I been saying? Not about the twins, surely? Not about the box and Charlie Swainbank and Richard. Yes, she'd remembered his name early on, hadn't she?

She swallowed the soup obediently.

'What are you smiling at, Ma?'

Me? I'm thinking of . . . oh, what was her name now, Molly? Remember the black horses with plumes, the whole street following the hearse? Blue. Old Mother Blue and that tube. Frightened the daylights out of me, she did. Saved my life, much as you're saving it now. I looked after her just as you're looking after me. Life's a wheel. Molly . . .

'You're not dribbling as much. And there's the odd twitch on the right hand side – I reckon you'll look yourself again, Ma.'

227

'Mo . . . ll . . . ee?'

'Yes Ma? Oh, God love you, you're trying so hard! Except for my kids, you've been the best thing in my life, Ma Maguire. I've not forgot Mam and Dad, but I'll never be able to pay back what you gave me. But for you, I'd have been for the orphanage. I need you. Don't be lying there thinking you're not needed no more. They need you too – the kiddies. And as for Paddy – well, you can manage him and I can't. But I've no regrets, Ma. Specially about turning. The Faith, you, my children – all I've got, all I need—'

'D . . . on c . . . ry Mo . . . ll . . . ee.'

'Come back to me, Ma! I shall never cope else! You've been tipping up more than wages these years, haven't you? I thought the extras were from your cures, only I know you nearly give them away. We've been living out of yon box, haven't we? Haven't we?'

Ma sighed and averted her gaze.

'It's not just the money, Ma! Money's the least of what you've given me. You've loved me. Except for Mam and Dad, you're the only one as ever loved me just for meself, no questions asked. Kids love you 'cos you're their mam, not for the person you are. Paddy cares about me on a different level altogether, I'm his wife and he expects . . . things. But you're different, I've seen past your rages and I know you've looked out for me always. Come back to me. I've lost one mam and I don't want to let another go.'

'S . . . soo . . . n.'

'Janet's caught you talking, gabbling away like you used to. I suppose you're having to learn things again like a child. Do you keep going back in your mind? Back to Mayo and your mam always shouting, your dad and his still hidden out at the back in the trees? They're dead, love. You don't have to keep worrying about the past. You don't need a past. You're here in Bolton, Lancashire. It's 1937, middle of June. Here.' She pulled a rosary from her pocket and threaded it through Ma's fingers. 'I never thought to give you them last month, month of Mary. But you weren't up to much. Now say your prayers, same as I've been doing.'

228

She picked up the soup bowl and walked towards the door, pausing on the way. 'While you're at it, say one for me because that son of yours has me fair flummoxed.' She faced the bed once more. 'He's back on pobs again, says his stomach won't take owt else only bread soaked in milk. Well, he's stomached a bottle of rum and enough brown ales to refloat the Spanish Armada. Our Joey sneaks it to him. Best suit's gone again, likely down the pawnshop with my gold cross and chain.' She nodded. 'Yes, I know. It was your wedding present to me and you'll kill him. But to kill him, you'll need to be up and about, won't you? So get shaping.'

'Pa . . . dd . . . ee. Ne . . . ver co . . . me—'

'I know! I know he doesn't come to see you. He's too busy drinking himself to death and concentrating on having some fancy illness with a big name what he can't get his tongue round. I feel like pouring the bloody pobs over his soft head – oh, I know I'm swearing. If I didn't swear, I'd bust me corsets. Well now, are you laughing? Just keep it that way, carry on smiling. I'm going upstairs to crown the king of the castle. If you hear any screaming, don't think about it.'

After Molly had left, Ma Maguire reached down with the good hand and dragged the other stiffened limb up to her chest. An inch at a time, she eased the closed fist upward until it rested on Uncle Porrick's brooch. She prayed then to the Blessed Virgin, Saints Patrick, Columba and Jude to come to her aid at this dreadful time. Just before sleep claimed her, the arm twitched involuntarily.

The time to return had almost come.

Chapter 6

Sarah Leason flung the door open. After standing for several seconds in the street, she marched into the kitchen with an expression on her face that might have stripped paint at forty paces. 'What is becoming of this household?' she cried.

Molly studied this odd creature, wondering, just as she'd wondered so often in the past, whether or not a normal person should take Sarah Leason seriously. Here she stood, arms akimbo, wellies up to her knees in the middle of June, light-weight men's overalls over a collarless striped shirt, a shifty-looking mongrel fastened to her hand with a bit of rope, her hair sticking up like the contents of a manger. Taken all round, Miss Leason bore a strong resemblance to an unmade bed that hadn't had a change of sheets in months.

'Come in,' said Molly.

'I am in. Where is the rascal?'

'Who?'

'That bloody man of yours. He who forced me to sell up my land and come to live here in this tasteless conurbation.'

'Oh. Him. He's in bed.'

'I see. And Ma Maguire?'

'In bed.'

Sarah Leason bent down and fastened the dog to Ma's best table. 'Stay,' she ordered unnecessarily as the animal cowered, unable to move much anyway with just a few inches of play left in its tether. 'Right.' She straightened. 'First things first. Where's the old one?'

Molly pointed towards the best room, her other hand coming up to hide a smile. The old one? Miss Leason was seventy if a day.

With Molly on her heels, Sarah flung open Ma's door and strode to the foot of the bed. 'Time you stopped feeling sorry for yourself, woman. The longer you lie, the tighter you'll set. Like a jelly or one of those blancmange puddings. Left long enough, they go mouldy. We'll have you up in a chair, I think.' She glared at Molly. 'Bring through some appropriate seating, if you please.'

'But—'

'But what?'

'Well . . . she's big – tall, I mean. How are you and I going to manage a woman this size?'

The tiny visitor clucked her tongue in irritation. 'All right then, we'll do it the other way round. Wait here,' she said to Ma who winked at Molly as if to say 'where would I be going?'

The two women walked through the house and up the stairs, Sarah muttering all the while about people having no sense and animals knowing better than to lie in a hole longer than necessary.

Paddy was snoring fit to raise slates off the roof.

'He's not been well,' said Molly lamely.

'Hasn't he?' Tap, tap went the rubber sole on the oilcloth. 'What he needs is a good five mile hike across the moors, get some colour in his cheeks.'

'He's had a bit of TB. In his hand, like.'

'Really? I've seen cows with that and they don't go to bed. Leave him like this and it will kill him. Get him up chopping wood and he'll have as good a chance as any man. Mind over matter.' She drew a whistle from the top pocket of her overall and delivered a shrill blast in the direction of the bed.

Paddy sat bolt upright, mouth and eyes round with shock. 'What the hell's up? Is it fire or war or what?'

'Worse than that,' declared Sarah firmly. 'It's me.'

'Oh heck.' Paddy pulled the sheets up to his chest and looked accusingly at Molly. 'What are you thinking of, bringing a lady up to me room like this?'

'I didn't bring her. She just came.'

'That's right, Paddy. All by myself. This family's going to pot and your wife's becoming worn out. So we'll have you out of the bed and doing something useful in two shakes of a lamb's tail.' She paused. 'Won't we?'

He fell against his pillows. 'I'm not meself.'

'Oh, I see.' Sarah sat on the edge of the bed. 'Who are you then?' The tone was friendly and conversational.

He rolled his eyes dramatically. 'I'm a victim, Sarah.' Aye, she'd like that. She went in a lot for victims, did Sarah, was always on their side. 'A victim of life is what I am. Tossed about like a bit of wood broke off a boat. It's going up me arm and into me brain.'

'What is?'

'TB.' His tone was appropriately mournful.

'Oh. I thought for a moment you had splinters.'

'Eh?'

'Wood. Tossed about on the tide of life, cracking at the seams and getting spiles.'

'Spiles?'

'Big splinters, lad.' Molly hid a grin. He was looking better already. Confused, but better. 'Miss Leason thought you'd been chopping firewood.'

'How can I chop firewood in bloody bed? Am I going soft in the head like I thought, or is it you two?'

Sarah jumped up and heaved back the bedcovers. 'He's right, Mrs Maguire. He can't chop wood in bed. Whatever were you thinking of to suggest that he might? Come on now, Paddy. Let's get you dressed and downstairs.'

He leapt from the bed. 'I'm not being dressed by no bloody women! I can still dress meself, still tie the bloody clog-laces on me own.'

'Good. We'll wait for you on the landing. Don't be too long now, because we're going to get Ma out of her bed too.'

Several minutes later found the three of them in the best room with Ma. Sarah surveyed the situation critically before deciding on a plan of campaign. 'Right,' she said finally. 'Swing her legs out over the edge, then sit one at each side of her. Paddy – you take the bad side.'

They complied with these barked orders, sweating with the exertion of lifting the half-dead weight of Ma's body.

'Stand her!'

'What?' Paddy stared incredulously at the fierce little woman. 'She's nobbut one-footed! If we stand her up, she'll keel over like one of our Daisy's peg dollies!'

'Paddy! Were you born without a brain, or have you worked on getting rid of it? Hold her up! That's it, she won't break. Don't look so worried, Ma Maguire. We'll have you chasing children from your doorstep in no time at all.'

Paddy looked across at his wife whose head seemed to be tucked somewhere beneath Ma's arm. 'Are you all right, lass?'

'She's got me hair, hanging on like beggary, she is.'

Sarah Leason suddenly dropped to the floor and began to crawl under the bed.

'What the bloody hell—?' began Paddy. He clung on to his mother's waist, trying to look for the disappearing visitor. 'Is she searching for the jummy, or what?'

'Paddy!' Molly's voice arrived strangled.

'What?'

'Shut up, for God's sake!'

'Ma?' This word floated up from the oilcloth.

Paddy swore under his breath before answering, 'She can't talk, Sarah.'

'She can hear, can't she? You can hear, Ma Maguire! I'm not going to treat you as if you're not here just because you're slightly incapacitated.'

'Slightly? She's about as steady as a bowl of porridge without the flaming bowl. Can't we put her down? Me hand's badly—'

Both women ordered him to shut up, their voices mingling with Paddy's exaggeratedly laboured breathing.

Sarah continued undaunted. 'I am your right leg.'

'Well,' said Paddy. 'I'll go to the foot of our stairs.'

'What a good idea!' The voice from beneath the bed was depressingly cheerful and optimistic. 'We'll take her through to the kitchen, sit her by the fire.'

Ma, realizing what was required of her, hung on to her uncertain companions and pushed her left foot forward. Sarah, still crawling, moved the right leg accordingly. Thus

233

they travelled across the room, through the door and into the kitchen. When they reached the table, Sarah jumped up and cursed loudly. 'You'll not bite me again,' she spat at the poor little mongrel. 'This is the hand that feeds.'

'Sarah!' screamed Molly. 'Sarah – look!'

Still depending heavily on her supporters, Ma moved the right leg fractionally, pulling it along in short spurts until both slippers stood side by side. With a small cry of triumph, Paddy lifted his mother into his arms and placed her in the carpet chair. 'Pack her in with pillows, Molly,' he gasped. 'There's life in the old girl yet! And she weighs a blinking ton and all.'

The three of them stood and stared at Ma once she was safely wedged. She was shaking fit to burst, trembling like a leaf.

Molly fell to her knees. 'What's matter, lass? Did we hurt you?'

Ma's head shook slightly.

'What is it, then?'

'Un . . . Porr . . . '

'Uncle Porrick – yes?'

'Sa . . . id litt . . . peo . . . ple. . . . ' Ma looked from Molly to Sarah. Neither of them was more than five feet tall. 'Tr . . . ue!'

Molly clapped her hands in childlike delight. 'She says it's come true. Uncle Porrick said if she wore the brooch, then the little people would help her. Well, Sarah. They don't come much littler than you and me—'

'What about me?' asked Paddy. 'I'm not little.'

Sarah looked him over. 'No. You can be an honorary member. There are many ways of being small, Paddy. One is to lie in bed while your wife runs around silly. From now on, you will pull your weight. Understood?'

'Yes, Miss.' He touched his forelock mockingly. 'Any more orders?'

'A cup of tea and a scone would not go amiss. And a few scraps for this miserable hound.'

Ma looked at the dog and the dog looked at Ma. A thin tail

wagged hopefully. Somehow, the animal empathized with Ma, realized that he and she were underprivileged, not fully furnished, not quite up to the mark.

Sarah, watching this silent communication, released the dog from its moorings and it leapt across the room, flinging itself in abject obedience and adoration at Ma's feet.

'Keep him,' said Sarah magnanimously. 'I've too many cats, have to get rid of him anyway. He's a difficult character, was almost drowned as a newborn, can't seem to trust me. He likes you, though. Name's Yorick, took it from Shakespeare, you know. Yorick was a mere skull and this fellow was all bone when I got him. He'll help you recover, believe me. There's nothing like a dog for keeping a person up to the mark.'

Molly's jaw dropped. A blinking dog to look after on top of everything else! 'Are you sure?' she asked, hoping against hope.

'Yes. Take him, he's yours.'

They sat by the fire drinking tea. Ma could manage a cup all right, though she still needed a pot towel on her chest to catch dribbles from her one-sided mouth.

Paddy sniffed the air gingerly. Something stank, that was for sure. And it wasn't even the blinking dog, it was Miss Sarah Leason, all horse liniment and cat hairs, she was. He wondered if she'd ever heard of lavender water or Evening in Paris. Likely not. That was what they sprayed round at the Rialto between performances, California Poppy or Evening in Paris, just to take the edge off one lot of sweaty leavings before letting the next crowd in. He couldn't go to the pictures no more on account of the pongs. It was the kids, he knew that. If some poor little soul wanted the lav, big brother or sister made them squat on the floor so they wouldn't miss any of the story. Then it all ran down the front. Hence the need for lavender water and the like.

'What are you thinking about, Paddy?' Molly asked. She could tell when he was actually thinking, because his face looked occupied for a while.

'The pictures. Haven't been for ages.'

'I've never been,' said Sarah proudly. 'And I never shall.

235

Don't read the papers, no idea at all of what's going on in the world. Not interested, you see. Enough to do walking from here to the Hollies just to see my horse.'

'You've missed a treat with the pictures,' said Molly, grinning widely. 'Remember him with the long pole when we were kids, Paddy?'

He laughed loudly. 'Do I? Aye, he marched up and down that aisle clocking us, didn't he? The pole was just long enough to reach halfway from either direction. Had them made to measure, he did.'

'And her on the piano playing sad music at the happy part and the other way round.'

'Sh . . . ee wa . . . dea . . . f.'

Molly nudged her husband's arm. 'She's talking, lad.'

'Pa . . . dd . . . ee rea . . . d for me.' Her face was contorted with the effort, but the sentence came out well towards its end.

'That's right,' agreed Paddy. 'I used to read the captions for you. Some lads got in free every week as readers, paid for by somebody who'd never learned. Them were the days, eh Ma?'

'Y . . . es. G . . . ood day . . . s.'

'Better than these, what?' snapped Sarah. She turned her attention to Paddy now. 'I should never have allowed you to talk me into it. There isn't room in that house to swing a cat – and I've enough of those if I chose to swing them. I should have stayed on the moor.'

'You'd have died,' he said baldly. 'And been well rotted afore anybody found you. Swainbank was your nearest neighbour and when did he ever put in an appearance, eh? No, we did the right thing. And you got a fair price for the land, so stop your moaning.'

'I miss the space and I miss Samson.'

'Get away with your bother! Them's nice folk what have took over the Hollies. It's a grand house again and Samson's got his own stable. Good horse, that. Look what you've had out of him for stud. Mind, you'd have made a lot more if you hadn't been so choosy.'

'I wasn't having him fathering hunters. Carriage and show horses I don't mind. But hunters?' She shivered. 'Still, I suppose it wasn't the same after Fergus left me. Perhaps you're right. But I do hate living down here. It's like Dante's Inferno at times . . .'

'Who's he when his mother shouts him in for his dinner?'

'Oh, never mind, Paddy.' She jumped up with all the agility of a child. 'I'll leave you with your dog, then.'

Paddy and Molly stared unenthusiastically at the latest addition to their family. Although he was a great lover of animals, Paddy had never seen anything quite like Yorick before. The young animal was asleep, curled up at Ma's feet with his head tucked up to his tail. 'I hope he doesn't bite the kids,' said Molly. 'If he does, you'll have to take him back.'

'If they don't bite him, he won't bite them,' she pronounced.

'He bit you.'

'He doesn't like me. Obviously a discerning animal. No-body with any sense likes me.' She touched Ma's shoulder. 'They think I'm a witch because of the cats. It suits me. They leave me alone.'

She swept out, leaving behind her an aroma that was not quite savoury.

'Nee . . . ds a goo . . . d wa . . . sh,' said Ma. 'And a de . . . cent fr . . . ock.'

Molly glanced at Paddy. 'I think your mam's on the mend. So you'd best buck up, hadn't you? And don't be sneaking off, I'll need you to help me get her back to bed later on.'

Yorick stretched, yawned and struggled into a sitting position, his solemn brown eyes fixed firmly on his new mistress's face. First a paw, then a muzzle rested on her knee. The pink tongue began to lick her right hand and she smiled at her canine friend, giving him the odd conspiratorial wink from time to time. It was her secret for now, hers and the dog's. Because Ma could feel the roughness of his whiskers, the wetness of his tongue, even the heat of his breath. But she wouldn't hope too much, not just yet.

He was a mess of a dog, looked as if he'd been put together with the nuts and bolts in all the wrong places. His feet were

237

huge and he'd probably finish up enormous. But for some reason she couldn't quite work out, Ma loved Yorick right from the start. And she knew that he loved her.

'I wonder what it's like being dead?'

Joey stared at his sister in amazement. 'Like nothing on earth, I'd say.'

'Aw, don't go all funny on me. I was just wondering, like. Specially at our age.'

He looked up at the sky and sniffed noisily. Sometimes, he just couldn't catch their Janet's drift at all. 'You can't be dead at our age.'

'Course you can. It was in the paper, that there Mr Swainbank's boys – they're dead at sixteen and fourteen.'

'Then they've stopped being sixteen and fourteen, haven't they? Once you're dead, you stop having an age.'

'Do you?'

'Yes.' He leaned nonchalantly against Miss Leason's wall. 'Dead means finished, so don't think about it. We haven't hardly started living yet. I'm going to have a good life, I am. Plenty of money and a car.'

Janet thought about her brother. He'd always been on the make, had their Joey. Almost as soon as he could walk, he was into things, taking empties back for the odd penny, helping the clogger out by picking up spilled nails with a big magnet, collecting with the ragman on a Saturday for tuppence. Lately, he'd started on a paper round, though his shoe and clog cleaning business seemed to have fizzled out. He was up to something, she could sense it.

'I've thought of a way we can get a bit of brass put together,' he said now.

'What for?'

Joey sighed deeply and dropped his shaking head. Women. There was no following their trail at all. It was like they were a different species from another world, a law unto themselves with their daft way of reckoning. Still, their Janet was different, wasn't she? She was his, born on the same day, sharing everything with him since before the start. He would make something of himself for Janet. One day, they'd both have everything . . .

'What do you want to go making money for, Joey?'

'What do you mean, "what for?"? For things, is what for! I don't want to be starting me apprenticeship in clogs, do I? Oh no, I'm after a pair of boots, proper leather with irons on the toes and heels for good wear. Cost a bob or two, do boots. And you'll be wanting a new frock once you get set on. See, Janet – you've got to have a goal, a dream, a thing you want, or a few things.'

'Why?'

'Because . . . because otherwise, life's daft. I mean, you don't want everything to stop the same, do you? We shall get our own place, just thee and me, away from Granny and Mam, away from Dad with his booze and bad turns—'

'You get him the drink, Joey.'

'I know. It shuts him up, keeps him out of the road.'

'But Mam says it's killing him, eating away at his innards—'

'Good!'

She stepped back. 'Our Joey!'

'Well, I mean it. We'd be better off without him – aye and the old girl too. No, I'm not talking about Mam, I mean the owld dragon in the front room. All the street's bloody scared of her, but I'm not, oh no. She's a pain in the bum and so's our Dad, waste of Mam's time the pair of them.'

Janet opened her mouth to speak, but was stopped by the sudden arrival of Miss Leason. 'Just left your house,' announced the sprightly old lady. 'Ma's up in a chair and I've managed to resurrect the dead from beyond the stairway too. Yes, as I've always said about a lazy horse, a swift punch on the rump gets the bugger going.' She studied the two children's faces. It was obvious that they were in the middle of a disagreement. 'Quarrelling?' she demanded. 'No time for that! Shouldn't be allowed.'

'It's nothing much,' said Janet quietly.

'Isn't it?' This pair didn't belong with the rest somehow. There was something about them, a faint resemblance to another litter altogether. Still, no matter. 'I've balls and books for you,' she announced. 'Exercise for mind and body, that's what you need.' She shot up the path and into the house.

'Follow her – go on,' challenged Joey.

'She's weird.'

He laughed. 'Aye. Black cats and funny brews, just like Gran.'

'Gran never had a cat. And Miss Leason's no witch – she's just odd.'

'Go in, then.'

'No. Joey, don't you love our Gran? And Dad too? Don't you care about your own family?'

His face was brick-red. 'I care about Mam and you. But—'

'What about Michael and Daisy?'

'I'd see them right, but they're not like us, Janet. We're twins, we belong together. Michael and Daisy are . . . responsibilities, people I'll have to look after being as I'm the oldest. But you're my sister—'

Miss Leason dumped a bag of books and a metal bucket on the pavement by their feet. 'Books and balls,' she announced before stamping back into the house.

'Bloody hell,' cursed Joey. 'All the years she's kept our rounders and cricket balls and hidden them in the scullery. All lined up by the back door, they were. Now she decides to be nice when we're nearly too old for games.'

They looked over their shoulders. Miss Leason's house was terraced like theirs, but bigger, with gates, a garden, bow windows and fancy patterns in the brickwork above the front door. The houses at each side of hers were pretty, painted in greens and blues, nice crisp curtains in the windows, vases of flowers and pot dogs on the sills. But Sarah's house stank, waves of bad air wafting out into the garden. It was terrible inside, Joey knew that. Five years she'd lived here, during which time she'd turned it into a right mess. Once, on a dare off Colin Shuttleworth over a bag of ballbearings, Joey had climbed Miss Leason's wall and had a real good look, not just for the balls they'd kicked over, but through the windows and past filthy rags of curtain. The ashes under the range were raked out to the middle of the floor, never cleared from one month to the next. The slopstone had been filled with decaying food, tea leaves and half a dozen yowling cats.

He swallowed hard. In spite of the contempt he felt for Miss Leason, he somehow understood her. There was no meaning in her life, nowt to aim for. Though she was clever, he knew that. Likely rich too. Rich, but without the sense to know how to spend her money. Aye, clever was one thing, sensible another matter altogether.

Janet fingered the set of books. 'Look, Joey! Aren't they lovely?'

His face lit up. 'By, they'll be worth something, they will. Leather bound and all. I wonder how much we'll get?'

'Don't you dare!' screamed Janet. 'Don't even think about it! These are little encyclopedias – I'm keeping them.'

'They stink.'

Janet squared up to him for the first time in her life, fists bunched, eyes wide and angry. 'I'll put them in the washhouse to air. Touch these, Joey Maguire and I'll never talk to you again. That's after I've knocked your blinking head off!'

He gaped at her. God, she meant it and all! 'Okay, I'll not step within a mile of them.'

'Better not.'

They walked slowly homeward. At the corner of Delia Street, Janet placed a hand on her brother's arm. 'Hang on a minute.'

They paused beneath an unlit gaslamp, Joey bouncing one of the balls from the bucket.

'What you were saying before – about Granny and Dad – you didn't mean it, did you?'

'I did. Life's not a bloody fairy tale, our Janet. Nobody can care about everybody in their family and live happy ever after. Truth is, our dad's a drunk and Gran's a bad-tempered old biddy. There's nowt in this world to change that. So, what can't be changed must be walked away from. I'm for clearing off as soon as we're working, get a couple of rooms down town. We could save up, get our own house. See, money's the answer. And that's what I wanted to talk to you about before

241

Witchie Leason came along. I've got this . . . this arrangement starting up.'

'What arrangement? Who with?'

'Mr Goldberg.'

'The pawnie?'

'Aye. Business has dropped a bit. Seems that some people who used to go to Uncle's have got a bit proud. They want the stuff pledged, only they're scared of being seen in his queue of a Monday with the best suit and of a Friday with the money and the ticket.'

'So?'

He shrugged. 'We provide a service, do the business for them. We'll be helping them, Mr Goldberg and ourselves. Can't see nowt wrong with that.'

'Oh. So how do we go about providing this here service?'

'Well, we get out of bed at the crack of a Monday. Mr Goldberg gives us a list of regulars and we knock at the doors and say, "Anything for charity today Mrs So-and-So?" Then we take the stuff down the shop. Mr Goldberg gives us the money and the tickets, then we go back to the houses and deliver. On a Friday after school, we do the same thing only backwards. Got it?'

She nodded thoughtfully. 'What do you want me for?'

'To help me carry the stuff! Can you see one lad on his own lumping fourteen suits and a dozen pairs of boots? Not to mention the odd wireless. And it has to be done quick. Some of them need the money for Monday's breakfast. Most folk will be that happy to see half-a-crown on a Monday, they'll more than likely give us the odd penny. So we get paid both ends. Wages off Uncle, pennies off the customers.'

'And you'd take their pennies?'

'Aye, I bloody would!'

Janet fixed her eyes on her new blue clogs. Mam had had them made special, leather roses stitched on the sides and a pearl button for the ankle-strap. She felt uneasy, didn't want to look at him. And he was getting on her nerves, bouncing that ball all the while he was talking, carrying on about how brilliant he was. She glanced up the street towards their own

242

front door at the top. She wasn't going to leave Mam, not even for Joey. Especially not for Joey.

'Well?' he asked.

'I'm not doing it. Any of it.' She forced herself to meet that penetrating black gaze. 'Sometimes, I don't like you, our Joey. There's no . . . forgiveness in you, no kindness or charity.'

'What? I've always tret you right, haven't I?'

'Yes.' She pushed the fringe off her forehead and tucked it behind her ear. 'Yes, because you've always thought about me like something . . . something you own, like I'm your property. But I've got a mind of me own, Joey. I don't object to helping folk borrow food money, only I'd take not one penny in tips. It would be like stealing. I know I've always backed you up before and if you're ever in bother, then I shall likely stick up for you again. But I'll not go against me and what I believe in.'

'Hoity-bloody-toity!'

'Say what you like, I shan't take notice.'

He replaced the ball in the bucket with the others. 'You've no head for business, lass.'

'If a head for business means cheating people, then I'll do without.'

'How do you think the mill bosses make all that brass, eh?' His voice was raised in pitch now. 'By treating folk right and paying good wages? Never. They get where they are by taking and not giving, that's how. You can't change things, Janet.'

'No, happen I can't. But like you said before, what can't be changed must be walked away from.'

'That was different – I meant family.'

'Oh. I see. Well, I don't want to leave my family. And working folk are our family too, our big family. There's us on one side and them on the other. You're after becoming one of them and I'm going to stay one of us. Parting of our ways, I suppose.'

'Aw, Janet—'

'It's all right, we shan't quarrel. We never have and I hope we never will. But we're different. We can be different, you know. It's all right to be different. I mean, we won't always be together. I'll get wed and so will you—'

He grabbed her arm fiercely. 'But we'll still be twins and best mates?'

'Oh aye.' She smiled feebly. 'No doubt there.'

They walked up the street together. To an onlooker, it might have seemed that the Maguire twins were enjoying that companionable silence that so often existed between them. But Joey felt disturbed, alarmed almost. She'd always done his bidding; he'd led the way at all times. Now, a warning bell was sounding in his mind, a message from the future – if such a thing could be possible. She wouldn't always be here. It was hard admitting, even to himself, how much he depended on her. There'd never be a wife good enough, not while Janet lived. No girl could match her beauty and cleverness, no girl could ever make him feel so proud. Heads turned when Janet passed by with her dark gold hair and big grey eyes. Not that he felt desire for her – oh no – she was his sister. What he felt for Janet went way beyond all that. He worshipped her, loved her as his other half. One day, a head too many would turn and take her away from him. No!

Janet, on the other hand, felt strangely calm. Things needed sorting out in Joey's mind, especially now they were near fifteen. She loved him dearly, couldn't help admiring all that clear thinking and single-minded determination, but he'd smothered her all their lives, never letting her out of his sight if he could help it. Soon, she'd be working away from him, meeting new friends, learning a trade. In a way, she felt as if shackles were being removed from her ankles. Sometimes, when they'd been little, she'd tried to imagine what it must be like to be a single like Michael and Daisy, to be born alone, separate and individual. Yes, Joey had looked after her and she was grateful for that. But she wanted her own life, her own way of living it. And she was glad that she had expressed this need, at least in part.

Mam was setting the table. 'Where've you two been?'

'Witchie Leason's,' replied Joey.

'Don't call her that!' said Molly. 'She's of a good family, is Miss Leason—'

'She let us have some books and a few balls for Michael and

Daisy.' Janet gave her brother a withering look. 'They smell a bit, so I've left them in the wash-house to air a while.'

'We've a dog,' announced Molly. 'She gave us that and all – I'm doing me best to be grateful. It's in the front room with your Gran, won't leave her side. It's called Yorick and Ma likes it. Rhymes with Porrick, I suppose. Great lump of a thing it's going to turn out to be.'

'I've always wanted a dog.' Joey grinned and turned towards the best room.

Molly held up her hand. 'Leave it! It's there to get your Gran better. You can take it for a walk after. Gran's been up, by the way.'

'We know. Miss Leason said.' Janet's face glowed with pleasure. 'Will she start getting right now, Mam?'

'Aye. I reckon she will.'

'Good God.' Joey dropped his head. 'The eyes, ears and gob of the world shall rise and walk again—'

'Joey Maguire!' Molly clouted him hard across his back. 'You bad little beggar, you! That's your grandmother in there flat on her back and nearly helpless. She's kept this family going many a year, put the bread in your mouths, she has. You just don't understand her, that's all. Come to think, you don't understand anybody except yourself, grabbing little swine, you are! Never refused the pennies, did you? Would you work as hard as she has, just for other folk?'

He looked her squarely in the face. 'For Janet, I would.'

'Why just Janet?'

'Because she and I are . . . different. Separate from the rest of you.'

Molly staggered back fighting for air and Janet rushed to her side. 'Mam, are you all right?'

But Molly's eyes were fastened on her son's face. 'How do you mean – different?' she whispered.

Janet rounded on him. 'Look what you've done! This is her nervous asthma back and after she was doing so well. Get the kettle—'

'No! I'm all right! What did you mean by that, our Joey?'

The boy studied his mother carefully, aware that he had

245

touched a raw nerve, unsure of how he'd achieved that.

'Different in what way?' she persisted.

He allowed a few seconds to tick by before answering. 'Twins, in case you'd forgotten.'

'No, I've not forgot, Joey. You first, then her. That's the order you were born in. But that doesn't mean you've to lead her by the nose through life! And you're the same as the rest of us, no matter what!'

He grinned mirthlessly, his eyes still cold and angry. 'We'll see about that. I'm off out – you coming, Janet?'

'No. I shall look after Mam. You can start managing without me. Anyway, what about your tea?'

For answer, he walked out and slammed the door.

Molly found herself sobbing in her daughter's arms. It was as if he knew something – everything, in fact. Was it possible to start hating your own child? Oh, if only there'd been just Janet and not him with his near-black eyes always reminding her . . .

'I'm sorry, Mam.'

'What for? Why should you be forever apologising for him? You're not responsible just because you arrived in the same batch! Don't let him take you over, lass. Don't let him! Promise me!'

'I promise. Calm down now. You've not to get excited, specially in summer. Didn't the doctor say that grass makes asthma worse?'

'What? We've got no grass, love. And this isn't asthma, it's bloody heartbreak . . . '

How many times could a heart be broken before it disintegrated altogether? It was like papering over cracks, they always showed through at the finish. Just as she always cried and let her own cracks show . . .

'Come on, Mam. We'll get the tea on.'

Molly followed Janet into the scullery. There was something in that lad, something cunning and not a mile short of bad. Where had he got it? Not from the Dobson side, that was for sure. And not from the Maguires by example either. Paddy might be a bit daft at times, but there was little malice

246

in him. Bloody Swainbanks! She threw the vegetables into the pan, not heeding the splashes of water on her clothes.

'Mam? Mam? Whatever is it now?'

Molly's hand was fastened to her chest. She stared down at the table where lay the peelings all spread out over an old newspaper. They were dead. Dead. Both of them. It was there, thick black print with a border, made to stand out, a declaration of their family's position in the community. The words jumped about all over the page as she struggled to focus on this incredible and terrifying truth. His sons had been killed in a motoring accident.

'Mam!'

'What?'

'Shall I get some steam to you?'

'No. No, I should never have eaten that bacon at dinner time. I eat too fast and all. That's always been my trouble, doing things too fast. Without thinking, like. You can pay all your life for a few minutes of not thinking.'

'Joey's upset you.'

'It's not that, love. I like bacon but it doesn't like me. Go through and set the kettle on the fire, 'cos I'll be using the gas rings. Make a nice cuppa just for the two of us.'

'And Gran?' She was dying to get in there to see this new dog.

Molly braced herself against the table's edge and looked at her pretty daughter. That's not your granny, love. Your granny was a bad old bugger with a tongue like snakebite . . . 'Yes, take Gran a cup. And fetch your dad's tray down. He wore himself out getting her back in the front room.'

After Janet had left, Molly reached down, picked up the paper and screwed it round the peelings as tightly as she could, as if trying to deny the words it contained. But even when she'd tossed newspaper and contents into the ashpit, she still saw the black border and the thick fancy lettering dancing in front of her eyes.

Why hadn't she heard before? This news was at least two days old. Aye, but there'd been no time to read the paper, had there? And with Paddy in bed most of the time and Bella

247

Seddon not talking, there'd been little contact with the outside world. Miss Leason never took notice of much. And Janet, who was doing the shopping after school, wasn't the age to bother about this sort of gossip. Thank God.

Why his sons, though? Why couldn't it have been somebody else's? No, that was a sin. Wishing anybody dead – even some poor anonymous soul – was a sin, though a part of her wanted to go out right this minute and kill Charlie Swainbank. And he was a long way from anonymous, wasn't he? Nay, it wasn't his fault. He couldn't be blamed for the death of his kiddies. And there was no need for her to feel so bloody furious, so worked up and worried. There was no connection between him and her any more, no need for him to be in her life ever again.

Why this fear, then? Where was the anger, the dread coming from? She steadied herself in the wash-house doorway. No! They were hers! Janet and Joey were hers! And anyway, surely he wouldn't . . . But oh dear God in heaven, Joey was his living image! Yes, she'd been married all right and the twins had been born in wedlock, all properly documented, registered by their father. Only he wasn't their father. Had Charlie Swainbank done his sums ever? Did he know she'd had twins almost exactly nine months after that night?

Molly Maguire fell in at the scullery door and grabbed a glass of water. There was no point in wondering and worrying. No point at all. She must get a grip on herself, stop all this stupidity. And she must surely pray for those poor dead boys.

Janet stared down at the figure on the bed, a scream frozen in her throat. Slowly, she reached down and touched his hand. It was warm, but his eyes were fixed glassy and unseeing on something behind her head. She shook him. 'Dad! Dad!'

His whole frame shuddered as he inhaled deeply.

'Oh, Dad.'

'What?'

'Never mind. You all right?'

'No, I'm not, but who's bloody bothered over me, eh? Your mam doesn't care whether I live or die, stuck in here on me own all day, nowt to see, nobody to talk to—'

'We do care!' Janet relaxed. This was more like the dad she knew. 'It's just that Mam's got so much to do.'

'Rubbish, Jan. It's Ma that set her off with all this housework lark, keeping one jump in front of the neighbours all the while. Daft, it is. Molly's at it now, just like me mother, time to donkey the step before her next door, don't be the last one in with the washing – barmpots, the lot on 'em.' He paused, completely breathless.

'Dad, you sound like Mam with her bit of asthma.'

'Bit of asthma? I've been blessed all me life with a chest, love. Your Granny used to send me to school wearing that many clothes I wasn't recognized some days. They thought I was a new fat lad. I went through the first twelve years of my life reeking of camphorated. Every time I went near her, she covered me in camphorated.'

'You should have learned to duck. Can I get you anything?'

'Bottle of stout.'

She shook her head. 'No. You've not to drink, the doctor said. Tea, milk, water – you can have them, but no beer, Dad.'

'Christ. It's you that sounds like your bloody mother! Fetch us a proper drink, lass. Joey does.'

'It's killing you. You know it's killing you, so why do you do it?'

'Because I'm stupid.' He grinned at her boyishly.

'No, you're not. It takes a clever man to act as daft as you do.'

'Aye. And a clever girl to know it. Get me a drink.'

'No. I think you'd best get up and stop crying wolf.' Was he crying wolf? After all, he'd looked so ill when she first came in. But it was no use telling him that, he'd just linger in the bed for ever.

He was studying her. 'I've often wondered how I come to get a lass like you. You're beautiful, our Janet. I reckon as how you could be in the pictures like one of them there film stars—'

'Don't talk so daft! You'll not get round me!'

'Nay, I'm serious. Now listen while I tell you, 'cos I'm not one for speeches. I haven't been a good dad. I'm not what you'd call a good person, see. When I was little, I plagued the

249

daylights out of me mam and I've not changed over-much. But I don't tell lies, never did – except to get out of a tight corner. So if I say you're as pretty as a picture, you can take that as gospel.'

'All right. I'll get you a glass of barley wine.'

'What?' He sat bolt upright. 'I'm not laying a finger on that muck. You've not seen what goes into your Gran's wines, have you? I reckon she goes through the ashpit for some of the makings.'

She smiled and reached out to ruffle his already disordered hair. 'You win. If Mam goes to Confession, then I'll nip down with the jug to the outdoor – just half a pint, mind.'

'Couldn't you . . . stretch it to a pint?'

'Don't push your luck, Paddy! Mam would have me flayed.'

'All right. Have it your own road – same as you women always do.'

She made for the door.

'Jan?'

'What?'

'I love you, lass.'

He'd never said that for ages. Her eyes misted over as she looked at this lazy great lump of a man who was her father. No matter what he was, she adored him, always had and always would. 'I love you too, Paddy Maguire,' she whispered.

'Wish I was worth it!'

'You are! You're my dad, so you must be worth it! It's not every feller can have a film star for a daughter, is it?' She posed in the doorway.

'Oh, get gone for me ale.'

'I'm going, I'm going . . .'

At the foot of the stairs, she paused, tray in hand. He'd eaten almost none of his dinner. Was he really ill this time? She tutted quietly under her breath. He'd been swinging the lead for so long now – it wouldn't matter whether or not his illness was real. Nobody would ever take him seriously. They were hard women, Gran and Mam. Perhaps they'd had to be? Mam hadn't drunk her tea. The meal was ready, left to warm in the range. But she hadn't drunk her tea, which was unusual.

250

She must be at Confession early, must have a special sin to tell. Janet couldn't imagine her mother having sinned.

She washed her father's dishes then went out to fetch the young ones in from play, hoping there'd be enough time to nip out for Dad's beer. After all, a promise was a promise. And Mam was so hard on him at times.

Molly Maguire was feeling anything but hard. With her equilibrium slipping fast, she howled her pain and confusion into Father Mahoney's ears. She couldn't see his face, what with the grille being there and her eyes filling up all the while. But even the man's vague outline was comforting, while his gentle Irish voice was as good as any of Ma's herbal sedatives.

'Aw now Molly. Don't be getting yourself into one of them flat spins. Himself may have no interest in your children – why should he have? I dare say if he met them in the street, he'd pass by and never a thought to it. And if he did put in an appearance, wouldn't he have meself to contend with? I may not be quick on me feet, Molly Maguire, but I can cut the legs off any man if it comes to a battle of words.'

'But . . . but if Paddy ever found out . . . ' She blew her nose noisily.

'Look, child. Has this man sent money ever for support purposes? Has he fed, clothed and warmed those children, paid their doctors' bills, sent them a gift at Christmas or on their birthday?'

'No. Never. I've not seen hide nor hair of him since I left the big house.'

'Well then, be sensible. What proof does the man have at all?'

'None. His sort doesn't need proof. With the other kiddies gone and Joey his rightful son – happen he'll want somebody to carry on in the mills.'

The shape behind the wooden grille tut-tutted loudly. 'What? Can you see Joey Maguire with his finger on the pulse? Sure, I'm not being critical of your son now, Molly, for he's a fine boy in his own way. But he hardly fits the bill, does he? Can you see him in a fancy hat? I can't.'

'I bet our Joey would like a fancy hat to wear though, Father. He's got ambitions . . . '

'Away with your bother! The man's wife may well bear him another child.'

'Aye, she might. But they'll be getting on now, happen she's past childbirth. And his other two sons were reared – ready for business, they were. They'd be about sixteen and fourteen. That's right, the older one wasn't born when he . . . he—'

'When he raped you?'

'It wasn't quite—'

'Seduced you, then. Sure, you were a young girl without the sense to realize what was afoot. He took advantage of you. Isn't that a fine carry-on for him to be advertising, now? The fact that he molested you while his wife was expecting his first son?'

She mopped her face with her handkerchief. 'He can always say I was willing. It wouldn't really be a lie. And at the end of the day, it's the word of a servant against that of a master.'

'Dry your eyes now, Molly. Go out into the church and pray to Our Lady. Didn't she have a child she'd never have explained in a month of Sundays except for Joseph? You're not alone, my dear. And you're a good woman. Mary takes a special interest in converts, keeps them under her wing. And I'll pray for you like billy-o—'

'Oh Father – you're a terrible caution!'

'I know. Me mother was glad to see the back of me the day I disappeared into that seminary. "Bernard," she said. "If they can make a priest of you, then there's hope for sows' ears." I think I stuck it out to spite her.'

Molly giggled.

'That sounds a little more like yourself. Now compose your face and away back to your children. Your children, Molly. Nobody else's. Tell Paddy I'll be along.'

'With the whiskey, I suppose?'

'That I won't answer on the grounds that it might incriminate me. Also I cannot lie in me present capacity and wearing blessed vestments too.'

'I'm glad you're so . . . so ordinary, Father.'

'So am I,' he whispered. 'Wouldn't it be desperate if they made the terrible mistake of turning me into a bishop? Or worse still, a cardinal?'

'What about Pope?'

'Ah, now you're being silly, Molly Maguire. Which means you're back to normal. Say your penance and get home.'

He intoned the blessing while Molly made her Act of Contrition. He always made her feel better no matter what, did Father Mahoney.

Outside the church, she found Joey pretending not to wait for her. He tagged along behind, hands thrust into pockets, brow furrowed into a deep frown. At the corner, he caught up with her.

'Are you mad with me, Mam?'

'A bit.'

'Been crying?'

'No. Just one of me turns. What's up with you these days, lad? Is it part of growing up, I wonder?'

'I don't know.' He sparked a clog-iron against the pavement as they walked homeward. 'I want things, Mam. A different life, a good job—'

'Money?'

'Aye. I want money. Janet doesn't seem to want the same as I do.'

'Happen that's with her being a girl. And you have to give her some space, Joey, room to find out what she does want. I know you've always looked out for her and I've been grateful for that – never had to worry over my daughter while you were with her. But she's near a woman now, love. I know you want success – she likely just dreams of contentment, a nice husband and a couple of children—'

'I want me own business.'

They stopped simultaneously outside Tommy's Tripe, each pretending to stare at the display of manifold, black puddings, cow heels and pigs' trotters spread out on the white marble slab.

'What sort of business?' she asked eventually.

He grinned. 'Not tripe, I know that much. Maybe a shop or a little engineering works.'

'Selling what? Making what?'

'I've not thought that far. I just know I want to make me own road.'

'I see.' They continued to walk. 'What about your apprenticeship?'

'Oh, I'll take it till something comes up. It'll not be wasted. Even Gran says education's never lost. If I can get to grips with a lathe, then happen I might get me own workshop one day, mend cars or something.'

Yes, there was a lot of the other feller in him. Even if Charlie Swainbank hadn't been born to money, he'd have made it, perhaps breaking the odd back on the way like his forefathers had. And here was his spitten image with the same ideas. She must stop it! All this resentment and ill-feeling – it was bad! Charlie Swainbank had done wrong by her, but that didn't make him wicked. And she shouldn't be looking for such 'evils' in her son.

Aye, but it might suit Joey to find out he was a Swainbank. He'd jump at the chance of all that brass. Not Janet though. No. Janet had a strong sense of family, a need to identify with a close-knit group. But if the worst did come to the worst, would this one eventually persuade Janet to go with him, manipulate her as he had in the past?

Molly glanced sideways at her son. She didn't hate him. She loved him all right, in spite of the fact that he riled her to bursting. Sometimes she didn't like him, but he was her son when all came to all.

Yes. And he was somebody else's too . . .

Chapter 7

Charles Swainbank stood in the large hallway, elbows resting on the oak mantel shelf, head in his hands, eyes staring down unseeing at the heavy marble slab which formed the hearth. He could not take this in, never would. Both of them gone? With his teeth grinding to hide the pain and defeat threatening tears, he turned and began to pace the area between door and fireplace, every nerve in his body jangling and screaming as he waited for the hearses.

The boys were in the games room, one trestle each end of the billiard table at which they'd spent so many happy hours. He couldn't go in there, not yet, not until it was time to carry his sons out of their home for the last time. Everything in that room was in pairs, two cricket bats, tennis rackets, two sets of darts, one with red flights and the other with blue, twin school sports' caps, a pair of polished boxes now, each covered in flowers and wreaths. Both coffins were closed, the contents of one so disfigured as to render his son barely recognizable . . .

No, he couldn't go in there. And he couldn't go upstairs either, would not expose himself again to Amelia's frail fury. She blamed him, that was plain enough. He'd let them loose on the estate in the car, why – he'd positively encouraged John to drive when the poor child was scarcely sixteen! Yes, time after time during these dreadful days, she'd turned on him, berated him for the fool he was.

Oh Peter, Peter! What would he do without him? The younger son, yes, but of the two, Peter had shown the better head for business, that streak of calculated detachment so vital in a mill owner. John had been softer, gentler, concerned for his fellow man, committed to the improvement of working conditions, canteen facilities, first-aid and the like.

Charles beat his fists against a wall. Oh to have John here at this minute to hug and reassure, to be able to tell him how he'd loved him, that John had not been a disappointment! After all, which man wanted his children all the same, peas out of a pod, mirror images of one another?

What price the carefully made will now, eh? A will engineered painstakingly so that the two brothers might run the mills together. Peter would have kept John in line, Peter would have kept things ticking over in the good old Swainbank tradition. What now? Everything was wiped out, nullified, made into a nonsense. What the hell was he going to do?

Yes, at last Charles understood his own father, realized that old Richard had been far-seeing in getting rid of poor Harold. Harold was dead, yes, but the vulture had arrived and Charles saw her now for what she was – a scheming, grabbing scavenger with an eye to the main chance. Harold's shares and dividends, currently held in trust for his son, would no longer suffice. Not now. Not with the whole uncut cake waiting on the table. She'd brought the brat along with her. Considerably grown, long, lanky and lethargic, that was Cyril, with his steel-rimmed spectacles and the brain of a stuffed tortoise.

He stared through the hall window and down the length of the drive to a pair of wrought-iron gates, opened now against twin gatehouse walls. Open and waiting like Alice's hands. The Swainbanks had been sparse breeders, so there remained just Cyril now that the unthinkable had happened. The future of the line rested with that acne-spotted beanpole who'd never be capable of running a tap, let alone a thriving business. Peter could have managed it, leading the elder brother from behind, knowing, as Peter had always seemed to know, that business was a flirtatious and wayward mistress, ever vulnerable, demanding constant attention.

God, he wished he'd never bought them that bloody car with its paper-thin roof and fierce little engine! But they'd wanted it, begged for it – and hadn't they always got round him every time? Yes, they'd known their father's weakness, had recognized that he too was fascinated by fast cars.

With a huge roar of animal rage, Charles crossed the room and swept a vase of flowers from a table, hurling it against the wall where it smashed into a thousand shards, leaving the oak panelling weeping flower water, tears he himself could not release just yet.

Emmie rushed in with pan and brush. Her face was swollen with constant crying and she cleared the mess hurriedly in case she set off again in front of Mr Swainbank.

'Emmie?'

'Yes, sir?'

'Sorry about the mess, lass.'

' 'S all right, sir.'

'You're a good girl. Take no notice of my rages – they'll burn themselves out in their own good time. Send Nurse Fishwick in, will you?'

Emmie scuttled off to do his bidding. She didn't blame him for smashing things, didn't care about all the extra cleaning just lately. If them two lovely lads had been hers – why, she'd have smashed every pot in the house and every bloody window and all.

The nurse was on the landing, just closing Mrs Swainbank's door.

'He wants you, Nurse. Will I sit with the Missus?'

'No need. Her sister-in-law's with her. Doctor Blunt has administered a strong sedative to keep the mistress quiet till it's all over.'

'She won't be going, then? To the funeral?'

'It wouldn't do her any good, Emmie. She's fought us all morning, but now she'll probably sleep till they all get back from the churchyard. I'll stay with her. Mrs Alice will be going—'

'Mr Swainbank says we've to call her Mrs Fenner with her getting married again. I don't think he likes her much—'

'Shush, dearie. Keep your thoughts to yourself, especially now.'

'He's like a bear with a sore head,' warned Emmie in a whisper as they descended the curved stairway. 'Suppose it's only to be expected.'

Nurse Fishwick entered the hall. He stood with his back towards her, gazing out across the lawns. 'How is she?' he asked without turning.

'Not good. The doctor's put her out, given her an extra-strong dose.'

'That's best. Sit down, will you?'

He joined her after a few moments, lowering his solid frame into the opposite armchair. 'How long has she got?' he asked bluntly.

She hesitated fractionally. But no, there was no point in beating about the bush, not with Mr Swainbank. He wanted the truth and he wanted it yesterday. Not like some relatives who just couldn't accept what was evident to the least experienced of eyes. 'That's a difficult one, sir. It's probably travelled all through her by now, but she could linger for months – even longer.'

'I see. Is she . . . is she suffering?'

'There's some physical pain, some discomfort. But most of her misery is . . . well, the accident will more than likely make her worse. They kept her going, you see. She looked forward to their visits every day. I've seen cancer patients go on for years if they've had . . . well . . . an incentive. But we keep her dosed up, make sure she's as comfortable as possible.'

'And she still doesn't know?'

'Hard to say. I get the feeling she's not quite aware of what she's got. Later on, towards the end, she'll probably catch on. Most do when they realize they've been in bed for so long without showing any signs of improvement.'

He ran a hand through thick brown waves. 'Would she be better away – in a nursing home or a hospital? It's obvious she can't stand the sight of me—'

'No.' She shook her head vigorously. 'Not yet. To send her away just now, after what's happened – well, she'd be losing everything at once, wouldn't she? Mr Swainbank, if you've no objection, I really think we should talk about this some other time. You've a lot to go through this morning. Perhaps we could discuss Mrs Swainbank's condition in a week or so?'

'I suppose you're right.' He stared hard at her. She was a fine figure of a woman, fifty if a day, but strong as a horse, loyal and good-hearted too. And she knew her place, always wore her stiffly-starched uniform and an encouraging smile, always spoke to him properly, not like some medical folk who treated every person as if he had brain damage and couldn't understand the simplest thing. 'I appreciate your concern for me and mine, Nurse. Whatever happens, don't let her suffer. She's suffered enough with one thing and another. I couldn't have let her go with us today.'

'I understand.' She knew the real reason why his wife was being confined to quarters. Even if she had been fit to go, he'd have left her behind, terrified in case she screamed at him from the wheelchair, cursed him as she had these last days. 'I think they're here, Mr Swainbank.'

His face blanched as he rose slowly to his feet. 'Get me a brandy, Molly,' he whispered.

'Pardon?'

He gazed at her without comprehension.

'You called me Molly, Mr Swainbank.'

'Did I? Must be in a world of my own. Why, Molly's been gone fifteen years or more. She was a servant, a housemaid. And you look nothing like her. No. No.' He shook his head. 'Nothing like her at all. Get me a brandy, will you? A very large one.'

Yes, Molly had been gone for a long, long time, Molly with the laughing eyes and cheeky grin. Whatever had he been thinking of?

Nurse Fishwick brought the brandy and he swallowed it in one huge gulp, shuddering as it scalded his parched throat.

Perkins opened the front doors and eight burly men in black entered, the undertaker with his shiny black hat behind them. Charles' eyes skimmed over this solemn group. 'Shan't need all of you,' he said gruffly. 'I'll be carrying my own.'

The servants lined up in the hallway while the two coffins were carried through. Perkins, who had been butler, valet, part-time chauffeur and jack of all trades for some time, bit hard into his lower lip. He'd seen some funerals in his time, but nothing as downright tragic as this. They'd been fine lads, right enough, solid Swainbanks through and through, though Master John had allowed his mam to soften him a bit.

Perkins and Mrs Marshall, who was usually called Mrs M, were attending the funeral as representatives of the house staff and neither looked forward to this dubious honour. Mrs M, the cook-housekeeper, had cried into her bread dough all morning while Perkins himself had taken it out on the Master's favourite car, polishing the thing to within an inch of its existence. And Mr Swainbank looked terrible, like an old man as he tried to bear the weight of his own children – aye – in more ways than one.

Perkins took the two servants' wreaths and laid them on the coffins in the hearses, then he and Mrs M waited for the third car, watching as Mrs Fenner and her son got into the first with the Master. The manservant glanced sideways at his friend and companion. 'God help us if that one takes over,' he muttered from the corner of his mouth.

'Shush,' she answered without moving her head. 'We can't do nowt about it, so just frame yourself not to think on such things.'

Perkins grunted his disapproval. She was likely over the moon, that Mrs Alice, or Mrs Fenner as she was called now. Hardly a brass farthing to her name since her spendthrift husband upped and offed. No sign of him, was there? Oh no, he'd not be bothered attending the funeral, but he'd get back sharpish if he knew there might be money about. Aye, she'd be all right now, that one. And her chinless son would want for nowt if things went as Perkins dreaded. There was no one else, was there? Cyril was the end of the line and what a bloody end, eh?

In the second car, Perkins caught sight of the managers and their wives, faces white with shock because no doubt they'd taken in the implications by this time. Not that the Master was old – nay, he'd be around for a while yet. But what about after him? Yes, they all looked grey-faced and weary-worn this morning in spite of the sunshine.

Charles Swainbank saw little. Alice kept patting his hand

and muttering words of encouragement while her son sat as still as stone next to her, but Charles wasn't really aware of any of it. The cortege pulled out of the estate and turned right for the town. Although the church and cemetery were well out of Bolton, tradition must be maintained and all three mills would be visited before the service.

When they pulled up outside the gates of number one mill, Alice had to push him out of the car. It seemed that everyone was here and Charles wondered, very briefly, who was working the machines. Ah yes, it was a family funeral. Family funerals meant a near stop to everything. Not a word was spoken as Charles took the wreath from a young breaker and passed it on to the undertaker. Caps were doffed and heads were bowed while the procession moved on.

Then, as one man, the massive crowd followed round the corner to number two, doubling in number when it arrived. By the time the cortege left number three, it had collected a thousand mourners who stopped the traffic as they pursued the slow-moving vehicles along Bury Road.

It was then, when the cars turned, that Charles saw the speechless throng and his heart suddenly burst when he noticed all the tears being shed for his sons, pouring down the faces of work-toughened men and women who stood ten and twelve abreast in the road with no thought for their own safety. And he heard John screaming at him, 'They're people, Dad. They're not bloody work-horses! They need unions, they've got to have protection, otherwise we'd be running them fifty-five hours a week like in the bad old days . . . '

They were people all right. That was real grief, genuine concern for him and his poor dead boys. A girl of about fifteen was sobbing inconsolably in the arms of a woman who might have been her mother. But Charles wasn't sure, had never been sure. Too many of them for him to take more than a passing interest.

'You don't care where they come from, do you? As long as they keep coming, you don't care, Dad! And when they threaten to strike for a few pennies an hour, you lock them out! Don't you realize that most of them haven't a bath in the

261

house or a proper lavatory? Have you been in their houses? Have you . . . ?' Oh John, I will, I will go . . .

Alice pushed a handkerchief into his hands and he suddenly realized that he was crying, blubbering like an infant.

'Bear up, Charles. Do try, you must make an effort . . . '

'What for? Two fine boys I've lost, two of the best. A whole future's gone down the drain . . . '

'No, no. There's Cyril, your own dear brother's son.' She patted his arm in what was meant to be a comforting way.

'You bloody fool of a woman!' Yes, Father had had Alice weighed up well enough. 'I'm not talking about the future of the Swainbank mills! I'm talking about a pair of fine and intelligent boys mown down before they've even ripened!' He rubbed his eyes fiercely. 'And even if I were to discuss the Swainbank so-called empire, that damn fool boy of yours isn't good enough, do you hear? Not good enough! I'd sooner sell out this very day to old Leatherbarrow than have that lad of yours touch one frame, one spool . . . ' Yes, he was taking it out on her and yes, she probably deserved it. But he must stop. This day was for his sons, the very last day for them.

'You're upset, Charles. It's perfectly understandable.' She closed her mouth firmly. There was no point in pursuing the matter just now – this was hardly the appropriate time. But she knew as well as Charles did that Cyril was next in line. Even if the mills were sold, the money would eventually revert to Harold's son. Ah well. It was a sad way to achieve some comfort, but she was relieved to think that her old age might be easier than she'd expected. Harold's shares paled into insignificance by the side of the real inheritance. There'd be no more children from Amelia, that was certain. The only real danger would arrive once poor Amelia passed away. Charles was young and healthy enough to start again with a new wife. But no, she would not think of that. Amelia might last for years yet . . .

As the boys were being placed in the ground after the service, Charles was somehow not surprised to see a large contingent from the mills standing well back from the grave, far enough away to show they knew their place. He beckoned silently and they drew nearer, placing their individual floral tributes at the side of the newly-dug hole. 'Thank you,' he mouthed and they turned almost in unison to walk back to the gate where stood two charabancs, probably paid for out of union funds. Life seemed to be an interminable and insoluble mystery. They fought him, worked damned hard for him, made unreasonable demands, bought him cigars at Christmas, spat on his name, swore that Swainbank's goods were the best, reviled and cursed him. And above all, they loved him. They cared. His eyes misted over again. They might lose a morning's pay for this – perhaps a day's pay, for many of them would probably go and get drunk now, drown their sorrows in some town centre pub. He smiled sadly. No money would be docked; there'd be full packets this week, he would see to that personally.

When all had left, a lone figure stepped from behind a tree and walked towards the grave. The diggers looked up from their task. 'Too late, lass? Never mind, you can put your flowers over there with the others. We'll stick 'em on top when we've finished filling in.'

Molly placed the roses on the heap with the rest. She didn't really know why she was here. To make sure? To confirm or deny her own worst fears, to look at him again, work out what he was made of? Or was she simply paying tribute to these two kiddies who had been half-brothers to her own twins?

She shouldn't have come. He looked terrible, did Charlie. Not that she'd seen him since . . . well, since all that bother. But his photos in the paper, right up to lately, had been of a younger man. Poor Charlie. He'd done wrong in the past, but so had most people if you just reckoned it up. And he was paying, by Christ he was! Happen he'd leave her alone. Happen he wouldn't want Joey after all, because Joey hadn't been fetched up right, hadn't been trained for power and ownership and suchlike, didn't even talk proper. And there was always Harold's lad. Even if old Richard hadn't thought much of his younger son, perhaps the next generation had turned out a bit nearer to what was wanted. But she felt sorry for Charlie, she really did. There could be nowt worse than losing your child. Losing them all must be beyond all bearing.

Back at Briars Hall, Charles poured himself a third liberal measure of brandy. There was no gathering after the funeral. Had Amelia been well, things might have been different, but he hadn't wanted a crowd of well-meaning hangers-on and curious acquaintances enquiring after her health and offering empty words of condolence. Because no words could describe how Charles Swainbank felt at this moment – the dictionary that contained them had not yet been invented.

Strangely enough, the most immediate emotion was anger. He was angry with himself for buying the car, angry with the old oak for simply being there when the vehicle swerved, almost angry with the boys for dying like that, going off without a word of warning. But if he could have directed his wrath, it would have been aimed straight at Mrs Alice Fenner, his dead brother's wife. She was walking around the house with an air that bordered on the proprietorial, fingering ornaments, running her hands over drapes to feel their quality, ordering the staff about. She probably wasn't even aware of what she was doing, but what she was doing made Charles Swainbank's pores open so that the hairs on his arms stood to attention as if ready for a fight.

He watched her now across the table. Her spotty-faced son sat between the two adults, where Peter used to sit.

' . . . of course, it would have been easier if she'd had another to turn to now. But then she might improve in time.'

'Pardon?'

'I was just saying that it's a pity you had no more children.'

Charles stared at her. She looked like something that had fallen from the top of a Christmas tree. Well, a negative photograph of such an item, at least. Black frills and ribbons, black shiny beads, even a black handkerchief threaded through her watch strap. What a bloody mess. Father had been right. Again. This one was dangerous. Not because she had brains – oh no, no sign of higher intelligence here. But she possessed that female cunning, an instinct never fully acquired or understood by the male of the species. It was like an extra sense with some of them, Father had said. The same fatal trait that caused a spider to eat her mate once she'd finished with him. Charles shivered.

'Are you cold, dear?'

'No.'

She sighed loudly. 'Yes, it's a shame that you didn't have a third.'

'Even if we had had more, nothing could replace John and Peter.'

'No.' She dabbed at her face with the napkin. 'But they're such a comfort, aren't they? My Cyril's always been a comfort to me.'

Charles turned to stare at the youth in question. 'You'll be going on to college, then?'

'Er . . . no.' The thin face reddened. 'I thought I'd rather get some business experience.'

'Really?' Charles fiddled with the stem of his glass. 'In which sphere?'

The boy looked anxiously at his mother who cleared her throat delicately before saying, 'Well, we thought – especially now – that he could start in one of the mills?'

'I see. Especially now, of course. And what do you have to offer, Cyril?'

'I beg . . . I beg your pardon?'

'If I'm to employ you, what will you do for me?'

'I . . . er . . . well . . . '

'He could learn,' said Alice with forced brightness.

'Right.' Charles pushed his chair back and stretched long legs. 'If this were an interview, Cyril, you'd never get on the shortlist. Do you think I owe you a living because you're my brother's son?'

'No! I . . . that is . . . my mother . . . '

'Ah yes. Your mother.' He looked directly at her. 'After my money, are you?'

'Well! What a terrible thing to say! Cyril has the right to a position – he would have had the right without this terrible accident.'

'Ah yes. But this makes Cyril's road a lot clearer, doesn't it?

265

You've amazed me over the years, Alice. Coming here to see Amelia when the money ran out, when your husband ran out – coming to see what you could get. For years we kept you because you were Harold's wife, but when you married that Fenner, our obligation ceased.'

'There's still Cyril,' she snapped, teeth bared now. 'He is the only Swainbank left.'

'I'm not dead yet, Alice.' His tone was very quiet. 'When did you last come to see "poor Amelia" who has been such a wonderful sister – I'm using your words now. When did you last visit? She's been bedridden for months and what consideration have you shown for the woman who pleaded for you, gave you money, paid your bills? None!' He clicked his fingers sharply. 'None at all, because you knew you didn't stand to gain. I stopped her giving you money. You've a husband – let him keep you! But now, the world's your oyster, isn't it? You've only to see Amelia in her grave quickly followed by me, of course, then it's all yours, lock, stock and mill chimneys. Clever. Just one word of warning, though. I'll not be shuffling off just yet and although Amelia can have no more children, the mills and any monies from them will be otherwise bequeathed!'

'What?' Her mouth fell open.

'That took the wind out of your sails, Alice Fenner. Look. I don't like you, I don't like your husband and this son of yours is about as much use as a pint of pee on a volcanic eruption!'

She rose from the table, a hand to her breast. 'There is no need for vulgarity!'

'What's the matter, lass? Hasn't little Cyril heard any language yet? Did he get to seventeen and never a cross word?'

She steadied herself against the table. 'He is the next in line! Whatever you put in your will is of no importance. We shall contest it. Cyril's claim will not be denied. And I repeat, there is no necessity for common and vulgar behaviour . . . '

'Really?' he roared, jumping to his feet, taking the cloth and everything that occupied the table with him. He flung the lot across the room, tureens, plates, glasses, cutlery.

'There's a definite necessity for me to tell you to get out! Get out and stay out!'

'Wait till I tell Amelia of your crass behaviour—'

'You'll tell her nothing! She's looked after you for long enough. Go near my sick wife and I'll have you sued for . . . for harassment!'

Cyril, covered in vegetables of various denominations and colours, stood foolishly against the wall, dabbing at his stained clothing with a napkin. Charles experienced a sudden fierce desire to laugh, but he checked it, knowing only too well that he was on the verge of hysteria. But the pathetic lad looked so ridiculous wearing asparagus and peas . . . Charles turned abruptly and faced the window. 'Go and pack your bags, Alice Fenner. We have no need of you here.'

'But I only . . .'

'You only wanted to get Cyril's feet under my table. My table, Alice. Never forget that. Now go, there's been enough upset for one day.' Yes, he'd buried his sons as well as smashing a vase and half the Crown Derby, hadn't he? But he wanted this pair out of the house as quickly as possible, even if he had to throw them out. He glanced over his shoulder and saw Emmie hovering in the doorway. 'It's all right, Emmie. Just another accident.'

Alice and Cyril continued to linger. 'You still here?' shouted Charles.

Alice bristled. '*Pas devant la domestique!*' she muttered.

'I'll say what I like in front of whoever I choose in my own house! She's my bloody maid, isn't she? Emmie, who pays your wages? Go on, tell her.'

'You do, Mr Swainbank.'

'See?' he bellowed. 'My house, my servants, my bloody mills! Emmie?'

'Yes, sir?'

'Go and stand outside my wife's door. This woman is not to see Mrs Swainbank. Understand?'

'Right, sir.' Emmie fled gratefully from the room.

'You are uncouth, Charles Swainbank. I've always thought so. Your father was rough and ready too, no education, few

267

manners . . . ' It was obvious that Alice's carefully constructed facade was slipping.

'I know all about that!' roared the furious Charles. 'Consider my beginnings, eh? My great-grandfather used to spread his lengths on the moors for sun-bleaching. Poor stock, you see. No breeding, not like your lot. Only who's got the whip-hand now? I have. So put that in your pipe, Missus. And don't come back here unless you get a written invitation. I reckon you're more likely to get asked to take tea with King George. Now bugger off, the pair of you!'

Cyril led his mother to the door. She turned, her features rearranged to demonstrate a semblance of grief and deep hurt. 'I hope you never need me, Charles. And Amelia is sure to discover that you intend to cut poor Cyril off without a penny.' She straightened her shoulders. 'Still, I'm sure the legal system will attend to the justice of this matter.'

'Oh take him home and get him cleaned up! If you boil that jacket, you'll get soup enough for a week!'

He stormed out through the French windows and began to pace about the small courtyard. Good God, he'd sell up, he would indeed! Sell up and take Amelia on a long cruise or to Switzerland where she might last a bit longer. He'd spend every penny, he would that! Or perhaps he could give it away now, hand it over to widows and orphans because it was too late for Amelia. Aye, no amount of money would help her now. But he must get rid of it, make sure that grasping bitch and her whelp didn't get their sticky paws on it!

How was he managing to think like this and his boys barely cold? He stopped in his tracks. Because he was a business-man, that was how and why. He'd been raised for it, weaned on it, trained for it. And business meant responsibility come what may.

He had debts. Debts to those who had travelled towards work all those years ago, many of them covering miles unshod and dressed in rags and tatters, the forefathers of today's workforce. Debts to his own ancestors who had lifted the trade out of the cottage and into the spinning and weaving sheds. Morally, emotionally and actually, Charles was caught in a cotton web whose fibres must hold, must remain intact because so many people hung from those delicate threads.

No, he couldn't throw all that away. And he couldn't leave a portion, let alone all of it, to the Fenners. Apart from anything else, if Cyril's stepfather got wind of the possibilities, he'd be back quick as a flash from whichever racecourse or gambling den he was currently haunting. No, he'd sooner leave it to the workers, give the ones who toiled a chance of a share or two in a back pocket, a vested interest in what they sweated for. Or was that John talking, softening his dad's brain from beyond the grave?

He sighed, hands folded across his chest as he surveyed his property, vast lawns bordered by long and perfectly sculpted hedges, a small lake, a glen full of trees and shrubs left deliberately wild when the boys were children, somewhere for them to play. There had to be a meaning to all this! It couldn't just end, fizzle out like a candle with all the wax used up! Amelia would die soon. Could he start again after her, take a new wife, rear more sons? The thought sickened him; the idea that he might entertain such a concept sickened him even further. No. He might be a young man by most standards, but at forty, he knew he had not the stomach to begin again, turn to a clean page and rewrite the whole thing. Better to give the lot to charity than to make more children and worry about their survival.

He marched round to the back of the house where Perkins continued to assault the car.

'You'll have all the paint off her, man. Come on now, leave it alone.'

'Aye.' Perkins straightened from his labours. 'It were just summat to clear me mind, sir.'

'Yes, I know what you mean. I've done a bit of mind-clearing myself this morning.'

'And a bit of table-clearing and all, sir. From what I've heard, like.'

Charles managed a tight smile. Perkins was one of the few he could really trust, a man he'd depend on for his life if necessary. 'Have they gone?' he asked.

'They're on their way. Only she's demanding a lift back to Preston. Will I take them?'

'I suppose so. After all, she brought enough luggage for a long stay, didn't she? Use the Singer – I'll drive myself today.'

'Nay.' Perkins took a step forward. 'You're never going to business, sir? Not today. I reckon they'll manage without you this once.'

For answer, Charles opened the door of the car. 'I'll have to see that those who attended the funeral don't get penalized—'

'Use the phone!'

'No. It must be done personally. It touched me deeply, that they would come out to the cemetery and risk losing pay. Devotion must always be rewarded, Perkins.'

The man swallowed audibly. 'They were grand lads, sir, and everybody knew it. A credit to you and the Missus. Whatever will we do without them, Mr Swainbank?'

'I don't know. And that's the truth, I really don't. I keep expecting to see them running about the tennis court or playing cricket on the lawn. It's so damned quiet, isn't it? No, I'm not sure what we'll do. But I'll sort something out – for the mills, I mean. For us, for the way we feel, I can do nothing.'

He drove quickly down country lanes, not fully sure where he was going. Yet somewhere inside himself, he knew his destination. Thoughts only half-formed were taking root in his mind, seedlings too young to flourish just yet. Number three mill. He left his car in the cobbled yard and made his way to the manager's office on the first floor. Tom Bishop looked up in surprise as he entered.

'All right, Tom?'

'Er . . . fine, Mr Swainbank. Sit down here.' He cleared some samples from a chair. 'Didn't expect to see you, not today.' When no answer was forthcoming, he decided to switch to business matters. Happen the boss needed his mind shifting off things. 'Good batch in last week, best raw we've had in months, it's carding up a treat.'

'Yes.' Charles stroked his chin thoughtfully. 'Nice little

mill, this. Always has been my favourite. I expect you're proud of all this refurbishment?'

'Oh aye. And they're fighting to get taken on here with the conditions and all. Very attractive compared to most.'

'Master John had a deal to do with that, Tom. Remember him eating here the day we opened the canteen? Then he went out there and worked in every bit of the mill, carding and winding all day. He was over the moon when he saw the new machines spread out with space between. And look how he took to ring-spinning.'

'Yes. Like a duck to water, eh? We all remember, we do that.'

Charles gazed through the window at the large Swainbank sign painted vertically on a chimney. 'There's nothing will bring them back, Tom. Thanks for coming this morning – thank your wife too.'

'Aw, it was only because we wanted to come. Them lads meant a lot to us. I keep thinking back to when they were little and up to mischief, pinching tubes for guns and getting in a right tear for messing in the skips. I clouted the pair of them many a time—'

'Only because I told you to, Tom. They had to learn—'

'Aye.'

Learn what? For what reason? Both men stared at the floor.

'Give everybody ten per cent bonus. Every last one of them. Those who attended the burial are to have no stoppages. Even if they failed to return . . . ' Charles cleared his throat. 'The people who remained here and kept the wheels moving are to be similarly treated. Ten per cent all round. Management included.'

'Right. Thank you, Mr Swainbank.'

'Let the other mills know, will you?' He shifted uneasily. 'Tell me – does Ma Maguire still work here?'

'Ma Maguire?' He shook his head sadly. 'No, more's the pity. We used to move her about between all three mills, she was a good teacher for apprentices. One of the best weavers I've ever met, that one. Had a feel for the cloth, you see. Like seeing a bit of poetry, it was, looking at one of her lengths – if

271

that doesn't sound too daft, like. Nimble-fingered and sharp-mouthed was our Ma. Mind, we never heard her in the sheds with the machines going. Thankful for small mercies, eh?'

Charles placed his hat on the desk. 'Where is she now?' he asked carefully. 'I'm taking an interest because she looked after my father for years, something of a herbalist—'

'Oh aye, she's as good as most doctors. Only she's taken a stroke by all accounts. Oh – a couple of months ago, it was. Her daughter-in-law came up and told us.'

'Molly?'

'That's right, I believe she is called Molly.'

'She worked for us as a housemaid, left to marry Ma Maguire's son.' He cleared his throat. 'How are they all faring, then?'

'Not sure. There's four kiddies, I think. I dare say Ma will come back to work given half a chance, only I don't know how the stroke's left her. They're still living in the same place near Leatherbarrow's mill, corner of Delia Street. Come to think, he likely owns their house.'

'I see.' Charles rose and picked up his hat. 'I'll not be calling on the other managers today, Tom. They'll under-stand why. Just pass on my messages, will you?'

'I will.'

Tom stood at the window and watched the boss driving away. This had been one of the few times he'd known Swainbank to ask about a worker. Mind, if she'd looked after his dad, it was understandable. Though rumour had it that old Richard had wanted a bit more out of Ma, not just her medicines, but that was all in the past now. Poor Charlie was likely just reminiscing, looking back over better days.

Charles drove around aimlessly for an hour or more, up and down Bradshawgate and Deansgate, past the Town Hall, over Trinity Street bridge, along Manchester Road and back again.

Eventually, inevitably, he found himself on School Hill, the car parked outside Leatherbarrow's which formed the top of a T across the end of Delia Street. He stared for a long time at the corner house until he noticed four children making their way along the pavement.

The smallest, a girl, was a pretty little thing with bouncing yellow curls. A slightly older boy, darker in colouring, walked by her side, clogs sparking as he scraped the flags.

Behind these two came the others, the twins. Even from a distance of thirty yards or more, Charles could see that the boy was his, the same brown hair and near-black eyes. The girl was unbelievably beautiful, golden-haired and with lighter eyes of a shade he could not determine from so far away. Long before they reached the door and turned the knob, thereby confirming it all, Charles knew that these were his children.

A tremendous surge of hope filled his chest, only to be squashed immediately by the mental images of John and Peter whom he felt he was betraying by his very presence here. He started the car and shot away at speed, leaving the four children gaping after him from the front of their house.

He slept badly that night, tossing and turning in the bed, his mind a tangle of confusing and often conflicting thoughts. Awake, he considered John and Peter, the brevity of their lives, the abruptness of their departure. Asleep, he dreamed of a dark-eyed boy and an incredibly attractive girl, flesh of his flesh, Swainbank blood in their veins. He woke with a start, sweat pouring down his face. What where they like? Who were they like?

A nightmare followed, Rivington Pike, laughing eyes that matched the green of surrounding fields, all that tumbling and bumping down, down to the bottom, down to the bed where she did not struggle. Molly. Seventeen, too young to know. His daughter was just two years younger than Molly had been. Would some man do the same to her . . . ?

'No!' He found himself standing beside the bed, his legs shaking so badly that he tumbled to the floor, the loud exclamation still echoing round the room. He was their father. The 'Maguire' twins had been supported all along by Swainbank money. Surely, that would be proof enough?

He crawled on hands and knees to the window. The slow seconds of dawn ticked by. Did he want to be their father? What would it do to Amelia if she discovered that he had two illegitimate children? Could he announce his claim to this boy and girl, shout it from the rooftops of a town which, though large, was the size of a village when it came to gossip?

So many people to hurt. And the twins were on the list, right at the top. What must he do?

Instinct prevailed in the end, instinct that was blind and deaf to reason and common sense.

He rose at eight and took breakfast in his room. After a bath and a shave, he picked up the telephone and spoke first to his lawyer, then to a man of dubious background, a person who had helped him more than once to spy on rival concerns.

By ten o'clock, Charles sat in his solicitor's office, hearing, though hardly willing to listen, as Philip Charnock ranted and raved.

'Bloody madness,' he was saying now. 'Why don't you think about it, Charlie? You buried your sons only yesterday – can't you see you're still in shock? This is absolute and utter lunacy . . . '

'They're my children.' There was a stubborn note in his voice.

'Ah yes – now that it suits you. Until today, you haven't shown the slightest interest in them. For all you knew, they might have been at the other end of the world starving to death. Your lack of interest would not look good in court—'

'Stop being judgemental. They have not been starving, Philip. The whole family's been kept.'

Philip Charnock walked round the desk and sat on its edge, studying his friend closely. 'Have you had any sleep?'

'Not much. But that's hardly the issue—'

'Go home. Have a rest, then think about all this, please.'

'No. I want to see what they're made of, these two. How old are they now? Precisely, I mean?'

'Fifteen in a few weeks. Look, Charlie. I'm going to be straight with you. Until now, the arrangement this firm made between your father and the Maguires' solicitor has not been significant, but if you are intent on pursuing this course of action, then I must warn you that there is a great deal more to it than meets the eye.'

274

'Really? Well fire away, I've got all day.'

'It's complicated. You were never put fully in the picture. There was no need to—'

'Come on! Stop beating about the bush, for goodness sake!'

'All right then! But keep your hair on! Now, my dealings with the actual family amount to nil. I communicate from time to time with Barton – he's Ma Maguire's representative, but everything is done on an impersonal basis, all very formal and legal. I must tell you now that Molly Maguire is not aware of your involvement. The children are, to all intents and purposes, Patrick Maguire's.'

'What? That buffoon? Have you seen my children?'

'No, I haven't.'

'Or him? Have you seen him?'

'No. Listen to me, Charlie. All four children are properly registered as Maguires.'

'Well, two of them are Swainbanks.'

The lawyer sighed deeply. 'You'd have a job to prove that.'

Charles laughed, a humourless sound that made his friend shiver. 'Let her face me in court and say those twins are not mine! Let her swear that my family has not supported them—'

'As far as she is concerned, they have received no support.'

Seconds passed. 'What?' yelled Charles. 'She thinks I just left her to cope . . . that my father didn't pay . . . did nobody tell her? And where's the bloody money gone?'

'Straight to Mrs Maguire – the grandmother. Apparently, she agreed to allow her son to marry the housemaid in exchange for certain securities. The mother of the twins is completely unaware of all this. As far as the younger Mrs Maguire is concerned, nobody but herself knows that the children are not her husband's.'

Charles shook his head slowly. 'No. Molly will be aware. Any discerning person can see that those two are not Maguires. She must see my face every time . . . The boy in particular looks so much like me.' He paused. 'I wonder what she's thinking now? Does she realize that I might be looking for them?'

'Probably not. She'll believe that you, along with the rest of the world, have been fooled into thinking the children were Patrick's. If you had paid maintenance directly to her, if you'd admitted paternity, then you might have had a case.'

'But I do have a case! All that money and the property deeds too – I wouldn't be giving those away to just anyone!'

'Charlie, the old girl has kept her side of the bargain. When the shops are turned over to her as the twins' financial guardian, she will say she's had a windfall from a distant branch of her family in Ireland. This was all agreed with your father. Nothing was ever said about you claiming the twins.'

'They are mine!' His face darkened with anger. 'I've a lot to offer.'

'Not to them, Charlie. They wouldn't understand your life, wouldn't want it. The working class has its own pride, you know. They've no time for velvet drapes and crystal chandeliers. If you tried to claim those children, it would be like . . . like taking a polar bear and putting it to live in the tropics. You can't do it, Charlie. You simply can't—'

'We'll see.' Charles rose and picked up his hat and driving gloves.

'Don't do anything foolish, I beg you . . . '

'I've only done one foolish thing in my life, Philip. And even that could turn out to be a bonus. We shall see.'

'Charlie . . . ' But he was gone.

That night, a shabby figure in a black overcoat and with a hat pulled well over the eyes visited Charles. They sat in the conservatory, well out of reach of servants' inquisitive ears.

'Well?' asked Charles. 'And take that damn fool hat off, Lucas. You're not following some gangster through the East End now!'

The man placed the offending item on the floor.

'Well? Out with it. I'm told you're so clever you could even find out what the PM says in his sleep if the price was right. Surely the assignment was not too much for you?'

The visitor took a notebook from his pocket. 'Joseph Arthur Maguire,' he read. 'Born July 1922. Address, 34 Delia Street – a house consisting of two downstairs rooms plus scullery, an outside lavatory of the tippler variety, a small wash-house and three upstairs rooms. The house is well-kept. Let me see – one of twins, the other's a girl, Janet Edith. Local Catholic school, due to leave next month. Joseph's work record is fair, the girl's is excellent. Good attendance. Healthy and robust according to my sources and on personal observation I found them both to have strong limbs, no sign of rickets or poor nourishment. The girl is exceptionally pretty.'

'You spoke to them?'

'To him, yes. She walked off, said she hadn't to talk to strangers. But the boy is made of sterner stuff, Mr Swainbank. Quite a character, in fact.'

Charles smiled grimly. 'Oh yes? In what way?'

'Very amusing, sir, an inventive chap. He's already attempted several small business ventures . . . but I won't bore you with anecdotes.'

'Tell me what makes you grin.'

The man rearranged his features. 'The most amusing was a vegetable round. He and a couple of other boys bought a metal bin which they placed on a cart, then a few potato peelers and a stone of spuds. They peeled the things and flogged them around School Hill. Joseph decided to branch out into carrots and swedes, but after finding the market to be poor, he reverted to potatoes until business collapsed.'

'I see. What caused the collapse?'

The mouth twitched. 'Well, the cart fell to bits and his colleagues lost interest. He's never forgiven them and swears the enterprise was sabotaged. As I said, quite a character.'

'It would seem so. Anything else?'

'He's currently a pawnbroker's runner, bringing in pledges for customers who want to save face. The idea is to put a bit by in the Post Office, though he's highly offended because his sister won't join him in the venture.'

'Why won't she?'

'Bit of a socialist, I'd say. Won't take tips, doesn't like the idea of living off ill-gotten gains. She seems to have some high-faluting principles.'

They were just like Peter and John! One with a business head, the other with causes to fight for!

'Anyway, it seems that Joseph – he's usually called Joey, by the way – is going into engineering while Janet's for the mill.'

'Really? No mention of a shop or two in the town?'

'None.'

Ah well, perhaps Ma hadn't broken the news yet, the news about her Irish legacy. If she'd suffered a stroke, then she might not be well enough to tell them what was about to happen. And if Molly didn't know . . . how were they going to find out?

'The boy is worried about his mother, says she seems to have had something on her mind these last couple of weeks.'

Oh Molly, Molly! 'He's no idea of what she's worrying about?'

'Apparently not. Though her husband is terminally ill.'

Charles sat bolt upright. 'Are you sure?'

The man tapped the side of his nose. 'I didn't get that from the lad, Mr Swainbank. Medical records—'

'But how do you get access to—'

'Don't ask, sir. I've seen it in black and white. What can't speak can't lie. So perhaps Mrs Maguire is concerned for her husband's health.'

'What's the matter with him?'

'Caught bovine TB years ago. Mind, from the sound of him, his liver will go before the rest of him.'

'Poor chap. He's worked for me. When he's sober, the man's a damned good driver. I know the rest, I think. Ma Maguire with her stroke, boss of the street, herbalist and midwife.'

'Lost her power of speech, but it's returning.' The man hesitated. 'This boy . . . he's all right, I suppose. But there's a streak in him. I reckon he'd sell his own granny for a small consideration. His father he'd give away, but that may be understandable. Paddy sounds about as straight as a nine-bob note, bit of a police record for drunken behaviour. But Joey's . . . hard for his age. He loves his mother, worships his twin sister, but I reckon the rest of us could go to the devil and he'd not notice.'

'Ambitious?'

'Definitely.'

Charles paid the man off, shaking his head as he watched the almost comically discreet exit with the hat back in place. But he had his uses, did old Lucas.

He sat up pondering well into the night. He had relatives, that was certain. They might not be as well-born as Cyril, but they sounded a far better gamble. For now, Charles would do nothing but watch and wait. Poor Amelia would soon be too far gone to care what was happening outside her own bedroom. And if Paddy Maguire was dying too . . . What a terrible way to think! But was there a real alternative?

When he eventually got to bed, he slept well. John would have approved of this new-born scheme, he felt that in his bones. As for the niceties and proprieties – well, time would surely show the way, fill in the massive gaps, help Charles to do what was right. Yes, whatever Philip Charnock's opinion, he could help that family.

And in helping them, he might just solve some of his own problems too.

Chapter 8

Yorick was also known as Alas-poor. This second naming had been performed by no less a person than Miss Sarah Leason, who, during her more poetical phases, had a distinct leaning towards the great English bard, whom she was given to misquoting when chiding inferior beings.

Yorick was an inferior being. It was in his nature to be inferior and he had no ambitions with regard to improvements or elevations in status. It suited him well enough to act as doormat, draught excluder, foot warmer and fetcher of half-chewed slippers. These latter items were a constant reminder of his low calibre, for he was the one who had masticated the nice fluffy bits into pulp while getting rid of his puppy teeth. At sixteen weeks of age, Yorick was already an old dog, a wise dog with an eye to a full plate and an ear ever cocked for Ma's call.

She looked fondly at him now, recognizing how much they had both changed since his arrival just a couple of weeks ago. Although the dog was far from a trier and a long way from industrious, he had altered in spite of himself, had become calm because he was in the company of an old lady. So they had both improved, both by accident. He because he was a little older, she because the thing in her head was mending itself – and Yorick had had a lot to do with that. Something about the way he just sat and existed had encouraged her, while his devotion was touching and very comforting. None of her faculties had been taken permanently. All along, she'd been able to think and calculate clearly once she'd got the words sorted out in her mind. And now she could almost walk unaided, while her speech improved daily.

'Stop chew . . . ing your tail. It's like a fea . . . ther duster al . . . ready.'

She picked up the wooden walking frame that Paddy and Miss Leason had thrown together in the wash-house, a rough item constructed from the remnants of a wrecked chair and a snapped broom handle. With grim purpose dripping from every pore, she dragged herself across the room, bed to window, window to bed, the dog at her heels each time she turned. If she hadn't picked up on yesterday's performance, then Sarah Leason would raise the roof again. It was terrible. She was so bossy – why, she'd get anybody's back up, would Sarah. Ma grinned ruefully. Perhaps she was getting some of her own back, some of the stuff she herself had dished out over the years.

Janet put her head round the door. 'Is he ready for his walk, Gran?' There was little enthusiasm in her tone. Taking Alaspoor Yorick for a walk was a bit like leading an innocent man to the gallows, all pulling and persuading and sad eyes. And when he went on sit-down strike, especially in the middle of the road, life could get a bit unusual to say the least.

'You want to ta . . . ke him?'

'Not really. Nobody in their right mind would want to be seen out with him. Miss Leason says he's got a complex, something to do with not being loved. And he's so ugly!'

'I lo . . . ve him. He's a good do . . . g.'

Janet came in and flung herself on to the bed. 'I've been trying to work out what he is, Gran. I reckon his tail's spaniel, only thinned out a bit. The legs are definitely greyhound, but those feet are more St Bernard. His in-between bits don't seem to have made their mind up yet, but for now he's a Spangreynard. Do you think we've invented a new breed?'

'Sh . . . ush. He's sensi . . . tive. Don't up . . . set him.'

'Upset him? I can't get through to him! He sat at the edge of Butler's rec yesterday and I couldn't budge him. It took four of us at the finish, one leg each. Come on, then,' she sighed. 'Let's get it over with. Show me up again and I'll strangle you with the lead.'

She pulled him out of the room while Gran just stood there laughing.

It wasn't an easy journey, because she had decided to kill

two birds with one stone and return Miss Leason's property at the same time. So she struggled along with bag, bucket and reluctant animal until she reached the corner of Lever Lane. Here she stopped and placed Miss Leason's things on the pavement. It was time to come to grips with Yorick.

'Why can't you be nice? Other dogs don't need pulling along, because they like walkies. Walkies are a good thing. Look at me when I'm talking to you!'

Yorick had never gone a bundle on eye contact. Ma he could cope with, but these younger ones with so much life in their faces terrified him. He wagged his tail weakly, realizing that as he was off his home patch, he had better co-operate before he got abandoned in unfamiliar territory. With this awesome possibility in mind, he picked up the bag as a gesture of good will. If he made himself useful, then he might get home in one piece.

Janet patted his head. 'Good dog. I reckon we might make something of you yet.'

He grinned widely and the bag fell to the floor. Life was a very confusing thing. Whatever he did was wrong some-how, because she now snatched up the bag and dragged him away with his rear scraping painfully along the pavement. Resignedly, he raised his hind quarters and walked. It was easier in the end to take the line of least resistance.

As they neared Miss Leason's house, they met Joey who was pushing a heavily loaded handcart, furniture piled high and fastened on with strings and ropes. 'House clearance,' he breathed, pausing to greet his sister.

'Dog,' she answered, jerking a thumb towards her own burden. 'Who are you clearing out?'

'Somebody called Mathieson, died last week, next door neighbour of Witchie Leason's. Seems the old girl had no family, so Mr Goldberg's selling her furniture off for charity. Soft bugger, he is. She left some sort of message with him about orphans, so he's giving it all to a children's home.'

'Fair enough.' She cast an eye over the cart. 'That looks better than your pram, doesn't it?'

Things had got a bit strained between Janet and Joey lately, especially after she'd refused outright to help him with the pawnie's round. Course, Joey was managing fine on his own, didn't need her to fetch and carry now he'd got that big pram. In a way, she could only admire him. Not many lads going on fifteen would dare be seen pushing a pram full of pledges round twice a week. He'd taken a fair bit of stick for it from the other boys, but he'd sorted them out, threatened them with a clouting if they didn't leave off. So they'd left off. Nobody tackled Joey Maguire lightly.

'Mr Goldberg says I can use the handcart whenever I want, so I'll get rid of the pram, clean it up, see if anybody wants it.'

She smiled. Nothing would ever go to waste, not with Joey, not if it could put a penny or two in his back pocket.

'He says this used to be Gran's cart. She sold it to him years ago after she stopped going round the streets with her medicines.'

'Family heirloom, then?' She tugged at the dog's lead as he began to show a meagre interest in a passing cat.

'Suppose so. Where are you off to?'

'Just taking Miss Leason's things back. I know she comes round nearly every day, but she always forgets them. I reckon they might be a bit heavy for her.'

He laughed. 'Heavy? For her? She could raise the Titanic single-handed, that one. Anyway, why bother giving them back? She'll never miss them.'

'Because they're hers, Joey.'

'You're daft, you are. Why worry over a filthy old biddy like her, eh? You're never going in her house? It's crawling, covered in muck. I'll bet there's rats and mice as well as cockroaches in there climbing the walls. Happen she catches them and uses them in her spells at midnight, rats' eyes and ground-up spiders all minced in a pot with bits of toad and castor oil.'

She rounded on him, not for the first time lately. 'Shut up, you! They used to say our Granny was a witch and she wasn't! It's cruel, that sort of talk, no need for it! All you care about is money and where you can get it, who you can take it from next. Oh . . . go and push your pram round, leave me in peace!'

He looked down at his clogs, a frown creasing the tanned forehead. 'Sometimes I think you hate me, Janet.'

'That's rubbish! You talk a lot of that lately, Joey Maguire! I don't hate anybody. I'm not the one who wishes me own dad dead and me granny out of the road!' She took a deep breath after this outburst. 'I've told you before, it's not easy to like you at times, but I don't hate you.'

He sighed loudly. 'Do you want me to take old Alas-poor home? He can sit on top of this tallboy, king of the castle. I've got to pass the end of our street anyway.'

'No, it's all right.' She knew he was trying to be nice, trying to get round her. 'I'm going to train him. If it's the last thing I do, Joey, I'll have this lunatic walking in a straight line on all four feet like a proper dog.'

'I wouldn't lay odds on it, Jan.'

'We'll see.' She gave him an appeasing smile, then continued along to Miss Leason's. It was awful. Filthy windows, cracked and peeling paintwork, gutters hanging at impossible angles from the roof's edge, dirty lace curtains all full of holes where the cats had caught them.

Cats. She glanced down at her passive companion. He looked angelic enough in a sombre sort of way, but you never could tell with dogs and cats. So she tied him to the stone gatepost.

After knocking several times without getting a response, Janet pushed against the door. Most people left their doors on the latch when they went out. Rent money, insurance, milk and coal payments would remain lined up on a dresser or a table, each resting on the appropriate book or bill slip in readiness for various callers who were trusted to take only what was owed to them.

The door swung open, thirsty hinges screaming for a drop of oil. Janet stepped into the vestibule, gagging immediately as the smell of the place filled her nostrils. And it was a lovely house, she could see that in spite of the dirt. Once her stomach had settled, she found herself opening the interior door. Oh, it was grand, that vestibule, like something you might find in a real posh house up Chorley Road. Their house in Delia Street had the front door in the living room, just a single stride off the pavement. But this was grand. The floor had black and white tiles in a pleasant pattern, all squares and diamonds. Well, it was supposed to be black and white, only the white bits were grey and the whole area was covered in a sort of greasy skin.

This inner door, which led into the hall proper, had Janet fascinated. The top half was glass, but you couldn't see through it, partly because it was filthy, but mostly because the glazing was patterned and had leaded bits round the edges, all red and blue crinkly glass. She closed this door, noting that the handle was of tarnished brass, then rubbed at a red patch and stared at the rosy world outside, all bright pink through the open outer entrance. Even Yorick managed to look cheerful with his dull yellowish hair coloured in. It was beautiful, like something out of a story, a piece of magic right here in Miss Leason's house. She longed to clean it up properly so that she might enjoy the distorted and tinted view, but she was keenly aware of being an intruder, so she walked further into the wide hall.

'Miss Leason? Hello? Anybody in?'

When no answer came, she began to look around for a place where she could leave the bucket and the bag. The smell didn't seem so bad now. Happen you got used to it after a while, she thought. But her breath was taken by what she found in the hall, a veritable treasure-trove of books piled floor to halfway up the walls on both sides. They smelled old and mouldy, as if they'd been stored for ever and some of the dirtier piles were festooned with garlands of cobweb on the tops. Cats crawled in and out of boxes, jumping from atlas to encyclopedia, from Austen to Dickens. Shakespeare's works were almost hidden beneath the latest litter of kittens, the mother cat hissing at Janet from behind the crate containing her family and a full collection of plays.

After spitting back at the harassed cat, Janet examined some of these volumes before walking through to the back living room. The condition of this was so bad that she had to steel herself before stepping inside. There was cat-soil on newspaper, fire-ash raked out well beyond the hearth's boundary, a table covered in rotting food and dirty clothing. And there were cats and books everywhere, messes piled upon messes.

Instinctively, Janet set to work on the ashes, using the bucket to carry the debris out through the cluttered scullery and into the yard. After five trips, she was exhausted, but the grate was empty. She placed bag and bucket under the table, screwed up the worst of the decaying foodstuff into an old paper bag and dumped it in the ashpit down the yard.

Although her fingers itched to tidy the rest of the room, she forced herself not to begin. For one thing, she wouldn't really know where to start and for another, Miss Leason might well take umbrage at such high-handed behaviour. Perhaps the old lady liked living in a mess, happen that was how she wanted it. And people had a right to live how they pleased. Yet Janet felt that Miss Leason really didn't know how to take care of herself, hadn't had the right education for it. After all, she'd likely been waited on right up to her mam and dad dying, wouldn't know the first thing about lifting a hand to housework.

Anyway, something had been achieved, because a fire would be wanted sooner or later and nothing could have got burning in that choked-up range. It was posh too, the fireplace, moulded patterns on the oven door and little plaques set into the surround, all flowers and leaves on them. With a bit of leading on the black bits, it would be really pretty, welcoming and homely on a cold night.

Just as she was about to leave the room, Janet noticed that a box beneath the table had been overturned, probably by herself as she pushed the bucket under out of harm's way. Well, there was no point in adding to the mess – she'd better stand it up before she left. Her heart almost stopped when she picked up the container, because it was stuffed to the brim with money – notes and coins packed in any old way. She gathered up the scattered contents and piled them back inside, shoving the money well down so that it would not spill again. There must be hundreds – thousands even!

When the rotting cardboard treasure chest had been

replaced, she straightened, her mind still not fully capable of taking in what she had just seen. All that money and the door not locked? She shivered. There it stood under the table, 'Crawford Biscuits' fading on the side, a dozen or so five pound notes sticking out of the seams where the sides were giving way. Why? Why did Miss Leason keep all that money here when it should be in the Post Office? This wasn't safe – it wasn't right!

She stepped back into the hall, realizing that the floor in here was parquet, zig-zag blocks of wood covered in fluff and grease-spots. 'Oh dear,' she muttered. 'What a shame! What a blinking stupid shame!' The front room likely had the same floor – it would look lovely washed and sanded down then a bit of polish on it. Aye, this was a posh house, flags at the back and wooden floors at the front just like the rich folk had. And Miss Leason was rich, wasn't she? Oh yes, she could afford to get this house set to rights if only she'd put her mind to it. 'For God's sake!' Janet exclaimed now to the surprised mother cat. 'Even if she's a miser, soap and water costs nowt. And I'd have you lot cleared out for a kick-off!' Janet was not a cat person. Was she a dog person? She raised her eyes to heaven before going outside to collect her charge.

Yorick greeted her joyfully as she untied him and led him out to the pavement. He had just suffered ten minutes of sheer hell. Surely he wasn't being brought back here to all those sharp claws, all that flying fur? Gratitude as deep as this must be demonstrated, so he walked nicely by Janet's side, keeping pace, maintaining a satisfactory distance to heel. She grinned at him, somehow understanding how he felt. 'Good boy,' she said.

He woofed politely. They walked homeward and dinner-ward, Yorick pausing just once, very apologetically, to leave a marker on a lamp post. After all, if he should ever pass this way again, he'd be wanting his bearings. And anyway, being a 'good dog' made him feel all warm inside, like after finishing Ma's porridge in a morning. They turned into Delia Street and he held up head and tail with something approaching pride. It promised to be not a bad life after all.

*   *   *

Sarah Leason, after pummelling Ma's leg and arm in much the same way as she might have massaged a healing horse, pushed the hair from her own damp face and helped Ma into her chair by the window. 'Great show,' she said brightly. 'Have you up and running in no time now.'

'Good.'

'Right. Now say "a pound of onions, please." '

'A pou . . . nd of oni . . . ons please.'

'Again!'

The elocution lesson continued for another five minutes, then Sarah pulled an envelope from her pocket. 'This was given to me a few weeks ago by my next door neighbour, a Mrs Mathieson. Pleasant woman, made good scones and had an affection for cats. Died last Thursday, unfortunately. Used to be housekeeper up at Briars Hall. Remember her? Something to do with feet?'

Ma nodded. So old Cissie had gone at last.

'Anyway, she instructed me to pass this message on to you in the event of her death.'

'I don't re . . . ad.'

'Yes. I'm aware of that. There was a verbal message too, for you to trust me to open this and tell you its contents. But if you'd rather someone else . . . ?'

'No.' Ma studied Sarah Leason. A rough and ready soul, a lady deep down, kind, dependable, definitely not a gossip. 'You do it.'

'Sure?'

Ma jerked her head quickly. 'Where . . .'s Molly?'

'Shopping.'

'Read it.'

Sarah tore at the envelope and skimmed the contents quickly.

Dear Ma,

You was always good to me over me feet and I have not forgot. I was there the nite of all the bother only I never dared say. The boss pays the rent here and I have not got nowere else to go to. So I will be in the grave when you get this Ma.

288

Molly come in dirty and I told her off. Master Charles come in all mucky to. There were nowt I cud do over it with the job. I never had no mony of me own see. His clothes was spoilt.

Later on he went in her room I saw him come out. It were gone one in the morning. She were crying but I never went neer I am sorry Ma.

She had them twins what I have seen in town I know they are his. It has sat in me mind all the years but I were to scared. Ma beleeve me this is the only thing I can think to do about it. I never said nothing. So nobody else thinks them kids is his.

Pleese find it in your hart to forgive an old woman. But I wood not rest in the grave till you got this letter.

From Cissie.

'I knew they were from a different batch,' muttered Sarah before reading the letter to Ma.

A single tear ran down Ma's cheek. 'P . . . oor Cissie. I knew. I al . . . ways knew. No nee . . . d to tell me. Poor C . . . issie.'

'What? You knew the twins were his?'

'Yes.'

'What about Paddy? Does he know?'

'No.'

'And Molly?'

'Thinks it's her se . . . cret.'

'Well.' Sarah screwed the note into a ball and pushed it deep into her top pocket. 'Best get rid of this, then. What a bloody pickle, eh? Does Swainbank know he has these two children?'

'Yes. He kno . . . ws.'

'Bloody hell fire!'

'Wh . . . at?'

Sarah began to pace about the floor, her black Wellington boots quietly padding to and fro between Ma's chair and the bed. She pulled a hand through stringy grey hair and turned to face her friend, this poor dear woman whose family had made her so welcome in a world that still remained alien. 'His boys are dead, Ma! They were both killed a few weeks ago in a car.

Never did like bloody cars. Rather trust a good horse any time . . . '

'Sa . . . rah?'

'Only found out myself a couple of days ago, didn't realize the significance to you. Now, I'm not saying for one minute that he might start taking an interest in the twins, but fore-warned is forearmed. Are you in pain, Ma?'

'No.' Her face was white and strained. 'Do . . . es Molly know his bo . . . ys are dead?'

Sarah shrugged. 'She said nothing to me. But there again, this is not the sort of thing she'll want to draw attention to, is it? If she's had this secret for fifteen years, she's hardly going to blurt it out at this point. This is complicated. Tell me, does Molly know that Swainbank is aware of the children's exist-ence? Did she tell him she was pregnant?'

'N . . . o. I told him, just me on m . . . y own. But Joey loo . . . ks like him. Mo . . . lly will be fright . . . ened.'

'Surprised Paddy never noticed.'

'Padd . . . ee sees what Padd . . . ee wants to s . . . ee.'

'True.' Sarah continued to pace the room. 'There are several possibilities here. Firstly, Swainbank may not give a damn about Molly's kids. After all, he is supposed to be gentry and I know well enough about that sort of thing with my own stupid family. Secondly, he may decide to have more children – after all, Amelia's not forty, so it's still feasible. And young Harold had a son, you know, so there is a rightful heir.'

'B . . . ut Molly may be worry . . . ing.'

'Indeed she might, but there's nothing we can do about that, Ma. Not without telling her you've known all along. What would that do to her? I really think you should have let her know before now. Before she married Paddy. That might have been easiest all round.'

'I want . . . ed to leave her s . . . ome pride!'

Sarah laughed mirthlessly. 'And what's pride worth, Ma? Is it worth all this agonizing now? I imagine that Molly too is suffering, hypothesizing about the future, wondering whether or no he's seen the twins and recognized his family's features. And here you sit with a burden an ox couldn't shift, filled with guilt because you failed to protect Molly against this eventuality. Yes, it's a rum do. Don't know how to advise you. Except to say best do nothing. Nothing's been done for years, so I don't see the benefit of a change in tactics now. Just hold on and wait. And don't let this impede your progress.'

'No. I sha . . . ll have need of stren . . . gth now. Things to do. Ma . . . ny things to do.'

When Sarah had left, Ma sat for a while as if drawing breath after a race. This was it, then. The time was here and now. The time for her to begin working on a new set of lies, to lay the foundations for a Maguire business. Aye, and built on Swainbank's money too. Should she tell Molly the truth now? No, best to wait like Sarah said, best leave well alone. If only she could get to Mr Barton! The shops would be available any minute for the twins to run. There was so much to explain, like getting Molly to help the children start the shops, like discussing what kind of shops they would be, there was stock to buy, there were deeds to sign.

Was it best to leave it all, forget the shops, give the deeds back? After all, the opening of a couple of shops in Bolton would draw Swainbank's attention, help him remember that he had supported the twins. But if the deeds were returned, that too would bring Molly into his mind, make him wonder . . . It was a maze, an endless maze with no escape from the centre. So she must go ahead. With all of it, just as she'd always planned.

Mr Barton had better stick to the story come the day. She didn't want Molly and the kiddies finding out from him where the money was really coming from. If anybody should ever be forced to give away the truth, then it should certainly be herself.

Janet fell in at the door. 'Where's Miss Leason? Has she been?'

'Been and go . . . ne.'

'She must have gone the back way, 'cos I never saw her. Guess what? He can walk proper, like a real dog.' She patted Yorick's yellow head. 'I've trained him.'

'Good.'

'What's wrong, Gran?'

Ma sighed sadly. If Harold had left a lad, if Charles had managed to forget Molly and the babies . . . Surely it would all work out? There was no cause for concern, none at all. A mill owner had lost his sons, but that should not affect the family of a part-time drover. They were registered Maguires. And a Maguire was not a Swainbank, just as day was never night.

'You all right?' asked Janet again.

'Yes. Up and about soo . . . n.'

'I've got something to tell you, Gran.' Janet dropped to the floor beside Ma's chair and sat hugging her knees. 'I've been in Miss Leason's.'

'Why?'

'I took her bag and bucket back – she was always forgetting them. Anyway, she wasn't in, so I put them under the table.'

'Good.'

'I knocked a big box over. It was full of money, stuffed to the top. I've never seen so much in my life. Why doesn't she put it in the bank, Gran? Me dad always said she had plenty after the sale, but I didn't know she kept it in the house stuck in a biscuit box under the table.'

'She doesn't belie . . . ve in banks. Doesn't believe in any . . . thing except her moo . . . rs and her horses. And her cats.'

'But it's just sitting there! Anybody could take it, anybody!'

Joey, who had left his heavy handcart on the corner while he got a drink of pop from the scullery, pinned his ear to Gran's door and listened hard. In a biscuit box under the table, eh? Christ, what he could do with a nice pile of money.

'Why doesn't she get the house done up, Gran?' Janet was saying now. 'They're posh houses down Lever Lane, there's only a few rented. Hers is the worst, yet she's all that money doing nothing.'

'She's not inter . . . ested,' came Gran's stumbling reply.

Joey stepped back silently. He could find a use for it, he could that! A nice house, a car, some proper boots and clothes – no! People would notice, it would take brains to cope with a windfall like that. He'd emigrate. He'd get boat tickets for America and force Janet to come with him. They could have a ranch – he'd get a horse like the cowboys had in the pictures, go for a drink in the saloon, ride over the mountains and look for gold. Or they might go to New York and make a fortune, or to California and get Janet in the films – she was bonny enough ...

No, he wasn't planning anything. It was just an idea, just a daft idea. Wasn't it?

Nay, what did old Witchie Leason want with a load of cash? She'd likely not long to go for all she was strong. And who would she leave it to? Somebody with a rest farm for old donkeys, a cats' home? He needed it and so did Janet, only she hadn't the sense to see what was staring her in the face, daft lass. How could he get it? He thought about this for a while. Wait till Witchie was asleep, then in and out like a shadow, nobody to know it was him. Yes, it would have to be at night. Even if the crazy old bat did leave her door open at times, a boy creeping in during the day could well be remembered once money had gone missing. It was one thing to climb over and look for balls, another entirely to do a proper robbery like what they sometimes wrote about in the papers.

He moved well back from Gran's room and sat pondering by the fireplace. Getting out of here at night was not going to be easy, not with the four of them sleeping in the one room. And Janet and Daisy's half, at the other side of the folding screen, was nearest the door. So, not only would he have to get out of bed without disturbing their Michael – he'd also need to get past the girls. And with two double beds in that small space, there was hardly room to move without bumping into something.

Aye, this was what it meant, being poor. Four kids in one room, no bath, clogs instead of shoes. He hated it, felt little but contempt for those who endured it year in, year out, never a question, never a thought to betterment. Like sheep they were, waiting for the masters to set the dog on them, grateful for a handful of spare fodder. The unions couldn't do nowt, not really. Load of windbags, they were – it was still them and us no matter what the stewards tried to do. Well, Joey didn't want the crumbs that fell off the top table. Oh no, he wanted the whole bloody loaf and the gravy that went with it. He wanted to sit at the head of that table today, not tomorrow or next flaming week!

He jumped up and stood on the peg rug, feet tapping, his mind demanding that his body should keep pace with its swift activity. It would have to be tonight, get it over and done with. If he didn't do it right away, then he never would.

'What's up with you?' Janet startled him as she entered from the best room. 'Twitching like a cat on hot bricks, you are. Something on your mind?'

'No. No, I just wondered if you wanted to go to the pictures tonight.'

'I thought you were clearing that house next door to Miss Leason?'

'Nearly finished. Just one more trip.'

She stood in front of the dresser and stared at him. 'You're up to something, Joey. I can always tell when you're working on one of your schemes. You nearly had the rug worn out when you were planning that doorstep round, reckoning up how much sandy stone and how much white you'd need. Yes, you're up to something, I can smell it.'

'I'm not!'

'Tell that to the pigeons, Joey. You're like a clock with no back on – I can spot your workings from a mile off. What is it this time? A rag and bone round, window-cleaning, singing to the picture queues?'

He knew his face was brick-red again. If only she wouldn't read him so easily and so often! To cover his discomfort, he asked again, 'What about this film tonight, then?'

'No thanks.'

'Why not?'

She shrugged, her grey eyes downcast. 'Don't feel like it. I'll help Mam and Gran with the exercises. And whatever you're thinking on, Joey, is best left alone.'

'What do you mean?'

'I don't know! But stop dreaming, will you? One of these days, your plans will get you in real trouble. You've that shifty look on you again, that look you always had when you'd been caned at school and I had to cover up for you in case Mam gave you another clout.'

The shade of Joey's skin had darkened to beetroot. 'You don't half talk rubbish, our Janet! It's all in your imagination!'

'Is it? I thought I had none of that, according to you. Didn't you say last week that I was too easy satisfied, no ambition, couldn't imagine me way out of a wet paper bag?'

Molly broke the mood by bursting in at the front door with the two younger children in tow. 'Get up them stairs,' she screamed at Michael. 'Shown me up good and proper this time, he has. He run off from the dentist's! While our Daisy was having her teeth looked at, he shot out of that front door like a bullet from a gun! You'll end up with pot ones like your Granny's,' she yelled at the boy's disappearing back. Molly threw her aching body into a chair. 'Where have I gone wrong, eh? I'd half the street out last week with him tying door-knockers together and chucking rice at folks' upstairs windows six o'clock of a Sunday morning. Honest, you do your best, try to keep them healthy and well-fed with a full set of teeth and all – what do they do? Turn on you, is what.'

Janet tried not to grin. 'He's scared of the dentist, Mam. It's ever since somebody told him about getting teeth taken out with a pair of clog nail pincers. He'll not admit it, him being such a tough lad. But he whimpered all night in his sleep – he can't help it. It's only like you and spiders. Shall I make you a nice cup of tea?'

'Aye. That'd happen be a good idea. And where are you sloping off to?' This question was directed at Joey who was making for the door.

'I've a job on. After that, I'm going to the pictures without them that are too good to come with me. When I've took the cart back, I'll find somebody sensible to go to the Odeon with.' He went out and slammed the door.

'What's up with everybody?' asked Molly of no-one in particular.

Janet closed her mouth firmly and brewed the tea. No point in discussing any of it, really. Miss Leason's money, Joey's strange moods, Michael's naughtiness. She pushed Joey's blue mug away inside the dresser cupboard. He wasn't here for tea. It was as if he wasn't going to be here again. In his mind, her brother was already miles away and she knew it. And he wouldn't come back until he was ready.

Joey balanced on a couple of bricks and peered over Witchie Leason's high back gate. Just a quick look, that was all he'd need. They were sash windows, not easy to open if the butterfly was clipped from the inside, but they were rotted right through, most of the putty flaking away to dust. Happen he could lift a pane out in one piece without making any noise. The back door had long rectangles of glass in its top half. If he could break one of these quietly, he might be able to reach in and turn the key. One way or another, he would get in tonight.

He stepped down on to the pavement, his eyes darting this way and that to make sure nobody was watching. Not that they'd think much of it – loads of people went looking for their ball back from over Witchie Leason's. And he was working next door clearing out, had been hanging around for hours.

Joey walked home slowly, deliberately working on a way to straighten his face. Whatever he felt, whatever excitement he held inside himself, it must not show.

Fortunately for him, there was so much going on when he got home, so much noise and movement that not one of them paid him much heed.

Paddy stood swaying on the bottom stair, his voice raised in anger and self-pity. 'Where's me bloody pension?' he was screaming, obviously the worse for drink, drink Joey had smuggled to him earlier in the day.

'It's not a pension!' shouted Molly. 'It's a retainer, a few paltry bob! I'm feeding seven mouths with it!' She'd got extra of course, from Ma, from the box beneath the bed. 'What do you expect, Paddy, when you won't work?'

'I expect gratitude, that's what!' He fought to maintain a dignity already depleted by a sudden and total lack of co-ordination. 'I got this hand feeding mouths! The hand that feeds has got bit, near bit off altogether and me no more than a lad at the time.' His eyes were bright with unshed tears. 'Don't start telling me about filling mouths, Molly Maguire! This hand, this poor hand . . . ' He waved an arm, then, realizing that he was displaying the wrong limb, made the necessary adjustments and stumbled down the last stairs. 'This hand died so others might live! This hand is a monument, that's what it is. A monument. So where's me bloody bit of pension?'

'Gone.' She stood, hands on hips, her attitude challenging. 'Will you take the bread from my babies' mouths so that you can pour filth down your throat? Will you?'

'Quarter of a thumb, I've bloody got . . . '

'A half.'

'Oh, so we're going to argue over flaming fractions now, are we? You'd have me working till I dropped, you would. What about this better or worse and sickness and health, eh?'

'Don't forget richer or poorer, Paddy.'

'I'm not likely, am I? Can't even have a drop of milk stout out of me own pension, a pension what I earned, a pension what I had bits cut off me for. Burned my bloody hand away, they have! Give it here! Come on, pass it over woman, afore I lose my rag.'

'Pa . . . trick Maguire!'

'Oh heck.' Paddy sank to the floor as his mother entered from the best room.

'Get up those stairs now! Th . . . is minute!' She watched her son as he turned and crawled through the stairway door. 'Con . . . fession!' she said grimly. 'For swearing!'

A great fuss was made of Ma as she took her first meal with the family. Paddy kept well out of it, cursing Molly quietly when she took up his tray. But the one who must truly, for ever and immediately be obeyed had risen, not only from her bed, but also against all odds and probabilities. Even from upstairs, Paddy could feel her power. Like an invisible gas it soaked through floorboards, penetrating every pore of every brick, curling and twisting its unseen tentacles around everything that moved and everything that stood still. Or lay still.

He sighed. His long rest was over. Swainbank's tomorrow, look for a bit of droving. Other folks didn't have mothers like his. Why was he so blessed?

Throughout the animated conversation downstairs, Joey managed to maintain his distance, bolting his food before escaping through the back door. Better keep well out of the road till bedtime, think up his plan properly, then sneak back in late, too late for any questions or funny looks off Janet.

After spending the evening at the pictures watching a film he didn't really see, Joey lay in the bed he was condemned to share with his little brother, who seemed to have more legs than a flaming octopus. And he was bonier than an octopus, thought Joey as he pushed Michael nearer to the wall. God, it had to be midnight by now! He listened to his sisters' breathing, trying to calculate whether or not they were properly asleep.

'Joey?'

Oh Christ! 'What?' he whispered.

'Why aren't you asleep?'

'I could ask you the same question.' He turned on to his side and spoke quietly to the screen that stood between the two large beds. 'I'm not tired.'

She yawned. 'You should be. After emptying that house for Mr Goldberg.'

'Well, I'm not.'

'You're up to something.' Her voice was slowed by sleep.

'Leave me alone!' He knew his teeth were gritted with fury. 'You don't want owt to do with me, I've reckoned that these past weeks. Just let me get on with my life. You'll be glad enough when I'm rich . . . '

There followed a short pause, then she mumbled, 'Don't do it, Joey. Whatever it is, don't . . . '

Although he knew that sleep had claimed her, Joey waited for an hour or more, until all the breathing in the room was even and heavy. Then he crept furtively from the bed, every sound magnified by darkness and stillness as he pulled on his clothes. With his clogs held one in each hand, he began the perilous journey round the edge of Janet's bed, flinching with every creak of old flooring.

The stairs were murderous, each step seeming to echo round the house as he inched his way to the bottom. He left by the scullery door in order to avoid passing Gran's room, pausing to breathe for what seemed like the first time as he stepped into the back alley.

The walk to Witchie Leason's was eerie – Joey had never been out in the middle of the night before. He stopped at the end of one street, watching members of a family as they moved about like grey ghosts, hardly a sound while they loaded furniture on to a cart. More evidence of poverty and what it did to people – this was a midnight flit, all done under cover of darkness because rent had not been paid. Well, that would never happen to Joey, not bloody likely.

It was frighteningly easy. Once he was over the gate, he simply took a penknife and removed a pane from Witchie's back door, manipulating it carefully out of its space and placing it on a pile of ashes in the yard. He reached inside and turned the rusted key, retching almost as the stink of the place filled his nose.

He was in! A few cats escaped, rushing out into the night to join a choir further down the street. Christ, what a stench! He went out and filled his lungs with good air before passing through the scullery and into the living room. It was as black as hell in there except for near the window – he should have brought some matches! The table stood below the window – he remembered that from the last time he'd had a close look, or as close a look as he could get through those rotten dirty panes.

He cursed inwardly as his fingers made contact with a bucket – probably the one their Janet had brought back. Metal clashed sharply against metal until he stilled the handle. Then he found himself smiling when his hand touched the inside of a large box. Yes, this was money all right! Money didn't feel like any other kind of paper and anyway, here were some coins too.

Right. What must he do? Take the lot or leave some so that the old girl wouldn't notice? Nay, he wouldn't know how much he was getting in this light, couldn't count and make it halfy-halfy. And she'd notice her back door broken, so he might as well take the bloody lot. He dragged the box out, standing the bucket in the hearth where it could not cause further trouble.

Suddenly, the hairs on his neck stood on end. He could feel them as they prickled against the back of his collar. There was somebody here, somebody in the room with him. A cat? Just another of her horde of moggies? A match was struck and he jumped to his feet, turning to find the tiny old woman standing there with an expression of great sadness on her face.

'Why?' she asked quietly. 'Ask and I'll give you if the need is real. Why, Joey?'

'I . . . ' He stumbled backwards against the scullery door. 'I didn't . . . I mean, I was just—'

'Just what? Just what are you doing in my house in the middle of the night? Is this a social call? Shall I put on the kettle, make a pot of tea?' She stared hard at him. Yes, this one was Swainbank to the core, with Charles' features, the cunning of old Richard and – oh, she hoped he hadn't inherited Harold's weaknesses! It was the same with horses. You never could tell. Put a good sire to a fine mare and the slightest shared flaw would be magnified. Though Molly seemed an excellent dam . . .

His mouth opened, but no words were framed as the matchlight dwindled away.

She lit another, applying the flame to a nearby candle. Her movements were slow while she raised the horsewhip and brought it down hard across his shoulder. As she tried to deliver a second blow, Joey's temper erupted with force, his mind clouded by the pain she had inflicted. No way would he allow an old woman to beat him! Why, she must be seventy-five, just a little old crone, no real strength except in her gob.

He grabbed the whip and pulled it sharply from her hands, causing her to fall against the mantel, her head cracking loud as a pistol fired into the black silence of night. Miss Leason lay like a crumpled heap of dirty clothing, just another pile in a room filled with such messes.

Although his heart was beating erratically, fear pounding

in his ears like a jungle drum, Joey found the sense to extinguish the candle. The house next door was empty – he'd emptied it himself. But the other side was occupied by a family, people who cared about and protected their property, all new windows and a showy garden. He listened. Except for the cats, there came no sound.

On hands and knees he crept to her side, placing his head against her chest, trying to hear some sign of life. Silence again. Except for the sound of his own laboured breathing. He sat back on his heels. If there had been a heartbeat, what would he have done? It was beyond him, too much to think about. But as she was dead, he might as well take the money. With his eyes riveted to the dim shape of her body, he backed out of the room, the box clutched tightly to his chest.

Janet watched as her brother disappeared up the back street. She'd lost him ages ago and didn't know what had prompted her to look for him here. But yes, she did know. Somewhere inside herself, Janet had realized that Joey was going to do something bad, something really bad. He'd likely been listening when she'd told all that to Gran, all that about Miss Leason's money. What now?

Moments later, Janet found herself stumbling through Miss Leason's wide-open door. Inside, it was very dark and she almost fell over the little lady's prostrate form, so still she lay, right next to the range in the living room. Cats crawled on to their mistress' motionless body; Janet could feel little paws touching and clawing for some response.

'Miss Leason?' Her hand reached out and made contact with the woman's head. 'Miss Leason?' This was blood on her fingers – she needed no light to identify the sticky substance. Quick as a flash, she tore down the ragged curtains, thereby allowing a meagre glimmer to enter the room. At last, she saw some matches on the floor and, with shaking fingers, she managed to light a mantel.

If Miss Leason wasn't dead, she was hurt very badly, that was for sure. And Janet knew with a blinding certainty, a clarity of mind fuelled by fury and disgust, that she had protected Joey for the last time. With sobs racking her chest, she covered the old lady with the curtains and a few clothes from a chair. Joey must pay for this. He really must.

She raced home, her feet barely touching the flags as she flew for help. It was like a dream, a nightmare. The faster she ran, the further she still needed to run. And he was ahead of her, well in front. She wanted to reach home before he did. But she took the faster route past all the house-fronts, knowing that Joey would be slower round the backs and with the box to carry too.

At last she burst into her parents' bedroom, tearing back the quilt as she spoke, her voice rising in pitch when the response was not immediate. 'Wake up! Mam, for goodness sake, get up!'

'Whatever . . . good God, Janet! You frightened me out of my skin . . .'

'You have to come!'

'What? Why? Set a match to the nightlight, will you?'

Janet obeyed, her teeth chattering as she put flame to the squat candle on the mantel. 'I followed him. I followed him, Mam. Thought I'd lost him—'

'Who? What are you on about, lass?'

'Our Joey! He's killed Miss Leason and took all her money, I think.'

'Eh?' Paddy rubbed his eyes.

'Go back to sleep, you.' Molly pushed him on to the pillows, jumped from the bed and dragged Janet out to the landing. 'Where is he?'

'I don't know! He's likely hiding the money! She's hurt, Mam. She might even be dead—'

Molly ran into the children's room. Only Daisy and Michael lay sleeping in their beds. Swiftly she dashed out again and down the stairs, beckoning Janet to follow.

'Please, Mam – she needs the hospital.'

'Right. How do you know all this, lady?'

'I followed him – I told you before—'

'Middle of the bloody night?'

'Yes.' Janet hung her head. 'See, I thought he was up to something, but I hoped I might stop him before he got in bother with you again.'

'And she's bad ways?'

Janet nodded quickly.

'Right. You get to that there phone box down yonder – or break the glass in the old emergency box on Saint George's Road. Ask for the ambulance. Don't say who you are or nowt like that. Just say her address and that she's hurt bad. Tell them it's an emergency so's they'll hurry up.'

'I will.' Janet turned at the front door. 'What about our Joey?'

'Just leave him to me. He'll be dealt with. Now get gone.'

After pulling on a coat to cover her nightdress, Molly put the fire to rights and set the kettle, just for something to do while she waited. It couldn't be true – not this! Aye, he'd a streak in him – plus that determination, that Swainbank single-mindedness – but murder? After the road he'd been fetched up in a good Catholic house?

She gazed into flickering flames as they struggled for life around fresh coals. Did Charlie have murder in him, or old Richard before him? No! Not murder, not direct actual murder. Was Joey so frustrated by his station in life, did some instinct dictate that he ought to be among finer, richer and more powerful surroundings? Did he feel so thwarted that he had to go out and steal, whatever the cost? Even if it meant taking human life? Dear God, what had she brought into the world? What had she carried in her belly, nursed at her breast, nourished in her home? And what had she inflicted on the rest of this innocent family?

But Janet was all right. It hadn't come out in her, not yet. God forbid . . .

Janet ran into the house, white-faced and panting. 'Our Joey's in the wash-house, I think. Why are you sitting in the dark, Mam?'

'I want him to think we're in bed. Did he see you?'

'No. I just heard him. I tiptoed round and—'

'All right. Stay there and make not one sound.' Molly crept out into the scullery and peered through the window. As quietly as possible, she opened the back door, sped down the yard and collared him just as he was making for the gate. With a blow that might have unsettled a man twice his size, she sent him reeling towards the house, kicking him into the scullery with the brass-capped toe of her workday clog.

When they were both inside the house, she grabbed him by the hair, dragging him through to the kitchen. The firelight flickered on his ashen face. 'You bloody little swine, you!' She threw him on to the sofa beneath the window. 'What have you done now, eh?'

He glanced quickly at Janet. 'Nowt! I've done nowt!'

Molly fixed a steely stare on her son. 'Nowt?' she breathed. 'You're nowt a pound, our Joey. Scum of the earth, if what I hear's right. And you'll go down for it, lad. Oh aye, there'll be nowhere for you to hide once the bobbies start looking.' She paused. 'Well?'

'I don't know what you mean.'

Molly stood by the fire, her hands straying for support along the guard. 'Tell him, Janet.'

The girl swallowed hard. 'You stole Miss Leason's money and after she's been so good to us and all! She must have caught you at it and you . . . you killed her!' She burst into tears. 'It's my fault! If he'd never heard me today telling Gran about the box, if I'd told somebody he was up to no good—'

'Rubbish!' Molly's tone was dangerously quiet. 'Why do you always cover up for him, girl? He's no good! And why should it be your fault? I'm the one as brought him up! Now stop your snivelling!' She turned to Joey. 'Where is it?'

'Where's what?' His voice faltered.

'You hard-faced little bugger, you! Now, either you tell me where that money is, or our Janet runs down for the police.'

Joey eyed Janet who was still dabbing her face. 'She wouldn't do it!' Fear distorted his features. 'She wouldn't—'

Janet sniffed noisily. 'I would, Joey! You've gone for a poor little old lady tonight and I'll never forgive you for that! Never!' She seemed to regain some strength as she spoke. 'I'll tell them! I'll say I saw you coming out!'

'No, Janet.' Molly spoke firmly. 'If he admits it and gives the money back—'

'But he's a murderer, Mam!'

'That's as may be, Janet. And they hang murderers, don't they? They'd probably not hang him, not at his age, but he could go to one of them reform places, then on to prison the rest of his life.'

'Like Grandad,' said Janet quietly.

'What?' Molly thought for a moment, then remembered Ma Maguire's husband who was currently serving a third term. 'Oh yes. Like your grandad.' Their real grandad was dead. Long dead. Like many of those who'd worked for him, worn out, gone to dust . . . What a daft world. Their real grandad had died with their adopted granny by his side, yet . . . She shook herself visibly. How was she managing to think about all this rubbish while her son was a thief and a murderer? 'The rest of your life, Joey, in prison with a lot of other bad men. Is that what you want?'

'He should go!' Janet's chin jutted forward. 'He should pay for what he's done! I hate you, Joey Maguire! You were right all along – I do hate you!'

Ma's door opened and there she stood, toothless and in the long white nightdress, a dark net holding to her head what was left of her hair. Yorick loitered by her side, the usual lugubrious expression on his yellow face. 'Speak!' This single word was spat from Ma's mouth like venom.

Joey hung his head in the face of such adversity. 'It's in the wash-house,' he muttered.

'What?' Molly's eyes widened in disbelief. 'You fetched it here to your own family, trying to get us all involved in theft and bloody murder? I can't believe . . . ' Her voice faded away.

'I . . . didn't know what else to do with it.' His head still hung in shame.

'And why did you hurt her? Why?' asked Janet.

'I never! She hit me with a big whip – I pulled it off her, that's all! And when I pulled, she fell against the mantel-piece.'

Ma studied this terrible scene. Molly must be tormented halfway to death with it, probably feeling it was all her fault.

305

After all, wasn't Joey one of the two cuckoos in this particular nest?

'Get that money in here, our Janet,' ordered Molly. 'I'll have to think on what to do. They'll likely come round questioning everybody if she's dead – wherever shall I put it?'

'With me.' Ma's voice was clear and firm. 'Let him ta . . . ke it from me. If he dares.' Her head nodded wisely. 'Yes. If he da . . . res.'

Janet left to fetch the box. Molly now turned the full force of her wrath on Joey. 'Keep away from the rest of my children, do you hear? Because they're too good for your likes. I don't want them all copying you and turning out criminals. And if that woman is dead, may God help you. The same if she isn't, because then she'll go for you, will Sarah Leason. Powerful woman in her time, knows all the topknobs, all the posh folk.'

'Molly!' Ma raised an arm. 'Do . . . n't be carrying on, now—'

'Hush, Ma! This is nowt to do with you! You're supposed to be ill in bed, so shut up!'

Ma, unaccustomed to being told to shut up, sat in a dining chair with the dog by her side.

Molly wagged a finger in Joey's face. 'Even if you get away with it this time, I've no doubt you'll be in bother again, Joey Maguire. It's in you. I don't know how, but it's there. Pure and simple bloody bad, that's what you are. And you didn't learn that from me, or from Ma, or from your dad.' She swallowed audibly. 'God alone knows how it got there, this wickedness, but I've a mind to kick it out of you. I'd rather see you dead than this!'

She turned away to pull the steaming kettle off the coals, then leaned against the range, arms outstretched along the mantel, head bowed as if beneath a great weight. 'The only reason I'm saying nowt to the law is because I have to think about the rest of this family. Who wants to admit to a son or a brother like you, eh? We don't. And don't be thinking on running away, for the police will be looking for anybody as does something unusual. This country would not be big enough to hide you.'

'If—' he began.

'If what?' Molly straightened and swivelled to face him. 'If what?'

'If I had some money . . . well . . . I could go abroad . . . '

In spite of her disability, Ma had to jump quickly to her feet, because Molly had thrown herself at the boy, was swearing, clawing, punching and spitting just as Edie would have done. 'Stop it!' screamed the older woman.

Janet entered, dropped the box, then dragged her mother away from Joey. 'Don't, Mam. He's not worth it, not worth anything.'

Molly sobbed inconsolably in her daughter's arms. 'Get up the stairs,' snapped Janet. 'And stay there until you're told different.'

Joey slunk out of the room.

'Mam . . . come on now, sit down till I make a drink. Gran, make her sit still. Mother – will you stop it? We've made enough noise already – Mrs Seddon will be sending for the police next news! Gran, reach in that drawer and get her an Aspro. Stop shaking, Mam. It's not your fault . . . '

'It is! You don't know – any of you! You just don't know—'

'Be quiet!' snapped Ma. Not now, dear God, let her not say it all now, not on top of everything else. And Janet was coping so well, organizing tea, wrapping a shawl round Molly's shoulders, forcing her to swallow the tablet. Yet the girl was near to breaking, Ma could see that.

'I'm not a good mother,' wailed Molly. 'I'm not a good woman! It's me – can't you see, it's me!'

Ma raised her good hand and delivered a sizeable blow to Molly's cheek. 'Sorry,' she said straight away. 'But we don't want the hyst . . . erics.'

Molly whimpered quietly into her teacup.

Now that the drama was over, Yorick indulged in a good scratch before settling down in front of the fire. He would never work them out, the way they carried on. And he was too tired to care anyway, too full of dinner. Yet he kept a weather eye on Ma. She was still the best of the bunch, the most predictable. Wherever she went, he would go.

They carried the money to Ma's bed, peeling back blue

and white striped ticking to reveal a plain flock mattress bag beneath. Between these two layers the coins and notes were lodged, right at the bottom of the bed so that Ma would suffer no discomfort.

'I'll sew it up proper tomorrow, Ma.' Molly was calmer now. 'I wonder how that poor old soul's getting on? You did send for an ambulance, Janet? They did say they'd go to her?'

Janet laid a hand on her mother's arm. 'Yes. When they asked who I was, I kept on screaming her address and saying she was hurt bad. They got the message. She'll be in hospital, Mam.' Just in time, she managed to bite back, 'or with the undertaker'.

'And what about our Joey?' Molly looked from Janet to Ma. 'What about him?'

'As far as I'm concerned, he doesn't even exist!' Janet's voice was cold.

Ma shook her head. 'Your brother. What . . . ever, he is your brother.'

'And Seamus Maguire's your husband, my granddad. But you wouldn't have him back, not after what he did.'

'Not the sa . . . me! Joey did a bad thing. My hus . . . band is a terror . . . ist. Joey will settle down.'

Janet took the cardboard box and tore it into tiny pieces, pushing them one by one on to the fire. 'Look at us, covering up for him.' Her eyes shone angrily in the flickering light. 'Just because he's family.'

'That's right,' said Ma clearly. 'Joey is your family. Never forget that.'

Chapter 9

'I have nothing to say to you, young man.'

'But – Miss Leason! You're lying here with a cracked skull and enough bruises to cover a blackboard—'

'Feed my cats!' She glared at him with the one unbandaged eye. 'It was all my own doing. I slipped, fell, must have banged my head against the fireplace. Old women do that sort of thing, constable. It's called having an accident. Now. Where are my cats?'

'The neighbours are seeing to them.'

'Good enough.' She heaved herself into a sitting position. 'Then you will bring my clothes and allow me some privacy while I dress myself.'

'You what?' He turned and waved frantically at the ward sister. 'She's for going home,' he shouted.

Sister arrived at the bedside, starched apron crackling, eyes flashing with barely contained temper. 'You will remain exactly where you are, Madam.'

'Miss.'

'You cannot go home. This is the only place for a person with concussion . . .'

'I think I am the better judge of that. The food is not edible, the bed is obviously made of bricks and mortar – I am therefore returning to my own house.'

Sister's face hardened further. 'If necessary, I shall fasten you into that bed, Miss Leason. Your home is unfit for human habitation and you will go back to it when it is cleaned and fumigated.'

'I beg your pardon?'

'You heard me! Now, I have no wish to get you certified . . .'

'Certified? How dare you! Do you realize who I am?'

'We know who you are, all right. But you can't carry on living like that no matter what your name is. If it comes to a fight, then I'll get two doctors to sign you in as mentally unfit.'

'Don't you dare threaten me, woman!' Her head was banging like a drum as she lay back against rock-hard pillows and surveyed the other occupants of the large ward. 'What's the matter with you all?' she screamed in spite of the pain. 'Are you afraid of this creature? She's just another bloody woman, wears knickers like the rest of us. And I am not insane!'

The policeman bent over the bed. 'Look, love . . .'

'Miss Leason, if you please.' She fixed him with a steely eye. 'Get me out of here.'

'I can't.' He raised his palms in frustration. 'You won't tell us anything, won't co-operate – is it any wonder Sister thinks you're crackers? It's obvious you were thumped over the head while you were horsewhipping whoever broke in—'

'Nobody broke in! Are you deaf as well as bloody stupid?'

'Then why have you only got half a back door, eh?'

'I broke it.'

'Broke it?' He passed a hand over his prematurely balding pate. 'The glass was lifted out in one piece!'

'Oh.'

He folded his arms and arranged his face into what he hoped was an encouraging and patient expression. 'Somebody removed the glass, came into the house, pinched all your money—'

'Which money? Who said anything about money?'

He floundered for a second. 'Well . . . we thought . . . as there was no cash in the house . . . we thought you'd been robbed of every penny.'

'You were wrong.'

'There wasn't even the price of a loaf and a bowl of dripping! Where is your money, Miss Leason?'

'Safe.'

'Safe where?'

'That's for me, my bank manager and my lawyer to know.

And unless you have any more questions, I suggest you leave and let the dragon get on with her job.'

The blue-clad figure of the nurse stiffened. 'My name is Sister Cornwell.'

Miss Leason nodded. 'Yes. I dare say you need no matches to light the fire! Well, you don't frighten me, Nursie! Try to get me certified and I shall sue you, the doctor and the bloody hospital too! We'll see who comes out of this saner, you or I! However, I am prepared to admit to a slight head-ache, which even you are probably capable of treating.'

'You were unconscious for hours,' said the sister. 'And you will behave yourself while you are here on my ward.'

'If I don't, might I get thrown out by any splendid chance?'

The nurse turned on her heels and marched into her office.

'Touchy bugger,' said the patient. 'Are you sure my cats are being cared for?'

'Are you sure you've nothing to tell me?'

'Absolutely sure.'

He sighed. 'We'll see to the cats until you get out of here. But you're wrong, you know. I think you're protecting some-body. Why? What for? What if he does it again to somebody else?'

'Go away.'

'Miss Leason, please . . . '

'Go.'

He picked up his helmet and left, head shaking slowly as he wondered anew about the vagaries of human nature. She'd been clobbered, right enough – and she knew who'd done it.

Sarah Leason lay on the rigid bed, her mind going over the events of the previous evening. Joey bloody Maguire! It occurred to her that this boy had every penny she owned, every last farthing of the money. If he didn't bring it back, then what would she live on? And how long were they going to keep her in this terrible place, all trussed up like a chicken and in a bed with sides like an infant's cot? Could they really detain her against her will?

She was in pain, though she'd never tell the dragon that. Her head felt as if it had been flattened by a tram, while every

311

bone in her body ached continually. Poor Ma Maguire. There was no explaining this at all. How could Joey be delinquent when the rest of the family was so well-behaved? Apart from Paddy, who was merely lazy – and even he had his better side, was soft-hearted and easy to coax.

Across the room a row of crones stared back at her, each contained in a cot similar to hers, each with all the marks of age cut deep into withered features. Did she look like that? Very probably. Of course, they'd all be having visitors this afternoon, children, grandchildren, perhaps even great-grand-children. She had no-one. Until now, she had needed and wanted nobody, had chosen to be alone. A husband might have proved an encumbrance, especially when it came to the mines. Which man would have got rid of them as she had, which man could have given up the promise of such an easy income? But now, in this disadvantaged state, she wondered whether or no she'd done the right thing all those years ago, turning away suitors, backing off from the mainstream, iso-lating herself so completely. A grandchild or two would have been such a comfort.

The future held little promise – none at all if she didn't retrieve the money. But she couldn't have informed on Joey. Policemen were not on Miss Leason's list of favoured people. She'd had her own encounters with them, arguments about rights of way and hunt sabotage, the odd row when she'd tackled a hunt head-on, often scattering dogs and unseating riders by the indiscriminate firing of a gun, the throwing of exploding fireworks. She smiled grimly as she remembered her favourite court appearance after baptizing the Master of Hounds with a pan of hot custard. Yellow for cowardice.

Was she a coward now, lying here and letting Joey Maguire get away with near murder? No! She would have her day with him. It was, after all, only money.

Amelia Swainbank watched her husband walking up the drive-way, his shoulders rounded and bent like those of an old man. She lay on the chaise longue in front of her full-height window, a warm wrap about her shoulders, a rug spread over her knees. Charles was suffering, that was plain to see. He would be coming up soon, paying his evening visit before settling down in the study with orders and accounts. He was a strange man, because although he employed an army of clerks and accountants, he still insisted on overall supervision, particularly of the financial side.

Of course, that was probably typical of a tradesman. Her own father had been a professional, a doctor of medicine, had always worn an air of one not quite in touch with his fellow man, an aloofness that precluded direct approach. So different, these two men who had dominated her life, but Amelia had few regrets. Charles had been such a wonderful husband, a loving father . . .

'Amelia! You're up – what a marvellous surprise! Feeling better?' He bent to kiss her cheek. 'Yes, you look almost well today.'

'I'm much stronger thank you, dear. Pull up a chair and keep me company for a few minutes.'

She studied him while he fetched a dressing stool from the opposite side of the room. He was still a fine figure of a man, still handsome as long as he didn't stoop. She chided him now. 'You're becoming round-shouldered. One of the few things I admired about your father was that he carried his height well. I'll have to force you to walk round with a pile of books balanced on your head. That's what I had to do at finishing school.'

'I see. And what else did they manage to teach you in the middle of the Alps?'

'Nothing meaningful. Except for the naughty girls who got friendly with the ground staff – they learned a bit of yodelling among other things. We goodies spent a lot of time doing embroidery, gossiping, speculating about the husband market.' She paused, her voice cracking. 'Oh Charles – what are we going to do without them? I try so hard to be cheerful when you come home—'

He reached across and patted her knee. 'No need. Don't put on an act for me. You're entitled to be heartbroken.'

'Even so – the things I said, the way I blamed you for

allowing them the car – that was dreadful of me. I didn't mean all that. You must believe me.'

'I know. But anger is a perfectly normal emotion and you had to throw the book at somebody. Still, I don't mind you throwing the damned things as long as I don't have to go walking about with a pile of Oxford dictionaries on my head. Now come on – don't cry . . . ' He couldn't bear her tears, never had been able to cope with her sudden swings of mood. Now, of course, such changes were inevitable – apart from the boys' deaths, there was her condition to be considered. But underneath her fragile facade, Amelia had always been a woman of great power, a manipulative creature with a fine brain and the skill to use it whenever necessary. He loved her. Over the years, the initial passion had lessened, only to be replaced by something stronger, a sense of comradeship and respect, a need for her to simply be there at the end of a working day. Soon, he would lose her too . . .

'Number three's looking good,' he said, desperately seeking to alter her train of thought. 'The whole place has been upgraded and rewired and most of the new frames are in.'

'Many of them went to the funeral, so I'm told.'

He inclined his head; she would not be diverted. 'Yes. They . . . they cared, Amelia. They've probably always cared in their own way—'

'Their way's no different from ours, my love.' She sighed her exhaustion as quietly as she could. Such an obvious snob, this dear man. Like many who had risen through trade, he remained haunted by humble beginnings, kept a false distance between himself and those designated as truly working class, manufactured a space so that any similarities between himself and those who served might pass unnoticed.

'Have you had a good day?' he was asking now.

A good day? She could scarcely remember one. Something tore at her insides, ripping them apart it seemed, allowing her pain beyond measure until Nurse Fishwick decided to allocate a portion of relative peace, doses whose frequency needed to be increased daily now. She smiled up at him bravely. A brave wife was a good wife – and she would be good right up to the end. 'Yes, I've had a good day.' The illness was terminal, of that she had become absolutely sure. She had always been slim, but now she was positively skeletal, like some poor starved viçtim of war. Yes, she was just skin and bone, nothing left but spirit – and that too would be quenched soon enough.

So. There remained several delicate matters, subjects about which Charles must be approached while her faculties remained intact. Life was becoming hazy these days – on occasion, she was forced to positively reach out in order to make true contact. Although she was about to leave the world, it was as if the situation had been reversed and the world was slipping away from her, abandoning her gradually. In her head there was little pain, but whatever sat in her chest and stomach had gone on a journey, tentacles extending into new areas as it decided to claim more territory for itself. Like an invaded and unarmed country, she was forced to simply lie there while the aggressor established himself, her own defences too diminished for any real resistance.

'How long have you been out of bed?'

'Oh, an hour or more. I have to make an effort, Charles. It isn't easy, not without my boys to cheer me on. But I still have you and you're more than worth it.' She blinked rapidly as his face swam out of focus. 'We need to talk, dear.'

'We are talking.'

'I meant we should really talk. About the future.'

'I see.' He touched her hand. 'You sound very . . . serious. What is it?'

'I'll try not to cry, Charles. The days for weeping, for myself at least, are long past. Yes, death is a serious business, but it must be faced sensibly. The loss we have suffered will lessen my time with you. No – I beg you – don't tell me I am going to recover. I'm not a stupid woman and I should prefer to be treated as intelligent until my senses desert me completely. That is going to happen, Charles. Gradually, I shall stop being myself. My hearing, sight and balance are already affected and it's getting worse. However, while the recognition of one's own imminent ending is a test of sanity, it does

315

not deaden reason completely. Not at this stage. My powers of reason will no doubt disappear in their own good time.'

'Amelia . . . please!'

She held up her hand to cut off whatever he was about to utter. 'I just want you to know that I don't blame you for the death of our sons. I think that's very important for both of us. We feel so guilty when a loved one dies – things we ought to have done, ways in which we might have prevented such tragedies. When a child dies, all that is intensified because life has somehow got disordered. Parents die before their children. That is so regularly expected that it's become an unwritten law. Please don't blame yourself, Charles—'

'It's hard not to.'

'Yes. Yes, I expect it is. So it will take an act of mind, even an act of will and faith to change your attitude towards yourself. I must have made it so much worse those first few days when I screamed at you constantly. But in blaming you, I was also blaming myself – because that's how close a family we have always been. If I hadn't confined myself to bed, if I hadn't given in so easily and so early to my illness – don't you see? I accused myself of being a neglectful mother. Not now, though. Neither of us is to blame for what happened. I've a lot of time to ponder, so I've done the thinking for both of us. Absolve yourself, Charles . . . '

He took a handkerchief from a pocket and wiped his streaming eyes. 'So I must face losing you too?'

'Yes. But that will be so much easier than losing John and Peter.'

'No! No, it won't!'

She placed a transparent hand on his knee. 'We shall work to prepare you for this.'

'How? There's no way . . . none . . . '

She drew as deep a breath as tired lungs would contain. 'Life does not begin or end with us, my darling. When we go, someone takes our place. It's the ultimate proof that each of us is totally dispensable. So, the future is always protected in one sense. However, preparation for the time after us cannot be a bad thing.'

'How do we get ready for this?'

She could see that this was cutting him deeply, breaking through his brusque reserve, that down-to-earth manlinesss he employed as a cover for emotion, a defence that would surely crumble once he was truly alone in this enormous house. She feared for him, knew that he should rather break down now while she was still around to comfort him. If he continued to sit on his feelings, wouldn't they build up like the heat in the earth's core, then find a weak spot through which they might escape? She could not leave him to such madness, must do all she could to preclude it, force him to feel pain now! 'We get ready by examining what is left,' she said quietly.

'What's left is sweet Fanny Adams!'

She smiled at this outburst. 'No. What's left is a strong young man with three mills and a great deal of property.' There was a long pause while his face receded then returned as she narrowed her eyes to encourage the arrival of a clearer picture. 'You must remarry,' she whispered at last.

'What? Never! There was only one wife for me, Amelia. I couldn't find another like you.'

'Don't the locals have a saying – 'a change is as good as a rest"? For goodness sake, Charles, anybody might think I'd suggested you go out with a pistol and commit mayhem! The nicest compliment you could pay me would be to take another wife. A happy marriage often breeds a second after the death of a partner. And we have been happy, darling.'

He fought back the tears as he spoke. 'I have been more than content with my lot, Amelia, more than lucky. But I couldn't go through it again, I simply couldn't do it! I don't want any more children, don't want to watch them grow, couldn't bear to hope that they'd match up to John and Peter, that they'd be healthy . . . that they would survive . . . '

'In time, though . . . ?'

'No! I am sorry if this upsets you, but I refuse to think about remarriage! The only thing I know is that I shall not marry again.'

She leaned her head against the curved arm of the chaise.

317

'Alice came to see me today, complained that you have threatened to cut poor Cyril off. Is this true?'

'Where did she park her broomstick? On the roof? Oh, I'm sorry, love. No, I can't cut him off, not completely. He still has a share in the profits . . . '

'But you would if you could?'

'He's a buffoon!'

'Exactly.'

'What? I thought you were Alice's champion?'

She shook her head slowly. 'No. I felt sorry for Alice because she could never put a foot right in your father's opinion. I did not like your father, didn't care for the callous way in which he treated Harold and Alice. But I agree, Cyril's hardly the most presentable of beings.'

'A slight understatement—'

'Be fair, Charles. The boy is interested in accountancy and will probably succeed in his own area and in a limited way. But Alice is determined that her son should inherit the Swainbank mills. After all, there would appear to be no other heir. So, if you don't intend to remarry, then who will get the mills?'

He stared at the floor.

'Charles?'

'Yes dear?'

'Who?'

He shrugged his shoulders in a gesture that bordered on the impatient.

'Will it be Molly Dobson's child?' Her voice was soft. 'It's all right, Charles—'

He shot up from the stool, mouth agape, hands waving uselessly by his sides.

'Oh sit down – do!' she said. 'Stop attempting that very poor imitation of a windmill and pass me some water.'

He complied like a large dumb child, stumbling across the edge of the carpet as he handed her the glass. 'Sorry,' he mumbled, stooping to mop up the spillage with a handkerchief already sodden by tears.

He returned to his seat, head bent in an attitude of shame and despair.

She took a sip of water then pushed the glass into his hands. He placed it on the floor and sat staring down into it, every sinew aching as he took in what she had just said, digested the significance behind her words.

'I've known for a long time, sweetheart. Your mother was too vindictive a woman to keep a gem like that to herself. She found it out by listening at doors, hearing you arguing with your father. Yes, she enjoyed my fear, told me she was letting me know "for my own good", advised me to keep an eye on you in the future. It hurt at the time, but I would not allow that terrible mother of yours to come between us. I have never, before or since, had the misfortune to meet anyone quite like your parents. Sorry – I know you loved your father, but I found the pair of them to be remarkably unlovable.'

'Oh, Amelia—'

'I've known about Molly for a long, long time.'

'What? You mean she actually told you – knowing that you might lose the child, her own grandchild?'

'Yes.'

'Why? Why would she do such a thing?'

Amelia shrugged painfully thin shoulders. 'If your mother had a favourite, then it was Harold – merely because he looked like her. Beatrice was an unhappy woman in an unhappy marriage and she believed in fair shares for all. If she was miserable, then she spread it around a bit, made sure everybody suffered.'

'But that's inexcusable!'

'Your mother never asked to be excused, Charles. Don't forget, she was married to a much older man with a very short fuse on his temper. This was all a part of paying him back. I'm not apologizing for her – I'm merely trying to explain why she was so vicious.'

He rose from the stool and paced about in front of the window. 'Good God – if she were still alive, I'd . . . I'd—'

'No! Please – no more hatred! I lived with that for long enough! Don't make me die with it! Your mother was shaped by circumstance, just as we all are—'

'It's me I hate! Me!' He pounded his chest with a closed fist. 'I loved you, Amelia, yet I went out and . . . and . . . '

'Took some comfort? Does it really matter at this point? This knowledge is not new to me – it doesn't hurt any more. Only your suffering can hurt me now.'

'It wasn't just comfort! Oh my God – how can I explain this to my wife of all people? Believe me, I loved you! Always, always, I loved you!'

'And you loved Molly too.'

'I don't know! Yes . . . for a while, a very short time.'

'Do you think of her now?'

'Sometimes. Yes, yes, I think of her. I don't want to, I try not to . . . She hardly knew what was happening. I betrayed your trust, hers, my father's. Above all, I sickened myself.' He turned and flung his tormented body at Amelia's feet, burying his head in her lap.

She stroked the thick brown hair. 'Tell me – was it a boy or a girl?'

'Both.' His voice arrived muffled by the rug. 'She had twins.'

Her hand paused momentarily. 'So you have a son and a daughter, Charles! What more could you want? Bring them here! Let me see your children!'

'I can't.' He leaned back on his heels. 'They don't know they're mine. She married a chap called Paddy Maguire and he believes the twins are his.'

'But Molly knows they aren't.'

'Probably. The boy is . . . well, obviously not a Maguire. But Molly found her safety, her own way of coping. It is not going to be easy to claim them, to prove that they are my children.'

'But surely you have supported them?'

'Only indirectly. Remember Ma Maguire – used to look after Father's leg—?'

'One of his mistresses, wasn't she?'

He shook his head. 'Oh no, she was never one of his women. That's a separate story altogether, a very long one. Father worshipped that impossible creature, set her on a pedestal, even wrote poetry about her—'

'Poetry? Old Richard?'

'Yes. Theirs was a real love story. Anyway, Ma's son married Molly without knowing about the pregnancy. But Ma knew. She came down to the mill and "sold" her son to my father, used Paddy to protect Molly's name. You see, Molly was adopted by Ma after the death of her parents – almost a daughter, in fact.'

'What was the price?'

'A future for the unborn child – or children as it turned out – then a weaving job for herself and some comfort for the family until the children were due to leave school. That's where the promised future comes in – they are to have a couple of shops in the town centre.'

Amelia's head nodded slowly. 'How will Ma explain these shops?'

'A legacy from Ireland.'

'Difficult. What a mess, Charles!'

'Exactly. In order to reclaim those children as mine, I have a hell of a lot to prove.'

'I can see that. Obviously, you've given this some consideration?'

'A little, yes.'

'Thank God we are finally open and honest with each other! When you just now admitted your association with Molly, I thought we would be bringing home a needy child, someone Molly would be glad to give over to better prospects.'

Charles bit his lip while he pondered. 'He probably wouldn't be suitable anyway.'

She swung her legs over the edge of the sofa and raised herself into a sitting position. 'Who wouldn't?'

'Joseph . . . Joey.'

'Your son.'

'Joey would never make a Swainbank. He's an alleycat from the sound of things. Plenty of nous, earns money wherever he can—'

'Sounds like your father. What about the girl?'

He passed a hand across his forehead. 'Pretty as a picture, but a girl nonetheless. If I were to nominate one of them, it would have to be the boy.'

She stood on uncertain feet, then began the perilous journey towards her bed. Charles rushed to her side, knowing only too well that he must not offer immediate support. This little lady intended to keep her limited independence for as long as possible. He pulled the covers over her body, noticing that the swelling on her stomach had increased, as if the filthy thing were feeding off her, nourishing itself while depriving her of vital sustenance. He hated this pale invader, this insidious and cowardly killer that sucked away life without showing its hideous face until the end, until its victory was assured.

She sank into feather pillows, her breath shortened by the recent small exertion. 'What makes a Swainbank, Charles?' she managed at last.

'Breeding.'

'He has your blood.'

'Yes, but it's been diluted. I can't bring a lad from the slums and turn him into a gentleman overnight.'

'Molly was a spirited and intelligent girl, my dear. If your blood has been diluted, then at least it wasn't polluted as well. Yes, I rather liked Molly. And so did you.' She looked straight into his eyes. 'Are you tempted?'

'Of course I am! It would be . . . interesting to observe him at first hand, find out what he's really made of.'

'And it would hurt poor little Molly all over again. I've thought about her often, Charles, wondered, hoped she'd been taken care of, compensated—'

'Yes.' He looked tenderly at the ashen face on the pillow, so frail and damaged, so ill. 'All these years . . . all these years, you've known what I am.'

'I have known, yes. That you were a good husband, a very honest man. I wasn't going to waste my life blaming you for one mistake. If I had, then your mother would have been delighted.'

'Thanks, Amelia.'

'It's nothing.' She achieved a tight smile. 'Just think about the future, about that boy. And the girl too. A creature cannot be at fault or substandard simply because it's female.' Her face suddenly twisted with the agony she had fought so long to hide. 'Get me the nurse, darling. I need some relief from this . . . '

After bending to kiss her, he left to summon help for his dying wife.

Charles brooded for a long time in his study after supper. It was a real bloody mess and no mistake. All that damage he'd caused for one night of . . . no, he couldn't even call it pleasure. The girl's fury, the resulting marriage to a man hardly fit to rear an orphaned sparrow, let alone a child. Then the murderous weapon Beatrice had picked up and wielded. Ah yes. Mother was not one to leave a sword idling long in its sheath. And poor Amelia, all this time a wronged wife and never a word had she uttered. It was the fact that she had known and kept silent that hurt him most.

What to do? He'd have had it out with Ma Maguire pretty damned quickly if the old girl had been at her looms. To think she'd pocketed the money year after year without telling Molly! Was it really about protecting Molly, that elaborate charade thought up by Ma? Or was she salting the money for her own purposes? Probably not. No, she'd likely kept the whole family, his own offspring included, in a decent enough style. She wasn't a bad old stick.

He moved across to his desk and lit a cigar. Yes, he would have to make a decision soon. If he were to die intestate, then that chicken-livered idiot would get the lot – why, that went beyond all reason! Cyril in a Swainbank hat? The thought was more than ridiculous.

Should he pursue his instincts, approach Joey directly? Perhaps he could offer him work, a good salary and a decent post? No. That wouldn't do either. The boy was going to start his own business once Ma was up and running again. From the sound of Joey, he would choose to be his own master rather than another's minion.

Other alternatives arrived stillborn as soon as he thought of them. To face Molly would be more than difficult after all this time. Paddy would have to remain where he was – strictly in the dark, while Ma, the one he really needed, was out of commission for now.

Patience was a virtue foreign to Charles. Even if he were to pray for it, he'd probably beg for it to arrive by return of post. But he must continue to watch and wait until the time was right. Right to do something that might turn out to be so wrong.

Slowly, he pulled from a drawer the new will, a document ready to be signed and witnessed in Philip Charnock's presence in spite of loud protestations. The way he had worded it – well, it seemed more a confession, a testament to all his sins. But Molly must be protected. Molly with her cheeky grin and laughing green eyes should suffer no more. It was his fault, his guilt. And the will was written accordingly.

Molly stood glowering in the centre of the rug, her face twisted by anger as she looked down at Joey who was cowering in a fireside chair. 'So it looks as if you've got away with it, then. She's alive at least – happen we should be grateful for that! According to what I've heard, she's saying it was an accident. Seems you hit her that hard she's lost her bloody memory or summat!'

'I didn't hit her! I keep telling you—'

'Tell me nowt, lad! When it's your turn to speak, I'll let you know. Right.' She placed her hands on her hips and leaned forward, her face almost making contact with the top of his head. 'How do we get the brass back to her? Come on, clever lad – you were wanting a turn to use your voice – how do we manage that, eh? Stick it in our Michael's go-cart and trundle it round the bobby shop, cod on as we've found it at the back of Leatherbarrow's?'

'I don't know, do I?'

'Aye well, it's your problem. Except of course we're all involved now. Janet and me – we both know who did it and we're sheltering a criminal. Do you realize that your sister, who'd never hurt a flaming fly if she could help it, could finish up in prison over this? Me too 'cos I hid the bloody evidence! Me! Good job your dad was bad ways that night, otherwise he'd be in it too!' Aye, right up to his neck, she thought. Paddy would have had the stolen money spent by now. No, he wouldn't. Even a chap as selfish as Paddy wouldn't pinch poor old Miss Leason's money.

'I can put it back,' said Joey lamely.

'Put it back? Put it blinking well back?' she screamed. 'How? Break a window and chuck it in? That house is crawling with the sanitary folk – how are you going to get past them? And I wouldn't trust you to do it anyway – I'm not that daft, lad. Nay, I've met some bloody fools in my time, but you take the whole bag of biscuits, you do! Aye – and the Crawford's box with the money in and all! Well? What have you got to say for yourself?'

'Nowt.'

'Right. You just listen to me, you little rat! I know Sarah Leason. She's a decent sort for all she's a bit on the peculiar side and I reckon I'll have to go and make my peace with her. It shouldn't be up to me – this is your bother, not mine. Only I fetched you up and it's me as'll get the blame for you going wrong. So I'll have to find out a way of getting the money back to her. That's unless she changes her mind and wants to get the law in. If she does, then there'll be nothing I can do for you.'

'You're going . . . to see her?' His face was white. 'Down at the infirmary?'

She nodded. 'And I'm telling you now, this is the last time I'll be cleaning up your leavings. I dare say your sister feels much the same road.'

'I wouldn't know. She doesn't talk to me any more—'

'What did you expect? Hero's welcome and a band, happen a few flags strung up between doors? It's you as wants flaming stringing up! Nay, you'll be lucky if that girl walks the same side of the street as you from now on. She's disgusted with you! And so am I!'

Molly stepped back, turned and took her coat from a peg on the stairway door. Dear God, how could it be possible to despise your own child while all the time you knew you still loved him? She wanted to open her arms and draw him close, comfort him, lessen his pain. Like another pain years ago – sobbing and weeping in a courtyard, moonlight on stable roofs, shadows, a thin coat and nowhere to go . . . Except here. To all this. Charlie bloody Swainbank! She pulled the coat on angrily.

'Mam?'

'What?'

'Tell her . . . tell her . . . oh, I don't know—'

'Neither do I. I don't know what to tell a seventy-odd year old woman with a broken skull. She could finish up like your gran did after that clot – you might have crippled her for ever. No, I can't think of one single sensible word to say.'

'Then . . . don't go.'

'Take the coward's way out, is that it? Shut me eyes and pretend nowt's happened, carry on as if we were just a normal family with a nice lad as the eldest? I can't. It's not in my nature, Joey Maguire.'

'Then create it, Molly!' They both turned to find Ma in the doorway of the best room. She walked slowly forward a few paces and lowered herself into a dining chair. 'Whatever, you can't let the boy down.'

'What?' yelled Molly. 'After what he's done?'

'He is your son!' The voice arrived strong and firm. 'Fifteen years old next Wednesday! They make mistakes, Molly! Did you never make one?'

Molly stared hard at Joey. 'Yes, I've made mistakes. And I've paid for them.'

'Got round them, you mean. Just as we all do. Forgive him, Molly.'

'I'll do me best. Just like I've always done me blinking best!' She grabbed her bag and flounced out of the house.

Ma gazed across the table at her grandson. No matter who Joey really was, no matter what his name should have been, he was still her grandchild. From the day in the church with her hands covered in soda, these twins had been hers morally and actually. 'Follow your mother, Joey.'

'Eh?'

'Go to the hospital, see Miss Leason. It is your duty.'

'I can't. I daren't . . . '

Carefully, she removed the tiger's eye brooch from the front of her shawl. 'Take this, Joey. It's not magic, but it helps somehow. I mind the times it's helped me . . . ' She placed it on the table. 'Go and do what must be done.'

He picked up the brooch and stared at it. 'You're talking proper now.'

'Yes. Look at me, Joey Maguire. I am going to tell you something now, something I have kept from the rest of this family. Before I had the stroke, I was alone one day in this very kitchen when a knocking came at the door. I found a man from the prison over to Manchester. He had with him several policemen who were dressed in ordinary clothes. They carried a paper allowing them to search my house from top to bottom.'

Joey swallowed audibly. 'What . . . what were they looking for? I hadn't done nothing . . . '

'They were searching for Seamus Maguire. Do you want to be like him, Joey? Running all your life, escaping from prison on the back of a muck-cart with all the pig-feed in your hair, hiding, stealing, doing wrong? The worst part is that I don't really care what happens to my own husband. If you continue, then nobody will mind you or look out for you. Is that any way to live at all?'

A tear made its way down the boy's thin cheek. 'No.'

'Then go and make your peace. If Sarah had wished it, you would have been with the police long before this. There is nothing to fear except fear itself. Start today with the truth and do the best you can with all the tomorrows, see each morning as a clean start with no black marks to it. I ask you to do this in return for my support, Joey. And if you need to get back your mother's respect, then go down now to that hospital.'

'She . . . hates me—' He was sobbing now.

'Away with your bother, man! Molly Dobson never had a hateful bone in all her body! She loves you. 'Tis love that took her this day to the infirmary with the pride swallowed, love makes her fight and hope for you. Sure she's a bag of wind at times, sounding off about this, that and t'other thing as if the world was about to finish in a puff of smoke. But I tell you

327

honestly now, your mother got that from me and from her own mother too. We were a right pair together, meself and Edie Dobson, plain-spoken and hurtful at times. You've a good mother, so away now this minute and make peace.'

'I'm . . . I'm sorry, Gran—'

'For what?'

'Calling you an old biddy, cursing me dad as useless, stealing all that money—'

'But you didn't hit Sarah Leason. I know you didn't, son. Go on now. Take Uncle Porrick's brooch in your pocket and keep your hand on it. The little people are on the side of whoever holds the brooch – and aren't Sarah and Molly knee-high to a grasshopper the both of them?'

He stumbled to his feet. 'Thanks, Gran.'

'Don't mention it.'

He was gone, the tiger's eye tucked safely into his trouser pocket.

Ma stared at herself in the brass-framed mirror. An old lady gazed back at her and smiled grimly. She must find her black dress, the teeth, the good black shoes, that box, all the papers. Tomorrow had finally arrived, nothing could be put off now. She was armed, shielded by the almost complete return of her faculties, stronger, wiser, richer in spirit because of this latest brush with death. She exhaled loudly. It was time to take on the world.

Chapter 10

They stood outside Cowley's General, the grocery store that used to be Freddie Chadwick's clog shop. Molly dabbed a suspicion of moisture from her eyes, then turned as if to study a pyramid of soapflake boxes in the window. 'I'll just nip in here for a quarter of potted meat.'

'Didn't our Janet fetch some this morning?'

'Aye.' She grimaced to hide her emotion. 'Bloody Yorick ate it – paper and all. That was for your dad's butties. He's fetching a herd over from Chorley tomorrow. Flaming dog!'

Joey grinned, though his eyes remained sad. 'You shouldn't talk about your husband like that, Mam.'

'Don't start! You know what I mean, Joey Maguire. Are you waiting or walking back home by yourself?'

'I'll hang on.'

She touched his arm almost hesitantly. 'I'm . . . I'm proud of you, lad. Prouder than I was this morning anyroad. It took guts, did that, coming down and facing the woman . . . '

Pleased and embarrassed, he tapped the ground with the heel of his clog. 'What was she going on about though? All that about sleep and knitted sleeves? Have they got her making jumpers through the night?'

Molly began to giggle quietly, the sound echoing an inner hysteria that had simmered all day. 'Eeh Joey! That was her bit of Shakespeare, love. It's summat to do with a good kip making things better – and she's getting no sleep. According to that there Sister – the one as Miss Leason calls Dragon – old Sarah sat up till all hours in the lavvy singing Rock of Ages. She said it was an appropriate hymn 'cos it matches her bed. They'll be chucking her out any day, can't cope with her. She makes your gran look like the Archangel Gabriel at times, does Miss Leason.'

'Gran's on the mend, isn't she?'

Molly nodded. 'Aye. Fur and feathers will fly any minute, Joey, you just mark my words. She'll launch herself with a bang, not a whimper. I've never known her do anything quiet. I'm told she used to be a bit on the shy side as a girl, a bit backwards at coming forwards, but I've got me doubts about that. Happen we should pin a notice on the front door to warn the neighbours.'

'Mam?'

'What?'

'I'm going to ... well ... try and put things right.'

'How?'

'If you straighten it with Miss Leason, I could use some of her money for a bit of distemper and paper – get the house nearer to scratch. And our Janet might help me.'

'She might.'

'Will you have a word?'

'I will. Now wait there till I get a few odds and ends.'

While Mr Cowley patted butter with two wooden bats, Molly made polite conversation, her eyes straying towards the door where Joey lingered, a look of despair and self-loathing on his usually mischievous face. Yes, he'd had a hard lesson, but – God willing – the lad had learned from it. With his right side in shadow, he was the spitting image of Charlie Swainbank, the same expression too, the way Charlie had looked that night in the stable yard . . . Mr Cowley dashed round the counter and helped her to pick up the dropped change. 'My, you fair shivered then, Mrs Maguire. Somebody walk over your grave, lass?'

'Aye. Thanks,' she stammered.

'Got everything you need?'

'Yes, I think so.' Yes, she had everything. Except peace of mind . . .

When they arrived back at the house, Molly and Joey found almost total disorder. The two younger children spilled out at the front door, yelling and pulling at their mother's coat.

'Wait till you see, Mam! Just you wait!'

'Wait for what? What the blinking heck's going on, Michael?'

Bella Seddon stepped on to the pavement, arms folded, lips clamped together beneath the blackest of frowns. 'There's been a fair din from your house just lately, Mrs Maguire,' she pronounced. 'Happen I'll have to have a word in the rent-man's ear – old Leatherbarrow doesn't like rumbustious tenants in his houses.'

Molly pushed her children away. 'Hang on a minute while I get this sorted,' she muttered before turning to face the offending neighbour. 'Have you nowt better to do, Bella Seddon? Nothing in the pot, no fish to fry?'

The woman's mouth fell open. She wasn't used to a lot of backchat from Molly Maguire, though lately there'd been a thing or two said out of place . . . 'How do you mean?' she asked eventually, her back straightening with self-righteousness. After all, them bloody Maguires needed fetching a peg or two down.

'What I mean is, Bella Seddon, how come you're always watching me and mine when you should be keeping an eye to your own business by rights? Have you nowt at all to be getting on with, no lodgers to cater for?'

Bella Seddon blushed a deep and rather unbecoming purple. God, would she never live that down? Just a couple of paying guests for a week or two twenty years back? 'There's things going on in your house,' she said loudly. 'Like living next door to bloody bedlam, it is, what with your old feller singing his head off half the time and them kids out of hand all day long. I don't see as how I should have to put up with it! Now. I've said me piece and I'll say no more.'

A head appeared at the open upstairs window of the Maguire house. 'That you won't, ye old besom! And move out, why don't you? Get off on a midnight flit over to the grand end of town with the toffs, see will they put up with you! Whatever – leave us in blessed peace, woman!'

Everyone stared skyward as if fascinated by some unprecedented phenomenon. Molly stepped back and shielded her eyes. So this was the cause of the two youngsters' excitement. 'What are you doing with that bucket?' she shouted.

Ma put her head on one side. 'Breeding goldfish,' she snapped.

'You shouldn't be cleaning windows!'

Ma muttered something inaudible, then fixed her eyes on poor Bella who slowly backed away, a fist clenched over her heart. Dear God – she was up! The woman's magenta hue faded slowly to a sickly white. Now there'd be hell to pay, right enough. Why, when Ma Maguire got her paddy up, there was no doing anything to mend it. It had been said, over the years, that dogs stopped barking, birds stopped singing – even the bloody fleas gave over biting once Ma kicked off.

With her bucket balanced on the window ledge, Ma leaned out, her eyes skimming the street methodically – no doubt looking for evidence of bad housekeeping – and Bella shot a quick glance over her own day-old donkey-stoning. She was back! No more slacking, no more gossip – not with her coming home from the mill every night to look for dirty curtains or neglected flags, nosey old cow!

'Things have not improved,' said the voice from on high. ' 'Tis as well I am out of me bed at last.'

'You're . . . better then?' Bella managed with some difficulty.

'I am mending, Bella Seddon. And I suggest you do the same, for I have not seen a step so bad since the Zeppelin came over and left us a bomb or two. I think herself the other side of you could do with a wipe at the same time – is she ready for confinement? In which case, Missus, you should better go and see does the poor girl need a hand. Howandever we have not the time to spend here talking over the what's-to-be-dones and the wheres and whyfores with the likes of you.' She turned her attention to the children. 'We shall go this minute and thank the Lord that your Granny is spared and has not left you to the sort who takes in lodgers ten to the bed and never a mind for the neighbours.' She slammed the window and began to polish its inner surface furiously while the rest of the Maguires ran indoors, leaving Bella Seddon with her face almost down to her chest.

She looked furtively along the street to assess how many had heard the heated exchange, but all the doors remained closed. The old troublemaker! Ten to a bed? Never more than two and then it was just to help the war effort, giving them as made uniforms and bullets somewhere to put their heads at night. Aye, that one needed no bullets, did she? Mouth on her like one of them automatic machine-guns, she had. Oh yes, the stroke had slowed her down a bit, but she could still rattle off nineteen to the dozen, that nice soft Irish voice – like a velvet cover over barbed flaming wire, it was! They could have done with her during the war. She'd have broken through the lines for them – there'd have been no need to get them there tanks invented, because any sensible German would have run up a mountain to get away from that!

Oh well, nowt else for it, she thought as she went in for bucket, scrubber and stone. Best get on with it before she got reported.

Inside the Maguire house, joy reigned supreme. Molly, overcome completely after her outing to the hospital, sat howling her eyes out at the kitchen table. Daisy performed an impromptu clog-dance in the scullery doorway while Janet poured a glass of parsnip wine for Ma who glared across the table at her daughter-in-law. 'Would you ever take a look at that now, Janet? If that's a picture of happiness, sure I'd settle for a pig-killing every time.' She glanced over her shoulder at Joey and Michael. 'And behind me I've a pair of apes grinning like they've found out which dock the banana boat comes into. Pull yourself together, Molly Maguire, or I'm away just now to have another stroke and a bit of quiet!'

Molly looked up. 'Oh Ma. You don't change, do you?'

'Would you rather I should? Will I go out and come in again as the organ-grinder's monkey and cheer you up? Where's me other animal?'

Yorick pushed his large head on to Ma's lap and she fondled the soft yellow ears. 'The dog has you all beaten for sense,' she declared. 'He takes me as I am, doesn't mind whether me legs

333

are back to front or dropped off altogether. Daisy, would you stop that clogging? You're wearing out the floor and me head's bursting with the noise of it.'

'You talk a bit slower, Gran.' Janet refilled the ample glass.

'Ah well, there's a reason for all that now. In the first place, I had a clot in me head the size of a tennis ball and in the second place, where's me snuff? I have not had a good clear-out of the nasal passages in all this long while.' Janet dashed off to find the box as Ma continued, 'During which long while not every-body came to see me regularly. Those who did will be remembered. Those who did not will also be remembered, but on a separate list altogether.'

'Oh Ma . . . Ma . . .' Molly didn't know whether to laugh or cry. 'I've missed you!'

'I can see I've been missed, for isn't the place in a sorry state and me just off the critical list? Where's the Zebo for heaven's sakes? When did that grate last see a bit of spit? And me brasses have a bloom on them like the flowers in June. Ah now, 'tis a good girl you are, Janet Maguire.' She took the tiny box and emptied a liberal portion of yellow-brown powder on to the back of a clenched fist. 'See? Both hands!' she proclaimed before inhaling deeply. The pepper-like substance caused several sharp sneezes followed by a long sigh of relief. 'There now, isn't that better? I can walk, talk and breathe at last, so we must get on with things. Joey – away and do the grate. Janet can clean me brasses while you two little ones might help your mammy by scraping some praties. Molly – you and I have matters to discuss.'

Ma rose and walked towards the best room, the damaged leg trailing slightly as she moved. Molly turned towards her children, shrugged in a gesture of helpless submission, then followed her mother-in-law into what had become her bedroom.

They sat in twin straight chairs by the window.

'Well now, Molly. And how was Sarah Leason?'

'Causing bother.' She wiped her eyes. 'Won't stop in bed, has the poor ward sister up the pole and the rest of the patients on strike over their food. There's talk of force-feeding and Sarah's got everybody to sign a petition or summat.'

'Good. Sounds like she's on the mend.'

'Joey came. Did you send him?'

Ma studied her wedding ring. 'Joey does what he wants to do.'

'Happen he'll get over his bad ways, Ma.'

'Indeed. Give the money back after she's home from the infirmary.'

'I will.' Molly dropped her voice to a whisper. 'I reckon Joey knows where it is, though.'

'He'll not touch it.'

'No, I suppose you're right. So, you're up for good, eh? I'd never have thought it, even last week. It's like a miracle.'

'Nonsense! It was time to get better, so I got better. These things cannot be hastened or slowed. But I have a reason to be about my business again, so I suppose I have tried extra hard just lately.' She paused for a second or two. 'The box under me bed,' she continued slowly. 'There's a deal of disorder in it and I shall need things setting to rights by a lawyer. It seems that not all the Gallaghers were poor tenants. Some feller over to Sligo left me a piece of money and I'm taking a shop or two with it. Himself – the uncle – has willed everything to my first grandchild and as I seem to have a pair, then it must be split evenly between them.'

Molly's jaw dropped. 'Shops? For Janet and Joey?'

'That's the size of it. I thought a couple of shops would give them a start in life, but they'll need help in setting up the trade. There's money for stock too—'

'Well!' Molly's face was a perfect illustration of the term 'gobsmacked'. 'How long have you known about this?'

Ma considered her next untruth. 'A fair while. Only I said nothing because I didn't want Joey getting out of his boots and him still in clogs too. Can you imagine the face on Bella Seddon when she finds out we are people of substance? And Joey would never have kept this to himself. Neither would you, Molly.'

'That's true enough.' Molly pondered. So that was why Ma had had the twins trained for book-keeping and the like! Aye, Molly would never have sat long on a piece of information this size – she'd have been bursting to tell somebody! Shops in town? By, they were about to come up in the world.

'And that son of mine – may God forgive me for saying so – would have tried to take the lot to spend on a desperate pile of foolishness. How is he, by the way?'

'Daft as ever. He's supposed to be droving tomorrow, only he's taken a fancy for a night on the town, him and a few cronies. Fever's been up and down, but he's drinking that much – well, he makes himself ill. I noticed today he's a bit yellow again.'

Ma sighed and dropped her grey head. 'His liver is pickled, sure enough. After he's gone, they'll put him straight in a jar and he'll keep as he stands, for there's more whiskey than blood in his veins. He has been a sore disappointment to me, Molly, as was his father before him.'

Molly fixed her gaze on the box, a corner of which peeped out from beneath Ma's bed. 'Do you want me to take the papers down to a solicitor then?'

'No. I've me own arrangements. What we'll have to do soon is talk to the twins, see what do they want to sell. Joey will no doubt go into something mechanical, though I don't know what Janet would like. Of course, I've a few ideas in me head, but the young ones will have their own thoughts on the matter.'

Molly's eyes remained fastened on the box. 'What are your ideas?' she asked absently.

'Well, before I came to England, I had the privilege of seeing some real shops, Irish shops, proper emporiums with souls, they were. Not so much shops as meeting places for many a social gathering. I remember me Uncle Porrick taking me down along to some little town and showing me these fine businesses. They'd a feel to them, do you see? Like the one called Duggan's Stores. Now, there was a proper shop! Three doors it had, three separate establishments under the one roof. You could buy your groceries, go through and get a penny dinner, then on into the last shop to order your granny's coffin. Wonderful, it was. A grocer's, an eating place and a funeral parlour all in the one house. Mr Duggan was the owner of no less than three hats. He'd a yellow straw for the grocery, a flat white cap for the sit-down-to-eat and a tall black topper for the funerals.'

At last Ma had Molly's full attention. 'What?' cried the latter. 'You're not suggesting that our twins turn to undertaking?'

'Indeed I am not. What I'm saying is there's no need for just the one thing to be sold. I found that out when I worked with Freddie – they come for one item and buy another because it's on show. And why have one place for tripe and another altogether for bacon? Why walk a mile when you can cater for many needs in the one shop?'

Molly shifted uncomfortably in her chair. 'There's other problems, Ma.'

'I know. They're not talking to one another. And while Joey's no angel, that Janet of yours is as stubborn as a donkey in an orchard of windfalls. She'll not work alongside of him until she's ready and a bit of sense in her head. Ah now, take the look off your face, Molly Maguire! Weren't you a determined little madam in your time? Don't be travelling through life thinking Janet is perfect, for did not the good Lord put a flaw in every flower? I believe Janet will go for the mill in spite of this legacy. Another thing – she needs to escape Joey for a while, find her own bearings. A spell in the sheds will do no harm and whatever Joey makes of the shops, half will always belong to his twin.'

'But – hey, hang on a minute? What about Michael and Daisy? Won't they have a say in time?'

'Now Molly, I cannot be responsible for the terms of a will, can I? Sure, I never even met the man! It states that the money is for my first grandchild, so I invested it in the two shops I mentioned. No doubt the twins will take care of their own kin.'

Molly studied her mother-in-law closely. Something about this didn't ring quite true, but she weighed her words before tackling Ma. Even when she was in the best of moods, this matriarch was a force to be reckoned with. 'Ma?'

'Yes?'

'How did you . . . get this will? And when you did get it, how did you manage to read it?'

'Are you doubting my word, Molly?'

'No – but—'

'Ah. An attack of the no-buts, is it? For your information, it took British justice many a long year to find me. In the end, a solicitor got hold of me on account of the marriage lines—'

'But—'

'But what?'

'How did he find you? There's a lot of Maguires and Gallaghers – and some of your family didn't even know you'd come to England. If they're spread out all over Ireland . . . '

Molly sighed. It was no use. Ma's face was closed and bolted like an iron door with chains and padlocks holding it.

Behind the facade, Ma's heart was beating erratically and she knew that a cold sweat had broken out on her brow. Could she go through with this? And if not, wasn't this the time to get the linen washed? 'Janet's for Swainbank's is she?' The tone was deliberately light.

Molly jerked her head in acknowledgement. 'She says Leatherbarrow's is a bit old-fashioned. Mind, I'm hoping she'll change her mind now and stop out of the mill altogether . . . '

'Especially Swainbank's?'

'Not particularly. I don't want her going in any mill at all . . . '

'But she's determined to make a weaver, Molly. Swainbank has some good sheds for training in.'

'Yes.'

Ma glanced from Molly to the box and back again. With a blinding clarity of mind, she suddenly knew that this thing must be stopped, stopped now before the children heard about the shops, before hopes were raised and dashed . . . 'He's . . . lost his sons, I'm told. Didn't they die in a motor accident?'

Molly's hands were clenched tightly round the braided edges of her flowered wrapover apron. 'Aye. A few weeks back.'

'A terrible sad business.'

'Yes.'

There followed a very long pause, then Ma reached and

338

pulled the curtain aside as if to stare out into the street. 'Is something troubling you, Molly?'

'No more than usual. Joey's had me fair flummoxed with that robbery and I've been worried past meself in case the old lady upped and died . . . ' Her voice tailed away.

'You're a very pretty woman still, Molly. The worry on your face will set in lines unless you share it out.'

'I don't set a lot of store in me looks, Ma. It's what's inside a body that counts.'

Ma dropped the curtain. 'True enough. There's many a blessing arrives disguised. Take young Joey. If he hadn't failed with that burglary, who knows what might have become of him? There's grief on his face, but inside he's a much better person.'

'Aye. Happen he is.'

Ma clicked her tongue impatiently. This was the hardest moment of her life so far, worse than Paddy's birth, worse even than any loss by death, certainly harder than the stroke, than a million illnesses or shocks. 'Tell me, girl! Tell me!'

'Tell you what?' Molly's eyebrows shot upward. 'What am I supposed to say?'

'Either you say it or I will.'

Ma beat her breast with a closed fist before folding her arms as if to force back some rising inner tide. That two women could live together all these years with a shared secret that was not shared at all! Now there was himself to worry over. Swainbank might just choose to prove in spite of scandal that he had supported the twins, that they were his! Surely a mother had a right to such knowledge? If he came for the children – what then? There was Paddy who would throw a fit if he was sober, Molly with the shame to face all over again – not to mention a pair of youngsters who would find out that they were not Maguires at all.

But then again, he might not come. Perhaps he didn't want the twins even now, even with the others dead. Why, he'd not be much more than forty – couldn't he begin again? Whatever, Molly should know. And until she knew, the box and its contents would have to remain untouched.

'I think you're the troubled one, Ma.'

'We're both troubled. And it's time we aired all the nonsense in this house.' She paused, each hand gripping tightly on to the opposite elbow. 'Molly, I know.'

'What do you know?' Her face was white and strained.

'A story. About a young girl fresh as dew who fell into great difficulty. There were few she could turn to. Yet she has a wonderful family now, though she was for the streets not sixteen years ago. Or she would perhaps have been given a cottage by the man who brought her down. Who can say what might have become of her?'

Seconds passed. Molly slumped against the back of the chair, her face full of questions.

Ma took a deep breath. 'I have always known, child. And yes, we are in some danger, for the deeds under that very bed are from him – or from his father. I fought for the sake of your unborn child, Molly. Rightly or wrongly—' She blinked away the stinging tears. 'If his sons had not died, then I would have stuck to my lies about an uncle. Perhaps I should have done that anyway. But I can't. Suddenly, even after all the waiting and planning, I can't. Not today . . . '

Molly jumped to her feet. 'Paddy?' she whispered, a hand to her mouth.

'He knows nothing and seems to care even less. If he'd eyes in his head, wouldn't he have seen that Joey is the image of the other feller? Molly, the time for truth between us has come . . . '

The younger woman backed slowly towards the door. 'Money? You've took money and deeds for shops off . . . off him?'

'For you, Molly! You deserved compensation! What would have happened to you without meself and Paddy? An orphanage for the children, no place for you to turn! Or would you rather have been a kept woman? I had to do it! If you were in my place, could you stand by and watch a daughter fall?'

'I am not your daughter!'

'Ah, but you are. I was there at your birth, I minded you after Edie died. When I looked at you I recognized my own self, no mother, no father to care should you live or die. Whatever I have done, good or bad, has been for you and your children.'

Molly's eyes blazed with fury. 'That is the most high-handed bloody thing I ever heard of in my life! All these years I've worried about you finding out! And you knew! Damn you, you bloody knew! And what about your son, eh? What about the way you've pulled the wool over his eyes? You made sure we got wed!'

'Didn't you deceive him too, Molly?'

'There's a difference between desperation and . . . and calculation! You saw a way for yourself, Ma Maguire! A bit of comfort, a few extras! You have used me and my twins to feather your own nest!'

'That is not the case! I did it all for the love of you, Molly.'

'Rubbish!' She paced the floor, her arms flailing in the air. 'You've laughed at me! All I cared about was that no-one should know! For years I've worried in case Paddy ever noticed that they don't really look like either of us. And you've laughed up your bloody sleeve.' She paused, her shoulders straightening. 'Aye well. We'll see about that, Missus. They say the last laugh is the longest! How could you? Taking money off Swainbank, giving him a hold on my family—'

'The money has kept all of you—'

'And it will take two of us away!'

'How was I to know his children would die? And he may have others . . .'

'Right! Shut up, will you? For once, shut your flaming gob! That box is going back where it belongs if I have to walk or crawl on hands and knees every inch from here to Blackburn. And I'll pay him back the last penny! You're not the only one as can work in a mill. I'll get took on as a tenter, you'll see. If it takes me to retirement, I'll give him his money back!' She covered her face with her hands. He knew! He knew about Janet and Joey!

'So. You'll see your children with their backs broken in mills and factories when they could have their own shop?'

341

Molly's hands fell to her sides. 'My children and my decision,' she snapped quietly before bending to grab the box. 'Don't you ever forget that! And if you breathe a word of this to Janet or Joey, if I hear them going on about shops and the like, you'll wish you had died with your stroke! What's matter? Feels strange, does it, somebody shouting the odds at you for a change? Well, get used to it, because your reign's over. You just abdicated, Ma Maguire!'

Molly flounced from the room, the box gripped tightly against her chest.

The four children watched in amazement while their mother rooted about under the dresser for her best shoes, dragged a comb through her hair, threw her apron to the floor and pulled on a coat. It was teatime. Where would she be going at teatime?

Daisy sidled along the table's edge, hands and face covered in soil from the potatoes. 'What are you going out for, Mam?'

Molly rounded on all of them. 'Have you been listening at that door?'

Janet shook her head. 'No. Joey's only just in – he had to go for blacking. I've been in the wash-house doing brasses and these two were peeling in the scullery.'

Molly gazed hard at them. 'Right. Well carry on minding your own business and you'll not go far wrong.' She picked up her shopping bag and pushed the box inside. 'I've . . . I've got to go out. Janet, you get the tea and make sure your father eats something for a change. Don't let him out, Joey. Hide his pants and braces – just keep him in. If you have to take a jug to the outdoor-licence, then do it. As long as he stops away from Bobby McMorrow.'

Janet placed the gleaming brasses in the centre of the table. 'What's the matter, Mam? And where are you going?'

'Out! I don't have to explain meself all the time, do I? Give her in there a tray – happen she's still not up to sitting at the table.'

'Mam! Have you had a row with Gran?' Janet's voice faded as Molly opened the door, stepped outside, then slammed the latch home loudly.

Joey pulled at his twin's sleeve. 'Let her go, lass. There's been bother enough.'

She dragged herself away from him. 'Yes. And you should know all about that!'

Joey pushed her through the scullery doorway. 'Now listen, our Janet. I went up the hospital today and saw old Witchie . . . sorry . . . Miss Leason. She's more than willing to forgive and forget and I'm going to look after her in the future. I thought you'd help me—'

'Oh, if only I could believe you meant that, Joey Maguire.'

'I do – honest! Cross me heart and hope to die. I don't know what came over me, Janet. I just . . . well . . . thought about Dad and how useless he is, thought about slaving the rest of me life just to keep going on bread and marge. And yes, I took her money. It was wrong. I was wrong, but I stole it.'

'And hit her!'

He hung his head. 'No. I pulled the whip and she fell. If she can care enough about me not to tell the police, surely me own sister . . . ' He turned away from her, shoulders bent in an attitude of hopelessness.

Janet remained still and silent for several seconds as she thought about this. She would never trust him again, not completely. But for the sake of family peace – a peace that seemed to be growing more tenuous with each passing day – she concluded that an effort must be made. 'OK. We'll help her together. But you do anything like that ever again, our Joey—'

'I won't! I won't!'

'Right. Let's get the tea going.'

He piled vegetables into a large blackened pan. 'Hey, Janet?'

'What?'

'There's something going on, isn't there? Between Mam and Gran, I mean.'

'I don't know. They might be working out how to get Miss Leason's money back to her—'

'No. No, it's something else, something just as big, though. I think they've had a fair old bust-up.'

She nodded. 'Whatever it is, it's got something to do with Mam going out all of a sudden like that. I've never known her go out at meal times before. She'd Gran's private box with her and all.'

Ma Maguire lowered herself into a seat at the table, her eyes fixed on the open front door through which she could watch Michael and Daisy playing. She heard the two in the scullery talking and she called out now, 'Mind you put some turnip with the carrots. There's been no taste to anything just lately.'

Janet poked her head into the room. 'All right, Gran?'

'No, me darling – I'm still half left.'

'Your jokes haven't improved then?'

'So fetch me snuff!' And pray to God, she said silently, for your mammy not to do anything foolish. The hopes of a lifetime could be dashed this day. And not a thing could Ma Maguire do about it.

Molly began the long walk up the drive to the big house, her movements, still fuelled by temper, continuing swift and determined. She wasn't going round the back, no – not bloody likely. Long enough she'd been a servant here, eating the leftovers that old Bea had allowed the minions, begging for a set of new pinnies, jumping every time a bell rang. Well, she was going to use the big doorbell this time like a proper visitor and she couldn't care less if King George himself opened the door! Or Mrs Amelia, come to that! Aye, the time for worrying over what folk in this house thought was long past! She walked past terraced gardens and between the two crouching stone lions that guarded the paved path to the main entrance. God, the size of this house just for a family of three or four! Big enough for the Irish Guards including horses, it was.

She paused for a moment on the top step, just to make sure that the seams on her coarse stockings were straight. No fine hose for Molly Maguire, though the lady of this house probably bought such items by the drawerful. Not that Molly wanted fancy clothes and the like – oh no – all she wanted was her children. She rang the bell loud and long, feeling the hackles rising on her back, recognizing in herself the symptoms she often noticed in that daft dog at home when he was unsettled and the hair stood on end along his spine. Perhaps she should have brought him. He didn't take kindly to strangers, didn't Yorick, would have stuck up for her in his own dumb way. Yes, she was reacting just like an animal, though she could hardly compare herself to Ma's canine friend, because at this moment, she felt more like a tigress ready to pounce when cubs were threatened. Not that the threat was visible – she'd no proof that Charlie might be interested in the twins. All the same, just to make sure, she'd let him know where he stood, she would that!

A man opened the door. 'Yes?' His tone was pleasant and polite enough.

'I want to see Mr Swainbank, Mr Charles Swainbank. And it has to be private like – just him and me.'

'I see. Are you expected?'

'I've no idea.' She refrained from adding 'and I couldn't care less.' 'If you tell him Molly Dobson's here, I don't doubt he'll see me quick enough.'

The man stepped aside and allowed Molly to enter the wide hall, which was in itself a room big enough to accommodate a sizeable family. She stood by a large oval table, the first seeds of uncertainty taking root in her mind. It was one thing feeling righteous and angry out on the road, but another matter entirely here on his patch with all the surrounding grandeur. What was she going to say to him? Was she being a bit on the hasty side, coming all the way up here on the bounce without a ha'p'orth of proof or solid evidence to go on? After all, he'd kept his distance . . . But no! The money, all that cash handed round behind her back year in and year out – it wasn't right!

As soon as Charles entered the hall, she turned on him, the full force of her frustration stopping him dead just inside the doorway.

'You conniving bugger!' she spat. 'All this time I've thought I was rid of you. Even felt sorry for you, I did – why, I come up to that cemetery to see your poor lads going under! I've

345

been bothered a time or two, worried in case you'd done your sums and worked out that happen my twins were yours, but I felt you had no hold, no say. Then I found this.' She hurled the box across the floor and it skimmed over the highly polished surface until it rested at his feet. He bent slowly to pick it up as she continued, 'You and her, you and Ma Maguire—'

'What about me and Ma Maguire?' He straightened. 'I've never seen the woman for years—'

'You've sent her money though! Money I thought she'd earned fair and square in that mill of yours! You weren't meant to know about the children – she had no right to tell you! But there you've been, plotting away without me—' She pounded her chest to emphasize her words, 'without me – their mother – knowing what was going on.'

He walked across the room and placed Ma's box on the mantelpiece. 'This was none of my doing, Molly.'

'Oh, I know that! It was that old devil, that father of yours! I reckon he'd have been happier if I'd had my babies killed with a mucky knitting needle and a bottle of gin!' She walked to within a few feet of him now. 'I saved them – me! Not you that put them there, not Ma Maguire who sold her son for thirty pieces of filthy silver. Me! On me own with no help from you, no help from anybody! I wanted no help and I still want none. Nine months I carried my twins, fifteen years I've raised them. Proud of that, I was. Grateful to Ma too for working so hard for us, glad we never asked for a penny piece from your sweatshop hands—'

'I don't run sweatshops—'

'Don't you? Well, I've never seen a dry back coming out of one of your bloody mills!' She knew she was being unreasonable, but wanted the chance to carry on venting her feelings, needed to let it all pour out, the worry, the tensions of nearly sixteen years caused by this man. 'You're a rat, Charlie Swainbank, a cowardly good-for-nothing sewer animal. Why didn't you tell me you knew about my kids, eh? Why?'

'Molly—' He reached out to touch her arm. 'Calm down for Christ's sake—'

'Keep away from me!' She backed towards the corner. 'You're dirty, you are. When I think back – there I was, straight from school and into your mother's clutches, passed from her hands into yours . . . oh God, I feel sick! Treated me like horse-muck, she did. Then along you came with your fancy white scarf and your fancy black car, carrying on as if you thought I might be half-human after all—'

'Stop this, Molly! Stop it now! I will not have behaviour like this in my house. I loved you! All right? Does that make any difference? I bloody loved you! Half of me wanted to walk away from my life here just to find you and be with you. But we don't do that. Swainbanks don't walk away, aren't allowed to. Don't tell me you're the only sufferer, don't carry on like a wretched martyr. I'm sorry. What more can I say?'

She squared up to him. 'Sorry? What's sorry worth to me, eh? Nowt a pound!' She clicked her fingers under his nose. 'Now I find out you've got shops lined up for Joey and Janet – what next, I wonder? A king's ransom, a bucket of gold? Huh!' Her lip curled. 'Are you coming after mine because you've lost the other two? Can't you get yourself some more? If your wife's not having them, surely you can find some other daft bugger of a servant to carry your kids. You are the scum of the earth, Charlie Swainbank – for all your swank and posh furniture, you're no good!'

'Have you finished?'

'Oh aye, I have that! But I'm here to make sure you've finished as far as me and mine are concerned. I tell you now, if you come within a mile of my children, I'll kill you. Right?'

He leaned against the oak mantel, his head shaking slowly from side to side. 'I didn't have much say in the bargain struck between my father and your mother-in-law. If shop premises are available for your children, then all that was arranged by others. Any money sent to Ma Maguire was never handled by me – this has been a matter between lawyers.'

'I'll pay every penny back.'

'How?'

'I don't know.'

'I suggest we sit down, Molly.'

347

'You can do as you like. I've not come here to show off me manners.'

'I gathered that,' he said grimly as he seated himself in a fireside chair. 'Have it your own way then,' he said after several moments' consideration. 'I'll go to court and claim the twins as mine – I think there's enough documentary evidence to support such a declaration. If you want a fight, I'll give you one.'

'What?' In spite of her resolve, Molly fell crumpled into the chair opposite his. 'So. You were thinking of it then! I knew it – I felt it in me bones! How can you do that to me? Haven't you done enough already? You and that old witch at home . . .'

'That old witch cares for you, Molly. I firmly believe that she has always had your best interests at heart. In fact, I'd wager that she has not taken one penny for herself or for her son. But that is not the point just now. I wish to make provision for the twins and you are in no position to deny me. If you do, then I shall take the matter further.'

'Don't do it . . . please, don't do it!' She gritted her teeth. She'd come here to shout the odds, not to beg like a hungry hound. 'Why? Why can't you have some more kiddies? Or find a relative to take over after you?'

'There is no-one, Molly. And my wife is upstairs dying of cancer.'

The ormolu clock ticked as she stared into his haggard face. Tears sprang readily to her eyes. 'Oh no! Not Mrs Amelia! She can't be much older than me!'

'Thirty-six,' he said gruffly. 'And in a great deal of pain.'

She swallowed hard. 'I'm sorry, lad. See, I'll go now—'

'It's all right. Amelia has been a long time dying, poor soul. Your going or staying will not alter the situation.'

Molly stared down at her cotton gloves. Her voice quieter now, she said, 'Charlie, I don't want them rich. I don't want them having shops and certainly not mills. I've fetched them up and now you want to turn them into something else—'

'We could compromise.'

'How do you mean?' Her eyes were round with surprise.

'They're either yours or Paddy's – there's no way to get round it!'

'Just leave it all be, Molly. Look. Take the shops and let Ma say they're from an Irish uncle – yes, my lawyer put me in the picture. I don't want to fight you, really I don't. What would be the point of a legal battle when I don't even know Joey and Janet? Think about it. I get two children delivered to my door . . . '

'One at most. My Janet would never come . . . '

'All right – one child. Will he like that, will he want to be a Swainbank? Don't push me into doing something we could all live to regret. But I will take no money back because I wronged you and I have a debt to pay, so I insist on continuing to maintain the situation you have provided for the twins. When I die, they will inherit all my property. The will is made, Molly. But you could well be long dead before it is ever implemented.'

'But . . . my children will think I was a . . . ' Her voice died away.

'A whore? No, it's all in the will, the whole story. Well, what do you say?'

'What can I say? Whichever road I turn, you'll do what you want and never mind anybody else. Anyroad, haven't you a nephew? Didn't Master Harold have a lad? Why can't you shove it all on to him? He'll likely have been fetched up nearer the mark than my two – more gentrified.'

'He's useless.'

'So might Joey be! Haven't you thought that my lad has no idea of how to go about being a boss?'

'I've thought. I've thought endlessly – believe me. If he proves himself in a shop, then he might be capable of bigger things. Joey is an unknown quantity. Cyril's failure I'm sure of already—'

'I'm so . . . so scared though—'

'Don't be. Please try not to feel threatened. But I shall be getting to know the twins and I'd advise you against trying to put a stop to that. They won't learn yet that I'm their father – not from me, not unless it becomes absolutely unavoidable.'

Molly rose stiffly to her feet. Something about his tone annoyed her all over again. So controlled, so domineering – even though his wife lay dying, Charles Swainbank Esquire could go on discussing just about anything. As long as he had the upper hand, of course. 'You're not their father, Charlie. You're a self-centred creature with no thought for anybody except him you see in the mirror every day. Yes, you're a Swainbank all right. But you have never been a father to my children, wouldn't have cared about them at all if the other two had lived. If you'd been a proper dad, happen them poor lads might have survived.'

'How dare you?' He leapt from the chair.

'How dare I? Easy, that's how. Because I know what you are, because I know you've spent your life up to the eyeballs in cotton and money, no thought for folk. Struck a nerve, have I?'

'My sons died by accident . . .'

She nodded grimly. 'Aye. But my two survived in spite of you and well away from you. They don't go in cars, you see. I don't want them going in cars and sitting at fancy tables with silver spoons stuck in their gobs! I want them to be real people, not names on a bloody tombstone—'

'That is cruel, Molly Dobson!'

'Is it? Well, I think you're a failure. As a father, as a husband and as a human being.'

'You are being so unreasonable, so unfair!'

Molly took a few paces towards the door then swivelled to face him once more. 'Unfair? What's fair about any of it, eh? I didn't come up here to play fair, Charlie. I came to fight tooth and nail to protect my children. A wounded female doesn't know what fair means – and neither do you, come to that. What's fair about getting a girl in trouble while your wife's six or seven months gone? What's fair about your dad and our Ma plotting behind my back with you in it and all? And what's bloody right about that poor girl upstairs suffering while you carry on living?'

'Molly, shut up!'

'Oh aye?' She laughed mirthlessly. 'Keep your box of tricks, Charlie. Shove it where it fits!'

She stood, hands on hips, eyes flashing green fire, hair still soft and silky, the tiny body as straight and true as it ever was. He turned to face the wall. 'The box will be returned to Ma Maguire. Go home, Molly. Stop tearing at me for pity's sake.'

She hesitated, a hand to her throat. 'Hey?' she said eventually. 'Are you . . . are you all right?'

'I'm great, Molly.' His voice arrived muffled. 'I'm cruel, unfair, a failure as a father, my wife is dying . . . ' He sniffed quietly. 'I'm just fine, thanks.'

'Charlie—'

'Go, Molly.' He was sobbing now and the feeling welled up in her again, that old need to run to him and offer comfort.

She opened the door softly. 'Stop . . . stop stable-yarding me, lad.'

'Pardon?' He blew his nose before looking at her.

'Nothing.'

'What's stable-yarding? Molly!'

She ran down the six steps.

'Molly?'

'What? Bloody what?'

Their eyes met across the threshold that divided them. 'Molly?' he said again.

'I mustn't pity you, Charlie. I've not to feel anything for you, nothing at all. You're just a thing that's trying to stand between me and my twins, a bit of a wall or a fence! Nothing I can't jump. You are not to be a person!' Her tone rose hysterically. 'Go in! Go back in the house!'

Their eyes locked for several seconds before she turned and fled as if running for her life, running all over again, just as she'd run from Rivington Pike. There was a bench on Stitch-mi-Lane and Molly sat on it for a long time before going to find her bus. She was all mixed up inside, stomach churning, mind spinning like a kiddy's top after a solid whipping. The man was arrogant, infuriating, stupid too in his own way. Why then did she want to turn back and apologize for such bad behaviour, to make sure he'd had a proper dinner, to tuck him up for the night and tell him everything would be fine tomorrow?

She sighed. Because she was a mother, that was why. Because any injured creature stirred these emotions in her, turned her all protective and flappy like an old hen. Yes, she was a mother all right. And as a mother, Molly Maguire, née Dobson, walked into the dusk to find some transport. Her children were waiting at home.

Ma sat up late after the youngsters had all gone to bed, her head in her hands as she waited for Molly's return. Paddy had escaped, of course, was out on the rampage somewhere or other, likely up to a power of mischief.

Dear Lord, hadn't she always followed the prescribed path, a route dictated outside of herself? Hadn't she ever known that Molly and the children were her reason for going on in a way that was not strictly honest? And now she'd blown it all away, cast it out to the winds to be scattered by Molly, doubtless all thrown back in Swainbank's face by this time. It was late. Soon the pubs would empty, Paddy would return and there'd be little enough chance of getting Molly on her own.

Then the latch creaked and Molly stepped into the house, weariness plain on her face and in the slope of her shoulders.

'Where have you been, child?'

'I'm not a child – I'm thirty-three years old. And I've been out walking the streets of Bolton if you must know, pacing about like a cat on hot bricks.' She tore off her coat and went to hang it on the stairway door. 'Are they all in bed?'

'Except for your man. He got out by pretending to go twice to the lavatory – I think he must have carried the best suit with him the first time and then he probably changed into it on the second occasion. He's been gone a fair while.'

Molly came and sat at the table, her hands twisting together with anxiety. 'Happen I shouldn't have gone for you before, like. Not so hard anyway.'

' 'Tis no matter. The more I've thought about it, the more I've understood your point, Molly. Mind, I've always understood, always worried about this day. I know how it must seem to you, but I took only what I thought was owed to you and the children. Never a penny did I use for myself – except for a coat and some work clothes.'

'I know. But I wish you hadn't done it. He's named them in his new will, Ma. And there was me hoping he didn't even know the twins existed! Mind, I have mithered meself since his lads died, wondered what he'd make of Joey if he ever clapped eyes on him. If only you'd told me years back, I'd never have let you take his money.'

Ma gazed at Molly. 'Are you sure? Would you not have been tempted when Paddy lay in his bed too ill or too lazy for work? Would you not?'

Molly sighed. 'I don't know. There were some bad times, but nowt as bad as this. And to top it all, his wife's on her way out with cancer.'

'God bless her.'

'Aye. Unless he gets wed again, our twins stand to gain three mills and about four dozen houses – not to mention the big estate. Paddy'll hit the roof! I mean, what if Charlie Swainbank died sudden, eh? It's all in the will, all written down that he's their father. What'll happen to us, Ma?'

The older woman reached out and took hold of a chilled hand. 'It might have been me, Molly. In your place. Yes, it might easily have been me.'

'Eh? What are you going on about?'

'Me and Charlie's dad.'

'What? I thought all that was rubbish. Didn't you just look after his leg?'

'I trounced him from Delia Street to kingdom come on several occasions, Molly. You see, I loved him.'

Seconds ticked by. 'You what?' asked Molly finally. 'That miserable old bugger?'

'Yes. He wrote me poems, sent me fruit when I was ill, followed me through town just to catch a glimpse of the back of my head. Of course, I wouldn't let him touch me, wouldn't ever consider being a kept woman. But oh my Lord, was I tempted? And I hated him, Molly. My hatred for him was so strong that I had to pray for my soul's very existence.'

'Yet . . . yet you loved him?'

353

A solitary tear made its way down Ma's haggard face. 'I worshipped the very ground on which he stood. Aye – another sin. His presence in a room was like physical torture, for I wanted so much to touch him, love him, be with him.'

'Oh . . . Ma!'

'I know! That's why I shielded you and protected your pride. It was like looking at my own reflection – there but for the grace of God and all that kind of stuff. He died in my arms, Molly. I let him slip away without knowing him as a woman should know a man. Yes, look at my list of great mortal whoppers! I was cold the night he died, chilled to the bone. Nobody has ever warmed me like he did. Nobody.' She began to shake with sobs of self-pity and regret.

'You'll . . . meet him in heaven, love.'

'Will I? Is that where I'm going, is it where he's gone to? And would heaven be big enough to hold the pair of us fighting like a couple of gutter children? At least you had the courage to love your man, Molly.'

'Yes. But I love Paddy too.'

'Do you?'

'He's gentle, Ma. There's things about Paddy you can't know, not as a mother. There's more to Paddy than meets the eye, a lot more. I don't want him hurt.'

Ma dried her eyes. 'What was it like seeing Charlie again?'

'Not easy.'

'So. You'd not leave Paddy for him?'

'I wouldn't leave Paddy for any man. But—' She shook her head slightly.

'Sure there's no need to explain. I know what comes after the but, for didn't I live with it all those years? Whatever, let's hope we come out of this terrible pickle in some kind of order.' She turned her head and continued, almost to herself, 'The houses are joined – I've always known that. Aye, there's a bit of old Granny in me after all—'

The door flew open and Paddy fell in, his arms wrapped around the neck of a red-faced young policeman. The constable nodded tersely at the two women, then dragged his untidy charge across the floor.

'Me legs have gone,' announced Paddy as he found himself being forced into a fireside chair.

The policeman straightened and fought to regain breath and composure. He looked accusingly at Molly. 'Can't you keep him in, Missus?'

'Why? What's he done now?'

'I found him on St George's Road having an argument with a lamp post. The subject of discussion was a bike – he reckoned the lamp post was trying to pinch it off him.'

'He hasn't got a bike,' said Ma.

'I know he hasn't, Ma! It was my bloody bike!'

Ma looked at Molly and Molly looked at Ma. The offending party slid down from his chair and landed gracelessly on the rug where he lay singing:

> 'If you ever go to Ireland
> Will you kiss my dear mother for me . . . '

Ma turned away from this scene, outwardly engrossed in a statue on the dresser, the figure of a boy holding a bunch of cherries to his lips. She dried her eyes of recent tears and fought the laughter that threatened in her chest.

Molly gazed down at her husband. 'Shut up, Paddy! We'll have her next door banging on the wall again.'

The policeman edged away towards the front door. 'If he carries on, I'll have to take him in for drunk and disorderly.'

'And no visible means of support,' interposed the voice from the floor. ' 'Cos me legs have gone . . . '

This proved too much for the women. With one voice they began to laugh loudly, each clasping herself round the middle as if trying to contain such disobedient and unseemly mirth. The policeman, aware of the hysteria in these sounds, beat a hasty retreat from the house.

'I am a sick man!' moaned the sorry bundle on the floor. 'Death's door is where I'm at, yet me own mam and me own wife—'

'Oh, get up the stairs, eejit,' shouted Ma. 'Go and sleep it off, won't you?'

Molly slumped against the wall. 'He'll never make it. Not without visible means . . . '

With great difficulty, Paddy focused his eyes on his wife's face. 'You'll be sorry when I'm gone,' he said mournfully before beginning to crawl on hands and knees towards the stairway door. 'No stomach for me food, me thumb on fire, a terrible disease filling me veins—'

'That's milk stout, not TB,' yelled Ma. 'Get out before I take a broom to your backside!'

Alone once more, the two women rested in the pair of chairs that flanked the grate, each staring into the dying fire as sobering thoughts arrived to obliterate the memory of Paddy and his antics.

'Funny how we've both loved Swainbanks,' said Ma quietly. 'I looked at Richard one afternoon in town – and it was as if I already knew all of this. Oh I cursed him many a day, laid so many bad wishes at his door that I frightened meself at times. All to protect my precious virtue. So. It happened to you instead, to my own dear girl.'

'Don't blame yourself. I don't believe in all that stuff anyway. I had free will, Ma, same as the priests have always taught me since I turned. It was nowt to do with you and old Richard. Me and Charlie got in this mess without any help from you.'

'Strange though.'

'Yes.'

'So. What do we do, Molly?'

'We open shops. He's twisting my arm that far up my back – well, there's no alternative. It's blackmail, Ma, but I can't fight it clean or even dirty. Aye. He's paying the band, so we dance to his tunes. Charlie Swainbank has agreed to be your Irish uncle. For a while, at least.'

'I'm sorry, Molly.'

'So am I, love.' She sighed heavily. 'Aye, so am I.'

Chapter 11

On a balmy summer evening, Amelia Swainbank slipped into her final drug-assisted sleep, emerging now and then to reach feebly for her husband as the last agonies racked her emaciated body. For days he had remained by her side, a constant guardian and companion at the grim gate towards which she journeyed in spite of his staying hand. At the end, he prayed inwardly for her death, begged that she might be released from the unendurable. Not a word was spoken as Dr Blake inserted the needle, administering a dose that would push her gently and mercifully into an oblivion that had never been discussed, a decision made without the uttering of a single syllable. Nurse Fishwick and Charles bore witness to this, hanging on to each other like brother and sister while the doctor performed his invaluable act of kindness.

It was over. The two professionals managed, at last, to drag him away from the cooling corpse. He wandered out to the landing and howled like a baby, eventually allowing himself to be led to his own room.

The doctor addressed his colleague. 'Stay with him, Nurse. Don't leave his side for a minute – get help for your own rest times. This will be his undoing if we don't take care.'

'I'll not leave him, Doctor Blake. Not till he's right. And . . . thanks. God bless you.'

'Does He approve of me?'

She blinked rapidly to clear the wetness from her eyes. 'There's law beyond the strictly legal. You're a good man and a damn fine doctor.'

He went away to attend to the paperwork. Just another signature, a brief list of causes primary and secondary, date and time, dot the I, cross the T, close the file. Just another beautiful and agonized soul delivered prematurely to its Maker, very probably not the last to travel on an assisted passage ticket.

The doctor's main concern was not for Amelia whose sufferings were over, nor for what he himself had perpetrated in order to ease her exit from this world. His mind was fixed on Charles Swainbank, a man who, until recently, had seemed to have everything. True enough, Amelia had been on her way for some time, but to lose the boys and his wife so quickly – how would the poor chap cope? The swift deterioration in Amelia after her sons' deaths had come as no surprise, but what would happen now to Charles, alone in the world except for employees and a few business contacts? He'd never been a great one for friends, hadn't Charles, wasn't an easy man to get to know. Ah well. The doctor drove slowly towards the main gate, his head shaking sadly as he thought of the big man and his great tragedy.

Charles lay on his bed, eyes travelling over moulded ceiling covings, along the picture rail, down the length of a rosewood wardrobe and on to the substantial figure of Nurse Fishwick. The doctor had administered something to slow him down, yet his senses remained alert to the point of pain. She sat beside him in a wicker chair, a piece of neglected needlework resting crumpled on her knees.

'Nurse?'

'Try to relax, sir.'

'Stay with me.'

'I shall. If you get a nightmare, somebody'll be here all the time, so don't you be worrying about dropping off.'

'No.' He pushed himself further up on the pillows. 'I didn't mean that. When it's over – if I survive all this . . . ' He waved a hand towards the door. 'Stay with me. I'll give you the rate and half again for you to take charge of number one as State Nurse and Welfare. You can see to them when they get hurt, help judge their fitness for work, go on home visits when there are problems.'

She pulled the covers to his chin. 'We'll discuss it tomorrow—'

'You could wear a smart suit instead of that uniform. And you can carry on living here as a staff member – nice rooms and full board laid on . . . ' He was gabbling now, chattering like one trying to make his way out of a maze of shock by dwelling on matters mundane.

'All right. Whatever you say.'

'You'll do it?'

'Yes, I'll do it. I've nowhere else to go, Mr Swainbank, nowhere definite. I just wander round in circles looking after incurables – a change would do no harm.'

'Haven't you a family – parents?'

She plucked at the embroidery silks, her face a mask over submerged emotions. 'No.'

'What happened to them?'

'Cancer.'

'Both?'

She nodded quickly. 'My mother was widowed, died two years ago. I nursed her to the end. It was then I decided to work in people's homes, help them to stay out of hospital if possible. She hated hospitals, did my mother.'

'And your father?'

'A brain tumour when I was fifteen.'

Charles reached for the large strong hand. 'Then you know how I feel at this moment, Nurse?'

'Nobody can know that, sir. But you're not by yourself. I remember my own private grief, so I can meet you halfway. It's personal, everybody takes it differently. The one common factor is that there seems to be no reason for going on, especially when you've been through a few bereavements. But there is a reason – always. At first, you can't see it, but it's still there, very strong and enduring. Mine was helping folk get by, seeing they were all right before I moved on to another case. I've never left right off after a funeral. When you nurse the terminally ill, you nurse a whole family.'

'Except here. There's no family here, is there?'

She patted his arm. 'There's you. Whether it's a brood of ten or a person on his own, I see the job through.'

'And what's my reason for going on?'

She smiled patiently. 'I could say your mills and your work-force, but I won't. Your reason is that you're here – it's as simple as that.'

'I don't want to be here. Not without them, not without a future.' He paused for a while, deep in thought. 'Is suicide such a terrible thing?'

'Not always, no. If you're at the end of your rope and tormented to the point of mental illness. But it's not for you, Mr Swainbank. Yours is a bright light, too healthy to be snuffed out on an impulse. You'll go on living your life as best you can because you fear nothing. More positively, I'd say life clings to you and won't let go. Anyway, the reasons outside yourself will just arrive. But it's the inside ones that count.' She pushed his hands under the counterpane. 'I'll pop down and make us both a drop of cocoa now.'

In the kitchen, she found the cook, Perkins and Emmie deep in grief, the two women sobbing at the table, the man sitting on the floor in front of the open fire, his arms wrapped around Klaus, the black labrador which had been Mrs Swainbank's pet for many a year. The dog raised his soft muzzle and whined pitifully. 'He knows,' said Perkins sadly.

'They always do.' The nurse crossed the room and stroked black satin ears. 'You'll have to look after your master now,' she said to the unhappy animal before turning to observe the three servants. 'Listen to me, all of you. I know I've not been here long and you might think I'm talking out of turn, but he's in a bad way up there. I don't want to cause any more upset, but I believe you ought to know he's not thinking straight.'

'How do you mean?' Mrs Marshall made an attempt to dry her streaming eyes on her sleeve.

'Well, planning for the future one minute, carrying on with the next breath as if there is no tomorrow. He might just damage himself, try to . . . oh, you know what I'm talking about. He's lost all his loved ones – it's unhinged him. Now, I realise I'm the nurse, but I can't keep my eyes open all the time. We shall have to work shifts. So I suggest you all pull yourselves together and help me, otherwise we might well lose what's left of this family.'

'No!' Emmie jumped up from the table. 'Will I go to him now, Nurse?'

'Yes. Take him some cocoa and a biscuit – he's had nothing solid since about Thursday.' She fell wearily into a chair. 'This is one of my days for wondering about God. I mean, what can I do for Mr Swainbank after the things heaven's allowed to happen? And why did this family arrive at all that trouble – two boys and a lovely lady snuffed out in a matter of weeks? People think I'm hard because I'm a nurse and I see things – but oh no, that's not the case. It gets to me! It does!' She hugged herself and began to rock back and forth, her own tears dangerously close. 'It was the boys that finished her, Mrs Marshall. She might have gone on without too much pain if—'

'Nay lass.' Mrs M dashed round the table, her own sorrow set aside for the moment. 'Her would have died anyroad, love, with or without her lads and with or without a nurse. Well away before you ever came near, she was, 'cos I watched her fading with me own eyes! Don't take on! There were nowt in this world you could have done, girl, nowt this side of a miracle!'

'I feel so . . . useless!'

Perkins leapt up and came to the table, throwing a heavy arm around the nurse's trembling shoulders. 'What's thy name, lass?'

'Caroline – Carrie for short.'

'Well look here, Carrie for short, we shall "Carrie" thee out next news if we're not careful. You don't look so good yourself. Aye, it's right enough, we did cod ourselves as you'd be used to watching pain without it bothering you. You should have come to us before, love. Not a one of us here would have turned a back on a worker in this house. Now, you just listen to me. Will you be stopping on?'

'I'm not sure. He's for putting me in the mills as welfare – says I can live here if I like – but he might not be talking sense—'

'Yes he is, 'cos he's mentioned it to me before this, asked me and Mrs M here our opinion of you, like. You live at Briars if you want. There's none of us has family apart from one another. Mrs M's never married, gets called Missus on account of her job. Me and Emmie – we're on our own too, so we stick together – safety in numbers. And him upstairs is no bad master. You could do a lot worse than throw in with us.'

'Thank you. I'll stay if he asks me again. I'd like to settle and I've no home apart from a couple of rooms in Bradford Street.'

Mrs Marshall poured a large drink and pushed the glass into the nurse's tense hands. 'Put yourself outside of that, lovey. It's only cooking, but it'll take the sharp edges off. We mun stick together from now on. Emmie can do the first shift while midnight, then I'll take over. Jacob here will sit with him in the morning, give you a rest up to dinner. Nay lass, we'll not let our master go, not without a damn good fight . . . '

And so it continued until well after the funeral, the four of them dogging Charles Swainbank's every step as he made his uncertain way through a second bereavement while the first had not yet served its time. Rules in the house slackened; at first, the master took his meals on a tray in the study because the isolation of the dining room was too chilling to bear. Most weekends and evenings he spent walking with Klaus and Perkins, pacing through his mourning in companionable silence with servant and dog.

Then, one unseasonably cold Sunday, Charles announced his intention to dine in the kitchen, nominally to save fuel, actually to escape from solitude and the negative thoughts that plagued lonely moments. So began the gradual erosion of that fine divide between the residents of Briars Hall and while Charles remained indisputable master, an enduring comradeship was born between the five of them, often extending to daily workers who ceased to express their surprise on finding Mr Swainbank doing his accounts by the kitchen fire when they arrived for a tea-break.

After his return to full-time work, Charles came home in the evenings and read the Bolton papers while Mrs M bustled around him with pots and pans, while Jacob Perkins cleaned silver and polished shoes, while Emmie chattered on about the latest film or a new kind of lipstick. As the weeks passed, Charles Swainbank remembered his dead boy's wisdom, learned for himself that there was, at the end of a day, no division between peoples, that master and servant could sit at the one table, that crossing the invisible line had proved, for himself at least, not only painless but also necessary.

He taught his companions bridge and chess, discovering an agility of minds that had previously been unlooked for, unnoticed. From Perkins he learned to play a vicious hand of poker, while many of his spare coins were lost in games of pontoon and find-the-lady. As long as he lived, he would never forget the four people who had dragged him out of the mire and back on to the safety of firm ground.

As Nurse Fishwick had predicted, reasons for continuing began to arrive. He bought most of Delia Street, paying old Leatherbarrow a price that left the man gaping. After studying plans, he sent in a workforce to renew plumbing, wire the houses for electricity, treat walls and roofs against the eternal damp and decorate the homes to a high standard. He consulted lawyers and accountants, moved tenants from the two shops on Bradshawgate, found them decent premises elsewhere, then had the shops cleared and cleaned in preparation for the twins.

Nurse Fishwick was duly installed as Medical and Welfare with number one mill as her base. After a while she was accepted, though at first she was treated like a spy – something to do with time and motion – because she lived at the big house. While she practised what she called her 'union smile', Charles spent many an hour crawling on hands and knees over oily floorboards, measuring every inch of numbers one and two, trying to work out how to keep up profits while installing machines with safer space between them. He was aware of cutting a comical figure, especially after hearing on the stairs, 'Did tha see yon Charlie afore? All mucked up like a bloody greaser he were. Tell thee summat, Jack. Them there 'ighborns is too inbred, it gets ter t' brain at t' finish.' But he didn't care. Even if he had been 'daft in th' 'ead', the Bolton folk would have forgiven him. They were straight, unnervingly direct, but very warm. Had he noticed that before? Probably . . .

Thus Charles's life, while empty in a personal sense, became meaningful once more. The truest meaning though was his interest in the Maguire family whose progress he monitored daily. It was a brave attempt they were making, an assault on a buying public set in its ways and still suffering financial depression. But whoever had dreamed up this audacious concept had imagination and an eye to a better future, that much was plain, for the shops even before they opened displayed a vigour that attracted comment from many quarters. In his bones, Charles felt that an old head had birthed this idea, that Ma Maguire was its true inventor. Three shops in one, three different businesses under one management – the novelty and daring amused him. And because of its uniqueness, the venture would probably succeed.

Behind the scenes, Charles orchestrated many a miracle, greasing the odd palm, bending the ears of the influential to make the way easier for the Maguires, smoothing out legalities and licences whenever it looked as if the path might roughen. Each day he drove past the site, watching as workmen carried in shelving or chairs and tables, supervising from afar while painters brightened the weather-stained exterior. But even he was ill-prepared when the big day arrived, for the sign was so commanding that it shortened the most nonchalant breath. A bright emerald-green rectangle was erected above the three doorways and the signwriter worked painstakingly in black and gold for several days before the message became fully plain.

MAGUIRES' MARKET was printed out in high-case copperplate, while underneath, in smaller lettering, the building's new purpose was explained.

Enjoy our Irish kitchen (Ma Maguire's famous herbal teas and remedies also available)

Hand-trimmed clothing – wools and cottons – patterns and yarns

New and secondhand bicycles – also repairs and maintenance

Charles closed the door of his car and grinned widely. Ah, she had the right idea – get them in for a bowl of stew, let the ladies browse through hats and trimmings while the men and boys studied bikes. And if the stew didn't suit their digestion, a remedy would be on hand! He found himself laughing aloud as he drove away. Why, if the old girl stayed alive long enough, there'd be Maguires' Markets from here to Timbuctoo!

He made his way back to number one. For the first time ever, he would be there to interview the new intake, trainees straight from school, the workers of the future. The manager had been shocked at this intention, believing that his own abilities were being questioned, but Charles had pacified the man by explaining that Nurse Fishwick needed some interview experience and that Charles himself wished to supervise her induction.

The real reason for Charles' sudden interest in these school-leavers was invested in a single name halfway down the list, one Janet Maguire who had submitted an application for a weaver's apprenticeship. Yes, he wanted to meet the little madam who had obviously turned down the chance to work in her own family business. There was going to be more to this one than just a pretty face, he suspected.

He was right. When summoned, she stepped into the office with a firm stride, gloved hands folded neatly at her waist, head held high, eyes making bold contact each time she was addressed. Nurse Fishwick filled out the standard questionnaire with its endless enquiries about health and family situation, then Charles dismissed her to her own office, using as excuse the fact that several absentees had not been accounted for on that day.

He faced this new grown-up daughter and his heart nearly burst when he saw those straight Swainbank brows above a pair of smoke-grey eyes that were almost too beautiful to describe. He cleared his throat nervously. 'What do you know about cotton then, Miss . . . Maguire? Did you learn anything at school?'

'A bit. Only I've read more in books out of the library. I think

365

it's . . . well . . . really funny. Not for laughing at, I don't mean that. But it's like a story, isn't it? You get a plant grown hundreds and thousands of miles away, pile it on a boat, sail it halfway round the world, then we make cloth of it.'

He was suddenly smiling. 'Yes, if you put it that way, I suppose it must seem a bit odd.'

'I think it's unbelievable. I mean, if it wasn't actually happening here in Bolton, you'd think somebody had made it all up! Course, it's been round donkey's years, long before we got hold of it. When we first did, it was called vegetable wool 'cos they'd all been used to getting their clothes off sheep.' She leaned forward, clearly warming to a favourite subject. 'Anyroad, this here Roman feller called Pliny – I think he was one of their poshknobs – he decided that cotton pods looked a bit like quince. That's a fruit. Have you ever ate one?'

'No.'

'Well it is a fruit, it was in the book. Now the Latin for quince is cotoneum, so cotton could have got its name there. Only I found out it's likely Arabic, k-o-t-o-n what sounded something like gooten. It's dead interesting, though.'

It was in her blood! From both sides she'd got it, from himself genetically, also from the experience of being reared by a cotton family. Though the interest she'd taken in research could only have come from him, he told himself somewhat smugly. No ordinary girl would know so much about the industry and its history.

'Am I talking too much?' she was asking now. 'I get in bother over that off me mam.'

'Do you?'

'Oh aye. She reckons I have more to say than the BBC Home Service.'

'And you want to be a weaver?'

'Yes. My granny's a weaver – a good one too.'

'You'll not be able to talk in a weaving shed, Janet. It's too noisy and far too busy.'

'I know. I'll have to shut up and learn to lip-read.'

Charles moved a few papers on the desk and placed his elbows on its surface while he studied this personable young woman. 'I believe your family is about to open a shop in the town centre. Have you no inclination to work there?'

She sucked in her cheeks while considering the reply to this. 'I don't want to sell things – I'd sooner make them. I thought if I learned enough about different cloths, I could happen make some dresses and that for the shop in me spare time, but for full-time, I'd rather come in the mill. I . . . I don't really want to work with our Joey . . . '

'I see. Do you mind if I ask why?'

'Well, Mr . . . er . . . er . . . what did you say your name was?'

'Swainbank.'

She swallowed. 'You mean . . . you're the boss? Ooh, I never thought—'

'I own the mills. But I'm still an ordinary chap, wouldn't you say?'

'I wouldn't know, sir.'

'Oh, come on! Why don't you want to work with your brother?'

She sighed resignedly, then looked him straight in the eye. 'Might as well hang for a sheep, I suppose,' she muttered. 'Have you ever been a twin, Mr Swainbank?'

'No. No, I haven't.'

'Well, you've missed nowt, I can tell you. It's murder at times – like having your shadow with you all the while, even in the dark, somebody you're fastened to through no fault of your own. I love my brother, Mr Swainbank, but I want to be . . . oh, I don't know—'

'Independent?'

'Aye, that's it. I want to make me own way. They're all mad with me at home, mouthing off 'cos Gran's got these shops and I should know which side me bread's buttered. Only I need to be . . . separate.'

Charles stared at her. These were the things he would have known, should have known about his own daughter. That she was free-spirited, imaginative, bright. Fifteen years he had missed. Now she came to him, a grown-up new baby with her character formed by circumstances he might have altered or improved. 'It's a hard life in a cotton mill, dear.'

367

'I've no fear of work. And it's not as hard as it used to be.'
She lowered her lashes and, for the first time, averted her
gaze. 'My mother doesn't want me working for you. Happen
she's read the same books as I have, though she doesn't really
have a lot of spare time for reading. I don't know why, but she
doesn't seem to like you, Mr Swainbank. Perhaps she doesn't
like mill owners.' She shrugged and drew a deep breath.
'Your great- or maybe great-great-grandfather had men
hanged for croft-breaking, sir. That doesn't happen any more,
so nothing's as bad as it was.' She looked down at her gloved
hands and continued, as if to herself, 'They got hanged on
Bolton Moor for stealing half a dozen yards of cloth.'

'They were similarly punished for a loaf or a cup of milk,
Janet. You seem to read a lot.'

She suddenly looked at him again, her face filled with a
kind of excitement he had not witnessed in years. 'Half of me
wishes I'd been alive then, before the bleachworks, when
Bolton was surrounded by miles of cloth left out in the sun to
whiten. I bet it looked like snow in the middle of summer.'

He hid a grin behind an outspread palm. The girl was
plainly a romantic at heart. 'And what would you have done
with the croft-breakers?'

'In your lot's place, I'd have given them a good hiding and
got me cloth back. As a worker though, I'd have stuck up for
them and fought back . . . '

'And you'd have given my lot a good hiding?'

'Aye, I would.' Her chin jutted forward. It was clear that
though she wanted the job, she would air her views nevertheless.

He cleared his throat again. 'My mills are being renovated.
You'll find conditions here will improve gradually and your
mother can hardly disapprove of that. Number three is almost
finished – work begins on one and two next year.' Dear God,
was he apologizing to this child?

'About time too, Mr Swainbank – if you don't mind my
saying so. Happen you should have a word with Leatherbarrow, 'cos he's still in the Iron Age. Arms and legs have
been lost, not to mention lives. I want the mills great because

they're a part of our town, but I don't want them cruel.'

Yes, this was a cheeky young imp. Her mother was right, too much to say, too careless about choosing her audience. Any other mill owner in the town would have seen her off as a possible troublemaker. But he wouldn't. And not only because of who she was, but because she fascinated him with her clear thinking and brave expression. 'Would you not prefer to work in the offices?' he asked. 'I've an opening for a clerk—'

She shook her head vehemently. 'No. I can't see meself happy pushing a pen and wading through lists. I want me own looms and me own patterns – I like what they call fancies – all them brocades and such. One day, I want to invent a cloth of mine, something a bit Chinese or Indian with squiggly bits on. Me school reports were all good. I never missed, never got in no trouble. Ooh, I do hope I've not got on your nerves talking out of turn.'

'No, you haven't. I'm pleased to hear you speak your mind, though I should expect loyalty at all times if I were to employ you. If conditions are not perfect as yet, all my workforce is well and fairly treated. I'd be happier to hear less about lost limbs – we do try to send our staff home in one piece at the end of the day.'

She hung her head. 'I'm sorry.' Then, as suddenly as she had dropped it, she thrust her jaw forward once more. 'I love the mills, Mr Swainbank. If they weren't mills, some of them would be the most beautiful buildings I ever saw. We've a photo at home of Buckingham Palace – it's dead plain, all square and flat. I always thought the king would live somewhere special – a grand posh house with castle walls and stuff. But it's ugly and ordinary, right disappointing. If we had a garden outside this mill, it'd be like a palace, a proper one.'

'And where would I keep the princess? In the north-east or the south-west tower? Yes, that might present a problem, having two towers. Prince Charming wouldn't know where to look.'

Her mouth spread into a wide and extremely becoming smile. Her mother's smile. 'I know. I'm proper daft, aren't I? Me mam's always told me to keep me gob shut except for

369

answering questions. She says me imagination runs away with itself and unless I can make a bob or two out of writing me soft tales, I'd best keep them to meself.'

'There's nothing wrong with pride in your town and the industry that supports it, Janet.'

'Oh I'm not that proud, sir. Black people got put in chains for us. We shoved them on ships and sold them like animals. Them that lived through the trip got stuck in boiling cotton fields till they dropped dead. Then there was us here, spinners and weavers from way back, all living in cellars with no drains, dying of fevers, nowt to eat.'

'And you blame my kind for that?'

'Somebody's to blame for it, sir. But you didn't invent slavery, did you? And I can see you're trying to put things right, proper wages and canteens, welfare to see to us. No. You can't be blamed for things as happened before your time.'

'Thank you.' He smiled wryly. This fifteen-year-old was about to turn forty if he wasn't mistaken.

'Oh heck.' She slid an inch or two down in her chair. 'I bet I haven't got the job. I was warned – it's me own fault. I haven't got what me granny calls tact. Mind you, neither has she. Oh well. I'd best go to the dungeons and see old Cowcart.'

'Who?'

She gritted her teeth against this latest faux pas. 'That's what we call Mr Leatherbarrow, sir. Well, it's one of the names we call him anyroad. Cow as in leather, cart as in barrow.'

This was too much. He leapt from the chair and made a mad dash for the window.

'Mr Swainbank?' She stared at the shivering back.

'Yes?' The voice was strangled.

'Are you ill, sir?'

'No.' He mopped his eyes with a large white handkerchief. The seconds ticked away. 'Mr Swainbank?'

'Just . . . just a moment, my dear . . .'

She tapped the edge of the desk with the tips of her fingers, then examined the newly-washed white gloves for dust marks. 'Are you killing yourself laughing, Mr Swainbank?'

'Shut up, Janet!'

'Yes, sir.'

Charles returned to the desk, mouth clamped against merriment. He spent a moment or two going through the motions, applying the odd tick or written comment in the margins of the questionnaire. 'Your grandmother is the best weaver we ever had,' he managed eventually. 'She won't be coming back, then?'

'I don't think so.'

'A pity. She might have taught you.'

'No thanks! I've trouble enough – hey! Does that mean you'll take me on?'

It occurred to Charles that the boot was on the other foot, that this commanding little personality might well 'take him on' in the future if he didn't watch his step. If she followed Ma, then she'd be sleeping under a union banner rather than a bedspread! But this was too bright a button to put back in the box. Yes, the slender waif with her polished blue clogs and thin cotton gloves was his only tangible link with the future – she and her dark-eyed brother. 'Start next Monday. Stay behind for the guided tour – it's part of your education.'

She jumped up from the chair, her eyes bright with victory. For one terrible moment, he thought she would grab his hand and shake it, or worse still, run round the desk and hug him. Had she done the latter, he would surely have been reduced to a pool of tears. But she hung on to her pride, gabbled her thanks, then fled from the room to send in the next candidate.

Charles remained where he was, determinedly seeing the task through to its end, trying to conceal boredom as he talked to other pale-faced applicants, a sombre group all scrubbed and dressed as if for Sunday school. Not one of them asked a question; few replied to his in better than a monosyllable. But then, none of them was a Swainbank and every last one had probably been terrified by teachers, perhaps even threatened by parents who desperately needed another worker in the house.

During the tour which followed, Charles found himself looking at this, his oldest mill, with eyes opened by Janet Maguire. Oh, he knew every inch of the place, but he could not help wondering how it looked to her.

371

He stood in the opening and blending rooms where the process began, watching her as she questioned a foreman closely. All around, groups of men were breaking bales and feeding raw cotton into blenders. The foreman explained as best he could above the noise that this was to guarantee uniformity, that even a single bale from one field could vary according to soil and sun. They followed the raw down the line from blending, through opening and picking, then right down to carding.

She arrived at Charles's side, exclaiming over the large spikes protruding from a carding drum. 'They look dangerous. Scalp you in two seconds, they could.'

'Ah, but this is probably the most important single operation,' he answered while she read his lips. 'All the dirt comes out here – and you'll notice cotton in a recognizable form at the end – see?' He pointed to the cylinders that stood ready to receive thick strands of carded material. 'After drawing and slubbing, this will be fine enough to spin.'

'And I'll finish up weaving it into cloth!'

He laughed. 'Not yet, you won't. You must walk before you can run.'

'I'll learn, Mr Swainbank.'

'I reckon you will, child. But it's still a very hard life in here.'

After following the cotton to its inevitable end in the weaving sheds, the party left for number three mill. As this had the only canteen, each factory used it in turn throughout the day, staggering meal-breaks so that all might be fed a decent cheap dinner. Refreshments for the new recruits were served by older apprentices, boys and girls with a year or more under their belts.

Again, Charles felt himself drawn to the table at which she sat with several of the silent ones, children used to the mindless discipline of a classroom, people who seemed scarcely ready to launch themselves into the world of work. She stood out as one who ought to have been educated properly, a candidate for management rather than manual labour. But he would train her from the bottom. This girl and her brother would come up in the world if he must drag them by the boot-laces.

He sat opposite her and accepted a mug of tea from the trolley.

'Why isn't it all done in the one place, Mr Swainbank?'

'Pardon?'

'Well, I just wondered – why can't you do your own bleaching? Or do we need to be near a stream for that? Only if you did the bleaching and dyeing and printing, happen you could make things like frocks and curtains. Then everything would be cheaper at the finish.'

Goodness, she talked like some kind of bloody economist! Here she sat, fifteen years old, expounding a concept that had been pushed around many a cotton meeting – hadn't they all been warned about over-specializing, about the possible danger of cheaper imports? 'Bleaching's an art, Janet. So is dressmaking – we can't do everything.'

'It'd be good though, wouldn't it?'

'Yes, I don't doubt that it would be good.'

She stirred several spoonfuls of sugar into the thick brew, then dipped a biscuit into the beaker. There was little of the lady about her, much of the woman. He sighed. Ah well, any fool could learn to crook a little finger while holding a cup, but what she possessed had not arrived through a drawing-room, was not a copied pattern taught by elders and so-called betters. Janet would make her own pattern – and not just at the loom. The girl had raw brains, fertile, unspoiled, she displayed vivacity, enthusiasm, breadth of vision. Her faults he skimmed over. Her faults would be ironed out.

'This is a nicer mill,' she announced while those around her gaped and nudged one another.

'Would you rather work here?'

She gazed around thoughtfully. 'No. You've bigger sheds at number one and a lot of old weavers near retiring. I shall get me own looms faster there. Everybody wants to work at number three, so there wouldn't be as much room for us learners. Mind you, that weaving looked a bit complicated. And you were right about the din! I think I'll make meself some

373

ear-muffs. I noticed it's mostly men in them sheds, isn't it?'

'A master weaver was traditionally male. It's a very taxing job.'

She glanced sideways at the other two recruits who had opted for weaving. 'Not too hard for us, is it? This pair were at school with me Mr Swainbank. They're not really shy and daft – I think they're having you on. Ronnie here were dead good at drawing – weren't you, Ron?'

Ronnie blushed a deeper red and muttered something unintelligible.

Unperturbed, Janet continued, 'And Lizzie were the best at embroidery – she even did some of Father Mahoney's vestments in gold. Can you imagine that? Thread made out of real gold? Her mother does lace-making for the church . . . '

A Catholic, of course. There'd never been one of those in the Swainbank clan – a few corpses would be turning if Charles left the inheritance to a pair of papists! Still. Better that than pathetic Cyril with his grasping mother and all her airs and graces. Even Amelia had agreed . . .

Good God, he'd almost forgotten! Alice and Cyril would be up at the Hall now waiting for him! He took the watch from his top pocket and glanced at the time. Five to four – they'd been expected at three! He jumped up from the table. 'Goodbye for now,' he said to the awestruck group. 'I'll see you next week.' He turned to Janet. 'As for you, young lady – we shall make a boss of you yet. Your mother's right – you do chatter like a cageful of monkeys. No bad thing. Tell your parents – all of you – that I'm very impressed.'

Charles left for home, more than satisfied with what he had seen in his daughter thus far.

Back at Briars Hall, Alice Fenner was pacing about, her face twisted by a rage she deemed to be self-righteous. 'He's gone too far this time, Cyril. Not only was I deprived of seeing my poor dear sister-in-law during her last days, not only were we left ignorant of her death until after the funeral – we now suffer this indignity! It is twenty minutes past four, Cyril. And take your hands from your pockets, or the suit will be ruined before it's been worn twice.'

Cyril obeyed, leaving long arms to dangle uselessly by his sides. This was going to be so embarrassing, having to listen while his mother begged for items of jewellery, for money she'd been promised by Aunt Amelia, for a job for himself. He didn't want a job, couldn't have cared less about filthy cotton mills. He was quite happily engaged now as a junior in an accountant's office, and would be more than pleased to work his way up in the firm. Cyril liked figures as long as they were disembodied, as long as he didn't have to handle the items he accounted for. If only he could find the courage to stand up to her!

'And you might make more of yourself,' she snapped now, her tone accusatory. 'Do you realize how much Charles is worth? Tens of thousands – if not more! And there you stand, ready to allow it all to pour through your fingers—'

'I . . . don't want it, Mother . . . I . . .'

'What? Do you think my life has been easy? The money from my parents is almost gone – the little your stepfather left behind when he sought pastures new. What next? For years I have scrimped and saved so that you might have an education. Even if John and Peter had lived, there would have been a place for you at Swainbanks' had you shown some interest. Now, it could all have been ours! Yet you repay me in this way, by allowing everyone to see that you don't want the mills . . . oh!' Exasperated beyond words, she turned her back on him.

'It will come to me whether I want it or not – there's no-one else.'

'I wouldn't be too sure of that! He might leave you with a fight on your hands, Cyril, because he can't stand the sight of either of us . . .'

'Very perceptive of you, Alice.'

She swung round to face Charles. 'How could you?' she muttered between gritted teeth. 'How could you keep me away from the funeral?'

'Quite easily. I simply made sure that Amelia's death was announced only in the local papers.'

'You are . . . unfeeling! And now, to keep us waiting for hours after we have travelled so far—'

'Your journey has not been in vain, I assure you. The terms of my wife's will are being observed to the letter.' He thrust a sheet of paper into her hand. 'Much of the jewellery is yours. Amelia felt you had a right to it because you were Harold's wife. She also left a thousand pounds each for you and Cyril. That should keep the wolf from the door for a while.' He passed a large brown envelope to Cyril. 'You know, lad, with a different mother you might have done quite well.'

'How dare you?' she cried, twisting the will into a ball between her fingers. 'We are your only living relatives . . . '

'Hmm.' His eyes swept over her.

'Who will follow if you don't re-marry?' she cried. 'Why don't you train Cyril in case he's needed one of these fine days?'

'Because Cyril does not wish it. Neither do I.'

She turned her attention to the unfortunate boy. 'Tell him!' she screamed. 'Tell him that you wish to go into mill management!'

For answer, the youth simply bowed his head.

'Tell me,' whispered Charles. 'Tell me you want to work in cotton.'

'Cyril!' She arrived at his side and shook his sleeve fiercely. 'What is the matter with you?'

'The matter is quite simple, Alice,' said Charles. 'You have orchestrated every movement of his life so far, held his hand for too long, made him depend so that he would eventually feel obligated and guilty enough to indulge your every whim. But Cyril has his own opinions and his own life to lead. You made a laughing-stock of him, turned him into a mother's boy, dragged him around like a dog on a leash. He will still be a wealthy man – don't worry, his interests are being catered for. No Swainbank will ever be poor, certainly not my brother's son. The lad has a head for figures, a brain that should do well in accounting. But he would never make a direct living from cotton.'

The young man flashed a look of gratitude in his uncle's direction.

'He will leave you soon, Alice.' There was a trace of sadness in Charles' tone. 'And you'll be alone. So take this money

376

and enjoy it – there will be little else from me except for Cyril's dividends in the trust fund.' He grinned. 'Which can't be touched yet. Now, I must return to my business. A meal has been prepared – if you wish to partake of it, Emmie will serve you at the small table in my study.' He came forward and shook Cyril's hand solemnly. 'More to you than meets the eye, son. I wish you all the best in your chosen walk.'

'Thank you, sir.'

'And I'll put work your way. You know, I could grow quite proud of you.'

'I'll do my best.'

Throughout all this, Alice stood glowering, her hands clawing at the paper containing Amelia's last wishes. Now she stepped nearer to Charles. 'Who will get the mills if you have no children?' she asked, her voice cracking with temper.

'My will is made. It's a private matter between my lawyer and myself. Nothing you can say will undo it, so I suggest you hang on to your pride and ask no more questions.'

'But I—'

'No more, Alice. I believe we shall not meet again.' He strode out of the room, leaving her standing with her mouth agape.

'You fool, Cyril!' she finally muttered as Charles's footsteps faded away across the hall floor.

'I think we should go, Mother—'

'Oh no! We shall take the meal in his office. His office is precisely where I want to be!'

She strode across the hall and into the small book-lined study where Charles kept his desk. Cyril followed at a slower pace, instinctively aware that his mother was up to no good. They sat at the tiny central table until Emmie had served them with fruit juices and a roast meal. 'This will suffice,' said Alice, her voice saccharine-sweet. 'Don't disturb us by bringing another course – I shall rest in Mr Swainbank's chair after we have eaten. It's such a tiring journey home.'

As soon as the servant had left, Alice leapt up and took a little key from behind the curtain. 'He doesn't change his habits,' she said almost to herself. 'We must be grateful for such mercies.'

Cyril's mouth fell open as he watched his mother undoing a small drawer in the bureau. She lifted out a pile of papers and brought them to the table.

'Mother! What are you doing? Those are private—'

'Oh for goodness sake – eat your roast beef – enjoy it while you can, because there won't be a great deal of that on our table unless I can work something out! I need to see if this is a will we can fight—'

'Uncle Charles is not dead!'

'It is as well to be prepared.'

Both meals grew cold as Alice pored over the papers while Cyril jumped at every slight sound in the old house. At last she found her goal, a copy of Charles Swainbank's latest testament among all the deeds and bonds. These latter items she waved at Cyril. 'The man's practically a millionaire,' she declared. 'Shares in Australian and African minerals, British stocks, the mills—'

Cyril rose to his feet, his face reddened by embarrassment. 'I will not stay to watch you do this thing.'

'Don't be a fool, boy! We'll be finished if we're not careful!'

'I am finished now, Mother!' When no response was forthcoming, Cyril crept out of the room. He stood in the wide hallway, his heart beating so fiercely that it seemed to be trying to escape from his chest. Whatever any will contained, he had no wish to know about it!

Alice Fenner folded the papers as exactly as she could, taking care to keep them in their original order. No-one must suspect that she knew; no evidence of her behaviour must remain. It was perhaps a good thing that Cyril had left the room – this information was too precious to share, too valuable to dilute by distribution. Everything must look right, no hint of what she had learned must be passed on or even suspected. The immediate thing was to keep cool, give the impression of normality. She forced herself to eat as much of both meals as she could manage, shuddering as she swallowed congealing gravy and cold potato.

While everything was fresh in her mind, she took a small pencil and a notepad from her bag and began to scribble. So.

He had two children, the result of a liaison with a servant. Could she blackmail him with this fact, force him to either pay up or name Cyril as his successor? No. A man who could bare his breast so freely on paper would not be averse to bringing all out into the open if pushed.

What else? Yes, the alternatives were terrifying, even to someone as angry and desperate as she was. But the truth stared plainly from her pad – if the Maguires were eliminated, then nothing could stand between Cyril and what was rightfully his. Unless Charles were to take another wife, of course. Yet that would be at least acceptable, a defeat she might face with dignity. But to be disinherited by the offspring of a housemaid, a pair of urchins from the wrong side of the blanket?

In those moments, Alice felt so much hatred for Charles Swainbank that she wanted to rush down to the mills and scream his inadequacies for all to hear. He would suffer for this betrayal! She paced the room, her agitation increased by the discomfort of an overloaded stomach. She must compose herself, act as if nothing were amiss.

Angrily she pulled at the bellcord until Emmie, breathless from running, arrived in the doorway. Alice turned on her. 'I need a remedy for my stomach,' she snapped. 'I have never before eaten such an ill-prepared meal!'

Cyril entered the room as the flustered servant left. 'Have you done what you came to do, Mother?'

'How dare you address me in that tone?!'

He shuffled about, badly co-ordinated limbs jerking as he moved towards her. 'I am . . . ashamed,' he said quietly. 'I've always known you valued money above all else, but I never thought you'd resort to—'

'You ungrateful fool! This was for your sake!'

He shook his narrow head, Adam's apple sliding up and down his thin neck as he fought the great tide of anger that welled in him. 'This is terrible,' he whispered. 'And it was for your own sake, not mine. If these are the depths you'll sink to for the sake of money . . . I'm sorry, but I shall be seeking lodgings after today.'

'What?!'

'I can't live with you any more. Aunt Amelia's thousand pounds will get me a place.' He straightened his over-long spine. 'I've a good mind to tell Uncle Charles what went on here today—'

'Very little went on. There is no copy of the will – it must be with his lawyer. So, I know nothing of Charles' intentions.'

'And you have returned the key?'

'Yes! Don't judge me, Cyril! Can't you see – after your stepfather went off with most of my money'—

'That's wearing thin, Mother. You could have worked – honest people do.'

'And you would condemn me to that? After all I've done for you?'

Emmie entered with a glass of milky liquid on a tray. 'For your trouble, Mrs Fenner. Mrs M sends her regards and apologies for the meal. And she says to take care, Ma'am, for the mistress started off with what she thought was indigestion.'

Alice opened her mouth to reply, but Emmie was closing the door before the words were framed.

'I'm leaving now.' Cyril moved towards the hall.

'Wait for me! We're going in the same direction.'

He turned and stared at her. 'Not any more, Mother.'

Again the door was closed. Alice picked up the large envelope of jewellery – the man hadn't even bothered to leave it in the inlaid case where Amelia had used to store it. The plain brown package was a visible token of his contempt, a final gesture of dismissal. Now she was also rejected by her own son, cast aside as unimportant, a thing to be discarded after long use.

Why should she bother now with Cyril gone? Why not leave it all to these Maguire twins, let the town laugh while a fortune was dispersed on fripperies? No! She smiled grimly. Cyril would thank her one day, would have to take care of her. And for the first time ever, she felt glad that she had married Marcus Fenner, that infamous charmer who lived with one foot on the racetrack and the other in some seedy den of

gambling thieves. Tonight, she would write him a letter –
a letter which might take months to find its wandering
addressee – but a message worded so skilfully that Marcus
would eventually arrive home with winged heels.

Alice had been born a lady, had lived as ladylike an existence
as reduced circumstances would allow and was determined,
above all else, that she would spend her last years in comfort.
Life owed her that. And Marcus Fenner would help her
achieve this goal. At last, she had found a use for him.

Chapter 12

Ma and Molly fixed their eyes on the white porcelain bowl with its seat of polished wood. It had been an interesting few days, what with the plumbers, plasterers and decorators in and out by the minute, a chap on the roof replacing slates and another running round like a cat with its tail on fire trying to be the boss. Molly nodded to Ma. 'Go on – you can have the first try.'

'Sure, I've never set eyes on one of these things except in the mills. Unhygienical, they are. Whatever possessed decent law-abiding folk to have such an item on the inside of a house? Isn't the world a desperate upside down place all of a sudden, Molly? Here we are with the outside conveniences on the inside, then there's me forced to sleep downstairs when I should rightly be up! 'Twas little difference for the rest of the houses in the row, for didn't they already have just the two large bedrooms and a bit taken off for the bath? Whereas now that me own bedroom's a bathroom, I am condemned to sleep downstairs the rest of me life . . . '

'Never mind – you can still use the outside tippler if you want. Anyroad, plumber reckons as how it's healthy enough to have a lavatory inside – as long as you keep it flushed and a bit of bleach down. He says the water in the bowl stops germs rising. And just think, Ma, we've no need to fetch the tin bath in no more – running hot water off the back-boiler.'

'And a mountain of coal to heat it!' Ma looked glumly into the gleaming white tub. 'I shall surely drown in that. Imagine if I took a turn up to the eyes in water! 'Tis not natural, any of it.'

'You don't need to fill it! There's nowt to stop you having a bath in half an inch of water if that's what you want, you old misery! I can't wait meself, a good long soak in a hot bath. That's luxury, that is. Go on – pull the chain.'

'We'll be flooded inside a minute and us with the new decorations! Can you imagine the state of the downstairs should this thing take it into its head to overflow?'

'That'll be the landlord's problem.' When Ma showed no sign of performing the christening rites, Molly reached out and tugged at the chain, stepping back as water cascaded into the bowl. They held their breath and listened while the cylinder refilled, then Ma came forward to perform the second flush. 'The miracles of modern science,' she declared, her tone lacking enthusiasm. 'And not a penny piece on the rent. I wonder does our new landlord have his head screwed on at all?'

'It's Swainbank.' Molly's voice was devoid of expression.

Ma staggered back, a hand to her breast. 'By all the saints! Getting nearer by the day, is he not?'

'Aye. And there's none of it my doing!' She paused as if deep in thought. 'Nay, we can't go on blaming one another for ever, I suppose. You shouldn't have done this, I should have said that – it's the same tune over and over. But honest – if he ever tells my twins the truth, I'll die of shame! Trouble is, there's nowt in this world I can do about any of it – shops, bathrooms – whatever next?'

'Just make the best of it, Molly. Can you imagine himself now, walking up to Janet at her loom and saying "I'm your daddy."? Can you see him going into the shop for a yard of knicker elastic or a bicycle chain and "by the way, Joey, you're a bastard"? Never. There's not a thing he'll do while he lives and breathes.'

'Don't be too sure. Sounds like he's took a right fancy to our Janet. Most of the new ones are out on the trek – going about the mills doing odd jobs till they're settled. But not Fancy Nancy. Oh no, her's on a right cushy number – studying time and bloody motion from the looks of it, getting a back or two up, I shouldn't wonder.'

'Language, Molly!'

'Well – there she is, titti-fal-lalling around with a board and a bit of paper stuck on it, watching folk work and writing bits of sums. Mind, he's boxing clever – she's not the only one with a pencil. He reckons the best way for them to learn is by watching all the jobs, seeing what's done and how long things take. She's down for management, Ma, and she can't even see it.'

' 'Tis as well she can't, or she'd tell him where to put his pen and paper. Howandever, I think it's time for me to have a word with Mr Charles Swainbank. I can fill his pipe for him if anyone can. Too big for his boots by a mile or more, is that feller.'

Molly stared at her mother-in-law who seemed to have shrunk since the stroke – as if she'd been in a hot wash then bleached white in the dolly-tub. 'You're not fit, Ma. Haven't you took enough on with the shop and all? You're going to be up dawn to dusk as it is – why go tempting fate and fetching another bad do on, eh?'

Shrewd blue eyes travelled over the new bathroom with its white tiles and Greek key border pattern. 'All this he did for the twins. A whole street gutted so that we would not stand out as favoured. Aye.' She nodded knowingly. 'Richard had a soft centre, but there was a four foot layer of granite on the outside of that old devil. This one's manageable.'

'Eh?' Molly's eyes were round. 'Manageable? Charlie Swainbank?'

'Compared to his father, he's biddable. Yes, I must see him, for there's a thing or two he has not considered.'

'Like what?'

'Like . . . oh God, if only I could read! There's a paper with Mr Barton; something to do with rights. Now, if I understand properly, I put me cross to say I'd never bother the Swainbanks, never take the twins to their doorstep no matter what the situation. Surely that should work both ways? I kept our side of the bargain, took the money and the deeds, took the job in the sheds – glad enough they were then to be rid of us. And above all else, I've not bothered him. If his rightful sons had not died, then Janet and Joey would have been left alone.' She straightened visibly. 'I am going to fight this man, Molly.'

'It's no use, Ma. He's got power – the sort of power you and I don't understand—'

'We'll see.' Ma turned to see Paddy passing the doorway, hair slicked back, face ruddy from recent shaving, tie fastened neatly, shoes polished like black glass. 'And where do you think you're off to done up like the dog's dinner? A wedding? A funeral?'

He stopped to adjust the handkerchief in his top pocket. 'While you two stand there blethering, I'm going down for a look at our shop, see how it's coming along.'

Molly folded her arms and put her head on one side as she studied her husband. Obviously, he had not overheard their conversation, though they'd have to be more careful in the future. 'Isn't that the best suit? Anybody would think you were setting off on a visit to the Mayor's Parlour! You're going to work in the shop, Paddy, help to mend bikes and put oil on chains. That'll need an overall—'

'Not today. We aren't open yet, anyway. And I'm not up to much what with me thumb and me stomach – then there's me dizzy spells – fair mazed with them I am at times. Aye. Happen I should stick to the counter stuff – deal with the customers and that.'

'And put your hand in the money box every time you've a mind?' There was acid in Ma's tone. 'Every till is locked, Paddy. The only keys will be with me, Molly and Joey. We can't have you soaking up the profits!'

Paddy shook his head sadly. 'Oh ye of little faith! Do you think I'd sink so low?'

'Yes!' replied the women in unison.

He mumbled a curse under his breath then descended the stairs noisily. Ma and Molly followed, taking great care not to brush against newly decorated stairway walls.

In the kitchen they found Daisy with her paints, brush poised above the paper, her whole body stiff and straight, eyes staring unseeing from beneath a shock of yellow curls. 'She's gone again,' remarked Ma. 'Won't have noticed a thing, not in this world, at least. No doubt Paddy's away out of the back gate by this time. Daisy?' She bent towards her small grand-daughter's shoulder. 'Come back, child.'

Molly ran to the little girl's side.

'Don't touch her!' snapped the older woman. 'We never touched me granny when the sight came.'

'Sight?' Molly's voice was shrill. 'Do you want her putting

away as daft, not right in the head? It's not bloody sight, Ma! She's just being stubborn again. Flaming sight, stupid brooches and leprechauns – would you have us all as crackers as yourself? Daisy!'

The child remained motionless, as if time had stood still for her. Both women knew that when she came out of her trance, she would continue as if nothing had happened. The frequency of these episodes was increasing, causing many an argument between Ma and Molly. The former, who had witnessed such behaviour long ago, held to her view that the child was gifted beyond the norm, while Molly adhered to the opinion that Daisy was seeking attention by holding her breath like a naughty two-year-old, that she had never outgrown the tantrums of infancy.

'She's having visions,' insisted Ma.

'Then why does she never remember them? What's the point of visions if she can't tell us owt after, eh? Why don't you go the whole pig and run up for Father Mahoney, tell him we're having a miracle twice a week? Daisy Maguire, you'd better pull yourself together afore I clip you one! Sighted? She's as sighted as yon daft dog!'

Yorick crawled under the table. It was simpler to go for invisibility once Molly kicked off. He licked Daisy's shin until it twitched, then flattened himself against the oilcloth. As an experienced student of the human animal, he knew when to make himself scarce. This was one of their odd games, another session of to-ings and fro-ings with a bit of shouting thrown in. He closed his eyes and thought of bones, marrow bones with plenty of meat stuck on. But one ear remained cocked, just in case. Just in case of what – well, he'd never worked that out yet.

Daisy resumed her painting. 'I've run out of brown,' she complained, 'so I'm using the scrapings out of the treacle tin.'

'Daisy!' Molly's voice was stern.

'What?'

'Why do you keep doing that?'

'Eh?' The child's face wore a puzzled expression. 'I haven't done nothing. Except for pinching the treacle and there was hardly none left, Mam – honest!'

Molly folded her arms tightly. 'You know what I mean, Daisy! Frightening us all to death, sitting there hardly breathing.'

'When?'

'Just now!'

'But—' Daisy's eyes filled with tears. 'I've been painting.'

Ma reached out and ruffled the already tousled curls. 'Didn't you hear us talking to you, child? Did you see us come in – and your daddy too, all done up in his best suit?'

'No. I didn't see him. And you and Mam must have crept in, 'cos I looked up and . . . and you were there. Have I been day-dreaming again, Gran? I get in trouble for that at school.' Yes, school was very confusing at times. She'd be all right one minute, doing her writing, listening to the teacher, then the next minute there'd be somebody screaming at her for not paying attention. 'I try not to daydream.' The little girl fought back the tears. 'But it just happens, then I get in bother.'

'It's all right, child,' soothed Ma. 'Don't be carrying on all upset on a lovely day—'

'No need for any of it.' Molly turned and stalked out to the scullery. 'Kids!' she muttered, her voice reaching the pair at the table. 'Bloody sight! I'll sight her if she starts showing me up all over the place going stiff and stupid!' Pots clattered. 'Thought you'd got away with it, didn't you, Molly Maguire? With the last one, at least. But oh no. Joey's as naughty as they come, Janet's gone high-faluting with time and motion, Michael's got the neighbours round by the minute. And now . . . ' A pan lid fell and shivered to a standstill on the flagged floor before she continued. 'And now we've got bloody visions! We shall be charging entrance next, tuppence for a look at the queer folk!'

Daisy stared at Ma. 'What have I to do, Gran? How can I make it all go right?'

'There's nothing wrong, pet. You've taken after me old granny, that's all.'

'Did she do . . . like I do?'

'Sure enough. She'd be halfway across the yard with a bucket of swill, then all at once, she'd be as still as a statue, not a word or a move out of her – and not a drop lost from the bucket. After that, she would carry on as if nothing had happened. Tell me, child,' she dropped her voice. 'What do you see?'

'Eh?'

'When you go – what do you see?'

'Go where?'

'Away. By yourself.'

'I never go nowhere by meself. Our Michael or our Janet's always with me.'

'No. I mean in your head.'

'Oh.' Daisy nodded. 'I do sums in me head now. Sister Vincentia said I could be right clever if I didn't dream half the day.'

'Ah. And what do you dream about, Daisy?'

'Nothing.'

'So. You just go and come back with no memories. Perhaps you're too young just yet.'

'I don't know what you mean, Gran. And I don't know what me mam means either – or the teachers. I keep getting in trouble for something I haven't done!'

'Don't you cry now, little one. They'll all be glad enough of your gifts one day.'

'What gifts? I haven't bought no presents! What gifts, Gran?'

'The sight. You have the sight.'

'Oh.'

'It's very precious, Daisy.'

'I know. We did it at school. We've to be glad of our eyes, Sister says. And our ears and our legs—'

'Your sight is special.'

Daisy smiled. 'Is it? I'm glad. I don't never want to wear glasses. Mrs Melia at school wears glasses, dead thick ones.' She picked up her brush and dipped it into the water. 'I hate glasses.' Mollified slightly, the child carried on with her painting. Mam was still upset, but she'd come round in the end. Mam always came round.

With the child showing signs of settling. Ma went to sit on the outside stool to the left of the front door, placed there deliberately so that it would not mark Molly's stoning. She did a pretty pattern, did Molly, not just the usual twin stripes along the sides of the step and the line across the front of this heavy stone slab. Molly took pride in her donkeying, had developed a design all her own, a trademark that made her area stand out in the street. All six flags, property of Bolton Corporation, were scrubbed daily. Each 'clean' house recognized its own six flags, adopted them as part of the tenancy. Molly's began the day edged by the white stone she had lately preferred, while her house step was decorated at each side with a pair of triangles, one upright, the other inverted, apexes joining exactly as if executed by some master geometrician. By the end of a day, the six flags would be clog-scraped and ruined, but the start was what really mattered.

During clement weather, ladies of the street would sit out in the evenings, each with a mug of strong tea and something to occupy her hands – knitting or a pile of socks and a darning mushroom. While the women sat, children provided their entertainment, often getting up a concert party or a game of hopscotch under the eagle eyes of female parents.

Ma rested in the sunshine, her mind filled by Daisy and her strange absences. It was early for street-sitting, but since the stroke she had spent much of her time out here, regaining her strength for the task to come, the opening and running of her Irish Kitchen. Ah well, perhaps Daisy was sighted or perhaps she wasn't. No matter. Time would tell.

The rest of the youngsters began to arrive home from parks and playgrounds, many of them sent out again immediately to the street while meals were prepared. From open doorways drifted the mixed perfumes of boiling ribs and cabbage, onions with tripe and manifold, stews, cowheels simmering on hobs, the smells of newly-baked bread and cobbler toppings. This was home. Sun-warmed bricks to lean on, the sounds of family life all around, movement and colour for old eyes to rest on. Except for Charles Swainbank, things would be as near perfect as they could ever be.

This was the end of Bolton September wakes, so few were working and not many could afford the price of a trip out, let alone a holiday. But there was a festiveness in the air, a relaxing of rules and a mellowing of tempers. Bella Seddon poked her head round the door. 'Out already, Ma? That's it – you take your ease while you get chance. I've a spot of apple pie over if you'd like it for afters.'

Ma nodded. It was the unspoken commandment – even amongst enemies – that nothing should ever be refused. A refusal meant pride and pride was universally condemned. 'I'll take it now, thank you kindly, for the meal will be late this evening.'

'Drop of custard with it?'

'That will go down a treat, Mrs Seddon. And if you've a minute, fetch a stool, why don't you, for I have need of a word with you.'

A few minutes later, the woman arrived, best dish balanced on a stool fashioned by simply removing the back from an old chair. This pair of adversaries sat in silence while Ma relished her apple pie. She placed the empty dish on the deep stone window ledge of her own room. 'That was nectar, Mrs Seddon. Yes, a piece of heaven on a plate, sure enough. I could scarcely do better meself, for you've a hand with the custard sauce – I shall have the recipe from you one day.'

Bella's face widened as she beamed broadly. 'You wanted a word, Ma?'

'Aye, right enough.' Yes, she would need this awful person on her side, for she was at least a dependable sort – and surely nobody on God's blessed earth could be completely bad to the bones? 'I shall be grateful for your support, Mrs Seddon.'

'Me? What for?'

'To look after my two youngest grandchildren. We shall be away, the rest of us, working in town – Janet at Swainbank's number one, the rest of us in the shop.'

'Oh.' There followed a short pause and a clanking of curlers as Bella Seddon patted her head in pretended disinterest. But curiosity overcame her, just as Ma had felt it would. 'What shop?' she asked after a few seconds.

'Have you not been to town lately, Mrs Seddon?'

'Not for a week or two, no.' All this politeness was getting to Bella, chewing away at her insides like a badly cooked black pudding. It was as if both of them had put the claws aside – or sent them away for sharpening was more likely.

'Ah well, that would account for it. We open next week – Maguire's Market, we're to be called. It's a café and a bike shop with another part where Molly can sell fabrics and such. Of course, once the two little ones return to their schooling, they'll need caring for. And I can think of no one more suited to the task than your good self.' And a great big lie that was, for hadn't Bella Seddon's children flown the nest almost as soon as they'd left their learning? Still, at least she was on hand, being right next door. And Michael and Daisy were resilient enough.

The woman's jaw dropped, displaying bare gums where she had left out the lower set. 'But . . . er . . . if you don't mind me asking, like—'

'Not at all! Ask away!' Ma's voice dripped honey.

'Well. How can you afford to open a shop, like?'

'A legacy.'

Bella swallowed audibly. 'Oh. Were it a lot of money?'

'Enough.'

Both women took a sudden close interest in the street, each staring at a fixed point as if riveted by some unusual happening. Ma studied a bit of loose guttering where the renovators had not finished, while Bella fixed her attention on a window of Leatherbarrow's mill. But Ma knew she had won this particular round; the line was baited and Bella would rise any minute now.

'So.' There was a slight stiffening of shoulders. 'I'm . . . right glad to hear about your good fortune, Ma.' The tone conveyed little of this verbally expressed delight. 'But I'm not so sure, like. I'm not used to kids, not since me own lot left.'

And no wonder, thought Ma, though she continued to smile at the section of detached rainwater troughing. 'They can come in their own house, Mrs Seddon, no need for you to keep them by you all the while. Michael can be a sensible lad when he chooses and Daisy has a fine head on her too.'

'What about her turns?'

Ma could no longer pretend to be distracted by the buildings across the way. 'What turns?' Her eyes narrowed.

'She goes all funny and still, can't hear you!'

Ma Maguire fought with her tongue, using every bit of her strength as if holding back a rampaging stallion. 'They pass,' was all she said now. 'All I'm asking is that you watch over the pair of them, give them a meal at your table. And having tasted your cooking, I'd say my grandchildren would be privileged.' She closed her mouth firmly.

This new feather sat well in Bella Seddon's bonnet. 'Very kind of you.' she muttered, pleased beyond measure.

'Three pounds a week?'

'Eh?' The mouth opened and closed rapidly, putting Ma in mind of a baby practising for the first time on solids. 'Ooh! Ooh, I couldn't!'

'Then I'll have to find somebody else, which is a great pity—'

'No.' Bella touched Ma's arm. 'I'll have to think on it. But three pounds is a right lot of money—'

'Away with your bother! For one thing, I want this on a proper business footing. And for a second, I know the cost of food. Then there's your fuel for cooking and the inconvenience of staying in to mind my family. No, 'tis well worth the three pounds. A great weight off my mind, this would be.'

'Well—'

'Another matter – I'm tired out now, so how will I be when I'm cooking and serving all day? Who's going to watch her at number seven with her filthy ways? Did you know she was seen emptying the contents of the child's chamber pot in the ashpit last week?'

'What? She never did! The dirty little madam—'

Ma placed a finger to her lips and pointed along the row to warn her companion about ears and tongues. 'You and I have set the standard in Delia Street, Mrs Seddon,' she whispered. 'I could eat me dinner off your scullery floor and you could do the same in my house. It took years to make these people clean. So. From now, you must take complete responsibility for tenants, because I shall have no time. Furthermore, included in the three pounds, I'd be asking you to stone our step when you do your own. Is it settled, then?'

Bella Seddon went through the motions of considering the pros and cons. It would not pay to refuse, but to jump at the offer would be equally ill-advised. 'Right,' she said eventually. 'You're on.'

'Good. It's pleased I am to hear it. Will we shake on that?' The two enemies shook hands gravely while several children from neighbouring streets gaped at the sight of this unprecedented event.

'Off with you!' screamed Ma. 'Go ride a kench up to the wall, for we could used something to smile at.'

Bella Seddon and Philomena Maguire hugged their sides throughout this game – an advanced form of leapfrog. Half a dozen boys bent low one behind the other, while the rest ran a great distance to see how many backs they could clear without tumbling to the floor. When seven were on the kench, the whole collapsed with the front boy, who had been leaning against the wall, emerging last from the tangle of arms and legs.

Ma clapped her hands together. With sights such as this, who needed the theatre for entertainment? The boys regrouped and began to produce diablos and tops, balls, jacks and bobbers. A game of cops and robbers broke out at one end of the street, while at the other kick-a-ball-out seemed favourite for the day.

Then a parade advanced along the front of Leatherbarrow's, an answer to last May's display of female finery by May-queens. 'Hippy-chippy-Charlie, round and round we go . . . ' sang this discordant group of miscreants. The boys carried a crude Maypole, probably some poor mother's decapitated yardbrush. To this were nailed several pieces of rope, each with a boy attached to its end. These lads were dressed in their fathers' old clothes, trousers rolled to half-mast, tattered coat hems sweeping the ground in their wake, shirt tails flapping, caps back to front. Faces, decorated with Zebo, shoe-polish, cocoa and coal-dust, were twisted into deliberately silly expressions and a separate boy, his face completely blackened, carried a tin for contributions. Ma threw a penny, thereby forcing the travelling players to attend her door, where they performed a travesty of the Maypole dance, clog-irons sparking against the cobblestones.

Ma and Bella dried streaming eyes. 'Did you see the feller with the great gaping hole on the backside?' roared Ma. 'And him without a stitch between fresh air and nature!'

'Aye. His mam'll kill him when he gets home. The others won't tell him, you know. They'll let him carry on with the bare bum on show – eeh, I've not laughed this much since the war finished!'

They sobered up gradually, then Bella asked, 'What do you think to our houses, then? All done up and not a penny on the rent. Baths and 'lectric lights – getting to be posh, aren't we?'

Ma reached for her dish and handed it back. 'Swainbank's bought them. Perhaps he's gone soft in the head with his wife and sons gone.'

'Funny though. They're not worth much, these houses. I reckon he's spent more on them than they cost in the first place. Nowt as queer as folk with too much brass, eh?'

'I wouldn't know. It may be because we've always been a decent street. This could be our reward for good housekeeping.'

'Except for number seven.'

'As you say.' Ma rose stiffly and made for the door. 'Well, I'll see does Molly need a hand. And I'll be calling on you about the details of that other little matter.'

The two antagonists parted as near friends as they had ever been, each hopeful that the treaty would last. Inside, Ma found Daisy still at her painting, much of which had spread itself over the green between-meals table cover. 'Oh Daisy!' She tutted and placed her hands on her hips. 'Whatever have you done to the new cloth? And why did you not come out to see the hippy-chippy-Charlies?'

'When?'

'Just now – in the street. Oh, have you been off again?'

'I don't know.'

'You heard nothing?'

'No.' The child hung her head. 'Sometimes a long while is just a minute for me. I missed four catechisms last week.'

'You're a remarkable girl, Daisy.'

Blue eyes looked up hopefully. 'I know that. Sister Vincentia said I was remarka-bubble. She thinks I could learn fast but must not become proud. Pride is what she calls a deadly sin – so she'll go to hell for a kick off.'

'What are you saying, child?'

'She's always looking in the mirror, forever bending down in the girls' toilet to straighten her veil and see how pretty she is in the glass. She's proud, so she'd best watch out.'

Ma threw back her head and laughed. 'Never lose that, mavourneen. 'Tis a sense of humour carries you through this life.'

Janet and Joey burst in simultaneously, obviously in the middle of yet another argument. The girl threw her schoolbag on to the table, almost upsetting Daisy's jam jar of dirty paint water. 'I'd never have come if I'd known! You said you wanted advice over the colour scheme.'

'I'm not having powder blue in a bike shop!'

'So there I was with me bag full of pictures and colours – and you'd already made your mind up! Bottle green? It'll look like a school or a flaming hospital!'

'At least it won't look soft.'

'Well, what did you need me for, then? To give me another lecture about how I should be working in the shop instead of going in for weaving? You're wasting your time, our Joey. That there Mr Swainbank thinks a lot of me, I can tell. I shall do all right in number one, you just mark my words.'

Joey flung himself into a fireside chair, propping his feet on the fireguard so that he might admire his new shoes. 'I think you should be grateful to Gran, that's all. She got us these shops and now you're . . . '

'After what you said? After what you said only weeks ago? About certain people being . . . ' She looked at her grandmother. No, she couldn't say it, not now, wouldn't upset Gran by coming out with that lot. He was two-faced was their Joey. He'd been for getting rid of Gran and Dad, calling them useless and a waste of time. Not now though. Oh no, he was getting his own road at the moment.

'I've learned me lesson, Janet,' he said quietly.

'By practising on deaf old women!' Janet could not resist this barbed remark.

'Enough of that!' shouted Ma. 'Hasn't he suffered enough already for it? Stop judging everybody in your path, Janet Maguire! A person would think that you were perfect – or that you believed yourself so! There's many a wrong you'll do, madam! I agree in part with Joey – you should be helping this family establish a business. But no. You want your own way as surely as your twin wants his.'

Janet grabbed her bag from the table and glared at everybody in the room. 'Why are you all picking on me, eh? He was the one who wanted to leave home! He was the one who nearly fetched the police to the door! I don't want to work with him!'

Ma lifted up Daisy's soggy work and draped it over the guard away from Joey's feet. 'Climb down off the horse before the saddle slips, girl,' she said quietly. 'One of these days, you'll take a tumble from the pedestal and then you might be needing us to pick you up. And you can wipe away the tears, for they don't fool me for a minute. He did wrong – we all know that. And the less said about that, in front of your little sister, the better. Stop condemning him.'

Molly came in from the scullery with a pie for the oven. 'What's going on now?' She opened the oven door and pushed the dish on to a shelf. 'Are they fighting?'

'Your daughter has not a forgiving nature, Molly.' Ma removed the cover from the table. 'She'd have Joey doing penance the rest of his days.'

Molly slammed the door and straightened. 'The thing he did takes a bit of getting used to, Ma.'

'What?' Paintbox and brush were banged on to the highly polished dresser. 'Jesus Christ hung there on that Cross with six-inch nails in his hands. And what did He say? Lock them up and swallow the key? No! He said, "Forgive them, for they know not what they do"! Are you above all that, Janet Maguire? You too?' She glared at Molly. 'Did you never make a mistake? Have you gone through life with a sheet so clean that you needed no priest to get it washed? It's quick enough you are to tell me what I did wrong, just as your daughter now tells Joey.' She glanced at her grandson. 'Take the smile off, lad, before I shift it meself! Your debt will be repaid when you-know-who gets out of hospital. But I will not have these carryings-on in my house!'

Molly, her face reddened by temper and embarrassment, stalked across the room and pulled a white tablecloth from a drawer. With quick movements that expressed her state of mind, she began to throw knives and forks on to the table. It had always been Ma's house, Ma's table, Ma's flaming street. Yet Molly had been the one who'd kept things going, cleaning, shopping, washing and ironing day in and day out, never a moment to herself. And him upstairs with his stomach and his thumb . . . A thought struck her suddenly. 'Where's your dad? He was for coming down to the shop today.'

Joey shrugged. 'We never saw him, did we?'

'No.' Janet placed her bag at the foot of the stairs and came to arrange the table properly. 'Don't get wound up, Mam,' she whispered.

Molly turned to her son. 'Happen you'd best get out and look for him. He's got a few shillings and if he meets up with Bobby McMorrow, there'll be trouble from here to Barrow Bridge. The police have had enough of your dad's caperings.'

'Aw Mam – I'm hungry! I've been stacking shelves and counting stock all afternoon.'

Janet lifted salt and pepper from the dresser shelf. Now was as good a time as any to try for a level of peace with Joey. 'I'll go with you. There's no pubs open, so we might just catch him before the bother starts.'

'And we'll save you some pie,' promised Ma.

Molly stared past them all to where Daisy sat on the sofa. 'Dear God!' Her hand flew to her mouth. 'She's gone blue! Daisy!' While Molly remained riveted to the spot, Janet and Ma forced the child's stiff body into a prone position. Her lips were pale with chill, though the evening remained fine and warm.

Paddy was forgotten in the frenzy that followed. Janet filled hot bottles, Joey ran for the doctor, Molly and Ma heaped blankets and coats on to the tiny form. An icy sweat broke out on Daisy's cheeks and Molly began to wail.

'Hush!' chided Ma. 'This child is not for death – believe me, Molly. She has much to do because she is chosen.'

'Don't you start with all that now! Mumbo-jumbo, it is, a load of rubbish and at a time like this too! Can't you see she's hardly breathing? Janet – shove them old bricks in the oven and fetch a couple of towels to wrap them in once they're warmed. Oh God – where is that flaming doctor? Daisy? Daisy, love? It's your mam – can't you hear me? Look at her little face! Daisy!'

Joey and the doctor burst in at the front door. 'Leave her with me,' ordered the black-suited man. 'Go – all of you – into the other room. This child needs all the oxygen she can find.'

The four of them went reluctantly into Ma's bedroom, each locked in private thought as the crisis hit home. Daisy was universally loved; wherever she went the child brought laughter and happiness with her pretty smiling face, those little songs and dances and that disconcerting way she had of suddenly becoming grown-up while only five years old. Daisy had learned to read and count long before she started school. A child of great promise, sometimes a dreamer, sometimes present in body though not in mind . . .

'It's my bloody punishment,' muttered Joey through clenched teeth. 'Why her, eh? Why not me?'

'It's nowt to do with you.' This from Janet who wept quietly in a corner. 'I started the row when we both came in, I got her all worked up and worried.'

Molly, perched tensely on the edge of the bed, cursed herself inwardly for the dishonest woman she had been. Now her precious baby was suffering. Would God pay Molly back in this cruel way, punish her so viciously for pretending that the twins were Paddy's? Would He reach down His almighty arm and snatch the most loved, the most adored of all her children?

Ma gazed through the window, her mind reaching out towards a heaven she was doubting for the very first time.

If Daisy had been granted the gift of second sight, surely it should not hurt like this? Granny Gallagher had never fallen sick with her sight. Was the sight a sickness then, an illness that varied in degree from one to another? No! This was a fever. The child had something identifiable, no doubt, some childhood disease that would pass after running its course.

The doctor opened the door. 'Mrs Maguire?' Both women leapt to their feet. 'Come with me, please. It would be best if the young ones remained here.'

Doctor, mother and grandmother looked down into Daisy's ashen face.

'She'll be fine,' said the man, placing his stethoscope in the brown leather bag. 'It's something we don't know a lot about, a mild type of epilepsy.'

Molly staggered back, her face as pale as her daughter's. 'Fits? My Daisy's never had a fit in her life.'

The doctor placed a steadying arm around Molly's shoulders. 'They're not real fits, love, not the sort to leave her thrashing and foaming. It's just that she . . . well . . . goes away from time to time. Haven't you noticed that? And you'll find that she won't even fall down – she'll simply stand where she is, lose a few seconds, then carry on as before. Unfortunately, these shut-downs can happen anywhere without warning – even in the middle of a busy street. She must have someone with her at all times. And she shows no sign at all of brain-damage.'

'Brain-damage? Is that what's down for her? Not my little flower, not my Daisy! No! No!'

She fell into the man's strong arms, her whole body racked by sobs.

He patted her back in a comforting way. 'Look, Mrs Maguire – I've seen kiddies with this condition come out of Oxford and Cambridge with qualifications that would shame the rest of us. It's nothing, nothing at all. In time, she'll even learn to manage these episodes – predict them, if you like. But just now, the main concern is for her safety. Keep her away from the fire and the kettle, get young Michael to see her back and forth from school.'

'It's not fits,' said Ma quietly. 'My family does not have fits. Daisy has a vision beyond ours, an ability we've lost or failed to develop. When she goes missing, she leaves the rest of the world trailing behind. We are the losers, not Daisy.'

Molly raised her face to look at Ma. 'You old fool! She's ill – can't you see?'

'Then my grandmother had the same disease.'

The doctor nodded. 'Yes, it can be hereditary.'

Michael stumbled in at the front door, muddied from head to foot after a day's fruitless fishing and paddling in the Croal. 'I fell in, Mam. Hey – what's matter?' he asked, concern about the unusual situation plain on his dirty face.

Molly detached herself from the doctor. 'Get up them stairs for a bath, Michael Maguire.'

'Not till you tell me what's up with her.' He waved a hand towards his sister.

The doctor squatted on his haunches in front of the small boy. 'What a pong, eh? You're as black as the ace of spades, lad. Mind, the time to worry about a boy is when he's clean. Now, your little sister's had a kind of fainting spell and there could be more to come.'

'Oh. Did she go all still again? Can't budge her sometimes – like a brick wall, she is.'

'Ah. So you know all about this, son. Will you look after her at school?'

'I always do! Can't have folk skitting her just 'cos she's different. Our Daisy is dead clever, Doc. It's just these turns what come and go, like. But I'll see she's minded.'

'Good.'

' 'S nowt to worry over.' Michael looked at his mother, the person he worshipped above all earthly beings. 'I'll get cleaned up. Are you all right, Mam?'

'Aye. Go on, tough guy – take the scrubbing brush with you, 'cos that muck 'll take a sight of shifting.'

Michael grinned and shot off upstairs to baptize the new bath.

The three adults turned to the sofa and saw Daisy's wide eyes staring up at them. 'He went and fell in the river again, didn't he?'

Molly dropped to her knees and clutched the child's hand. 'Thank God,' she mumbled. 'He did that, Daisy. Can you imagine Bolton holidays without our Michael coming in wearing half the river bank? Part of our celebrations, is that.'

'Where's me dad?'

'I'm not sure, lass.'

'It's so cold.' Daisy looked at her grandmother. 'Where is he? All that . . . all that shivering . . . '

'Meat!' yelled Ma, a look of triumph on her face. 'I told you! All of you! Perhaps you'll listen to me from now on! Stupid eejit, that Paddy Maguire. How did I come to have a son so . . . so . . . ?' She shook her head impatiently. 'Janet? Joey? Get yourselves in here this instant!'

The twins arrived together from the best room.

Ma looked everybody up and down before speaking again. 'Right, the lot of yous. I may be a daft old woman with the head only half screwed on, but I reckon I know where Paddy is.'

'Eh?' Joey's black eyes were fixed on his little sister.

Ma pointed to the sofa. 'She's seen him! Doesn't remember, but she knows he's cold. That's why she was shivering, because her father's in difficulty. You can laugh at me all you like, but Patrick Maguire is likely locked in the cold store behind Jones's butcher's shop. That's where Bobby McMorrow works. The pair of them will be after a bit of extra beef this Sunday, mark my words! So away the pair of you, rescue your daddy before he freezes to death.'

The twins ran out and Ma glanced at the door. 'Mind, he should keep well enough at that low temperature.'

The doctor coughed politely. 'You believe that this child . . . ? No. She has what we call petit mal, Mrs Maguire. How you can put your faith in all that nonsense—'

'Wait and see, why don't you? Paddy will be back any minute to thaw out on the paving slabs.' She took the man aside. 'The girl goes out of her body. Just because you don't understand it, you think it can't happen. But it does. Paddy was cold and she felt it. And you call it what?'

'Petit mal.'

'What's that when it's at home?'

401

'Translated, it means little illness.'

'Does it now? Well, we could be doing with a great deal more of these little illnesses, for they are a gift, not a curse.'

'I won't argue.'

'No point, for you haven't a leg to stand on.'

'Ma!' Molly's voice was stern. 'No more of it! Even if you're proved right, I want no more! This is my daughter, not yours and I won't have it said that she has visions. Are you hearing me?'

'Yes. Yes, I hear you.'

'I'll not be shown up with it. And I won't have her pointed at! I mean it, Ma. Any more of this nonsense and we'll find a house of our own, just me and Paddy and the kids. I don't want to leave you, but I will if you carry on. Daisy's got little fits like what the doctor said. All right?'

Ma studied the firm set of Molly's jaw. There came a point when arguing with Molly was useless. It didn't happen often, but Ma knew that she must concede now. 'Have it your own way,' she said quietly. 'What will out will out. In its own time.'

But neither of them was surprised when, ten minutes after the doctor had left, Paddy arrived home supported by the twins and closely followed by yet another policeman. Police in the house had become a part of life over the years, a part that shamed all except Paddy himself, who was usually too drunk to notice who brought him home.

'You were right, Gran,' puffed Joey. 'Him, Bobby McMorrow and half a dozen dead pigs all locked up safe and cosy for the night. Is our Daisy all right?'

'She's fine.' Ma looked at the policeman who lingered in the doorway. 'Get inside here this minute! You make the place look untidy and in broad daylight too!'

The constable stepped inside. 'Is she ill?' He pointed to Daisy.

'Just a turn, thanks for asking.' Ma dragged Paddy over to the fire and pushed him into a chair. 'Well?'

'Well what?'

'I require something of an explanation. So does this police-man.'

'We was just sweeping up, me and Bobby, when the old devil went and locked us in the cold room.'

The constable took a notebook from his pocket. 'Mr Jones, the butcher, says they were lying in wait to steal—'

Ma turned on him. 'Steal? My son? What proof have you at all? Has he half a pig up his vest and him in the best suit? Would you care to go through the pockets, see can you find a few cowheels and a pound of tripe?'

'No, but—'

'Ah. So we're back to the no-buts, are we? No but what?'

'Well – it's happened before.'

'With my Paddy involved?'

'Er . . . Mr McMorrow is under suspicion.'

Ma straightened. 'Under suspicion? Bobby McMorrow should be under six feet of something or other. He is a bad influence and gives a poor impression of all decent Irish folk! His name is not to be spoken here . . . '

'Bobby's lost his job,' said Paddy mournfully. 'I'll say his name, say it proudly, I will! Where is the justice? Won that war near single-handed, he did, over the top day after day . . . '

Janet and Joey fled to the kitchen. Once Dad started on about Bobby McMorrow's personal triumph over the Kaiser, things often got too hilarious to bear. They stuffed pot towels in their mouths to stop the laughter, unaware that half their hysteria was caused by seeing Daisy well again, all rosy-cheeked and smiling on the sofa.

The policeman placed his helmet in the centre of the table next to salt and pepper. 'Now look here, Mr Maguire. Past the eyeballs with you, we are. How many times have you been carried home near paralysed, eh? We've better things to do than keep hauling you out of hot water.' He smiled in spite of himself. 'Or cold as it turned out today. Mr Jones had no idea that you and McMorrow were in there.'

'Left us there to die, he did!'

'Rubbish! Now listen to me, Paddy. Look at me while I'm talking to you. One more foot out of line and you're up with the beak for time-wasting.' He glanced at Molly. 'Can't you keep him in, Missus?'

Molly bridled. 'What do you want me to do? Fasten him in the wash-house or the lavvy, stick a ball of string to his pants so I can drag him out of the pub at closing? Or do I keep him sedated?'

'I don't know, do I?' The constable retrieved his helmet. 'Only we've had more than enough! Twice we've fetched him out of the Temperance and him as puddled as a mad dog. Then there's been all this trouble down the Masonic, him and a couple of other heroes asking for a lend of a trowel and a pinny—'

'I don't like Masons,' announced Paddy to no-one in particular. 'The anti-Christ incarnate, they are, with their handshakes and ho boys let's roll up our trouser legs. Daft buggers—'

'Shut up, eejit!' yelled Ma. She turned to the guardian of the law whose face was now severely contorted as he fought back a laugh. 'Sorry for your trouble, officer,' she said sweetly.

'I wish . . . I wish your Paddy'd have a word with our Chief.'

'And why would you be wanting that now?'

'He's—' The voice was strangled. 'Worshipful Master this year.'

Ma nodded sagely. 'Our congratulations to him, young man. Now, this boy is drunk – as you can see – so I'd be glad if his silliness went no further than your good self.'

'Fair enough, Missus. Only keep him off the streets for a week or two, will you? If he walks in that Lodge again, he'll be coming back out with a few bits missing.'

The policeman left, his broad back shaking with mirth.

Ma sank into her regular place at the table. 'Molly!' she cried. 'What are we to do with them all? We've one in the river, another locked up with the bacon, the child with petty whatever the doctor said and twins at each other's throats. What'll we do?'

'We either laugh or flaming well cry!' Molly walked to her husband's side. 'Come on lad. Bed for you and no messing. You must be frozen through.'

Paddy got up and stood swaying dangerously by the fireplace. 'Hang on a minute,' he said carefully. Janet and Joey arrived in the doorway just in time to notice what followed, then disappeared quickly when they saw what was happening, returning to their pot towels to stifle chuckles which threatened to explode any second.

Like a conjurer at Bolton Fair, Paddy produced quarters of boiled ham and corned beef from his inside pockets, a greasy package of bacon from the shirt front, then two pork chops from his trouser pockets. These latter items he studied closely, brushing and picking odd bits of fluff from their surfaces.

This was all too much for Ma and Molly. They screamed their mirth into the room, both women gasping for breath between bouts of laughter.

Paddy rounded off his performance by discovering a sheep's eye in his waistcoat and he impaled this object on an index finger. 'Poor sheep,' he mumbled sadly. He tried to fix his family with a steely stare, failing completely due to lack of focus. 'Never say . . . ' the finger wagged. 'Never say I don't look out for me own folk.' Then he staggered upstairs, sheep's eye and all, to sleep it off.

Daisy giggled. 'He's naughty. Will it be a sin to eat the meat, Gran?'

But there was no getting a sensible answer from anyone. The twins entered from the scullery and joined in the merriment at the sight of Paddy's ill-gotten gains. Joey gathered them up and was just about to take them through to the meat-safe, when a rapping at the door put a sudden end to all the cavorting. He bundled the stolen goods into the dresser and tried to look casual while Ma went to answer.

They all watched as she gasped and stepped back a fraction, her hand straying along the wall for support. 'Molly?'

'Yes, Ma?'

'It's . . . it's Mr Swainbank.'

Chapter 13

Charles Swainbank surveyed the group of people in the cramped room. They looked terrified, all of them. Molly and Ma for obvious reasons, Janet because he was her boss, Joey because his sister seemed nervous, while the little girl was already out of order, lying on a couch covered in blankets and coats. He removed his trilby and stood awkwardly in the doorway, the hat twisting between restless fingers. 'I'm . . . er . . . your new landlord.'

Ma tutted under her breath before speaking. 'We know that, Mr Swainbank.' There was an edge to her voice – little short of a note of warning. She was recovering from the initial shock, that was plain to see.

'I just came round to check the quality of workmanship – I've been to several of the other houses too. If this is an inconvenient time, I'll call again—'

'No!' Molly approached him, her face white with terror. 'You own the house – you look at it!' She didn't want him coming back again, didn't like the idea of him getting a foot in the door more than once. Oh aye, he'd said he intended to get to know the twins – but here? In their own house? 'Do you want to go all through?' she asked, her voice not quite steady. 'Only our Michael's still in the bath – he's been up there hours – and me husband's in bed with a chill.'

Janet and Joey, discomfort forgotten as they realized that the caller was in no way connected with them, hid their faces, mirth threatening to arise anew. In bed with a chill? More like a big freeze, it was, though no doubt the brandy under the bed would hasten the thawing process.

Charles stared at Molly in her washed-out flowered apron. Had he switched off the light in those green eyes, turned it

406

out like an electric lamp? Molly! He forced himself to walk further into the room. It was about the size of one of the pantries up at the Hall, not much bigger than a cupboard with a window, really. And his children, his own flesh and blood had spent their short lives here. 'No, I don't need to go poking about the place, thank you. I just wanted to make sure you were satisfied with the improvements.' He paused. 'Is this your son?'

Molly nodded, her face stripped completely of expression. 'Yes, this is our Joey. Joey – Mr Swainbank, Janet's boss and our new landlord.'

The boy grunted a curt greeting. So here was the feller who thought a right lot of their Janet, who had courted her away from the shop. He decided there and then not to like this uninvited guest. If it wasn't for bloody Swainbank, their Janet could have had a counter all her own, ribbons and buttons, a ladylike kind of business. Instead, she had condemned herself to drudgery and this chap here was encouraging such stupidity. 'I'm off out.' His face wore a dark frown.

'But you've not had your tea!' Molly rushed to the oven. 'Pie's nearly ready.'

The boy glanced pointedly in the direction of the intruder. 'I'll come back when there's a bit more room in the house!' He walked out past Charles, not bothering to meet the man's eyes as he left.

There followed an uncomfortable silence. 'Well,' ventured Charles at last. 'Are you happy with the alterations?'

'Yes, thank you.' Molly's tone was as cool and dismissive as she could manage. 'It's very good of you, I'm sure.'

'Right. I'll . . . er . . . I'll be going, then.' He took a backward step towards the door.

'Would you hang on awhile, please?' said Ma. 'There's a thing or two needs doing and as the rent-book is in my name, we should perhaps discuss the business privately.' She looked meaningfully at Molly. 'Serve the tea up. I'll take mine later. Mr Swainbank and I will go into my room.'

Janet remained fastened to the spot, her eyes wide with disbelief as the boss followed Ma like a little lamb into the front room. Gran was a powerful woman all right, a force to be reckoned with – but to see Mr Swainbank doing as he was told, so meek and mild – well, it took her breath away!

Charles looked hard at Ma. She had changed greatly. His early recollections were dim, just a glimpse from a carriage, a shock of near-black hair, a pale Irish skin and, on closer inspection, piercing blue eyes. He remembered his own father's excitement whenever he caught sight of Ma Maguire, the quickening of hooves, a mad dash on foot through the market sometimes. Yes, Ma had remained a handsome woman right up to Father's death. She'd been a big girl, very tall, especially for one of her generation. Now she seemed shrivelled, as if her body had shrunk while the skin had remained the same size, rather wrinkled and sad like a punctured balloon. That famous dark hair of which she had reputedly been so proud was reduced to a few wisps of grey scraped tightly against her skull. But the eyes were the same, twin blue flames that crackled with life and energy. 'You've been ill, Ma. I'm sorry about that – are you better?'

She attempted to straighten the rounded spine. 'Improving, thank you. Sit yourself down, for I'm not going to strain meself looking up to you all the while.'

They sat down simultaneously, Charles allowing himself a tight smile. She'd look up to nobody if he remembered correctly. 'Well – what's wrong?' he ventured, half knowing the answer before it arrived.

Ma drew her chair closer so that their voices might be confined. 'You walk in here bold as brass and ask me what's wrong? I believe my daughter-in-law has already told you how we feel – it's clear enough the poor girl had little effect! I warn you now, Charles Swainbank – this may be your house, but it's our home. As long as we keep it decent enough and pay our rent, you have no right to interfere in this place!'

'I came to look at the alterations—'

'In a pig's eye, you did! Why spend all that money on the one street, a street you've never owned, a street not worth the owning? Why go out and buy a row of decaying houses, then throw away a fortune on buildings that will doubtless tumble to the wreckers inside fifty years?' She glowered at him. 'Well?'

'You know the answer. For the same reason my father wrote poems to a woman who would not cross a road to speak to him!'

She laughed mirthlessly. 'For love, is it?'

'Love, hopelessness – what's the difference?'

This stopped her momentarily. Was he comparing Richard's hopeless love for her to this very different situation? 'Rubbish! You're doing this for a pair of babbies you took care never to clap eyes on! Aye, twins that should never have lived. I bet if Molly had agreed to abortion—'

'No! There was no question – ever—'

'Keep your voice down,' she hissed. 'There was no question because there was no necessity for knitting needles and gin! I saw to that!'

His mouth twitched angrily. 'Yes, you saw to everything, didn't you? I'd have looked after her! If she'd come to me in the first place—'

'She didn't need you! We don't need you! Look. You know I was . . . fond of your father. Yet in him I saw . . . what's the word now? Qualities, that's it. I saw in Richard qualities from centuries before. Bad stock, evil line – it all comes out—'

'Then it's in the twins too?'

She gritted her teeth. 'Don't twist my words! They've been reared apart!' Her mind cast itself back over Joey's misdeeds before she continued, 'The Swainbanks have a history that's unclean. People were left crying in the streets because of your lot, thrown into the gutters, they were, for resting on a wall between jobs! And that still went on in your father's time!'

Charles opened his mouth to reply, but she held up a hand. 'No! I will have my say! Long ago, before I became a weaver, I worked as a spinner in one of your mills. Almost up to Patrick's birth I worked, bent double just to make ends meet in more ways than one. Served some time as a side-piecer, I did – and backbreaking labour it was too! When I got my own mules, I watched a little-piecer lifted and thrown across a room when a belt flew loose. Fingers were swept up at night, thrown away as just a bit more waste. I have seen children at death's door from blood-poisoning brought on by filth and grease.

409

Remember? How they toiled barefoot and in a little work-shirt, sliding in thick oil all over the place? Infants, they were – babes in arms—'

'They were not babies! And everyone employed them!'

'Ah, so it's accuracy you're after! In my time they were twelve years old, some of them weighing three or four stones for lack of nourishment. A six o'clock start to a midday finish, then off to school to be beaten half to death for collapsing at their desks! I have talked to and worked with some of these victims! Victims of your father and others like him.'

'And you blame me for that?'

She looked down at her hands. 'Not quite, not entirely. But I blame you for displaying that same coldness now in coming here to inspect my grandchildren.'

He cleared his throat. 'They're not your grandchildren, Ma.'

She jumped to her feet and brought her hand viciously across his face, delivering a slap that seemed to echo through the whole house. 'Remember the last time I did that? And your father too? There you stood, not a word to say for yourself, not while the old man lived. But now you have it all, don't you? The power, the weight, the so-called wisdom! Never dare say to me that those are not my grandchildren! Never! Who nurtured them and saw them through the night with croup and scarlet fever? Where were you when we thought Janet had the diphtheria? More to the point, where was her real so-called grandmother, that nasty piece of work you called Mother? Well?'

His face glowed where she had struck him, but he remained where he was, feeling as if he were doing penance not just for his own mistakes, but also for the undeniable sins of his predecessors.

She sat down again. 'You and your kind – I spit on you! You never look upon what you don't want to see. But I've seen it all, lad! One filthy sink in a corner, all clogged up with grease and cotton waste – that's where you washed and dressed a hand when the mule trapped fingers. Children running with wipers to clean as a mule opened, fleeing for their lives to get out again in time! Grown women weeping because

410

they were refused a new broom to sweep the floor while the old one still had two or three bristles on its head. Were you there? Did you learn all that?'

The chair creaked as she leaned nearer to him. 'There's no love lost, Charlie, no love at all for you here. You're not one of us. Did you ever get a clout off a minder for breaking ends while you cleaned a machine that threatened to kill you? Did you ever have to beg for wages because there was no pay however good a job you made? Aye. You remember don't you? Piecers were paid by the spinner out of his own wages. And a spinner was rightly called a minder, for he kept many a child alive out of his own pitiful sum. Were you there when a good minder brought in a flour cake and a slice of ham to save the life of a thirteen-year-old little-piecer with legs bent by rickets? No. You know nothing! You were too busy sitting in the whited sepulchre counting the takings! Your fine cars and carriages, your house and all its trappings – everything you own was bought and paid for with blood. Our blood.' She beat a closed fist against her breast. 'You cannot ever belong with us, just as we cannot ever belong with you.'

'All the cruelties you speak of are out of the past! Surely you can see that things are improving all the time . . . '

'Really? Tell that to Mary Watson down in Vernon Street. She'll be sixty-odd now if she's still alive. Four fingers she left behind one day and her driven out of her mind when your father's monkeys poured raw iodine on to the stumps. I can hear that girl's screams to this day – locked up as a lunatic for a while, she was. And when you've seen Mary, go round to all those who were scalped in the carding rooms, to weavers who lost eyes when a shuttle went astray. Tell it to the man who was left dangling with a flying belt around his neck – go to his grave and post him a letter, why don't you?' She paused for breath and gazed at him thoughtfully. 'Do you realize what you've taken on in Janet? She's aware of all that, for I have made sure she knows the true price of cotton!'

He held on grimly to what remained of his patience. 'Then your indoctrination has failed. She loves the mills.'

Ma smiled in a knowing way, her head nodding pensively.

411

'Janet's an odd girl. The buildings fascinate her and she likes the feel of a length of good cloth. But she's no fool. That girl will pay her dues to a union just like all the other weavers do. In her bones, Janet is for the workers. She might even help bring you down . . . '

'Then she'll bring herself down, because she and her brother stand to inherit whatever I leave.'

Ma's mouth twisted into a grimace. 'She doesn't want it! Am I not getting through to you at all? We're not part of all that!'

'I am weary, Ma, sick of sitting here and listening while you prattle on about history that's almost as ancient as the Greeks! You're a bitter old woman. And the undeniable fact remains – those are my children—'

'Children of a crime you committed against their mother!'

'But still mine! Don't you see – they're all I have?'

'Then take another wife and make more!'

He dropped his head. 'No. I've done enough. My children – my sons – they died because I over-indulged them. Amelia suffered so much . . . ' Unable to sit still with his thoughts, he jumped up and began to pace back and forth between bed and window. 'The twins are already here, a fact of my life. They're my responsibility. I am their father, for goodness sake!'

'You've paid your dues over the years. Look, I promised never to bother your family if a future for Molly's child could be guaranteed. So why do you annoy us now? What about my son who has lived a lifetime believing that all four are his? Can you imagine his state of mind if he finds this out? Will you break us, Charlie, just as your father broke so many? Will you cut out our hearts and lay them in the streets – your own too, for you will surely be judged?'

He ran his fingers through thick brown hair, his head waving slowly from side to side. 'I don't know! I'm not like you! I don't have a list of answers to all the questions in the world. All I know is that those two children are my only link with life after a terrible couple of months.'

'Aye. And it's sorry I am for all your trouble, Charles Swainbank, for no mortal deserves what you have suffered. It is enough to push you to the edge of sanity. But please – I beg you – leave my family alone.'

His eyes swam with unshed tears. 'I can't. She is so beautiful – I love her already.'

'And Joey?'

He rubbed his creased forehead. 'I don't know him.'

'Sit down, Charlie, or you'll have me bit of oilcloth worn out. Come away now, there's nought to be gained from a flat spin.'

He sank on to the edge of the bed, head in hands, elbows resting on his knees. After a few seconds, Ma came to join him. 'Where's your pride, man?'

'Gone. Buried with them, cold in the grave.'

'Sweet Jesus! I wish with all me heart that I could help you, son! But I can't. Not without hurting my own! Charlie, don't you see the size of the sword you hold over Molly's head? The girl is terrified.'

'I didn't want that. Not for Molly—'

'No indeed. And what about young Joey – is he worthy of your fortune?'

'He seems an ordinary enough lad, no harm in him.'

'No harm? Will I laugh or cry? He's another bag of mischief, different altogether from Janet, not as clever. She'll go her own road and shame the divil, but he's a mixed-up boy with a desperate need for money. Remember your old neighbour – the one who took Samson after your brother died?'

'Sarah Leason?'

'The same. He almost killed her, Charlie, went into the house after her money, put the old woman in the hospital where she still lies with a headache the rest of us can almost hear! He left her for dead. I'm not saying he actually struck a blow, but when she fell, he ran off with a box stuffed with every penny she owned. Now. How about that for a Swainbank?'

An expression of shock and disbelief twisted his features. 'Good God!'

'Exactly. So, who's to say how he'll turn out, eh? As I said before, we've brought them up decent, given them good Catholic values, watched to make sure they did right. Yet

413

something came out in that boy, something I didn't want to tell you about, but—'

'But you'll use any weapon to keep me at bay?'

'Yes. Yes, if I'm to be honest, I suppose I will do just that.'

'It won't work, Ma. Whatever he is, it won't work. Not till I've talked to him and made up my own mind. Sorry.'

'Step back a way, man! Consider the situation properly. These children were not born for you to choose their path in life. No one owns them, not you, not meself, not their mother. No person ever owns another, whatever the relationship. You cannot bend and shape them for your purpose, nor will they ever accept you as a father. My Paddy may not be up to much, but he is loved, particularly by Janet. She will hate you if you lay a claim, Charlie.'

He nodded quickly. 'Yes, yes I see that. But do you recognize my dilemma?'

'Indeed. And very clearly too. I am not completely without sympathy, though my loyalty lies elsewhere. And I also see a bargain made many years ago, an agreement I've stuck to which you now break by coming here.'

'I've read the papers, Ma. They say nothing about my claim—'

'And plenty about me having none, I take it?'

His chin dropped again. This was obviously an unfair world, yet he was glad that the law would, in all probability, favour him should the case reach the courts. 'Yes, that's about the size of it. You can't name them as Swainbanks, but I can.'

'British justice!' She spat these words. 'I sold my worthless son – may God forgive me – to give Molly some peace of mind and a safe home. Now she turns on me for doing just that, for bargaining with you! We've come to terms, she and I, but sure nothing's the same as it was. And still you come back for your pound of flesh. Is there no end to it?'

'I truly am sorry. But I will know my children and they will know me – not necessarily as a father – not yet. But they will know who I am, what I'm made of.'

'I see. Then you refuse to leave us alone?'

For answer, he nodded just once.

'Then go.'

He rose slowly from the bed. 'Ma?'

'I said go! Go now before I lose me temper and bring in the street! No more words, no more apologies. Just get out.'

He left her sitting there and walked out to the kitchen where Molly, Janet and Michael were eating their evening meal. Unable to meet any eyes, he muttered a hasty goodbye before striding out of the house.

Perkins waited patiently by the car outside Leather-barrow's, but Charles hurried past him to where Joey lounged at the corner of Delia Street's back alley. For a reason he would never be able to explain, Charles placed a hand on the boy's arm. 'Take care of your family, Joey. Especially that twin sister of yours.'

Joey cast his black eyes over this man, temper threatening to erupt as he pictured Janet slaving at a loom, probably finishing up bent double like so many worn-out workers in this God-forsaken town. And Joey wasn't afraid of him, not bloody likely! He might own the house they lived in, might own the mill where Janet worked, but Joey Maguire was a man with his own business, a man with a future. He straightened his long spine and looked Swainbank squarely in the face. 'I don't need you to tell me how to carry on! Take your hand off me before I fetch you one across the chops! I'm not right pleased about my sister working in your mill, fetching and carrying for your likes. She had a chance of a good life down the shop, but no, you went and give her the job, eh? Well, she'll not be stopping long.'

Charles stepped back as the boy's anger hit him. 'Why do you dislike me, Joey? No-one asked Janet to apply for work, no-one forced her to accept.'

Joey kicked at the ground moodily, then stopped himself when he remembered the good shoes. 'What were you doing at our house? Why have you picked our Janet out as special? She's her head in the clouds because the big boss likes her. Do you fancy taking her on now that your wife's gone?'

Charles held his tongue with difficulty. The cheek of this young man – and how far from the truth he was! 'Janet's a gifted girl,' he muttered lamely. 'I'm privileged to have her in the business, but I haven't picked her out, Joey—'

415

'Mr Maguire, if you don't mind. Aye, happen I have only just left school, but I'm a businessman same as yourself – or will be once Gran signs the shops over when me and Janet are eighteen.' He paused and took in the man's stricken expression. 'There's summat not quite right about you, Mr Swainbank. I don't know why you're messing about round here, only you're not wanted – I can tell you that for nowt. Me mam doesn't like you, Gran can't stand mill owners and I don't like the way you've got your claws in my sister. So why don't you sling your hook while the going's good?'

Charles' patience had reached its limit. After all the abuse from Ma, this was too much. 'If I had spoken to my father in such a way—'

'Aye. But you're not me dad, are you?'

Seconds passed while the man studied this face, this younger version of his own features. 'I am old enough to be your father, Mr Maguire. And how would it be if I turned your family out of the house because of your lack of respect?' He hated himself as soon as these words were out, for wasn't he acting as Ma would have predicted, taking a swing with the weighty hand of a boss?

'Do what you want! We'll get a house somewhere.'

This streetwise urchin was playing with him, dangling him like one of those dolls on elastic that were given away as prizes at Bolton Fair. Charles grabbed his son by the collar. 'Listen here, you little dog,' he hissed between clenched teeth. 'Shall I tell you why I'm here? Do you really want to know?' He swallowed hard. 'My old neighbour – remember her? Eccentric, rather unclean, a lot of money in the house?'

Joey struggled to free himself, eyes wide with terror.

'Would you like me to go on, Joey? Shall I tell you what I intend to do if you ever threaten me again?'

'Leave me . . . alone!'

'Got away with it, did you? Must have, or you'd have been locked up by now. Didn't Sarah tell them it was you? I will. I'll help the police with their enquiries, lad!'

'Who . . . who told you? Our Janet? Gran? Me mam?'

'Nobody in the house told me. I just know. I have ways of

finding out most things.' It was easier to lie; nothing would be gained from Joey discovering Ma's 'betrayal'. 'Well? What have you to say for yourself, boy?'

Joey broke free and smoothed the creased jacket. 'I didn't mean to hurt her – honest. I just wanted—'

'Money? How badly do you want money?'

'Not that badly. Not any more. It was . . . oh, I don't know—'

'Tell me, Joey! Come on, I need to know. I have to be sure it won't happen again. That poor lady lived alongside us for many years and now I shall have to take care of her, protect her from thieves and vagabonds like yourself.'

'It's . . . It's a bit hard to explain, like I don't know the right words.'

'Then get into the car while we discuss the matter.'

The boy's face was livid with fear as he found himself being bundled unceremoniously into the back seat of the large black vehicle.

Perkins, who could sense his master's ill-temper, knew better than to ask questions. He pulled on his chauffeur's cap and sat silently behind the wheel as he waited instruction.

'Home,' snapped Charles.

The car turned into Delia Street, purring its way past a few inquisitive bystanders. A heavy silence hung over the passengers until Bolton was well behind them, then Charles asked again, 'Why, Joey?'

'To get me and Janet away from them.' His voice was a mere whisper.

'Speak up! No need to worry about Perkins – his loyalty is beyond question.'

Joey looked fearfully into the big man's face. 'I wanted me and our Janet out of the house and in a place of our own.'

'Why?'

Joey stared out of the window. Why? He could scarcely remember. None of it mattered now, not with the shop and all. Except this bloke here could ruin everything, tell on Joey over Witchie Leason . . .

'Well?' persisted Charles.

The boy shrugged his shoulders. 'You've seen it. Oh, it's

417

all right now, better than it used to be – but the place was a dump. I'd look at me mother, see how weary she was and I'd think to meself, "I don't want that for Janet." Me gran got ill 'cos she'd worked all her life and got wore out. Then there's me dad – he's about as much use as a cushion stuffed with bricks. It was a lot of things all piled up. Little things on their own, but big when they were all stuck together. It got me down, specially the way our Janet just . . . well . . . '

'Accepted it?'

'Aye.' He nodded with a wisdom far older than his years. 'See, we're different, me and her, not like the others.'

Charles rubbed a hand across his mouth. 'Different?'

'Twins, like. And I wanted to turn her into a lady, something a bit out of the ordinary, one as didn't have to stone the steps or do her own black-leading.'

'So. You stole and committed near-murder to get your way?'

'The road as Witchie . . . Miss Leason got hurt – it were an accident. It happened that quick I can hardly remember. But I didn't hit her. She came for me and fell when I grabbed that big whip—'

'She took a whip to you? The size of her? Yes, I suppose she would. That sounds very much in character. Still, it's no way to get rich, is it? How would you like it if someone broke into your house and took everything?'

'We've nowt worth pinching.'

'It's all relative, Joey. To some people, you are quite comfortable, chairs to sit on, a table to eat at.'

Joey thought about this for a while. Where were they going anyway? The man had said home, hadn't he? Wouldn't they be making for the bobby shop if there was trouble on? He dragged himself upright. 'Mr Swainbank?'

'Yes?'

'How did you get your money?' His voice trembled, but he still managed this impertinent question.

'From my parents.'

Again, Joey pondered. 'And where did they get it?'

'From their parents.'

'Right back to crofting?'

418

Charles heaved a great sigh. 'Probably. Look, I've had this lecture from your grandmother and from others like her. Yes, somewhere along the line we took charge, appointed ourselves collectors and dealers. It's all in ledgers at home, records of how many cottages we called at, what we paid the weaver. But somebody had to do it, Joey. Somebody had to lift the industry out of the houses and into bigger sheds.'

'Why?'

'It's the way of the world! I could quote the Industrial Revolution till I'm blue in the face, but the simplest explanation is that the cottagers were starving. Each weaver, usually the father, had to depend on his own family of spinners, some of them very small children and old ladies. He could never get enough yarn. Do you realize what my ancestors went through?'

'Never thought on it.'

'Well, consider it now, Joey. Cotton was forbidden at one time. A man could go to prison for burying his mother in a shroud that contained cotton fibres. By written law, a body had to be buried in fleece. Wool was the thing. Keepers of flocks didn't want us Lancashire lads getting fat on vegetable wool. So we fought unfair laws, taxation, farmers – even the weavers stood against us later on in history! You know, a very few hundred years ago, you would have been fined a year's wages for the shirt you now wear. My family helped achieve the freedoms we now take for granted. Imagine – we might still have been forced to wear just wool or linen!'

'Like I said – I never thought—'

'Very few do bother to think.' He took a large cigar from his waistcoat, nipped the end with silver cutters, then lit it slowly, filling the car with rich blue smoke and the perfume of expensive tobaccos. 'What would have happened without the mills? The town you know as Bolton would have remained not much more than a large village, no pavements, no shops, few schools or churches. Yet we are hated for bringing prosperity to a town that otherwise would have continued a Tuesday cattle market with a bit of fish brought in from the coast occasionally! Ma Maguire and your sister have each reminded me of how bad my family was, how many fingers were lost, how

419

many heads of hair. But do they thank us for the Market Hall and the finest civic buildings in England? Never! They don't pause to think about the alternatives.' He shook his head vigorously. 'And has the world ever been a kind and gentle place? Right back to Roman times – and before that too – there have been the bosses and the workers. My lot is no easier than yours. It's just different – an accident of birth.' Yes and some births were more accidental than others, weren't they?

Joey stared at the large house ahead. 'Is that . . . is that all yours?'

'Yes.'

'Bloody hell!'

Charles laughed heartily. 'Bloody hell is right, lad! Because it takes some looking after and is no use to me any more!'

For the next hour, Joey was mesmerized as he allowed himself to be led through the mansion, room after room of opulence, priceless rugs and hangings, furniture the likes of which he'd only ever seen in books or films. They ended the tour in Charles's small study, each bent over ancient manuscripts, accounts covering a hundred and fifty years or more. There were original mill plans, drawings of Kay's flying shuttle dated 1738, pictures of Hargreaves's spinning jenny of 1767, documents frail and yellow with decay. Joey was a slow reader, but he learned for the first time how these inventors had suffered for their genius, many of them driven from Lancashire to do their research in Nottingham because local people, fearful for their livelihood in the domestic industry, smashed each new machine as soon as it was built. He read about weavers who would accept only hand-spun cotton, about the bravery of Arkwright and others who set up mills in spite of acute animosity. 'It wasn't easy then,' he said eventually. 'That there Samuel Crompton could have made a fortune, but he never.'

'That's right. They named streets and roads after him, but some men need to be dead before their greatness is appreciated.'

Joey gazed round the book-lined room. 'I suppose what you're saying is you're a worker just like the rest?'

Charles held out his hands. 'No callouses, no arthritis. Earlier Swainbanks had the ruined hands – I get the benefit of their sweat. That's how it works. If you do well in your shop, won't you give your children a better life, a house with gardens? The only difference between us, Joey, is that you're just starting out while I'm following on. But how will you feel if your workers turn on you and call you a bad boss? Because they will! Once you get a new semi-detached on Crompton Way, a car, a telephone – don't you see? They'll curse you for what you have become. A success. Success is something they will not tolerate. While you're a worker, one of them, you are loved, cared for, unionized. If you alter your status, then you walk alone.'

'I don't care! Somebody's got to run a shop, else where would everybody buy their stuff?'

'With the money they make in my mills. And if nobody ran the mills—'

'Aye. Aye, I see what you're getting at.'

'The very simple politics of very simple economics, son. So don't hate me, Mr Joseph Maguire. In a couple of years, you'll be in a house of your own, making a life for your children. If you hate what I am, then you must by the same token hate what you are about to become.'

Joey glanced up at the mantel clock, just for somewhere to look so that he wouldn't have to carry on meeting that strangely familiar near-black gaze. Then he noticed the time. 'Hey – me mam'll be out of her mind! She's done potato pie with peas and I never miss that!'

'Is there peace between us, Joey?'

'I reckon so, aye. And thanks for showing me your house – it's right grand. But the other thing . . . Miss Leason . . . I'm sorry and I'll do what I can for her. We're going to paint her house—'

'No need, lad. If I know Sarah, she'll be like a fish out of water down there. I'll put her in one of the lodges.'

'Oh. Well, I hope it's a big house. She's got about forty thousand cats.'

'Really? Then you and Janet can find good homes for most of them and I'll get the other few thousand neutered.'

421

'Her won't thank us, Mister!'

'Sarah Leason never thanked anybody, Joey. She'll give us all a hard time, but hard times are part of life. Anyway, it's time she started doing as she's told. Drove her parents to drink, so I'm reliably informed. There's a woman who's stuck to her principles – can't help admiring the silly old bat.'

'Then . . . you won't tell on me?'

'No.'

'Thanks.' He heaved a heartfelt sigh of relief. 'Er . . . will that feller take me back to our house?'

'He will.' They moved towards the door.

'Mr Swainbank?'

'Yes?'

'I'm sorry about your Missus and all – the lads too. It were a bad do, that lot.'

'Thank you.'

They progressed through the high-ceilinged hallway, Joey studying the humourless faces of dead ancestors as they looked down gloomily from the staircase wall.

'Miserable lot, aren't they?' said Charles. 'They all look as if they're suffering from terminal constipation – especially my father. He's the one on the end, the newest. I haven't had myself done yet, though I'm tempted to wear a silly hat for the occasion, cheer things up a bit.'

Joey held out his hand and gripped Charles's outstretched fingers. 'You're all right, you are. Thanks for helping out over Witchie. She will be happier up here in the country.'

'Witchie?'

'Oh heck.' Joey hung his head. 'That's what folk call her.'

'Is it? Well, that's what you get for being a bit different, Joey, for having a mind of your own. Remember it.'

'I will.'

'Just you be sensible and stay out of trouble. I'll be down to your shop – my housemaid would love a new bicycle.'

Joey grinned from ear to ear. 'You're on, sir! I'll put a nice one away for you – it's not going to be cheap!'

'Nothing ever is, son. Nothing worth having . . .'

The car pulled away and Charles walked through his lonely

house, making immediately for the kitchen where warmth and friendship awaited him.

All the way home, Joey Maguire remained thoughtful. He was a right clever bloke, that Swainbank, knew his stuff plain enough. And there was a lot in what he said, a lot of solid sense. By, it were a good job he weren't doing anything about the other, though! No way could Joey have looked into those black eyes and denied what he'd done to Witchie.

He settled back to enjoy this luxurious journey. Charles Swainbank had treated him with a kind of respect, as if he expected the shops to do well, as if he recognized a man who would make a success. One day, there'd happen be a car like this, a chauffeur with a peaked cap, a stairway with paintings climbing up the walls. Janet could have a fur coat, Mam could get her portrait done in a ball gown – she was still bonny, was Mam. If it all came quick enough, Michael and Daisy could go to proper schools and Dad – well – happen they'd buy Magee's brewery to keep him happy!

They stopped outside number 34. 'Here we are, sir. Stay put, I'll get the door for you.'

Perkins held the door wide while Joey stepped on to the pavement. 'Er . . . ta,' said the boy, embarrassment in his tone. 'It were good of you to fetch me home, like. Only I'm not sure of trams and buses from up yonder—'

'It's nothing, sir. Glad to be of service.' The uniformed man stood and watched as Joey entered the end house. What a turn-up, eh? As sure as he lived and breathed, Perkins recognized that walk, knew the face almost as well as he knew his own. He climbed into the driver's seat. Surely the rest of this family had noticed the resemblance? Perhaps not. Not the younger ones anyway. People only saw what they needed to see. Whatever, he would keep his counsel, hold the thoughts close to his chest. If the master wanted things known, then all would be revealed in time. But Perkins had seen Master Peter's double this day and he sensed that Charles Swainbank had found a basket where all the eggs could lie until required. The lad might be from the wrong side, but he was definitely a Swainbank.

Inside the house, Joey was being assaulted from all quarters.

'What did he want?' Janet hopped from foot to foot, eyes bright with anticipation. 'Did he say I'm a good tenter 'cos I've mastered all me knots? Did he tell you I know some patterns?'

'We didn't talk about . . .'

'Where've you been?' Molly's face was white. 'This pie crust must be like concrete—'

'What were you thinking of to get in a car with him?' Gran's voice was stern. 'The neighbours are four to a door and eyes on stalks! Bella Seddon has been sitting this last hour on the upstairs windowsill with the head out in the street. If she polishes that glass any longer, she'll surely wear it through! She's had the leather dropped twice and the bucket only missed some poor innocent feller by inches and him half drowned! Have you no sense but to go and set tongues wagging like a row of dogs' tails? This will be the talk for a month now!'

Michael pulled at his brother's jacket. 'What's it like in that car? Can I have a ride? Will he take me next time?'

'Did he send me some sweeties 'cos I'm poorly?' This from Daisy who looked about as poorly as the next robust five-year-old.

'Where did he take you? Where?' Ma Maguire dragged Joey to one side.

'To his house.'

'To his . . . ? Oh my God!' Molly collapsed into a chair. 'Whatever for?'

Joey looked meaningfully at his little brother and sister. 'I can't say now.'

Ma and Molly turned to each other. 'Send them upstairs, Ma,' said Molly, her tone heightened by anxiety.

When the two protesting youngsters had been dispatched, everyone joined Molly at the table.

'Well?' Janet kicked her brother gently. 'What did he want?'

Molly's hands twisted this way and that on the white tablecloth. She couldn't stand this any longer! What if he'd told Joey? What if Joey knew that Paddy wasn't his real dad? She longed to send Janet away . . . but no. If he was going to come out with it, they might as well all be together.

'Did you leave your tongue up to the big house?' Ma's sarcasm hid her fear. Had Swainbank changed his mind and told the whole story? 'Or is your head turned completely by what you saw?'

'No.' He cast a scathing glance at his annoying grandmother, then his head dropped with the shame he still felt. 'It's me own fault, I know it. He wanted me over the bother.'

'What bother?' Molly gripped her son's hand tightly. 'Tell me! Tell me now!'

'Witchie Leason used to be his neighbour. Anyroad, he found out what I did – I reckon she must have told him to teach me a lesson. So he's going to look after her in future, give her somewhere to live near fields.'

'And that's all?' gasped Molly. 'Nothing else?'

'It's enough, isn't it?' he cried. 'Frightened me to death, he did. Then he showed me all around, taught me about cotton and being a boss—'

'Did he now?' Ma leaned back, arms folded against her chest. 'Giving you big ideas, is it? Filling your head with nonsense and how to get rich quick?'

'No! They never got rich quick, Gran! He showed me, laid it out on a desk. We've had it all wrong – he's just the same as us! All of them are just the same as us!' He hadn't the words, couldn't express things as clearly as Swainbank had. 'They were common folk like everybody else, Gran. And—' he struggled to remember. 'They built the Market Hall and churches . . . ' There was more to it, but he hadn't the skill to cope verbally with what he really meant.

'They built graveyards too, lad.' Ma's voice was quiet. 'Graveyards with their names on them, plots of land given generously to the town for the burying of the industrially murdered.'

This was all way beyond Joey, big words, all that fighting talk Gran had learned while helping the unions. 'He's a nice man – that's all I know. He tret me right, carried on like I were important even if I did do that thieving! He's . . . just nice.' Aware of his inadequacies, Joey allowed his voice to tail away.

Janet stood up and leaned against the dresser. 'Joey, you are such a blinking hypocrite!'

'Eh?'

'You couldn't stand the man this afternoon! You've more tunes in you than an Irish fiddle! First off, you don't want me working for him. Now you change your mind as easy as changing your socks, all because of a ride in a posh car!'

'It weren't like that!' Joey jumped up and threw back his chair. 'He explained things, things I'd never thought on before. We blame him for all that's wrong because he's rich, only he comes from poor stock way back, folk as dragged theirselves up same as what we're trying to do now. And he thinks a right lot of you, our Janet, says you're a gifted girl.' He turned his attention to the women now. 'And you two sit here either frightened to death or calling him! Why?'

Ma Maguire rose slowly to her feet. 'If you employ a man in your shop, Joey, a man who misses work when his wife or mother dies – will you cast him from your door?'

'No, but . . . '

'He did. Or he let his managers do it, which is dirtier yet.'

'They were following the old way, doing what Swainbank's grandad would have done . . . '

'Could you walk between mules, see a man with his arm ripped off and say "have him replaced"?'

'He never! That were all before his time!'

Ma thrust her face closer to his, 'Blood flows from one generation along to the next.' She glanced at Molly's stricken face, knowing that these words were cutting her daughter-in-law deeply, yet she continued, 'The sins of the fathers, Joey. That's in the Bible. Don't be letting yourself get taken in by this man.'

Janet took up where Ma left off. 'Gran saw things in the mills, heard how people were treated, so she feels strongly. And Mam doesn't like him because she's worked in his house, remembers how nasty his mother was. As for me – well, I don't care either way – he can be good or bad, no difference to me. All I want is to be a master weaver. But what really upsets us is you, the way you change every time the wind blows.

426

First you hated him because he was a boss, now you like him because you want to be as successful as him. It's as if you've no mind of your own—'

'No! I mean I have! I listen to folk, hear them out. I don't make me mind up in a flash, then stick to it like glue no matter what!'

'You do. Till somebody changes it for you. I saw how you looked at him before, listened to you ranting this afternoon over how I should be in the shop and not working for him, the slave-driver. Your mind was made up then. There was no shifting you. Till he came with his fancy car and his big posh house . . .'

'You're jealous! You're jealous 'cos he never took you up to Briars Hall!'

'I'm not!'

'Oh yes you are!'

Molly slammed Joey's dried-up dinner on to the table. 'Shut up, both of you. It's like having a couple of cats in the house. Eat it if you want – it's well past its best.'

'I'm sorry, Mam,' he mumbled. 'It was just dead interesting, all them books and pictures. I never thought people really lived in places like that—'

'Well, they do!' Molly turned and walked out to the scullery, slamming the door in her wake.

Ma viewed the twins, her heart almost breaking for the pair of them. Joey sat and played with his food while Janet, her face still pale with righteous anger, seated herself by the fire. Ma chose her words with care. 'Keep a distance from him, both of you. These people are not our kind, we have no business with them.'

Joey threw down his fork. 'Will you tell him that when he comes in the shop for a bike, or when he sends somebody for a few shirt buttons? Will you? At least he talks some bloody sense, summat to do with economics and . . . and trade! At least you know where you are with him! Here – it's flaming mad, like a loony bin! Don't go in a car, you'll have the neighbours talking – I don't give a tuppenny damn for the blinking neighbours!' He stared mockingly at his grandmother. 'And you? With your precious brooch and your old Granny Gallagher's sight that you're wishing on poor little Daisy – honest! If we listened to you, really listened for more than five minutes on the trot, we'd all be head cases!'

'Don't you dare talk to me in that tone . . . '

'When will you let me grow up, Gran? That's another thing – he talked to me like I was a man, a real person! I'm not a little lad for you to push and shove around, "Joey do this, Joey get that." No! You expect me to be old enough to order me own stock, keep accounts, run a bike-mending shop – yet you want me young enough to boss about! Well, I can't be both. I can't be a man and a kid at the same time, so make up your mind what I'm supposed to be, will you? And when you've decided, happen you'll let me know so I can pick me trousers, long or short!' Pleased with the way he had finally expressed himself, Joey smiled tightly.

This was the second time Ma's authority had been questioned of late. Her rein on this family had been tight – necessarily so. But now Molly and Joey were both champing at the bit, she out of fear and frustration, he because of his haste to break free. She held tight to the brooch, her eyes swimming with unshed tears, tears she would not allow to fall. 'Remember, Joey, that I stood by you in your trouble. Always remember that. And above all, I am your grandmother. Whether I am right or wrong, I ask for respect at all times.' She left the room as quickly as the dragging foot would allow.

There followed a long silence, then Janet looked up at her brother. 'What's going on at all?' she asked, almost of herself.

Joey fixed his eyes on the fire. 'I don't know. But we'll not get to the bottom of anything till she thinks it's time.' He pointed towards Ma's room. 'Thing as bothers me is Mam being so upset. What is it about this Swainbank chap that gets everybody's backs up, Jan?'

'I don't know. Shall I ask him next time I see him?'

'And get an answer? From any of them? Nay, we're fifteen, still in nappies according to some folk. Don't bother asking. It'll come to us in time.'

Chapter 14

'I don't like cars!'

Charles gritted his teeth and bit back a ready answer. If he told her to get out and walk, then she probably would, even while the car was doing twenty-five miles an hour. She'd never been easy and age had done little to improve or soften her attitudes.

'Stupid great beasts with no personality, nothing to get to grips with. And the speed of everything. Did you have to go round that bend on two wheels? Watch out for the man crossing the street! See? You'll have us all dead! There's nothing can touch a good horse—'

'My brother died on horseback, Miss Leason, just as my sons were killed in one of these things. It's a matter of handling.'

'Is it now? Bloody high-handed, fetching me out of hospital in this . . . this coalcart, telling me where I'm going to live, how I'm going to live. It's me you're handling, isn't it? Me!'

'They wouldn't let you go back to your house. You know damned well it was either me or the asylum. So shut up and enjoy the ride even if it kills you.'

'Bloody men!'

'Pardon?' He grinned, having heard her plainly enough. 'Did you say something?'

'Why can't I go home? I've got my own place, don't need your charity.'

'You can't go home because you live like a tramp. Eccentricity's one thing, infestation's another matter altogether. You need watching. I've had to stick my neck right out to get you released after all the trouble you caused.'

'Trouble? I caused no trouble.'

He coughed to cover a laugh as he remembered the vivid picture Matron had painted. 'You were not supposed to get them all out of their beds for a hunger march—'

'It wasn't a hunger march, it was a bid for freedom.'

'In their nightgowns? Halfway down Chorley New Road without a coat between them?'

'It's the principle of the matter, Charles. They're old, they're useless and yet they still refuse to do what society requires, which is to die gracefully, quietly and with as little mess as possible. I showed them the sun, the wind and the rain—'

'And gave them arthritis, sore feet and pneumonia!'

'I gave them a day out!'

'Ten minutes at the most. Sarah, you are a bloody nuisance. They won't have you back. No matter how ill you become, you're blacklisted, banned, persona non grata.'

'Good.'

'They were going to put you away as crackers.'

'The word is senile, Charles. My mind is supposedly gone. That brain chap tried to explain it to me, but he was a remarkably stupid and odd character. Said the brain is rather like a loaf and that mine is down to the last slice.'

'To which you replied . . . ?'

'I suggested that his own grey matter seemed somewhat unleavened, as if it had never risen in the first place. This observation of mine was not well received – I was assessed insane right away. He'd no sense of humour, you see – and there's the first sign of insanity. Isn't it amazing that the queerest doctors are interested in the queerest medicine? Had a dreadful speech impediment, poor man. I gave him some written diphthongs to practise on, but he failed to appreciate my good intentions.'

Charles burst into loud laughter. 'God Almighty! You emasculate men as accurately as the vet dealt with your cats!'

'What? You've had my cats tampered with? And who gave you permission for that?'

'Don't need permission – cats are vermin. And there are too many of them, so the fewer reproductive organs, the better.

We've given most of them away to good homes – names and addresses on file if required. You have to learn to live a more normal life, Sarah.'

'How dare you?'

He stopped the car abruptly. 'Right. Shall we turn round and go back to the hospital, let them transfer you to the madhouse? Because those are your two choices – me or the loonies. Well?'

'Frankly, I don't know which is worse.'

He glanced at his watch. 'Make your mind up – I've a business to run.'

She went through the motion of considering the options. 'I suppose it will do no harm for me to look at the lodge—'

'Very kind of you, I'm sure. So. In case you do decide to live among us – grace us by your presence, as it were – these are the house rules. You'll make your own breakfast and lunch, then an evening meal will be brought to you each day. Catfood will come from the farm, also from the fishmarket every Tuesday. Don't get it mixed up with your own.'

'I'm not daft!' The small head jerked upward. 'Why do you talk to me as if I were a few pennies light of the shilling, eh? Because I'm not, not at all!'

He moved the car forward slowly. 'You've always been odd. If you start acting too reasonable, perhaps people will believe you have finally hit the floor. But moderate your tendencies, for heaven's sake. I can't watch you all the time and I don't want to come to visit you in the rubber room, do I? Padded cell, arms tied behind your back, terrible screams—'

'You're enjoying this! Trying to frighten a poor old woman!'

'Poor old woman? I'd have a better chance with a rogue elephant! Nobody scares you, Sarah Leason. No man, anyway. Faced with a wild animal, you might show some slight respect, but humanity holds little threat for you. I don't know why I'm bothering with you, really I don't. My staff spent days cleaning out the gatehouse for you – Perkins even went to the trouble of making five scratching posts, one for each cat! And all you do is moan about interference. I've gone so far

431

as to arrange for your friends to visit this afternoon – a nice cosy tea-party for you and Ma Maguire.'

And that had taken some manipulating, mostly through Janet at the mill.

'Is Joey coming?'

'I believe so. Why?'

'None of your business. What about my house?'

'Sell it.'

'Bloody men!' she cursed again. 'While we're up here, you might as well run me past The Hollies, haven't seen the old place in a while. I've a horse or two there—'

'Oh – another thing. I've put a goat and some chickens down at the lodge for you. Keep the cats out of the hen-run.' Something for her to look after, think about, care for. Yes, he was managing her, that was true enough. And compared to Miss Sarah Leason, the three mills including workforce were easy meat.

They drove slowly past Sarah's old home, the place where she had been born and raised, where her family had lived for three generations. Sun-streaked and mellowed by age, The Hollies sat smug and cared for by its present owners, barns rebuilt, stables painted and re-roofed, the house itself splendidly tended. 'Any regrets?' asked Charles.

'None. The house deserved life – children – a future. I gave nothing to it, just let it rot. My way of paying back the old man, I suppose. He was grim, Charles. The day he died, I felt like a creature in my own right for the very first time. Parents can be a dreadful trial. But no matter – I won. I wasn't having him dictate whom I should marry. Never forgave me for being a girl, never forgave Mother for producing no more live ones. Seven times he put her through childbirth – rather like a horse being driven at a fence which got higher and higher. But she outlived the old devil, got five years to herself. It was from her I learned that I must never be manipulated by the merely male, though she said not a word. She didn't need to, Charles. I just looked at her and saw—'

'Yes.' He reached across and patted a tiny hand. 'Had enough, old girl? Shall we go home?'

She nodded. 'Did I . . . did I do it all wrong?' This was the first time she'd admitted uncertainty – as far as he knew, at least. 'All gone. No pits, no house, no child . . . '

'There's no right and wrong, love.' His voice was gruff. 'You followed your own star. Even if no-one else could see your particular light, you bloody well stuck to it and to hell with all questions. It's not a matter of doing it this way or that – we just cope the only way we can. Anyway, it's a bit late for you to fret now, isn't it?'

'It is indeed.'

He turned the car round and made for Briars Hall, pulling in at the right of the main gate. This, the smaller of the two gatehouses, was indeed tiny, a pretty dwelling made of warm stone in a dusky pink shade except for all four corners where large blocks of sterner stuff supported the whole building. Mullions were also of this yellower fabric, while the windows they contained were stained and leaded, their patterns copied from various Tudor discoveries made in this part of Lancashire, finds thought by many to be the only genuine coloured glass from such early times.

Charles opened the solid oak door and sighed loudly as the ancient timber swung away from him. 'It's all disappearing, all the grace and elegance. Look at Smithills. Did you ever see a finer house than that, eh? It's to be sold to Bolton Corporation, Sarah. Nobody can afford to keep these old places going, ceilings as high as church spires, roofs falling to bits, money needed every day just to make them habitable. No matter that you might have a Tudor sovereign's arms in your window-lights, or Thomas Cranmer's crest over the dining table – it's all got to go. Still. No doubt Smithills will become a museum or a place for the public to go and poke round. Thank God Briars is not so important.'

'It is to you – obviously.'

'It's my home. And now this is yours.'

'How much a week?'

'For God's sake, Sarah . . . ?'

'How much?'

'A pound.'

'Fair enough. It's not the amount, you see – it's the—'

'Principle of the thing,' he finished for her. 'I know. I've

433

heard that song before. Right. This is the living room – no hall to worry about. The kitchen's through that door with a staircase leading out next to the pantry. Upstairs there's a bedroom and a bathroom. Three sheds outside for cats and other company, nice big garden for you to run riot in. All right?'

She swallowed. 'I know I'm a bloody old woman, more prickles than an injured hedgehog – but I can't tell you what this means to me. Never did settle down there, you see.' She waved a hand towards the road, the other arm coming up to wipe a little tear from her eye. 'I'm country. This is what I mean, Charles. It's fine to have principles, but look what mine cost! There's only one word for where the townspeople live – and that's hell. I was lucky in Bolton, bit of a garden at the front, an extra room, a bath. But what did I leave behind up here, what did I sacrifice in selling off the mines? That beautiful house, my horses, my freedom . . . '

'Given your attitude to mining, there was no alternative! Good grief, woman, Paddy Maguire saved your life by forcing you to come to a decision when you got too old for the place. Why didn't you call on me then, eh? I'd have given you a lodge! I know there aren't many rooms, but there's plenty of land and the big house nearby if you need help. Too proud, you are! Too proud for your own good!'

She grinned widely at this. 'Where's all my stuff?' she demanded.

'The Maguires brought it round. Perkins shelved the bedroom – all your books are in there – just. Don't buy any more! Borrow mine if you want to read. Dishes and so on will be in the kitchen cupboards. Items of value – those Chippendale chairs, the good china, the Stubbs paintings – they're stored up at the Hall.'

'Hmm. So now I have to learn to live properly.'

'Your cleaning will be done twice a week. Come to terms with it, Sarah. The days of splendid isolation are past. And you'll get more privacy here than you did at the hospital. You'll stay?'

'Of course I'll stay! I'm just not very good at being grateful!'

'None of us is, especially we who have been privileged.

It's hard to accept help when none's been needed, hard to take after giving charitably as you have done. But this is your turn. Grab it and be damned.'

'I will.'

'Bet you never thought you'd say those words to a man!'

'Charles Swainbank! Do you have a priest hidden in a cupboard?'

He gazed about the room. 'There are some priest holes around here somewhere . . .'

She chased him out of the house.

It was lovely. A beautiful fireplace with a large cat basket in front, two comfortable armchairs, a small sofa covered in chintz. The table was tiny, just big enough for one – two at a pinch. In the kitchen there was a gas cooker, a white porcelain sink, some substantial cupboards and another small table with a pair of stools. But it was the view that gripped her, trees and hedgerows, fields leading out to rolling moors, her own large garden with apple and pear trees, bushes of raspberry and blackcurrant, borders filled with wild flowers, a goat tethered to a sturdy pole, familiar cats sunning themselves in a small enclosure before a wooden hut. Home. Home at last.

Ma and Molly, each exhausted after the trip to Sarah's new house, collapsed on to the horsehair sofa under the window in the kitchen. 'She seems well enough settled,' commented the younger woman. 'Though I'd sooner not have gone. It's as if he's edging closer by the minute – coming in the shop, making up to Janet at work—'

'What was the alternative?' Ma leaned back, eyes closed against the bright electric lamp that now hung in the centre of the room. 'Should we have let the twins go up alone? He might have liked that, Molly. All his family together on his estate – though I dare say Sarah would have kept a rein on things.'

'Why should she?'

'Because she knows the whole story. And before you start kicking the ball at me, Molly Maguire, it was Cissie's doing. She realized the twins weren't Paddy's years ago, left a letter for me with Sarah Leason.'

'But . . . !' Molly's eyes were round. 'But she'll be telling everybody! If she's gone a bit doo-lally like they said at the hospital—'

'Sarah Leason is no more doo-lally than you are. She knows when to keep her mouth shut, believe me. Just relax, for goodness sake!'

Molly rubbed a hand across her brow. 'It's all a bit much, Ma. I'm whacked out! The shop's doing so well, I'm beginning to wish the customers would go away. Now this—'

'Don't be wishing any such thing. We're open only weeks and a handsome profit showing already. Sure, things won't always be like this, Molly, coming home to make stews and pies for the next day. Soon, we can take on staff and sit back. Then we'll be away from School Hill, get a nice new house of our own.' She placed an arm across her daughter-in-law's shoulder. 'Look, he's going to see the twins anyway. Isn't he like a daily dose of salts on Bradshawgate, running almost to time – every servant in his house must have at least one bike by now! And doesn't he take his midday meal in my kitchen, him and his cronies exclaiming over how quaint it is with the bread rising before the fire? Then with Janet carrying on as stubborn as a daft donkey in the weaving sheds – well – he'll get to them come what may.'

'Oh, Ma . . .'

'What?'

Molly's head dropped low before she spoke. 'Listen. I think we should tell them before he does, or before Sarah slips up.'

'Whatever for?' Ma pushed Molly away and looked into her troubled face. 'Why on earth should we be thinking on those lines?'

' 'Cos I can't stand it! I'm sick of watching and waiting, tired of looking at Janet when she comes in from the mill, wondering if she knows and what she knows! At the shop I'm on edge every time he goes anywhere near Joey—'

'Shush, girl! Where are the children?'

Molly shrugged listlessly. 'The twins are out with Lizzie and Ron – that pair from school as went in for weaving alongside Janet. I think the little ones are in the back yard dressing Yorick up.'

436

'Ah, he'll like that. Loves a nice frock and a bonnet – hey – do you think he's one of them funny fellers? For heaven's sake, give us a smile!'

'There's nowt to smile at, Ma! Nowt at all! I'd rather we told them now – get it over and done with—'

'Molly! Get yourself all of a piece, will you? Have we not known all this for years, the both of us? Aye, we weren't honest with one another, but each of us knew the truth. Can we not live with it a little longer?'

'It was all right before! He had two sons!'

'I know that. I'm not daft, Molly. But we must carry on taking our chances and hope he'll keep quiet and leave the money elsewhere. If we do well in the shops, if we can get Janet out of the mill and into the business – then himself might see that we need him not at all. So don't you dare say a word, Molly Maguire!'

The scullery door opened and in walked Yorick on his hind legs, a straw bonnet perched on his silly panting head, a garish frock trailing along the floor behind him. 'Would you ever look at that?' exclaimed Ma. 'We should put him in the circus, for he's crazy enough to do anything in order to keep the peace. Michael! Daisy! Get this poor beast out of the clothes. He puts me in mind of old Mother Blue, a terrible character who saved my life then stayed on to torment me afterwards.' She studied her youngest grandchild. 'Have you had any turns recently, child?'

Daisy unbuttoned the dog's dress. 'No. I've given them up,' she pronounced. 'I'm going to constant trait.'

'She means concentrate.' Michael was Daisy's interpreter whenever she tackled bigger words. 'She doesn't want no visions and shiverings and she's not having no fits.'

In spite of herself, Molly smiled. 'That's the spirit, Daisy.'

The child straightened as Yorick made off beneath the table with the hat and a mind filled with destructive intentions. 'Do you mean Holy Spirit?' she asked innocently.

'No. I mean attitude.'

This chance to air a family joke was too tempting to resist. Michael looked at the dog, heard the ominous sounds of

tearing. 'No, Mam,' he said gravely. 'It's not Daisy's attitude
– it's your 'at 'e chewed!'

Yorick wagged bravely, spitting straw as he emerged from
his hiding place.

'You see, Molly?' said Ma. 'There's ever something to
laugh at—'

In the cool of that evening, Molly sat on an upturned
orange box in the yard, a bucket of peeled potatoes at her feet.
The two young ones continued to torment Alas-poor Yorick,
but he was a patient dog, no malice in him. She watched their
antics, her chest filled with a panic that approached sickness.
It wasn't just the twins that worried her – there was this pair
too, little innocents that would suffer simply by association.
Then there was Paddy. All the names under the sun she'd
called that lad during the fifteen years of their marriage. Theirs
was a common enough relationship in these parts, the woman
seemingly strong and dominant, the man browbeaten.

She remembered Mrs Shipperbottom from number nine,
long moved on now. The Shipperbottoms had been the star
turn on a Saturday night, especially in the summer. Long
hazy-gold evenings would be spent in the street, children
playing and singing until well past bedtime. The ice-cream
man always came on his bike-cart and the kids would perform
their tricks for the promise of a penny cornet.

Then he would arrive home, little Mr Shipperbottom from
number nine, too full of booze and bonhommie to notice how
hushed the street became as he made his entrance. The door
would be flung open and there she would stand, all six feet
and nineteen stones of her, a yardbrush in her huge hands.
While the women held her back, the poor little man crawled
into the house and underneath the dresser for the night, his
life saved yet again by the usual group of self-appointed
guardian angels. At this point, most children would be sent
inside, because Mrs Shipperbottom's language was as colourful as a summer rainbow.

But that was all a part of the Shipperbottoms' lives, a part
they could not have existed without. The big woman would
cry in the end, sit and weep copiously in a neighbour's house

while the yardbrush was taken away in case she might go poking under the dresser with it.

Molly glanced up at the clear blue sky. She hadn't expected it to happen, had never let it show except in privacy between the two of them. But she loved Paddy, loved his foolishness, forgave him for his idleness. He was such a gentle man, not once had he hurt her knowingly. He annoyed her thoroughly – sometimes, she could scarcely bear the sight of him. But no love could be perfect, no marriage arrived without its troubles.

The fact remained that Paddy Maguire did not deserve this terrible thing that was coming to all of them. And not a hand's turn could she do. If she ran away from it all, if she died – whatever she did, the truth would eventually come out. And all the forgiveness in the world, all the blessings from Father Mahoney – or even from the pope himself – none of it could wipe out the fact that she, Molly Maguire, was a terrible sinner.

'Smile, Mam!'

She picked up her youngest child and held the little body close. 'I'm doing me best, Daisy.' That was all she could do. And it wasn't going to be enough.

Janet was very lucky with her teacher. His name was Jim Higgins and he had spent all his life in the sheds, was a master weaver with a fine reputation because of his knowledge of the craft. Jim was a character, an exceptionally intelligent man with a wicked humour and a gift for music that endeared him greatly to his colleagues. During these fine autumn days, the workers did not always use the canteen, preferring to sit out in the mill yard while Jim played his melodeon or his fiddle. Completely self-taught, he won many prizes for these amateur talents and always drew a large crowd when he chose to entertain the spinners and weavers at Swainbank's mills.

He and Janet sat now on the top stone step in the courtyard, sharing opinions and sandwiches until the others would return from shopping or from a quick lunch in the canteen.

'What have you got today, lass?'

'Cheese and home-made pickle.'

'Ma Maguire's pickle? That yellow stuff as makes you pull

funny faces because it's on the tart side? That yellow stuff as runs down your chin and isn't very suitable for a fashionable young lady on account of it being a bit untidy, like?'

'Yes. It's lovely.' She grinned mischievously. 'What have you got, Jim?'

He hung his head sadly. 'From a lad, I have been one of life's unfortunates. And since Bridie died, I've been left to me own devices, Janet, a poor starving man with nothing but me talent to keep me warm.' He sighed dramatically. 'Bread and jam again.'

'What a shame about that!' She grabbed his tin. Jim was renowned not just for his music – he more than adequately provided for himself and his motherless daughter. 'Look at that, Jim Higgins – a miracle! Leg of chicken and two tomatoes.'

He scratched his head. 'Funny, that. It tasted just like tinned plum jam to me. I'll swap you me leg for half a butty.'

'No. I've had enough, you can have a butty for free if you let me run a loom this after.'

'Can't do that, love. We're only one between the two of us as it is, what with your lack of experience and me with one eye.'

'Give over – you've got two! See, I can count – one, two. So eat your butty and shut up.'

He took the proffered sandwich and bit into it hungrily. 'Manna from heaven,' he declared. 'We miss your old granny – will she not be coming back?'

'No. They've got the shops now. Jim?'

'That's me.'

'Can't you see proper?'

'Depends.'

'What on?'

'Which way the wind's blowing, how Bolton Wanderers are getting on – oh and the colour of me socks.'

She punched him on the arm. 'Are you never serious? I can't get a straight answer from you – ever! You've got to be Irish!'

'Course I am. Me dad landed in 1880 with me mother, a

bucket of spuds and a big fat smile. Trouble is – he's always thought he was in America – only found out last year that the boat fetched him to Liverpool. Terrible thing for him to latch on to at the grand age of eighty, eh? He's been wandering round for years looking for yon lady with the torch – you know – that big lass as France give to the Americans. Sad, isn't it?'

'Jim Higgins! I'll clout you in a minute for all you're me boss!'

'Stop nagging, woman! You're as bad as me daughter! "Have you got a clean hanky, Dad, where's your good shoes, you're never going out in that old hat." I get enough of it at home. She's always on about how I should pack it in.'

'The weaving?'

'Aye, she knows I'm blind some days.' He paused and stared down at work-worn hands. 'I started this lark over forty year ago, Janet. Come on at six, half an hour for breakfast at eight, worked right through to dinner then. Weeks about, we did, so we'd be on afternoons sometimes. I don't know which was worse – school first or work first, but I do know there was never enough sleep. By thirteen, I was full-time and me no bigger than a nine-year-old today. Anyway, a shuttle flew off and hit me in the eye one day – I'd be about twenty at the time. Nowt happened at first, except it hurt like blazes. Only it troubles me now and again lately. Good job I know them pattern cards like the back of me hand, eh?'

'Oh Jim! Does Mr Swainbank know?'

'No! And you'll not tell him, neither! I want a few more years in, get a bit put by for me and our Eileen. I never told a soul before, so keep it to yourself. Don't be worrying, I can manage well enough most of the time.'

The rest of the workers began to arrive and Jim picked up his melodeon. Within minutes, everyone was singing 'It's a Long Way to Tipperary', followed by 'Pack up your Troubles'.

Janet wandered into the shed and leaned against a wall. What about poor Jim? He was one of the nicest, kindest men she had ever met, a man who never missed work, one who always lent a hand gladly when a weaver lost a pattern or hit a

snag. Why couldn't he have a pension, stop at home and play
his music? Perhaps he wouldn't like that. Perhaps his need
for work was essential, an inbred part of him, nothing to
do with shortage of money. But if his bad sight led to an
accident . . .

The hooter wailed and everyone piled in at the door, some
grinding cigarette ends into the cobbles before entering.
Smoking was absolutely forbidden – it was still possible, in
spite of union representation, to be sacked on the spot for
being found with a lighted cigarette. Most recognized the
sense in this rule, because the mills were a terrible fire-hazard
with all the dry cotton, the piles of waste, the oil that kept
machinery moving.

There was, of course, one exception to this regulation and
that was Mr Swainbank himself. He frequently travelled about
with a cigar, usually unlit, stuck between his teeth. These
days, he often paused to speak to his workers, asked them
about their families, lip-reading as well as any of them in
the awful din. For the older generation, this behaviour came
as a shock, because they had spent their lives being ignored,
expecting at best a telling-off from a tackler for bad work – or
the odd cursory nod from an owner after thirty or forty years
at their looms.

Janet and Jim set to work on their six machines, he setting
patterns, she keeping an eye on the flow of cloth as it poured
out like a magic carpet. Then Jim dragged her to one side.
'Right, I'm letting you loose. Tell anybody and I'll smack
your bum,' he mouthed. He inserted a fresh cop into an idle
loom that awaited servicing. 'Warp's done, card's in – get on
with it.'

With a huge smile of pleasure, Janet got on with it, watching the shuttle fly as she made her very first length of cloth.
When the spool was emptied, Jim lifted the small piece off
and presented it to her with a flourish. 'Hide it – take it
home. In years to come, you can tell your grandchildren that
this was your first.'

'Thank you!' She folded the cloth and stuffed it into her
pocket. In old Swainbank's time, she'd have been thrown out

for this – even for stealing a handful of waste she would have been dismissed.

They continued to work the looms, backs and faces wet with sweat, ears deafened by the constant clatter of heavy machinery. The boss came through at about three o'clock, the usual cigar protruding from his mouth. Janet frowned when she noticed this, because the whisper of blue smoke above his head told that the cigar was actually alight. But knots and breaks seemed to abound this day, so she and Jim were too busy to pay attention to visitors and onlookers. Swainbank walked across and had a word with Jim, no doubt asking about her progress and she prayed fervently that the boss wasn't going to put her back on the study project; all that standing around and watching, nothing to show at the end except for a load of writing. She sighed her relief as Swainbank walked away, then caught a further glimpse when the large man left by the corner door. Something about him made her uneasy, but she was too embroiled with some difficult ends to let anything take her mind completely from the work.

The fire broke out at about three-thirty, spreading in seconds across oily floorboards, licking the edges of looms and swallowing everything in its path. Someone slid open the great door to the yard, thereby feeding the flames with the oxygen they craved. Within minutes the air was thick with greasy black smoke and Janet felt herself being dragged across the shed and into the yard. It was eerie. The few faces she saw were wide with screams, yet nothing could be heard above the noise of looms which clattered on in spite of the consuming fire.

Jim threw her on to the cobbles and went back inside.

She jumped to her feet. 'Jim! Come back . . . Jim!' But he had disappeared into that terrible blackness, a blackness punctuated now by areas of high red flame.

Several others staggered out, coughing and choking, fighting to heave breath into lungs scalded by hot smoke. Jim appeared again, a length of cotton sheeting wrapped around his mouth and this time carrying Lizzie, Janet's friend from school. 'Look after her, lass.'

Janet grabbed Jim's arm. 'Don't go back – please! Think of Eileen with no mother and her wedding coming soon. Who'll give her away then? And what about your old dad?'

Jim hesitated. 'Swainbank's still in. I've got to get him out, lass, else there'll be jobs for none of us! He's running about in there like somebody demented—'

'Leave him! Let him find his own way out! Look – it's too bad now. No-one could live in that, Jim! If he's still inside, then it's likely too late for him already.' The man gave in to reason and they stood together comforting Lizzie while she fought for good air.

Charles Swainbank appeared at a run from the opposite direction – he had obviously escaped through the side door. His eyes met Janet's and he slumped against the wall, a hand to his chest.

The fire brigade arrived and cleared everyone away to the other side of the yard where they all remained, some silent, some choking as they watched their weaving shed going up in flames. Those worst affected, including Lizzie, were herded into ambulances and mill lorries, but most stayed with eyes glued to their disappearing livelihood. By this time, the whole of number one had been evacuated and people arrived in droves to stare at the fire.

'Is everybody out?' asked a man by Janet's side. 'There's not much alive in there now, I can tell thee that for nowt.'

'I don't know. I don't know how many were in and some have gone to the infirmary.'

Jim laid an arm across her shoulders. 'That's me decision made for me, then.'

'No! You can still work if you want to! There's other sheds, other mills . . . '

He shook his head sadly. 'Nay, lass. Man and boy I've worked in this shed. I know where I am here – I was even looking forward to getting me automatics – I'd like to have tried one of them new-fangled battery looms. But it's not to be, Janet. You can start afresh, but not me.'

A quiet crowd had gathered on the road outside, not out of curiosity, but because this was the way when disaster struck.

A fire, a collapsed pit, a road accident—all these melded people together, brought them to stand shoulder to shoulder like a human wall of support for unfortunate victims and their kin. Then a great sigh went up as a brave fireman carried out a charred body, laying it with reverence on the cobbles in the centre of the mill yard. Janet burst into tears and threw herself against Jim. There was little to recognize about the blackened remains, but she knew those clogs. Nobody in the world had feet as big as Ronnie's.

Jim patted her back. 'Aye, it's your mate, lass. I always said his feet would give him away come the day. But not like this, dear God . . . ' And Jim began to cry, his weeping interrupted by a dry, smokey cough.

'The price, Jim! Gran always said about the price of cotton.' She took from her pinny pocket the length that had been her first, the length that would also be her last. 'It costs too much,' she said to herself.

'I've had enough, love. I'm fair sickened now.' He dried his eyes. 'They can do without me from this day. When I think of the sights I've seen in me time – but young Ron? Not a bad bone in him – and there were only him and his mam at home . . . '

Ronnie was wrapped in a large sheet and carried out through the gates, the crowd drawing aside to allow this sad procession through.

Janet raised her eyes and stared directly at Charles Swainbank. He stood at the top of some steps across the yard, face and clothes made filthy by smoke, hands resting for support on the cast-iron rail. Yes. That was what had bothered her before in the shed. He came in with a cigar and left without one!

She walked unsteadily across the yard and stood at the bottom of the flight. Jim followed. 'Whatever are you doing, Janet? Come away – you mustn't go near the buildings. Fire spreads, you know.'

Janet threw back her head and stared up at the boss. 'Swainbank?' Her voice was high and clear. 'Where's your cigar?'

The crowd studied this insolent young girl, eyes and mouths widening in amazement. They were not used to such direct confrontation – if the lass had anything to say, then it should rightly go through a steward.

'You came in our shed at three o'clock smoking. There's a sign in there as says you can't smoke, but you're above all that, aren't you? Or can't you read?'

The man flattened himself against a door.

'You dropped a cigar end, didn't you? Happen you thought you'd put it out, but it seems you hadn't. My friend has died today, somebody I've known from nursery. You killed him.'

A murmuring broke out among the crowd as Janet pointed an accusing finger. 'We all have to sneak out for a smoke, them that need a cigarette. We could get sacked for smoking – even the unions agree about that. But who sacks you now, eh?'

A group of angry men approached Charles. 'Well?' asked one. 'Can't you answer her? She's nobbut a slip of a lass – she'll not bite thee. Are you feared?'

The crowd began to roar its demands for a reply. 'Answer her!' 'Get on with it!' 'Come on, Swainbank!'

'I can't.' His voice arrived strangled. 'I don't . . . don't remember.'

A spinner joined Janet on the bottom step. 'You'd best remember, Boss, 'cos we want to know. Were you lit up in that weaving shed? Well, were you?'

'Yes!'

The spinner turned to his colleagues. 'We've all seen him smoking, haven't we? Do we smoke at our mules?'

'No!' shouted a hundred voices.

'What would happen if we did? Sack on the spot, thrown out for behaviour likely to threaten lives. Yet he smokes, Mr Charles bloody Swainbank with his airs and graces.' He looked at his employer. 'You didn't just threaten lives – you bloody took at least ore! So you can stop here till you tell us where you put that fag-end!'

The crowd was no longer quiet. Someone picked up a stone and threw it at Charles, missing his head by no more than an inch. Jim ran up the steps, his arms outstretched as he covered

Charles Swainbank's body with his own. 'Listen to me!' he cried. 'Do we want to sink to that level? Don't forget, any of you, that we are human beings and not blinking animals.'

'He's an animal!' screamed a hysterical woman. 'Ronnie were from our street . . . '

'Charlie's dad were an even worse animal,' shouted a man from the back.

'Aye,' came an anonymous cry. 'And his grandad were a flaming dinosaur!'

Jim held up a hand. 'Look lads – and lasses too. We all make mistakes. I've been for a crafty smoke in the lav before now and so have most of you. He's done wrong, has this feller. Aye, I know how you all feel, 'cos I'd scalp him meself given half a chance and a dark enough night. But where would it get me? Would I want to go dangling and dancing at the end of a rope for his likes? No, he's not worth it. Let him suffer knowing what he's done. Now go home, all of you.'

'Why should we?' asked the spinner at the bottom of the stone steps. 'He should be done for murder, he should!'

Jim maintained his precarious stance in front of Charles, the latter apparently dumbstruck by what went on around him. 'Hang on!' screamed Jim. 'That's if they ever prove he started the fire. It could have been owt – a total accident for all we know. And you can't form a lynch-mob whether he did it or not. So I'm telling you now – all of you – get home before this goes out of hand.'

When a few policemen entered the yard, the crowd began to disperse. As soon as there was enough space, Jim bundled Charles down the steps and round the corner to number two mill. Janet followed at a slower pace, catching up with the two men outside the ground floor office. 'Mr Swainbank?' she called.

He turned to look at her.

'I shan't be coming back, not tomorrow, not ever. Ronnie was a good lad, good at school – talented, like – and kind to his mother. He was special. I've no real idea whether or not you started this lot, but in me bones, I feel it's your fault. So I don't want to work for you no more.'

Jim reached out an imploring arm. 'Nay lass. Don't be hasty. You'll make a fair weaver in time.'

'If I wanted to carry on, there's other mills, Jim. Mind, I'll never find a better teacher, will I?'

'You'll do all right. Anyway, I'm leaving meself what with one thing and another.'

Janet fixed a cold grey gaze on Charles Swainbank's stricken face. 'Mr Higgins is going blind,' she said quietly. 'Because of one of your shuttles. I think it's time you paid him off, don't you?'

Jim's face was white with grief and anger. 'Janet! Don't you be minding my business now! Anything between him and me will go through the union—'

She straightened her weary spine, holding herself tall, literally and actually growing up in that moment. 'No, it won't, Jim. Like a lot round here, you'll just put up with it because old injuries are hard to prove. Fight him! For God's sake – have some pride!'

'Not you, Janet.' Charles' voice was weak with smoke-damage. 'Don't turn against me – please.'

'Why not? What does it matter to you, eh? I'm just an apprentice weaver, ten a penny. Why should you care what I think?' She smiled at Jim. 'I'll not be going in another mill. Me mother wants me in the shop in town, so I'll give in to her. Like you, I feel it's all been decided for me—'

'Janet!' Charles' tone was stronger now. 'Do you realize who I am?'

She looked him up and down. 'Oh yes. I know who you are, all right. We all know who you are. In time, it won't matter a jot. Government will keep you going for a while, put taxes on cheap cloth from abroad. But the only road as you lot will survive in the long run is if you all stick together. Names are probably the first thing for the chop. I came into cotton hoping that a few takeovers would give me a good wage. It won't be a case of who you are – it'll be who you used to be.'

This was Ma Maguire all right! Ma Maguire talking through the mouth of a fifteen year-old babe! 'Janet!' he called. 'I am your f—' He dropped his head. What was he doing? What price would she put on herself now if she knew whose daughter she really was? Cheaper than ten a penny? Dear God, what had he done with that dead cigar? And had it been dead? Questions, questions, all unanswerable. He lifted his head. 'I am your friend,' he muttered.

'Then I'd best keep me eyes open for enemies, hadn't I? Make sure you give something to Mr Higgins to cheer him up now you've sent him near blind—'

'Shut up!' shouted Jim.

'They've got away with too much!'

'Janet.' Jim's tone was quiet and serious. 'I've seen a lot of life and a lot more of death than I wanted to. There's a pattern to things, lass. If it wasn't him' he jerked a thumb towards his employer, 'it would be some other clever bugger flying battle colours and shouting the orders. Don't be taking so much on yourself and you not that long out of nappies. If you're not careful, you'll turn out a bitter woman.'

'Then I'd best leave present company. Oh, I don't mean you. You were the greatest thing about this job. But I'd get bitter if I stopped too long near him.'

'Wait!' Charles stepped forward. 'Listen to me. I don't know how the fire started and that's the honest truth. Perhaps it was my fault and if that's the case, I am very sorry. Ronnie's mother will be compensated . . . '

'Oh aye? Pounds shillings and pence? How much for a life, Mr Swainbank? Ten bob, a hundred pounds – two hundred? What's the bloody difference? How much for Jim's eye, what about them that lost arms and legs, what about bald old women who left their hair in a carder? You can't do anything for Ronnie's mam, nowt at all! There's no fetching him back, is there?' Her eyes blazed with fury.

'He knows that, Janet,' ventured Jim. 'Two sons and a Missus he's lost these last weeks . . . '

'Really? Then he'll know it's nowt at all to do with money. Though I dare say Ronnie's mother would be glad of a few bob now her wage-earner's been snatched. Do as you like, Mr Swainbank. I'm off to my family, must let them know you didn't kill me too!'

449

Janet marched out past the smouldering remains of the shed, her eyes brimming with tears. She had loved the mill, so had poor Ronnie. He'd been a good laugh once he'd got his bearings and stopped being shy, always joking and pulling folks' legs, was Ron. Why, if he'd lived, they might have finished up wed to one another, 'cos they'd got on great.

She turned into a dingy street at the back of the mills and walked unannounced into a house. Ronnie's mother, her face white with shock, sat by the fire surrounded by neighbours.

'Mrs Bowles?'

'What? Oh, hello love. Get a brew, pot's full.'

Janet led Mrs Bowles' next door neighbour into the scullery and closed the door quietly. 'I'm Ronnie's friend,' she whispered. 'Now I know Mrs Bowles won't be up to much for a while, but when it's all over, send her to my shop on Bradshawgate.'

'Your shop, love?'

'Maguires' Market – it's owned between me and me brother. There'll be a job for her, fair pay and a good dinner on top. She can start whenever she's ready.'

'I'll tell her. What happened at the mill, lass?'

Janet shook her head wearily. 'I'm not sure.'

'They say Swainbank were smoking. Is it right?'

'Yes.'

The woman dropped on to a stool. 'There'll be bother – I reckon they'll kill him! Her at the other side of Mrs Bowles – she works at number one, says their blood's up.'

'They'll have to catch him first.' Janet smoothed her tangled hair, noticing how it still reeked of oily smoke. 'Yes, they'll have to catch him. And there's no easy way to catch a snake, is there?'

Chapter 15

He had been shut away in the study for a week now. Food was left outside the door and untouched trays would be picked up within the hour, while very short shrift was meted to anyone who dared to put a head inside the room when it was unlocked for brief periods. Perkins marched into the kitchen and banged Mr Swainbank's breakfast on the table. 'That does it!' he announced. 'I'm for getting the doctor in.'

Mrs Marshall tutted as she scraped eggs, bacon, toast and marmalade into the slops bucket. 'I wouldn't care. There's folk who'd give an arm for a meal like this.'

'Aye well. There's no use saying them sorts of things to him just now, is there? That's what it's all about – how his workers are bad done to. He blames himself for that lad's death. And God knows there's been more than enough dying round here lately.' He fell into a chair and stretched aching legs in front of him. 'Happen he's stopping out of the union's road till after the investigations. Only that's not like him – he's never been a-feared of facing music. I don't know how to snap him out of it – he won't listen to anything like sense.'

Mrs M threw the pots into the sink, then removed her capacious apron. 'You're not the only one, Jacob. Me, Emmie, Carrie Fishwick – we've all fell out of the same boat, all drowning 'cos yon feller won't try and swim. Damn foolishness! Carrie's usually good with him and you'd think her nursing training would help, but she's pleaded with him all night through that door, begged him to come out and eat, she did. Might as well talk to herself! Anyroad, I'm nearing the end of me rope and you can come with me and all.'

'Where?' He sat bolt upright and stared at the bustling

451

woman as she dragged a comb through her hair. 'What the hell are you up to?'

'Me? I'm up to nowt much! I'm ground that far down with cooking meals what folk don't eat – I feel as if I'm not a full shilling any more! I've tried boiling, frying, poaching – you name it – I've stood on me head and done it. There's more food in that pig-swill bucket for the back farm than there's ever been before, even when we had a full house. So, I'm putting a stop to it, that's what. I just wish Carrie was here to back me up, only she's past the armpits down the mill what with him stopping here a week and no sign of going back. We are getting in that room, Jacob Perkins, even if it means taking an axe to the door.'

His jaw dropped. 'We can't do that, Mary!'

'Course we can! Shut your mouth, there's a tram coming! No use sitting there looking gobsmacked and gormless.' She smoothed the dark dress over her heavily corseted frame. 'It's either thee and me or the bloody fire brigade. Coming on a treat, he were. And now where is he? Back to the kick-off is where. We have to get him out of that study, lad.'

'You're not wrong.' He puffed out his cheeks and exhaled loudly. 'When did he last eat?'

She scratched her pepper-and-salt head. 'I'm not sure. Only I count the spuds and that, I even know how many carrot rings or peas to the nearest and it looks as if he's touching nowt apart from tea, coffee and whatever he's got in them there decanters on his desk.'

Perkins leapt to his feet. 'All right, lass. Can't let him drink himself to death, can't let you tackle him on your own. Only we might need help – he's a big feller and there's a fair amount of whisky in that study.'

'You mean there was.'

He nodded grimly. 'There's more to this than meets the eye, Mary. There's summat up with him, summat as were there long afore the fire. Always either excited or deep in thought, he was. Only I'd be better saying nowt—'

'Jacob! When did we last have a secret, eh?' She strode across the room and placed herself in front of him, hands on ample

452

hips, feet apart, head wagging from side to side in an attitude that demanded an immediate answer.

'Oh it were . . . well . . . I don't rightly think I should say much—'

'Out with it, Jacob Perkins, before I fetch you one with me rolling pin! Whatever it is, I'll keep it to meself!'

Perkins walked round the table and stared into the fireplace, hands thrust deep into trouser pockets. 'There's a lad, the one he turned up with not long back – him as got the guided tour.'

'Well? I never saw him.' A foot tapped on the floor while thick arms folded themselves beneath a heavy bosom. 'What about him? I've not all day to be stood here gassing with you!'

'I reckon . . . I could be wrong, like . . . ' He took a deep shuddering breath. 'I reckon that one's his son.'

'You what?' Her mouth opened and closed several times. 'Wrong side, you mean?'

'Aye.'

'Eeh, heck!' Visibly deflated, Mary Marshall fell against the table, fat hands outspread on its bleached wooden surface. 'Who's the mother?'

'I could have it all wrong – there might be nowt in it!'

'Who though?'

'Somebody called Maguire. She's been up here lately and all – on the bounce from the look on her face. Used to be housemaid before our time, when Cissie Whatsername was cook-housekeeper. Old Ma Maguire – you'll have heard of her with her creams and potions – well, she had a son called Paddy who married this here maid. They've four children, I think – well – I've seen four. Only I reckon Mr Swainbank's had a hand in it somewhere.'

'More than a hand, ask me! Sorry – I didn't mean to be so crude, only this is a right turn-up, isn't it? So you think this woman had Mr Swainbank's child?'

'Happen she did. The boy's been in bother, summat to do with Miss Leason.'

'Eh? Her in the lodge?'

'That's right. Took her money, I'd guess. Anyroad, I caught the resemblance, you see. And it all fits, doesn't it? Fetching

453

a strange lad up here to look round – well, it didn't seem right to me, specially if he were a bad 'un. I'd say the boy knows nowt. Mr Swainbank were likely just looking him over, seeing what he's made of. You'll not let on, I know that, but I've had to tell somebody 'cos it's been going round in me head like a spinning top since I got wind of it. Like I say, I could be up the wrong tree altogether . . . ' He shrugged. 'Only there's two of them.'

'Two? You mean the master made a habit of it? Dear God in heaven, the poor Missus!'

'Nay, it weren't that. Twins as far as I could work out from what the lad said in the car. Anyroad, the more I think on it, the closer it fits. Master's been motoring on his own a lot lately, then when I've driven him the odd time, we've always had to go along Bradshawgate. They've opened a shop, these Maguires. All them bikes for Emmie and the dailies have come from there. Till this week, Mr Swainbank hasn't been able to stop away from Bolton.'

Mrs M straightened, adjusted the belt of her black dress as if to pull herself together, then moved towards the door. 'I suppose, come the day, it'll be nowt to do with us. Main thing is to get this one on his feet. I can't work out why he's took it so bad – this is not the first mill fire and it likely won't be the last either.'

'Mary?'

She turned in the doorway, 'What? You coming or not?'

'There's talk. Some say he started it.'

'Deliberate? For insurance? Never, it's not in his nature – specially with folk in. He's too honest, Jacob!'

'They say he were smoking a cigar in that weaving shed.'

'But . . . in the *Evening News*, it were reported as likely accidental, no mention of anybody smoking . . . '

Perkins shrugged. 'Same ones are saying that Swainbank has enough clout to write his own account for the paper. I reckon there's folk after yon feller's blood.'

'Nay – he wouldn't hurt a flea—'

'He smokes in them sheds, Mary. There's nowt to get away from it – he breaks his own factory rules regular, like. And

454

now he can't live with what he might have done.'

She put a hand over her mouth and nodded slowly. 'Yes,' she mumbled. 'Specially after the boys and the Missus. This must feel like the last flaming straw—'

'Flaming is right, lass. There's jobs threatened, people with smoke on their chests, one dead. And a load of others that would swing for him given half a chance.'

'Eeh Jacob!' Her voice was cracking. 'What the hell do we do for the poor lad?'

Perkins moved closer to her. 'We get him out of there afore he starves hisself to death.'

'That's it. First things first, eh? But listen – before we go – do you reckon he's for naming these Maguires? What about Alice and Squirrel?'

He smiled weakly at the old joke they had made so often about Cyril's name. 'I've no idea. Same as you said before – it's none of our business. But he'd perked up a right lot – seemed to have been setting some store by these twins if I've got it weighed proper. Now, we're back to square bloody one—'

The doorbell rang sharply and Perkins poked his head into the hall corridor. 'Who the hell's that at this time of day? And he won't talk to nobody—'

'Oh, just go and see whoever it is on their way. We've more to bother about than visitors. Go on.' She pushed him out of the kitchen.

Perkins opened the heavy front door to find a man in a suit that had seen better days, a scrubbed and polished person with a flat cap twisting nervously between work-gnarled fingers. 'Is the boss in?' The tone was controlled, though the speaker was plainly ill-at-ease.

'I'm afraid he's not available. Who shall I say called?'

'The name's Higgins – Jim Higgins. I'm from number one, worked there man and boy, I have. And I've heard as how Mr Swainbank's took it bad – the fire and all – so I come up to see him. Is it true he's never set foot over the step since it happened?'

Perkins looked the man up and down. Was this one of those after Mr Swainbank's blood? Had he come up to make bother?

'I saved him from a stoning. They'd have gone for him but for me. Let me talk to him – please.'

'Well, I don't know. He's not seeing anybody.'

'He'll see me. I promise you he will.'

Jacob Perkins scratched his chin thoughtfully. Happen this chap might be the key to the locked study door. On the other hand, would there be trouble for the staff if someone got let in against orders? It was all getting a bit much for Perkins to handle, all these decisions about right and wrong, working out what would be best or worst. And the time for desperate measures had definitely arrived. He stepped back and allowed Jim to enter the hallway.

'How the other half lives, eh?' Jim gazed around before permitting the manservant to relieve him of his cap. 'Where is he?'

'In here.' Perkins led the visitor to the study door. 'And I hope you have better luck than we did.'

Jim tapped lightly. 'Mr Swainbank? You in there?' He turned round. 'Are you sure he's here?'

'Oh aye. He'll start cursing at you any minute. The language can get a bit ripe at times—'

'Bugger off!' A chair scraped across the floor and the voice came closer. 'Go away and leave me alone! I've told you, Perkins, if I get disturbed at all, you're for the high-jump. And where's that claret I told you to fetch from the cellar? Will you leave me in here bloody parched?'

Perkins smiled wryly at Jim and approached the study door. 'You're getting no more, sir. Not off me anyroad.'

'What?' The voice shook with temper. 'Who the hell do you think you're talking to?'

'I'm talking to you, sir. If you want to drink yourself soft, then you can do it without my help.'

'Aye – and without mine!' This from Mrs M who had arrived at a run from the kitchen with a tea towel clutched tensely in her hands. 'I'm fed up with cooking meals for chucking out,' she shouted. Turning to the two men, she lowered her tone. 'Last time I saw him – on his way to the bathroom – he looked like something dragged out of the gutter on a Saturday night.' She pushed her face against the door.

'Either you come out or we come in. Mr Swainbank? Are you listening? If you'd prefer it, we'll go off – all of us! That there Beddows chap as owns the bleachworks is looking for good staff.'

'Then go! I can manage without you!'

A long silence followed. Mrs M and Perkins crept away to the fireplace while Jim continued his efforts. 'Mr Swainbank?'

'Who the bloody hell are you?'

'Jim Higgins – weaver from number one.'

Several thuds informed the small audience that the news had not been well-received. 'He's chucking books again,' whispered Mrs M.

Jim placed a finger to his lips.

'Higgins?'

'Yes sir?'

'There's a job in another shed if you want it. As for the eye – take the hall clock, it's worth a couple of thousand. Then go away and leave me in peace!'

'I'm going nowhere, Boss. But you are and that's for bloody sure. They'll be here in a bit with the cart, shove you in the loony bin with the other daft folk. So. You can either open up now, or you can wait for them in the white coats to kick it in.'

'How dare you?' Another loud crash followed this rhetorical question.

Jim cast a glance over his shoulder at the two servants who were hanging on to one another in trepidation while furniture hit the walls. 'Thank God it's Emmie's day off,' mumbled Mrs M. 'She'd likely go into one of her hystericals if she saw this! Get him out, Mr Higgins – he'll damage hisself afore long.'

The visitor concentrated his attention on the solid oak door. 'Are you asking me how I dare, Mr Swainbank? Well, I'll tell thee! I've got the upper hand now, you see. You're stuck in there like a dog in a kennel and I'm out here coming and going as I please. I'm telling you what to do and you're having to listen, like it or not! So stick that in your wineglass and see how it tastes.'

457

Perkins raised his eyes to heaven. 'Careful, lad. Don't rile him—'

'Shush! I know this man near as well as you do. He'll be out before I've done with him, never bother.'

'How long have you worked in my mill?' roared Charles.

'Since you were in nappies, son!'

'Well, you're bloody sacked!'

'Am I? You can shove your job and your clock and all! Now stop acting like a big kid and get out here. I'm sick of talking to a blinking door.'

Two or three ominous crashes confirmed that Charles was smashing items in the room.

'That's right!' yelled Jim above the din. 'Take it out on the furniture – it can't answer back, can it? That's what your father did, took his temper out on us that didn't dare look him in the face for fear of the sack. That's all we were to him, bits of chairs and tables! Are you practising for turning into what he was, a bloody tyrant? Anyroad, you listen to me, Mr Boss-man. You killed nobody, nobody at all! The firemen have traced what they call the source. It were that black box in the corner, that thing with all the wires in. Melted past recognizing, it was. And your cigar was stubbed out in the back half where the fire never reached – dead as a dodo in an enamel dish on the window ledge.'

In the silence that followed, one might have heard a feather floating on the breeze.

Jim came to join the others by the fireplace. 'I've done what I came to do,' he said quietly. 'I'll be off now.'

'But he's still not out!' shouted Mrs M. 'You said you'd get him out!'

'I'm out.'

Everyone stared at the dishevelled figure as it emerged slowly from the study.

'Good God!' exclaimed Jim. 'Who got you ready for the party, eh? I'd sack the bloody tailor for a kick-off!'

Charles looked down at himself. The clothes hung on his thinner frame, shirt undone to the waist, cuffs hanging filthy and limp without studs to anchor them, socks covered in dirt from a week's wear. Irrelevantly, he wondered briefly what had become of his shoes. 'I'm not a pretty sight, am I?'

'I've got to say I've seen better,' admitted Jim. 'Mostly up Breightmet in the gypsy caravans. The beard suits you, though. Your old feller had a beard, right proud of it, he was.'

'Yes. Yes, he was a proud man altogether. And not a completely bad one, Mr Higgins. He'd a hard life, a lot on his mind.'

'If you say so.' Jim turned as if to leave.

'Hang on!' Charles made some small effort to tuck the trailing shirt-tail into his trousers. 'Take him to the kitchen and give him a hot drink,' he snapped. 'I'll get cleaned up.'

When the others had moved out of the hall, he climbed the stairs wearily, his heart still heavy with grief and pain. No, it hadn't been his cigar, but the fire was still of his making. Hadn't he known that the wiring was not completely safe? Wasn't it on the agenda for checking . . . yes . . . just before the boys' accident? Everything had gone from his mind at that time, had been pushed back even further by Amelia's death. Yet he had done so well! Except for this one forgotten thing! But he was responsible for those three mills no matter what happened in his personal life, responsible too for the people who worked for him.

He dragged a desultory razor across his stubbly chin, trying hard to look at the positive side. The week had not been totally wasted. By telephone, he had arranged compensation for the dead boy's mother, had instructed his managers to battle on in spite of this setback and the resulting animosity. But everything else seemed so negative! Janet was gone. Her obvious hatred for him had made Charles turn inward, had forced him to see himself as she and others surely must. What could he do to put things right?

He sat in his dressing room after pulling on a clean set of clothes. Should he sell the mills, cut his losses and retire to obscurity? Was there any real point in continuing with no-one to follow, no Swainbank to take up the slack once he was gone? And even if young Joey did come through with flying colours, was there any real future in such a bottom-heavy concern, hundreds of employees and one small family at the helm?

Charles retained just about enough sense to realize that this was not the time to make major decisions, simply because he was not thinking straight. All kinds of ideas had bounced around in his head these last few days while he sat in the study, his body starved of food, his brain befuddled by exhaustion and alcohol. According to sources, Paddy Maguire was at death's door. Charles had even caught himself dreaming of marrying Molly, of adopting the twins and changing their name to his. And he'd been so haunted, the scenes of his past life floating before his eyes like a newsreel at the picture house – Molly, Amelia, John and Peter, Father dying with Ma Maguire as his only company, Mother screaming at the servants, Sarah struggling against the inevitable, the twins rejecting him, a terrible fire consuming everything . . .

Like an ostrich, Charles had buried his head, vainly hoping that he would not be seen simply because he himself could not see. But he must go back. To do that, to face angry scenes and humiliation, to face himself and the guilt he must suffer – this would take a courage beyond any depths he had plumbed so far. And did he really care, was he capable of that? Was he genuinely concerned for the childless widow, for those whose lives had possibly been shortened by exposure to such terrifying danger? Or was he merely out to protect himself from the barbs he would definitely feel?

He entered the kitchen and joined the solemn group at the table. 'Get me an egg, Mrs M – and a bit of toast.' He sat with the two men while she bustled off to cook this first requested meal. 'It was still my fault,' he said quietly. 'I knew the wiring was worn.'

Jim nodded wisely. 'I know how you feel.'

'How can you?' Charles buried his head in his hands. 'How can anyone know?'

'Easy. It's not just gentry as gets in bother over decisions. I've been a bundle of contradictions all me own life, Mr

460

Swainbank. I know what it's like being dragged that many ways at once – sometimes, you can't work out whether it's Tuesday or breakfast time. Question of priorities, see – and I know all about them, nobody better.'

'Really?' He lifted his head and gazed at this conscientious, quiet and dependable employee, a man who, until today, had been almost anonymous.

'Really. I wouldn't fight in their war. Didn't matter at first, but when conscription started some time in '16, I got more than white feathers, I can tell thee. They come up to our house and asked me if I'd kill a man as raped me wife and daughter. Well, I had to think about that one, didn't I? So I said I might, being as the grudge would be on the personal side, only I weren't going traipsing round sticking bayonets in no Germans. They didn't like it, Mr Swainbank. Happen I were wrong refusing to defend me country. Happen we're all wrong at times—'

'But you went!'

Jim nodded. 'Aye. Bit of Red Cross training, then out to the front lines with half a dozen bandages and a bucket of mucky water. But I never touched a gun, sir. Bridie got that many white feathers she were thinking of starting a pillow factory. But I stuck to it all through.'

'Brave man.'

'Nay, I were judged a coward all the way, but I've never cared tuppence what folk thought. You've got to stop caring too, lad.' He reached out a hand and covered Charles's blanched knuckles. 'There's several ways of travelling the distance. You can sit on a bus and do nowt, let some other bugger do the driving. Or you can leave a mark or two by setting the pace like you have, or by dragging your heels like I did. Stick to your own way and you'll not go wrong.'

'But I killed that boy! I neglected the mill's safety!'

'And I killed a few by not standing in their place, little lads shot to bits, bits I couldn't stick back together because I couldn't find them! Do you think I were going to lock meself away worriting over that the rest of me life? No! There's men in yon mills who know they dodged a bullet for the next feller

461

to take it! Just stop it, man! Look what you've been through, eh?' Two sons and a wife gone – how the hell can you be expected to think on electrics when you're spending your time up the graveyard? Bloody hell – are you after being perfect? Far as I can work out, there's only been one perfect and we blinking well crucified him with a couple of thieves!'

'Thanks, Jim.'

'Think nowt of it. I just wanted to let on as they're not all gunning for you. Them with sense knows it were an accident and they all remember what you've suffered lately. Every last man jack of them came out for your lads. Working folk are not without heart, Mr Swainbank. Education might be lacking, but feelings run much the same. They don't want you a saint, they only want you fair.'

'Have I not been fair?'

'You're all right. There's many – meself included – as think you're a vast improvement on what we had before. And I'm not kicking your dad 'cos he's dead – him and me had a couple of fights in our time – I weren't feared of him. But he were hard, harder than you. You've done your best. Nobody can do more than that.'

The back door flew open and Sarah Leason stepped into the room, a basket of eggs in her hands. She put her head on one side. 'And friend to friend in wonder said, the Lord is risen from the dead,' she pronounced.

Charles stared at her. 'That's blasphemy, Sarah.'

'Is it? I thought the blasphemy was you stuck in your room sulking like a boy with no lollipop. Time you were up and about, you great soft pudding! Here are some eggs, Mary. Any more trouble with this man, just send for me. I still have my horsewhip!' After glaring at Charles for a second or two, she strode out with the agility of a young woman.

Mrs M arrived at the table with a boiled egg for Charles and sandwiches for the visitor. 'Eat,' she commanded. 'Or I pack my bags this very minute.'

Charles picked up the spoon, 'Is that a promise? I've known some bossy women in my time, but you take the biscuit.'

'Never mind the biscuit – eat the egg!' She dropped into a chair and watched eagle-eyed until every crumb of toast had been consumed. 'I don't want no more trouble with you. Them pigs round the back are as big as houses – they've had a birthday party every day this week! Now. Wipe the egg off your chin and take this nice man for a walk.'

Charles cast a despairing glance at Jim. 'See what I mean? Give her an inch and she takes three miles.'

Mrs M grinned. 'I never said owt about three miles – gate and back'll do for now. Get some colour in your cheeks, you look about as healthy as boiled rope.'

The two men ambled side by side along the drive, Charles tall and still quite straight, Jim slightly bent after more than forty years of hard manual labour. 'What's it like?' asked Charles. 'All that time in the shed – how does it feel?'

'It doesn't feel like anything. I've never known owt else. But my job were always satisfying. I'd see a row of quilts up an alley hung out to dry and I'd wonder which were mine. There's folk all over the shop sleeping under my quilts – aye – they'll last longer than me, that's for sure. Made to last, they were. You can boil a quilt of mine every Monday from here to doomsday and it'll come up smiling.'

'You're proud?'

'Took pride in me work, didn't like things shoddy or finished bad.'

'What will you do now?'

'I'll manage, ta.'

'How?'

'Pubs mostly. Piano, melodeon, bit of fiddling down School Hill where they still like the old Irish music.' His back straightened slightly. 'I'm self-taught, you know. You hum it, I'll play it. It's a gift, a talent as runs in our family.'

They reached the twin lodges at the end of the drive and Charles stopped, a hand on his companion's arm. 'Wait. I want to thank you for taking the trouble to come out. I've always been a positive thinker, always prided myself on that. And I shall be again – because of people like you.'

'Glad to hear it. There's families depending on you.'

'Yes. But part of my thinking includes you, Jim Higgins.'

Jim turned away and looked back up the driveway towards a lifestyle he had never before witnessed at such close quarters. 'I'm not coming back to me trade. I've had enough, see—'

'Can you?'

'Can I what?'

'Can you bloody see, man?'

Jim faced the man who, until a week ago, had been his employer. He seemed smaller somehow, as if half the spirit had been beaten out of him. Aye, there was no escaping it. Rich or poor, life got to you in the end one way or another. There was no divide between himself and the 'Big Feller' now, for each had been ground down by the inexorable forces that surrounded them, invisible, silent, deadly. 'I see well enough.'

'Then look at this empty house. It's yours for as long as you need it.'

'Eh?'

'Deaf as well?' Charles managed a smile.

'Well I wouldn't be the first to be deafened by weaving. Are . . . are you offering me a home?'

'And your daughter. How old is she?'

'Old enough to be getting wed next month.'

'Then live here and do my gardening.'

'Me? I wouldn't know a weed from a prize-winning rose!'

'There was a time when you didn't know warp from weft, Jim Higgins, but you learned. What do you say? Meals up at the Hall if you like – I could see that you and Perkins got on well together. Think of it. Good fresh air—'

'I don't know owt about good fresh air! There's no shops, no pubs, nowt happening!'

'There's plenty happening! Give a hand at Chase Farm, come to grips with a bit of ploughing and milking—'

'You what? Get a grip on a cow?'

'Yes. Keep an eye on old Sarah Leason in the other lodge, help her with the chickens. And there's a pub down the road – the walk will do you good.'

'Well! Well, I'll go to our house!'

'Good. Try it for a month, see how you get on—'

'Wait a minute! Go to our house is just an expression—'

'Try it. I dare you. Let's see if we can transplant you from town to country.'

Jim looked longingly at the pretty little house, all sandstone and funny shaped windows, a tall chimney stack and a low dry wall marking its boundaries.

'This one has two bedrooms,' said Charles coaxingly.

'Aye. I could fetch me old dad up – he lives with our Vera down Parliament Street. He were country, me dad. Come over from the West of Ireland. Mind, he's a right bloody pest.'

'He'll be welcome.'

'But I don't reckon your garden's chances if it's down to me.'

'Don't worry. I've daily gardeners – you can do the job for which the lodge was originally built – keep watch on my property.'

'Right. You're on. Ta.'

They shook hands on this bargain, then Jim wandered off to find his bus. Charles watched the figure as it receded into the distance, realizing, not for the first time lately, that he had never had a friend. There were acquaintances, business associates, necessary contacts. But friendship had somehow eluded him all his life and now he suddenly needed it, needed more than the warmth of Mrs M's kitchen and homespun philosophy, more than Perkins' devotion and camaraderie. In Jim Higgins, Charles had spotted a man of great character and intellect, a brain which had miraculously survived undiminished by the clatter of the loom, a smile never overshadowed by tall chimneys. But he was unused to acting so impulsively, and still felt uncomfortable about following instinct rather than reason. He had just offered home and board to a man he scarcely knew, and had for some time considered leaving a hard-won fortune to a pair of children who were almost strangers to him.

He strolled up the drive towards the empty shell which had once been home, where even now he caught echoes of Amelia's laughter, where he continued to be plagued by sweet memories of boys' voices raised in companionable argument. This was a house built on sweat and tears, though no generation within living memory had truly paid for it. Long ago, in a little stone cottage, a Swainbank had watched his wife and children working at wheel and loom, had walked out to collect and sell cloth. And so it had begun, a long-ago father and son trailing up and down the country, London, Manchester, Liverpool, Bolton, taking the finished with them and returning with the raw. For this house to stand, trade had been carried on beneath a blanket of darkness on moonless nights, laws had been passed, while fearful assailants with narrowed vision had languished in prisons for smashing machinery.

He entered the house and closed the door. Why then should this not pass to the toilers of today, those who resembled so closely the ones who had begun it all? Perhaps there was some poetic justice in the recent turn of vicious events, perhaps the wheel had come full circle as a wheel inevitably must. He leaned against the hall table, knuckles whitening in tightly clenched fists. Ma Maguire was right. Cotton had a price. And the Swainbanks were now paying it with interest.

Janet was surprised to find, within a fortnight of leaving the mill, that the shop more than fulfilled her need to be creative. She didn't like the idea of selling, still felt the strong desire to manufacture, so she settled on a compromise that promised to be the making of them all. From a small seed sown in the form of a four-line advertisement in the local press, the girl rapidly developed yet another business, thereby doubling the shops' takings within a matter of weeks. 'Maguire's Made-To-Measure Curtains' took off instantly and Janet found her days filled with cutting and sewing, while her evenings were heavily booked for measuring and hanging. The rest of the family almost gaped in wonder as they watched the miracle happening – the girl had a head for trade – there was no denying that. Maguires' Market was doing so well that by October Ma was looking for a house to buy, a nice little semi with a bit of garden and a shed for Joey's bikes.

Although Molly had little to say about the proposed move,

Daisy was the one who seemed slightly disturbed just now. Michael apparently didn't care a jot – wherever he lived was all the same to him as long as there was somewhere to kick a ball. But Daisy had become lethargic yet tense all at once, as if she must accept the inevitable and would not fight it, although she obviously worried about the outcome. She sat obediently now at Bella Seddon's table, a disinterested eye sweeping over the food before her.

'Aren't you having any tea then?' asked the woman. 'Seems to me you don't know good food when it stares you in the face. How about a nice bit of steak and kidley with a few peas, eh?'

The child nodded and stared unseeing at the heaped plate.

'Hey! You're not having one of them turns, are you?' Bella's face was taut with worry. She'd heard about fits, and didn't want any in her house. Why, that Tommy Weir down Isabel Street had some shockers by all accounts, finished up many a time foaming at the mouth and jerking about like a wild animal in the gutter. They weren't right, people with fits, shouldn't be allowed to mix with normal folk.

Michael looked at his little sister. 'She don't have turns,' he said, his mouth full of steak and kidney pie. 'She sees things like what our gran's gran could see. When she grows up, Daisy's going to be a desperate powerful force, Gran says.'

'Ooh aye? So the doctor's wrong when he says she's got the epileptics? Tommy Weir's got them.' She shivered visibly.

Daisy's eyes focused on Bella Seddon. She didn't like Bella Seddon. If she were to draw a picture of her – which she never would anyway – it would be a scribbly picture all black and empty, not coloured in like a drawing of Mam. 'I haven't got the same as that Tommy,' she said clearly. 'Even if I had, it wouldn't be my fault. And some right clever people have fits and I don't like kidney in my steak pie!'

'Well!' Bella folded her arms tightly. 'Not good enough for you? Rather have bread and scrape?' She stamped across the room towards the scullery and turned in the doorway. 'What do you see then, Daisy Maguire? What's all these visions?'

Daisy got out of the chair slowly, her bright blue eyes fixed on Bella's bitter face. 'You go too fast in here, Mrs Seddon. Boom-boom . . . ' She beat her little chest with a closed fist. 'That might make you poorly.'

Bella Seddon's mouth opened and closed around words that refused to come out. Not yet six and with enough cheek to talk to her elders and betters like that! Never had been a kid, that one, always did have a head on her like an old woman. But it was all true! These palpitations were getting her down and no mistake. And there was a look in the child's eye, an expression seldom worn by a face under sixty years old.

So. Had it come out then, the so-called magic Ma Maguire's grandmother was reputed to have known? Could it do that – leap across the sea, across a generation or two? Nay. It was rubbish, all of it! A load of stuff for the muck-cart, nowt else. With a sigh of frustration, Bella left the room and slammed the scullery door.

Michael finished his own meal, then polished off Daisy's as well. 'Coming out?' he asked as his spoon clattered on to the plate. 'What's up, Daisy? Are you sickening for something or what?'

'I'm fed up.'

'What of?'

'They all think I'm daft 'cos I fall asleep stood up! I can't help it! And I have these dreams . . . '

'When you're asleep stood up?'

She cast a withering glance in his direction. 'No, don't talk soft. I don't remember nothing when I go still. It's when I'm in bed. I keep seeing our Joey all quiet. Joey's never quiet. Same as I dreamed about fires before our Janet's shed burned down.'

'Then tell somebody!'

'I have done! They won't listen to me 'cept for Gran and she's too busy making pies all the while. But Joey—'

'What about him?'

'I don't know!' She was almost shouting now.

He grabbed her hand. 'Look, you come with me. We'll fasten one end of the rope to the drainpipe and I'll turn. You can play run in run out.'

Daisy hopped about on the spot, her face brightening with gratitude. All she could feel now was joy because a game was promised, because her big brother would demean himself by playing with her. For a while, she could live in this sixth year of her life without being different, without fits or remembered nightmares. With that superior single-mindedness common to all infants, Daisy cast aside her worries and ran into Delia Street. A red October sun bounced off windows and echoed its brilliance across the way, turning much of the glass bronze and radiant. In such a world, there was no room for visions . . .

The shops had been the making of Paddy too. He wore a suit with a stiff-collared shirt, treated the customers with deference and charm, kept a set of overalls round the back for dirtier jobs. The family had never known him so industrious and clean-living. Each evening, he sent Michael for a jug of draught black, then set to work with paring knife and apron, sleeves rolled up to the elbows as he peeled spuds or kneaded bread dough for the following day. Not once since the opening had he gone astray, not once had he been fetched home by police or by comrades too inebriated to negotiate a sensible direction before the early hours.

Janet and Molly worked the haberdashery side of the business, though Janet spent much of her time in a back room where she made curtains and chair covers. The orders arrived thick and fast; soon, anyone who was anyone at all bought Maguire's soft furnishings because the quality was good while prices remained competitive.

Ma's kitchen was a sight for sore eyes. The walls were of thick stippled plaster and the open fireplace was flanked by a pair of Irish dressers covered in brass, copper and clay cookware. Pies were brought straight from the huge fireside ovens and served steaming hot to hungry customers. A pan of Irish stew sat eternally on the grate while bread dough rose in white enamel pans on the hearth. Often a line formed as people waited for space at one of the six tables where two young waitresses, hair scraped tightly under white caps, took orders

469

and gave out meals. Ma, noticing that the queue grew daily, took to serving 'carry-outs' to those who brought their own dishes for spare ribs, baked potatoes, slices of pie. The box of herbal remedies would make an appearance once the dinner trade slackened and Ma sold cures while the waitresses washed dishes and took their own meal.

Faces became familiar after a time. Ma, remembering the lesson learned in Freddie Chadwick's clog shop, took a careful interest in her regulars and their daily problems. When a customer came in for advice or escape, a space was made next to the sink in the small scullery and here Ma listened and nodded while keeping a weather eye on the staff through the open door. Thus the shop became a place of refuge with Ma as unofficial Mother Confessor, a woman who might be trusted with secrets. It paid off. They came in to moan, went out with nothing more than a lighter heart, then returned days later with a friend or two and an order for ham and eggs all round. Things were going well, everything according to plans laid fifteen years ago.

It was a Friday evening at the end of October. All the shop signs showed 'closed' and the five of them sat at a table polishing off the day's leavings. Paddy leaned back expansively and picked his teeth with a matchstick. 'I never thought as how I'd feel so well again in me life!' He beamed at his family. 'No sign of me fevers – even this here hand feels on the better side just lately.'

'And your stomach improves too!' Ma clattered the plates into a pile. 'You've eaten more than the rest of us put together!'

Molly smiled at her husband. 'And we all believed he was at death's door, the road he carried on. Still, coming off the drink has done you good, lad.'

'He'll outlive us all,' pronounced Ma. 'Like a creaking gate, he'll carry on and never mind the rust.'

Janet glanced down at her new wristwatch. 'I've a big order on. Happen I'll stay behind and get it done. If I make a good job of it, I'll likely get more work off Chorley New Road and they go in for velvet and brocade up there, pelmets too.'

Molly tutted impatiently. 'You'll make yourself ill, mark my words. There's no need to go hammer and tongs all the while. Leave it till tomorrow.'

'But Mam—'

'Do as you're told for once,' snapped Ma. 'And you'll be needing to take on help, child, or you won't manage at all. That's a desperate big order now, isn't it? How can you hang curtains nine feet long without an assistant?'

'I know. I will take somebody on. Ronnie's mam's going to start soon and I'll set a girl on, somebody young and hefty.'

'Aye.' Paddy grinned. 'Somebody with arms six feet long eh, lass?'

Ma and Molly went through to the scullery to wash dishes while Paddy, who was now considered fairly trustworthy, wandered off to count the day's takings in the bike shop. For the first time in weeks, the twins were left alone together.

'It were electrical!' began Joey without preamble. 'I'm glad you're here with us, Jan, glad you're not still in the mill. But what happened – that fire – don't go on blaming him. He's a nice bloke in his own way—'

'In a pig's eye! He's one of them, one of the takers who'd stand on your face for a chance of an extra tanner in a back pocket! Just 'cos he showed you round his house—'

'Stop being so damn stupid!' Joey's face was reddened by anger and indignation. 'He took me up there on account of what I did – the break-in and that. He wanted to make sure I wouldn't do it again.'

'Don't talk so daft! He was showing off, enjoying being powerful while he frightened you. He doesn't care about Miss Leason, doesn't give a damn! He's just doing what he thinks looks right by giving her that little house and a few hens. I reckon he's bothered about nobody but himself.'

'That's not true!' Joey jumped up from the table. 'He cared about his kids and his Missus. He's lost everybody, Jan. Now, he's even lost one of his sheds—'

Janet rose quickly and leaned across so that her face almost touched his. 'Don't worry, he'll be well insured against fire, Joey. I bet Ronnie wasn't, though. There'd only be a penny a

471

week on Ronnie for a decent coffin. But he doesn't matter, does he? Who gives a damn for a penny a week lad, eh? I'm telling you now, I don't want to talk about this. If he comes in my side of the shop, I'll walk out till the air clears up a bit.'

'You're a right hard-faced bitch at times, you are . . .'

'Me?' She chuckled humourlessly. 'You two-faced beggar! I wouldn't leave me mam or me gran. I wouldn't write me dad off as useless and stupid. You were the one as wanted that, Joey! You were the one for getting away till this money turned up.' She beat her breast with a closed fist. 'I know how I feel. I don't change with the wind.'

He nodded slowly. 'You said I were unforgiving. Can't you forgive either? Me for robbing Witchie Leason, him for something as wasn't even his fault? He's paid Robbie's mam, hasn't he?'

'Not enough!' she spat. 'I'd like her to sue bloody Swainbank, drag him through the courts for leaving that place dangerous. Ronnie was in my class ten years – yours too – only you seem to have forgotten your mates all of a sudden. Have you ever seen a burnt body, ever caught a whiff of one? 'Cos I have and it's not something I can live with easy. And it's not just Ronnie! It's the fact that Swainbank can just walk away! I want his name dirt in this town. If it takes me all my life—'

'But that's not fair!'

'Tell me what is fair, then. You hated him for taking me on in the mill, didn't want me slaving. A ride in his posh car and all that's changed. I've no time for you, Joey! And I think we'd be best not talking about this any more.'

She moved away and began to stack the chairs. After a few moments, he came to stand behind her. 'We're going up, Jan. Soon, we'll be like Swainbank ourselves, nice new house, a van – happen a car in time. Why do you think we're working so hard, eh? To give it all away, to worry over other folk?'

'Not to trample on them, that's for sure. Anybody as works here will get a fair deal, a bonus on profits if we make good. This business is not just for our pockets – it's for decent working folk to come and buy a bargain or earn a living wage. Don't you ever say we're like Swainbank!'

'And you're buying curtain linings wholesale from a mill?'

'Not from his mill!'

'What's the difference? They've all been the same!'

She stood, cheeks flushed, feet apart and arms folded, an expression of fast diminishing patience on her face. 'Not to me, they haven't. Leatherbarrow didn't kill Ronnie.'

He sighed heavily and turned away to look through the lace-curtained window. 'You're going to be what Gran calls a bitter woman. You know what she always says – "Don't carry a grudge because it's an awkward shape and has no handle." I've been wild and grabbing, I know that now. Whether I'd have learned to behave without this chance at me own shop – well, I'll never know. But you're worse than me, our Janet. You've picked on a man to hate without even getting to know him proper. He's done nowt to you, nowt to this family. I know I didn't like him meself at one time, only it didn't go as deep as what you feel now.' He gazed at her over his shoulder. 'It'll eat you up. And I'll tell you summat else – Mrs Bowles won't go to court and sue him, 'cos he'll see she's looked after. Please, Janet—' But she was already out of the shop, coat trailing from a hand along the pavement behind her.

Paddy arrived and placed an arm about his son's shoulders. 'Let her go, lad. Women is a thing we can never understand, 'cos we're only men. They're all the same, son – not one to mend another.' He shook his head. 'Yet they're all different. Even one on its own can be half a dozen all at once. As long as you know that, as long as you can predict that they'll be unpredictable, then you'll keep in front. Well – alongside, which is the best you can hope for really.'

Joey stared in amazement at this man who had always been labelled daft, who seldom had anything interesting or meaningful to say.

Paddy grinned sheepishly. 'I know, Joey, I've ever been thought on as a few butties short of a picnic, but I'm not. Nay, I'm all there with me lemon drops as me Ma says, though I get away with murder when it suits. Acting dumb can get you a long way. But about our Janet – she's had a right bad shock

473

with her friend dying like that and him nobbut fifteen, poor beggar. Death's never what you might call acceptable, Joey. Best we can hope for is that we'll stop being angry. She will. In time, she'll learn—'

'No, Dad. There's something in our Janet – I can't pin it down, only it's as if she's always going to be mad about something or other.'

'Nay, it's her age. Most are a bit rebellious at fifteen, some do odd things, things they grow out of towards twenty—'

Joey's chin dropped. 'I did a burglary, Dad.'

'I know.'

'You . . . you knew? You knew and you did nowt?'

Paddy stood his ground, the only sign of discomfort showing in his hands as they twisted together on his chest. 'Not because I don't care, lad. Never think that. Only I've lived that long in a house of women, folk who reckoned to know better than I did – well, I've had to keep me place to keep the peace! When you get treated as stupid, you act stupid. And there's no two ways, Joey – I was fair pickled at the time, knocked out with drink and fever. But I knew what was going on – or had a fair idea. And I've been a lazy sod, I admit that right enough. I knew your mam would see to things. Yes, you did wrong, but you're never a wrong 'un. No lad of mine could ever be that bad.'

'Thanks, Dad.'

Paddy moved towards the scullery. 'Are you coming home with the rest of us?'

Joey glanced at the wall clock above Ma's range. 'No. It might get to about half past ten – I've had a fair amount of stock through and it needs checking. Then I said I'd have that kiddy's trike ready by morning. Customer's got to come first, Dad.'

'That's right. See you later, then.'

Joey Maguire watched his family disappearing round the corner, Paddy pushing a small handcart containing all the dishes and pie plates for tonight's cooking session. It was a long walk along Bradshawgate, through Deansgate then up to School Hill, especially for the old one with her dragging foot.

Yet they managed it daily, found the strength somehow, drew on this newborn promise for a better future and channelled all energies into making the business work.

Tomorrow would be brighter. Tomorrow, he'd make his peace with Janet, give a bit of ground in the hope that her anger and hatred would begin to burn out as Paddy had predicted. Whatever had gone wrong could be put right.

He walked into the back yard, took up his brush and began to paint the small tricycle. Yes, there was always tomorrow . . .

Chapter 16

Paddy Maguire was a truly contented man. It occurred to him from time to time that he was forgetting to be ill, that his various wounds and disorders should perhaps be troubling him more, that everything would surely catch up with him in the end, make him suffer twice over. But the opportunity to ail was now denied him, the need to hide away and drink was suddenly absent, for he found himself caught up in a project so exciting as to leave little space for self-indulgence. He felt proud of his family, proud of what they were making of the shops and, most importantly of all, Paddy was happy with himself, enjoyed a sense of usefulness and fulfilment at last.

He sat alone in the kitchen, the proof of his worth spread out before him on the table in the form of account books and receipts. He had rediscovered his good head for sums, was given the weekly task of balancing the sheets, took great care to keep his work neat and legible.

'Paddy? Have ye the ledgers filled yet?' called Ma from the scullery.

He scratched his head with the end of the indelible pencil, then licked the point before inserting a final digit. 'We're more than eighty quid to the good this month – that's clear profit after Janet's paid off her materials and the butcher's bill's seen to. Next month, we might hit three figures.'

Ma came to stand at her son's side. She stared down at the rows of meaningless hieroglyphics on the page. 'Humph!' she muttered. 'Daisy is showing me the reading – or trying to, at least. It's a jumble of nonsense at the best of times. What's this?' She pointed to an item on the list.

'Linings – best cotton.'

'Ah yes.' She moved her eyes downward. 'And there's cotton

476

again and here's . . . no . . . don't you be telling me now! B – U – T . . . that must be buttons. If it were butter, sure it would be on another page altogether. Turn over to the next and let me see. Well now, there we have eggs and lard. I'm improving, am I not?'

'You are that, Ma. We'll have you reading out the news on the wireless before we know where we are.'

She sat down opposite him, rubbing floury hands on her apron as she studied this new man who was her only son. ' 'Tis a fine boy you're making, Paddy, a person a mother might take pride in after all. Not a penny piece have you taken from the business and you're after becoming a decent sober man at last.'

'Happen all I needed was a chance, eh?'

'Aye well, good man yourself – I have never before seen you make an effort the size of this. By the way – where is Joey?'

Paddy piled the takings into a green drawstring purse. 'Stopped behind to do up a trike and check his stocks. They've had another row, them two. Over Swainbank, I think. Poor old Charlie. He never did me no harm – I got many a laugh out of him and a few bob extra for droving and mucking out. Anyroad, far as I can work out, our Janet's for having him tarred and feathered while Joey wants him knighted down the palace. Like chalk and cheese – I don't know about twins. Who'd have thought they'd turn out so different from one another?'

Ma pushed a few grey wisps off her face, leaving behind a large smudge of flour on her forehead. 'They're stubborn, the both of them. 'Tis the sameness, not the difference that comes between them. Molly thinks Janet's a saint, but young Miss falls well short of the mark for canonization. Sure, there's good and bad in the pair of them, but Molly won't have it that her darling girl has faults like the rest of us. As for Joey – well, I hope he's had his slate wiped good and proper. But she's the deep one, Paddy. Mark my words – she's the one who'll leave a stamp on life.'

'She's a fair talent, Ma—'

'I know. And the ruthlessness that goes along with it. Anyway, reach me down a pinch, son, then away for your drop of stout – the jug's here on the dresser ready. We've a stone of praties still to peel and the chickens wait plucking . . . '

After Paddy had left, Ma remained a while at the table and took an extra portion of snuff, sneezing prolifically to 'clear her head'. Ah well, there was enough now, ample funds for a deposit on their own place, a nice newish semi off Bury Road with a long back garden to grow their own herbs and veg, a little greenhouse for tomatoes, that good big wooden shed for Joey's bits and pieces.

She glanced up at the clock. Janet was out, of course, had gone against her elders' advice as usual. Hanging curtains in Plodder Lane, carrying heavy bundles on and off buses, burdening her young back to maintain that self-imposed breakneck speed, doubtless out to prove something without even realizing the fact. Molly was down in the wash-house with a barrel full of water and a paring knife, likely working and worrying herself to a standstill. The only two safely in place were the little ones, in bed for an hour or more now.

Howandever, this would never get the baby's head washed, would it? All this daydreaming and with the earth waiting to be moved! She replaced the snuff box and took a batch of hotpots from the oven, checking rising dough in the hearth at the same time, then pausing to taste from a pan of broth that sat on the open range. Tomorrow morning, all this would have to be loaded on to the handcart to be pushed down for reheating in Ma's Irish Kitchen. Then Paddy would return home and bring down the makings for more batches of bread and pies. It was a hard life for all of them, yet Ma knew in her bones that not one of the family, with the possible exception of Molly, could bear to ever lay it down and go back to how things were before. Though Daisy seemed . . . well . . . a bit distant. Yes, she'd have to make time for a talk with Daisy one of these days.

She piled bread dough into tins for baking. Swainbank probably had a point, she thought as she pushed the loaves to one side of the table. At the bottom, everybody was after first-class

478

travel through life, most would work past themselves to achieve it. So what was the difference? The fact that he had arrived while the Maguires were still in the queue at the ticket office?

Molly entered through the scullery door, her face flushed after an hour or more of concentrated labour. 'I've done the spuds. Sliced for Lancashire pots are in the two big pans. Scrubbed for baking are in the buckets and I've cubed the rest for pies and stew. All right? Where's Paddy?'

'Gone for his pint of black, God love him – doubtless having a chat with the feller in the outdoor, gossiping on what it's like to be in business these days. You'd think he was a tycoon, so you would! Sure, I never did see such an improvement in a man.' She looked at her daughter-in-law's haggard face, the black smudges beneath the eyes, those worry-lines around the mouth, lines that seemed to be setting deeper with each passing day.

'Aye, he's better.' The voice arrived devoid of any expression.

'Molly, cheer up, why don't you? Look, we're out of here by Christmas – isn't that great? I'm going to put down on that corner one in Withins Lane. Ah, we could stop here and use the money to hire staff, but they'd never cook like we do, for we're the best. And it would be wiser to carry on with the hard work a while more, get a nice place as long as the twins agree on it. We're to have a van too – imagine that! We'll be the only small business in the town with motor transport.'

Molly lowered aching bones into a fireside chair and fixed unseeing eyes on the row of blue-rimmed enamel dishes that contained tomorrow's rising bread. It was all the same to her. The source of the original money meant that she could take little pleasure in whatever was achieved unless they somehow managed to pay it all back. But he wouldn't take it, might even be riled enough to come out with the tale if she tried to stuff the money down his throat where it rightly belonged. 'Do what you want, Ma. It makes no difference to me.'

'But you liked the house! Didn't you say yourself what a pretty place it was with the bay windows and that French door to the back garden? Wouldn't most people be delighted to get the chance?'

Molly shrugged her drooping shoulders. 'It won't be ours. It'll belong to the twins – or to their father, more like. When all this comes out, there'll be that many tongues wagging – why – they'll feel the draught in Manchester.'

'Let it be, Molly!'

'I can't.' Her tone remained quiet. 'I'd sooner tell them myself what happened, that it weren't really my fault. Only there's Paddy – he'd never forgive me—'

'Molly Maguire! Are we walking that same old ground again? Haven't we been down this road so often that our clog-irons are rusted through with it?'

'Then we must choose another road. I'm for selling up and moving away – London maybe—'

'What? Do you think he wouldn't notice the shops on the market? Wouldn't he find out in two shakes from Joey where you were for? And you cannot run from him, girl! He'd find you wherever you went! You must just wait and see—'

'I am waiting! I am seeing!' At last she reacted, jumping up from the chair, arms waving wildly in the air to emphasize her words. 'My twins are at one another's throats because of him! I want to be free, I'd rather be clean even if it means losing my husband! Look at me! Look!' She held out shaking fingers, thrusting them to within an inch of Ma's head. 'I'm a bag of nerves and there's grey hairs all over me head and I'm only thirty-three! Long enough I lived with what happened to me, thinking only meself knew! It hurt, but I never worried 'cos I thought nobody would ever find out. Oh, I cleared it with God, went through Father Mahoney, told my sins. But that was then and this is now! Paddy loves them kids – they're his! If he's got to lose them, I'd rather he got the truth from me, not from bloody Swainbank! I tell you now, this is killing me! And you can't make me feel any better, no matter what you say. I watch that shop front like a hawk, feared to death every time I notice a big car. At the finish, they'll find out anyway, so why not get it over or clear off out of the road? Why do I have to carry on like a sitting duck?'

Ma rushed round the table and pulled Molly into her arms. 'Things do change all the time, mavourneen. In me heart, I nurse this very fierce hope that Janet and Joey will never know, that something will happen to stop the wagon rolling down the hill. But please pull yourself together! He could re-marry. He might leave all to his nephew or simply cut the twins out as unsuitable. Remember the burglary? Hang on to the knowledge that Janet near went for him with a sledge-hammer the day of that fire. Would you leave thousands to someone who half-killed an old woman? Or to a girl who hates you fit to burst? Would you now?'

Molly rested her throbbing head against Ma's thin shoulder. 'No, I wouldn't. But I'm not a Swainbank, so I don't set store by the bloodline.' She sighed, her breath trembling as if broken by a swallowed sob. 'Oh, I'll try to hold together. Only some days I feel like running, taking Daisy and Michael out of here before it's too late. I'll be all right. Just give me a minute—'

Aye, a minute and then another. An hour or a day at a time got through in pain and anguish – how much more would the poor girl take? Ma felt as if a knife were being twisted in her own breast as she held on to the stiff, tense body of this woman she loved so much. What to say, though? Molly was right, there was no making it better, easier. They clung to one another for several seconds, then, without further conversation, each set about her nightly tasks.

Paddy returned with his milk stout, cleared the table and began to deal with rolling pin and pastry. He was proud of his pie crust, pleased with the way he'd taken to cooking as easily as a duck to water. Weren't some of the best cooks in the world men, after all?

Janet arrived at about nine o'clock and immersed herself immediately in calculations, samples and price lists. The kitchen was filled with the aroma of new-baked bread and cooling pies by the time everyone settled down for cocoa. Too tired for small talk, the four of them sat in silence as the clock ticked its steady way towards bedtime.

It happened with Yorick first. One minute he was lying across the rug, apparently trying to take up as much space as possible, then he was suddenly up and howling, the large yellow head raised as if baying at some unseen moon.

'Whatever—?' began Ma. The dog looked at her sadly – but Yorick was always sad – then fled beneath the table. He shivered violently. It was one of them, he knew it. One of them in trouble. Not here. Somewhere away from the house.

'Daft hound,' said Paddy. 'He's about as much use as a chocolate fireguard – I reckon if we had burglars, he'd run a flaming mile. Now he sets off hooting like a late train with too much steam—'

'Leave him!' snapped Ma. 'There's more to a dog than meets the eye. And he was no doubt having a bad dream, poor lad.'

The stairway door flew open and Daisy swayed dangerously on the second step. 'Joey?' she cried, her voice strangled.

Paddy leapt forward to catch her before she fell. 'Another one with bad dreams,' he said as he lifted his small daughter. 'What's matter, lass?'

'Joey. Where's Joey? All still now, Mam. Our Joey's all still . . .'

'It was a dream,' Molly cried as she ran to Paddy's side. 'Just a nightmare, love.'

'No.' The lower lip trembled just as it always did before the tears came. 'It was real.'

Ma struggled to her feet and placed the cocoa mug on the mantelpiece as a car screeched to a halt outside. She stared hard into Daisy's eyes, her own grandmother Gallagher's eyes, before going to the door. The ultimate proof of Daisy's sightedness was probably outside the house right this minute. Ma Maguire laid a hand on the gleaming brass latch just before the knock arrived. She should have listened to Daisy. They should all have listened to Daisy . . .

He worked hard on the trike for an hour or more, replacing distorted mudguards, oiling and tightening the rusted chain, fiddling with a small brush to paint all the tiny nooks and crannies. Aye, the job was a good 'un. He stretched stiffened limbs and smiled at his handiwork as he thought of the delighted child who would receive this gift tomorrow. Joey would have given an arm and a leg for a toy like that when he was a kid. His grin broadened. With no arm and no leg – he'd not have been able to ride it, would he?

Now for the stock. He walked through the back door and into the shop where he set about checking small equipment before improving his displays. People looking for a bike, whether new or secondhand, liked to handle the merchandise, have a good prod at a saddle, get their fingers round the handlebars for an idea of the feel of a machine. So he began to reorganize things, spread everything out, mount a few bikes on metal stands so that folk could get a better look at what they were buying.

When the back door burst open, Joey stood dumbfounded, almost rooted to the spot by what he saw, three large hooded men wielding knives and bike chains – the latter likely picked up in his own back yard. 'What do you want?' He edged stiffly towards the front of the shop. 'We're shut and the takings are long gone – there's nowt in the tills . . . ' He looked over his shoulder and through the window out on to the main road, hoping against all hope that someone would glance in and notice the bother.

One of the three sprang forward and flicked off the lights, then they all surrounded him, legs apart and arms outstretched to discourage any attempt at escape.

'Joey Maguire?' asked one.

'Eh?'

'Is your name Joey Maguire?'

'What if it is?' He knew his voice was shaking while his legs threatened to give way at any minute.

'We'll ask the questions!' The accent was Southern, possibly London. 'We got orders, see? Some bleeder wants you done in, Joey. Booked a place in the great bike shop in the sky for you, they have. Shame, ain't it? Only we got to do as we're told. Nothing personal, old son. But orders is orders . . . '

Joey heard himself blubbering, 'Why? What for? I've done nowt, far as I know. Who—?'

'Don't need to have done a thing, mate. Just the fact that you're here is enough, just the fact that you was ever born.

See, Joey . . . ' He leaned against a wall, his tone conversational. 'Fact is, you stand between Mr Fenner and a lot of dough.' The man shrugged carelessly. 'No contest. And where's the other one? Usually here making curtains, ain't she?'

'I don't know what you mean—'

'We was expecting two of you – one in this room and the other through there. But yours was the only light.' He jerked his head towards the door that connected Joey's shop to Janet's. 'Your twin sister. Where is she? Only we're on a double according to Fenner—'

'But . . . hey . . . hang on a minute! I don't know anybody called Fenner. Who the hell's he when he's at home? Never even heard the name. And I've got no twin sister.' A bus rattled by and Joey glanced over his shoulder again, praying that some eagle-eyed passenger would notice what was amiss in the shop. But he held no real hope. The room was in semi-darkness now, illuminated only by the meagre glimmer borrowed from street lamps and a narrow beam from behind the shop where the door remained slightly ajar. 'There's been a mistake made,' he went on, heart in his mouth. 'You've come after the wrong Maguire.'

'Naw.' The spokesman shook his hooded head and pounded a black-gloved fist into the flat of his other hand. 'Fenner don't make mistakes – except when he backs a lame nag about every other meeting. It's a fair cop, Joey. We gotcher and we ain't gonna let go. More than our lives is worth, see? But it's not personal, like I said before. It's a contract. A question of my word what I gave in good faith. And me being a gentleman – well – I never break my word.' He raised a huge arm.

'No!' Joey cowered against the door, hands coming up automatically to shield his face.

They laid into him systematically, fists, boots, bike chains, then finally, a single slash of the blade across his neck. And all the time, Joey's main feeling was one of absolute confusion and disbelief. Why him? Oh God, it hurt like hell! Why him, though? A steel-toed boot caught him in the groin and he folded instantly to the floor. Then a knife flashed in the miserly light, slicing neatly through the flesh of his throat. Bikes tumbled and crashed down as Joey writhed in agony, his world collapsing about ears already dulled by pain. As complete darkness descended, a last disjointed thought flitted across his tormented mind. This was retribution. For Witchie Leason . . .

Charles sat in the conservatory, a sheet of plans laid out before him on a white-painted wrought iron table. The insurance was cleared and, with a bit of juggling, he'd have the latest looms installed within six months. He sighed deeply and stretched long legs. Things in general were not looking good. For a start, there was this Hitler chap promising to stir up trouble by trying to take over half of Europe. And the last cotton meeting had gone on for hours, a roomful of old men speculating gloomily about Eastern imports and whether or no the government would keep a rein on them. Would there be a flood of foreign cloth within five or ten years? Would Lancashire be able to compete, was this the beginning of the end for Bolton traders, should everyone think not of expanding, but rather of cutting costs and drawing in horns? Miserable old buggers, they were, all cotton and no fun, having the bloody wake before there was a body to bury. No guts, no imagination.

He heaved himself to his feet and wandered about among Amelia's plants, all lovingly tended now by Emmie, all thriving and healthy in spite of their mistress's absence. Why should they live their stupid immobile lives when those of real value had been taken? But no, he wouldn't smash anything else. And she'd loved those plants, he could never hurt or destroy things so dear to Amelia's heart.

He paced the narrow area, listening to the hollow sound of his shoes against the red ceramic tiled floor. Life was becoming no easier. Since the fire, some hadn't wanted to know him, had treated him as something of a Jonah. Even with the noise of machinery all around, he sometimes sensed a layer of silence as he entered a shed, could almost reach out and touch the atmosphere created by his presence in their midst. It wasn't all of them, just a group here and there, the odd few who seemed to think he was some kind of bad luck charm.

Klaus growled and Charles stroked the animal's head absently. 'Are memories so short?' he asked his canine companion. 'All behind me when the boys died, sympathetic when I lost my wife . . . but now?' He shrugged and looked down at the dog. 'One of their own has died, Klaus. One of their own.'

A sharp rapping at the window caused the dog to growl again while Charles peered out into the darkness before opening the door. 'Who's there?'

Out of the shadows stepped the familiar man in black, the same hat pulled well over the eyes, that perennial raincoat belted tightly against his thin body.

'Lucas?'

The man crept forward and entered the conservatory, pulling the door tightly behind him. 'Don't say my name, sir. I've brought some information you might need.'

'Oh yes?'

The visitor glanced quickly over his shoulder and through the window into a blackness too heavy for any human eye. 'I'm not really being over-cautious, Mr Swainbank. I'd be no use to anybody if I got noticed. And what I've found out could affect me as well as others—'

'Then I suggest you pass it on quickly.' Charles could feel his patience slipping. This caricature of a spy was almost laughable, though Charles had not been inclined towards hilarity for some time now. 'Well? What is it? Is old Leatherbarrow about to undercut me by a mile?'

Lucas flattened himself against a wall and reached for the light switch. Then he whispered into the dimmed room, 'The boy you were interested in – Joey Maguire—'

'What about him?'

'There's a contract out on him and his sister.'

Seeds of fear quickly rooted themselves in Charles's mind and he felt a chilly finger travelling the length of his backbone. 'Contract? What do you mean by a contract? This is hardly Chicago—'

'Money. Some quite big London money. I took the liberty of

paying high for this information on your behalf, sir. The name's Fenner, Marcus Fenner. Seems he got his hands on a largish gambling win and chose to spend it this way. They're after a couple of corpses, Mr Swainbank. Cash on delivery, I understand.'

Charles backed away from the carrier of this news. 'But . . . but this is ridiculous! Why would Fenner . . . ? How would he . . . ? Oh no! Dear God, no!' Like a white-hot knife, the assessment of what must have occurred cut into his brain, burning through fear and confusion instantly. He shook his head frantically. 'That scheming conniving bitch! I left the bloody thing in my desk! She must have gone through every-thing . . . '

Lucas stepped closer and placed a hand on Charles's arm. 'Sorry I couldn't let you know earlier, but I've been away and only found out myself this evening. It cost me . . . '

'I'll pay! What the devil's going on?'

'They've arranged for him to work late, sent in a rush job for him to do. The girl usually stays behind on a Friday night, but they wanted the pair. He works with bikes?'

'Yes!'

'They've given him plenty to do, probably watched them both till it went dark—'

'Christ! What if Janet's there too? What if—'

'I think we should get down there, sir, try to put your mind at rest. Because I phoned the police, rang in anonymously with the tip-off. I'd rather not get too involved, you understand.'

They dashed out of the house and through the grounds. Charles started up the car engine as soon as they were seated, screeching off down the drive almost before the doors were closed.

'Slow down, Mr Swainbank! The police are on to it – and there's no point in arriving dead, is there?'

'How much?' The voice, unlike the driving, was cold and controlled.

'Pardon?'

'How much are they paying for my . . . for those two lives?'

Lucas hung on grimly as they careered down the road on the

wrong side, the vehicle brushing against overhanging green-ery, tyres spinning on the verge from time to time. 'A couple of thousand, I reckon. Could be more.'

Charles screamed round a corner on two wheels. How much for a life, Mr Swainbank? Yes, he could hear her now, what price a life, what price an eye . . . ? And it was his fault, all of it. How many children would he kill? His boys in a fancy sports car, Ronnie Bowles in a mill fire, Joey and Janet Maguire because of a will he'd failed to conceal.

Janet. He shivered convulsively. Let her be alive, he prayed, shoulders hunched over a tightly gripped wheel. Spare her, let it not be her! So much store he'd set by sons, carriers of the line, the great makers of continuity. But a daughter? Yes, that particular daughter had made him think, filled him with hope, despair, love. Janet Maguire had restored his ability to feel, had caused his blood to warm and flow, had allowed him to remember pain and joy in a heart so completely deadened by misery.

He shuddered to a halt on Bradshawgate just as an ambu-lance pulled away, a loud bell proclaiming that its cargo was alive. Hurt, perhaps dying . . . With his head in his hands, Charles began to rock back and forth, unable to contain in his mind the knowledge that he had arrived too late. Lucas crouched down in his seat as a policeman approached the car and knocked on the window.

'Sir?' The constable's voice arrived muffled by glass.

Charles turned the handle and took a deep breath of air once the window was lowered. 'What happened?' he managed.

'Not sure, sir. Oh, it's Mr Swainbank, isn't it? Friend of yours, this lad?' He jerked a thumb in the direction of the shop.

'Yes. A friend. Was he alone? Was anyone else in there with him?'

The policeman shuffled uneasily from foot to foot. 'Not supposed to discuss it at this stage. But being as it's you – yes, there was just the one.'

Charles swallowed. 'The ambulance bell – he isn't . . . ?' Sweat poured from his brow as he waited for an answer.

The officer drew a thoughtful hand across his chin. 'How did you know about this, sir – if you don't mind me asking, like?'

'One of your superiors. I've an . . . interest in the shop, you see.'

'Aye well. I don't know as how your investment will pay off, Mr Swainbank. There wasn't a lot of that boy left, just hanging on, poor beggar. We must have disturbed whoever did it, else they'd likely have stopped on to make sure he was out of it altogether. It was plain enough they meant to finish him off, I can tell you that for nowt. But I reckon they got away over the backs when they heard us coming. Likely after what was in the till, then decided to clobber the lad in case he recognized them. Shocking, it is. I don't know what this world's coming to at all. Good kid, that. I got a nice bike off him for my daughter only a few weeks back—'

Charles nodded. 'Where have they taken him?'

'Infirmary. They'll have a go at stitching him up, see what's wrong inside—'

'Stitching him up?'

The constable nodded sadly. 'Throat cut ear to ear, sir. Only they've happen missed the main artery or he'd have been well away by now. Bloody bastards. I wish I could get my hands on them.'

'Thanks, officer. I'll be on my way—'

He dropped Lucas at the corner by the Swan Hotel. 'I'm grateful,' he whispered before the man could do his disappearing act. 'I'll see you right in a day or two – there'll be a package of money at the Post Office, usual box number. And . . . stand by, will you?'

'I will.'

Charles sped off towards School Hill, his eyes darting this way and that as he searched for whoever had committed this terrible crime. But how would he recognize them? Fenner would never do his own dirty work, probably worried too much about lily-white hands and years of imprisonment. 'Don't worry about prison, Marcus,' he muttered beneath his breath. 'I'll keep you out of jail, old son.'

He burst into number 34 without even pausing to knock. A lone figure sat hunched over the fire, body trembling, head in hands. On the couch lay a child, the same girl who'd been there last time, while a large yellow hound occupied the space beneath the table. 'Paddy?' Charles rushed to his side. Paddy!'

The man looked up, eyes red-raw, cheeks tear-stained and haggard. 'Mr Swainbank? Charlie?' What was he doing here? Aye, they'd been in touch on and off over the years, bit of droving, bit of chauffeuring, a pie and a pint once in some country pub. But Charlie wasn't really a friend, not what could be called a mate. 'What do you want?'

'Just to help. Where is everybody?'

Paddy's hands twisted in his lap. 'All gone. Police took them. Our Janet screamed that much, they had to take her in the car and all before she brought the house down. Infirmary, I suppose.'

Charles let out a heartfelt sigh. She was safe.

'Course, I've been left here to mind the young ones.' Paddy waved a hand towards the sleeping child. 'I always get left. No matter what happens, I get left. Charlie . . . Charlie? Was there ever a God?' He began to sob, his mouth wide and gaping.

'I don't know, Paddy. Sometimes, I think He got invented to tide us over. I . . . er . . . passed the shop, noticed the ambulance. The police told me what had happened. I'm so terribly sorry . . . '

But Paddy continued between sobs, 'When they were born, I got shut out of the house, shoved in the street like a dog, I was. I stood at that window listening like a child sent to bed early, then I fell asleep on the flags. That's how you get treated in a house with two women, like you've got no say in anything. But when Ma told me I had a son and a daughter both together . . . well . . . I were that proud . . . ' He wept copiously, pausing only to draw a shirt sleeve across his streaming eyes. 'My lad, Charlie. My bonny lad—'

'Don't wake the little one, Paddy. Hush now—'

The door flew open and a black-robed figure fell in, cassock swinging wide, biretta slipping to the floor as the man crossed

490

the small room. 'Patrick! I only just now heard from Mrs Seddon – she ran all the way to the presbytery to let me know. Paddy?'

'What?' The single word arrived strangled by a sob.

'I've phoned through for the Extreme Unction, just in case. 'Tis as well to be on the safe side.'

'What for? What the bloody hell for?' screamed the tormented man. 'He'll not die, not my Joey!'

'He might. And you'd be wanting him to go in a state of grace now, would you not?'

'No! I'd sooner he stopped in this world with a soul blacker than hell!'

'Ah now – Patrick—'

Charles stepped forward. 'He doesn't want to hear that sort of thing, Reverend. Leave him some hope, for God's sake. And it might be as well to keep our voices down.' He indicated the couch where Daisy moaned softly in her sleep. 'No point in disturbing the little girl.'

Bernard Mahoney stared hard and long at the man whose face he knew so well from pictures in the paper, he who had already brought so much trouble to this particular door. 'What's your business here? Were you invited?'

'No.'

'Then I suggest you leave. This is no time for casual callers.'

Paddy struggled for breath and composure. 'Hang on, Father. This is my house, not yours. That's the one thing about being a Catholic – you lot just walk in and shout the flaming odds as if you own the place! This man were passing the shops, that's all there is to it. And I've worked for him, so has my wife. He's only come to see what he can do—'

'And what can you do, Mr Swainbank?' The priest's lip curled into a sneer. 'Have you the power, the ability to make things come right?'

'No. Have you?'

Paddy dragged himself from the chair and squared up to his Father Confessor. 'Shut up, Father Bernie! He's only doing the decent human thing!'

'Is he now?'

Charles straightened his long back and looked down on the small priest. 'The boy is hurt. I came to see what I could do for the family.' Their eyes locked and Charles could tell that Molly had confided in this man, probably in the privacy and safety of the confessional. 'The Maguires have worked for me – and Ma was like a second mother the night my father died.' That was a lie, for he'd never had a first, had never learned love and generosity from the ideal source, from a maternal breast. 'Paddy's children are my children, sir. All four of them. He and I have broken horses together – and we've broken bread together. Now we grieve in unison, because I too have suffered some great blows of late and I understand what he's going through.'

'Is that so?'

'It is.'

Paddy began to stride back and forth about the room, his lips moving in what looked like silent prayer. Then he swivelled on his heel in the scullery doorway. 'Father?'

'Yes, Paddy?'

'Do me a favour – stop here and watch the kids. I have to get down to that infirmary and see for myself. I can't just sit here waiting. Long enough they've left me sat here waiting for a tram that never comes. I've got to do something.'

Father Mahoney put his head on one side and raised his arms in an imploring gesture. 'But what can you do, man?'

'I can be there! I can be with my son, whatever happens!'

'I'll drive you down,' offered Charles. 'Go up and change your shoes and wash your face, then I'll give you a lift. Go on! There's nothing to be gained by arriving with your face tear-stained.'

Paddy dabbed at his eyes, looked down at his carpet slippers, then left the room by the stairway door.

The priest turned on Charles as soon as the coast was clear. 'Why did you come here? Will you put the finishing touches on what you started? Are you come to interfere at this desperate grievous time?'

Charles stood his ground. He wasn't afraid of this black-coated New Testament thumper, this flightless crow that cawed doom on everything it imagined to be beneath it. 'Do you think you've cornered the market on charity just because you wear the collar back to front?'

'Indeed I do not. But I don't trust you, Mr Swainbank.'

'Then that's your privilege. Why aren't you on your knees counting beads for Joey Maguire?'

Bernard Mahoney's tongue flicked nervously to touch his upper lip. This was a man of strong mind and great intelligence. 'Ah. So Maguire's the name, is it?'

'Yes. Maguire is his name. Why aren't you praying for him? Isn't that your job? Instead of attacking me, shouldn't you be talking to God or the Virgin – or perhaps another of your pot saints? And in case you still think it's your business, I didn't come here to hurt Paddy, Molly, or anyone else.' He paused, his eyes sweeping up and down over the man's short body. 'Yes, nod your wise old head – make your judgements – because they are of no significance. I don't need you to stand between me and what's supposedly right. None of us really needs your kind. You hang on to people by playing on their guilt, adding up sins like a dossier for blackmail, making them ashamed of the slightest human thought, need or desire. That's the only way you can hang on, by moral blackmail. And all the time, there's a boy lying in hospital with his throat cut and the life beaten out of him! So get your priorities right, priest, before too many others start to see you for what you really are. A total bloody sham!'

Charles walked out of the house, his whole body shaking with shock, anger and a strange relief. He was trembling at the thought of what had befallen Joey, felt he might never recover from this latest tragedy. Yet the relief at knowing Janet was safe – that was so sweet as to be almost another pain. But beneath these two emotions flowed a river of rage, a torrent that no dam could ever hold. At its deepest point, it was cold and clear, would be easy to direct at a specific target. Fenner. Yes, old Marcus would get his dues. Yet the hot anger, the shallower and more immediate fury, had caused him to turn on the priest, to make of him a whipping boy, a bullseye to practise on. But the man had made Charles feel doubly guilty

493

and he needed no reminder of his various crimes, certainly not from the Catholic clergy. All incense and not much common sense, they were!

'I see you've a conscience then, Mr Swainbank.'

He didn't turn, didn't bother to answer the figure in the doorway.

'God bless you and stay with you, my son.'

Charles swallowed hard and fixed his gaze on a lighted window across the street. 'I'm . . . I'm not of your faith, Father.'

'We are all born under the one sky; we all walk the same good earth on the same one-way journey. Like yourself, I have little time for the divisions between us, so let us not fight. You will do the right thing, Charles Swainbank. I may be just a daft old priest, but I've brain enough to spot a good man in a crowd.'

Charles cleared his constricted throat. 'Is this some kind of apology, then?'

'What do you want, man? Blood? Out of an Irishman? Better to try the paving stones! And I am praying for that boy—'

Paddy pushed Father Mahoney to one side and joined Charles at the car. As they pulled away from the house, Charles noticed the old man's hand raised in blessing. 'Not a bad stick, is he?'

'Eh? Oh, you mean our Bernie?' He blew his nose noisily. 'Salt of the earth, that one. Spent two years in no-man's land, so I'm told, blessed them all whether they were Catholic or Protestant, German or English, came back with a leg full of shrapnel and enough stories to write a book. Are you coming in the hospital?'

'No. I'll go home, Paddy. I can always use the phone to find out how the boy is. Just hold together for everyone's sake.' He bit hard into his lower lip. 'But mainly for your son.'

Paddy's voice broke as he whispered, 'If I have a son any more, Charlie. I know how quick yours went, I know what you must have gone through. It's bloody awful, is this. No rhyme nor reason without your kids, is there?'

'No.' He watched Paddy as he ran through the front door of

494

the infirmary. If what Lucas said was right, if Paddy was truly dying, then this could finish the man. None of it bore thinking about. And there were things to do, arrangements to be made.

He drove quickly through the town centre. What price a life? He knew the answer now. Father Mahoney probably wouldn't approve, but Charles had his own gods to appease. And wasn't it in the Book somewhere – an eye for an eye? He smiled grimly. Jim Higgins wouldn't get his eye back, but he'd been given something in return, a little house, a second chance at marriage from the look of things, from the way he and Carrie Fishwick were getting along. So the owner of the loom had paid in the end, just as surely as Fenner would now.

Charles shivered as he travelled through the countryside towards Briars Hall. He'd never had a stomach for killing, had always been glad about avoiding the war by staying to manufacture vital cloth. And he would surely make a mess of it, get it all wrong. So, he must do as Fenner had done, take the rich coward's way out, appoint anonymous killers.

As soon as he arrived home, he made for the study and picked up the telephone. When the connection was made, he spoke briefly to the party at the other end. 'Alice? Read any good wills lately?'

He heard a sharp intake of breath, though no answer was forthcoming.

'I suggest you get out of the way pretty damned quick, my dear. The money to travel will be with you tomorrow.' He slammed the receiver into its rest. Why had he done that? Because she was his brother's wife, because he wanted her safe? He shook his head. No. He wanted her frightened to death. But he would need to move fast, or Fenner would be on his guard.

He made a second call. 'Lucas? The contract. Can you arrange the same for me?'

After a slight pause for consideration, the answer came. 'Yes. A couple of thousand plus expenses.'

'Fair enough. You know the party – he who instigated the original?'

'Easy enough to find, I'd say.'

'When?'

'Within a week. Will that do, sir?'

Charles sighed. 'Yesterday wouldn't be soon enough. Understand?'

'Consider it done. I'll contact you by Monday, let you know how things are progressing.'

The line went dead. Charles stared down at the instrument, this tool he'd used to condemn a man to eternal damnation. Had he been a fool, putting Alice on edge like that? She'd probably have her dear husband across the Channel by morning. Still. Lucas's cronies would find him wherever he went. And there might be something to be said for having him killed abroad, well away from Lancashire.

He phoned the hospital, his hand shaking so violently that he almost dropped the receiver. Joey's condition remained critical, no visitors except family.

Charles stared through the window until dawn arrived with its false promises, all azure sky and birdsong. When he finally slipped into a fitful doze, the words continued to echo through his tortured brain. No visitors. No visitors except family.

They brought home what was left of him at the end of November. Paddy was drunk, of course, needed help to get up the stairs before his son's broken body could be wheeled into the house. Ma saw to everything, arranged for a bed in the kitchen, organized furniture so that most items might be squeezed in. Molly watched the horsehair sofa disappearing off down the street to some poor family, the sofa already moved once to accommodate Ma's bed in the front room. That piece of furniture had been in the best room years ago, when Molly had first moved in with her mother after her dad's untimely death at Pretoria. It had meant something, that sofa. But it was gone now. Not that it really mattered. She was like a zombie these days, going through the motions of being alive, seldom speaking or listening to anyone. She sat now on one of the straight-backed chairs, elbows on the table, chin resting on folded hands.

Ma and Bella Seddon lifted the twisted creature out of the wheelchair and struggled to lay him flat on the bed. 'Won't he go any straighter?' puffed Bella. 'His knees are up to his chin – we'll not get the lad comfortable this road!'

'He must lie as he is, I fear. 'Tis the paralysis. Just swing him over on to his side, Bella. That's it. Good boy, Joey. Who's a lovely boy, then? If only you'd give us a smile or a word—'

'Parrots are called Joey,' said Molly to no one in particular. 'Like talking to a bird.'

Janet entered the house with Joey's bag of pyjamas and towels. She had followed the ambulance in a taxi and she rushed to her brother's side, anxious to be of assistance. 'Is he all right?' Her voice was taut with fear and pity.

'He'll never be right. They said that plain enough at the hospital, didn't they? Never walk, never talk again.' Molly's voice was completely devoid of expression. 'He used to be all right, though. All my children were born perfect, not a mark on them. If he hadn't had that shop, he'd still have been all right. But there you go . . .' She smoothed her hair then sat back, arms folded tightly as she watched the three women trying to settle Joey in the bed.

Ma turned from the task. 'Are you going to carry on sitting there like a secondhand wardrobe up for sale? Molly Maguire, I'd take the flat of me hand to you just now – except it's otherwise engaged! Get off your backside and away to warm up the lad's soup!' She tutted her anger when Molly failed to move. 'Janet – get Joey some soup from the scullery – it's on the gas ring. Bring an old towel to make do as a bib—'

When Bella Seddon had gone home, Ma went through to the scullery to help Janet prepare the meal of slops, leaving Molly alone with Joey for the first time since the accident.

Molly stared at the wreckage, taking in every last detail, her mind strangely detached from what she was seeing. One eye was permanently closed, the lid drooping after severe haemorrhage in the brain. His limbs were stiff and rigid, legs jackknifed, hands clenched and at an unnatural angle to the spastic arms. But the ugliest thing was the mouth, forever wet, wide

497

and gaping, the skin around it red and roughened by the constant drip of saliva which seemed to spread in a never ending river all over his chin and down to the chest. A scarlet line around his throat made him look like a handmade monster, something built out of bits with the head sewn on last. He was revolting. And whoever he was, he certainly was not Joseph Arthur Maguire.

She jerked her head away from the sight, instinct dictating that she must escape. But where? The best room was now Ma's, the scullery was too small. Upstairs? With Paddy raving about his son? Huh! And this was her kitchen – hers! Not Ma's, for all she paid the rent. Molly was the one confined to this room, the one who would likely be condemned to sit here with this thing, this doubly incontinent object that required changing every five minutes. And why should poor Michael and Daisy give up their sofa and be forced to live with the unacceptable?

After Joey was fed and the two young ones were in from school, Ma called a conference. 'There's no need to ask you to the table,' she said scathingly to Molly. 'Since you've never moved from breakfast!' Janet was duly dispatched upstairs to fetch her father who started blubbering the instant he set eyes on Joey.

'You can stop that before you start!' chided Ma. 'We've a deal of sorting to do. Yes, you can stay,' she told the little ones. 'This is your life as much as it's ours and as you can all see . . . ' She waved a hand in the direction of the sofa. 'Nothing will ever be the same as it was. That, Molly, is a fact.'

They sat round the table, all four of them, the younger pair hovering by the dresser.

'Right,' began Ma. 'We're moving. Janet and I have decided on it, for we shall need more room with me-lad-o to take care of. To begin with, we re-open all the shops. Paddy, you will pull yourself together, hire a boy and continue with the bikes—'

'I couldn't go in there again! Not without him, not without Joey!'

'You are going! Molly – you and I will run the kitchen

498

between us. We'll take turns about – stay with Joey one day, go into work the next. I have arranged extra help both in the shops and at home. Mrs Seddon will give a hand here for a small consideration—'

'No.' Molly looked Ma straight in the eye. 'I'm not stopping here with . . . with him. He's not Joey. I don't know who he is, but he's not my Joey . . . '

Daisy frowned. 'Then why is he in our house? Don't talk so daft, Mam! Course it's our Joey.'

Ma decided to let this pass for now and she turned her attention to Janet. 'You and Ronnie's mother can see to the haberdashery, pick up on the curtains when you're ready.'

Janet nodded her assent. 'Mam – we've been shut down weeks now. Please – we have to get on with life!'

'Life?' Molly shrugged her shoulders carelessly. 'How can we have a life with that in it?'

Michael tugged at his mother's sleeve. 'Mam! That's my brother. He can't help the road he is.'

Molly smiled wanly at her younger son. 'No, Michael. He can't help it. But it's never Joey, never my lad. That's just a shell, like an empty house not fit to live in. My Joey was a fine boy. Wayward, but fine. Whatever that is in my kitchen, taking up room so's we can't sit down proper – whatever it is, it's nowt to do with me, for I reared a strong healthy boy.'

Daisy wandered over to the bed and stroked Joey's hair. 'Hiya, Joey. We know it's still you, don't we? Hippy-chippy-Charlie, round and round we go, I am the leader don't you see . . . Remember that song? And Janet in trouble for using Mam's best curtain as a train for May-queen? Come here, Mam. Come and talk to him.'

'Do as you're told!' snapped Ma.

'By a blinking six-year-old?'

'She's no ordinary baby, Molly! You know what she saw! We all know what she saw!' Ma gripped her daughter-in-law's hand. 'The child is sighted!'

'Rubbish!' screamed Molly. 'She's just like the next, nowt wrong with her.'

Daisy stood by the bed, her hand still resting on Joey's

head. 'I am nordinary,' she declared. 'And if I've said that wrong, our Michael, they know what I mean. I just know a few little things, things what can help us sometimes. There's a lot of people like me, isn't there, Gran? Only they don't know they're like me. Please come to Joey, Mam. Please!'

'Just do it, woman,' yelled Paddy. 'You'll not turn your back on the lad! Only a cruel-hearted bitch could do that!' He rose and dragged his wife from her chair, pulling her across the room, forcing her to face the boy on the bed. 'Look at him, for God's sake! Have you no love in you, no charity at all?'

'Paddy!' Ma arrived at his side. 'It's not heartlessness, son. That's shock and depression – she's been like this weeks. I know we've to reach her somehow, but don't push her too hard.'

Daisy took her mother's hand and guided it to Joey's disfigured face. And the miracle simply happened. The single eye lit up as if a switch had been turned on. A solitary tear made its way to the pillow while the mouth, twisted though it was, managed to frame a syllable. 'Mam.' It was enough. Just one word and Molly was on her knees, all the grief she'd ever known pouring out of her, wetting the bedspread as she hung on to what remained of her boy. 'Dear God, what have they done to you? Oh, Joey . . . Joey . . . Joey.'

There remained not a dry eye in the room. Michael, too young to cope with the shame of weeping, ran to the scullery to howl alone. The two girls clung together for comfort while Ma held on to her drunken son.

'He'll talk again, Mam,' Daisy cried between sobs. 'We can learn him, I know we can. Specially after I've passed for a doctor – then I'll know what to do, how to help him.'

Ma fell against Paddy's chest. So that was the end of Daisy's road, was it? The fourth generation of doctors in this family would be properly certificated, oaths sworn, books learned, papers written. Little Daisy was already dictating her own special path. 'You'll have to go to Mount St Joseph's then,' said Ma. 'Pass exams, get to one of them universities.'

'That's right.' The little girl dried her eyes. 'No more dreams, Gran. I don't get them now. And I haven't fell asleep stood up since Joey's accident.'

Molly lifted her head from the quilt. 'Ma – take Janet down and sort that new house out. Paddy – get to the corner for some boiled ham to save us cooking. Michael!' He ran into the room drying his eyes on the cuff of the school jersey. 'Get some coal in, son. I'll set the table. Everything's going to be all right. Isn't it, Daisy?'

'Yes, Mam.'

'So put the kettle on, child. We could all do with a nice strong cup of tea.'

They dispersed to carry out the various orders.

Molly looked down at her boy and noticed the gleam in his eye. 'We'll stick it out together, son,' she whispered. 'I'm sorry for what I said. I love you, Joey.'

The mouth quivered. 'Mam.'

'That's it, lad. I'm your mother. I'll never forget that again, not as long as I live.'

Part Four

Chapter 17

1940

They had lived in the corner house for almost three years now. It was a substantial semi-detached in red Accrington brick, well-built, a great improvement on Delia Street. Janet wished with all her heart that she might feel grateful, interested or even settled. But she didn't. Not since this rotten war, at least. She sauntered into the long back garden, her eyes drifting skyward as if she expected Adolf himself to arrive at any minute to drop his personal bomb on their home even though this was Sunday. But Janet had always taken the war personally, treated it as some kind of affront, a terrible blemish on the face of her life, something that would alter her destiny, leave her scarred and powerless for ever. Unless . . .

She paused by the familiar mound, staring down at the air-raid shelter, a corrugated object half-buried in the ground. Almost angrily, she dropped on to this item, kicking her heels against the ugly green-painted metal. Most of the family spent nights in the cellar when the siren went off, but Joey was easier to wheel outside, so Dad endured many a long hour interred here with her twin brother.

Oh, it wasn't fair! Gran and Mam had gone all clucky like mother hens since Joey's terrible accident – nobody could move without handing in a full report about destination, estimated time of arrival, intended time of return, name rank and flaming number of anyone likely to be encountered during an expedition to the grocer's or to a friend's house. Since last year, the two of them had become even more neurotic, often forcing Janet to stay at home 'in case the Jerries come over'.

Mind, they did have their troubles. There'd been food rationing since January and Gran was struggling with the Irish Kitchen, working hard to make a pound of meat feed a dozen, doing clever things with egg-powder and tinned jam. But as for Janet's side of the business – well, it was a laugh a minute, wasn't it? With folk worrying over their ration points and where could they get a bit of extra on the black market, few were interested in renewing their soft furnishings. Thus Janet had become just another salesgirl, half a yard of knicker elastic and a card of shirt buttons, please!

She was restless. Especially since reading in the paper that the Metropolitan Police were appointing women detectives at last. Not that she wanted to be a blinking detective. But she needed to do something – anything as long as it was useful. Of course, they'd hardly let her fly over Berlin and deliver her retribution, a nice neat stick of bombs to flatten some of their houses. And anyway, it wouldn't be right to kill kiddies even if they were only Jerries. But there must be a job somewhere! Joey couldn't fight, couldn't even walk or talk sensibly. Dad would always be exempt because of his thumb. And there was no bloody cloth to make curtains with even if anybody had wanted rotten curtains! So why couldn't she be in the war, make this family's contribution? After all, she'd be eighteen next birthday.

Eighteen. Eighteen and on the shelf. It was a stinking mess, this narrow life, these long days with no young men to turn their heads as she passed, no admiration, no excitement, no fun!

She looked through the French window to where Joey lolled in his chair, a rug spread over him to keep off draughts. He had the dining room all to himself – bed, wireless, special chairs, then a load of mirrors and bells hanging from the ceiling to draw his attention, make him focus. He took up a lot of space for someone who couldn't move, needed equipment, time and care. Fortunately, there was a fine big parlour at the front, a breakfast room running down the side of the house between hall and kitchen, an extra downstairs lavatory put in specially for the disposal of Joey's eternal mess. Upstairs there were four bedrooms, though Janet was still forced to continue sharing with Daisy. Gran and Michael had the two smaller rooms, while Dad and Mam occupied the biggest, leaving a moderate sized area for the sisters. Not that they slept up there much. The RAF might be knocking spots off the Luftwaffe, but the loud warnings still arrived almost every night, sending the two of them downstairs to shiver in the cellar beneath a pile of blankets while Mam and Gran brewed tea on a paraffin stove and argued about safety.

Daisy. Yes, Daisy looked as if she'd have it all, one way or another. And bloody good luck to her too! She was streets ahead of everybody else at the new school, was virtually sure of getting the Entrance. So she'd be educated, a doctor or some such fancy profession. Janet rocked back and forth as she fought with so many mixed emotions. Why couldn't it have been herself? It was her money that had brought them up to scratch, yet she was the one missing out! No qualifications, no hope for the future, not till this war was over. Why couldn't she go off to university and become something interesting? Her teeth sank sharply into the lower lip. Joey, poor Joey, she must never forget him. Janet Maguire should be grateful, shouldn't she?

She drew her knees up to her chin, folding the blue cotton frock around her thighs. It was a comfortable life except for the air-raids. Carpets, good furniture, money in the bank. Janet's money. Her eyes rested once more on the twisted figure in the wheelchair. The money hung round her neck like an albatross, because it was his too! And on account of that fact, Janet would have to take care of him for ever and ever. She hated herself for these thoughts, hated the knowledge that their last real words had been spoken in anger, disliked herself intensely for the slight resentment she held towards a brother who would always be dependent. But what were her chances of marriage now? No young men worth looking at, fewer still who would contemplate taking on her crippled twin . . .

Lizzie Corcoran stepped round the side of the house, a large brown envelope clutched tightly in her hand. 'Anybody in?' she called.

'Only Joey. They've all gone to church.'

'Oh. Have you been to early Mass?'

'No. I'm not going any more.'

507

'Why not?' Lizzie's face was a picture of surprise. 'I still go. Me mam would kill me if I ever missed. I went to seven o'clock – no sermon – it only lasts half an hour—'

'Good for you. But I don't see the sense in praying when half the world's trying to blow the other half to bits.'

'All the more reason – according to me mam.'

'We were made in His image, Liz. If this is part of His image, I'd sooner not stare too long in a mirror. I pretend to go, else Gran would have me guts for garters. Only I usually take a walk, enjoy a bit of freedom. Well, what have you found out? Is it in that packet?'

Lizzie joined her friend on top of the Anderson's roof. 'They need all sorts, Janet. There's drivers for ambulances, folk to do auxiliary nursing, land army girls, cooks, washers-up, laundry workers—'

'Are we old enough?'

'Well, we don't need to talk about our age, do we? And seventeen's likely all right – we're both near our birthdays too. With half the place wiped out and the rest waiting to be bombed, I reckon they'll take anybody willing.'

Janet jumped up. 'Right. Let's go then.'

Lizzie's mouth fell open. 'Just like that?'

'Yes! As soon as possible, anyway. Look, you can stop here if you want to, you can carry on with your weaving. But I'm going to defend my capital city.'

'Defend it? They'll not let you have an anti-aircraft gun, Janet!'

'Clean it up, then! Look after the walking wounded – anything at all rather than sell another reel of sewing thread or any more khaki wool for army socks! It's our war too, love! It doesn't just belong to the men, you know. That Hitler feller wants to take England over – Mr Churchill said so. Well, I'm blowed if I'm having him at Buckingham Palace with his funny flag flying on the roof! No bloody way! He's too ugly by a mile. Daft moustache and a walk like an egg-bound pigeon. Do what you want, but I'm going and that's for definite.' She strode towards the house, Lizzie running anxiously behind.

'Now? Are you going now, Janet?'

'Don't talk so daft. I've got to sort some money out, then get away while nobody's looking.'

'Eh?'

'I'm not telling them.' Janet swivelled in the doorway and faced her companion. 'They'll not let me and they'll not stop me. So why make them suffer twice over? They'll only worry till I'm gone, then worry again afterwards. This way, they get less bother.'

Lizzie paused by Joey's chair, her eyes misting over as she looked at him. They'd had hopes, dreams, ideas – well – the two girls had. Janet and Ronnie, Lizzie and Joey. All blown away with the dust now, Ronnie burnt to death, Joey a shrivelled old man. 'Hello Joey,' she said quietly.

He grinned in a lopsided fashion and mumbled something unintelligible.

'I might as well get some practice in.' Janet's tone was hard. 'This money from Ireland was left between the two of us. He'll be with me for ever, Liz. So I'm going to work in an army hospital or wherever they take bomb victims. That way, I'll learn how to look after my brother.'

'It's a shame,' said Lizzie.

'Yes.' Janet ruffled her twin's hair. 'It's a shame for all of us, but specially for him. That's why I have to do something, because he can't and I know he would have fought. Does your mam want you going to London?'

Lizzie shrugged. 'She's praying on it. But I think she'd like me to do what's right. So it's up to me, I suppose. If you go, then I'll go. It'll be easier if we've got each other.'

'It'll be an adventure! We've never been further than Blackpool, either of us. New people, a different place, a chance to have a go at something real. But you mustn't tell anybody. If this lot here finds out, there'll be ructions. I can't get past the front gate these days without having my passport stamped by somebody or other. Promise! Promise you won't tell!'

'I promise.'

'Right. I'll see you next week, get it sorted out properly. How we're going to travel, what we need to take. And I'll have

509

to give three days' notice on my own bit of savings at the bank—'

'Janet?'

'What?'

'You sound . . . all excited. It's a war, love, not a blinking holiday by the sea!'

'I know! But it'll change us, make us grow up. We'll never be the same again, not after this. And it'll all be over by Christmas, you'll see . . .'

Charles wasn't eavesdropping. It so happened that when Janet visited Sarah Leason, he was at the back of the lodge counting dead chickens after the local vixen's latest visit. Silly creatures, foxes. They killed a dozen, yet took only one, neither rhyme nor reason to this mass slaughter. Still. It was probably caused by all these flapping feathers getting up the animal's nose and driving her crazy. Just as the fear-filled chickens were driving him mad now. But Sarah would never let him take a gun to Mrs Fox. Though the old one grieved over her dead birds, she would doubtless insist that the responsible party should remain alive for the sake of what she termed 'the balance of nature'. Well, Sarah's idea of fairly weighted scales certainly involved a lot of blood and mayhem, that was plain.

Jim and Carrie Higgins ambled along the lane, arm in arm as usual. Now that Jim's daughter was securely settled and his old father had passed away, they had complete freedom to come and go as they chose when Carrie wasn't working. It had all turned out so well for them and Charles didn't like himself for the stab of jealousy caused by the closeness and obvious happiness of their marriage.

'Coming for a drink, Charlie? They've copped hold of a nice drop of Irish down at the Red Cat,' yelled Jim.

'No thanks. I'm up to my eyes in feathers and squawking hens. Have a double for me – and make sure you're back before blackout. Cheerio!' He watched as they disappeared along the road, each engrossed in the other, their world complete at last. After pacing the garden until the vixen's entry point was located, he sat on the step to make notes about necessary materials. Not that he held out much hope. Once a female fox made her mind up, there was no keeping her out.

It was then that he heard the voice. 'Miss Leason! There you are, a picture of what Gran calls rumbustious health. It's just a quick visit, 'cos I'm off to London in a few days. Don't tell Gran. You're one of the few folk I trust enough to say ta-ra to.'

'To London?' Sarah's tone was clipped. 'Whatever for? It's not a particularly healthy place to visit just now, Janet.'

'Well, I want to get in the war, do my bit.'

'Really? I should have thought you'd had enough of fighting. That family of yours re-creates Waterloo at least once a week – if my memory serves me correctly. Never before did I witness so much crossfire at a dinner table. How's Yorick?'

'Fine. Still a bit crackers, but not as soft in the head as he used to be. He thinks the Anderson's a kennel, though. Keeps burying his bones under Dad's emergency supply tins.'

'And everyone else?'

'Oh, he doesn't bury people, Miss Leason. At least, he hasn't up to now.'

'Very droll.' The sniff was audible even from the back door. 'I suppose you might make yourself useful by getting a pot of tea.'

Charles remained seated on the doorstep while she walked into the kitchen, heard the hesitation in her step once he was noticed.

'Oh.' She coughed quietly. 'I didn't realize Miss Leason already had a visitor.'

Slowly he rose from the stone step and turned to look at her. For almost three years he had caught no more than a passing glimpse, but now his daughter stood within feet of him, corn-coloured hair tied back with a bow, huge grey eyes staring solemnly at him. 'I'm not a visitor,' he managed at last. 'I'm just the landlord.'

'I see.'

'I was . . . ' He waved a hand towards the garden. 'I was just trying to protect Miss Leason's hens from the vixen. She must

511

have young to feed because she keeps coming back, the resolute little madam.'

'Yes.' Janet filled the kettle and lit the gas, her face reddened by embarrassment. She simply didn't know what to say to him, couldn't think of a thing. All that anger and nastiness seemed to have evaporated, as if it were nothing to do with her, as if it had come from another time, another person. He was bigger than she remembered, so big that the doorway was filled, his head bent awkwardly against the low lintel.

'Did I hear you say London?' he asked, his tone deliberately casual.

'That's right.'

Charles walked into the tiny room and stood by the table, just about two paces away from her. London. For no reason at all, the rhyme sang in his head over and over, "London's burning, London's burning . . .". Could he allow her to leave? If she got killed by a bomb, then all four would be gone. John and Peter, then Joey who was all but dead, poor soul. But this one? How might he stop her? Like the vixen, she was determined, possibly to the point of savagery if pushed. 'It's not . . . not a pleasant way to die, Janet. Falling masonry, explosions, fire—'

'I know all about fire, Mr Swainbank.'

'Ah.' His head drooped slightly. 'What will your parents say? Won't you be missed, won't they worry?'

'They'll worry.'

'Then . . . why?'

'There's worried mothers all over the place. At least I won't be fighting in the front lines or going up in a bomber. Worrying can't be helped. And I don't see why folk should bother more just because I'm a girl. Girls are tough, they can work long hours the same as men. Every bomb dropped is likely made in part by a woman.'

He drew a hand across his jaw. There would be no stopping her. The decision was made and once a Swainbank decided – well, nothing could change a strong mind. And the Maguires too were not without their particular brand of bloody-mindedness. 'Going alone?'

'With another girl. She's leaving your mill to come.'

'I see.' He paused for several seconds. 'Janet – about that fire and your friend who died—'

'Yes.' Her head nodded vigorously. 'I'm nearly eighteen now, more grown-up, a bit of sense in me head at last.' She swallowed hard and quickly. Pride was a bitter pill to consume. 'I was wrong. I was fifteen and I was wrong, sir. It's just that Ron was my mate from school – shared plasticine and books with him, I did. Him dying like that – it hurt me, 'cos I couldn't see the sense in it. Oh, I know he was a clumsy great lummox, but everybody loved him. You couldn't help liking Ron – he was as daft as a brush half the time. But even though I was so upset, I shouldn't have gone for you, not in front of all the mill. Me gran and me mam both taught us respect, so did our teachers. And everybody knows now that it wasn't your cigar. I'm sorry. I really am sorry for all the terrible things I said—' She stopped as he swivelled away abruptly to face the wall.

'Mr Swainbank?'

'Yes?'

She waited for a moment. 'You're not killing yourself laughing over old Cowcart this time, are you?'

'No. No, I'm not.'

Janet had seldom watched a grown man cry before. Except for Paddy – and his crocodile tears were usually more alcohol than saline. She took a hesitant step towards the distressed man. 'Sir? Can I help you?'

'I'm . . . I'm all right, love. Just a bad time, a very bad time . . . '

Her hands reached out to touch him, then dropped uselessly to her sides as she remembered who this was. Charles Swainbank, owner of three mills and a lot of houses, a big important man who didn't really need anybody, let alone a bit of a girl off Withins Lane. Happen his tears were not connected with the recent conversation. Perhaps something else had upset him, something she'd touched on without realizing it. 'I don't know what to say to you, Mister. I don't know what I can do to make you feel better. But all I wanted to tell you was . . . well . . . you can't be all bad after what you did for

513

Jim Higgins, eh? And . . . and a man who cries can't be hard, not inside. You're never a cruel man, sir. I've been wrong about you . . . ' Her voice faded away.

Sarah Leason beckoned from the doorway. 'Give him a hug,' she whispered. 'Every animal needs its fur smoothing from time to time. Go on – get hold of him.'

The old lady bit back her own threatening tears as she watched the daughter walking to her father for the very first time, saw how eagerly he turned to his girl, how tightly he clung. Never once had Sarah's own male parent touched her, played games with her. Sarah's existence had scarcely been acknowledged, yet here stood a man who would give his right arm to claim this child as his own. It was time. The old one knew it was time. This couldn't go on, the poor man fretting himself to death because of a simple lack of communication, a few missing words of truth!

She backed away and closed the door against a sight too moving for her lonely vision. Sarah leaned against the back of the sofa, her shoulders tense as she raised her head to the ceiling. 'If you're there, get it bloody right this time,' she snapped to the God she doubted. 'Stop making such a damned pig's ear of everything!'

In the kitchen, Charles drew himself away from the girl with reluctance. His affection might, after all, be misconstrued. This was a young woman now, someone strong enough to consider taking on the world, a fighting female with every intention of emerging victorious. Janet Maguire was not a candidate for unexplained manhandling. He gazed down at the straight eyebrows, the look of puzzlement beneath these perfect lines. A deep sigh shuddered its path along his calmer breath. The night of Joey's attack, Charles had vowed to say nothing while Paddy lived, to remain in the background for ever if necessary. 'Don't go, Janet,' he pleaded. 'Please don't go to London.'

'Why not?'

He took her hand and enfolded it between his palms. 'Remember your interview?'

She nodded quickly.

'I'd just lost my boys. And . . . oh, I don't know why . . . but when you walked into that office and gave me so much trouble, I realized how much I'd missed a daughter. Girls are . . . more argumentative, they have a special intelligence, a great deal of resilience and pride. You were the daughter I never had, Janet.'

Her face broke into a hesitant grin. 'Me?'

'Now it's my turn to ask "why not?" '

'Well . . . I'm ordinary. I never went to Bolton School for fancy education. There's nowt special about me, Mr Swainbank.'

He smiled. 'Oh, but there is. Look what you did for that business. Carry on there. This damn fool war can't go on for ever – they're only finishing off their tidying up from 1918.'

Janet shook her head again. 'No. This is nowt to do with the Great War, Mr Swainbank. Far as I can work out, the German folk have been pushed past desperation twice over. The daft ones among them see this Hitler as a sort of Jesus. I know that sounds awful, but I'm sure they think he's a saviour. Me dad says it's mass hysteria, like Rudolph Valentino's funeral, only bigger. They're sad, the Germans. Most of them don't want anything to do with this war, only he's clever. He's got them all riled up, made them join things, filled their heads with a load of Nazi rubbish. It's a war on its own, a special war.'

'And a very fierce one at the moment. Can't you find another outlet for your energies? Must you go into the thick of it?'

'Yes! There's not enough for me to do at the Market. And Joey would have gone to war. I know him – well, I used to. He wouldn't have carried on selling bikes and suchlike. Our Joey would have been one of the first to volunteer. Anyway, he's had a bad accident, can't walk, acts like a baby now. So I'm going in his place. And I've got to get away, else I'll burst, honest I will! Gran's had us all stuck together like a pan of treacle toffee since that night at the shop – nobody's allowed to be alone for a minute – even me dad. The only chance I get to be on me own is when they all go to the same Mass and I'm allowed to stop with me twin brother. It's awful. Gran even takes the dog to work for protection – it's all out of proportion, specially since the war. I have to get out of it. There was a time when I thought I'd always stay with me mam, never leave home. But I must find out what I want and they're smothering me! And if I don't go now, then I never will.'

'You won't wait for peace?'

'The war never waited for me, Mr Swainbank. It never asked me if I was ready, did it? There's no life up here—'

'We've munitions factories.'

'Aye.' She nodded wisely. 'Full of old folk and others not fit to fight. I need . . . I need people, Mr Swainbank, people me own age.'

'Hmm.' He released his hold on her hand. She needed a boy, a suitor, someone to make her feel alive, give her a sense of future. 'Won't Sarah Leason tell Ma of your intention?'

'No. Miss Leason can be trusted with anything. I'll work in a hospital – it'll be safe enough.'

Charles was suddenly aware that he was already halfway to giving his blessing, that he was letting his one and only child escape from him in this moment. Above all, he realized that she was going willingly into danger while looking for no more than excitement. Ah well. Perhaps she would be back within weeks. Terrified, traumatised, but home. 'I'll drive you down, make sure you're settled,' he said gruffly.

'There's no need—'

'I know people, places where you might stay.' Yes, he would find a way to monitor her safety. 'I shan't tell your parents what you intend, so don't worry. The trains are crazy at the moment and I've plenty of fuel for business. Consider it my contribution to the war effort.'

'Oh. All right then. It's next Wednesday, half past six in the morning. And thanks, it's very kind of you.'

'Fine. I'll pick you up outside the Man and Scythe.'

She pulled a wry face. 'Built 1251, the place where an Earl of Derby waited for his head to be cut off,' she recited parrot-fashion. 'Learned that at school. Ever since then, I've not been keen on the Man and Scythe.'

He smiled. 'Ye Olde Pastie Shoppe? Just a few doors down

and seventeenth century? Would that be more appropriate?'

'Thanks. There'll be me and Lizzie Corcoran.' He was doing so much for her, going right out of his way too. Why though? And shouldn't she take a polite interest in him, ask a question or two? After all, he'd been so upset a few minutes back. She groped in her consciousness for something sensible to say. 'How are the mills?' was the best she could come up with.

'Rayon,' he replied, a touch of regret colouring his tone. 'The only way to survive will be in man-made fibres. We've lost the cheap end of the cotton market, but then I've always done a lot of fancies. It's the export side we're losing. The government did what it could, put a levy on imports, but the Eastern countries are supplying elsewhere, markets that used to be exclusively ours. Cotton's a silly business, always has been. Still at least I've been lucky, haven't been threatened with closure for the duration. Things will revive after the war. But much of it will be this rayon and nylon.'

'Oh. Don't you mind?'

'A bit. But one must move with the times.'

'Aye. That's what I'm doing. Moving with the times.'

'It's a long way.'

She smiled mischievously. 'I'll be back, Mr Swainbank. You just mark my words. There's no keeping a good girl down.' The shoulders straightened as she performed a comic salute. 'I shall return.'

And he knew in that instant that she would.

It was a chilly morning. Janet pulled the scarf more tightly about her neck as she studied a bird flying across the spire of Bolton Parish Church. She stood on Churchgate, the site of the town's earliest market, where generations before her had haggled over sheep and cattle, where Puritans had gathered to sever the head of a royalist. So familiar, all of it, so dear to her. It was her town, hers! Why then was she leaving it? Because if she didn't, if everyone didn't try in his own way, then there would be no Bolton, no Lancashire, no England. The whole of Europe would be eaten away, that's what Mr Churchill

517

said. And as far as Janet was concerned, whatever Winnie said was gospel.

Nevertheless, she grieved almost to the point of tears, cursed herself inwardly for not having a handkerchief in her pocket. She bent to open the suitcase, lifting out the top items as she searched for a hanky. Her fingers made contact with an unexpected object and she lifted this out, her eyes widening with shock as she found herself staring at Gran's special brooch, the leprechaun's gift. After more careless rummaging, she came up with an envelope, her name printed roughly in pencil on the outside.

Quickly she tore at the flap and pulled out a single sheet. The writing was like that of a child, half lowcase, half high, while spellings and grammar were infantile and untutored.

MY Dere JAnet
I no YoU Are goin froM Us. This YoU Do with bLessin froM Me. cUM hoMe to Us. I wish I cUD rite More. TAke cAre of YoUr SeLf.
With Love FroM MA MAgUire.

Through a thickening fog of tears, she watched Lizzie Corcoran struggling towards her, a weighty suitcase dragging along the ground. Janet looked back at the words in her hand, then, after pinning the brooch firmly to her collar, she bundled everything under the already creased best frock. Oh Gran! The old dear must have found the case ready packed, must have decided to keep Janet's secret to herself. Oh Gran! Now, Janet really did need a handkerchief.

'You knew! You knew and you said nowt to me?' Molly stared open-mouthed at her mother-in-law. 'How could you do that? Just sit back and let her go? Paddy! Get down to that station and look for her.'

'Eh? What about the shop?'

'Kevin Wotsisname can manage. And anyway, what's more important – the shop or our daughter? Go on! Get in the van and down to Trinity Street. Mind, she might have gone on a chara if there's any running. What if she's at the coach station? Look there and all, Paddy! Hurry up!' She pushed her husband out of the room.

'We don't even know where she's for,' said Ma quietly.

'It'll be London. You know damned well it'll be London, the road she's carried on about bombings and what if they kill the king. She'll finish up sleeping under the ground with all them trains! She'll be killed! I just know she'll be killed!'

'Then bring her back, why don't you? Get her home so that she can run tomorrow or next week.'

'Eh?'

'She'll go whatever you do. We cannot hold the girl any longer, Molly. That's the truth of the matter – and the sooner you face up to it, the better for all concerned.'

'I feel sick.'

'So do I.'

'Aye well, happen you deserve it. I wouldn't have let her go, not without a fight.'

'And where would the argufying get you? You'd finish up with a daughter who hates you.'

'But . . . ' Molly sank into a chair, her hands straying across the table to pluck at a tea towel that covered a tray of scones. 'Why didn't she tell me? Why didn't she let me know she was going?'

'Because she realized you would try to stop her. Janet wanted no bad feelings between us. She is following her conscience, Molly.'

'She's looking for a bloody husband, more like!'

'Perhaps she's killing several birds with just the one stone. Howandever, we've held on a little too firmly—'

'You were as bad! You wouldn't let her go nowhere!'

'I know that. But there comes a time for letting go. Now. Get all the stuff ready for when Paddy returns with the van and Bella. She'll stay with Joey till after dinner, then I'll pop back and take over. We'll manage, Molly. Mrs Bowles can sell buttons just as well as Janet did. And don't be worrying, for Janet's a survivor if ever I saw one.'

'But . . . the bombs! And all them foreigners—'

519

'Foreigners?'

'There's all sorts in London. Australians, Poles, Canadians, even Americans—'

'And good luck to them too! If it's not their war and yet they still care enough, then surely they are welcome visitors! Just pull yourself into one piece, woman! Your daughter is almost eighteen years old, old enough to cope. Would you have her fastened down the rest of her life? Weren't you the one who wanted her to make her own way? Well, she is making it and good luck to her.'

'It's a bloody war!'

'I'm not deaf! Don't shout at me, girl – and less of the language, if you please! Do you think I haven't noticed the sirens and the bombers? I worry too, sure enough. Where will she live, what sort of work will she have to do, will she be safe? But she's gone. And we will do nothing to bring her back. If you want to keep her, then let her go.'

'Oh, Ma—'

'I understand, Molly. I do.'

They piled all the day's food into crates, then made breakfast for the two younger children. When Michael and Daisy had left for school, the women sat in silence waiting for Paddy. Bella Seddon burst in before he did, her face purple with excitement.

Ma sighed heavily. 'Morning, Bella.'

'He's took them. Him.'

'Who?' Ma's eyebrows shot upward. 'Who's taken who and where to?'

'The landlord. Swainbank.'

Molly jumped to her feet. 'Eh? What are you on about at all?'

Paddy fell in at the front door, a look of absolute amazement on his face. 'Mrs Corcoran flagged me down, asked what I thought of Charlie Swainbank being so good. He's give our Janet and their Lizzie a lift to London! They're going to work at a hospital or summat.'

Ma looked quickly from Molly to Paddy. 'Yes. I knew all about that. The man was already going down on business . . . er . . . to talk to the government about the cotton mills,' she lied hurriedly. After all, she didn't want Bella Seddon running round the old neighbourhood with tales of Janet making off with the landlord. 'I didn't say anything, for I knew the two of you would try to prevent the poor child going for a nurse. I'm very proud of my granddaughter, Bella. Very proud indeed. And yes, it was good of Mr Swainbank to take them.'

Bella, her sails collapsing for lack of wind, went to have a look at Joey. It seemed there was going to be little to gossip about after all.

'Get in the van,' whispered Ma between gritted teeth. 'No, I didn't know. But I wasn't giving you-know-who any advantage. Come on now, Paddy. The man likely thought she had permission.'

'Lizzie had permission.' Paddy continued to look confused.

'Well, our young madam certainly didn't.' Molly's face wore that closed look, the expression Ma recognized as 'I've made my mind up to get to the bottom of this and don't try and stop me'.

Ma called a farewell to Bella, then pushed the other two through the front door. They sat in the van, Molly on a pile of sacks behind the passenger seat. 'Get back inside for the stuff, Paddy,' snapped Ma. 'We'll be forgetting our heads next.'

'Bastard!' cursed Molly as soon as her husband was out of earshot.

'Don't you dare say one thing, Molly Maguire! Throw your weight about with Swainbank now and he'll tell Janet what you don't want her to hear. And how would she handle the news in the middle of a blitz, eh? Would she take care of herself with all that on her mind? Leave it alone.'

'He's already told her,' wailed Molly. 'That's why she's run away—'

'Rubbish! Stop talking a load of potato peelings, will you? Dear Lord of mercy—'

'I want to go to London,' Molly sobbed. 'I want to follow him and bring my Janet back.'

'In this boneshaker? You'd never catch him.'

'We could try!'

Ma swivelled as far as she could manage in the uncomfortable seat. Molly wept hysterically, her breath taken by violent sobs. 'Asthma next,' pronounced Ma before delivering a sizeable blow to her daughter-in-law's cheek.'Stop it! Stop it now, this very minute! You've other children to care for, a husband to think about and a business to run. We carry on as usual. We carry on so that there'll be something for Janet to come back for.'

'You hard-faced miserable old bitch!'

'And the top of the morning to you too, Molly Maguire. Here's Paddy with the food. Don't be weeping into the bread now.'

'Ma!'

'What?'

Molly swallowed hard. 'Oh, I don't know.'

'That, my love, makes several of us.'

It was Friday evening. Perkins was polishing the car, trying to achieve a decent shine with the cheap wax he'd been forced to buy. This was a damned shame. Money counted for nowt these days. You could have a drawerful and still get nothing with it because there was little to sell. He straightened from his task to find Molly Maguire standing quietly by his side, an expression of calm determination on her face. 'Oh.' Perkins stepped back a pace. She looked grand, all poshed up in a nice suit and with her hair done. But she was on the bounce again – he could tell that from the hard look in her eyes. The anger might be cold, even frozen, but it was there all right. 'I . . . er . . . ' he mumbled ineffectually, suddenly tongue-tied. If she was the mother of . . . eeh, it didn't bear thinking about, not with a face on her hard enough to stand clogging! 'I were just . . . cleaning up a bit . . . er . . . tidying, like.'

'Is he in?'

'Well, he was. I mean . . . I mean yes, I'm sure . . . Shall I go and find him?'

'It might be a good idea.'

'Bit of nice weather, eh?'

'Yes.'

'I'll . . . er . . . I'll just . . . Hang on a minute, will you?'
He flew through the house, bursting unannounced into the
study with a cleaning rag still clutched to his chest.

'Whatever's the matter, Perkins? You look as if you've seen
a ghost.'

'It's a woman. I mean a lady. Her as come to see you a few
years back.'

'Pardon?'

Perkins coughed. 'That one with the shop, her as used to
live up School Hill way in Bolton.'

'Oh.' Charles was suddenly bolt upright in the chair.

'She . . . she don't look right pleased with life – if you get
my drift, sir. In fact, I'd say she's got the whole bloody hive in
her hat, not just the one bee.'

'Show her in.'

'In here?'

'That's right.' Charles waited for the man to move. 'Preferably tonight, Perkins. Before it goes dark.'

'Oh. Right. Yes.' He backed out of the room and rushed
down the steps. 'He says you've to come in, Madam.'

'Thank you. Are you all right?'

'Me? Oh aye. Yes, I'm fine. Never been better. Touch of
rheumatism now and again, mustn't complain. Bit of nice
weather, see?'

'Yes.' Molly decided that Perkins was likely a screw or two
short, probably another of Charlie's charity cases, a conscience saver. Though he'd seemed all there last time when
he'd opened the door to her. Still. You never could tell. Perhaps he had something that worsened with the years, a degen-
erative disorder of some kind. Poor man.

Molly wasn't angry, not at all. What she felt was – well –
nothing, really. The ability to feel had disappeared these last
two days, had started to disappear once she'd found Janet's
farewell note in the bread bin. But she'd decided to come up
to the Hall all the same. Charlie Swainbank had never bested
her yet and he wasn't going to start now! And she wouldn't
show herself up, not this time. She walked slowly into the
study, her eyes fixed on Charles until the door closed behind

her. 'Well?' she asked as she placed her bag on the table. 'I'm not going to lose me rag, so there's no need for you to fetch the suit of armour. Just tell me what's gone on.'

'I was coming to see you anyway, Molly . . . to explain a few things . . . '

'That's easy to say now, isn't it? The bloody filly has gone and bolted!'

He shook his head slowly. 'Look. I promised not to tell you of her intentions, but I said nothing about presenting you with a fait accompli.'

She tutted quietly under her breath. 'It's all right, lad. I'm not thick, I do know what fait accompli means.'

'She's safe.'

'Is she? How can anyone be safe among that lot down there?'

'She's as safe as possible. I've placed her with some friends. They'll try to direct her into work that's not too exposed.'

'Janet's not a particularly directable item, Charlie. Even if she was a weathervane, she'd turn her own road against the wind.'

'I know.'

They stared at one another in silence for a while, then Charles rose to fetch a bottle and two glasses. Without asking, he poured her a hefty measure of port. 'Drink it up, girl. That must have come as a terrible shock.'

'It did. Ma knew, though. I think she'd been helping with the packing without even Janet realizing. Why did she come to you? I want the truth now.' She dropped into the chair opposite his.

'She didn't come to me, Molly.'

'So she . . . I mean, you didn't—'

'She doesn't know. She'll never know while Paddy lives – unless I die before he does. Even then, arrangements might be considered—'

'Oh. Why this sudden concern for my husband, eh?'

'The night of Joey's . . . accident, I sat with Paddy. I knew then that I had to back off, stay away from Janet . . . '

She fought to keep her composure. Bloody arrogance! Janet

wouldn't have let him within a mile, not while she was still riled over the fire. Mind, she'd got over that now, hadn't she? All pals together, jaunting off to London in the middle of a flaming world-war! 'That was a good decision, a really charitable thing to do. You've gone in for charity lately, I notice. So. If you were stopping away, how come you took my daughter and Lizzie Corcoran all the way to London?'

'She came to say goodbye to old Sarah. I was there. When I heard her talking about London, I knew she'd already made up her mind. Oh, I could have come to you and told you, but what would that have achieved? She'd have found a way, Molly. So I did what I could, put her with decent people in a good house with clean sheets. And that's all.'

Considerably deflated, Molly picked up the glass and drained it before sinking back into the chair. 'I called you a bastard on Wednesday morning. If I could have got my hands on you then, I'd have strangled you.'

'And now?'

'Oh, your luck's in now. I just feel numb.'

'The port will warm you.'

'It's not that kind of numb. It's like after Joey, like I've lost something precious, a thing I can't replace. She'll change, you see. When she comes back, she'll be different. And I'll have missed part of her growing up. Like I've missed my Joey. And by Christ, have I missed him!'

He squeezed hard on the glass until it threatened to shatter. This was one area in which he would forever remain a coward. As long as he lived, he would never tell Molly who had finished Joey's life. Fenner was dead, murdered by some unnamed gangster. But if Molly knew . . . No! It wasn't his fault. Time and time again he had gone over this. All he had done was to leave a will in a locked drawer. There was no need for Molly to hear the story, no need for her to be hurt even more. Or for himself to suffer further . . .

'What are you thinking about?' she was asking now.

'Joey.'

She nodded sadly. 'Aye. All that for an empty till, eh? And they never caught them. So that's your son out of the picture.

Just Janet now. And how long will she last with Jerries dropping tons every day? Happen it'll finish up with Cyril after all.'

'She'll come back, love. I know she will.' He reached across to refill her glass.

Molly gazed past him and through the small window. He was right about the port. It made her feel mellower, kinder. 'We could have been friends, you and me. If we hadn't had kids between us, I reckon we might have even liked one another. Remember your mam? Remember all the laughs we had?'

'I remember.'

'And Mrs Amelia with all her pretty frocks and Mrs Alice trying to look as nice. She never managed it, did she?'

'You should see her now! A face like parchment and a figure like a coat stand!' He shivered in an exaggerated fashion. 'She lives abroad on one of the Greek islands. I've sent directions to the RAF and the Luftwaffe. Between them, they might just find her.'

She drained the glass a second time. 'That's a terrible thing to say, Charlie Swainbank.'

'I'm a terrible man. You've always said I was a terrible man.'

'Aye. Happen I did and happen you are. But there's nowt we can do to change owt, eh?'

'Nowt at all.'

'I didn't know you spoke Bolton.'

'Fluidly.'

'Eh? Shouldn't that be "fluently"?'

'No. I speak it when I'm full of fluid, preferably alcoholic.'

'Oh. Well, being as you're drunk, I'd best be on my way.'

'Molly?'

'What?'

'That . . . numbness. That emptiness. I do understand. It's with me all the time, ever since the boys died. At least you have other children.'

She looked hard at him. It was difficult to focus, almost impossible to achieve a clear picture. Ah well. That would be the port – she wasn't used to port. 'Stable-yarding,' she muttered beneath her breath as she rose to leave. He came after her, placing his hand on the doorknob to prevent her turning it.

'I'm going,' she said rather unclearly.

'Not till you explain this stable-yard business.'

'You what?'

'Stable-yard.'

She grinned. 'That's a place where they exercise horses and groom them, I think.'

'You mentioned it the last time you were here. Has it some significance? Will you please explain it?'

She steadied herself against the oak-panelled wall. 'Charlie, it's inexpl— inexplic— I don't know how to go about telling you. You are not old enough to understand. Neither am I. We will never be old enough, not till we're dead.' She hiccuped politely, a hand to her mouth.

'That'll be a bit late.'

'Aye. That's why they call dead people late – you know – the late Mrs So-and-So and the late Sir Thingy Wotsisname. It's 'cos they're too late for everything. Too late for the bus, too late for the train—'

'You are drunk, Molly Maguire!'

'I know. Isn't it awful? Nay – hang on – I thought you were the one gone to fluid, not me. Tell you what, though . . . '

'Yes?'

'If I am tiddly – and I'm not saying I am – then I must be a disgrace. See, it's this way. Time and again I've told him what I'd do if he came home drunk ever again. I'm a right one to talk! Anyroad, thanks for that nice drop of port. It's made me worry a bit less. She'll come home. G'night then, Charlie.'

He pulled the door wide. 'Perkins!'

Perkins arrived at a trot from the kitchen.

'Get your jacket and take Mrs Maguire home,' said Charles.

Molly watched Perkins's disappearing back. 'Hey,' she whispered. 'Is he all right in the head? Seems a bit peculiar to me. Will he get me home in one piece? Only I'd sooner walk than be left with somebody who's got a degener— de— one of them illnesses what gets worse.'

'I would happily place my life in Perkins's hands, Molly.'

'Would you?' She made some small attempt to straighten her hat.

'Indeed.'

'Oh well. If he's good enough for the Lord of the Manor, I reckon he'll do for me. You'll do for me, lad,' she shouted at the returned and very startled Perkins.

Charles grabbed her arm. 'What's stable-yarding?'

Molly gathered what remained of her shredded dignity, drawing on her gloves with infinite care before pushing a stray curl from her forehead. 'I have no idea,' she replied with a dazzlingly sweet smile. 'If I find out, I'll phone you.'

'Promise?'

'Aso-blutely . . . ab . . . yes.'

She took a few uncertain steps.

'Molly?'

'Hello?'

'Your gloves. They're on the wrong hands.'

A look of saintly patience covered her face as she said, very plainly for one so obviously the worse for drink, 'These are the only hands I have, Charlie. Right or wrong, they're what God gave me. Ta-ra.'

She was gone. Charles walked back to the study and watched the car disappearing along the drive. It was still there, all of it. No change, no deterioration. Molly Maguire had survived the births of four children, had tolerated a domineering mother-in-law, a buffoon of a husband, the near brain-death of her older son, a great deal of adversity when it was all added up. More importantly, more significantly, Molly Dobson remained alive and very, very well. His little Molly had endured it all.

Chapter 18

1945

Janet didn't particularly like Sundays. But this was the quietest day for driving, so she had set out at the crack of dawn, waving a fond farewell to those who were close enough friends to rise at that ungodly hour. It was over. Part of her couldn't believe it, perhaps didn't want to believe it. So much to leave behind, most of it for ever, a great deal of it irretrievable whether she stayed or went.

She pulled in at the cemetery gate and turned to look at Paul who was still fast asleep on the back seat. There was no point in disturbing him. And this was something she wanted and needed to do alone. The Protestant side was nearer the entrance, so she pulled up first beside Sarah Leason's grave, following the map Mr Swainbank had sent a couple of years ago. Defiant to the last, Sarah had been interred well away from her parents – even in a different cemetery. The gravestone was an oddity, of course, an ornate carving of foxes and cats, then a short verse commanding those who passed by to care for the creatures of the earth. Good old Sarah. Janet prayed inwardly that there would be more like her, more people with enough guts and devilment to be fiercely different from the accepted and often tedious mould.

She drove slowly along to the Catholic side, passing the nuns' graves with their funny little crosses, pausing now and then to refer to the sketch. Both members of her family had died without much warning. And Janet had attended neither of the funerals. In the first instance she had been ill herself, struck down by some nasty bug brought home from the front by those she nursed. The message about the second death had arrived while she was in Cornwall for a brief holiday with one of the other girls. Joey had gone with pneumonia, just slipped away in the night with no unusual symptoms. Then it was Dad, poor Dad who had apparently been riddled for years with a particularly nasty and painful tuberculosis.

It was a simple stone, just a slab with a rose on one corner and a crucifix on the other, white marble, the names inscribed in black.

JOSEPH ARTHUR MAGUIRE
JULY 21 1922–AUGUST 4 1942
BELOVED SON AND BROTHER
ALSO HIS DEAR FATHER, PATRICK JOSEPH MAGUIRE
AUGUST 15 1904–JANUARY 7 1943

Beneath a large space for the names of future occupants were the words REQUIESCANT IN PACE. Janet placed her flowers in the vase and stepped back. 'Oh, Paddy Maguire,' she whispered. 'How often did you cry wolf? How often were you really crying? I love you, Dad. And you too, Joey. I had to go, because they needed me too and I didn't see your need, stupid girl, I was! But oh I wish I could have seen you both one more time. Just one more time. Paul's with me. You'd like Paul.' Tears poured down her face, but she was too miserable to wipe them away. 'I don't know how I'm going to face Mam, not after all that's happened. You would have been easier, Dad. You always forgave me everything. Remember how you said I was like a film star? Mam won't think I'm a film star, not now. I miss you. I don't want to go home, not without you. Joey, I would have looked after you, so would Paul. It won't be home . . . '

Two graves away lay Agnes Evelyn and Elizabeth Mary Corcoran, killed by a stray German bomb in 1942. Lizzie hadn't lasted in London. London had proved too big for Lizzie, too dangerous. So she'd come home and died in her mother's house just off Deane Road. They'd only lived there a fortnight too . . . Janet turned her face away from the row of graves. Even after all she'd endured, this was too much.

A terrible surge of hot panic suddenly flooded her veins. She could not go through with it! Wouldn't it be easier to turn round and go back to Paul's parents, back to that lovely big farm in Kent, to her own thatched cottage on the edge of the estate? Not now, not today. She could book a room at the Swan, set off again tomorrow with her extra petrol coupons. But there was Paul to think of. And Gran and Mam – even Michael and Daisy deserved some kind of explanation for her recent silence.

Resolutely she strode towards the car and glanced at the rear seat where he still slept. The small red vehicle crawled past the resting place of her dad and her brother, turned in a loop past Sarah and towards the gate. Almost of its own accord, the little Singer took the Bury road, the road to Withins. The two hundred miles since this morning seemed no distance at all. But this last mile was the longest in the world.

'Janet! Oh me darlin' girl!' As always when she was excited, Gran slipped into a very heavy brogue. 'We have missed you so! And you look great, a picture for me sad old weary eyes. Not a one of them here to greet you, for you were not expected. Sit down now – haven't we a deal to catch up on?' She fluttered about like an oversized bird, smoothing cushions, straightening a lace-edged chair cover, glancing in the mirror to make sure she was presentable enough for such a momentous occasion. 'And thank God you are safe! Wasn't London town in the most desperate trouble? Did you see the bombings, child? Were you hurt ever?'

'Where is everyone?'

'Daisy's away doing homework over to some girl's house. Top of the class in all subjects, is Daisy. We're very proud of her. She recovered from her petty whatever, no more dreams or visions—'

'Good.'

'And Michael will be kicking a ball with a dozen other lunatics.'

'My mother?'

'Well now, don't you talk all posh and Southern? Your mam's walking. She walks a lot these days, especially on a fine Sunday afternoon. I'd say she'll be on her way to Rivington

531

Pike. It's a place she's always had an affection for ever since she was a little child.'

'Oh.' Janet folded her arms and stared through the window. 'All the houses are intact, I see.'

'Yes. We were lucky just here. Luckier than poor Lizzie and her mother certainly. Did you hear?'

'Yes. I visited the grave just a few minutes ago.'

Ma Maguire studied this calm young woman. Beneath the exterior, something seethed, a great torment, some kind of terrible worry. 'What is it, child? You won't sit, you've hardly looked me in the face once. Do you have anything to tell me at all?'

'Plenty.'

'There's no blame. We know you had to go, Janet. Even Molly accepted that after a time. You went and did what needed doing—'

Janet turned on her heel and faced the old lady. 'I'm not alone,' she said at last. 'There's someone out in my car, someone I think you should meet. He's very important to me.'

'Then fetch him in! I'll set the kettle to boil, make a sandwich—'

'You fetch him, Gran. I'd like you to welcome him.'

'And why would that be?'

'Go and look in my car, Gran. It's up to you to decide whether or no he is welcome in your house—'

'But sure – it's your house—'

'Yes. And it's your home. You made it and kept it, you held this family together through the years. I know what you've done for us, Gran. No matter what happens, I'll never forget what we owe you, taking my mother in when she was an orphan, looking after us when we were small. You're the head of the family. If anyone comes into this place, then you should be the one to bring that person in.' There was little expression in her tone. She might have been reading a list of facts or a set of tables to be learned for homework. 'Most of all, I'd like to say a thank you for the brooch and the note that came with it. It meant a great deal to me at that particular time – and during some worse times later on. I'm grateful to you.'

Ma stared into the closed face. There was no point in further questioning. 'Right. I'll away and bring in the poor man. What's his name?'

'Paul.'

'Paul? That's a good Christian choice.'

'He comes of a good Christian family.'

Janet placed herself in the centre of the rug while her grandmother went out of the room. Several minutes passed. She heard the car door opening, then, after a long pause, the sound of footsteps approaching the house. The front door slammed.

'Janet!'

'I'm still here.'

Ma entered the parlour with a bundle in her arms. 'He's ... he's yours?'

'Yes. Four months old.'

The old lady gazed down into the white shawl. 'I think ... I think this is the most beautiful baby I ever saw. Look at the eyes! Near dark as Joey's, they are. And such wonderful soft hair ... '

'He has his father's colouring, Gran.'

'I see. Yes.' She sat in a fireside chair and rocked the baby back and forth. 'And where is his father?'

'Paul's dead. I named his son after him.'

Ma's face whitened. 'I'm sorry, my love. Did he ... did the poor boy live to see this child?'

'No.'

'Janet! Oh my dear girl! What have you been through at all? And why did you not tell us? We would have come for you, brought you home!'

'Paul's family looked after us. We've been well cared for.'

'But you never even asked us to the wedding!'

Janet glanced down at her shoes before speaking. 'That's because there was no wedding. My child is illegitimate.'

'What?'

'I don't need to repeat that, Gran. You heard me well enough. I'm a fallen woman, a woman with loose morals, a slut—' Her voice cracked very slightly.

'Never! Were you carrying on with a whole battalion?'

'No!'

'Just your man?'

'Yes!'

'Then how in God's good name do you manage to be a slut? I've seen sluts. They hang around on Bradshawgate on a Friday night, permed hair and the legs stained with gravy browning and a line drawn up the back. You have not the qualifications to be a slut, Janet Maguire.'

'Thank you.'

'There is one thing, though. I noticed just this minute that you wear a wedding ring—'

'That's for the child's sake. For the moment, I am a war widow. When the boy's old enough, I'll tell him the truth. I'm . . . very proud of his father. And young Paul has a right to know his true identity. More than that, he has a right to know his other family, his grandparents. They accepted me and loved me, they knew Paul was the father of this little one.' She swallowed hard, showing some emotion at last. 'I loved him, Gran! Oh God, how I loved him!'

Ma placed the baby on the rug, freeing tiny limbs so that he might kick and enjoy the warmth of the fire. 'You come to your old gran, now.' She held out her arms. 'Come, Janet. There is no sin in loving a man, none at all. I am proud of you, so I am.' Her arms closed around the trembling shoulders. 'Tell me. Tell me all about it.'

They sank on to the sofa, the younger woman clinging hard to the figure beside her. 'He was a fighter pilot. They flew missions, went out on escort with the bombers. Anyway, he just didn't come back one night. I waited to hear from him, but when I got the call, it was from Piggy.'

'Piggy?'

Janet nodded. 'He flew the leader plane in Paul's squadron. Anyway, he didn't say much on the phone, just that Paul was not accounted for. I think that was the longest night of my life.'

'I'm sure it must have been. Were you alone?'

'Yes. I moved away from Mr Swainbank's friends to be

nearer to Paul's base, took a little room of my own. Two nights later, Piggy came round. He told me he'd seen Paul hit. The last thing he shouted over the radio was a request for Piggy to tell Janet—' She sobbed loudly.

'That he loved you.' This was not a question.

When she was calmer, Janet continued, 'Mr Anderton came for me, took me down to the farm. They never once criticized me for being pregnant and unmarried. I think they were just glad that Paul was not completely gone.'

'He didn't know about the pregnancy?'

'No. I was going to tell him after his twelfth mission. He'd been offered a training job. That was his last flight, Gran—'

'In more ways than one. May the saints watch over his soul.'

Janet rubbed her eyes fiercely and pointed to the baby. 'He's Paul Anderton too. It's on his birth certificate, I made sure of that. And I don't really feel any shame—'

'Nor you should!'

'But I've been afraid of telling my mother.'

Ma nodded slowly. 'You feel strongly about this identity business, then? Strongly enough to tell your son about the circumstances of his birth?'

'Oh yes. I think everyone has a right to know who his parents are. Don't you?'

'But . . . but what if it hurts, Janet? What if it causes too much pain to the teller and to the receiver of such news?'

'The worst hurt is not knowing. I'd hate not to know or to be told a pack of lies.'

Ma rose from the sofa and stared down at the wriggling infant. 'So. If Paddy had not been your father, you would have wanted to be told?'

'Definitely.'

'Are you sure?'

'Yes.'

'I think it's time you and I had a little chat, my child. Time to get the history books straight, eh?'

'Gran – what is it?'

'Pick up your little boy and feed him. Sit by me and stay very close because you will need me now. And you'll need the

535

closeness of your baby. It's a long tale, child. When I've finished, you'll perhaps go back to the Andertons. But not before I've finished, Janet. This time, let me get it right once and for all . . . '

It was only two o'clock, plenty of time to get everything over and done with. She drove past the twin lodges, glancing at Sarah's house where she had last spoken at length with Charles Swainbank, then looking across at the pretty little house where her work master now lived with his second wife. It was a frighteningly long driveway, every yard of it reminding her of who she was, who she had always been, the terrifying responsibility that went along with this new knowledge. New to her, obviously not to others.

But was it new to her, was it really new? There'd always been something between herself and Charles Swainbank, a line of communication that would scarcely have been expected to run from boss to apprentice and back again. The anger, the special silliness, 'are you killing yourself laughing, Mr Swainbank . . . ?' And the grief, that hitherto indefinable expression on his face when he'd looked at her.

Strange how she'd decided instantly and instinctively what to do. Old Ma had taken the baby gladly, asking no questions about her granddaughter's destination. The car shuddered to a sudden halt. Maguire. Her name wasn't Maguire any more. Gran wasn't Gran, Paddy wasn't . . . Oh no! Paddy would always be her daddy, her real true daddy. Just as Ma Maguire would ever be the best grandmother a girl could have.

She stepped out of the Singer and strode towards the imposing house, past the lions couchant, past the carved stone balustrade and up the six steps. No-one answered when she rang the bell, even after the second time. His large car was slewed at a silly angle to the right of the front entrance, skid marks in gravel marking its path. But he might be out, he had other cars.

Down the six steps she walked, then along past the front of the house and round the corner. Dear Lord, the place was massive! She counted eighty paces before reaching the back, where she was greeted by screams and shouts. The area at the rear of the Hall was partly cobbled, though they were playing on a flatter patch, stumps chalked on an outhouse wall, a large lady striding forth towards the bowler, hands on hips, head wagging angrily.

'Now hang on, Mrs M . . . ' called the man with the ball.

'Don't you be telling me what to do, Mr Swainbank! You can't bowl and be the bloody umpire and all – that's not fair.'

'You were leg before wicket!'

'She was everything before wicket,' shouted a younger woman. 'We can't see the wicket with you standing in front of it, Mrs M.'

The fat lady turned on this latest speaker and another man who stood by laughing helplessly. 'Less of the cheek from you, Emmie Sharples! Jacob – whose side are you on, eh? I thought it was me and thee against these two. If you want to see the stumps, then I suppose you'd best draw them a bit bigger!'

Janet watched as Charles Swainbank approached the outhouse wall. He took chalk from his pocket and drew a set of wickets about seven feet high and as wide as the building. 'What do you think, Perkins?' he yelled.

The man who was Perkins threw back his head. 'I reckon . . . oh Lord . . . I reckon we need a wider shed . . . '

This proved too much for Mrs M. With the cricket bat raised high above her head, she chased her employer, driving him round the end of the house and almost into the arms of the single spectator. Emmie and Perkins followed, all four of them pulling up abruptly when they saw the young woman.

'Janet!' shouted Charles. He picked her up and swung her round until both were dizzy. 'Welcome! Welcome home!' He turned to his companions. 'This is that dreadful runaway I took to London five years ago. Nasty little ingrate, too! I found her a good home, but what did she do? Went off and lived elsewhere, not a word for over a year.' He placed her gently on her feet. 'How are you?'

'Fine thanks, Mr Swainbank.'

'Go and make tea,' he said to the servants. 'And a few sandwiches.'

Emmie, Perkins and a very sweaty Mrs M turned and walked away towards the kitchen door.

'Don't bother on my account,' Janet called after them. 'I shan't be staying.'

His face fell. 'Oh. I rather thought you might like a cup of tea, at least. You've never seen the house before, have you?'

'Only from the outside. I used to visit Miss Leason and Jim.'

'Ah yes. Sad business, the old girl popping off so suddenly. Her heart gave out in the end. At least it was quick, very little pain.'

They strolled along the side of the Hall, Charles taking the odd covert glance at this beautiful young woman. Her face was so . . . serene . . . so calm! 'Your brother and your father too. I'm terribly sorry, Janet.'

'So am I.'

They stopped beside her little red car. 'Fine piece of machinery,' he commented, just for something to say.

'It belonged to a friend, a close friend. He died. His parents gave me this.' An awful sadness coloured her tone. 'I saw . . . a lot of death, Mr Swainbank. Boys younger than I was. Those who survived will continue suffering in their minds. War is so bloody stupid!'

He took a deep breath to cover a stab of pain, a great sense of regret and uselessness caused by her hidden suffering. 'So. London was a handful, eh? I knew what you were going into, Janet. And I also knew that nothing would dissuade you.'

'London is beautiful. The people – well, they defy description, really. So damned proud, so strong. I met the queen. She came down to talk to the patients twice, no thought for her own safety or any infection she might catch. Saw King George too one day, doing a balancing act on a pile of rubble where people used to live. Everybody was worried in case he got hurt, but he didn't give a tuppenny damn. An ordinary man and woman doing an extraordinary job. The place is . . . in me now, as if a bit of it belongs to me. Or perhaps it's the other way round – part of me belongs to London.'

Her accent was almost gone, only the odd flat vowel betrayed her true origins. 'Going back?' he asked as casually as he could manage.

'That depends on a lot of things, Mr Swainbank. I've friends there now, ideas for starting up a business here and selling down there. That way, I'll keep in touch with everything, won't I?'

'What sort of business?'

'Fabrics, soft furnishings, other things to match like pottery and wallpaper. It's all very much in the future.'

'But for the moment you're staying with Mo . . . with your mother?'

'That's right.' She looked directly into his eyes. 'Get in the car, please.'

'What?'

'I want you to get into my car.'

'But where . . . I mean why . . . ?'

'You drove me to London, remember? I trusted you to drive me, so now you can repay that compliment. Please! Don't ask any questions! I just want you to come with me.'

He watched her hand as it came to rest on the door handle. 'Is that . . . is that a wedding ring?'

'Yes.'

'Who did you—?'

'Get in the car!'

Her face wore a strange mixture of expressions. The mouth half smiled, while the eyes showed mischief, shock, sadness and a kind of resigned happiness all at once. Slowly and not without a degree of reluctance, Charles climbed into the Singer next to this enigma who was his daughter. Like himself, she was a rapid driver, one who let the car do the work, a confident woman with an eye for the road and a mind on her eventual destination. Yes, she would get there. Wherever this little lady had decided to go today, tomorrow, for the rest of her life, neither distance nor obstacle would deter her.

'We're almost there,' she said at last. 'And you will do exactly as I tell you. Right?'

A shiver of fear touched his spine briefly. 'What's going on, Janet? What the hell is all this?'

'Shut up, Mr Swainbank. Just bloody shut up for once, let someone else do the thinking and driving!'

'Janet!'

The car shuddered to a halt. She turned to face him. 'I've been away for five years. One of the things I missed is here, just around the corner. I'm sure you've heard of Rivington Pike?'

He nodded dumbly.

'I'm going to walk right to the top, have a quick look at my home town. After five minutes, you will follow me. Have you got that?'

'Yes.'

She touched his hand briefly. 'Everything's going to be all right. Stop worrying and asking why and where and what. I stopped asking those things almost a year ago. Trust me. OK?'

'I'll try.'

Janet Maguire stood at the foot of the hill and looked up at the lone figure next to the folly. Even from this distance, she could tell that the shoulders were hunched, that sadness, grief, even loneliness hung heavily around her poor little mother's neck. With the agility of a young deer, she launched herself at the steep gradient. 'Mam!' she called as she paused for breath. 'Mam! It's me – Janet!'

Molly sank to the ground, her arms outstretched to receive this precious girl. 'Oh, love. Where have you been? Where the bloody hell have you been all this long while?'

They clung together, then Janet pulled away to look at the careworn but still pretty face. 'Like Pussy, I've been up to London to look at the queen!'

'It were a long flaming visit, then!'

'A long flaming war, eh?'

Molly's tears flowed freely. 'Joey . . . and Paddy—'

'I know. I went to the grave earlier on.'

'Have you seen Ma?'

'Oh yes. I had to report to base first. She seems in good order, no bits missing, still as sharp as a razor.'

'You look lovely, our Janet. And don't you talk nice?'

'I had to. They didn't understand proper English down there, Mam. Thick as two short planks, they were. When I asked did they want a butty, they all fell about laughing, specially the Americans. Well, it was no good having patients dropping out of their beds like that, was it? So I had to mend my ways.'

'But you're still the same girl, aren't you?'

'Why? Did you want a new one?'

Molly dried her eyes. 'Nay, lass. Never. I don't want anything now.'

'Don't you?'

'No. What would I be wanting? I've got three lovely children, a nice house, me mother-in-law to drive me mad. There's nowt missing in my life, lass. Nowt worth having.'

'But I'm sorry I left you. If I'd known they were going to die—'

'Not your fault, love. And how would England have got through this war without my daughter? Nay, they'd be frog-marching all over the shop but for you. Mind, I did miss you. So did Paddy. I felt so guilty – there I was, thinking he was playing me up again—'

'We all thought that most days. It's no use blaming yourself.'

'Aye. Well, there was more to it than that, our Janet. A lot more.'

Janet knelt in front of her mother as the man began his ascent. 'Whatever that lot more is, Mam, don't worry about it.'

'Eh?'

'The past. Don't dwell on it.'

'Easy advice to give, lass. Not so easy to follow.'

'He's here.'

'Who's here?'

'The one who's been at the back of your mind all these years. Somebody I think you should talk to, Mother.'

'Janet! What have you been up to? I can hear somebody coming – get out of me road! Have you gone crackers or what? Janet!'

The younger woman rose slowly to her feet, her hands still clinging to her mother's. 'Here's Mr Swainbank,' she announced clearly. 'Mr Swainbank, I believe you've met my mother?'

He stood awkwardly on the rim of the hill. 'Yes. Of course I know your mother.'

Molly's hands fell away as Janet released her hold. She stared up at the two of them, her face creased by shock and the brightness of an afternoon sun. 'What the blinking heck . . . ?' she began hesitantly.

Janet pushed Charles nearer to the Pike. With her eyes meeting his boldly, she said, 'Paddy will always be my dad. I know you understand that, Charlie. But you are my father.'

Molly gasped audibly. After a long pause, she managed to spit the words, 'You told her! You went and told her . . . '

'No!' He gaped at the two women, his hands straying along the tower for support. 'I did no such thing, believe me!'

'Be quiet, both of you!' Janet's eyes shone with determination. 'You've a grandson, a sweet handsome little boy. My boy. He'll get no shocks like this one. I'll make sure he knows who his father was, even though I never married him. Stop looking at me like that! I'm not angry, not upset! And I understand why you never told me before. I loved Paddy Maguire and I'm glad you didn't hurt him.'

'A grandson?' Molly's hand was pressed tight against her chest.

Janet's chin jutted forward defiantly. 'From a man I cared about, someone who made my life worth living! I loved him. Just like you've always loved this fellow here. Gran knows. Gran knows you still care about one another. There's more wisdom in that woman's little finger . . . oh!' She almost screamed her exasperation. 'If just one of you had half Gran's sense . . . !'

'Eh?' Molly's eyes strayed from Janet to Charles. 'Ma Maguire! I'll kill her—'

'Please youself,' said Janet, her tone deliberately sweeter. 'Only I think you should both shut your mouths. You look like a pair of clocks waiting for cuckoos to jump out and sing the hour.'

Charles stepped forward to help Molly to her feet. 'There's

a lot of you in this girl,' he said quietly. 'She's not completely Swainbank, Molly.'

'Thank God,' came the quick response.

Janet raised her eyes to heaven. 'Here we go. I was warned. Gran said you'd probably kill one another one day. Kill one another or get together and fight the rest of your lives. Anyway, just make your own minds up about that. There's nothing more I can do.' She looked around furtively. 'Hey?' she muttered in a stage whisper. 'Is anybody watching?'

'No,' they replied in unison.

'Good. Last one down's a cretin. Oh – by the way – you'd best hurry up, you two. I told Gran to make a special tea. We'll only suffer if her butties are curled up!' She flung herself on to the grass and rolled away from them, disappearing fast down the side of the hill.

They stepped towards the edge and watched the flash of moving colour that was their daughter. 'Well.' Molly groped for something to say. All she could feel was a sense of blessed relief and freedom, something she hadn't known for more than twenty-three years. 'A grandson, eh?'

'That's what she said.'

'We'd best be going then.'

'Yes.'

She glanced at his handsome profile. 'Charlie?'

'What?'

'How are we going to get down this time?'

He took her hand and held it tightly. 'Together, Molly,' he said, his voice roughened by emotion. 'We go together.'

THE END

Author's Note

Particular thanks and appreciation are due to those who maintain our few remaining cotton mills. I must also express heartfelt gratitude to some visionary men of business who have occupied, enhanced and found a purpose for old cotton factories, thereby holding intact a display of our heritage.

On a larger scale, I pay homage to every soul who tended cloth, to breakers, carders, piecers, winders, weavers, doffers and bleachers. And I must mention those who toiled beneath the ground, especially the three hundred plus who did not survive Pretoria. God bless them all.

And last, but never least, I recall with great fondness my uncle, James Higgins. He is portrayed in this novel as he actually was, though I managed to improve his lot in life by imagining what I would have chosen for him. To his daughter Eileen Riley, I say thanks for lending me this wonderful character, for allowing me to use his name..

We all remember your music, Uncle Jim.

Ruth Hamilton